CW00497565

THE FLYBLOWN CRUSADE

THE THIRD NOVEL OF THE THELENIC CURRICULUM, REVISED SECOND EDITION.

T R PEERS

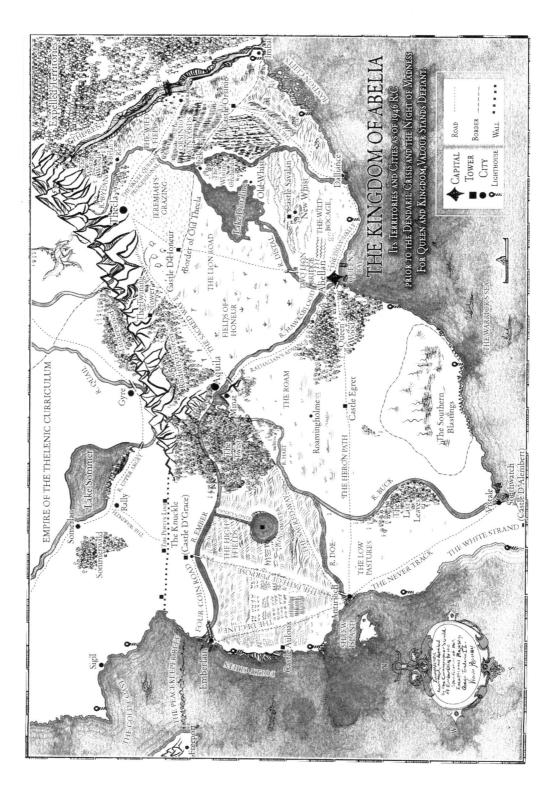

THE KINGDOM OF ABELIA

Its Territories and Cities as of 1946 R.C.
prior to the Dendaril Crisis and the Night of Madness
For Queen and Kingdom, Valour Stands Defiant

Copyright © 2019, 2022 Timothy R Peers
All rights reserved.

ISBN-13: 9781521583746

Cover art by Sean Harrington (seanharringtonart.com)

Map art by Tiffany Munro (feedthemultiverse.com)

For more information about the world of the Thelenic Curriculum, short stories and news visit
thetcbooks.co.uk

The Thelenic Curriculum Novels
The Wake of Manadar
The Third Mirror
The Flyblown Crusade
The Fire in the Wind

Short Stories (free to read at thetcbooks.co.uk)
The Oath of Sherenith
The Sins of the Mother
Leverage
Assignment: Chechnya
Foundation Day

❀ Created with Vellum

For Gail and Lyla. One journey ends, another begins.

PROLOGUE

*J*oniah awoke at first light, and knew immediately that today was the first day of his daughter's life.

She had, of course, been 'born', to use the word that those who did not know the Blessing used for the moment a child's wailing shell entered the world, some twelve years ago. He didn't know the exact day, and it didn't matter. That day was unimportant, a moment to be forgotten, merely a single necessary step on the road to the Blessing. It had been a simple act, though one that stood as a stark example of how lucky the Blessed were, for the child's flesh-mother, Dendris, had simply retired to her bed one afternoon and emerged a few minutes later with the fruit of her labours. Amongst the Other, it was known that the process of childbirth could be painful or even fatal for both mother and baby. Truly, they were deserving of pity.

He rolled off the bed, the swelling bulk of his stomach not encumbering him as much as an observer might have expected. Dendris was already up- a mother knew these things, he supposed. He patted his belly affectionately. He was only thirty as the Blessed measured time, so it would be at least ten years before his Ending. He wondered which of them the Blessed would use as the Vessel.

Downstairs at the breakfast table, Dendris awaited with their daughter. The child's long, golden hair shimmered in the dawn sunlight, matching that of her mother. They ate a simple meal of bread and fruit, and if the child knew that today was special, she gave no sign of it. As with all children who were yet unblessed, she was quiet, dutiful, knowing that she had yet to take her place in the world.

Once the meal was finished, Joniah strode to the door and threw it wide open. As he had known there would be, a large crowd had gathered, led by Pilgrim Ronald. His daughter ran to his side, looking at the assembled throng with wide eyes.

"Father!" she gasped, excitedly. "Is it time?"

He turned to look down at her. "Yes, child. The whole village is here to witness your Becoming."

Before the girl could reply, Pilgrim Ronald's voice boomed out. "Fellows! It is time for an Ending, and a Beginning. Yathik, step forwards!"

An elderly man was helped to the front of the crowd by a pair of younger, stronger men. Dressed like the rest in a simple white linen robe, his body was grossly swollen, but his eyes rolled in his head and his face bore an expression of beatific joy. Swiftly the attendants removed the robe, leaving the old man naked from the waist up. Suddenly he threw back his head and screamed, a sound of such volume and intensity that whether it conveyed agony or ecstasy was impossible to tell. With a wet tearing sound, his belly split down the middle, releasing a shower of pale amniotic fluids and no small amount of blood, which spattered over many of those nearby. Even as the husk that had been the man called Yathik sank to its knees, a mass of flies erupted from within him.

They flew arrow-straight, not swarming or deviating from their path as a common insect might, towards Joniah and the child. Swiftly, he stepped out of the way, allowing the race to take its course unhindered. His daughter stood her ground, eyes shining, and he read approval on the faces of the watching crowd. Sometimes, though it was rare, the ancient instincts of a child overrode their upbringing and they attempted to flee from the Blessing- this brought no shame upon them, but was considered to reflect poorly on their parents. The mass of insects reached the girl, and finally the swarm broke. Mercifully, she remembered to close her eyes- when the Blessing came from so well-seasoned a Vessel it was not unheard of for some of the Bearers to be strong enough to attempt to burrow straight through the sockets, which was troublesome and an unpleasant start to a new life.

For a single moment the child's head disappeared from view completely. She gave a single, convulsive gasp as her body spasmed, and then the creatures were streaming away from her. Blood poured from both nostrils and her right ear, but not the left, and Joniah nodded in satisfaction. When the Blessing took root in the ear, the Becoming was generally swift and painless. The girl's eyes snapped open, and her hands snatched savagely at some of the last Bearers to emerge, these bloody from their own attempts to bond. The new-born would not suffer these invaders to live gladly, and she seized several and dashed them against the wall of the daubed house that her forbear had been born and raised in. The rest made good their escape, swarming loosely now to flee to the fields and live out the rest of their short lives on the blood of sheep and cows.

"Welcome, Daughter," said Joniah, as the girl wiped her bloody hands down her white shift. "What is your name?"

For a moment, confusion showed in the child's eyes, as the new mind drove out the last vestiges of the old. If the Becoming was successful, the child would know in moments the name that her parents had chosen for her, even though they had never spoken it to her out loud. Such was just the merest part of the Blessing.

"I.. am Maria, Father," she said, slowly, a smile spreading across her face. From behind him, Dendris gave a shriek of joy and ran forwards, pushing past her husband to sweep her new daughter up in her arms, heedless of the blood that stained the girl's clothing and matted the blonde hair. The watching crowd broke out into applause and cheering, and even Pilgrim Ronald beamed.

"You have done well, Joniah, Dendris," he said, as the attendants bore the remains of Yathik away for disposal. "Maria shall be a fine addition to the Blessed, and some day.." he trailed off, his head suddenly cocking to one side. Joniah was about to ask him what was the matter, but then he felt it too, dimly. A feeling of.. of release, as if a distant danger had suddenly receded.

"I must go," said Ronald. "The way has been opened, and the Pilgrims must walk once more. Be one in the Blessing, my Fellows."

Without a further word, the crowd parting reverently before him, he turned, and began to walk west.

1

The spy walked casually down the hallway, nodding and smiling to friends and acquaintances as she passed. Nobody who saw her, not even the famed Operative Amanda Devereux, had any reason to suspect exactly what she was, and with good reason. Indeed, even the spy herself would certainly not have regarded herself as a traitor to the Vigilants, as the men and women who garrisoned the eastern border of the Empire of the Thelenic Curriculum were known. For that matter, given that the Eastern Vigil took in those who for whatever reason were unwelcome in their homelands providing that they were prepared to take up sword or bow in the bastion's defence, several of them held far more claim to infamy than she ever could. That Jandallan woman, for example, tall, slender, skin of pure white, sheltering even indoors from the sunlight under a large, wide-brimmed hat- she had been caught running *Tok'sla*, the potent narcotic Jandallan warriors relied on, into the Empire through Abelia. Not only had her induction to the Vigilants kept her out of prison, she had even been allowed to keep her wares, for the few of her countrymen who served with them needed the stuff as much as anyone did.

The whole thing had gone into one of her reports, of course, just as everything else did. The spy didn't know exactly who she worked for, and didn't care, and only in the very rarest of circumstances did she receive orders from the shadowy figure she knew only as "The Boss". For the most part, all she had to do was send a report each day, and make sure it included everything even remotely out of the ordinary. Considering that she owed The Boss her life, and that of her young son, she didn't consider making the reports to be any sort of imposition. Not that she was under any illusions as to the motives of her 'employer'- The Boss controlled people, and hoarded secrets and information, and it was merely a happy coincidence for the spy that saving her life had been part of a larger scheme to acquire another, more capable piece in the game.

The spy was not in the first flush of youth, having reached her thirty-fourth birthday some months previously, but the long, brown hair that framed her attractive, friendly face still retained all of its original colour. Her figure was perhaps more curvaceous than was encouraged amongst the more martial Vigilants, but in a place of work that featured so many stairs she had kept in shape almost by accident. More than one considerably younger man- and, flatteringly, several women- had been undeterred by her known status as a widow and had had to be gently rebuffed. Nor had the fact that her previous marriage had left her with a young son who followed her everywhere discouraged attention to any great degree. Of course, as an entertainer the dresses she wore to perform didn't exactly help the situation. A depressingly large number of Vigilants seemed to think that just because something was in the window, it was on the market.

Not that she was *off* the market altogether, of course. It just wasn't the right time. The loss of her husband was still too fresh.

The sight of the High Vigilant approaching jolted the spy out of her reverie. For most intelligence agents, direct contact with someone as important as High Vigilant Wilhelmina, the military commander of the fortress, would have been either a risk to be avoided, or an opportunity to be exploited, or both. To her, it was nothing more than a chat with Isla.

"Hello, Chania, Young Dorik," said the sturdy brunette, her armour creaking a little as she squatted down to make sure Chania's son could see her lips. "Making plans for the evening, are we?"

Young Dorik Steine, Chania's son, had recently turned five years old, and like his late father, who he was named for, he was almost completely deaf. For Chania, a Bard, this was difficult to take but she had already begun to let Dorik visit the Vigil's forge, in the hope that he might become a Smith in his turn. Dorik senior had always maintained that his poor hearing was practically an asset in his profession, and of course it had saved his life. For a while.

"Hello, Auntie Izzie," said Young Dorik with a shy smile. Like his father, he spoke slowly and carefully and often louder than people expected, but Chania was proud of how well his language skills were developing, all things considered. "Mama was going to do Burny Face tonight."

"*Born in Fire*, Dorik," laughed Chania.

"Burny Face," insisted the child.

"A fine choice, whichever title you use," said the High Vigilant, diplomatically. "I should mention, though, that His Roy- that is, Sir Matthew, has been feeling a little homesick lately. Perhaps if you could slip in an Abelian ballad or two?"

Chania made a face. "Ugh. The short ones are ten minutes long and everyone dies in them. Maybe.. *The March of the Wooden Men?*"

"Stompy Feet!" laughed Dorik. Chania rolled her eyes at him.

"Well... it's certainly a crowd-pleaser and it's... *about* Abelia," said Wilhelmina, doubtfully. The song they were discussing was about the Stickmen, the wooden automata that had replaced much of the Kingdom of Abelia's standing army, and had a simple march rhythm that the audience were encouraged to stamp along to. "But do you think reminding him of the plague that killed most of his homeland's population is the best idea?"

"The last time we played it he bought everyone in the Great Hall a drink," pointed out Chania.

"Good for morale, if nothing else," smiled the High Vigilant. "Still, maybe-"

Further discussion was cut short by the sound of a loud horn-blast which reverberated through the fortress. The watch had spotted something in the Expelled Territories that alarmed them, and were calling the Vigilants to action stations.

Without saying another word, Wilhelmina span on her heel and dashed for the stairs, her heavy silver armour encumbering her no more than a silk nightgown. Chania took a firm hold of Young Dorik's shoulders, and squatted down to look him in the eyes.

"Dorik, Mama has to go with Auntie Izzie. You go down to see Uncle Jals at the forge, all right?"

Dorik nodded at her, his face a mask of seriousness. "Yes Mama."

"Off you go, then,"

Young Dorik lumbered off, running with the exaggerated heaviness of a toddler. He was already turning into a large child, and Chania found herself hoping his deafness would disqualify him from taking the Seal of the Soldier. Putting such concerns out of her mind, she turned to follow Wilhelmina. The High Vigilant had always been reluctant to let the Bard watch the Vigilants in action, but Chania had pointed out, completely truthfully, that she needed to witness their heroic deeds in order to compose songs to celebrate them.

And, of course, to report them to The Boss.

2

By the time Chania arrived, slightly winded, at the upper battlement of the fortress, her Seal being of no help where physical exertion was concerned, both Wilhelmina and Sir Matthew were already there. As always, the Abelian Ambassador was accompanied by his ambulatory armour, which the Vigilants referred to as The Butler. The duty Sentry was just concluding his report, and the man looked more than a little flustered.

"So you saw nothing threatening at all?" snapped Wilhelmina. "No Expelled warriors, no Dragons, nothing?"

Chania thought Isla was being a little unfair about the Dragons. Antorathes, one that was known to roost in the mountains north of the Vigil, had recently awoken from slumber and had been seen so frequently that the watch would be unlikely to raise the alarm even if they had seen her. The exception had come almost two weeks ago, when the creature had alighted on a mountain that had dominated the eastern skyline for as long as anyone could remember and seemingly caused it to at least partially collapse. There were whispers that Magister Thalia Daran, who had passed through the Vigil shortly before that with Amanda Devereux and a small retinue, was somehow involved.

Sir Matthew, his finely-groomed moustache as impeccable as always, spoke up. "Come now, High Vigilant. Your sentries are experienced and capable men and women. If something caused Davin here concern, it is only right that he should raise the alarm- I had rather ascend the stairs a hundred times for no reason than fail to once when I should have."

"I-" began the Sentry, before a shout from behind him caused him to whirl. "There he is again!"

The figure was well into the forest which stood at the extreme of bow range from the Vigil, and at such a distance all Chania could see was that they seemed to be wearing white. The Sentries, of course, could enhance their vision with their Seals even beyond what an Archer or most Magisters were capable of. For the rest,

8

there was a large telescoping spyglass, which Wilhelmina had swept up and was peering through.

"Hmm.." mused the High Vigilant. "Yes.. he's picking fruit. One unarmed man, picking kalaberries, khile and apples. Truly a dire threat to our security, well done, Sentry Davin."

The Sentry made an irritated face that Wilhelmina couldn't see with her eye screwed to the telescope lens. "Yes... but where did he come from? He doesn't look like any Expelled I've ever seen. Anyway it's too early in the season to be picking.."

Behind them, Sir Matthew, who had been squinting even worse than Chania, gave a grunt of annoyance. Clearly, though the Royal Knights of Abelia stood at least equal in status to Magisters, they were unable to use magic in the same way. A clumping sound, followed by a clang, heralded the approach of The Butler, which had moved to stand directly behind its master. With no command apparently being issued, the suit seemed to unfold as Sir Matthew stepped backwards, and in less than a second he was encased in the armour. A moment later a startled oath escaped from the closed helmet, given an odd, metallic timbre by the suit.

"Sacred blood of Thecla!"

"Sir Matthew?" said Wilhelmina, whirling. "What-"

If the armoured man heard her, he gave no sign of it. The Abelian braced his feet, and slammed both gauntleted palms together with a loud clang. Silver light blazed out from between his hands, and he slowly moved them apart again, the dazzling brilliance coalescing into a long, solid object. Once Chania had blinked her eyes back into function, she saw that he was now holding a massive, silver bow, some six feet in length.

Everyone stationed at the Eastern Vigil knew that once, before the Vigilants were established, the Expelled Territories had been blasted by the Foundation Wars. The aftermath of the conflict that led to the birth of the College had left the Territories populated only by the followers of the Warlocks who had fled in defeat, and over time the Expelled had allowed thick forest to cover much of their domain. When the threat from the savages had been deemed to great to ignore, the ancient fortress had been rebuilt and pressed into service, and the forest cut back as far as an Archer could shoot from the top of the battlements. Any Expelled warrior knew that in the forest, they were safe, whereas to leave it exposed them to deadly danger.

That knowledge, it was now evident, was no longer valid when Sir Matthew D'Honeur of Thecla was Gifted in residence at the fortress. An arrow of pure silver light sprang into being as he drew back the huge weapon, and before anyone could do any more than gape in shock the shot was released. It hurtled, neither arcing nor plunging, towards the white-clad figure and struck home with the force of a thunderbolt, not only smashing the target asunder but also shattering the tree behind him. The crack of detonation reached the ears of the stunned watchers a split-second later.

"Well," muttered Davin into the ensuing, shocked silence. "*He* thought it was important..."

"I must.. investigate the body, High Vigilant," announced Sir Matthew. "No-one else is to leave the Vigil by the East Gate until I return."

"Very good, Sir Matthew," replied Wilhelmina, a little stiffly. "I shall arrange an escort and-"

"NO-ONE ELSE IS TO LEAVE!" roared the Abelian, the blank face-plate of his armour flaring with light as he fixed its eyeless gaze on the woman. Even the High Vigilant, who had served in her post for twenty years and faced down an entire Incursion, took an involuntary step backwards.

"Y-Yes, Your Excellency," she replied. Without another word, Sir Matthew turned and strode off to the stairs, the bow dissolving into a swirling mass of light as he went.

"Runner," said Wilhelmina, once the tramping of the Abelian's armoured feet had faded to silence.

"Aye!" replied the duty messenger.

"See that the order is relayed. Once Sir Matthew leaves, we're locked down until his return. And have the Operators prepare the Messaging Crystal. Whatever else he said, that silver-plated lunatic didn't forbid me to tell the College what just happened."

"What... what *did* just happen, High Vigilant?" asked Davin, as the runner dashed off.

"Other than our fearless leader murdering an unarmed man in cold blood in neutral territory?" said Wilhelmina, mildly. "Sherenith do me with a silver tool if I know. But I'm going to do everything I can to find out."

They stood in silence for a while, watching as Sir Matthew, mounted on Nemesis, his massive, silver-armoured horse, rode out to the site of his kill. Mere moments after he dismounted, fire blazed as the ruined corpse was reduced to ashes.

"Not much material for one of your songs here, I'm afraid, Chania," said the High Vigilant, softly.

No, thought Chania. But plenty for her other work.

3

By the time Magister Thalia Daran came into sight of the huge stone bridge known as the Farspan, she was in an utterly foul temper. Almost two weeks previously, she had been forced to flee the collapse of the Mountain Halls, the ancient ruins of the city that had once been known as Xodan and then served as the capital of the Expelled. That she was in no small part responsible for their collapse had not helped the situation, though in fairness the destruction of the stronghold had been necessary to prevent an overwhelming invasion by the Celestial Harmony of Daxalai. Along with Sergeant Athas, Amanda Devereux, and inevitably, Delys Amaranth, who was increasingly becoming as inseparable from the Operative as her own shadow, they had first rescued Dokan, one of the Mighty Ones who led the Expelled, and then kept him as a potential hostage.

Bringing Mighty Dokan along had proved to be both a master-stroke, and a blunder of immense magnitude. On recovering his wits from exerting a dangerous amount of Aether during the battle at the Mountain Halls, the Expelled Warlock had been immensely grateful to Thalia for saving his life for a second time, and had once again promised to grant any boon that might be in his power. Just as she had done when Dokan had accidentally creased himself with a bullet from one of Amanda's guns, Thalia chose to use the boon to accomplish a greater goal rather than the immediate one. So rather than ask Dokan to help get her little party safely to Abelia, she instead requested that he explain to the other Free Tribes, as the Expelled called themselves, that their visitors from the Lily College had acted as they had to save the continent from invasion, rather than out of malice towards them. This was no easy task, for the Mountain Halls were the only major settlement the Expelled had and were used as the venue for the Moot of Kings- the exact sort of meeting that Dokan explained needed to be called for Thalia's goals to be met. Worse, the Mighty One insisted that the others of his kind would not be likely to believe his story unless Thalia herself were there to corroborate it.

It took an entire, tooth-gnashingly, hair-pullingly infuriating week to arrange the Moot at a temporary venue on the mountainside above what had once been the Mountain Halls. The Mighty Ones turned out to be every bit as prickly as senior Faculty Magisters about status, and the wrangling about which tribe's representative would be seated where, and how close they would be to the position of greatest honour, and where the position of greatest honour even was in the first place, had been interminable. The loss of Mighty Thror, who according to one of the serving girls had sacrificed himself to prevent the advance of the Daxalai, delayed things still further, since Thror had been the incumbent guardian of the Halls and would ordinarily have been placed in charge of the arrangements their destruction had necessitated. Overall, Thalia swore that if and when she finally got home, she would never complain about College politics again.

What made things worse was that, for the most part, only Thalia seemed concerned by the delay. Athas, though barely understanding anything that was going on, was content to stay by her side as her protector, and seemed to be rather enjoying the reputation he was building among the Expelled. They called him 'The Shield That Strikes' after his habit of employing his massive tower shield to bash in preference to his sword if at all possible. Whilst the big man's instinct was to subdue, rather than kill, the almost six foot tall steel and silver shield, propelled by his prodigious muscles, was an exceptionally dangerous weapon in its own right.

Devereux, for her part, was happy to observe. Occasionally she would mention to Thalia that Anneke Belus, the Vice-Chancellor, had sent yet another message through the crystal in the hilt of her sword demanding that Thalia and her party make for Abelia with all haste to report. Since the crystal could basically only be used to respond with simple pulses for 'yes' and 'no', the College's spymaster was probably climbing the walls with curiosity by now. Meanwhile Delys was a constant source of mischief, playfully teasing Athas and doing her best to unsettle the Expelled warriors without actually provoking violence. Since the Free Tribes did not use Seals, instead relying on mystic tattoos to control their power, all of them had some level of magical sensitivity and all could sense just how dangerous the little Swordmaster could be, if she wanted to. Oddly, though, Delys had struck up something of a rapport with the Second of the Tree-Searchers, a warrior of Dokan's own tribe who was one of the rare Expelled to be able to turn herself into a large wolf, and Thalia would often come across her fussing over the creature's fur. Or the woman's fur. The shape-shifting made things more than a little confusing.

Finally, the Moot convened, and despite all the complications went off surprisingly smoothly. The painstaking preparations proved not to be in vain, and apart from one minor incident involving a scuffle between a Tree-Searcher and a Blackblood, the latter being from a tribe renowned for their truculence, the matter was resolved without conflict. Thalia, still wearing the scandalously revealing outfit of leather straps that all Mighty Ones wore in the interests of fairness towards those not blessed with Aethersight (or, as the Expelled called it, The Third Eye) was recognised as an honorary member of that class, and explained enough about the operation of the Stepping Mirrors to satisfy them that the destruction of the Mountain Halls had been necessary. Further, it was agreed that the Guardians of the Halls, the tribe formerly responsible for the security of the stronghold, would now ensure that the curious or foolish did not dig around in the area in the hope of uncovering the portal stone the Daxalai had been using, or any other remains of the collapsed Halls.

With the business concluded, there were two further days of festivities to sit through, which Dokan hinted it would give grave offence for them to avoid. Fortunately, even though she chafed at the delay, Thalia at least found this part of the whole affair quite enjoyable. There was good food, freshly-roasted game and preserved fruit salvaged from the stores of the Halls, along with a concoction of fruit, honey and dried meat that Amanda declared to be similar to something called 'pemmican'. To go with the food was strong drink, though Thalia also brewed up the last of her tea, which several Mighty Ones sampled with solemn, and almost certainly insincere, appreciation.

There were songs and stories and numerous contests and tests of prowess. Athas, always reluctant to hurt anyone, passed up numerous invitations to wrestling or boxing contests- the latter especially causing Thalia to shoot him a sharp look in remembrance of the Miser's Fists incident- but finally agreed to arm-wrestle and take part in a lifting competition. He acquitted himself nobly in the former, though he was undone in the semi-final by poor technique, but walked away with the latter. This involved a race, in which the competitors had to carry as many of the watching spectators from one mark to another within a time limit as they could, and not only was Athas considerably stronger than most of his opponents, he seemed to attract a large number of attractive, young, and helpfully light women to his mark. Thalia was pleased to note that the big man at least kept his hands to himself as much as he was able whilst carrying them three at a time, one under each arm and another clinging gleefully to his neck.

Delys, finally let off the metaphorical leash, enjoyed herself immensely playing what the Free Tribes called the Circle Game. Twenty warriors surrounded one competitor in the middle of the circle, each with a number assigned to them and all armed with staves, whilst another called out numbers at random. Each warrior took the calling of their number as their cue to attack their target until the victim was struck, or struck a blow in return. The game was similar enough to the Dance of Eight Blades that formed the final challenge of Swordmaster training that Delys breezed through it like a child playing skip-rope.

Even Devereux found herself reluctantly roped in to the festivities. Though she declined any of the challenges thrown her way, protesting that despite her sword she was no duellist, she had to admit when pressed by Dokan that she had a unique capability unseen by almost all those present. After securing a supply of materials to make some lightweight training rounds for her two HP-50 automatics, she had several of the village children hurl handfuls of spoiled, bruised fruit into the air. Keeping her eyes closed and starting with both weapons holstered, she set the Hercules combat-support suite to use the fruit as targets for a point-defence calibration test, and the guns flashed into her hands, discharging fourteen rounds for fourteen perfect hits in under two seconds. Shrill screaming from the children caused the Operative to open her eyes in concern, only to find that the youngsters had been liberally drenched with the pulpy shrapnel of her handiwork.

That had brought the evening to a close, with several sticky, but awestruck, children trailing off with their parents for a late night scrub-down at the lake that had once served as the freshwater supply for the Mountain Halls. The next morning, after a late start brought on by tiredness for much of the party and a murderous hangover for Thalia, who had once again been misled by a fruity beverage's sweetness concealing the strength of its alcohol, they had finally set off for Abelia. In truth, with their status among the Free Tribes improved, returning directly to the Eastern Vigil would not have been out of the question, but according to Anneke's messages the College authorities had expended a significant amount of diplomatic effort arranging their passage through the Kingdom, and to then spurn the offer would have offended the Abelians at least as much as skipping out on the party would have the Expelled.

They were guided, or possibly escorted, most of the way by Second, in her wolf form. The Stone Paths which allowed the Expelled to move quickly around their domain seemed to have been largely unaffected by the fall of the Mountain Halls, and Second was as skilled as any at finding them, though only one stone lay in the direction in which they needed to go. That left them travelling the last sixty miles or so by mundane means, through some of the thickest forest Thalia had ever seen, which coupled with a throbbing head she had been too foolishly proud to ask any of the Mighty Ones to cure had left the young Magister firmly committed to a state of high dudgeon.

Second left them as they reached the edge of the forest. The great wolf slunk behind a tree, and Thalia felt the surge of Aether as the woman reverted to her human shape. Since the wolf form could not wear or easily carry clothes, even the simple leathers of the Expelled, she did not offer to step out of her concealment, but spoke from it.

"You are delivered, Mighty Thalia. Beyond these trees lies the Great Rent, and across it, the Farspan. Soon you shall once more be among the Deluded, with their silver armour and their silk robes. I do not envy you."

"Thank you for your assistance, Second of the Tree-Searchers. Please convey my thanks to Mighty Dokan as well." Thalia noticed Delys was trying to creep up to peek around the tree, and scowled at her.

"Your thanks will not be necessary. Mighty Dokan owed you a life-debt, and you asked only that he cause the truth to be known. There is much honour in such a path, Mighty Thalia. Know that you and your companions are welcome in our lands as members of the Free, but only you. Do not seek to bring other Deluded with you, unless they wish to buy their passage in blood."

"I understand," said Thalia, feeling another surge of Aether just as Delys slipped around the tree to find Second had returned to her wolf-shape. The little Swordmaster gaped in mock outrage, the limitations of College battlefield sign-language restricting her complaints to *bad dog!* Thalia wasn't even sure the Expelled could understand her, but Second's mouth fell open in a lupine approximation of a laugh before she loped off into the trees.

"Well," said Devereux. "Time to see if Sir Matthew's homeland is as weird as he made it sound. Not that everything else in this world of yours is exactly normal."

---

a n ominous sound echoed from the Impose board, though Magister Ollan's blushes were saved by the privacy spell that all private booths in the Senior Common Rooms featured as a matter of course. Arch-Chancellor Derelar Thane allowed himself a moment of satisfaction at the result of the timing of his news.

"A dead man's rattle, I think, Magister Ollan."

The older Magister looked at him as if he had just turned bright green. "You think I care about a game of Impose when you have just delivered news like *that?*"

"Perhaps not," admitted Derelar, "but I confess I took some small pleasure from seeing its effects."

Ollan sighed. "I suppose there's no chance that you were lying just to throw off my concentration? If so I would compliment your ingenuity, if not your integrity."

Derelar shook his head, slowly. "I am afraid not, Magister. The High Chirurgeon does not make such mistakes in her field of expertise- she would hardly be the Chair of Sherenith if she did. Moreover, I only asked her to compare the samples- the fact that both came from a Dragon was volunteered by her in the full expectation that I already knew it. I must confess that keeping the shock from showing on my face was no small feat."

"And you have known this now for... two weeks?"

"Indeed. I was, as you can understand, more than a little discomfited by Magister Gisela's revelation. I decided to allow myself ample time to process it before I shared it with anyone else. In that time I have also observed the Vice-Chancellor for any behaviour that might suggest she was aware of my enquiries. I have seen none."

Ollan still seemed unwilling to accept the facts. "You are sure- absolutely, completely sure- that both samples came from Anneke? I have called her many names in the past, spider, snake, harridan and vixen, but Dragon is one I had never considered."

"I am certain," said Derelar, firmly. "And given the source of the samples, were they *not* from the same... being... our situation would be even worse."

"Worse?"

"Indeed. For then we would be dealing with not one, but *two* concealed Dragons."

Ollan stared at him for a moment, and then chuckled. "Arch-Chancellor, did you or did you not just make a *joke?*"

"Your frivolity is clearly rubbing off on me," replied Derelar, completely deadpan.

"So," said Ollan, after taking a moment to take a bite of his meal. "What do you plan to do about it?"

"That is the pertinent question. Ordinarily, the discovery of such a.. politically inconvenient situation would see me place the matter in the hands of the head of my intelligence service. The implicit irony in this case aside, I think we can agree that that option is off the table."

"Magister Jarton?" suggested Ollan, referring to the Chair of Walanstahl, a post which traditionally took responsibility for the Imperial Service.

"He has agreed to take a more active part in such matters, yes," said Derelar. "But as you yourself have pointed out, he operates most effectively in the light, and this is a matter best kept in the darkest shadows. You know how poorly the man lies."

Ollan grimaced. "Aye. It is a sad fact of politics that simple truth is a sword often turned upon its own wielder. Jarton knows truth, and he knows swords, but he holds the former as over-tight as a novice Guard might the latter."

"Agreed. We might use him to gather information, but he cannot know the reason for it. For now, I believe we must learn more of this Dragon, specifically when she, or indeed it, began to impersonate the Vice-Chancellor."

"Impersonate? Ah, of course. There are enough living Magisters who remember Anneke as a Twig to confirm that she was born in the conventional manner," said Ollan. "Therefore you are suggesting that at some point, this Dragon... disposed of the original and replaced her. I wonder..."

Ollan trailed off. Derelar took a moment to sample his own meal, which today was venison hunted in Lydia Grove at some expense, before raising a questioning eyebrow. The older man grunted.

"Sorry, Arch-Chancellor, you caught me picking amaranth. You are aware of what Anneke did to.. my family?"

"I am aware of House Dane's officially unproven claims in the matter," said Derelar, carefully.

"Hmph. Well, I was just wondering which Anneke it was that did it."

"Would it matter?"

"Practically? Not particularly. To me? Indisputably."

"Well, in our investigations we may well discover- Thelen's breath!"

Ollan turned to look in the direction Derelar was staring in. On the threshold of the Senior Common Room, and advancing in some haste, was Vice-Chancellor Anneke Belus.

The Arch-Chancellor, for one of the very few times in his life, was thrown into a state of near-panic. A carefully-nurtured rumour that Ollan was helping him with a personal existential crisis brought on by his attendance at the Committal service for Magister Fredus Dane would explain the other man's presence, but he could not actually admit it publicly. Anneke would expect a face-saving lie, and her appearance was so utterly unexpected that he had not prepared one.

In the event, it proved unnecessary. Anneke hurried over to the booth, and stepped across the threshold of the privacy spell, which muted sound and blurred the vision of those looking from outside of it. She ignored Ollan utterly.

"Arch-Chancellor, you must come at once to the Messaging Chamber!"

Despite his surprise, Derelar rallied to the dignity of his office. "Vice-Chancellor, this intrusion-"

"Now, Derelar!" hissed Anneke. "It's the Dendaril!"

5

*D*erelar trailed behind Anneke, feeling for all the world like an errant Acolyte despite being senior to the Vice-Chancellor in both age and rank. *At least apparent age,* he mentally corrected. Not wanting to raise any undue alarm, they walked briskly, rather than running.

"Wilhelmina doesn't understand the full import of what she saw, Arch-Chancellor," said Anneke, quietly, "and given that she's reporting on the main Crystal I've made a point not to explain it to her. As far as she's concerned, she's simply making a complaint about the conduct of Sir Matthew."

"You are sure the report is correct?" asked Derelar, more to fill the silence than out of any expectation of a useful answer.

"My own sources have confirmed it. Nonetheless, I thought you should hear it first-hand."

Almost half an hour later, having heard the High Vigilant's report, Derelar sat at his desk, an untouched coffee in front of him. Though his every instinct had screamed at him to do so, he had not bothered to ask the woman to keep her news secret- the Vigilants were officially neutral, acting only to protect the Empire from threats from the east, and that neutrality had been preserved throughout the War of Rule. Even if he had given such an order, there would be no way of seeing it obeyed unless a suitable Magister could be dispatched to relieve Sir Matthew.

The post of Gifted in Residence at the Eastern Vigil was an unusual one. Since joining the Vigilants led to an amnesty for all but the most heinous of crimes, some renegade Magisters had taken the post in the past, but for most, the idea of spending the rest of their lives in the middle of nowhere was abhorrent. It was more usual for the Gifted, who took responsibility for all matters of magic at the Vigil, to be a temporary posting, and whilst it was occasionally used as a convenient way to get rid of a troublesome Magister for a while no House would suggest one for the post who was not capable. For an Abelian to serve in the manner Sir Matthew currently did was unusual, but not unprecedented.

Derelar only wished the man had been somewhat more subtle in dealing with the threat.

There was a discreet tap at the door, and Anneke opened it to admit Gisela Dar. A brief thrill of anticipation washed over Derelar as she walked past the Vice-Chancellor, whose blood she had so recently examined, but the High Chirurgeon gave no sign of recognition other than what would usually be expected.

"Welcome, High Chirurgeon," said Derelar. "Please, sit down."

"Arch-Chancellor, I really must protest," said Gisela. "I have several borderline critical cases in the Infirmary and leaving at such short notice is-"

"Sit down, Gisela," said Anneke, gently. "If you don't, you'll wish you had."

The High Chirurgeon blanched, and flashed a quick glare at Anneke, unsure whether she had just been threatened, warned, or both. Nonetheless, seeing the looks on the faces of the two most senior Magisters in the College, she did as she was bid.

"Now, Magister Gisela, please tell us all you can about the Dendaril Shrive-Tick and the Hegemony," said Derelar.

Gisela went pale. "What? Why? What has-"

"In good time, High Chirurgeon. Please."

"V-Very well, Arch-Chancellor. The Dendaril Shrive-Tick is a small creature, no more than a Demisemital in length, or slightly smaller than the common fruit-fly. They were first documented as being discovered in the area of the Eastern Empire now known as the Shriven Marshes, which lie to the east of what we now call the Expelled Territories, and are mentioned in passing in the Book of Sherenith. Before the rise of Thelen, they were considered to be a mere parasitic pest that infested the large wading beasts that dwelt in the Marshes. At that time, the nomadic tribes that existed as little more than slaves to the Dragons roved over the entire continent, and the land to the farthest east, beyond the Whitepeak Mountains, was known as Den-Dar."

"*Land of the people*, in ancient Yotan," put in Anneke, absently.

"Er, quite," said Gisela, non-committally. Derelar glanced at Anneke, who didn't seem to have noticed she'd said anything unusual. "Anyway, the tribes east of the Whitepeaks were uninvolved in the wars against the Dragons. Those native to that part of the world appear to have slept through the war, though in light of what happened later there may be another explanation for that. After the death of Thelen, magic-users began to appear amongst the tribes of Den-Dar and a city bearing the same name was founded on the south-western coast. Trade and diplomatic contact was established with what was then the Southern Empire, as well as with other nearby powers, the tribes of Jandalla, and even the Har'ii and Daxalai."

Derelar nodded. Most of this was well covered in the official histories, but he had not specified that Gisela start in the middle of the story. It was what was coming next that he was most interested in.

"By the time of the foundation of the College, after the Expelled Territories and Abelia had split away from the Old Empire, the Dendaril Hegemony had expanded to fill much of what had been called Den-Dar. Diplomatic contact was firmly established, and the northern city of Hyphan continued trade with Mernas even as Abellan and the other Abelian ports did with Dendar itself. Then, one day in 11C.C., all communication from the Dendaril abruptly cut off. There was no warning that anything was wrong, and ships sent on the usual trade routes reported that everyone seemed to be fine.. except none of them were quite the same any more."

Derelar finally remembered his coffee, and took a calming sip.

"The traders were quite unable to get the Dendaril to honour any of their existing agreements, and most left empty-handed, swearing never to return. One crew of Toskans, however, refused to take no for an answer and, in the manner of their people, raided Hyphan, carrying off a significant amount of gold and silver as well as several young men and women for use as.. slaves. Their Captain, recorded by history only as Karik The Bastard, laired on an island some way to the east of what we now call the Toskan Coalition, and fortunately for everyone was famously antisocial. It was some weeks before anyone realised that Karik's crew, in their turn, had suddenly gone silent and broken off all their usual contacts. At this point Magister Keshalina Thule, who was the first Chair of Aurantus due to her trading acumen, took a personal interest in the situation and led a Seminar to Karik's lair."

"I've always wondered how Keshalina knew where those pirates were based," said Anneke. "I suppose even in those days, trade was as dirty a profession as spy-craft."

"Regardless of exactly how the Merchant Queen found Karik and his men, history does not record what happened at their lair, other than that when the Seminar left, they burned the place to ashes behind them. They brought back a single survivor, one of the kidnapped women, who they kept in strict quarantine. Instead of returning to Lore, Keshalina had the woman and her Seminar unloaded at Highpoint, ordering the workers building the lighthouse there to evacuate. What they had discovered was that the girl, along with every one of Karik's crew, was host to a single Shrive-Tick, which had burrowed into her brain through her ear. The result was extraordinary."

"The creature controls the host body?" said Derelar. He had read old reports, but the archaic language had been vague on the details.

"Not.. exactly, Arch-Chancellor," said Gisela. "Rather, the Tick fuses with the brain of the host, in effect slightly expanding it. It becomes an inextricable part of the host, leading to the creation of an entirely new personality. This new being has none of the memories of their previous life, though they do seem to retain much of their skills and knowledge. Worse than the effective death of the original person, however, is the role the new one plays in the life-cycle of the Shrive-Tick. Once mature, the Tick begins to secrete larvae, which make their way into the stomach and... reproductive organs of the host. The former simply embeds itself into the stomach lining, where it matures and then begins to secrete more larvae, whilst the latter ensure that any sexual contact with the host will lead to the larvae infecting the partner, whereupon they move from the sexual organs to the stomach and brain. By the time the parasites in the stomach begin to reproduce, the Tick in the brain is usually indistinguishable from the original tissue."

Gisela's voice had faded to a near croak, and Anneke brought her the carafes of water and wine from the sideboard, along with a glass. After a moment's consideration, the High Chirurgeon went with the wine. She took a decorous sip to moisten her lips, and continued.

"As Keshalina and her Magisters eventually discovered, very nearly too late, the life-span of a Dendaril host is distinctly limited. The gestation cycle of the parasite varies from victim to victim, but usually some forty years after infection the stomach of the host becomes grossly swollen with live Ticks. By this time the host is usually unable either to move or even eat, but will spend their time in a permanent state of euphoria. Eventually they die, at which point a swarm of fresh Ticks, usually numbering in the hundreds, emerges. Indeed, the death of any host who has been infected for more than a day will result in at least some newborn Ticks being discharged, so quickly do they multiply."

"Which is why any and all contact with the Dendaril is strictly forbidden," noted Derelar. "What measures have proven effective in preventing infection?"

"Quarantine is obviously the simplest, Arch-Chancellor. Not being physically anywhere near a Shrive-Tick remains the most certain way to avoid infestation. Armour is largely ineffective unless completely sealed since the Ticks are so small-that of the Scholastic Guards and the Abelian Royal Knights is thought to be proof against them. Most shielding spells, including Gandel's Ward, are similarly ineffective since the Ticks do not seem to present a threat to the magic."

"What about something like the flame-wreath of Ixilinath?" asked Anneke. "That surrounds the caster in a sphere of living fire. Admittedly it's hard on the carpets."

Gisela nodded. "That would work, yes. Any spell that actively destroys the Ticks as they cross the threshold is viable so long as it is maintained long enough. Unfortunately the insects have an instinctive fear of destructive magic, and will tend to simply remain at bay until the caster runs out of Aether."

"Surely the parasite, by its very nature, cannot live for long outside of a host?" asked Derelar, hopefully.

"That is not entirely true, Arch-Chancellor," said Gisela. "Though the modern Shrive-Tick has evolved considerably from the simple creatures that live in the Shriven Marsh, it is still capable of feeding on lower life-forms for extended periods. Even those as small as a mouse can sustain several Ticks for some time. Oddly, though, such creatures are immune to the mind-altering effects of the Tick infection, and the Ticks cannot reproduce in such hosts. Once they begin to feed on a lower animal, they are effectively inert."

"So Aether is the key, then," mused Derelar.

"That is the conclusion of those in the Infirmary who have studied the condition, yes, Arch-Chancellor. No less a High Chirurgeon than Gandel himself met with some success in counteracting the infestation in the early stages by draining the would-be host of Aether altogether or physically removing the symbiont."

"I would have thought that obtaining more test subjects would violate the Oath of Sherenith," said Anneke, with a thin smile.

"Gandel wrote it," pointed out Gisela. "I think he always considered it to be more of a philosophy than a rigid rule."

Derelar finished the coffee, and set the cup down with a click. "So, we have established that direct contact with the Dendaril is most undesirable. High Chirurgeon, Vice-Chancellor, have you any reason to suspect that spreading the parasite is something that they actively attempt?"

"Other than...?" said Anneke, raising an eyebrow.

"Other than that, yes."

"Other than what? Arch-Chancellor, what in the name of Sherenith has happened?" snapped Gisela. "I refuse to simply blunder in the dark with only half of the puzzle agai- ah, er, against my, er, better judgement."

Though Derelar showed no outside reaction, for the second time that day he was seized by extreme alarm. In her irritation, Gisela had nearly said *again*, a clear reference to the delicate task she had recently completed for him. He decided the High Chirurgeon needed all of the facts before a further slip was provoked.

"Magister Gisela, today the College received a most disturbing report from High Vigilant Wilhelmina at the Eastern Vigil. Earlier today, the watch at the fortress reported seeing a single, apparently unarmed, white-robed man picking fruit on the edge of the Expelled Territories. We cannot yet be exactly sure why, but when Sir Matthew D'Honeur, the Abelian Ambassador who is currently serving as Gifted in residence, saw the man, he killed him almost immediately with one of the magical bows some Royal Knights can summon."

"I would dearly like to get hold of one of those suits of armour," mused Anneke. "So would half the College, at that. It's a pain that as soon as the suit's master is killed the damn things discorporate themselves."

"Quite," said Derelar. "Having made his kill, Sir Matthew forbade any of the Vigilants to leave before riding to the corpse and immediately burning it to ashes."

Gisela had turned pale. "The white robes.. a caste of Dendaril society is believed to wear simple white cotton robes. They call them Pilgrims. It's mostly unsubstantiated rumour, of course, but they seem to be involved in some sort of coming-of-age ceremony. What would clinch it is if the robes bore the design of an open hand. It was the traditional sign of the Dendaril, signifying friendship."

"*Kara'sla retik tän, heril linfa tôl,*" murmured Anneke. "My hand is open, as is my heart."

"The High Vigilant reports seeing what looked like a hand-print on the robes." said Derelar, after a pause.

"Thelen's breath!" gasped Gisela, gulping back the rest of the wine in one go. "Arch-Chancellor, to answer your question, the Dendaril Hegemony covers an area slightly larger than our Empire and Abelia combined, though much of the interior is uninhabited desert. They have never seemed to be interested in expansion before, and in general the new personality created by the Ticks is usually fairly docile. Gandel used convicted murderers as some of his test subjects and reported a marked reduction in their aggression once they were exposed to the parasite."

"That could simply be due to the loss of the memories of whatever turned them into murderers in the first place," pointed out Anneke.

"True, the age-old nature versus nurture debate," agreed Gisela. "Almost seven centuries old, in this case. Nonetheless, Gandel noted a reduction not only in violent tendencies, but also in reaction to violent stimuli in his tests, unless the parasites themselves were threatened."

"So, it is your opinion that this.. Pilgrim was not a scout for a larger Dendaril force?" said Derelar.

"Truly? I don't know if the Dendaril even understand such a concept, Arch-Chancellor. The Hegemony certainly maintains some sort of army to protect their cities from roving beasts and the like, but I've never heard of them undertaking any sort of military campaign."

"Then perhaps we worry unduly," said Derelar. "Sir Matthew dealt handily with this Pilgrim, and there is no reason to suspect that he will fail to do so again if necessary."

"With respect, Arch-Chancellor, I think you are missing the true threat," said Gisela, looking if anything even more worried. "The Pilgrim had already travelled across the entirety of the Expelled Territories. He could potentially have passed Ticks on to any number of them. Should hosts approach the Vigil in great numbers, slaying them will not help matters. It appears Sir Matthew was able to destroy the corpse of this Pilgrim before any further Ticks could be released, but should, say, a hundred approach the Vigil potentially several thousand of them might be spawned on their deaths. If even a handful make it into the fortress undetected..."

Derelar nodded. "I understand, High Chirurgeon. What I do not yet comprehend is what precipitated this event in the first place."

"Blood, ice and fire!" hissed Anneke, suddenly. "I can hazard a guess, Arch-Chancellor. Thalia Daran and Amanda Devereux. We know that they were involved in the destruction of Xodan, which stood at the heart of the Expelled Territories. I suspect that has caused some sort of shift in the balance of power in those lands, and the Dendaril have moved into the gap."

"Amanda Devereux does seem to have been at the centre of many.. remarkable events since her arrival in our world," said Derelar.

"And then some!" snapped Anneke. "The fall of Manadar, including the destruction of half the Eighth Volume and the deaths of an entire Seminar. The subsequent escape of the Red Witch from self-annihilation, the weakening of the Worldshell to the extent that the Daxalai were able to attempt to invade via the Third Mirror, and now this! That woman is a veritable mother of calamities!"

"She did also have a hand in resolving most of those crises," pointed out Derelar. "Including saving my own life, and then helping stop the invasion she had inadvertently facilitated."

"And I suppose she's going to save us all again this time as well?" said Anneke, still clearly annoyed.

"Actually," replied Derelar, "I think it quite possible that she might."

6

The Farspan proved to be every bit as awe-inspiring as Thalia had made it sound. As they emerged from the trees, the Magister remembering just before they did so that she could finally change back into her robes, Devereux studied it. Not for the first time, the Hercules suite took one look at the construction and objected violently to the fact of its existence.

The massive chasm that the stone bridge crossed, which was known only as The Rent, was almost twenty miles across at the widest point. The bridge-builders had clearly decided that to be too much of a challenge, and had instead chosen a spot where the canyon was only some ten miles wide. They had then, as far as the visual evidence went, simply laid a single continuous slab of solid rock across it and built a bridge on top of that. Over the entire length of the huge construction there was no sign of any sort of support, arch or cable. There was, in short, no way whatsoever according to the laws of architecture, or for that matter physics, that the thing should be standing, and Daniel was making a point of saying so.

"That's... some bridge," said the Operative, slowly. There were bigger ones where she came from, of course, but they were rarely approached on foot and none displayed such blatant disdain for the properties of their materials.

"It's a bit vulgar," sniffed Thalia. "A pretty classic example of pre-College design. No subtlety, just materials browbeaten into doing what the builder wills by the application of sheer, albeit magical, brute-force."

"Like the Royal Keep?" said Athas, with a slight shudder. Thalia grimaced.

"In part, Sergeant. Later buildings were at least designed to be able to stand up on their own, but structures like this, or the Royal Keep, were meant as a statement. The Rent itself is believed to be the result of some sort of disaster that occurred during the Great War, when Thelen defeated the Dragons, and it stands on a site of some magical potency. Whoever built the Farspan tapped that power and channelled it into the structure- and not gently."

"Whoever built it?" said Devereux, as they approached the bridge. "Doesn't anyone know?"

"As with any great achievement of antiquity, there are competing claims," said Thalia, pausing just before stepping onto the bridge. Her eyes took on the unfocused look that told anyone who knew what to watch for that she was using her Aethersight. "In this case, several factions are eager to *avoid* responsibility. For one thing, the Weavers are adamant that Walanstahl, with his keen eye for structure, would have had nothing to do with something as.. brutal as this. Some historians still give him credit, or maybe blame, whilst others say that one of the Warlocks who fled the Southern Empire before it became Abelia created it. It's safe, by the way, the magic is still strong."

"Didn't you trust it?" asked Devereux, mischievously.

"With our recent history with ancient, magical structures? Not as far as I could throw Athas."

"You could probably throw him some distance with your magic," pointed out the Operative.

"Yes, I could. And accordingly, since it still has *its* magic," said Thalia, banging the stonework with her staff, "I trust the bridge."

Delys laughed and hopped up onto the wall of the bridge, seemingly uncaring of the drop of several hundred feet that yawned below. For a moment, Devereux's heart leapt into her mouth, but the wall was some five feet thick and flat at the top, and it would probably be more dangerous to try to get the little daredevil off it than to leave her up there. Here and there the space was decorated with grim-looking statues of ancient heroes, which Delys accorded absolutely no respect whatsoever.

So far did the bridge span that it was almost an hour and a half before their pace brought the far end into view on the horizon. Devereux zoomed her eyesight in to look to the other side. "Looks like there's a welcoming committee."

"I hope they haven't been waiting too long," said the Magister, sourly.

"From the looks of it, I doubt they'd care," said Devereux. What she could see awaiting them in the distance didn't appear to be capable of having any emotions at all. They looked a lot like The Butler, Sir Matthew's ambulatory armour, but they were taller, almost ten feet according to the Hercules suite. There were eight of them in all, standing at regular intervals across the entire width of the bridge, huge, heavy, silver figures that looked to her a lot like the toy war-robots that children had collected before nano-manufacturing made the idea of physical collectibles largely obsolete. Each bore a massive tower-shield on its left arm that made Athas' seem small by comparison, whilst the right ended in an ominous-looking double-headed weapon that boasted an axe-blade and a hammer.

"War Golems," breathed Thalia, taking a look herself. "An entire Demolition of the things."

"A what?"

"A Demolition. The standard battlefield unit of War or Siege Golems, eight strong. The Abelians don't usually deploy them in that strength except in full-scale war."

Athas shifted his shield on his arm, and glanced at Thalia nervously. "Learned Magister, should we be worried?"

"I *am* worried," admitted Thalia. "Not that they're going to attack us- you see the two towers on either side of the far end of the bridge? Each of them mounts a heavy siege crossbow that covers the span and fires an enchanted bolt. If the Abelians wanted us dead, we'd be dead by now. No, what worries me is that with those towers, and the gate between them which they can close at the far end, someone thought it was necessary to also deploy that Demolition."

Without consciously discussing it, they began to walk a little faster.

"They're configured in anti-personnel mode," mused Thalia. "See the weapon-arm? The axe-heads are rotated into striking position. If the Golems are being used against fortifications, they rotate the 'wrist' to bring the hammer forward."

"I doubt it'd make that much difference which bit they hit you with," said Devereux, sourly. The Hercules suite was running some impact-damage simulations based on the assumed strength and weight of the constructs and was distinctly pessimistic about the ability of her armouring to withstand even a single blow from one of the Golems. A dedicated military cyborg or autonomous drone-tank would probably be able to deal with one, but the Office existed in no small part to stop such things ever being deployed, not to use them itself. She shuddered inwardly at the memory of the one time she had encountered an 'Agamemnon'.

They drew closer, and Thalia's eyes narrowed. "Amanda.. you have ways of seeing through stone, do you not? Can you tell if either tower is manned?"

"Can't you?" asked Devereux, switching to thermal and scanning the towers at maximum zoom.

"Think of it as me asking for a second opinion."

"The short answers are yes, and no," replied Devereux. "I can see heat signatures through a fair distance of most materials, depending on their insulating properties, and I'm getting nothing but background heat from those towers. It's a pretty warm day, though, and if the stonework's thick enough it might be masking it."

"It *is* getting warm," agreed Athas. "My canteen's empty."

Delys whistled, and tossed her own canteen down to the big man. "Wow, still almost half-full! Thanks, Del."

Thalia sighed, and pushed a sweaty lock of hair out of her eyes. "I must admit, I'm beginning to regret putting this robe back on. Say what you will about the propriety of Expelled fashions, but they certainly lend themselves to the local climate. Anyway, to return to the matter at hand, Amanda, I'm not seeing any signs of life either."

"Are we worried now?" asked Athas, offering the canteen to the two women, who both declined before he passed it back up to Delys.

"I was worried before," said Thalia. "Now I'm very concerned indeed."

26

7

*I*t was well into the afternoon by the time they came into shouting range of the towers. Thalia tried calling out to the garrison a couple of times, the second time amplifying her voice with her magic to such an extent that Devereux could feel the vibrations in the air, but no response came. The Golems still made no hostile move, though their eyeless heads steadily turned to track the little party as they advanced.

"Should we... do anything?" asked Athas, nervously, as they approached the line of Golems. Delys, who had finally jumped down to join them, shrugged, and flicked a quick sign. *Not for us.*

"What do you mean, Del?" said the big man, his brow furrowing.

"Del seems to have a good sense for danger," said Devereux, watching as the Swordmaster sauntered past the constructs. "If she says they're not here for us, I think she's probably right." The heads on the silver giants kept tracking the Swordmaster until she passed them, before swinging back to face the rest of the party.

"They'd have done something by now if they were," agreed Thalia. "When a War Golem goes into action its Aether swells massively. These ones are merely idling at the moment. Wait.. do you hear that?"

Devereux did. From the road ahead came the sound of marching feet. From the sound of it, their step was almost completely perfect but a slight Doppler effect allowed the Hercules suite to identify sixty-four separate individuals. As the column came into view, the Operative's first thought was that she was looking at a unit of College Guards. The silver-plated armour was much the same, though the helmets bore extravagant plumes of something that looked like peacock feathers, and each warrior bore a large halberd very similar to those used by the First Volume of the Guard, who were stationed at Lore. What was wearing the armour, though, was a far cry from anything she had seen there.

It looked, to her eye, as if someone had taken a tailor's dummy, or perhaps a pose-able mannequin that some traditionally-minded artists still used, and dressed it up as a soldier. Each of the figures stood exactly six feet tall, and was made entirely of solid wood, cunningly carved with articulated joints that allowed them the full range of movement of any living human.

"The Stickmen," said Thalia. "Or Wood Golems, to give them the technical name that almost no-one uses. Probably the greatest achievement of the Abelian Artificers to date." ·

"Not those things?" asked Devereux, tilting her head back towards the larger constructs.

"Them? Though we're still not sure how the Abelians power them, the War Golems are simple enough creations. The shield is fused to the arm, and the weapon built in to the wrist. The College even has a few similar constructs, though a Magister is needed to control and power each one, much as Mighty Thror did the Eternals at Xodan. No, the Stickmen are far more impressive- able to move as fluidly as a living human, perform manual labour or march to war as the situation demands, mostly without direct control."

"Well, these ones don't look like they're here to till a field. They're looking for a fight," said Athas.

"I'm not so sure," said Devereux. "Look at what the ones at the back are carrying."

Before the big man could see what she meant, the block of wooden men slammed to a halt. The blank head of the automaton in the centre of the front rank lit up with silver light, and an incongruous feminine voice emanated from it.

"Magister Thalia and party, on behalf of Her Exceptional Majesty, Queen Tondarin II, I bid you welcome to the Kingdom of Abelia. I apologise for the manner of your reception, but since you left civilised lands there have been some significant developments. Please, you must be weary from long travel. I bid you ascend, and this Assemblage will convey you to Naxxiamor, where I will endeavour to offer you more fitting hospitality."

"Ascend?" said Athas, puzzled. "Oh!"

The exclamation was brought on by the rear ranks of the formation of Stickmen raising up their burdens, which proved to be thick, sturdy planks of wood. Other members of the unit were carrying chairs, and within moments the Golems had assembled a palanquin that they carried on their shoulders, expertly-designed interlocking joins creating a solid platform on which the four seats were placed. Finally, another Stickman placed a ladder at the side of the construction.

"I think I just got another candidate for my weirdest experience since I came to this world," murmured Devereux as they climbed.

"The Abelians have been like this for a while," said Thalia. "Ever since the Stickmen became commonplace, they've treated every situation as a reason to employ them, just as a carpenter who only has a hammer sees every problem as a nail."

"Can they.. hear us?" whispered Athas, settling gingerly into his seat.

"Of course," said Thalia. "They won't act on anything we say or do unless whoever's controlling them wills it, though. But we should certainly assume that anything that happens around them will get back to the Abelians one way or another."

With everyone seated, though in Athas' case his chair was a somewhat uncomfortably tight fit, the Stickmen wheeled in perfect formation, and set off back down the road by which they had come. The ride was surprisingly level and smooth, and despite her initial misgivings Devereux found herself quite enjoying the unconventional journey.

Something about all of this was still bothering her, though. She just couldn't quite tell what it was.

8

The Symposium was perhaps not quite as full as the last time Derelar had convened it over the enigmatic warning the Blue Council had delivered at Mernas, but enough of the Senior Faculty were present to show that they were taking the rumours from the Eastern Vigil seriously. The entire High Seminar were in attendance, even Anneke, though the Chair of Amaran remained vacant. That was something the Arch-Chancellor was going to have to deal with soon- the representative of Amaran was known as the Voice of the Voiceless, and was supposed to provide an important balance to College discussions. Already demagogues were whispering that the Chair was vacant because it was inconvenient. It was just typical of recent times that Magister Thalia, who Derelar favoured for the post, had been delayed in returning to Lore and might even be delayed further by the results of this meeting.

After order had been called by the traditional striking of the Senior Faculty's staffs on the floor, the Arch-Chancellor spoke. "My friends, and fellow Magisters. As you will have seen in the agenda, I have called this meeting in light of recent events at the Eastern Vigil. You will have heard, and it is true, that His Excellency Sir Matthew D'Honeur of Thecla, the Abelian Ambassador who is currently serving as Gifted in Residence at the Vigil, was witnessed killing an apparently unarmed and unthreatening man by the High Vigilant. Certain elements in the press and civil society are already seeking to turn this news into a tool with which to whip up new hostility against the Abelians, or even against the College itself. What you will not have heard from most sources is that we strongly suspect that the man Sir Matthew slew was a Dendaril Pilgrim. I will now invite the Chair of Sherenith to explain to us what that might mean."

A muttering of alarm rippled through the chamber as Gisela stood. On the huge Seminary Desk in front of her stood a cloth-covered object, though she did not initially refer to it. Clearly, at least some Senior Faculty were well aware of what the Arch-Chancellor's words implied. Swiftly, and as dispassionately as possible, the High Chirurgeon ran through the history and anthropology of the Dendaril as she had for Derelar and Anneke previously. With that done, she turned to the Arch-Chancellor.

"With your permission, Arch-Chancellor, I would like to ask Magister Ollan to assist me in a demonstrative experiment."

Derelar's eyebrows shot up, but he nodded. As Ollan, looking no more informed about what was going on than anyone else, descended the steps to the chamber floor, two of Gisela's Healers set up her demonstration. One placed a tall, wrought-silver stand on the floor some distance away from the Seminary Desk, on which he placed an apple. The other removed the cover from the object on the table, which turned out to contain a large number of winged insects. Several of the Senior Faculty uttered startled oaths and Derelar sensed more than one of the Chairs casting personal shielding spells. To his right, Magister Jakob, the Chair of Yar, half-rose to his feet before catching himself. The veteran strategist, one of the few members of House Adaran to remain loyal to the College, had always been a bit paranoid.

"It is quite safe, I assure you," said Gisela, casting a reassuring look at Ollan who had stopped dead in his tracks. "This sample jar was created by High Chirurgeon Gandel himself to study the Shrive-Ticks and has been used as part of the research into them for seven centuries. These Ticks are part of a small colony that the Menagerie has maintained without incident for that entire time."

Derelar didn't sense anyone lowering their shields, but he didn't cast his own. It would not do to be seen to distrust the High Chirurgeon. Of course, there was also the fact that she'd already explained that they wouldn't help.

"Now," said Gisela, motioning Ollan to stand a little way away from the fruit. "I should first clarify that since this colony of Ticks has been separate from the Dendaril for countless generations, it is quite possible that those in the Hegemony have evolved very differently with access to human hosts. That said, they seem to behave much as what reports we have been able to gather indicate the modern Dendaril symbionts do. You will observe that, at the moment, they are showing little interest in their surroundings. Now, if we bring the apple close enough that they can see it..."

The Healer in charge of the apple pushed the stand closer to the jar. When it had almost reached the Seminary Desk, the insects began to mass on the side of the vessel closest to the fruit.

"Obviously, the Tick primarily finds food by smell, as do most insects, but they recognise the fruit by sight nonetheless. If we move the apple away again..." the Healer did so, "they rapidly lose interest. Observe, however, what happens if we replace the apple with a particularly fine, Aetherically-ripened khile-fruit."

Once the food had been swapped, the insects seemed able to sense it from far further away, which the Healer demonstrated by moving it around the chamber.

"As you can see, food which is rich in Aether is particularly attractive to the Ticks, and they can sense that Aether from a considerable distance even from within a warded container." The Healer replaced the stand in its original position.

"Was there actually something you wanted me to do, High Chirurgeon?" asked Ollan, mildly. "Or am I here merely to demonstrate the creatures' marked lack of interest in elderly pipe-smokers?"

"Your time has, come, Magister Ollan," said Gisela with a small smile. "I would like you, in your inimitable style, to destroy the khile-fruit. Please, do not damage anything else."

"I shall be the very model of precision, albeit in a state of some confusion," replied Ollan. Turning to face the target, he raised his right hand palm-outwards, staff clutched firmly in the left, chanting softly. A chilling mist surrounded the khile-fruit, freezing it solid, before Ollan abruptly clenched his fist, shattering it. The instant he did so, the Shrive-Ticks darted to the far side of the jar with such force that the vessel moved a short way across the desk.

"How was that?" asked the elderly Magister. "I was tempted to merely eat it, but I imagine that wasn't quite what you had in mind."

"You did exactly what was required, Magister Ollan," replied Gisela. "As you can see, Magisters, the Shrive-Ticks were unconcerned by the initial manifestation of Magister Ollan's power, as well as by the theatrics which invariably accompany it." A chuckle went around the Symposium as Ollan gaped in mock outrage. The old man's habit of dressing up his magic in largely perfunctory gestures was well known, though he and several other Senior Faculty maintained that it aided focus. "As soon as the Magister released that power in a destructive manner, however, the Shrive-Ticks attempted to escape from its vicinity."

Magister Jakob flipped his hand out in front of him and conjured a small ball of flame in it. As the rest of the Chairs watched, he sent it floating towards the jar, moving it around and watching the Ticks react by huddling on the opposite side. With a grunt of satisfaction, he closed his hand and snuffed the flame out.

"A decent idea, Jakob, but I think flawed," said Elinda Daran, the newly-appointed Chair of Light. "After all, most insects instinctively fear fire. I wonder..."

She cast a similar spell, but created only a harmless ball of light. This, the Ticks seemed to completely ignore.

"As the Chairs are now most helpfully demonstrating," said Gisela, her tone once again completely unreadable, "The Ticks react to Aether in three ways. If it is contained in a potential food source or host, they move towards it. If it is bound into a destructive spell, they move away from it, and if it is being put to a harmless purpose, they ignore it. They are, for example, completely ignoring the power of Lore's Waycrystal despite our proximity to it."

Elinda tapped her staff on the floor gently to be recognised. She was still young for a Chair, only just over thirty, but had served as an assistant to the late Magister Tomas for some time and was noted as a talented researcher. Anneke had suggested, not subtly, to Derelar that her admittedly stunning looks, framed by long hair that she had magically coloured midnight blue, had not hurt her chances of getting the House Patriarch's attention.

"High Chirurgeon, I think there may be a flaw in your experiment as well. From what you have told us, the Shrive-Ticks are driven to infect human hosts, and as a rich food source as well as fonts of considerable Aether a Symposium-full of Magisters should be as appealing to them as a banquet to a starving army, and yet these little soldiers seem almost insultingly disinterested in us."

Gisela nodded. "Indeed, Magister Elinda. Our initial experiments confirmed it. My theory is that, since in the early days of the breeding programme any Ticks that escaped containment and approached a Magister attempting to infect them were immediately incinerated or otherwise destroyed, this colony has lost the instinct to infest magic-users- it has been bred out of them. The same seems to apply to our Healers. However, whenever Guards or other Sealed personnel approach them they become extremely excitable."

"Then they can not only sense Aether, but also tell whether the Seal of the victim might allow them to defend themselves," mused Elinda. "A Healer would obviously be able to at the very least destroy the symbiont before it could fully infest them. Intriguing."

"Pah!" snorted Jakob. "It would seem that the 'threat' from these creatures is largely imagined. If they're so frightened of destructive magic that they won't go anywhere near it, all we need do is move a few Petard Engines up to the Vigil. The spectacle of one of those charging to fire should send them skittering all the way to the Black Coast. I move that we recall Ambassador Sir Matthew to Lore to explain himself, and assign Kandira Dar to replace him at the Vigil to oversee the installation of a battery of Engines. We were planning to do it anyway. Do I have a second?"

"For your analysis? No," said Elinda. "But for your precautions, aye."

"If I might make an addendum," put in Magister Jarton, the Chair of Walanstahl, "I would make it clear in the order that Sir Matthew is not to leave until Kandira arrives. I doubt that he would storm back here prematurely in a fit of pique, but the stakes are too high to risk leaving the Vigil without a Gifted."

Jakob nodded his assent, but before Derelar could put the matter to a vote, Ollan spoke up. "Learned Magisters, at the risk of over-complicating matters, I would propose a further amendment. Magister Kandira is well known for her skill at siege-craft, but the Sixth are still a volume under reformation. The Vigilants, similarly, might baulk at the suggestion that striking down apparently harmless Dendaril might be necessary, as indeed Wilhelmina has. There is, however, a Magister available who not only has more relevant experience, but also commands a veteran Volume that is proven in this distasteful task."

"Thelen's balls, Ollan!" snapped Jakob. "You cannot seriously be suggesting-"

"He is, and he's right," said Anneke, quietly. "Magister Haran and the Wardens should be assigned this duty. The Second Volume is almost the perfect tool for the task."

"Yes," said Ollan, staring at the Vice-Chancellor with narrowed eyes. "They are, aren't they? How very convenient."

"Magister Jakob?" said Derelar. "It is your motion. Will you have Magister Ollan's amendment applied to it, or should we hold an opposed vote?"

The Chair of Yar ground his teeth angrily. "I.. I wish your reasoning were less sound, Learned Magisters. Too much has been placed on the shoulders of the Wardens already. Yar's tits, Ollan, Haran is your friend!"

"Yes, he is," agreed Ollan with a sad smile. "But he is also the man best suited to this task, and were he here, he would concur, much though it would grieve him. These times do not choose who they call with compassion, Learned Magister, but with the cold logic of war. You, of all people, should know that."

"Aye, that I do," said Jakob, sadly. "Arch-Chancellor, I do not oppose the amendment, but let the record show that the appointment is not made without regard to the pain it will cause."

Derelar nodded, and put the matter to the Symposium. A room-full of lit staffs signalled the motion passed.

Tapping his own staff on the floor and receiving the Arch-Chancellor's nod of recognition, Ollan spoke up. "These are fine measures for the short term, my Learned Friends, but they do not begin to address the scale of the problem. Magister Jarton, if you will humour me, what is the estimate for the population of the Dendaril Hegemony?"

Jarton looked confused for a moment, and Anneke leaned over and whispered something to him. "Ah.. we believe something in the region of fifty million, Magister Ollan. The territory is vast- it would be more than that but for the deserts."

"Indeed," agreed Ollan. "And High Chirurgeon, one host which is allowed to reach the end of the natural life-cycle releases roughly how many Shrive-Ticks?"

"It varies, but for an average, well-nourished man of six feet, several hundred."

A fresh ripple of alarm went around the room.

"I would suggest that merely holding them at the Vigil is unlikely to be enough," said Ollan, quietly. "If even a few manage to skirt the fortress and make it through the mountains..."

"He's right," put in Anneke, suddenly, agreeing with Ollan for the second time in a day. Derelar almost fell over with shock. "You must not underestimate the danger these things pose, Magisters. If we allow them to overrun the Expelled and mass up against the Vigil, with the amount of exploitable food in the Territories we could lose the entire Empire in a generation. They must be stopped before they leave their own territory in any numbers, and then we need to either deter them permanently, or.." she clenched her fist, "exterminate them."

"That would entail killing tens of millions of people, Vice-Chancellor," pointed out Gisela. "No method has yet been found to remove a mature symbiont without killing the host, and we must remember that the bonded pair is a living, thinking and largely non-aggressive being."

"Thelen's breath," hissed Elinda. "And there we thought the task we were assigning *Haran* was distasteful."

"Well, however we stop them, we can't use the Volumes," said Jakob. "I doubt that even the best Archer can keep those things at bay for long in the open field and even with Singers supporting them any Magisters trying to protect them would be drained long before the tide of these things abated, if your numbers are right."

"We need the Abelians," said Derelar, firmly.

"Blood, ice and fire!" snapped Jakob. "Those preening idiots? What use are a few high-blooded morons on oversized horses going to be?"

"He means their automata, Jakob," sighed Elinda.

"I- ah," murmured the Chair of Yar. "My apologies, Arch-Chancellor. I lost several friends in the last Abelian War and I dismissed your suggestion too lightly. It could work- certainly the Stickmen would be immune to infestation..?" he tailed off, looking from Elinda to Gisela for confirmation. They looked at each other, and then nodded to him. "As I thought. So, assuming they had the numbers, and assuming the Expelled at least stay out of their way and have the sense to avoid the Dendaril- neither of which is something I can comfortably assert, mark you- then the Abelians could potentially drive at least the human hosts back as far as the Whitepeaks. This all assumes that those blue-blooded bastards will co-operate, of course."

"We will discuss the matter with Sir Matthew," said Derelar. "And our own Ambassador in Abelia-"

"Ah, about that," put in Stalis Thule, the Chair of Mendarant, a thin, nervous-looking man who bore responsibility for foreign policy. "I was going to bring this up later, but events have forced my hand. Apparently our representative in Abellan was recently implicated in a plot to assassinate Queen Tondarin. He was acting in concert with the Daxalai Ambassador there, of all things. Fortunately the Abelians have accepted my reassurances that the College had nothing to do with it, and in fact the evidence points to a Daxalai faction, but at the moment our Embassy there is without a representative."

"As I was about to say, our Ambassador in Abelia is not available, so we will need the assistance of Magister Thalia," finished Derelar. "Hopefully her recent experience with the Expelled will aid her in securing their cooperation as well."

"This is potentially very advantageous, Arch-Chancellor," said Stalis. "An endeavour of this importance, undertaken by the Abelians, the Expelled and the College, could be the first step on the path to reunification of the Old Empire!"

"Or we could just let the damn things in and 'unite' the entire continent.." muttered Anneke, darkly.

9

The journey to Naxxiamor took a little over an hour, though the Stickmen covered almost fifteen miles in that time. It was hard to see from the platform exactly how they were moving, but from the sound of it they were practically running, albeit in such perfect step that the ride was completely smooth. After a while Athas, complaining that his chair was too tight a fit, stood up to stretch his muscles, and, finding that he could balance, stayed that way.

The countryside they travelled through looked much like that of the Empire to the north, but with a crucial difference. Whereas most of the land claimed by the College was put to use in some form of agriculture or industry, from the grain fields and cattle meadows of Sommerlan to the pig-farming country of Verge, the lands of the Abelians seemed far less cultivated. Of course, the area near the Farspan was very much on the fringes of civilisation, but even within sight of the Wake of Manadar there had been small farmsteads, horse and cattle ranches and orchards though many had been destroyed in the war. Here, there were simply trees and meadows, though on closer inspection some seemed to bear the marks of agriculture at some time in the past.

As they approached the town, the land did begin to show signs of farming, the wilderness giving way to neatly-arranged fields. Even here, though, much of the land seemed to be lying fallow, as if the farmer had decided to use medieval crop-rotation methods. Stranger still, there was barely a human being to be seen, with the work in the fields being done by yet more Stickmen overseen by a single foreman. These few people, who seemed too richly-dressed and well-fed to be common farmers, eyed the passing Assemblage and its charges with ill-disguised curiosity.

Devereux stared out at the latest farm, its crop of vegetables being tended by five of the wooden constructs. "I'd heard it from Sir Matthew, but I didn't really believe it. There're really this few of them left?"

Thalia grimaced. "Of the lower classes, yes. There are many who claim that the

Winnowing Ague, tragedy that it was, gave the Abelians an exceptional advantage. Of course that wouldn't be true without the Stickmen, but with them they have farmers who neither need to eat, nor to be paid, and builders who never sleep. Without millions of mouths to feed, they can afford to export almost everything they make and grow. At the same time, of course, they're terribly vulnerable to any further disease- if another plague came along that swept through the Royal Knights the nation would probably cease to exist."

"When my world fully embraced automation it initially caused a lot of problems," said Devereux. "Suddenly low-skilled workers weren't valuable any more, and as the AI and robotics-" Thalia looked confused "sorry, my world's version of these things- got more advanced even the skilled ones started to worry. In our case, it turned out that the automation freed people up to invent new jobs no-one even realised could exist, but even then some people got left behind."

"Not a problem here," said Thalia, sourly. "The only people left behind were shrivelled corpses. I've even heard a few Magisters mutter in private that we could do with our own outbreak of the Ague."

"What do you think?" asked Devereux.

"I think I'd be all for it if it only took blabbering fools who said that sort of thing," said Thalia, firmly. "You'd think the Howling Plague would have taught them a lesson. Anyway, I doubt even the Royal Knights really like the situation- it's put a lot more power in the hands of their Wizards and anyway, what fun is there in being rich and powerful if you have no commoners to show off to?"

"Sir Matthew would probably agree on that point," said Devereux with a smile.

The town they were drawing into was almost ridiculously pretty, like a painting on the side of an extremely expensive box of Swiss chocolates. Houses, each one looking freshly-painted and with a picturesque thatched roof, stood arranged in neat rows, faint smoke drifting from their chimneys. The town square, surrounded by municipal buildings, was dominated by a life-sized bronze statue that depicted an armoured Royal Knight driving his sword through the breast of a tall, severe-looking woman in robes surmounted by armour that was sculpted to resemble bones. From her posture, and the damage the sculptor had added to the Knight's equipment, his victim hadn't gone down easily.

"It's called *The Fall of the Skull-Queen,* by Delatorio," said a voice which Devereux didn't need the Hercules suite's confirmation to know was that of the person who had spoken to them through the Stickmen. This time, however, it was coming from a robust-looking woman in a blue satin gown who had emerged from the largest building. "I've always thought it was a little... overly literal, but I appreciate that Delatorio at least allowed Naxxia to have got a few good strikes in."

The armoured man at her side snorted. "A few good strikes? She killed most of a regiment and six out of seven of the Knights pursuing her before they finally took her down." The speaker, from the look of his armour, was clearly another Royal Knight, though he carried his helmet tucked under his arm. It struck Devereux that he rather resembled Sir Matthew in his features.

"Good for her, I'm inclined to say," sniffed the woman, tossing her long, black hair. "Especially since most of the pursuing Knights were Orsinios and there're altogether too many of them *now,* let alone then. Most appalling table manners, for one thing."

"Queen's grace, it's no wonder women are trying to get more involved in the military these days," muttered the man. "After all, you've certainly never mastered diplomacy."

"Are we interrupting something?" said Thalia. "Would you prefer that we return to the Expelled Territories for another week and come back when you're less busy?"

"I apologise, Magister Thalia," trilled the woman, as the Stickmen placed the steps for Thalia's party to descend. "I am Alizabeth Iliana D'Honeur, and this is my husband, Sir Jeremiah. On behalf of Her Most Exceptional Majesty, Queen Tondarin II, I welcome you to the Kingdom of Abelia." She executed an elegant curtsy.

"To the arse-end of it, at least," said Sir Jeremiah, bowing.

"Er, thank you," said Thalia, a little taken aback by the rapid switching between formality and familiarity.

"You must excuse our behaviour, Learned Magister," said Alizabeth. "It is so rare to have the opportunity to talk to someone who isn't either a scraping commoner or a fellow nobleman that one's manners are more than a little rusty."

"Not that commoners are all that common in this day and age," put in her husband.

"Are you members of the same House as Sir Matthew?" asked Devereux. Seeing Thalia wince, she shrugged. "What?"

"You must be Amanda Devereux," said Sir Jeremiah. "Wally's letter said you were a little uneducated in these matters."

"I'm.. wait, Wally?"

Alizabeth laughed. "He always calls his brother that. It's one of those childhood things that they absolutely refuse to explain."

"The Great Families aren't like the Houses, Amanda," explained Thalia, with a brittle smile. "If you have the name, it means you're either blood or you married into blood. Now, Lady Alizabeth, whilst I thank you for your hospitality I would very much like to be on my way as soon as possible. I must return to Lore and attend to pressing matters there."

The two Abelians exchanged a worried glance. "You- you mean you haven't heard?" said Sir Jeremiah.

Thalia's patience snapped. Devereux had noticed her jaw working with suppressed fury for much of the trip, and it seemed these two bickering nobles had pushed her over the edge.

"No, I have not fucking heard! I have been living in a forest for over two weeks with a pack of sweaty savages who dress in leather straps and turn into Thelen-fucking dogs! I nearly had an ancient fortress dropped on me for the second time in less than a month and the one time I managed to have a decent bath I was prac-tically groped by a pair of naked women before solving a set of nonsensical riddles for the privilege of nearly getting myself damn well killed! So no, whatever it is you two in-bred, aristocratic imbeciles think I should have heard, I have not fucking heard it!"

The two Abelians gaped at her for a moment. Athas cast a nervous glance around the square, but the few liveried Abelian servants were studiously ignoring their betters.

"Wally was right about her temper, too," said Sir Jeremiah, with every indica-tion of approval. "Damned refreshing!"

Alizebeth gave him a weary look. "I apologise again, Learned Magister. I'm afraid for a gentleman of Jeremiah's lineage being shouted at by an angry woman is rather water off a duck's back. I do hope you found the experience cathartic, though. As for what you haven't heard, the College was supposed to have informed you- a situation has developed that means you will be staying in Abelia for a while."

"This smells of Anneke," growled Devereux. "It'd be just like her to get her own back by not sending the message when she was supposed to."

Thalia sighed, and her shoulders drooped. "I suppose you have a Messaging Crystal I can use?"

"Of course!" said Alizebeth. "Oh, but first, there was another thing. Jeremiah!"

"Hmm?"

"The present!"

"What present?"

"From Wally, you tin-plated nincompoop!"

"Oh, that present. Drat it all, I left it in Abraxes' saddlebag. A moment, Lady Thalia."

The Knight hurried off, and despite the comical scene Devereux was struck again by how easily he moved in armour that made Athas' look like light mail. Alizebeth gave the fuming Thalia a somewhat nervous smile.

"He really is a thoroughly decent man, and very solid on the battlefield. Bit solid between the ears, too, unfortunately, but the Families haven't really bred for brains until recently."

"You're a Wizard!" gasped Athas, suddenly.

"Well done, dear!" said the Abelian, with exactly the same blank smile Devereux had seen Anneke turn on her staff. "Yes, it's only in the last few generations that a mere spell-flinger like myself could even *dream* of marrying into the Great Families, but we're making up for lost time- and speaking of which, the conquering hero returns!"

Sir Jeremiah had come back, bearing a small, but exquisitely carved, wooden box. He solemnly presented it to Thalia, and bowed deeply. "I, Sir Jeremiah D'Honeur of Thecla, present this gift to the daughter of the esteemed Talion Mountainbreaker on behalf of my brother, Wal- Sir Matthew D'Honeur."

"Oh good, a box," said Thalia. "I'm sure that will come in very handy."

"Er, perhaps it's what's *inside* the box that-" began Athas. Thalia turned a stare on him that was one mote of Aether short of killing him on the spot.

"Yes, *thank* you, Sergeant," she said finally, through gritted teeth. Nevertheless, she opened the box, and a moment later let out a gasp of happy shock. "Daxalai tea!"

"My brother informs me that this is no ordinary Daxalai tea," said Sir Jeremiah. "The tea we usually obtain is considered inferior by the Daxalai, according to Wally, but this is from a shipment confiscated from the recently-executed Daxalai Ambassador. It is called *Shan-Sho-Cha*, or Tea of the Heavens."

Thalia breathed deeply. "I-I can tell. This is a very thoughtful- wait, you said 'recently-executed'?" She closed the box, carefully.

Alizebeth nodded. "Yes, and then your own Ambassador a few days ago. The Daxalai tried to have Queen Tondarin assassinated, and it turned out your own man was also implicated. Don't worry, though, there's every sign it was something the two of them cooked up between them, the diplomatic repercussions have been fairly minor. It *is* part of the reason why you'll be staying a while, though, but you should probably get the rest from the horse's mouth."

"Whole thing was the source of some amusement at Court, truth be told," chuckled Sir Jeremiah. "The assassin tried to knife Queen Tondarin during the day's Audience, and the fool didn't realise her corset is armoured. She backhanded him across the room, stepped into her armour, and then she and the Guardian broke every bone in his body in alphabetical order. It was reckoned to be the best sport since Sir Anthony of Aquila tried to get away with sending his armour to a tourney without bothering to get out of bed to put it on and got shanked by a disgruntled servant halfway through the melee." He roared with laughter.

"I'm guessing you had to be there," said Devereux.

"He certainly should have been," said Alizabeth. "Now, Learned Magister, I already have a pot of my own portion of Wally's gift brewing, and then we shall see about that Messaging Crystal."

10

Second of the Tree-Searchers loped through the dense forest, keeping to the Stone Path and maintaining a speed no real animal could have matched over any distance. On her coat, the Stalking Wolf glittered, accompanied by the Dashing Elk and Defiant Boar. Each tattoo was in its own way directly responsible for her speed- the Wolf by granting her a more suitable form for running, the Elk by lending her its swiftness, and the Boar with its endurance. Few of the Free could manage to use three tattoos at once, and only a First would be able to control four.

It wasn't just speed that had led Second to stay in the wolf-shape for the journey back to the rest of the Tree-Searchers. A significant detail was the fact that she had left her clothes with the tribe, for although none of the Free considered nudity to be any great shame it was less than practical for forest-running. More importantly, the wolf's keen senses made finding the faint trail of the Stone Path considerably easier- not just by the flow of Spirit, which those who were not Mighty Ones could usually perceive only dimly, but by the scent of those who had used it before. It was possible, with some concentration, to use the Stalking Wolf to gain much of the animal's perception without taking its shape, but the form held so many other advantages that few who bore the rare tattoo bothered to learn the trick.

Yes, the senses of the wolf were the reason she still wore its shape, but then there was the.. other thing. A slender, lithe other thing with the most incredibly long, blonde hair and the instincts of an alpha predator. Whilst she held the animal's form such things were less distracting, for the wolf largely regarded procreation as a necessary duty to continue the species and little else. Overall, it had been easier, and less confusing, to stay in that shape around the Silent Blade than to be human and read a challenging invitation in every glance that quickened her heart and flushed her skin. In any case, to try to take things further would be forbidden for one who was yet unbound and did not know her own True Name,

41

not to mention that the Silent Blade was claimed by Steel Heart, she who carried fire at her hips. Or perhaps Silent Blade had claimed her. In either case, that bond was as clear to woman as to wolf, albeit for different reasons.

It suddenly struck Second that perhaps her own relationship had been the reason why Steel Heart had reacted so badly when Mighty Dokan had explained the rules of Joining to Mighty Thalia and her party. Among the free tribes, her bond with Silent Blade would have led to exile at best for one of them, or death at worst. But then, the Deluded shared their True Names freely and seemed not to care for the ancient rules of the Mighty Ones. Such a thing seemed incredible to Second, for was it not the purpose of life to continue and create new life to follow it, as the Free Tribes had been taught for generations? Did not all other creatures learn each other's true nature only through Joining? Other than Dragons, she thought, sourly, but the trees knew that Dragons were arrogant aberrations who had more in common with rocks than with anything that truly lived.

All through her distracted musings the instincts and agility of the wolf-shape had kept her on the Stone Path, leaping nimbly over tree roots and ducking smoothly below low branches, but suddenly something changed. Her snout wrinkled, and without conscious thought she switched from loping run to slinking prowl, belly low to the ground to both lower her profile and conceal the dim glow of the tattoos on her body from searching eyes. An alien scent assailed her nostrils- there was dung, which was nothing to be ashamed of though most self-respecting creatures would clean it off, but also something else. A salty tang, but lacking the coppery notes of blood and the sweetness of fresh man-sweat, and another, almost sickly-sweet aroma. Now her ears pricked up, and brought the sound of something moving through the forest, not exactly towards her but in her general direction. Something big and heavy, not man, nor wolf or bear. The wolf-body wanted to run, its instincts prizing self-preservation over knowledge, but the woman-mind knew better. Whatever this thing was, it was something that should not be here, and the Mighty Ones must know of it, what form it took and what threat, if any, it posed.

She crept forward, keeping to the thickest undergrowth and moving to stay downwind of the prey, if prey it was. If it proved to be a predator, then such precautions would be even more important. Perhaps in her human shape her heart might have been hammering, but the wolf knew what to do, her ears flattening against her skull and her breathing slowing to become nearly imperceptible. And then she saw it. The beast lumbered through the trees, shouldering all but the largest out of the way. It stood a little over five feet tall and was at least three times as long, with short, heavy-looking legs, and was almost completely hairless. Its massive gut was horribly bloated and distended, dragging on the ground, but its thick skin seemed uninjured. The huge head swung from side to side as the beast plodded on with deceptive speed, the mouth lolling open to reveal yellow, rotted teeth and a swollen, leathery tongue.

Second had never seen such a thing before, but her hackles rose. The words of one of Mighty Dokan's songs echoed in her mind:

"And in that place did the Golden One fall,
and in that place did the little ones rise.
Brackish womb of salt-water, a cradle of brine,
for those that grew fat on the flesh of the Great Waders.
When the Golden One rose again, and journeyed home to sleep,
rode with it the little ones, and from them was born
the Woe of a people.

Woe that writhed and bred and grew,
in the heart of the mountain until it was strong.
Woe that to the Free shall come,
should the Great Waders venture beyond their salt-water homes,
for where those that came before will go,
those who came after will follow."

No Tree-Searcher had ever seen a Great Wader, which the Mighty Ones said lived in the Shriven Marshes where the Free Tribes were forbidden to go, but from everything Second had heard she was looking at one right now. She wondered, briefly, if she should try to bring the thing down, but the wolf's teeth, though sharp, were not made for hide that thick and her spear slept in her tent. No, this prey would not fall to her today.

"Woe that to the Free shall come should the Great Waders venture beyond.." the last few lines ran through her head again. She had seen enough to know that the Mighty Ones must be warned. Even as she formed the thought, events took a horrifying turn. Abruptly, the huge beast stopped dead, though there was no sign it had reached anywhere particularly significant. A strange, low, roaring moan issued from its mouth as it slowly sank to its knees, and then subsided onto its side with a crash that shook the forest and bounced Second's paws off the ground. And then the thing's belly burst. Blood, guts and bile sprayed into the air, the vital fluids smelling both foul and appetising to the wolf's nose, but it was not that which set her scrabbling to flee full-tilt into the forest with the full consent of the woman who dwelt within. For from the crimson ruin that had been the beast's stomach, even as its limbs quivered in a gross parody of ecstasy, came a dark swarm of fat, noisome flies.

11

The Broken Skull was, for the most part, a fairly typical inn. A large, open-plan main room took up the majority of the lower floor, with a kitchen area behind the bar and privies out the back, whilst a sturdy wooden staircase led up to the rooms for guests. In most respects, it could have been the Bunch of Fives at Iken, the X on the Spot at Ratheram's Cross, or any of the other similar establishments Devereux had seen since her arrival in this strange world. Even the somewhat gruesome-sounding name was no more than a reference to the defeat of the ancient Warlock, Naxxia the Skull-Queen, a story on which much of the town's culture was founded. Before the Winnowing Ague, the place had probably been something of a tourist trap.

There were, however, two things that set the Broken Skull apart from all the other taverns the Operative had seen, and they did not take Level Ten training to spot. They were, in short, the staff and what passed for the customers. Behind the bar, a Stickman stood polishing glasses, which in and of itself was not greatly disconcerting to a woman who came from a world in which entire hotels and restaurants were run by robots and automated systems, though the rich still preferred old-fashioned human attendants. Far more incomprehensible was the fact that many of the tables were also occupied by the wooden golems.

Sir Jeremiah, who had taken charge of the rest of the party whilst Thalia used the Messaging Crystal in the local guard house, saw the Operative's confusion. "I confess, Lady Devereux, that this aspect of Homomancy is one I, too, find disquieting."

"Homomancy?"

"The art of turning an inert, human-shaped construct into a Golem possessing the ability to move under its own power," supplied Sir Jeremiah. "As I understand it- and I should warn you, as a man of war my knowledge of such things is greatly limited- though the Stickmen do not suffer fatigue as such, they do gradually exhaust their Spirit- what the Thelenics call Aether. Accordingly, they must rest when not working much as human beings do."

"Yes... but in an inn?" said Athas, slightly wild-eyed.

"The buildings were already here and suitable for the purpose, so it was simpler to have the Stickmen use them rather than create new facilities," said Sir Jeremiah. "You saw the houses? Each of them resides in one, maintaining it and keeping it ready for the day when the numbers of the living reach the point when they are needed again."

"So, what, there's another of those things back there cooking food? Robot- I mean, Golem shopkeepers?" said Devereux.

"Not as such," said the Royal Knight. "The High Wizards have never success- fully taught a Stickman to cook, and they cannot speak unless a Gifted speaks through them. Empty shops are maintained by one, and in the larger cities, human merchants oversee trade. The bartender here does pull a fair pint of Naxxia's Blood, however, since that is a largely mechanical task."

As if to illustrate the point, a Stickman arrived at their table with several tankards of a thick, reddish ale. Athas sniffed at his doubtfully.

"Fear not, Sergeant. The colour comes from a peculiarity of the ingredients and the roasting process, there's no actual blood in it," said the Knight. Athas gave a weak smile, and took an experimental pull. "At least, not any more," finished Sir Jeremiah.

"So, how.. many of these things are there?" asked Devereux, looking around slowly. A worrying thought was forming in her mind.

"Oh, millions by now," said Sir Jeremiah with a dismissive wave of his hand. "Don't worry, though, I know what you're thinking and it can't happen."

"What's she thinking?" asked Athas, who was well into the ale by now. "This stuff's pretty good, by the way."

"I'm thinking that with that many Stickmen that don't need to eat and can't get sick, the Abelians are building a pretty terrifying army," said Devereux. "You don't need conscription, you don't need to pay them, you barely need any officers."

Sir Jeremiah nodded. "You do, however, need competence, and in that regard the Stickmen you see here are woefully lacking. Those which brought you here are dedicated warriors, true, but most are merely labourers. I'd say it was a matter of lack of training, but you can't even teach them to do anything new- once the High Wizards have created one, that's it."

"So it's more like programming," mused Devereux. "These don't have the right.. software to fight, and they're hard-coded so it can't be changed."

"Er.. as you say, my Lady," agreed Sir Jeremiah, showing no sign he'd under- stood a word she'd said.

"I'm not a Lady, you know," corrected the Operative, mildly.

"Forgive me, my Lady, but you are no servant or commoner, and to a Royal Knight there are only those, and nobility- unless you are suggesting that you are not, in fact, a *lady-*"

Delys laughed, and dinged the Royal Knight over the head. For a single, heart- freezing moment Devereux thought the little Swordmaster had just started the next Abelian war, but after a blink of surprise Sir Jeremiah laughed too. "Just so. Then please, forgive my reflexive formality but my Lady you shall remain. Though what I should call this little minx, I am unsure."

"Just call her Del," said Athas. "Everyone else does."

Before Devereux could point out the significant inaccuracies of Athas' claim, Sir Jeremiah stood up and gave a short bow of his head. "Very well, Sergeant. Lady Devereux, Lady Del, I must leave you for the moment. Please, enjoy the ale and the meal which will be brought out when Magister Thalia returns."

When Thalia did return, she was grey-faced. Plates of appetising-looking food followed soon after her, but the Magister didn't seem very interested in them.

"I don't like the look of that expression, Learned Magister," said Devereux. "What's up?"

"I.. have just been temporarily appointed the Imperial Ambassador to the Kingdom of Abelia," said Thalia, slowly.

"That's great, Learned Magister, congratulations!" said Athas, earnestly, before taking a large bite from a slice of beef.

"Notwithstanding my.. well known antipathy towards the Kingdom, Sergeant, it's more the reason for my appointment that worries me," said Thalia.

"The assassination attempt?" said Devereux. "I'd imagine that would make things a little awkward."

"Not that, no. The Abelians seem happy to blame that one on the Daxalai Ambassador and apparently everyone at court greatly enjoyed the spectacle of watching Queen Tondarin deal with it. Plans were already in place to select a new Ambassador but events have taken a more urgent turn. What do you know about the Dendaril Hegemony?"

"I remember you mentioned them in passing as the only force that might be able to stop the Daxalai if they got out of the Mountain Halls. Dokan called them the 'Fly Lords' and he didn't seem very enthusiastic about it," replied Devereux, as Athas shrugged.

"And with good reason," said Thalia, taking a very small sip from a steaming cup of tea with hands that shook slightly. "Most Magisters know only that the Hegemony occupies the eastern part of this continent beyond the Whitepeak Mountains, and that they broke off all contact with the outside world centuries ago, shortly after the Foundation Wars. I've just been told rather more of the story."

She took a few minutes to relay the High Chirurgeon's information about the Dendaril and the Shrive-Ticks. The Arch-Chancellor had managed to trim it down to a fairly short summary, but each word landed like the footfall of a War Golem.

"That's why there were no people at the bridge!" breathed Athas. Thalia nodded.

"Yes, Sergeant. Sir Matthew would have reported what he saw to his own people and they took steps. The War Golems and Stickmen are immune to the Shrive-Ticks, so they could hold that bridge against significant numbers of Dendaril. The towers are manned by Stickmen as well."

"Yes, but surely these... Ticks could just fly across the Rent from anywhere?" pointed out Devereux. "I mean, if they're basically just flies."

"According to Magister Gisela, the life-span of a Shrive-Tick outside of a host is little more than a day, and she suspects the evolved form that breeds in the Hegemony might live for an even shorter time than that. They fly little faster than the average person moves at a brisk walk." said Thalia. "Given that it took us several hours to cross by a good bridge at one of the thinnest points, the Ticks would be unlikely to survive as far as Naxxiamor. The Abelians might have to evacuate a few of the farm overseers, but that's about it."

"OK, so the Abelians can hold these Dendaril off," said Devereux. "Where does that leave us?"

"The big problem is the Expelled Territories," replied Thalia. "If the Ticks infect them, within a generation there could be millions of them swarming around that forest. They could overrun the Vigil with ease. The College is planning to use Petard Engines to try to keep them at bay, given their instinctive fear of offensive magic, but if the hosts get around through the mountains then- oh, great Thelen!"

"What?" said Devereux, as Thalia gently set down her cup and took her head in her hands.

"Their fear of offensive magic! This is our fault. Specifically mine, but you and I both had a hand in it. We can blame the Daxalai too, I suppose, for all the good that will do us."

"I.. don't follow," said Devereux, truthfully.

"Remember Xodan? How we collapsed it to stop the invasion?"

"I'm hardly likely to forget, even without a computer-assisted memory," pointed out the Operative. "I can tell you every word everyone said whilst we were there, if you like."

"This is something you wouldn't know, unless Magister Fredus realised it and told you," said Thalia, shaking her head. "Xodan was created both to be Thelen's capital, and as a base for his war against the Dragons. To that end, not only did it have the magic that allowed it to fly, it also had potent defensive spells."

"You mean a shield, like the one at Manadar?" said Athas, who had cleared his plate and was eyeing Thalia's hungrily. "Er, are you going to....?"

The Magister sighed, and pushed the food over to him. "Be my guest, Sergeant. You're right, Xodan did have a shielding spell, though nothing as efficient or effective as the modern version that protected Manadar. But more importantly, it had offensive magic, designed to be used to repel the Dragons if they ever attacked the city, as they did in the final battle of the war. When I was using the crystal to try to destroy Xodan, I found several potent weapon-constructs, nothing complicated, merely simple crystal-augmented thaumaturgic annihilators, but even after two millennia they were still charged to fire. The power that Thelen and the Patrons must have poured into that place, and it was still very nearly not enough!"

"Okay, you're losing me now," said Devereux. "So a thaumaturgic annihilator is what, a magical weapons system?"

"A very simple and inefficient precursor of the Petard Engine, yes," said Thalia. "But Amanda, do you not see what this means?"

"Walk me through it," said the Operative, though she was beginning to get a vague idea of where the Magister was going with this.

"There were several very powerful offensive spells primed to fire, in the middle of the Territories, since before the Foundation Wars," said Thalia. "In that time, no Shrive-Tick or its host ever moved west of the Shriven Marshes. We destroy Xodan- with very good reason, I'll grant you- and two weeks later a Dendaril turns up at the Vigil. Tell me you think that's a coincidence."

"Oh no," said Athas, quietly, through a mouthful of bread.

"Shit," said Devereux. *"I knew an old woman who swallowed a fly..."*

"What?"

"Sorry, a very old kids' song from back home," said Devereux. "It's about trying to solve problems and just ending up creating worse ones."

"Then it is fairly apt for our circumstances, I think," said Thalia. "If we ever return to the Vigil, you should teach it to the musicians there."

"Funnily enough it was one of the first things we were taught, those of us who were trained from childhood," said Devereux. "It was drummed into us from the start not to improvise, to stick to the plan for an operation unless it was completely impossible, because even though our own ideas might look better to us we never had the full picture and our actions might have unintended consequences." *And I've done a superb job of proving that right,* she thought, bitterly.

"Anyway, the point is that the Symposium believes that simply sitting in a defensive posture isn't going to be enough," said Thalia. "They want to move into the Territories and stop the Dendaril getting a foothold, and they want the Abelians to use their constructs to do it."

"Wait, sorry, I'm confused," said Athas. "We only just persuaded the Expelled that we weren't all that bad and got made honorary Free Tribesmen and all that, and now the College wants us to get the Abelians to invade them? Isn't that going to, well, start a war?"

"It certainly could," sighed Thalia. "Which is why the Arch-Chancellor has appointed me as the new Ambassador. They want me to go to Abellan to liaise with Queen Tondarin and her War Council on how best to conduct the campaign without antagonising the Expelled. Meanwhile, the College and the High Wizards are going to be trying to work out how to repel the Dendaril without us having to potentially kill millions of them, assuming we even could."

"Er, Learned Magister, I hate to mention this..." said Athas, miserably. "But... didn't your father drop a mountain on Queen Tondarin's father and her brother? And isn't the anniversary of that coming up in a few weeks?"

Thalia nodded, her jaw tight. "Yes, he did, and it is. And in return, the Abelians killed him, most likely on the orders of the new Queen. And yet, they have great respect for Talion Mountainbreaker, as they call him- you saw how Sir Matthew reacted when he found out who I was. The Arch-Chancellor is calculating that that, as well as my experience with the Expelled, will be enough to make the Queen listen to me. I.. have my doubts."

Devereux shook her head, slowly. Not in her wildest dreams, even allowing for the insanity of this world, had she imagined this scenario. An Ambassador who had excellent reasons to have a personal grudge against the ruler of the country she was supposed to be negotiating with- a grudge that may well be mutual. At least once again she would be trying to nip a war in the bud, the exact situation she was trained for. Of course, that would usually involve some back-up and a plan, neither of which she had at the moment. She glanced over to Delys, who had somehow managed to get one of the Stickmen out of its chair and was dancing with it, or at least around it, accompanied by a small band of musicians the D'Honeurs had brought with them. Some back-up then, maybe. Even though the tune didn't fit what she was hearing, she couldn't get the end of that old song out of her head.

"I knew an old woman who swallowed a fly,
I don't know why she swallowed the fly.
Perhaps she'll die?"

12

---

*B*y the time Derelar got back to the High Apartments after giving Magister Thalia her new orders- orders to which she had reacted with exactly as much trepidation as he had issued them with- Anneke was already waiting for him outside. As he strode down the hallway towards her, he took advantage of the excuse to study the Vice-Chancellor at length, looking for some sign, any sign, that she was anything other than the somewhat voluptuous, dark-haired woman some seven years his junior that she appeared to be. That youth, coupled with a power that was certainly in excess of that which her six Leaves suggested she should possess, was the only thing about her that seemed in any way unusual. That, and those oddly deep, violet eyes.

Of course he wasn't really sure what he would have expected to see if the Vice-Chancellor really were, as the evidence suggested, a disguised Dragon. It wasn't as if she was likely to be hiding a tail and scaly skin under her robes. Thelen knew, enough people had seen her out of them if half of the stories about her appetites were to be believed. There was, however, one other thing- Anneke tended, at times, to know things that even someone in her position seemingly should not. Names like the Yotan, a people so ancient that Derelar had had to search the appendix of the oldest history book in his personal library to find so much as a footnote about them. And yet not only did the Vice-Chancellor know of them, she seemed to speak at least some of their long-dead language.

None of this was damning, of course. Anneke was a person who thrived on knowledge and had an exceptional memory. It was quite possible that she had heard the things she knew in some lecture that even the Magister who gave it had long since forgotten, or had come across it during one of her investigations. Nonetheless, Derelar couldn't quite shake the feeling that a chink of light had appeared at the edge of the door to Anneke's personal vault of secrets, and he intended, as subtly as he could, to see if he could push it open still further.

With a nod to the Vice-Chancellor, he dispelled the wards on his office door and strode past her, collecting a strong coffee from his sideboard on the way to his desk. His nerves didn't really need any further stimulation at the moment, but he was a creature of habit and Anneke would certainly notice if he broke with it. Anneke, as was her own wont, poured herself a glass of wine.

"I take it that Magister Thalia took her new orders well?" said the Vice-Chancellor, innocently.

"Dutifully," said Derelar. "And she restricted herself to only the mildest profanity, at least whilst the Crystal was connected. I doubt that she was as restrained in the aftermath of the conversation."

"I would have liked to have seen that," said Anneke with a grin. "I doubt any Abelians who were standing too close would still have flesh on their bones."

"On that subject," said Derelar, quietly, "it appears that the situation with the Dendaril came as a complete surprise to her. Until she met with the Abelians, she had no knowledge of it at all. I had assumed, erroneously it would appear, that you would use the Messaging Crystal in Operative Devereux's possession to warn her of the threat ahead of that time."

Anneke shrugged. "To be honest, Arch-Chancellor, that Crystal was not one of Jarton's better ideas. Since Amanda frequently operates in situations demanding stealth and silence, the Crystal Jarton attached to *Liberty* can only send the most subtle of notification pulses when a message is pending, and she is still at best a novice at working with magical devices. She generally only notices messages when she happens to touch the grip of the sword, and even then you run the risk of distracting her in a crisis. All things considered, I decided that the news could wait until they were safely out of harm's way- in fact, knowing Thalia, she might even have turned around and tried to save the day single-handedly again."

Derelar gave Anneke a long, measuring look. Ollan was right- it would be an extremely bad idea to play Chasten, or any other game of bluff, against the woman. If a single word of what she had just said was untrue, he certainly had not detected it.

"Very well," he said, finally. "On to other matters, then. What is the situation with the unrest in Kathis?"

"Still not good," admitted Anneke. "There was a fair amount of sympathy for the Tydasks in Kathis, old merchant families with long-standing ties to the Royals, that sort of thing. Now that they're out of the picture, we're seeing a rise in anti-Magister sentiment. The City Guard was stripped of many of its best men and women to help reform the Sixth Volume and Oberon Thane has always been a somewhat.. abrasive character, making him hardly the ideal Chancellor for the occasion. He's been trying to come down hard on the demagogues and rabble-rousers but the Guard is not a subtle implement at the best of times, and these are hardly those."

"Is there any danger of rebellion?"

"Not at the moment," said Anneke, with a sigh. "There aren't many citizens with the skills to make serious trouble- ironically because many of those ended up helping re-form the Sixth. The re-establishment of the vineyards and orchards is also keeping many of the able-bodied youngsters too busy for any mischief and putting Quoits in their pockets, which helps. But if Oberon cracks down or something else happens that the troublemakers can use to whip up more anger... it could get unpleasant."

"What steps have so far been taken? By the Service, rather than by Oberon."

"Small ones. My people have been keeping an eye out for secret meetings, anti-Magister graffiti, that sort of thing. I already have several in useful positions among most of the more active groups, so whilst I won't be able to stop them I'll get some warning if anything major is about to happen. I wish we had Amanda back, though- from what she's told me, this sort of thing is exactly what she's trained for."

"I have confidence that you have sufficient personnel for the task, Vice-Chancellor," said Derelar. "In fact, I would suggest you have Magister Jarton liaise with Oberon on how best to control the situation whilst your own efforts in the shadows continue. The advice of the Chair of Walanstahl will not lightly be ignored. Now, there is another matter I wish you to attend to."

"Oh?" said Anneke, with undisguised curiosity.

"The Daxalai are still a threat," said Derelar. "We know that they have attempted an invasion on at least two recent occasions, and that despite those apparent failures the clan responsible has managed to not only maintain, but improve its position in the Celestial Harmony."

"That Smiling Snake is a wily one, to be certain," agreed Anneke.

"I wish to distract them, at the very least, or better yet, seriously damage their ability to threaten us," said Derelar, giving no indication of the surprise he was about to unleash on the Vice-Chancellor. "To that end, I want you to look into weaponising the Shrive-Ticks."

Anneke's face went pure white with shock, and her mouth fell open. For a fraction of a second Derelar felt a massive surge in her Aether, as if she were marshalling all of her strength for a desperate attack. Then her colour returned, and the sensation was gone as quickly as it came. She laughed, though the sound was brittle.

"Oh, Arch-Chancellor, that was very good. For a moment I almost believed you were serious."

"I am," said Derelar, flatly. "We know the Whales will stop us sending any sort of weapon overseas, but if contained within a human host the Ticks should escape detection. You will have your 'people' procure a suitable candidate, or preferably several, from Hyphan or one of the other Dendaril ports, and ship them to Gwai'Xi in Daxalai. Once the Ticks are loose in the Harmony, the Daxalai will be far too busy containing them to trouble us for some time."

Anneke shook her head. "It.. it can't be done, Arch-Chancellor. The Whales would-"

"The High Chirurgeon assures me that the Whales have never intervened to stop ships carrying hosts." interrupted Derelar.

"But the risks of obtaining a host at all-"

"You have skilled and expendable agents, do you not? The Dendaril are not violent and are all too willing to spread to new pastures, especially now, it seems."

"The Daxalai would search the ship the moment it arrived!" protested Anneke, desperately.

"Then your agents will simply have to see to it that the hosts die and release a suitable number of Ticks. Unless one of their Sages is present for such a mundane task, the Daxalai would be unlikely to prevent the spread of the symbionts, if they even understand what is happening."

Anneke stared at him for a moment, a look of pure, slack horror on her face. "No," she said, finally. Derelar took a large sip of his coffee and set it down carefully.

"I'm sorry, Vice-Chancellor, what did you say?"

"I said no, Derelar!" hissed Anneke. "Those creatures are not to be trifled with, not a weapon to be wielded or a tool to be used! They are a plague upon the face of this world and I will not, and cannot, be party to any scheme that involves them!"

"Very well," said Derelar. "Then you will instruct your staff to take orders directly from me in this matter, if you lack the stomach to do what must be done."

"Fool!" shouted Anneke, springing to her feet, all semblance of control gone. "I will not see those.. those abominations spread one tal out of the lice-ridden lands they have overrun! After what they did to- I would kill every one of my agents with my own hands before I let any of them-" she suddenly mastered herself. "I.. apologise for my outburst, Arch-Chancellor, but my refusal stands. If you persist in this scheme, I will be forced to..." she trailed off, trembling.

Derelar regarded her coldly. "To do what?"

"To... resign my post," said Anneke. "Effective immediately."

"That will not be necessary, Vice-Chancellor," said Derelar, after a long, ominous pause. "I see now that your objections are deep-rooted and come from a strong conviction that the Dendaril are too dangerous to be employed in this manner."

Anneke blinked at him, and sat down heavily. "You.. you do?"

"I could hardly conclude otherwise," he replied. "Therefore, I would like you to consult with Master Yukan and see what suggestions he has for reducing the Daxalai threat.. if those orders meet with your approval, of course."

The Vice-Chancellor had brought the carafe of ice-water floating over to her from the sideboard and poured herself a large measure, which she downed in one gulp. "Of.. of course, Arch-Chancellor. I will arrange a meeting with Yukan at his earliest convenience." She stood up, still looking a little unsteady on her feet. "If there is nothing else?"

"I do not believe so, Vice-Chancellor, and thank you."

Anneke, on the verge of turning to go, blinked at him. "Ah.. for what?"

"For your refreshing frankness," said Derelar. "A Vice-Chancellor who simply agrees with everything I say is useless to me. Had I desired such a thing, I would have appointed the late Magister Tomas to the post."

"Now that is something I am very glad you did not do, Arch-Chancellor," said Anneke, firmly. She gave a small nod of her head, turned on her heel, and hurried out. Derelar watched her go with a lack of appreciation that would have mortified Magister Kaine had the subject of his gaze been any other woman with the same attributes. Once the door had closed and he had re-established the wards, he stood and turned to look out of the window as he finished off the coffee.

This had certainly been interesting. He had noticed in the Symposium that Anneke had a healthy regard for the danger posed by the Shrive-Ticks, and at first it had seemed to be merely the instinctive reaction of any Magister faced with the threat of losing their free will. But something about Anneke's reaction compared to those of the other Senior Faculty had stood out to him, and this little experiment had reinforced it. Anneke's fear- that was the word, fear- of the Shrive-Ticks was not merely based on intellect and knowledge, nor on instinct. It was a fear that seemed for all the world to come from bitter, personal experience, and a certain conviction that could only stem from the same source. *"After what they did to-"* to what? Or to whom?

Finding out was going to be intriguing, but also possibly the most dangerous thing Derelar had ever done in his life.

13

*I*t was early afternoon when Rya-Ki of Hono, the Great Sage known to friend and foe alike as the Smiling Snake, entered the command post of his brother Tekkan-Cho. Frowning Iron was clad in his customary blue lacquered armour, which his attendants were repairing and repainting even as he stood studying his charts. The General Who Subdues the East had spent most of the last two weeks either in battle, or preparing for one, but showed no sign of fatigue, his long, blond hair and beard still immaculate and his face unlined by stress. Such was the way with any true General- they seemed to live off war as a common man might live off rice.

"Brother!" boomed Tekkan-Cho. "It is good to see you! This campaign has been fiercely contested, but with the forces of the Doha now fully recovered we shall at last strike the killing blow against these White Turban dogs. It would be my most sublime honour if you would review my battle plan, for truly is it said that the Smiling Snake sees flaws which no other man could hope to grasp, were he to study for a thousand years."

Smiling Snake bowed, bearing the expression from which he took his name. "It would be my honour, Brother, for Frowning Iron brings only woe to his enemies and my small assistance would be but the polish upon a peerless blade. But I have come to you on another matter, and I beg your leave to discuss it first."

"My elder brother need beg nothing of me," said Frowning Iron, calling for tea. "Speak, for that which the Smiling Snake deems worthy of discussion is that to which the Heavens themselves would do well to listen." He sat, cross-legged, and motioned his brother to join him, removing his sword and reversing it in the traditional posture of peace. As was proper, they waited for the tea to be brought, presented towards Shan'Xi'Sho in thanks, and poured, before continuing.

"I have this day learned of a most disturbing and distasteful scheme, considered, and by the grace of Heaven rejected, by the Most Learned Derelar Thane, Arch-Chancellor of the College of the Lilies and first among the servants of the

Devil Thelen," said Rya-Ki. "He proposed that a method be found to introduce a colony of the Mind-Stealer Fly to the shores of the Harmony."

Tekkan-Cho had just taken a sip of tea, and for a moment his cheeks bulged with the effort of not spitting it out in shock, which would present an unforgivable breach of protocol. His eyes stared wide as he fought to master himself, and with an effort he swallowed. "Monstrous! Infamous! Is there no depth to which the Eastern Devils will not sink? Were it within my power, I would strike the vile head from the festering shoulders of this Derelar and his own robes would grow a mouth to thank me for freeing them of him!"

Smiling Snake took a moment to appreciate how close his brother had unwittingly come to a profound revelation, and to revel in the spectacle of his righteous fury. Truly, Frowning Iron was a hero of the old blood, and everything he himself was not. He felt no jealousy at the fact, merely quiet satisfaction that their father had chosen his successor as head of the clan well. "Calm yourself, Brother," he said, after this indulgence. "As I said, the scheme was rejected, in no small part due to the counsel of the Most Learned Vice-Chancellor."

"You have spoken of that one before," said Tekkan-Cho, stroking his beard. "I would not have thought her capable of honour or righteousness."

"She is not," agreed Smiling Snake. "But she is wise, in her way. Her schemes are like the still surface of a black lake- he who stares into their depths sees only his own confusion gazing back at him, and to break the surface is to invite the most dire peril."

"Forgive me, Brother," replied Frowning Iron. "But why, if the scheme was rejected, do you feel the need to inform me of it?"

"To.. illustrate a revelation I have been granted," said the Sage. "We have proceeded, thus far, under the assumption that the Son of Heaven wills the conquest of the Chaotic East under the banner of Harmony."

"For this task am I appointed General Who Subdues the East," nodded Tekkan-Cho. "It is fortunate for the retention of my unworthy head that Shan'Xi'Sho lies far enough in the West for the White Turbans to fall under that purview, and that they chose this moment to strike."

"Indeed," agreed Smiling Snake, who had after all engineered just that fortunate state of affairs. "And yet look what we have wrought with our armies and invasion. The Eastern Devils are so afraid that they countenance the most terrible of atrocities to deter us."

"None.. need fear the Harmony," said the General, slowly, as if remembering something. "Only the unjust must tremble at the coming of the righteous."

"The Most Learned Derelar Thane would not be calmed by this revelation," smiled Rya-Ki. "But I would ask you, Brother, to consider the exile, Yu-Kan Toha."

"The Cutting Wind, son of Slumbering Dragon?" said Frowning Iron. "What of him? He is named exile and traitor, the last scion of a slaughtered clan. What could such a one teach us?"

"Do you recall the post to which Yu-Kan was appointed by the Son of Heaven?"

"Of course. He was appointed General Who Brings Harmony to Chaos, a title he forswore along with his clan and his honour."

"Did he?" said the Sage, softly. "Consider, Brother. In his exile, Cutting Wind now aids the College of Lilies in teaching its greatest warriors. He has brought with him the knowledge of *imasen* and the *kamiken-tatai*, and teaches his students much of the Way of Water, as well as the Path of Lightning."

"An act of... base treachery.." mused Tekkan-Cho, a puzzled look upon his face. "Brother, you cannot mean..."

"The General Who Brings Harmony to Chaos," repeated Smiling Snake, firmly. "Perhaps the manner of the bringing is not what any would have expected, but the fact of the result is indisputable. Without spilling so much as a drop of blood or striking a single blow in anger, Yu-Kan Toha has brought more Harmony to the lands of the Devil Thelen than we accomplished with a magic mirror, hundreds of *rok* in gold, and thousands of soldiers. The wisdom of the Son of Heaven is truly humbling."

Frowning Iron stared at him, his mouth agape. Finally he forced it to speak. "But Brother.. what does this mean? Are we to abandon our task, and tell the Court we have changed our interpretation of the Will of Heaven? Such a thing would be both our heads!"

The Great Sage shook his head. "No, Brother, but we must approach our task differently. The Harmony, at its core, is not an empire, nor is it the dominion of the Son of Heaven. It is an ideal, and it is that ideal that may cross the seas when our armies may not. Yu-Kan of Toha has done so, and I believe another may have also begun her own work. It is those efforts that must be bolstered."

Frowning Iron slapped his knees in resolution. "As you say, so shall it be done. Where do we begin?"

Smiling Snake laughed, sadly. "I have no idea, Brother. This revelation came to be mere hours ago, and it is a new-born chick, freshly hatched from its shell. It will not be able to fly for some time, and for now merely chirps irksomely for worms."

"Then I shall content myself with winning this war, and allow you to nurture this hatchling," said Tekkan-Cho. "For I fear I have not mastered the art of pre-chewing food."

14

$\mathcal{T}$he late afternoon sun was beginning to dip in the sky when Second burst from the forest into the Tree-Searchers' camp. Still moving at a full run, she followed her nose, weaving between surprised warriors and labourers until she found the First. Caring nothing for her nakedness, she shifted back into her woman-shape as she covered the last few feet. The First gaped in shock and a little awe- it was rare for a bearer of the Stalking Wolf to transform in full view of others, and rarer still for them to do it whilst still in motion. As she straightened to stand on what a receding part of her mind still thought of as her hind legs, he swept the war-cloak from his shoulders and presented it to her. The fresh sweat on her bare skin was already cooling in the air, and she donned the garment gratefully.

"What brings you to the camp at such haste, Second?" asked the war-leader, a look of some concern on his face. "Was there some disaster on your journey with Mighty Thalia?"

She opened her mouth to speak, but after such long, panting effort her mouth was too dry. She coughed, croaked, and gratefully took the water skin Fire in Winter Sky passed her, drinking greedily. "Mighty Thalia is delivered to the lands of the Great Knights, First," she said, finally. "It was during my return to the Free that misfortune found me, and I it. I encountered a Great Wader."

A murmur of shock rolled around the camp. Most of the warriors had heard the songs of Mighty Dokan and the other Mighty Ones as they had grown up.

"Where is the beast now?" said the First, doing a fair, though not perfect, job of keeping his concern from his face and his voice.

"Dead, many strides from here." said Second. "I smelt it as I travelled the Stone Path." First gave a sigh of relief, but she carried on. "That is not the worst of it, First. The Great Wader was.. infested with a swarm of flies that burst from it. I fear they may carry the Woe from the old tales."

"They do not," came a loud voice from the edge of the camp. The warriors turned to see Mighty Dokan advancing on them. "The Little Ones which breed in the Shriven Marshes do not carry the Woe themselves- they are but simple creatures. But *where those that came before will go..*"

"*..those that came after will follow,*" said the First in response, echoed by several of the other warriors. "What does it mean, Mighty One?"

"It is a warning from the very earliest days of the Free," said Dokan. "passed down since we cast off the yoke of the Deluded and took possession of the Mountain Halls. There is a great tribe to the east, across the mountains, that men call the Dendaril. Much like the Deluded, they live in cities of stone and seek to bend the land to their will, rather than living at peace with it."

"The lands to the east are forbidden," said First. "All know of this."

"Aye." nodded Dokan. "But what is not so well known is the reason why. The Dendaril are the slaves of the Little Ones, who long ago rode to their lands in the flesh of a great, golden Dragon. To slay one is to release untold hundreds of those tiny conquerors, an onslaught that even the Mighty cannot withstand for long."

"Then perhaps the Mighty are not as mighty as they like to believe," said a woman's mocking voice. From the trees to the north of the camp emerged a figure, clad like Dokan in only the merest leather straps except for a long buckskin loincloth and soft boots, though from head to toe her attire was decorated with brightly-coloured seashells. From the lack of a cloak, her flowing, loose black hair, and the skull-topped staff she bore, it was clear to all who saw her that this was another Mighty One, and yet such an insult could not stand.

"You dare?" roared the warrior nearest the woman, levelling his spear at her. Before anyone could act, the woman gestured casually at him, and the wooden shaft of the weapon burst into flames. The man dropped it with an oath, and swept the knife from his belt.

"Hold!" shouted Dokan. "Third of Falling Water, allow our visitor to approach!"

The warrior glared angrily at the invader, but did as he was bid, contenting himself with stamping out the flames that threatened to spread from his smouldering spear. The woman stalked past him without a second glance, the silver bracelets and bangles adorning her arms and legs jangling discordantly as she came, and the sea-shells rattling. As she passed him, First recoiled in shock.

"Mighty Dokan- upon her wrist. The brand of dread Ixil!"

Second could see it for herself now, the twisting pattern of alien runes burned into the wrist of the other woman that was identical to that which Mighty Hyrko had borne. The mark of Ixil, a tyrant of ancient times. That his minions had appeared now could not be a coincidence.

"Mighty Lelioko, what is the meaning of this?" growled Dokan. "I received word that the Shorewalkers wished to discuss a matter of great urgency with me, but you come into an encampment of the Free bearing the mark of the Enslaver?"

"Free?" snorted the woman, sweeping a challenging gaze around the camp. "For how long? Already you have heard that the Fly Lords turn their multi-faceted gaze upon your lands. One even reached the Doors of Patros, where the Great Knight slew him."

Despite their antipathy towards the visitor, the tribe listened with bated breath. This was potentially disastrous news. "The Great Knight." said Dokan, slowly. "Was he..?"

"The armour of the Great Knights is proof against the Woe," said Lelioko, "at least for as long as their Spirit lasts. He struck down the servant of the Fly Lords from afar, and brought fire to the remains. Other invaders were halted by my Master and His servants."

"Your master!" spat the First. "Shamed are these trees to hear one of the Free call any by that name! Begone from here, lest Ixil require a new lackey to bring his poisoned words."

"Be calm, First," said Dokan. "Mighty Lelioko comes to us with purpose, and I would know it."

The woman smiled. "You are truly the wisdom of your people, Mighty Dokan." She raised her left hand, fist clenched, allowing the bracelets to fall towards her elbow so that all could see the mark upon her wrist. "You know this as the mark of Ixil, and you know it as a shackle that binds the bearer to His will. And yet you know little of the truth."

"We know enough," said Second, unable to stay silent any longer. "You said it yourself, thrall, those marks are a shackle and we are the Free."

"But what you do not know is how it comes to be upon my wrist," said Lelioko. "The Firebrand makes Ixil the bearer's Master, it is true, and none who bear it may oppose His command. And yet, it cannot be placed upon an unwilling bearer, nor forced upon them by coercion or blackmail. To bear the Firebrand, one must have already agreed to serve Ixil by their own free will."

The First spat on the ground. "More lies! None of the Free would ever willingly do such a thing!"

"Ignorant child!" laughed Lelioko. "You speak as if Ixil were the only one to gain from the arrangement. Mighty Dokan, tell your people what fate awaits those who the Woe takes."

"It is not unlike your own," said Dokan, stubbornly. "The Woe burrows into the mind, and the one who was is slain, replaced by a new being that lives only to serve the Fly Lords."

"And yet there are two crucial differences," said Lelioko, her challenging stare sweeping around the assembled warriors again. "When you swear yourself to Ixil, nothing of your former self is lost. Your memories, your life, your loves- all these are still yours to keep. Ixil does not require mindless slaves, only those who will agree to protect His lands and their people from invaders, as the Free have done for generations. And then, of course, Ixil takes only those who will willingly serve."

Dokan nodded, grimly. "Aye, that is different. It may even be preferable to the Woe, but it is still a shackle. I hear nothing in your words that tells me why anyone would willingly take this Firebrand of which you seem so proud."

"Then you have not been listening, Mighty Dokan," said the woman. "I told you, those who bear the brand are subservient to the will of Ixil, and *only* to that will. I told you that we, His servants, halted the rest of the Fly Lords when they tried to cross our lands. Surely the conclusion is obvious?"

"Nak's Skull!" gasped Dokan. "You do not mean- you cannot mean...?"

"I can, and I do," said Lelioko. "Hear me, Tree-Searchers! I tell you now, as truly as the sun rises in the east, one bearing the Firebrand of Ixil receives in return complete protection against the dominion of any other mind. Any bearer of the Woe that makes the attempt is consumed utterly by my Master's fire. Join us, pledge your will to us, and the doom the Deluded have brought upon you shall not be yours to suffer."

Dokan shook his head, firmly. "The Deluded brought no doom. It was the black demons of the west that sought to take our lands from us. Mighty Thalia saved us from their dominion, and I would not see us sleep-walk into that of another."

"She saved you from nothing!" shouted Lelioko. "My Master had already begun to turn the schemes of the dragon-slaves to His own ends. He was mere moments from wresting control of the Patron's Gate from the feeble grasp of the bald wretch that had subverted it when that Deluded witch and her lack-witted accomplices brought Xodan crashing to rubble! Already had the lives of eight of our best been spent to preserve the Deluded from the dragon-slaves, and more were lost when their ignorant tinkering brought an endeavour centuries in the crafting to ruin!"

"Eight of your best.. Mighty Hyrko and her party?" mused Dokan, thoughtful now. "It seems to me, then, that Mighty Thalia merely thwarted a different tyrannical scheme to the one we thought she had. I do not think it worth sending a warband after her merely to retract thanks for one rescue and then extend them for another."

A low chuckle went around the tribe, and to Second's surprise even Lelioko joined in. "You jest, Mighty Dokan, but you do not yet understand. It was within my Master's power to bring the Mountain Halls crashing down at any time, and yet He did not do so. For centuries, the terrible power that place commanded has held back the Fly Lords, but now that the Deluded have reduced them to rubble the Free have no defence. My Master knows well that not all will accept His gift or His protection, but it is only those who do that will be saved. They will watch friends and loved ones who were less wise be taken from them by the Woe, and in time may even be forced- by circumstance, if not by His will- to slay them. The Woe is a dark fate, Mighty Dokan. Wish it not upon your people."

"We must choose, it seems, between the fiery pit and the crashing waves," said Dokan. "Second, as soon as you are recovered from your exertions you will travel to the new ritual grounds. Tell the Guardians what has happened here, and what you have seen, and ask that the Moot of Kings be reconvened. Mighty Lelioko, will you accompany me and speak there?"

"Mighty Dokan!" gasped the First. "Surely you do not intend-?"

"We are the Free Tribes, First," said Dokan, sadly. "We cannot call ourselves such and yet deny others a choice, whatever decision we ourselves might make. Tree-Searchers! I would ask, if you are minded to accept Mighty Lelioko's offer of 'protection', that you wait until the Moot is concluded. If you are minded to reject it, I ask that you respect the decisions of your fellows and refrain from attempting to harm the emissary of the Enslaver, no matter how justified you might feel."

The First, who had taken up his spear, growled and slammed it point-first into the ground. "I do not like this, Mighty One, but it shall be done as you say. These are dark times, and the Free must not squabble like Deluded."

Second suppressed a shudder. From the look of sly satisfaction that passed over the face of the servant of Ixil, she began to fear that this day might be the beginning of the end for the Free Tribes.

15

---

*M*agister Haran Dar watched from his horse as the Wardens laboured to set up an evening camp. On the eastern horizon, the city of Verge loomed, the long shadows cast by the setting sun lending it a malevolent aspect to match its reputation amongst the men and women of the Second Volume. None would ever forget the shame of their actions there during the War of Rule, nor the feeling of paralysing dread that had come over them when they had approached the city during the Revenant crisis. Chancellor Pieter, the last scion of the Tydask family who had been tasked with overseeing the glorified refugee camp that the partially-ruined metropolis had been reduced to, had offered the hospitality of his walls to the Wardens, but even though a few brave Scouts had confirmed that Verge could now safely be approached Haran had no desire to do so any sooner than necessary.

At his side, Magister Ollan gave a low, mirthless chuckle. "It still casts a long shadow, does it not, Haran?"

"A shadow that will be on my soul until the day I glimmer into dust, Learned Magister," said Haran, softly. "You really didn't have to come with us, you know."

"Nonsense." replied Ollan with a snort. "I go where I am needed, and right now I am needed wherever I say I am. I bear no small part of the responsibility for the Wardens being assigned this task, and I will help you see it through."

"And you suspect that the Vice-Chancellor has had a hand in it, don't you?" sighed Haran.

"Oh, I know she did," agreed Ollan. "She would have suggested you instead of Kandira if I hadn't done it first. But it goes deeper than that, Haran. I don't just suspect that Anneke engineered this posting, I think she engineered the creation of the Wardens themselves."

Haran, in the process of dismounting, nearly fell off his horse in shock. "You-what do you mean? The Second Volume was founded-"

"I don't mean the Volume, man!" snapped Ollan, sliding from his own saddle with far more ease than a man of his years should have possessed. "I mean the Wardens, specifically, the events that shaped them. Consider- in order to stop the Dendaril, we require a force capable of shooting them down at extreme range, and capable of doing so without hesitation regardless of how innocent or harmless the target might seemingly be. Few Volumes of the Guard possess the necessary skill, and fewer still would be willing to accept the task. And yet, the twin tragedies of Phyre and Verge have presented us with the Wardens, a Volume so suited to the grim work at hand that Walanstahl himself could not have forged better. Tell me that you think that is a coincidence."

"I admit that you raise a troubling point," conceded Haran. "It is merely another in a long list of them, however, at least for the moment. Now, my command staff approaches and at least one of them reports to the Vice-Chancellor, so I would suggest you keep such musings to yourself for the time being."

The approaching group was led by the Captain of the Wardens, Damia Render, and accompanied by Magritte, Haran's personal adjutant and the most skilled of his Operators. Haran also recognised Choirmaster Jarthis, a tall, almost skeletally thin man in the plain, dark-green robe of his rank, which unlike some of his Role he had not chosen to decorate. Like all the other members of the Volume, he bore the callouses on his hands that spoke of long practice with a bow, which the common folk referred to as Warden's Lumps.

Captain Render saluted, smartly, the motion largely silent since as a Sword-master of the Second she wore enchanted leather armour rather than the bulky plate of a Guardsman. "Learned Magisters, the camp is secure for the evening. However, we have a problem with the Petard Engines."

"That's one way of putting it," muttered Jarthis. "Thelen-fucking disaster, is a more accurate way."

"Elaborate," said Haran, shortly. He had never liked Jarthis- the man had been one of the first Choirmasters and had always seemed far to enthusiastic in exerting control over his Singers for the Magister's tastes. Still, he had taken his place in the pickets with everyone else, and that counted for a lot.

"It's the wagons, Learned Magister," explained Magritte. "We've been moving at battle march all day with the help of the Singers, but the wagons that carry the Engines were designed during the War for siege-work and nobody expected them to travel at that sort of speed. The Weavers managed to hold them together until we stopped but all three are badly damaged."

"That will be due to the suspension system, I expect," said Ollan, conversation-ally. "Jarton mentioned to me that even on a smooth surface rapid movement strains the springs- and this route is hardly smooth. He called it an 'oscillation issue', if I recall correctly."

"Did your conversation happen to get as far as a remedy?" asked Haran, some-what tetchily.

"Regrettably not."

"Then the Weavers will have to deal with it," said Haran. "They can carry out the necessary repairs tonight."

"With respect, Learned Magister, most of the Weavers are exhausted from the effort of keeping the damnable things going this long," pointed out Captain Render. "They're not going to have the Aether to conduct the repairs, especially if they have to do the whole thing again tomorrow."

"We have a full crew for the Engines with us, do we not?" asked Ollan.

"Aye," said Jarthis. "Ninety Singers, thirty per Engine."

"Then perhaps the Gathering Hymnal?" prompted the elder Magister.

"That will sorely tax my Singers, Learned Magister..." protested Jarthis.

"Blood, ice and fire!" growled Haran. "Your Singers have been riding horse-drawn wagons all day, Choirmaster! Get to it, before I lose what is left of my temper!"

Jarthis bristled. "Yes, Learned Magister. But if the Singers are unable to properly charge the Engines when we arrive at the Vigil, you will know why." He span on his heel, and stalked off.

Magritte watched him go, before turning back to Haran. "He's right, Learned Magister. The Singers have been performing the Canticle of the March for most of the day, even if they were riding on wagons rather than walking. They can probably take the strain of performing the Gathering Hymnal tonight as well, but if we keep pushing them.."

"Very well," said Haran. "Captain, tomorrow you will assign a Dispensation to escort the Petard Engines at whatever speed Choirmaster Jarthis and the Weavers think is most efficient. No Archers, though, I want all of them with us when we arrive at the Vigil. The rest of the Volume will continue to march at battle speed."

"Without the Singers?" said Render. "That will slow us down- the Canticle is pretty effective."

"Then Haran and I will take up the slack," said Ollan. "It will be a sad day for the College when nine Leaves worth of Magister are of less use than Jarthis' gaggle of drones. In any case, once we get off this infernal dirt track and onto a proper Road at Verge, travel will become a lot easier."

The Captain nodded. "Very well, Learned Magister. I'll give Sergeant Tika the Dispensation, she's reliable and not afraid to use her initiative. She'll make sure Jarthis isn't delayed any more than he absolutely needs to be. Now, if there's nothing else, I'll return to the troops."

The two Magisters watched for a while as Captain Render, Magritte, and the rest of the Wardens' senior staff busied themselves carrying out their orders. Finally, Haran spoke into the deepening gloom.

"I do not know if you are right, Learned Magister, but I agree that something about this whole affair feels.. contrived, as if some greater design were behind it. And there is something else."

"Hmm?"

"Captain Render. I would have expected her to deal with that problem on her own, she is usually an exceptionally capable officer. Since we received orders to march to the Vigil, she has seemed.. oddly distracted."

"Perhaps she has received some orders from Anneke that trouble her?" mused Ollan.

Haran gave a short, mirthless laugh. "She would hardly be alone in that."

"What about this Jarthis fellow? Certainly as far removed from Uthiel as one could get, but I find I trust him little more," said Ollan, rubbing at his beard.

"His loyalties? He served capably during the quarantine of Phyre, though he wouldn't let his Singers take any part in it. That caused some friction in the Volume, so when we had no further use for him he was reassigned to a training post at the Academy."

"Ah, I wondered why I hadn't had the pleasure previously. He was in Lore during the Equinox business, then?"

Haran nodded. "Him and his Singers both. It's quite possible that the Vice-Chancellor has her claws in him, but I've no way of knowing- and in any regard, as I told Render I have nothing to hide from the College. If the Service wishes to spy on me, it's their time to waste."

"Claws, hah!" said Ollan, quietly. Haran gave him a quizzical look.

"Learned Magister?"

"I was just considering the aptness of your metaphor, Haran. Now, unless my nose deceives me your cooks have begun their work for the evening and I, for one, do not intend to miss out on the results. Let us attend to these horses, and then to our stomachs."

16

The carriage that thundered down the road towards Abellan was perhaps the most reassuringly normal thing Amanda Devereux had encountered for some time. True, it was maintaining a speed approaching seventy miles per hour, but in most respects it was otherwise a wooden stagecoach that would not have looked out of place in the Old West.

After receiving her orders from the Arch-Chancellor, Thalia had been insistent on making a start on the journey to the Abelian capital as soon as possible. Their Abelian hosts, having already witnessed the young Magister's temper in full flow, had wisely not contested the point, and had put their own personal carriage at her disposal. They had also, much to Thalia's poorly-concealed annoyance, insisted on accompanying her. In the end, most of the D'Honeur's personal staff stayed behind in Naxxiamor, with only the coach driver accompanying them on the journey. This left enough room in the richly-appointed vehicle for Thalia, Devereux and Delys, along with Lady Alizabeth. Athas rode beside the driver in what the Abelians called the Sentinel's Seat, which their fellow travellers in another time and place would have known as 'shotgun'.

The vehicle was pulled by two more of the massive Abelian horses, though these, according to Sir Jeremiah, were "not of the first water." Known as Chaffs, the powerful animals were those which had been rejected as mounts for the Royal Knights for a variety of reasons, which could range from being temperamentally unsuited to warfare to simply being of a displeasing colour. In the case of the team pulling the coach, the Knight had warned them to be particularly wary of the right-hand horse, which he described as "a cantankerous bastard of a brute who tried to have the leg of the last man fool enough to try to saddle him."

Devereux peered out of the back window of the coach, to where Sir Jeremiah rode behind them. Mounted on Abraxes, his massive, armoured warhorse, and with the heavy visor of his helm sealed tightly shut, he looked more like a living metal sculpture than a human being. The moonlight, still silver for the moment, glinted dully off his armour.

"Is he going to be all right out there like that? We've been going for hours without a break."

"Oh, of course!" laughed Lady Alizabeth. "Jeremiah's a Royal Knight, remember, they can ride for days if need be. The Great Families have always bred for strength. You should have seen what I had to go through to prove myself worthy to marry him."

"What?" said Thalia, who had been on the verge of dozing off.

"Traditionally, we Wizards are of much lower birth than the Royal Knights," reminded Alizabeth. "We make up for our comparative weakness by extensive training in the magical arts, but even then there's a risk that letting us in would weaken the bloodline. So when a Wizard- or anyone else who isn't a member of a Great Family already, for that matter- desires to marry into one, the family Castellan tests them to make sure they won't dilute the blood too much."

Delys, who certainly had been asleep, was still pretending to be but Devereux could tell that she, too, was listening intently.

"So, how did they test you?" prompted Devereux, after a moment.

"Oh, the usual," replied the Abelian, a slight shadow flitting over her cheerful features. "Some ritual duels with other prospective candidates, tests of endurance and pain tolerance, a full examination by the family Surgeon, that sort of thing."

"Wait," said Thalia, sitting up now and paying full attention. "You had to fight other women for the right to marry Jeremiah? That's... that's barbaric!"

"Well, that's not quite how it works," said Alizabeth. "As I said, it's a ritual duel, and the other 'candidates' are just other low-born who wish to marry into a family, not necessarily other women who wish to marry the same Knight. You don't even absolutely have to win- the Castellan is looking for strength of character as much as anything else and a valiant defeat can show more of that than an underhanded victory. In some families, the duel isn't even a physical confrontation at all, just a test of endurance."

Delys suddenly signed something, which met with a blank stare from the Abelian until Devereux interpreted it for her. "Del wants to know what happened in your case, Lady Alizabeth. I'm sure she won't mind if you tell her to mind her own business."

"Not at all!" trilled Alizabeth. "In my case, I gave the future Lady Ysabella Orsinio a black eye to remember."

Delys laughed delightedly, and Thalia snorted. "So much for the Abelian code of honour! Brawling like commoners?"

"For shame, Learned Magister!" chuckled Alizabeth. "Ours *was* primarily a magical contest- we each had to burn a rose held by our opponent to cinders whilst protecting our own. Ysabella was always very good at shielding spells, but she has a nasty habit of getting lost in her magic and closing her eyes, so when she did I took advantage in a way she couldn't sense coming."

"And that gave you an opening to burn the rose?" said Devereux. Alizabeth smiled.

"She was *very* good at maintaining shielding spells, so we ended up, ahem, brawling like commoners. Both roses got rather ruined in the ensuing fracas and the contest was declared an honourable draw, which served both of our purposes rather well."

Thalia's eyes narrowed. "Wait a moment... are you saying that you and this Ysabella-"

"There is, as the saying goes, more than one way to get the fur off a Red Bear, Learned Magister."

Thalia opened her mouth to say something, but seemed to think better of it. Before she could close it again, the expression turned into a huge yawn.

"Don't worry, Learned Magister, we're very nearly at our stop for the night," said Alizabeth. "I apologise in advance for the quality of the hosts."

"For the what?" asked Thalia, a thickness creeping into her voice as she rubbed at her eyes.

"Who approaches Castle Orsinio?" came a shouted challenge from outside. Lady Alizabeth rolled her eyes as Sir Jeremiah rode past the halted coach to answer.

"As I said, Learned Magister, I do apologise."

———————

17

*I*t was late by the time Smiling Snake returned to his laboratory. In the shadows of the far wall, the Stepping Mirror still stood quiescent beneath its covers, but he paid it no heed. The adventure to the Chaotic East had not gone as well as he could have hoped, but at least his contingency plans had borne enough fruit to keep the clan in favour- and the heads of its leaders still attached to their shoulders.

He locked the door behind him, and strode to the secret passage that lead to the Tapestry. Even though his eyes burned with fatigue, he felt compelled to commune with the device again, to reassure himself that he had not imagined the revelation that had sent him scurrying to his brother's side- a revelation that he had realised almost too late that he could not yet share, even with Tekkan-Cho. The Vice-Chancellor, a Dragon! Such a thing was unheard of, and for her to have escaped detection for so long was incredible. He wondered briefly if his brother had believed he meant what he had said about finding other means to spread the Harmony to the Chaotic East. The idea had come to him almost at the last second, but some of the points he had made might bear investigation nonetheless. Doubtless a warrior as valorously single-minded as his brother would soon forget about the whole thing.

Of course, his new-found knowledge in and of itself posed an immediate, and troubling, problem. Within a week, Frowning Iron would have trounced the White Turbans, and with that victory would certainly come an audience with the Son of Heaven. That was to be expected, and he had planned for it, but now he knew a secret that, should the Harmony learn of it, would have to be acted upon. A secret that would lead to many searching questions as to how it was acquired. A secret so terrible that he knew that even he, a Great Sage of six Rings, could not hope to keep it from the Son of Heaven if the Emperor should make even the vaguest of requests for a report from him.

He paused in front of the Tapestry, studying the new design. Recent events had affected it more than he would have expected. The overall design was still the same- a Daxalai General on the left still faced a Lily Magister on the right- but there were several changes. Where before the General had stood with his sword raised, now it was sheathed, though he still stood ready to draw it. The Magister, too, had drawn back, and stood in a more neutral posture. But there was something else, and the shock of it made him blink with surprise before stumbling back to sit, heavily, upon the lacquered floor. The Dragon that lurked behind the Magister was no longer silver, but instead golden, and there was more..

He pushed himself to his feet and looked closer, not pausing to achieve the usual state of mental stillness that communing with the Tapestry required. There was a black dot on the golden Dragon, near the head, a mark that seemed impossibly small on a being that stood over eight feet in length on a tapestry over twenty tall. What was it? Even standing almost dangerously close to the threads, so close that the *ki* flowing through them made his skin tingle, he couldn't quite tell. It could almost be a speck of dirt, but such a thing was unthinkable. Though none of his attendants knew the true secret of the Tapestry, those few who could access the chamber knew well the penalty for allowing it to become grimy.

Finally, in exasperation, he focused a minute amount of *ki* into his eyes, bringing his vision into perfect focus. Immediately, the mark sprang into clarity. It was a fly. He almost laughed at his own foolishness- even most ancient and powerful of devices, it seemed, was not immune to the attentions of this tiniest of invaders. And yet something nagged at him. The insect stood out from the Tapestry in relief, clearly resting on top of it, and yet he had been certain when he first saw it that the mark had been flat on the surface.

As if startled, the insect suddenly took flight, and Smiling Snake saw to his horror that the mark remained. It was unmistakably in the shape of a fly, nestling in the nape of the Dragon. And then, even as he blinked, the shape was solid again, a second fly seeming to emerge from the very fabric of the Tapestry before joining the first in the air. And then there was another. And another. Within seconds, before he could even begin to fully realise what was happening, a swarm of the tiny, ebony-black creatures filled the room, raising a terrible buzzing din and becoming so thick that it seemed at any moment he might feel them crawling upon his skin, or worse, entering his body.

He fought for control, closing his eyes and centring himself, forcing himself to breathe slowly and deeply. Even in moments of the most dire chaos, a Great Sage must be the calm at the centre of the storm, like a gull that rode upon the crest of the crashing waves. The buzzing grew so loud that it seemed that the sound itself was a physical thing but he blocked it out, marshalling his *ki* to build a fortress of silence at the core of his being.

It almost worked.

Then something touched his face as he took another breath, and what felt like a tiny, scurrying leg brushed against the inside of his nostril as he inhaled. Instantly, instinctively, he lashed out to defend himself, his *ki* blazing forth in a wave of flame that blasted out in all directions. The buzzing cut off, abruptly.

Not daring to open his eyes, he sank down to the ground, barely able to control the motion on trembling legs. *What have I done?* There was no way that blast could have failed to reach the wall upon which the Tapestry, a priceless relic dating back to the very foundation of the Hono clan, hung. Without the secrets it had imparted, many of his greatest schemes could never have been accomplished, and now it must be nothing but a few charred silken threads. He, Smiling Snake of Hono, had doomed his clan, and possibly the entire Harmony, in a single moment of unforgivable weakness. Better that the flies had devoured him from the inside out than this.

And yet, what was done, was done. In some way, all that happened was the will of Heaven, and if the Heavens had decided that Sage Rya-Ki must be brought low in this fashion, then so it would be. Taking a fresh, steadying breath, he snapped his eyes open.

The Tapestry hung there still, unscathed. The Dragon was once more silver, its scaled hide unblemished by any mark. Blinking in confusion, Smiling Snake offered a quick prayer of thanks and settled down to meditate, but his mind, for once, was a whirl of chaotic thoughts.

What did it mean? What *could* it mean?

18

By the time Anneke arrived at his office the following morning, Derelar was on his second cup of coffee. He usually prided himself on his excellent sense of time and would awake without fail some half an hour before the start of Dawn Watch, but his sleep the previous night had been plagued by dreams. It wasn't the first time he'd had them- his mother had always claimed that the talent for Dream-Scrying ran in her family's blood- but usually he would awake at his usual time and remember the entire thing in precise detail. This dream, or perhaps more of a nightmare, had woken him with a pounding heart and sweat-soaked bedsheets, and all he could recall from it was the sound of swarming flies. Even without knowing all the details, though, the broad message was obvious- the Dendaril problem was increasing in urgency.

He favoured the Vice-Chancellor with a short nod of greeting, waiting until she had sat down before doing so himself. Once again, he mentally cursed Magister Ollan for using the excuse of his friendship with Haran Dar to go gallivanting off to the far side of the Empire without warning him. He knew he shouldn't be surprised- Ollan's love of travel was well-known and his skill as a horseman had led to him being appointed command of a Dispensation of White Riders, the College's elite cavalry, during the latter stages of the War of Rule. The closeness of his friendship with Haran was similarly common knowledge, and there were few in the Empire who had yet to hear *"The Song of the Red, the Wise and the Redeemed"*, a somewhat fanciful bardic account of the two Magisters' stand against Jocasta at Equinox. He still couldn't shake the feeling that Ollan's absence was more due to him wanting to stay well out of this whole mess with Anneke, though, even if the old man was in no small part responsible for starting it.

"Good morning, Arch-Chancellor," began Anneke, mildly. "I trust you slept well?"

Derelar cursed inwardly. The dark circles under his eyes that had glared back at him from the glass of the High Apartment's windows had clearly not escaped the Vice-Chancellor's notice- not that he would have expected them to.

"Adequately. I trust you have the morning's reports?"

"Of course. The Wardens are making good time towards the Vigil with the aid of Magisters Ollan and Haran, though they've been forced to leave their siege train behind them to catch up. Apparently there's a problem with moving the wagons at speed- I've already passed it on to Jarton and he's working on it. Things would be a lot easier, though, if we had a proper direct Road between Verge and Phyre."

Derelar nodded. "Indeed. Perhaps in the present climate we might be able to gain the necessary votes in the Symposium. That particular weakness in the Empire's infrastructure has been an embarrassment for centuries."

"We might do well to leave out any mention of the lack of a Road inconveniencing the Wardens, though," said Anneke with a wry grin. "There are still plenty of families who lost kin in the... unpleasantness at Verge who would prefer to stoke that old grudge."

Derelar grunted his agreement, taking a sip of his coffee.

"On the subject of Roads," continued Anneke, "we also have a report from a Captain Yansen of the Sixth, currently stationed at the new fortress in the Wake."

"The new *what?*" said Derelar. This was the first he'd heard of any such thing.

"Ah.. Yansen and Kandira Dar were charged with securing the site of the first Daxalai intrusion at the Wake, Arch-Chancellor. Apparently they consulted with Elinda after she became Chair of Light and decided the surest way to prevent the portal, or whatever it was, being used again was to bury the site, so they dug out some more of the earth in the crater and used it to raise an artificial hill. I won't bore you with all the details of groundwater levels and all the rest of it, though a full, and incredibly dreary, report is in the Archives should you desire it, but what it comes down to is that the Wake was already beginning to flood, and so the hill rapidly came to be possessed of a moat. The Sixth built temporary bridges to connect it to dry land, and then found themselves in charge of an ideal location to build a fortification, so..."

Derelar sighed, massaging his temples and closing his eyes. "And what, exactly, is the purpose of this 'new fortress?' Assuming I understand correctly that if anyone should successfully open the portal again they will appear under several tonnes of tightly-packed earth, why is a fortification necessary?"

"As I understand it, to be the beginning of a new settlement to replace Manadar, and somewhere to garrison a new Ninth Volume," said Anneke. "They're still trying to come up with a name- New Manadar is one obvious suggestion, but Devereux's Landing is gaining some traction with the more whimsical."

"Fort Tarim," said Derelar, immediately.

"Tar- ah, the unfortunate First-leaf who Deleth and his cronies used for that mysterious ritual of theirs? I think we could work with that, and it would be a good idea to remind everyone that it was Royalist treachery that destroyed Manadar, rather than anything we did. Anyway, the reason the report is relevant to today's business is that Yansen claims work on the bridges is proceeding as a priority, and Kandira, along with a contingent of Weavers from Kathis, plan to have the Road to the Vigil re-established, at least partially, within two days. That should mean the Wardens can just march straight through."

"That is certainly helpful," agreed Derelar. "I think we should also make it clear that as far as the College is concerned, the Wake and the surrounding area are still the domain of House Adaran."

"*House* Adaran?" said Anneke, incredulously. "But the only surviving Adaran Magister is.. ah, I see. You plan to give Magister Jakob a claim on this new city before it is even built?"

"Not just a claim," said Derelar. "Responsibility. For the moment, I assume that Kandira and this Captain Yansen have been using local materials, so this fortress is made of Aether-reinforced wood and earth, yes?"

Anneke nodded.

"This, of course, will not be the case for long. Any real city will need supplies of silver and marble at the very least, as well as considerably more labour. House Dar would doubtless come cap-in-hand to the College for assistance, and with all the other rebuilding projects currently underway we could ill-afford such expense. But House Adaran's coffers were frozen when the House defected to the Royalists and since the end of the War, Magister Jakob has become an extremely rich man upon their release."

"You wouldn't know it to look at the man," groused Anneke. "Typical soldier- no taste for the finer things in life. Believe me, I've had a few of my people try vari- ous.. distractions on him and nothing elicited much more than a raised eyebrow."

Derelar decided he didn't want to hear any more details of *that* particular project. "Quite. This new settlement presents an excellent opportunity to get that money out of Jakob's pockets and into the wider economy where it can start to do some good. I-"

A buzzing noise distracted him for a moment. Derelar's eyes flicked around wildly, but he couldn't make out the source.

"Arch-Chancellor?"

"I, er, would like you to get started on that as soon as possible..." said Derelar, vaguely, eyes still searching.

"Very well, Arch-Chancellor," said Anneke, standing up. "There's been no word from Abelia yet, but I'll let you know as soon as we get a report from Magister Thalia."

Derelar nodded, only half-hearing, and stood up himself, starting to turn back towards the window. He was only halfway through the motion when a black blur flashed into his vision, moving too fast for conscious reaction. It was a credit to the Arch-Chancellor's self-control that even under these circumstances, he managed to avoid lashing out with fire magic within the tight confines of his office. Instead, he hit the thing with a blast of pure kinetic force. The shape hurtled away from him with such speed that it cracked the glass of the window as it slammed into it.

Anneke regarded the flattened form of the fly as it hung suspended in the middle of a spiderweb of fine cracks. "My, Arch-Chancellor, you certainly are touchy this morning!"

19

$\mathscr{B}$reakfast that morning was among the more memorable meals Amanda Devereux had consumed. It wasn't so much that the food was unusual- the Orsinios had laid an elaborate and well-stocked table featuring everything from simple grain cereals, yogurts and fruit compotes to eggs, bacon and toast- but the location took some beating.

Castle Orsinio stood a little over a hundred miles broadly south of Naxxiamor, and commanded impressive views of the surrounding countryside. A solidly-built concentric castle with a round keep standing a little over two hundred feet high, it lay at the edge of an extensive system of meticulously cultivated and irrigated vineyards. The view of the gently-swaying vines was greatly improved by the fact that Sir Hektor Orsinio and his wife, who with crushing inevitability turned out to be Lady Ysabella, chose to breakfast on an observation platform at the very top of the keep. Surrounded on all sides by battlements that were high enough to prevent too much disruption from any crosswinds, the wooden-decked platform was shaded from the early morning sun by a somewhat gaudy red canvas marquee.

Just as in Naxxiamor, the Stickmen were everywhere and seemed to be involved in every task. Several took the role of waiters, their wooden bodies elab-orately worked with carvings, though the team was overseen by a liveried human servant whose crimson silk uniform was more elaborate than the robes of most Symposium Magisters. Besides directing his charges, this servant also took the role of sommelier, taking careful note of the food chosen by each guest and suggesting a wine to match. Thalia protested that the hour was too early and was promptly presented with a sparkling white grape juice that the man assured her would leave her both refreshed, and clear headed. She sipped it warily, and gave a gasp of happy surprise. Everyone else had the wine, though Sir Hektor insisted on making his own selection.

They sat at a long table beneath the marquee, Sir Jeremiah and Sir Hektor facing each other across its length whilst their wives did the same across its width.

Thalia's party filled the rest of the seats at Jeremiah's end, whilst the Orsinios' two sons and daughter did the same at Sir Hektor's. Alert to the possibility of committing a social blunder, Devereux kept a careful eye on the table manners of their Abelian hosts but for all their finery they seemed surprisingly informal- a product, she guessed, of a society in which the 'lower' classes had practically ceased to exist.

"So, your Excellency, how are you finding your visit to our fair country?" said Sir Hektor. He was a tall, lean, fine-featured man with a long, drooping black moustache that was showing the first streaks of a dignified grey.

There was a slightly awkward pause before Thalia seemed to realise the Knight had been speaking to her.

"Oh! My apologies, Sir Hektor. This title is new to me and I do not yet wear it with any comfort. I had heard stories of the beauty of Abelia, and I fear they do not do it- URP! - justice." She covered her mouth with her hand self-consciously. "Thelen's breath! I am- URP! - terribly sorry.."

Lady Ysabella laughed. "Ah, the price you pay for missing out on the wine, your Excellency! The *piel-de-vitess* does rather carry with it the demons of wind, and if they don't escape one way, they do the other, as it were."

"Then I shall count myself fort- URP!- fortunate that they have chosen this route, Lady Ysabella," replied Thalia.

Lady Ysabella Orsinio was perhaps a little younger than both her husband and Lady Alizabeth, with long, silver-blonde hair piled upon her head in an elaborate fashion. Her figure, whilst curvaceous, showed little of the effects of bearing three children and was barely, though firmly, contained in a rich red velvet dress. Low cuts and daring décolletage seemed very much to be the fashion amongst the Abelian noblewomen from what Devereux could tell so far. Athas, she'd noticed, was finding it hard at times to know where to look.

"I only wish," said Thalia, setting down her half-full glass warily having taken a moment to master her breathing, "that my visit came under better circumstances.."

"Nonsense!" said Sir Hektor, loudly, waving a rasher of bacon in one hand and making Ysabella wince. "Any advancement must always come into a place of vacancy. Whether you create that vacancy by your own hand or merely take advantage of another's ill-fortune, you should always seek to take maximum advantage. To do otherwise is disrespectful to those who died that you might prosper, don't you agree?"

"*Cutlery*, dear, when we have guests..." muttered Ysabella, quietly. If Thalia heard her, she gave no sign of it.

"Of course," said the Magister, diplomatically. "I was referring more to the threat from the East- these Dendaril. I would prefer to be visiting your lands in a time of peace when I might have leisure to properly appreciate their beauty."

"Such as the *terribly* fine sheep-breeding country, for example," said Ysabella with a sly smile. Sir Jeremiah buried his face in his hand, his elbow resting on the table. "Oh blast it, here we go..."

"Your Excellency, Lady Ysabella is of course referring to the lands around Thecla, that form the ancestral estates of the D'Honeur family," said Lady Alizabeth. "*Some* people have never quite got over the fact that the D'Honeurs rose to prominence because during the Great Famine of 1725 our lands produced food, milk and clothing whilst certain *other* families could only grow withered grapes."

"Oh, I wouldn't say that, Lizzie," replied Ysabella. "After all, *some* families then got quite *astonishingly* rich after the Ague when those who survived needed some truly superb vintage wines to drown their sorrows."

"Those same families certainly needed the money," agreed Lady Alizabeth, smiling sweetly. "After all, they needed to rebuild the castle that they lost during a border war that they most *certainly* should have thought twice about starting."

"Well, if a certain *other* family hadn't diverted water from the Bylan in the middle of the worst drought in two centuries-"

"Wait, wait, your, er, ladyships, please!" gasped Athas, the tips of his ears turning pink. "Didn't you both marry into your families?"

"Of course we did!" laughed Ysabella. "And you should have seen the state I left her in after the-"

"Then why are you arguing about things that those families did before you had anything to do with them?" said Athas. "It's not Lady Alizabeth's fault that Sir Jeremiah's family... diverted your river or whatever they did, and who cares who knocked down who's castle?"

Thalia put her head in her hands. "Sergeant, this is not the time to be...."

Anything else she was trying to say was drowned out by the Abelians, D'Honeur and Orsinio alike, roaring with laughter. The youngest son, Garath, laughed so hard he nearly choked on a piece of toast, but his sister pounded him firmly on the back to dislodge it, still giggling. Even the sommelier, who until then had seemed unable to form any expression other than mild disinterest, failed to completely suppress a smile.

Athas looked from one to the other as if they had all gone quite mad. "What? What did I say?"

Finally, Sir Jeremiah regained enough self-control to reply. "Sergeant, you are a kind-hearted and wise young man. Do you often train with your men, teach them the art of the sword?"

"Er.. we make sure they know which end goes in the enemy and how not to drop their shield.." said Athas, not quite understanding where this was going.

"Quite so! You see, courtly intrigue is much like battle, and like battle, it requires training. So Abelians, especially our womenfolk since they traditionally deal with matters of diplomacy, take every opportunity to practice bandying words with each other to sharpen their tongues as you and I might our swords."

"Oh.. I see.." said Athas, slowly, looking down the table to where the two noble-women were managing somehow to keep glaring at each other whilst laughing.

"Of course, it adds spice to the proceedings that our own particular wives get on like two Razorpaw Bears in a very small cave," said Sir Hektor, brandishing a sausage on the end of a fork which he held defiantly in the wrong hand.

"Oh, quite so!" said Jeremiah. "Fire in the blood, vigour in the soul, as they say. The verdict of the Castellans was well delivered in both our cases, eh, Hektor?" His fellow Knight grunted in response as he chewed.

"So, your Excellency, will you and your party be staying with us long?" asked Melisa, Hektor's daughter. Just entering her twenties, she seemed to have inherited much of her mother's good looks and other attributes, which she concealed in a red dress that was similar to her mother's, except that it somehow managed to plunge even lower without outraging public decency. Devereux noticed that whilst the question had been directed at Thalia, the young woman's gaze was firmly on Athas, as it had been for most of the meal.

"I'm afraid not, Lady Melisa," replied Thalia. "As soon as we are finished here, I must leave for Abellan. My audience with Queen Tondarin cannot wait."

Devereux noticed that Melisa seemed more than a little put-out at the news. Her mother spoke up quickly.

"Of course, your Excellency. We will have our fastest carriage put at your disposal, rather than that *relic* Lizzie brought you here in. A mere two horses in this day-and-age, Lizzie?"

"That *relic* is a family heirloom, you over-inflated-" began Lady Alizabeth, but suddenly Devereux noticed a pleading look flash into Ysabella's eyes. It seemed Alizabeth saw it too.

"ah, that is to say, Sir Jeremiah and I should really get back to our post in Naxxiamor, now that I think about it," she finished, changing track so smoothly it seemed the beginning of the sentence had never happened.

Thalia shrugged. "It makes no difference to me, Lady Ysabella. If your carriage will get us to Abellan faster, I gratefully accept the offer."

Ysabella clapped her hands together. "Capital! Melisa, I think Sergeant Athas has finished his breakfast. Take him down and show him where to put Ambassador Thalia's luggage, and instruct the head groom to have the fast carriage prepared within the hour."

Melisa stood, and curtsied prettily to her mother. "Of course, Mama. Please, Sergeant, would you come with me?"

Athas looked down at his plate, which still contained two small sausages and half a round of toast. "I, er, haven't quite..."

In a flash, the young woman swept in behind him, snatching up one of the sausages and putting it in her mouth before shoving the other into Athas'. "Now you have. Do come along!"

With a helpless shrug, Athas trailed along after her. Devereux watched them leave, suspicion turning rapidly to certainty.

"Perhaps I'd better go along with-" she began, making to stand. Delys, meanwhile, took advantage of the distraction to pilfer the toast that had been left behind on Athas' plate.

"Oh, nonsense!" said Lady Alizabeth. "They'll be fine, and moving baggage around is no task for a lady, even a warrior such as yourself. No, we should use the time we have left to make sure Ambassador Thalia is fully prepared for her audience with Queen Tondarin. Our beloved Queen, may she reign for a thousand years, is a fine, wise and just ruler, but to be frank.."

"She has a temper like a thunderstorm over a cold mountainside," put in Lady Ysabella. "You'll need to walk barefoot on toadstools around her, your Excellency, if you want to keep your head on your shoulders."

"I really think I should-" said Thalia, starting to get up.

"Oh, we really must insist!" trilled Lady Alizabeth, placing a hand on Thalia's shoulder and gently pressing her back into her chair. "You need to be most *thoroughly* briefed. And of course then we will take you to the Messaging Crystal, that you might report your progress to the College.."

Devereux settled back in her own seat. She was sure Athas would be fine. Hopefully.

20

Moon Behind Dark Clouds, First of the Shorewalkers, watched the procession of his kin trailing out of the forest that was their home with a pang of regret. He wished Mighty Lelioko were here to shoulder this burden, but the Master had sent her on an important errand. On the other side of the ancient stone steps that led up to the half-ruined fortress known only as The Tithing, his wife, Night's First Raven, shot him a reassuring glance. As Second of the clan it was only right that she be here in any case.

Despite the morning summer sun, a chill breeze swept in from the north, borne from the cold seas towards the warmer air of the Shriven Marshes. It was no surprise, he thought, as he wrapped his war-cloak about him, that none of the Free had ever guessed the purpose of the ruin. Standing as it did on the edge of a blasted wasteland, seemingly devoid of all life, and bordered to the south by the stinking marshes, the Tithing seemed to stand in defence of something nobody would ever want.

As the group of Free approached- and this was perhaps the last day on which they could truly lay claim to such a title- Night's First Raven strode down the steps to greet them. He watched her jet-black hair bounce with the movement- once she had discovered her True Name she had washed out the spikes and set it instead into two crests that stuck up at an angle like wings. He watched her open-toed bearskin boots pick their way elegantly across the rubble, and remembered the day he had given them to her, and how happy she had been to receive them. He had nearly lost an arm to that bear, one of the big, black, angry ones the Free called a Bark Chewer, but it was worth it- they had learned each other's names on that same day. She was still wearing her war-cloak, which was probably just as well with the places his memory was trying to take him to. Such things were for another time.

"I greet you, Shorewalkers, in the name of Mighty Lelioko and of Master Ixil," said Raven. "Come forward, and follow us to a new life, a life of certainty and of protection from the Woe That Flies."

"Protection? In that pile of stones?" shouted a warrior in the crowd. "We are the Free Tribes, and the great trees are the only protection we need."

"You heard the words of Mighty Lelioko," said Moon Behind Dark Clouds, coming to stand beside his wife. "Against the Woe, the old ways of the Free will not help us. But this-" he held up his wrist to reveal his Firebrand "this will. Once your mind and Spirit have received the touch of Master Ixil, the Woe shall have no claim upon you. The machinations of the Fly Lords shall come to naught."

"To call any man Master is to no longer be Free," responded the warrior, sullenly. Night's First Raven stepped up to him, and laid her hand gently on his shoulder.

"Perhaps. But I know that even bearing this mark, I am still free. Free to live-" she shot a quick glance at her husband, "and free to love. All the Master asks is that we defend His domain, as the Free Tribes have done since the Arrival. There is nothing to fear, Third of Shadowed Mountains."

"But the bearers of that.... mark are bound to the will of Ixil the Enslaver!" insisted the young warrior.

"Aye, that we are," said Moon Behind Dark Clouds. "Such commands, irresistible as they are, come but rarely. It is a small price to pay, but pay it we must. But you already know this, for why else would you be here? Why would any of you be here?"

"There is one more thing I must know, First," said an older woman, as Third of Shadowed Mountains lapsed into sullen silence. "What of our children? You tell us that the Firebrand can only be taken by our own will, but what of those who are too young to know it?" A younger woman stepped out from behind the first, clearly heavily pregnant, and the elder gestured to her. "What of those as yet unborn?"

"The Firebrand can only be worn by those of fifty seasons or more, Shadowed Mountains," replied Night's First Raven. "Until then, they will be protected at our Master's fortress."

"This?" laughed Shadowed Mountains. "This could not protect a rock from the rains!"

"No, not this," said Moon Behind Dark Clouds. "This is but a step on the way. We travel to Ixildundal."

"But... that is a dark, evil place..." said Shadowed Mountains, taking an uncertain step back. "And it lies many days into the Wastes of Ixil. Many of us will not even survive the journey, and should the Woe come upon us-"

"Enough!" shouted the First, his Roaring Toad tattoo flaring and amplifying his voice so that it rebounded off the crumbling stonework. "Do you think I, First of the Shorewalkers, would bring you here simply to see you die? To see my *wife* die? Do you believe that Mighty Lelioko or Master Ixil wishes to see a trail of bodies strewn across the Wastes? No. The time has come for you to decide. Place your trust in us, or find a tree to hide in and hope that the Woe does not find you. There are many to choose from."

Without saying another word he turned and began to climb up the steps, heart hammering, not daring to see if any were following him. They walked up broken steps and under ruined archways, each threshold guarded by two trusted Shorewalkers who had already taken the Firebrand. Their route took them past shattered statues and halls with roofs long since fallen, until they finally found themselves in the shadows of an ancient, musty cellar. Within the gloomy depths they came to a large, gloss-black dais upon which stood a circular, finely-polished stone ringed with gemstones and flanked by burning braziers. Alone amongst the surroundings, this structure was pristine and undamaged. At the foot of the steps leading up to the raised platform, the First stopped, and turned. To his relief, it seemed most, if not all, of his people had followed him.

Night's First Raven carried on up the steps, taking a small pouch from her belt and arranging the stones within in a precise pattern in front of the circle. Her task completed, she stepped carefully away and took up a torch, lighting it from one of the braziers. "Now, Shorewalkers!" she cried, fitting the blazing mass into a stand next to the stones. "Witness the power and wisdom of Master Ixil!"

As the light from the torch struck the stones, the runes upon them glowed, before twisting symbols seemingly composed of liquid fire sprang into being above them. The gems surrounding the stone circle blazed in response, and suddenly the circle was gone, replaced instead by an opening that led to another chamber, this one undamaged and lit by gently-glowing sigil-lights. The Second led the way, and after exchanging nervous glances the Shorewalkers followed her, stepping across the threshold and unknowingly travelling almost four hundred miles as they did so.

Moon Behind Dark Clouds was the last to go, though a small contingent of guards would remain behind as a precaution. Stopping on the threshold, he turned, snatching up the rune-stones and stepping swiftly through the portal a moment before it closed.

21

*C*hancellor Pieter Tydask looked up in irritation as someone knocked loudly on the door of his study. He had given strict orders that he should not be disturbed tonight. Still, his work was finally almost finished. He made one final cut, set down the knife, and then strode quickly to the door as it banged again.

"Captain, I would remind you that I was very specific about- oh!" He wrenched open the door crossly as he spoke, falling back a pace and stopping dead with shock on being confronted with the scowling face of Magister Haran Dar raising his staff ready to strike again. "Ah, er, Magister Haran- and Magister Ollan! I apologise for my rudeness- I have been somewhat busy and completely lost track of time. Is it morning already?"

"Is it *morning?*" echoed Haran, incredulously. "We breakfasted some four hours ago, Chancellor! When Magister Ollan insisted that we pay you the courtesy of announcing our passage through Verge, I did not expect to be met with indifferent shrugs from a pack of ill-disciplined Greycloaks!"

"Nor...." huffed Ollan from behind him, "did we expect... quite so many... stairs.."

"Thelen's breath! Please, Learned Magisters, come in and take some refreshment!" said Pieter, hurriedly. "I have ice-water, some fresh juices and I can have tea or coffee brought up should you wish it. Come, come!"

Once the two Magisters were settled, Ollan cast an interested eye around the study. "So, made yourself at home, have you?"

"That's not all he's made," observed Haran, inclining his head to Pieter's desk.

Ollan chuckled. "Indeed. It would certainly explain all these shavings of khilewood. You certainly moved fast, Chancellor- if I remember correctly, the Symposium only approved your third Leaf two days ago."

Pieter nodded, as Ollan took a large draught of ice-water. "I confess, Learned Magister, I had been considering completing my staff for some time. When the

Symposium decided to reward me for my efforts here, contemplation turned rapidly to obsession. I have windows and even a balcony behind me, and yet until I opened that door I was firmly convinced it was still yesterday evening."

"That is to be expected," admitted Haran. "A Magister's staff is a deeply personal thing, after all, as well as an expression of their power, and for someone of your years to not have one must have rankled." Pieter gave a wry laugh.

"I still have my head, Learned Magister. Had my power been anything other than mediocre, I doubt I could have kept it down, or attached, during the War. But it will be... satisfying to finally have a staff. I wonder, Learned Magisters, could I prevail upon you to...?"

"Hmm?" said Ollan, innocently, studying the staff. "Fine work on this, by the way, Pieter. I particularly like how you've kept the imagery restricted to lilies and other College symbols rather than anything too... Royal."

"Indeed," agreed Haran. "Quite the most non-committal staff I've seen, but that's completely understandable under the circumstances."

"Learned Magisters, I don't wish to delay you but please..." said Pieter, some-what desperately.

"Delay us?" said Ollan. "My word, you're quite right, we really must be going. The Sixth are working like madmen to get the Road to the Vigil back into service and I fear your cousin will be most aggrieved if we arrive a day after they finish, eh Haran?"

"You're quite right, Learned Magister," agreed Haran. "I wouldn't want to be the man to make Kandira's efforts go to waste. I think as soon as you're fully recov-ered from the effort of tackling all of those stairs, we should be going."

"As soon as *I'm* recovered!" boomed Ollan in mock indignation. "I distinctly recall you stopping for a rest at least twice during-"

"Please, Learned Magisters, will you conduct the ritual to attune my staff?" blurted Pieter.

The two elder Magisters looked at each other. "About time, eh Haran?" said Ollan.

"Aye," agreed Haran. "Much longer and we might have run out of things to stand here talking about."

"Oh, I could have gone on for far longer, believe me," said Ollan, puffing out his chest. "They don't call me the Master of the Filibuster for nothing, you know."

"I am unaware of anyone ever referring to you by that title," said Haran, flatly.

"Nonetheless, long-winded recitals of reasons why you really, truly should be going as soon as possible are a critical tool in the hands, or rather the mouth, of any truly committed blatherer," admonished Ollan. "You would do well to learn that, Haran. Never use one word when fifty will do."

Haran gave him a long, hard look. "Quite."

Ollan rolled his eyes. "You see what I have to work with, Pieter. Amongst House Dar, I think that comeback qualifies as wit. Now, ordinarily we would assemble your closest friends and relatives for this ceremony along with at least one representative of your *Alma Mater*, but the only person I can think of who might possibly fit either bill would be Indiria Tydask and she's been dead for some time, unfortunately. We shall simply have to make do with us three, and an entire Campus Keep that has stood largely untapped for over a year."

"Will that be enough?" asked Pieter with some sincerity. The two senior Magisters exchanged another glance, Ollan deadpan whilst Haran failed to completely keep the smile from his face.

"I think it might possibly suffice," said Ollan.

22

The carriage that Thalia had been loaned by the Orsinios hurtled down the Road towards the port city of Dalliance, which lay next on the route to Abellan. As Lady Ysabella had promised, it was a considerably more advanced vehicle than the one they had arrived at Castle Orsinio in, and the team of driver and guard who rode at the front of the coach to control its four-horse team were shielded from the roaring wind by heavy protective gear as well as warding spells. This time, Athas rode in the vehicle with the rest of them, a situation that given recent events was less than ideal.

The warm summer sun shone down, but the atmosphere inside the coach was distinctly chilly. The seats were wide enough for Thalia, Devereux and Delys to all sit on one plushly-upholstered seat whilst Athas sat on the other, facing them, looking utterly miserable. Delys, on the other hand, had settled into a corner and promptly fallen asleep.

Thalia glared at Athas as if she was trying to turn him to stone with sheer willpower. "Sergeant, you will explain to me exactly what happened back there, and you will leave nothing out, or as soon as we get to Dalliance I will have you put on the first boat to Damisk. Do you understand me?"

"Y-yes, Learned Magister.." said Athas, miserably. "But I.. I really don't want to talk about it.."

"You do know I can see your Pattern, don't you?" snapped Thalia. "I can see her... on you. Her Aether is clinging to you like that cheap perfume did to her."

Devereux winced. "Thalia... just let him explain?"

"Oh, I'll *gladly* let him explain!" hissed Thalia. "I'm positively eager for him to do so! But all I'm getting is 'I got a little delayed' and 'I had to help out Lady Melisa.' Well, I think we can all guess what you helped her out *of*, can't we?"

"It wasn't like that!" said Athas, flushing.

"Athas, you need to give us something here," said Devereux. "I think I might understand what happened, but you need to tell us the truth." At her side, Delys snored quietly.

"All... all right, Amanda," said Athas. "Well, as you saw Lady Melisa took me to show me where to put your luggage, Learned Magister. But on the way down to the stables, she said we were passing her chambers and she wanted to go in and change out of her morning dress and shoes, because it was a bit dirty underfoot down there. She was in there a few minutes, and then she called and said she needed a bit of help."

"I bet she did," growled Thalia.

"I went in," said Athas, quietly. "She had a Stickman as a maid- or maybe you'd call it a stick-woman, because it was all carved with a dress and everything. It was holding the clothes Melisa had been wearing, and once I came in it went to the door and shut it and then sort of.. stopped in front of it. Melisa called in from the next room and said that the stupid thing couldn't find the new dress she was going to put on even though she'd laid it out on the table that morning, and could I find it for her and bring it to the bedroom door. So I looked, and there was another dress on the table that looked like the one she'd been wearing to me, but what do I know about ladies' clothes?"

"Other than how to get them out of them, you mean?" grumbled Thalia, but Devereux could see she was listening carefully.

"Carry on, Athas," said the Operative, gently.

"Well, I said I'd found it and she asked me to hold it out in front of me and close my eyes so she could come and get it, so I did, and I heard the door open and there was this ripping sound from right in front of me, so my eyes sort of snapped open on reflex and she was stood there, right in front of me, stark naked, holding my boot-knife! I didn't even feel her slide it out, Learned Magister!" said Athas in a rush, almost running out of breath before he could get Thalia's title out.

Thalia visibly bit back another angry comment. "So she, what, threatened you at knifepoint? *You?*"

"No, that's not it," said Athas, shaking his head. "She'd slashed the dress I was holding open at the front with it, really roughly. Then she said if I didn't do what she wanted, she'd cut herself with the knife and then scream loud enough for the whole castle to hear!"

Devereux imagined how that would look. A man of Athas' size, a ripped dress, a shallow cut that would look like it could have been inflicted as he slashed the clothing. Perhaps the evidence wouldn't have held up in court, but at the very least it could have been devastating for the outcome of Thalia's mission. It could even have started another war at the worst time possible.

"And what, exactly, did she want you to do?" asked Thalia, in a flat tone now devoid of all emotion.

Athas opened his mouth to speak, thought for a moment, and closed it again. Finally he shrugged and simply said. "Her."

"Blood, ice and fire!" shouted Thalia. "Are you seriously trying to tell me that that blonde Abelian.... *scrubber* forced you to... to... *fuck* her and risked causing a major diplomatic incident to do it? This is one of the richest families in Abelia and she's a beautiful young woman- why in Thelen's name would she want to do something like that?"

Thalia had gone bright red, and she looked to be on the verge of tears. Athas looked down at his boots, shamefaced.

"I- I'm sorry, Learned Magister. I didn't want to tell you, I knew you'd be upset, but-"

"I AM NOT UPSET!" screamed Thalia. The Hercules suite gave a tactical alert that the temperature inside the coach had increased by over ten degrees, and Devereux could feel heat radiating from the furious Magister. Where her hands were digging into the upholstery, it had begun to smoulder. Quickly, the Operative slipped in front of Thalia, taking a firm grip on her shoulders and looking straight into her eyes.

"All right, Learned Magister, let's back it down before you burn this coach to ashes with us in it, eh?"

Thalia blinked at her, seemingly realising what she was doing for the first time. "Wh-what? Oh... oh, yes." Her eyes flared angrily again. "After all, we are going to need it to take us straight back to that damnable castle so I can find Lady Melisa and-"

"No, we don't need to go back there, Thalia," said Devereux, quietly, flicking a quick glance at Delys. Amazingly, the little Swordmaster was still asleep. "I think I can understand what happened here."

"Oh we can all understand what happened!" snapped Thalia. "We've all seen him with his shirt off, after-" she clapped a hand over her mouth, the red flush of rage replaced by a crimson of embarrassment. Fortunately, Athas was still staring at his boots and didn't seem to have noticed.

"That's not what I mean," said Devereux. "Athas- Athas, listen to me. Are you going to be all right?"

Athas took a deep breath. "I.. think so. I mean, it wasn't exactly... *bad*, just... well, if she'd just *asked*..."

"You'd have said no politely, of course," prompted Devereux. This time it was Thalia's distraction that saved the situation.

"Uh, yeah. So what did you mean you understood what happened?"

Thalia had recovered her wits by now. "Yes, I'd like to hear that explanation as well, Amanda."

"They're dying out, Thalia."

"What? Who?"

"The Abelians. How many human staff did we see at Castle Orsinio, five? Even the family's only daughter has one of those Stickmen for a maid, and did you notice how much the guy serving us at breakfast looked like Sir Hektor? The Great Houses have all these rules and rituals about who can marry into them, but it's a sham. They're desperate for new blood- any new blood. I'll bet that the Orsinios have at least one maid who's mother to some of the other staff."

"And you think Lady Ysabella just.. looks the other way?" said Thalia, horrified.

"I think she encourages it. Athas got away lightly- I think if we'd stayed there longer than a day it wouldn't have just been Melisa trying to get her claws into him, it'd be her mother too."

Athas opened his mouth to say something, but a startled gulp was all that came out.

"So.. you're saying the whole family knew this was going to happen? That they engineered it?" said Thalia, her look of horror gradually shifting to sheer incredulity. "Why?"

"Oh, I imagine that all the rules were followed to begin with," said Devereux. "But you can only breed with such a narrow gene-pool for so long before... problems set in."

"Like the Tydasks," said Thalia.

"Erm, yeah, maybe. In my world the old European royal families did have a few brushes with insanity. Anyway, right now I'd guess that a man with Athas' obvious physical prowess who isn't related to any of the Great Families would be considered a pretty valuable commodity in Abelia."

"I'm not sure I want to be a commodity," said Athas, firmly.

"Well," said Thalia, firmly. "I can appreciate, Sergeant, that you were put in an impossible situation, even if you did blunder into it like an idiot. I think for the duration of our visit it might be better if you were to avoid being left alone with any of the Abelian noblewomen, just as a precaution, don't you?"

Athas nodded, eagerly. "Yes, Learned Magister. I'll make sure I don't go out of your sight."

Thalia looked him up and down. "Hmm. I think in addition to that, once we arrive in Dalliance you should wear full armour at all times. We'll make a big show of you being the overprotective bodyguard, make it clear that there's no way you're going to be... lured away again. What do you think, Amanda?"

She turned to look at the Operative, but Devereux had stopped paying attention. "Thalia, I think something's wrong with Del."

"What? Why?"

"She fell asleep a little after we started moving, but even when you were shouting she didn't so much as stir." Devereux tapped the little Swordmaster on the shoulder and recoiled in shock. "Ouch! What the hell?"

++Aether reserves at 72% and dropping++

"What happened?" said Athas, eyeing them worriedly.

"I don't know! I touched her to see if I could wake her up and it was like she... drained me. It was almost painful." Devereux frowned. That was the first time since the reboot at the Wake that the Hercules suite had displayed its inexplicable ability to monitor her Aether, but there were more important things to worry about.

Thalia was staring at Delys too now, her eyes unfocused. "Something's wrong, certainly. There's barely any Aether flowing through her Pattern. Right now, even Athas has more."

"What?"

Thalia reached carefully over, and pulled up the sleeve of Delys' blouse so she could see her Seal. "Hmm, the Seal isn't blackened, so it's not that." She gingerly poked Delys' arm. "Nothing happens if I touch her, either."

"Could it be that disease that the Abelians got?" said Athas, shifting slightly away from the girl on his seat. "The.. Argue?"

"The Winnowing Ague," corrected Thalia. "And yes, it's possible. It certainly had the effect of draining the victim's Aether and making them sleepy, which seems to fit Delys' symptoms. What I can't understand is how she could have contracted it."

"It could be all manner of things!" said Devereux, a feeling of helpless panic starting to rise within her. "The food, the water- maybe the Abelians carry it but the survivors are immune! We need to get her help, quickly!"

"Calm down, Amanda," said Thalia. "From what we know of the Ague it only kills those who are too weak to resist it, and we all know Delys is anything but that."

Devereux considered for a moment, and then impulsively clapped her hand firmly on Delys' shoulder. "Del! Wake up, damn it! Agh!"

++ Operative Alert: Aether reserves at 27% and dropping ++

It felt as if she had stuck her entire hand into a live power socket. The electric buzz shot from her hand up her arm, causing her fingers to convulse involuntarily.

++Operative Alert: Aether reserves at 11% and dropping. Left hand muscular control compromised. Organic and fibre-bundle actuators unresponsive++

"Amanda!" shouted Thalia. "Let go! I don't know what that's doing to Delys but it could kill you!"

"I- I can't!" replied the Operative, now truly panicking. Her entire arm seemed to be on fire now, and it wouldn't respond to her. She grabbed it with the other arm, trying to pull it off, but the instant her grip closed the paralysis spread to both limbs.

++SUCS emergency motive override engaged. Brace for impact.++

Without any command from Devereux, her legs suddenly kicked her backwards full-force. For a moment, Delys was pulled off her seat with her, but then her body collided with Thalia's and the Operative's grip was torn free. She had just enough time to be grateful that her hand hadn't been fully closed when it froze before she burst through the door of the speeding carriage into the daylight.

23

When Moon Behind Dark Clouds emerged into the portal chamber, most of the Shorewalkers were gasping for breath. It wasn't due to any lack of air, but rather because the heat and closeness of the chamber were so oppressive that they struck almost like a blow in the gut. Night's First Raven was helping some of the youngest, in particular First of Shadowed Mountains, the pregnant girl.

Her younger brother stood up from her side, and turned to confront Moon, sweat pouring down his cheeks and his breath coming in ragged gasps. "What is this place, First? It is hotter than the depths of Ignilandarath in here!"

Moon shook his head, wryly. "It is not, young one, for the depths of Ignilandarath are precisely where you are standing. Still, this ancient place is nowhere for our fragile flesh to linger. Come, Shorewalkers!"

He led the way, and the tribe followed, more hastily this time. Until now, the flaming depths of the ancient volcano known only as Ignilandarath had existed in the minds of the Free Tribes merely as a metaphor for the hottest place imaginable. Few had expected to ever actually go there. And yet it was high upon the slopes of that ancient, black-stoned mountain that Ixilinath had built his refuge, Ixildundal, after his escape from the vengeful forces of the newly-founded Lily College centuries ago. When Moon Behind Dark Clouds had asked her why, Mighty Lelioko had told him that the volcano stood on a place of great power, and the inhospitable location made pursuit by the Warlock's enemies extremely difficult. There was also the fact, made obvious by their passage through the twisting corridors, that in the event that an enemy gained access to the portal chamber it would be trivially easy to seal the access tunnels and leave them to either retreat back through it, or bake alive.

Finally they came to a place where the tunnel opened out into a plateau on the side of the mountain, and here the First called a halt. Other thralls of Ixil were there, some of them bearing the Healing Hands, and they were ready with cooling drinks and simple food to fortify the Shorewalkers for the last part of their journey. As a couple of the healers fussed over her daughter, Shadowed Mountains caught the First's eye.

"You would ask us to leave our children here, in this dread place, First?" she hissed to him, as he drew near. "This is no place for the young. Umba's teeth, it is no place for the living!"

Moon Behind Dark Clouds nodded. "Aye. But this is not Ixildundal. Rather, this is the defence that keeps it safe. Know, Shadowed Mountains, that here we stand more than two days' travel on foot from either the sea, or the Shriven Marshes, and further still from any other place food might grow. The Woe-bearers would find great hardship in trying to travel here, even if they did not fear Master Ixil's power- and fear it they do."

"But if we are so far from any source of food, what will become of us?" asked the older woman. "Are we to eat rocks?"

Night's First Raven gave her an encouraging smile. "All will be revealed in time, revered one. Be at peace."

"Easy for you to say with all your youth and curves and.. things that are still firm with promise," grumbled the other. "Some of us have to think about the children."

Once rested, they pressed on, up the steps cut into the side of the mountain. One of the warriors, Fire in Deep Woods, suddenly gasped in surprise, running his finger carefully across a small, glistening outcropping. "Blade-glass!"

"Aye," smiled Moon Behind Dark Clouds. "Did you never wonder where the stones that make our spears so deadly and our knives so sharp came from?"

"I had thought the Mountain Halls.." began the warrior.

"And that was what the Mighty Ones chose to let us believe," agreed the First. "In fact, the stores held there were mined here in ancient times. The mines are here still, and my Master's servants work them as needed. It is an unpleasant duty, but the Blade-glass is so resilient that it is necessary only rarely."

"And yet many arrows were lost when the Black Demons attacked the halls," pointed out Fire in Deep Woods. "And more weapons too when that Nak-damned wyrm chose to finish the job."

"Aye," nodded Night's First Raven. "It might be that there is pick-work to be done, unless we wish to face the Fly Lords unarmed or go empty-sacking to the Deluded. But were we not here, there would be no recourse for us at all."

"Enough talk," said Moon Behind Dark Clouds. "If there is breath in your breast for idle chatter, there is breath for walking, and we have some way to travel yet. Come!"

The stone steps cut into the side of the great mountain were ancient, but had been inscribed with runes of preservation and still stood as flat and sharply-defined as the day when they were first carved. Mighty Lelioko had told Moon that they had even survived an eruption of the slumbering volcano, which had seemed incredible to the First until he had seen more evidence of the Master's power. He smiled to himself as he recognised a familiar corner ahead, and waited for the gasps as the tribe rounded it. They came just when he expected them to.

"It.. it is wondrous..." whispered Fire in Deep Woods. "How is it possible?"

They looked up at a scene of verdant promise. The slopes of the mountain, barren and rocky no longer, swayed with green leafy plants, great trees, and flowers in an abundance of colours. Here and there, in terraces cut into the side of the slope, crop-fields and grazing pastures spread out before the eye, each different and each bursting with life. Even those who had seen the glories of Ixil-dundal before found themselves stopping to drink in the spectacle.

"These are the Master's gardens," said Night's First Raven. "Just as new life grows from the carcass of a dead beast, so does new vitality follow in the wake of the mountain's anger. The fire that comes from the depths brings with it the good-ness that lies buried deep within the earth, and that goodness will feed the people of Ixil and keep our children safe. And then there is the fortress itself."

She pointed, and as one the Shorewalkers looked up, above the fields, to see a glassy black wall, surmounted by squat, solid-looking towers. "There stands Ixil-dundal, stronghold of the Master."

"There?" said Fire in Deep Woods. "But we are still no more than half-way up the mountain. Would not the very summit be easier to defend?"

Moon Behind Dark Clouds chuckled. "Aye, it would. But mostly because at that height, the air lies so thin and so chill that only a Mighty One could survive for long. The Master does indeed have a bastion further up the slopes, but it is no place for the Free to go."

"Are we... are we to stay here?" asked Shadowed Mountain, glancing around. "It is pleasant enough, but even here there is a bite to the breeze that I dislike." She wrapped her heavy cloak around her, even though as an elder she wore simple linen robes rather than a battle harness beneath it.

"Only if you wish it," said Night's First Raven, "or if the Master decides you are needed. Mothers and fathers may stay until their children are old enough for the Binding, of course, Master Ixil has no desire to break up your families."

"Fathers, ha!" said First of Shadowed Mountains, bitterly. The father of her child had proved to be an ill match and it was likely it would be born Wretched. The warrior responsible had met his end on the tip of her brother's spear, after refusing honourable exile. Moon had a sudden, chilling thought- would the Master accept the service of a Wretched? What would become of the child if he did not? He looked at the young mother, trying to judge if her time was likely to come before he returned to the lands of the Free. It was cowardly of him, he knew, but he had no desire to witness what might happen.

"Where does the water come from?" asked Fire in Deep Woods, suddenly. "You said we were far from sea or marsh, and I know of no rivers in the Wastes."

"There are none," agreed the First, glad to be able to change the subject. "A deep pool lies in the heights of the mountain, formed by snow-melt and rainfall. Once it fed a river that flowed into the Wastes, but the Master diverted it to His own purposes to fill a hidden reservoir and irrigate his fields. Fear not, our bellies will not be empty, nor our tongues parched, while we are within His domain."

"Unless we forsake his 'gift' of course," said Shadowed Mountains. Night's First Raven rounded on her, swiftly.

"Do not speak such words! We are here under the Master's sufferance and He is benevolent, but do not seek to incur His wrath with an incautious or disrespectful tongue! Once you have seen the wonders of Ixildundal, there can be no turning back, no wavering in your resolve. If you believe nothing else we have told you, believe that!"

Shadowed Mountains glared back at her. "It is enough that we have agreed to call him Master in spite of all we are as Free, Second. If Ixil expects us to be happy about it, he shall be sorely disappointed."

Moon Behind Dark Clouds shook his head, sadly. She would learn. May the Ancestors help them, they would all learn.

24

The Wardens thundered down the Great East Road towards Ratheram's Cross, Magisters Haran and Ollan in the vanguard. It was fortunate, Haran thought, that the Road was now fully operational and neither the help of the Singers, nor of the Magisters, was required to keep the Volume moving at full battle march. After the events of that morning, he doubted that either he or Ollan would have been much use. Even now his strength was only just returning.

Riding at his side, the elder Magister had the hood of his robe up, something Haran didn't think he'd ever seen Ollan do before in fine weather. He was also, like Haran, holding his staff across the saddle of his horse, allowing the revitalising flow of Aether from the Road to pass through him into the device.

"Are we going to talk about what happened back there?" asked Haran, when he could bear it no longer.

"What *did* happen back there?" shot back Ollan, though his voice was far quieter than his usual bombast. "I have never felt anything like that, even when we helped young Thalia with her staff and things took a turn for the strange. This was something else entirely. It was almost as if the staff were... broken."

Haran shook his head. "For once, Learned Magister, I think you misunderstand."

Ollan pushed back his hood, revealing a face that was only just beginning to regain its full colour. Despite dark circles of fatigue under his eyes, he favoured the other Magister with a faint smile as he took out his pipe and lit it with a glance. "Really? This should be a tale worth telling."

"I think you are right, in that something involved in the ritual was broken," said Haran, ignoring the mild jibe in his relief that Ollan seemed to be recovering both health and humour. "But I don't think it was the staff. I think it was Pieter himself."

"Hmph," grunted Ollan. "I confess that given that I spent most of my time feeling like someone had turned my Pattern inside-out, I was possibly not paying

94

full attention to the details. Next time we do something like that you can take the lead on the ritual, by the way. That was not an experience I care to repeat."

"Mine was not much more pleasant," said Haran. "But to get back to the point- there was a.. hunger.. to Pieter that was not confined to his staff, even though we were standing on top of a barely-tapped Waycrystal. There was power aplenty there, even when we were done, and yet both of us left that room barely able to stand, whilst Pieter seemed stronger than when we started."

Ollan stroked his beard thoughtfully, before blowing out a large cloud of foul-smelling smoke. "Ahh, that is considerably better. You may have something, Haran, but I am not entirely certain what. Pieter did not seem to do anything unusual during the ritual, and had he somehow attacked our Patterns in some way I am sure we would have noticed."

"What do we really know about Pieter?" said Haran. "He was the only natural child of Emperor Adramion and Empress Hypatia?"

"That survived the war, yes," clarified Ollan. "There was at least one more child born to her after him, but it was horribly malformed and died almost immedi-ately- I don't think the Healers were even able to work out what gender it was. A sister and a brother, Dilna and Tiber, preceded him but both had to be Sealed. Then there were the twins, Filia and Maria, who scraped a Leaf between them. Whatever else one might say about Hypatia, the woman didn't give up easily."

"Would you?" said Haran. "On second thought, the images that places in my head make me forbid you to answer. So.. Dilna was a Healer, if memory serves, and was killed in Verge, and Tiber.."

"White Riders," said Ollan. "Made up to a troop leader more through blood than ability, and went down at the first battle of Sommerlan. I believe it was mostly considered to be a waste of a good horse at the time, though I doubt many appreciated what it must have been like to have that name and be serving in a Loyalist unit. The twins fled Lore at the start of the War and took ship for Freeport, but met a bad end at the hands of Toskan pirates. Was there some point to this grim litany?"

"I don't know," confessed Haran. "I was wondering if Pieter was... flawed in some way and the staff ritual was part of some plan to... heal himself? No, that doesn't seem right. Even with his talent for healing, the ritual is too taxing for such subtleties."

"The only other thing of note I remember is that he seemed quite promising as a child," said Ollan. "I remember remarking to old Indiria on the occasion of his gaining his first Leaf that his development seemed to have somewhat plateaued, rather forgetting that she was his grandmother."

"How did she react?" asked Haran, trying to imagine the scene.

"She nearly bit my head off," replied the elder Magister with a faint smile. "She was always very protective of her Twigs, especially those that were family. And yet she did not truly contradict me."

"Interesting," said Haran. "The received wisdom was always that all the Tydask children prior to Ullarth were weak-blooded, but then I suppose in that House a perfectly competent but unremarkable Magister could be considered a disap-pointment."

"Well," said Ollan, after a long pause. "I don't suppose it matters all that much. If all we have done is make the caretaker Chancellor of Verge strong enough to perhaps retain his post when some bottom-feeder comes along to try and take it, I for one will weep no tears. Of course, perhaps this was part of some grand scheme and Pieter will eventually reach such a level of power that he can unseat Derelar and restore House Tydask to power, or for that matter, existence."

Haran stared at him wide-eyed, not for the first time unsure of whether the older man was joking. "And what if he does?"

"Then we hope he has a short memory for his enemies and a long one for his friends," said Ollan. "Now, shall we make a push for the Cross? I have heard interesting things about the food at the 'X on the Spot.'"

Haran watched as Ollan rode to the head of the column and started to wave his staff in the air, chanting as he did so. Once again he was playing the character of the theatrical buffoon, acting as if his lunch was the most important thing on his mind, but for a moment, the mask had slipped. He had spent enough time around Magister Ollan Dane to know the old man was deeply worried.

25

*O*perative Amanda Devereux lay in an untidy, bloodied heap and regarded the odd angle the horizon was sitting at. It took her a moment to realise that what had initially seemed to be the sky was in fact the ground, and she was upside-down- or at least, her head was. She wasn't in any pain, which didn't necessarily mean anything because her medical suite was capable of shutting down the relevant receptors if necessary or administering a variety of pain-killers.

She tried to stand, and discovered she couldn't move. That was a more worrying development.

Status report.

++SUCS motive override in effect. Damage to external armour and skin layers: Level 1 62% compromised, Level 2 3.6% compromised. Level 3 intact. Skeletal and muscular structure at 98% integrity, upper limb actuators still unresponsive. Operative consciousness restored after 31.6 minutes of trauma-induced fugue state. Medical and self-repair systems operating, but self-repair so far ineffective on upper limbs.++

Daniel's impassive report was a cause for serious concern. The combat support system had stopped her from moving for her own protection, which was understandable, but whatever had paralysed her arms was apparently still doing so. The damage to her outer skin was not really a problem- level one was merely the organic layer that gave her the appearance, body heat and fingerprints of a normal human being- but if anyone found her at this moment they wouldn't have to look very hard to see the Kevlar and silk composite weave that lay beneath it. She was just considering overriding the shutdown so she could at least look for some cover when she heard the shout.

"Amanda! Amanda, where are you?"

It was Athas' voice. She tried to shout back, but the paralysis was so total that she couldn't even do that.

Deactivate SUCS override.

++Operative Alert: Repair cycle incomplete. Procedure not recommended.++

Understood. Deactivate SUCS override.

"Over here!" she called back, a moment later. After a few seconds, something she recognised as one of Athas' boots appeared in her vision.

"Thelen's balls, Amanda, are you all right? There's... there's blood everywhere!"

"I've been better," she admitted. "Don't worry about the blood though, that's mostly... well, just don't worry about it."

"Don't move her!" cried Thalia's voice as she hurried over. "At least not until I've had a look at... Thelen's breath.."

There was a pause. Devereux guessed Thalia was looking at her Pattern, though the Magister had confessed to her before that with all the augmentation and modifications her body had been subjected to she literally couldn't make head nor tail of it.

"Bah, this is no use," grumbled the Magister. "Your Pattern was inscrutable enough before, but with that fake Seal on you I have even less of a clue as to what might be going on. You have shown a remarkable resilience before- can you not restore yourself this time?"

Carefully, Devereux unfolded herself and made to stand up. "Give me a hand here, Athas, my arms are still frozen. I'm working on it, Learned Magister. Most of the damage can be repaired but I have no idea what happened to my arms when I touched- Del!"

To her great surprise and relief, Devereux saw the little Swordmaster standing behind Thalia. She was holding *Liberty* in its scabbard. She looked tired, but the mere fact that she was awake at all was the best news the Operative had received since waking up herself. Thalia glanced quickly between the two of them, and smiled.

"Yes, she woke up almost immediately after your... er.. exit. Draining almost every last scrap of Aether from you seems to have done the trick, and there's no further sign of the Ague or anything similar. I found your sword some way back through the Messaging Crystal attached to it, and then we just followed the trail of destruction in its wake."

"Trail of..?" started Devereux, looking around. Leading up to the large, flat rock she seemed to have crashed into at the end of her involuntary journey was a trail gouged in the earth, which from the spacing and depth of the impacts suggested she must have been bouncing and tumbling. "Oh."

"Yeah, we found both of your guns on the way, and most of your.. er.. blouse.." said Athas, beginning the sentence holding the battered weapons out to her before visibly realising firstly that she was unable to reach for them, and secondly that under the mask of blood and dirt the Operative's upper body was mostly naked. He flushed red to the tips of his ears.

"Don't worry, Athas, my underwear is made of tougher stuff than that silk you and Del wear," said Devereux. "I'm still decent under all this- probably. Anyway, I'm far more concerned about my arms than I am about maybe being bare-chested."

Let me. Delys flicked the words, suddenly. Before anyone could react, she had reached out and taken Devereux's outstretched hand, still locked into a grasping claw.

"Wait, Delys!" gasped Thalia. "It was that sort of impulsive action that caused all of this trouble in the first place!"

Delys shook her head. *No. Hungry dream.* She turned back to Devereux, and placed the other hand she had used to sign the words on top of the first. There was another electrical tingle in the limb, but this one was softer, gentler, more controlled.

"What do you mean, 'hungry dream'?" snapped Thalia, before letting out a gasp of surprise as Devereux's arms relaxed. "I.. I really am going to have to write a paper about that strange synergy you two seem to have."

"I'm just glad it worked," admitted Devereux, testing the movement of the limbs carefully. "Thanks, Del."

++Operative Advisory: Arm actuators restored to 100% functionality. Aetheric transfusion received: reserves at 22.3%. Phenomena outside understood operating parameters and added to ongoing database for analysis.++

Yeah, Daniel, I don't have a clue what happened either.

They walked back to the coach, which had been travelling at such speed that it had got several miles further down the Road before it had come to a halt. As they went, Devereux reattached her weapons and restored the storage webbing, her nanites having already removed the blood and dirt and restored the standard combat jumpsuit which she had been wearing beneath her shredded clothing. The devices could have replaced the other clothes too, but even those simple garments were woven with subtle magics to keep them clean and fresh on the road which the nanites could not replicate- and their absence might raise the wrong sorts of questions.

Instead, once they reached the coach Athas reached up and unloaded a couple of the sturdy trunks the Abelians had provided for their spare clothing. As Devereux swiftly pulled on a new blouse and breeches, ignoring the goggling eyes of the coachman and his guard, Athas took the opportunity to unpack his armour and change into it as Thalia had suggested. To do so, he first had to remove his tunic to replace it with the padded leather under-shirt, and as he did the Operative saw something that made her laugh out loud.

"Stop, Athas! Thalia, come take a look at this!"

The Magister, who had been waiting on the other side of the coach, came around the corner swiftly to find Athas' frozen with his tunic halfway over his head. "What's the matter- oh! Amanda, I hardly think that such a joke at the Sergeant's expense is appropriate given the circumstances."

"That's just it," said Devereux, pointing. "Look!"

Thalia looked at Athas' bare chest, doing her best to seem reluctant to do so, and then visibly did a double-take. "Sergeant! What, exactly, is that?"

"Mhpmghmgm!?" said Athas, his voice muffled by the tunic that was still covering his face before he pulled it off in exasperation. "What's what?"

"That," said Thalia, pointing at the skull-carved wooden button nestling in the big Guardsman's navel.

"Oh, this thing?" said Athas. "That's something Mar- Ar- a.. friend suggested I get when we were on layover in Lore after that whole business with the Red Witch at the Wake. Sh- they said it would help keep me safe."

"Did Ariel tell you what it would keep you safe *from*?" said Thalia, archly. Athas opened his mouth as if to deny her assumption, but then closed it again.

"No, Learned Magister," he replied after a moment. "She just said it would help prevent.. accidents. All of her friends have one."

99

Devereux could take it no longer. Athas was like a mouse stuck under a cat's paw and Thalia showed no intention of putting him out of his misery. "It's a Killer, Athas, or at least that's what the House Belus Guard who told me about them called it. It's a contraceptive device."

"A contra- what?" said the big man, his brow furrowing.

"Thelen's breath, Sergeant, those things have only been on sale for fifty years or so!" laughed Thalia. "It never ceases to amaze me how little attention young men pay to that sort of thing. It stops you making babies, Athas."

"Oh," said Athas, seemingly uninterested. "Oh! That means that Lady Melisa..."

"..needs to learn to allow the gentlemen she.. seduces.. to at least remove their shirts," said Thalia with a slightly cruel smile. "As it was, I hope she enjoyed the immediate fruits of her efforts because they will bear no others. Ha!"

"I hope she won't get into any trouble..." said Athas, quietly, shrugging into the leather shirt and buckling the plate armour over the top of it.

"I wonder what she would have done if she had noticed it," said Devereux, as much to stop Thalia reacting to Athas' concern as anything else. "Eri told me a Magister could defeat their magic if they really wanted to."

"True, but it usually causes the device to catch fire," said Thalia, confirming what the Operative already knew. "She might have known a way around it- I think those things were an Abelian invention in the first place. A huge number of them flooded the market after the Ague because after that they really didn't want them any more. Most of the modern ones are made in the Empire, though."

"So does this mean I don't need to wear my armour after all, Learned Magister?" asked Athas, sounding hopeful despite having only just finished putting it on. Thalia gave another slightly cruel laugh.

"Oh, of course not! Provided, that is, that you'd rather wander around bare-chested so everyone can see that thing."

Athas looked down at his stomach, now concealed beneath layers of metal and leather. "Er.. maybe I could cut a hole in my tunic?"

Devereux and Thalia looked at each other, and warmer laughter filled the early afternoon air.

26

$\mathcal{T}$he closer he led the Shorewalkers to the great gates of Ixildundal, the more nervous Moon Behind Dark Clouds became. Before, the supplicants to the Master had come in small groups, ones and twos, a few members of the same family or oath-sworn warrior bands, but this was different. This was the largest single number of people he had ever led on this dark pilgrimage, a journey which would, for all of the honeyed words of those who had preceded them on it, irrevocably change all their lives. The larger the crowd, the more likely some within it were to be harbouring doubts, and should one of the malcontents choose to express them at the wrong moment then dissent could spread like rot through a split-barked tree- with results that might be every bit as disastrous.

For all of His dread reputation, Ixilinath had not built His last redoubt to terrify. The old songs of Umba might speak of grinning skull-faced towers and moats of liquid fire, but they were not to be found here. Instead the black, glossy walls were smooth, devoid of all decoration and offering any invader no hand-hold. The two great towers that rose to either side of the main gate grew wider as they rose, spreading into a curving overhang that frowned down imposingly on the band of Free who stood beneath them. On each overhang, as well as at regular intervals along the walls, was set a large, flame-red gemstone. Mighty Lelioko had told Moon that these stones allowed the Master to cast both His vision, and His power through them, and it would go ill for any invader upon which either fell.

They stopped before the gate, and waited. To the Shorewalkers, this seemed a strange thing, for other than being framed by the towers of the gatehouse and lying at the end of a well-cut path, the section of wall they stood at seemed no different to any other, and bore no hinge or seam.

"What do we do now?" asked Fire in Deep Woods after a few moments. "Are we to knock, to let the Master know we are here? Does someone need to let down a rope for us?"

"No," said Moon Behind Dark Clouds quietly. "The Master knows. He will open the gate when He wills us to enter."

"But there is no-" began the warrior, but his words were cut short by a wave of flame that seemed to spill out from the gemstone set into the middle of the wall. There was no heat, no smell of burning, but after the fires had faded away it seemed they had taken the stonework with them.

"This... this is..." began Shadowed Mountains, but she seemed unable to finish the thought.

"The power of Master Ixil," finished Night's First Raven. Without another word, she strode forwards, boldly. Despite their obvious nervousness, the rest of the tribe followed her, several of the warriors pausing at the place where the wall had been to poke at the ground and the base of the nearby towers with their spears, as if to prove to themselves that the huge mass of solid stone had indeed burned away into nothingness, not leaving so much as a scorch mark or ash behind. Moon Behind Dark Clouds brought up the rear, satisfying himself that there were no stragglers, and moments after he crossed the threshold there was a second, bright surge of flame that left the wall restored as if it had always been there.

"Nak's skull," muttered Third of Shadowed Mountains as he helped his mother support his sister. "That such power should be employed where a simple door could suffice! Truly is this Master Ixil the mightiest of the mighty."

"Aye, He is that, young one," agreed the First. "And here, in the very heart of His domain, you would do well to remember it."

The great hall loomed ahead, its vast, open entrance lit from high above by more of the soft sigil-lights that had illuminated the portal chamber. From the depths of the room came a robed, hooded figure, faintly feminine in shape but concealed so deeply within the voluminous cloth that only its face was visible. Even that was covered by a white mask of enamelled silver, decorated to reflect the countenance of a stern-featured, but beautiful, woman.

"Greetings to you, Shorewalkers, new supplicants to Master Ixilinath," said the newcomer, her voice seeming as soft as the sound of rustling leaves on the wind and yet carrying easily to the very back of the group. *"I am she who is known as the Seneschal. You will follow me to the waiting-chamber, where you will be prepared for your audience with the Master."*

Not seeming to care whether the Shorewalkers were following, the figure turned smoothly on the spot, and led the way into the hall. They passed many corridors and hallways, each guarded by one of the gilded-bone Eternals whose fellows had once stood sentinel over the Mountain Halls. But these were different, and those few who dared look at them saw that these warriors stood upon their own feet and turned heads with eye-sockets filled with flame to watch the passers-by.

No-one dared speak. The silence of the halls seemed a living, solid thing, and even the sounds of their footsteps were muted to the point of inaudibility despite a floor that was as hard and unyielding as the black walls. Finally they came to the waiting chamber, and a long table filled with the fruits of Ixildundal's fields. High windows let in the late afternoon sun, and the floors were covered with fine carpets and rich rugs, giving the room a far more welcoming air. A few other

Shorewalkers who had previously been through the Branding were already there, and several of the new arrivals recognised friends and family amongst them.

One of the younger children in the group, Second of Sounds of Falling Water, saw her grandmother waiting for her by the table, and broke free of her mother to run to her. In the clumsy, heedless way of children, she careened heavily across the room, blundering into the Seneschal's robes as she went. The heavy cloths flew up, and all who watched could see that there was no body beneath them. For her own part, the creature seemed unconcerned.

"Nak's skull!" gasped Fire in Deep Woods.

"Yes," replied the Seneschal.

27

The burly, moustachioed man crashed down on his back, and this time, thank Yar, he didn't get back up again. There was a roar of appreciation from the watching crowd, a motley bunch of Toskan sailors, Abelian and Imperial traders, and other permanent or temporary citizens of Freeport. Maike Dain spat blood from her mouth, little caring that some of it spattered on the bare chest of her recumbent opponent, and grinned.

"That's five gold Raks you owe me, Kjôr," she said, realising immediately as she did so that talking was more painful than she'd expected. "Gah! Yar's tits, that hurts."

"Shit me breeches, ye took me to Gwai'Xi on that one, Red," groused the Toskan. "Helkin wiped the decks with yer last time."

Maike made to reply, but Gundala, the Jandallan herb-woman, took a firm hold of her jaw to stop her, eliciting an undignified squeak of protest. "Hush, you," she chided. "Victorious you may be, but at the cost of several teeth and at least a slightly fractured jawbone. Keep it still, may the Ground-Wyrms take you!"

"What about my man?" complained Blue Kjôr, gesturing to the groaning heap on the sandy floor.

"What of him? He is far less likely to move and do himself further mischief than this one is."

"He's startin' to stir, though," said the Toskan.

"Good, then he's not dead. Just make sure the idiot doesn't try to stand up until I've finished with 'Red Lightning' here."

"What do ye want me to do, knock him out again?"

"If you like," sniffed the albino, working fingers covered with some sort of foul-smelling paste into Maike's mouth. "Just don't blame me if you upset him."

The stuff in her mouth- not to mention the depth within it to which Gundala's strong, probing fingers were intruding- made Maike want to gag, but she resisted the reflex. Her methods might seem primitive, and the source of her supplies so far from her homeland questionable, but the Jandallan's ministrations were usually at least as effective as those of any College Healer.

"There. Now sit down with your... mistress and try not to talk for a few minutes whilst that works. Let's see if this dolt can be restored to his senses."

"That'd be the first time in ten years!" shouted a man in the crowd, one of the few punters to be collecting winnings from the ringmaster. Even those who had lost a few coins this time laughed- the informal fighting pit that operated behind the Last Anchor didn't take high-stakes bets for very good reasons.

Maike sat down next to Willow-Sigh Wen as she had been bid. The Daxalai gave her a slight nod of appreciation, though her face remained impassively serene. She spoke a quick sentence in her musical native language.

"Master Wen says your control is improving," translated Rat-Tail Lao, the exiled Daxalai trader who had been helping out as an interpreter. A small, wiry little man with furtive eyes, he was almost completely bald except for the long, thin, white ponytail that gave him his nickname. Though his coal-black skin gave his nationality away to even the most casual observer, he now dressed in the sleeveless working leathers of a typical Freeport dock-hand.

"Mhm," agreed Maike, carefully keeping her mouth shut. She could feel Gundala's efforts working, the damaged bone re-knitting and new teeth forming in the jagged, bloody holes where the missing ones had been. It hurt like hell, though.

"Improving!" snorted Blue Kjôr. "Deep's balls, I ain't never seen no-one fluke a fight as hard as that. When Red hit him that last time her cursed eyes was shut!"

Another soft-spoken reply. "Master Wen says that was *Ranlaou* preventing herself from destroying him. The rage-fires rose within her, but she cast her focus deep to control them and channel them only into the blow that was necessary."

"What a load of-" began the Toskan. "Hold hard- ye din't tell her what I said!"

"Master Wen has gained an understanding of the speech of the Chaotic East," said Rat-Tail. "She does not, however, choose to sully her tongue with it."

"But you do?" said Gundala, standing up from where Helkin was now sitting. The charms dangling from the rim of her wide-brimmed hat jangled, almost accusingly. Rat-Tail bowed.

"Indeed, Most Gentle Healer. I have long since abandoned the path of Harmony for the simpler pursuit of wealth, but it is good to speak the Highest Tongue with one so masterful." He gave Wen an expectant look, and the Daxalai flipped him a coin, which happened to be an Abelian silver Rubal. A bewildering array of currencies flowed through Freeport, and the economy was based so heavily on barter and haggling that the worth of any coin was based mostly on the skill of its bearer.

"On top of that," said the exile, "she does pay me well."

Kjôr laughed heartily. The blue-haired sailor visited the pits a lot, and always seemed to know when Maike was going to be fighting. He was still not above dropping less-than-subtle hints that he'd be quite happy to pay far more than she was making as a prize-fighter for a single night of her company, and more still if Wen herself were also part of the deal. Of course, even if Maike had been fighting solely for the money as the Toskan assumed, she would have rejected his clumsy advances, but there was far more to it than that.

When they had arrived at Freeport, short on funds and desperately in need of lodgings and food, Rat-Tail had soon found them and suggested that Willow-Sigh demonstrate her skills in the Pit. Reluctantly the Daxalai had agreed, and challenged the then champion, a huge warrior exiled from the lands of the Expelled who called himself Blood on Cast Stone. Unsurprisingly, given that the tattooed giant stood almost seven feet tall with his hair set into sharp-looking spikes with dried blood, the betting had been heavy against the slight Daxalai, with the exception of Rat-Tail and a few veterans of the Damisk Sea Guard. The fight was over in two blows- the lightning-fast hook from the giant and the spinning kick to the throat from the Daxalai that answered it. Even with Gundala's ministrations- the Last Anchor kept her on a retainer- the Expelled had taken a week to recover the power of speech.

The winnings had been enough to get the two of them food and lodging for a week at the inn, on the condition that Willow-Sigh did not fight again in the pit for fear of her driving away or crippling the other competitors. Maike had gone one day before her temper got the better of her in the main hall of the inn, and the resulting brawl had led both to a stern, if second-hand, lecture from Wen via Rat-Tail, and also to her new career as a pit-fighter. When Wen had offered to train her, Maike had eagerly accepted, expecting to learn the devastating fighting style that the Daxalai had employed to defeat all-comers, up to and including a Red Bear, but instead she had focused entirely on the red-head's self-control and state of mind. And yet all the physical and mental exercises, the seemingly pointless mundane tasks that she was expected to perform without a murmur of complaint, and the bruising defeats had somehow led to an awakening of sorts.

Since her capture at the hands of the Lily College, engineered in a way Maike still did not entirely understand by the Swordmaster, Delys Amaranth, she had been aware of a boiling fury deep within her. It was unquestionably powerful, but it was impossible to control, lending her sudden bursts of furious strength that fled just as suddenly and had repeatedly got her into serious trouble. It was this that Wen Lian-Shi had sensed within her, and this which the Daxalai Initiate, like her a fugitive from her own people, had sworn to help her control. Somehow, incomprehensibly, it was working. The more she endured in the pit, the more blows rained down on her and the more she struggled to land them in return, the more the power rose. Each time it did, whatever else might be happening at the time, she fought to control it, to harness it, to focus it from a raging, haphazard flame into a purposeful force. On several occasions, she had done so only to be sent sprawling by an unanticipated blow, the power scattering away with her consciousness. On one, she had lost control altogether and only Wen's sudden intervention had prevented disaster. But other times- perhaps even, she dared to hope, most of the time- she was able to master the power and unleash a single strike of such force that hostilities ended there and then.

And yet, even as she watched the next fight from the sidelines, the pain from her throbbing jaw and aching teeth gradually dulling, she couldn't shake the feeling that she was only just beginning to explore the power. There was something else, too, a recurring dream that she couldn't quite remember when she woke up. She knew only that it was always the same, and that there was mud and rain and anger. Of course, that perfectly described her fateful encounter with Delys but she was certain that wasn't it. Her thoughts were interrupted as a particularly good blow from one of the fighters- a dark-haired woman bearing the Seal of the Soldier on her bare shoulder- staggered her Toskan opponent, sending her reeling back in a spray of red blood and blue dreadlocks. The crowd cheered, and Maike joined in, hoping that one of these two might impress the mob enough that she'd get to fight someone her own size again. The blue-haired girl fell back against the single rope that marked the boundary of the fighting area, and as they always did the crowd gave her a firm shove forwards- not so much out of any malice, as because the flimsy barrier would never hold if they did not. The Toskan was ready for the push, and went with it, the runic brand on her exposed chest flaring as she threw a punch with the momentum. A solid thwack and another cheer immediately followed, but Maike's eyes refused to look away from the spot in the crowd where the Toskan had briefly come to rest.

She wasn't even sure what she had seen- a flash of blonde hair from under a hooded robe, perhaps- but suddenly the power flared up furiously. She wanted to scream, to throw herself forwards and to kill them, kill them all, tear them limb-from-limb and-

"*Ranlaou! Don!*"

Wen's voice snapped Maike back to reality. She realised she had clenched both hands into fists and was gritting her new teeth so tightly that they hurt. Wen spoke again.

"She says you nearly lost control again there," said Rat-Tail. "What did you see?"

"I- I don't know," replied Maike, her eyes scanning the crowd which was being whipped up into a frenzy by the desperate last moments of the fight. Whatever or whoever she had seen, they were gone.

ire in Deep Woods swallowed, hard. At his side, Moon Behind Dark Clouds gave him an encouraging clap on the back. "Courage, my friend! I have seen you face worse than this!"

"Have you?" replied the warrior. "Before, I faced foes I could fight with spear in hand- the blue-haired coast raiders, clawed beasts and warriors of the Deluded. Now, you ask that I defeat my own nature."

"The Master knows well the heart of the Free," said the Seneschal in her strange, whisper-loud voice. *"When you gaze upon his face and make your pledge, you will know peace."* The creature had not commented on its cryptic statement earlier, and simply ignored any questions about it.

The young man stared from his First, to the floating woman-thing, and to the Second who stood at his other shoulder. "Very well. If this is the price that must be paid to save our people, let us be about it."

They stood before the entrance of the audience chamber, some way down a wide hallway from the waiting room. There were more of the Eternals there, arrayed at regular intervals, clutching their ancient two-handed swords in gilded bone hands. The doorway itself was a single huge slab of jet-black stone, inscribed with the twisting sigil of Ixilinath that formed the core of the brands on the wrists of His thralls. As the small group of Shorewalkers watched, the sigil blazed into bright flame, and then vanished, taking the door with it. The scene within brought a gasp of shock from Fire in Deep Woods. That didn't surprise the First, because he had reacted in much the same way the first time.

The room behind the door was not exceptionally large, nor opulent. It held little except for a raised stone dais, upon which sat a huge, plain, black stone throne. There was no upholstery, cushion or other concession to comfort, but then the occupant hardly seemed to need one. Dressed in a rich, purple robe worked with threads that seemed to burn with their own inner fire, the figure was tall and imposing even when seated. He wore fine black leather boots that disappeared under the robes, and his hands were encased in soft gloves of similar make. He was also, as far as any observer could tell, long-dead. Though only his head was exposed, the skin was drawn so tight that it was practically a skull, and within his eye-sockets lay two of the same burning gemstones that were present everywhere throughout Ixilinath's domain.

Fire in Deep Woods stared for a moment, and then, despite being pale with shock, managed to laugh. "This? This is mighty Master Ixil, whose power will save us from the Woe? This is a corpse, First, at most a puppet of bone. I-"

Light flared in the gem-eyes of the thing, and it stood- not the motion of a corpse or a marionette, or even the stilted movement of an Eternal. It sprang to its feet with all the vitality and menace of a warrior whose honour had been insulted.

"I AM NO PUPPET! I AM NO CORPSE! I AM IXILINATH, THE PHYRE-SCRIBE, RULER OF IXILDUNDAL AND ALL I SURVEY. YOU WILL KNEEL."

The voice was like an avalanche, seeming at once slow and powerful and yet coming on in a rumbling rush that made every iota of the hearer's being vibrate. If Fire in Deep Woods had been shocked before, this display stunned him beyond all reason. Heedless of the hard stone floor he dropped to his hands and knees, head down, not daring to meet that burning gaze. "I- I apologise, Mighty One. I meant no disrespect."

"YOU DID," replied Ixilinath, flatly. "FOR YOU BELIEVED YOU FACED SOME RUSE, SOME TRICK OF A CONJURER. DO YOU BELIEVE THIS STILL, LITTLE WARRIOR?"

"N-No, Mighty One." said the warrior.

"SPEAK NOT THESE WORDS TO YOUR MASTER," said the thing, coming closer. "FOR YOUR MASTER, I AM. YOU COME TO ME AS SUPPLICANT, TO TAKE MY MARK, OR YOU COME TO BURN. CHOOSE."

Finally, Fire in Deep Woods looked up, managing to force himself to stare into the face of his Master. "I will take your mark, Master, and may the Ancestors forgive me."

"I CARE NOT FOR THE WILL OF THOSE FOOLS," said Ixilinath. "LET THE FLAME JUDGE YOU."

Then, suddenly, everything the young warrior knew was replaced with fire. A coruscating column of flame consumed him, reaching from floor to ceiling, and he screamed in agony, flesh already starting to blister.

"You must accept the brand! To resist it is to burn!" shouted Night's First Raven.

"I... I do accept it!" whimpered Fire in Deep Woods.

"In your heart, fool!" she cried back. "Believe it, do not simply say it!"

His skin charred almost black now, the young warrior stared wildly from the leaders of his tribe to the skeletal figure that stood watching him dispassionately. Even the inert mask of the Seneschal seemed somehow to be displaying more interest. As suddenly as it had come, the flame winked out, and the young man stood, gazing at his unblemished skin in wonderment. Unblemished, of course, but for the twisting sigils that now adorned his wrists.

"WELCOME, FIRE IN DEEP WOODS. I, IXILINATH, YOUR MASTER, GREET YOU TO MY SERVICE. KNOW THAT MY POWER AND MY PROTEC-TION NOW WALK WITH YOU."

"Y-yes, Master," croaked the warrior, still uncomprehending of what had just happened. "Am I... may I return to the others, now?"

"*FIRST, YOU MUST LEARN,*" said Ixilinath. "*I BRING YOU TWO GIFTS.*"

Fire in Deep Woods turned, and saw a young woman standing behind him and smiling. In her hands she held a sheathed knife. "Smoke in Dawn Sky! Wife, I did not know you had come here!"

She nodded. "I came to the Master's service some days ago, Husband. Please, take His gift."

Fire in Deep Woods took the knife from her, and drew it in a practised movement. It was a fine example of a weapon of the Free, its hilt carved from the dense bone of a Red Bear and wrapped in its leather, with a black, glassy, curved blade that drew a tiny bead of blood when he touched it. He turned back to Ixilinath, who had settled back onto his throne.

"I thank you for these gifts, Master. I-"

"*KILL HER,*" said Ixilinath.

Even as fresh shock registered on his face, Fire in Deep Woods whirled and opened his wife's throat in a single blow of the dagger. Moaning with grief, he dropped the weapon and sank to his knees. "Monster! Why? I pledged myself to your service, survived your test!"

"*RISE, AND LOOK UPON YOUR WORKS.*"

As if jerked on strings, Fire in Deep Woods stood, and opened his eyes. Of his wife, and of her blood that had sprayed on the wall, there was no sign. Nor was the dropped knife anywhere to be seen. "Wh- what? How?"

"*KNOW NOW THAT YOUR WIFE LIVES. SHE IS NOT YET SAFE, FOR SHE HAS NOT COME TO MY SERVICE, BUT SHE LIVES.*"

"I- then what was the meaning of this?"

"*NOW YOU KNOW MY POWER, FIRE IN DEEP WOODS. THERE IS NOTHING I CANNOT COMPEL YOU TO DO, NO DEED SO CONTRARY TO YOUR WILL THAT YOU WILL RESIST MY COMMAND EVEN FOR A HEARTBEAT. NOW YOU KNOW THAT DEFIANCE IS IMPOSSIBLE AND MY POWER ABSOLUTE.*"

The young man bowed his head. "Yes, Master. Your lesson is well-learned."

"*THEN HEAR NOW MY PROMISE, FIRE IN DEEP WOODS. I WILL NEVER AGAIN COMMAND YOU IN THAT FASHION FOR AS LONG AS YOU SERVE FAITHFULLY. FROM NOW ON, YOUR WILL IS YOUR OWN. BUT BETRAY ME, AND I SHALL KNOW, AND YOUR PUNISHMENT WILL BE UNIMAGINABLE, AND DELIVERED BY YOUR OWN HAND.*"

"I understand, Master," said the warrior.

"*THEN GO. THERE ARE MANY MORE TO BRING INTO MY FOLD THIS DAY.*"

They left, swiftly, Fire in Deep Woods marvelling at the way the brands on his wrist seemed to burn painlessly. "Was it like that for you, First?" he asked.

"Much the same, aye," replied Moon Behind Dark Clouds, suppressing a shudder at the memory.

"Must He be so... cruel?"

Night's First Raven smiled. "It is not cruelty, Fire in Deep Woods, it is wisdom. There are those among the Free who might believe their will strong enough to resist the Firebrands even after accepting them, and that foolish belief might lead them to acts that would bring them harm. Master Ixilinath's trial is simply to show you that the possibility of such resistance simply does not exist."

They walked on, and the young warrior suddenly seemed struck by a thought. "First- are not the Firebrands similar to the burning marks that the blue-hairs wear on their chests? Are they, too, servants of the Master?"

Before the First could reply, an odd sound, like silver coins tumbling into a pile, came from behind them. It took a moment for the Shorewalkers to realise that the Seneschal was laughing.

"Not servants of our Master, no. But they stole their fire from the same hearth."

29

The Wardens made camp outside the town of Ratheram's Cross in the early evening. Though the Volume was much reduced due to the fact that it had received no new recruits since the atrocity at Verge, and further by the detachment of the escort Dispensation for the Petard Engines, it was still a camp of almost two thousand that lay in the fields south of the settlement. Any other Volume might have considered allowing some of the troops to visit the small town, but for all the good they had accomplished recently the Second were still not looked upon fondly by the populace, especially in the eastern provinces which had broadly supported the Royalists. None of this, of course, stopped Magister Ollan from heading to the local inn, and despite his protests Haran found himself accompanying him.

"Captain Render is more than capable of overseeing matters in your absence, Haran," admonished the elder Magister, as they entered the well-lit tavern. "No-one will begrudge you indulging the tastes of an old fool with a rumbling belly."

"You have had nothing but praise for the provisions of the Wardens in the past, Learned Magister," pointed out Haran, as the innkeeper showed them to his best table. Magisters did not generally carry large amounts of money, but businesses were allowed to claim compensation for serving them directly from their House, or from the College itself if they were on official business. As such, even a lowly First-Leaf could expect excellent treatment in any establishment other than the very least reputable.

"And they are fine indeed- for field catering," agreed Ollan. "But when one has the opportunity to visit an excellent inn such as this, one should take it, Haran. Especially, as is the case this evening, when the College is paying. Ah, I see the special today is wild pork steaks with Lydia apple sauce. Two, I think, my good man," he said, with an inquisitive glance at Haran, who merely shrugged, "and something white and fruity... aha, Lek Silver Granâppé."

"Abelian wine?" said Haran, as the man hurried off.

"Forgive my lack of patriotism in my choice of beverage," smiled Ollan. "The wines of the Orsinio vineyards are particularly fine and still hard to find, so when I see one available I tend to seize it immediately. I'm sure they have a Kathian red if you'd prefer?"

"I defer to your judgement, Learned Magister," said Haran, simply.

"Ah, a wise choice in this case, but do not let it become a habit," replied Ollan with a shake of his finger. "Mine is not often a popular world-view, especially not in these times."

The food came, and Haran had to admit it was excellent. The wild apples that grew in Lydia grove- an outgrowth of Ratheram Forest cut off from it by the construction of the Great East Road and named for the wife of Emperor Ratheram- were well-known for their Aether-infused kick, and here accompanied pork steaks so tender that they melted in the mouth. The steaks, which were the largest Haran had ever seen and were also accompanied by forest mushrooms and sweet potatoes in a rich gravy, were also impressively fatty. Haran cut the rind from his, eliciting a tut of displeasure from Ollan, who swiftly and shamelessly transferred the unwanted morsels to his own plate.

"Ah, Haran, we cannot simply waste the best part!"

"I am trying to watch my figure, Learned Magister," replied Haran. It was true- a flabby man commanded less respect from trail-hardened College Guards.

"As am I," said Ollan, "and I find that the more of it there is, the easier it is to keep an eye on. Hmm, it seems we have some unusual visitors."

Haran cast his eye to the doorway of the inn where Ollan was looking. A band of rough-looking men and women were gathered there, wearing tough but flexible leather armour and extremely heavily-armed for civilians, each bearing a battle-axe or heavy mace on their back in addition to a standard issue Guard sword. It did not escape the notice of either Magister that whilst their weapons had been kept in fine condition, there were signs of recent blood on their grips, and on the armour.

Never a man to allow a mystery to go uninvestigated, Ollan was already halfway across the tavern floor when several more of the men came in, toting heavy sacks. The innkeeper was in the process of counting out a large pile of silver Quoits when the Magister reached him, Haran trailing along behind warily.

"Well, this is an impressive band of mercenaries!" boomed Ollan. "But I wonder what business you might have in such a reputable establishment. Though if you are here to eat, I do recommend the pork."

A grim laugh went around the group, none of whom, Haran was relieved to note, seemed concerned by the appearance of two Magisters. "Aye, and I am pleased to hear you say so, Learned Magister!" said the large, bearded man receiving the money. "After all, 'twas most likely us what killed the bastard."

Ordinarily, Haran would have treasured the sight of Ollan looking so completely stunned. The old man opened and closed his mouth a couple of times before managing to respond. "Ah.. really? You look somewhat... over-equipped for pork butchers, if I might observe."

"Not in these times!" laughed a woman who was taking a rest from hauling in the sacks to down a cheap ale. "Any fool with cleaver and apron tries to take on these tusk-wielding bastards, he's likely to end up turned into *Kallouris*."

"Kallouris?" asked Haran, despite himself.

"A Jandallan delicacy, Haran," said Ollan. "It translates roughly to 'meat on a skewer'. Are you suggesting, my dear, that the pigs are... *attacking* people?"

"Well, not so much that, Learned Magister," admitted the leader. "But the pigs in the fields around Verge went feral after the city.. died.. and a decent number started to roam in search of food. Thing with your pig is he'll eat just about anything given half a chance, and there were a lot of dead bodies lying about during the War, so some of them got a bit of a taste for the.. er.. the long pork, if you catch my meaning."

"Great Thelen.." murmured Ollan. "But still, surely hunting bows would suffice?"

"Nah," said the woman, shaking her head. "Once they get to this sort of size, you'd need a proper silver military arrow to take one down- normal wooden shafts or even steel heads won't penetrate their thick piggy skulls. You need something with a fuck-load of heft to do the deed, pardon me talking like an Expelled, Learned Magister."

"And of course such arrows are unavailable to civilians, even to veterans such as yourselves..." mused Ollan.

Haran could hear no more. The meat this place was selling- which he, Magister Haran Dar, had eaten with great enjoyment- came from creatures who could have grown fat on corpses. Possibly even the corpses of the innocent citizens of Verge he had helped to slaughter. His gorge rising, Haran blundered past the amazed hunters and staggered out into the night.

Ollan found him a few minutes later, being noisily sick into a bush.

"Ah, there you are. I must admit my own enjoyment of the meal was somewhat.. coloured by those revelations."

Haran straightened himself, wiping his mouth clean. "Somewhat coloured! What we just ate was practically cannibalism!"

"Second-hand, at worst," pointed out Ollan. "And I doubt any of those pigs travelled into the ruins of Verge. The fires would have scared them away."

"The fires we set!" hissed Haran.

"Quite so," agreed the elder Magister. "And yet, as I have told you before, I suspect strongly that the Wardens were manipulated into their actions. You were never supposed to even be there, Haran. None of you were. As for the dining habits of the creature that provided our meal, it is no more distasteful than many other farming practices. We spread dung on the crops- and even, in the case of my own House recently, the mulched remains of Gestalt Apes over the fields of Sommerlan. We even take into ourselves the Aether of our slain comrades when we Commit them, an act arguably closer to cannibalism than this meal was."

Haran blinked at him. "Your honeyed words do little to soothe either my conscience, or my stomach, Learned Magister."

"The first is good news, Haran, for any man as deeply affected by such revelations is no heartless monster, whatever he might think. The second... I have it on good authority that the inn serves a very fine Jandallan coffee that settles the stomach wonderfully. Shall we?"

Haran's shoulders dropped. His stomach was still turning cartwheels, but he had to admit that the coffee sounded like a good idea.

"Very well, Learned Magister. Once again, I shall bow to your wisdom."

"So I should hope!" laughed Ollan. He led the way back into the building, where the innkeeper looked up with an expression of relief. "Two of the Jandallan twice-chewed, please."

The man moved over to a long-necked coffee pot, and began to prepare the drinks. Haran watched him work.

"Twice-chewed?" he asked, quietly.

"Indeed. According to the merchant I learned of it from, the fruit containing the bean is eaten and excreted by first a large variety of snake, and then by a flight-less- oh, for Thelen's sake!"

Haran disappeared back out into the night again, heading for his bush.

30

The borrowed coach rolled into the Abelian port city of Dalliance late that evening. Given that so far, the only sight Thalia had had of an Abelian settlement had been Naxxiamor, the place was quite a surprise. Unlike the quiet town, or the echoing halls of Castle Orsinio, Dalliance teemed with life.

The coach-driver slipped down from his drivers seat and saluted. "Your Excellency, the Crown has arranged quarters for your party here at the Star of Gold, one of the finest and most luxurious establishments in the dock quarter."

"Not at that castle up there?" asked Amanda Devereux, looking up at the solid-looking fort that squatted above the rest of the city on a man-made hill.

"The Watching Keep is a purely military installation, my Lady," replied the coachman, somewhat stiffly. "The accommodations are not suitable for one of Ambassador Thalia's standing."

Devereux looked up at the building they had stopped outside of, as did Thalia. It certainly was a large, opulent-looking place, more a fully-fledged hotel than an inn. A huge golden star hung over the wide entrance door. Every floor above ground level boasted large balconies that overlooked the docks, with windows that opened to allow access and were framed by rich, red curtains. "It.. doesn't look all that secure," said the Operative, but something else was clearly troubling her.

For that matter, Thalia noticed that despite the fine evening and excellent views of the moonlit port, most of the windows were firmly shut, even though lights burned within. No matter. "It will be fine, Amanda. We are only staying here for one night, after all. I assume the coach will be brought around in the morning?"

The coachman nodded. "Yes, your Excellency. Will the stroke of Dawn Watch be acceptable?"

"That should be fine," said Thalia, not really paying that much attention. Now that she looked, there was certainly something unusual about the hotel. Almost everyone coming and going from the entrance was richly-dressed, and about half of them were clearly high-born Abelians. The rest were an impressively cosmopolitan bunch, looking mostly to be wealthy traders and ship's captains from the Empire, Jandalla, even as far afield as Daxalai and Har'ii- she saw a Chime-Mage coming out, the tiny silver runic bells that always accompanied them floating around him.

As they approached, Athas and Devereux carrying the bulk of the luggage, Thalia tried to work out what was bothering her. A man hurried out, dressed in a slightly ill-fitting suit of expensive cloth, and almost blundered into her in his haste.

"Oh, er, sorry... Learned Magister!" he mumbled, seeing Thalia's robes and staff. Before she could say anything, Athas loomed over the man, a huge chest perched lightly on one shoulder and still dressed, as she had ordered, in full battle-plate.

"Get lost," he said, simply. The man ran for it. "That's odd," said the big Guard as they entered the Star. "That idiot had a pretty thick Damisk accent."

"Why's that odd?" said Devereux.

"Well, it's just that the captains and merchants generally don't have one," said Athas. "They tend to come from high-born families and lose the accent at the Academy or wherever they learn their trade. But that man was wearing clothes that would cost a common sailor a year's pay."

Devereux gave a sudden laugh, and Thalia got the horrible feeling that she had deduced whatever it was she herself had not yet realised. "Not many of these guests seem to have much luggage, either," said the Operative with a smile.

They checked in at the main desk of the hotel, which was as richly-appointed inside as out. Every surface seemed to be covered in red velvet, adorned by a silver-framed mirror or topped by a richly-worked golden statue, with the *pièce de résistance* being a life-size marble of a pair of naked lovers in the entrance hall, which had been artfully posed to preserve some semblance of modesty. The lower floor boasted a large bar and common area complete with a smoking room, two restaurants, one favouring Abelian cuisine and the other more international fare, and a large casino at which games of Chasten and other, more chance-based card and dice games were being enthusiastically played. There seemed to be Abelian noblewomen everywhere, watching the games at the tables, dining in the restaurants and dancing to the musicians in the common area.

As a young woman in a particularly scandalous gown passed her, it suddenly struck Thalia that although about half of the patrons seemed to be Abelian, few of those were men. Almost every male visitor was from somewhere else. A horrible feeling of unease began to grow within her. The staff, however, were nothing if not polite and efficient, offering to take their bags (an offer Devereux accepted and Athas stoically refused) and showing them to a suite of rooms on the top floor. Closing the thick, oak-panelled doors behind them as they backed out, the porters promised to return with refreshments within the half-hour, Thalia having decided that the public scrutiny of the restaurant patrons was undesirable. And then, of course, there was the other thing.

They looked around the opulent suite, which consisted of three main rooms- two double bedrooms, and a massive, en-suite bathroom with a bath fully twenty metres square. Thalia stared at the enormous, comfortable-looking yet impressively sturdy bed, and the inevitable conclusion hit her like a thunderbolt.

"The Thelen-damned Queen of Abelia," she announced, "has arranged for us to spend the night in a brothel."

Athas, who had been testing out the bedsprings in his full armour, leapt up in shock. "What!?"

"It's a very high-class brothel, though," laughed Devereux.

"I don't find this funny, Amanda!" snapped Thalia. "This is a deliberate insult!"

"Think about it, though," said the Operative. "This ties in to what we'd already figured out about Abelia. Did you see those girls down there?"

"Those... those *strumpets!* What of them?"

Devereux shook her head. "No, I don't think so. Some of the other... customers might be pretty rough- I think that guy who clattered into you had borrowed his suit to get in- but those girls are Abelian noblewomen 'of the first water' as Sir Jeremiah might say. I doubt anyone is paying for them, they're just here for the same reason Lady Melisa went after Athas."

"You mean... all of this..." said Thalia, gesturing at the finery that surrounded them.

"All of this is just to lure in new blood, yeah," said Devereux. "Although given that I saw a pretty impressive mix of ethnicities down there I'm not sure how they expect anyone not to notice."

"Folding would take care of that," said Thalia, barely believing she was seriously discussing this. "Especially when the child is of mixed heritage, manipulating their Pattern so only the race of one parent is apparent is simple enough- it can even be done before birth."

"So, I'd guess that more than one Royal Knight at court right now has a parent in Daxalai or Jandalla," said Devereux. "I'm surprised none of the fathers seem to care."

"Hmph," said Thalia. "Since when have young men cared where the seeds they sow fall? I'd guess most of those girls even use glamours so that no-one knows who they really are. Even if one of the fathers did try to track down their bastard, it'd be hard to know where to start looking."

Delys chose that moment to yawn, pointedly. Before anyone could do more than look at her, a knock at the door heralded the arrival of the food. It was an impressive feast, floating on an enchanted litter that rested a few feet from the ground as solidly as if it had been laid flat upon it. There were sweetmeats, assorted breads with butter and jams, cold meats, pastries, fine cheeses and a large plate of fresh oysters in a rich wine sauce.

"Well," said Thalia, once the servants had left them. "I think that after this, we should retire- we've an early start tomorrow and I have no desire to linger here."

"These are good!" enthused Athas, munching on an oyster that he had slipped out of its shell and placed on a slice of bread in a manner that might well have had the chef who cooked it reaching for a boning-knife. "Oh, Learned Magister, I did notice a bit of a.. problem."

"There's only two double beds," said Devereux, with a smile. "Wow, he's right, Thalia, these aren't bad at all. Hey Del, leave some for her!"

Thalia took one of the oysters, eating it in the traditional way, letting it slide directly from the shell into her mouth. They had always been a favourite of her father. The thought made her eyes prickle even as the rich flavour filled her mouth.

"It's all right, Learned Magister, really," said Athas, spectacularly misinterpreting her suddenly miserable expression. "I don't mind using some of these cushions to make up a bed by the door. I'll keep my sword handy, too, Amanda is right that this place doesn't look all that secure."

Thalia laughed, surprised at how quickly Athas' simple kindness had cheered her up. "Thank you, Sergeant. Amanda, I assume you and Delys will be fine with the other room?"

Devereux flicked a quick look at the grinning Swordmaster, who had finished off the oysters and was making a start on the pastries. "If she ever stops eating, sure. Oh, that one's got Daxalai orangebread in it, I never got to try one the last time I- hey!"

A sudden, furious mock battle erupted as Operative and Swordmaster struggled to take possession of the pastry. Thalia thought of pointing out that as Delys had already eaten three of the things, she should at least let Amanda have one, but the two seemed to be enjoying the light-hearted play-fight, so she left them to it.

How have I come to be here, in such company? Feeling that I can trust these three with my life, even alone in a foreign land?

Until this moment, she had wondered whether she could truly go through with her mission- face the Queen of Abelia, a woman who had every reason to hate her and who she could be excused for hating back. Face her with smiles and curtsies, rather than staff and flame. Now she knew that she could. With these three by her side, she could face down the world.

31

Braziers illuminated the night with a soft, dancing orange glow as the Free Tribes convened an unprecedented third Moot of Kings in a single season. Of course, thought the Second of the Tree-Searchers, that was hardly the only thing about it that was unusual. There was the setting, for a start. Gone were the Mountain Halls, with their high-ceilinged chambers and oddly-aligned walls, hidden secrets and ancient magics lurking in their depths. Second would not miss those, and the few fools who had contemplated digging down into the mass of rubble higher up the mountainside to see what remained were swiftly dissuaded by the Guardians. That part of the history of the Free was over, and the new location for the Moot reinforced the point.

Once the dust had settled, the ruins first collapsed by the power of their own magic and then trampled by a Dragon for good measure, the Free had returned to find a much-altered landscape. Not only had the shape of the mountainside completely changed, but the Dragon had bathed it in her flames, leaving the rock fused and glassy. Never ones to impose their will on nature where it was not wanted, the Free Tribes had simply picked a suitably flat area a little lower down and used it as the venue for the new Moot. The various supplies- weapons, preserved food, and a few artefacts and relics- had been taken by the Guardians to hidden caches in the forest. Though much had been saved from the Halls, much more had been lost, including the Thinking Seats- six chairs that hosted the most prominent Mighty One from each tribe. Traditionally, each Seat was made by the Mighty One who sat in it, and on the occasion of the death of an incumbent they were generally burned, buried or magically discorporated in it according to the traditions of their tribe.

This night, then, the Mighty Ones sat in Seats that had been crafted at some haste for Dokan's prior Moot, and Mighty Renjka of the Stonesingers was still softly humming to hers, trying to get rid of an uncomfortable bump in the backrest. Each tribe created their Seat in their own particular way- that of the Tree-

Searchers, in which Mighty Dokan now brooded, was woven from still-living leaves and branches, and had immediately begun to thrust searching roots into the solid rock when put in place. For the Blackbloods, the giant known only as Black Skull lounged in a throne of bones, a grinning human skull forming the end of each arm-rest. The Shorewalkers had created a fresh Seat of driftwood and seashells, inlaid with pearls and cushioned with soft seaweed on which Mighty Lelioko sat confidently. The sight reminded Second that Lelioko had attended the last Moot without revealing her allegiance to Ixil, a thing she would not have believed possible.

The Seat of the Heart-Eaters, occupied by Mighty Xaraya, was a plundered armchair from Abelia. How the famously aggressive tribe had come by it was unknown, but the large, silver-bladed sword the muscular red-headed woman had reluctantly surrendered to the Guardians looked likely to have come from the same source, as did the battered silver diadem woven into her hair. Several other swords had been firmly rammed into the back of the chair, their hilts protruding from the top, but these had attracted no comment. Though weapons were forbidden at the Moot to any but the Guardians, no Mighty One really needed one. In the case of the last member of the Moot, Mighty Taris of the Hearth-Tenders, no weapon was needed for another, simpler reason- as the caretakers of the deepest part of the forest and guardians of the children of other tribes during conflicts between them, no Hearth-Tender had borne arms in centuries. His Seat was the carved-out husk of one of the giant malphan gourds that the tribe cultivated high in the branches of the most ancient trees. Typically of the Hearth-Tenders, they had brought sweetbark-flour pies filled with the sweet flesh of the plant as a gift for the Guardians.

The last of the Free Tribes, the Guardians of the Halls themselves, were represented at the Moot by Mighty Tyrona, the granddaughter of Mighty Thror, who had sacrificed himself preventing the leader of the black demons from breaking out of the Halls. Her position as chief amongst the Mighty of the Guardians was far from certain, but Thror had not had time to train a successor and his granddaughter had grown up watching him, giving her better knowledge of the rituals than any other. Traditionally, the Mighty One of the Guardians served as Ritemaster, recognising speakers and directing proceedings rather than actually making decisions. This was considered only proper, since unlike the loose territories of the other Free Tribes the area within the perimeter of the Harbinger Skulls was exclusively the preserve of the Guardians and they bore responsibility for that part of the forest and no other. Despite her relative youth, a mere eighty seasons, Mighty Tyrona had so far managed proceedings with some skill, but this Moot now threatened to spiral out of control.

Things had got off to a predictably poor start when the Blackbloods and Heart-Eaters had learned of the reason for the Moot. The two most feared warrior tribes of the Free, neither had taken the suggestion that a threat was coming that they could not repel through their own strength well. Dokan and Taris had at least persuaded them not to violate every ancient law by killing Lelioko on the spot, but as the Shorewalker was making her case Xaraya had made a point of loudly heckling and challenging every statement, whilst the Black Skull simply sat in silence, seemingly paying little attention. Matters had come to a head when Xaraya started demanding to know how many Shorewalkers had already 'taken the dead thing's bargain', at which point Tyrona had forbidden her to speak again until called, on pain of expulsion from the Moot.

To Second's surprise, Mighty Dokan cleared his throat, his Seat waving a leafy branch in the air to signify that he wanted to speak. Tyrona, to the exasperation of Lelioko, recognised him.

"With respect to Mighty Lelioko, and to the Ritemaster, Mighty Xaraya raises a wise point, though only as a lakibird might find a tasty nut." This raised a chuckle from the Free- the huge-billed lakibird was famous for its appetite and habit of eating everything in sight before being chased away. Dokan gave them a moment, and continued. "Mighty Lelioko, your people have been most open about the process of receiving the Brands. I shall leave aside my shock at learning that your Master appears to be Ixilinath himself, thought dead centuries ago, and ask- is it not true that the Branding requires a personal audience with your Master?"

Lelioko nodded. "Aye, it is. And a great honour it is to be granted it."

"I do not doubt it," said Dokan with a smile. "And yet, if you will forgive my turning to the talk of the Deluded, there is a matter of.. logistics to consider. Though our war-bands are only a few thousand strong-"

"Speak for yourself, weakling!" laughed Xaraya, holding up her hands in mock surrender as Tyrona shook the Speaker's Staff at her in warning.

"-there are tens of thousands of our people throughout the Forest Home, perhaps more."

"When last I knew, there were almost eight hundred thousand Free, Dokan," put in Mighty Taris.

"As my Mighty Peer says, let us assume there are eight hundred thousand Free," said Dokan. The Black Skull pointedly stifled a yawn, but Xaraya, Second noticed, seemed to be paying close attention now. "Perhaps it takes ten minutes for your Master to complete a Branding. One does not need to be one of the dust-covered scribes of the Deluded to reach the obvious conclusion."

"Maybe.. sixty seasons?" breathed Xaraya.

"My Mighty Peer is quicker of mind than I," said Dokan. "But even so, that is assuming that one as... high of status as Mighty Ixilinath is prepared to exert himself continuously in such a fashion. I suspect that is unlikely to be the case."

Everyone looked at Lelioko, who seemed to be struggling to find the words to answer. Eventually, she spoke. "You are correct, Mighty Dokan. My Master has been working to build His forces in secret ever since the lackeys of Thelen the Mad drove Him and His people into exile. He had planned to continue that process for many more years yet, offering His gift only to the worthy and those brave enough to seek it out."

"But now those plans have changed?" said Xaraya, her tone now more conciliatory.

"Aye," nodded Lelioko, her shells rattling. "My Master will offer the sanctuary of Ixildundal to any who will bear His Brand, and once the numbers are sufficient He will grant them His gift in a new way, a way that will protect thousands at a time."

"And why has he not used this method before?" asked Mighty Taris, stroking his long, straggly grey beard thoughtfully.

"I think Mighty Lelioko has already answered that," said Tyrona. "You said 'once the numbers are sufficient', Mighty Lelioko- I assume this is significant?"

"It is," said the Shorewalker with another nod. "The faster method of Branding requires at least six-hundred and eighty-five Free to be present and unmarked. Do not ask me to explain that!" she said, even as questions filled the air. "Know only that it is the knowledge that my Master has imparted to me. Know as well that for the Branding to succeed, the desire of all present to receive it must be sincere and unshakeable. Even a single doubter will corrupt the ceremony."

"Madness!" spat Xaraya. "This is the way of the Deluded, putting our faith in rituals and spells instead of the strength of our arms and our lands. No, Ritemaster, I have heard enough, and now I will speak!"

Tyrona, who had once again brandished the Speaker's Staff, took a quick glance around the circle. Satisfying herself that there were no serious objections, she recognised the leader of the Heart-Eaters.

"Mighty Peers," said Xaraya. "We have heard the talk of the Woe and of the coming of a Great Wader, but we have seen *nothing*. Not so much as a single fly has been presented, and yet this... *slave*.. asks us to forsake all we are, to subvert our very will, on the basis of hearsay!"

"The Woe is very real, Mighty Xaraya," admonished Dokan. "I-" he stopped in astonishment as Tyrona shook the staff at him, and then sighed. "Very well."

"You!" said Xaraya, pointing at Second. "You are the one who saw the Great Wader, you say?"

"I did. I smelled it with my wolf's nose and saw it with her eyes," replied Second, proudly.

"And yet you stand unharmed!" said Xaraya, triumphantly. "If even a mere Tree-Searcher wolf-runner can stand against the Woe, the Heart-Eaters have no fear of it. No, Lelioko, thrall of Ixil. You will begone from this place, and know that as soon as this Moot ends, the fangs of the Heart-Eaters will be nipping at your heels."

"Fool!" cried Lelioko. "Try, and my Master's fire will singe the fur from your bitch's snout! I will-"

"We have taken one of these Dendaril," spoke the Black Skull, suddenly. "I will have him brought before us for judgement." His voice was low and slow, but replete with menace, and for a moment the entire assembly lapsed into a stunned silence.

"Madness!" hissed Lelioko, and the proceedings immediately devolved into a shouting-match. Second and Mighty Dokan exchanged a worried glance.

What will become of us now?

32

*a*rch-Chancellor Derelar Thane was working late in his office when someone knocked lightly on the door. He frowned. He hadn't given orders that visitors should be refused, but at this hour he was rarely awake. It wasn't the Vice-Chancellor, that much he could tell by the relative timidity of the knock. Curious.

"Enter," he said, having dispelled the wards. The man who did so was a slight, dark-haired Magister who he did not immediately recognise.

"Arch-Chancellor!" said the man, hurrying forwards. "I thank you for seeing me at this late hour, I hope I am not disturbing your work on the appointment of the new Ambassador to Abelia."

Derelar frowned. The list of candidates he was sorting through had only arrived earlier that evening, and he had not discussed it with anyone. "You have me at a disadvantage, Magister," he said, though by reputation he had an idea who his visitor was, which was immediately confirmed.

"Of course, of course. Magister Julius Thule, at your service, Arch-Chancellor. You are, of course, concerned at my knowledge of the contents of the papers you are working on."

Derelar regarded the man silently. It didn't seem his contribution was required.

"Just so. On my way here I observed that a member of the Administration was returning to the records carrying a green ribbon worked with yellow- not golden, you understand, but yellow- runic thread. He had also, from the condition of his boots and the lack of any moisture in his robes, not been outside for some considerable time."

Derelar simply raised an eyebrow, wondering if he could get some more work done on the documents before Julius got to the point.

"Green ribbons with yellow decorative stitching are only used by the records department of the Administration to bind dossiers relating to international diplomatic postings," said Julius. "And since the man carrying it had not been outside, he must therefore have travelled from the Hall of Records directly to whomever received the dossier, since protocol demands that the ribbons are never left in the possession of anyone other than an Archivist. Given that no international diplomatic vacancy had arisen other than the much-publicised one in Abelia, the conclusion was obvious."

"Is it not possible," ventured Derelar, the intellectual puzzle appealing to him after an evening of dry reports, "that a vacancy had arisen that was *not* publicised?"

"In that case, as you are well aware, Arch-Chancellor, the ribbon would have been worked in *gold* thread, to signify that it related to a classified matter under the purview of the Imperial Service. But you are testing me, of course."

"Of course," agreed Derelar, who had known nothing of the sort. "You also therefore considered it likely that I would be working outside of my usual hours. However, Magister, I assume that your reason for coming here was not simply to show off your own cleverness. If it was, I shall be displeased."

Julius cleared his throat. "Ah, yes, Arch-Chancellor."

"*Gravely* displeased, Magister," Derelar added for emphasis, even though it wasn't entirely true. For the moment, in a day that had consisted largely of paperwork and waiting for various movements of forces to be completed, this was at least providing some interest. "There is tea and coffee, if it will help you to focus."

"Oh, er, thank you, Arch-Chancellor," said Julius. "In truth I find myself in such a state of excitement that such stimulants are the last thing I need. Arch-Chancellor, I have uncovered evidence that the Daxalai Ambassador, Silver-Tongue Yue, was murdered."

Derelar snorted despite himself. "Of course he was! He was found dead in a back-alley in Damisk, killed by the Midnight Tiger!" Even as he spoke the words, Derelar realised that they weren't entirely true. He and Ollan had suspected that the Daxalai's death had been caused by a third party, after all.

"I apologise, Arch-Chancellor, my wording was imprecise. Yours, on the other hand, was perhaps more precise than you appreciated. Silver-Tongue Yue may well have been *found* dead in Damisk, but I do not believe he actually died there. I believe he was killed elsewhere, with his body then mutilated in the correct fashion and dumped in a location where it was sure to be found."

"I also said he was killed by the Midnight Tiger," said Derelar, slightly petulantly. Something in Julius' manner irritated him and he felt the need to throw him off his stride.

"And this, too, is true, though I will accept it is less precise," said Julius. "The fact of the Midnight Tiger's presence in the Empire was certainly the reason for his death, so in that sense the *kagimaren* was responsible. But to return to the point- I was informed by the Vice-Chancellor's office that the alleged scene of Ambassador Yue's death had been spoiled for my investigation by a skirmish between a group of scavengers and a City Guard patrol, and since at the time I was involved in another aspect of the case, I took those words at face value. This, in hindsight, was a mistake, but an understandable one."

"You were on your way to the Daran Manse at the time, were you not?" said Derelar, casting his mind back.

"Indeed, Arch-Chancellor, I was just beginning my investigation there. To continue, once my duties at the Manse were concluded I resolved to visit Damisk and learn what I could. It was fortunate for me that the winds at this time of year make the journey from Damisk to Gwai'Xi, the principle Daxalai port on their east coast, somewhat difficult. As I am sure you know, the Daxalai prefer simple sailing ships to our oar-driven vessels, believing them to be more.. harmonious with nature. A man of Ambassador Yue's status must, of course, be repatriated on a vessel of his own nation, and thus his body was still being preserved in a vault in Damisk, waiting for the winds to change. The Watch Commander of Damisk owed me a debt after the affair of the Red Hand gang, and so allowed me to briefly examine the remains, on the condition that I did not visibly disturb them."

Derelar had not heard anything about the Red Hand gang, but decided that given the chance Julius would talk about the earlier case all night, and so instead applied a gentle prod. "I assume you found something?"

"I found something, and I did *not* find something. It was what I did not find that was the most singular piece of evidence. Firstly, the victim was still possessed of several very fine rings and a well-concealed money-belt. There was no evidence that anyone had tried to remove any of his jewellery. Secondly, I noted damage to his knuckles, as well as other bruising indicative of a struggle- a struggle in which there were two very active sides. Though the Pattern of the deceased rarely reveals much, I was able to discern that most of the bruising was pre-mortem."

"So, the Ambassador was not looted of valuables, and apparently fought back against an attacker," summed up Derelar. "What was it you did not find?"

"The wounds in his throat, Arch-Chancellor. From my examination of them, it was evident, as the Healer who examined the body surmised, that the cause of death was the removal of the Ambassador's throat with some form of bladed claws. However, there was evidence of clotting in the wounds, and the blood had dried quickly. The claws of the Midnight Tiger are in some way enchanted, Arch-Chancellor, they leave wounds which do not easily heal and remain fresh for some time after death. I could find no evidence, either physical or magical, of such properties in the weapon that killed Ambassador Yue."

Derelar remembered reading as much in Julius' report on the death of Keris Daran. "This is interesting, but as yet inconclusive, Magister."

"Indeed, Arch-Chancellor. I next took my investigation to the underbelly of Damisk, the corner-inns and drinking cellars in which the criminal element gathers. Such men and women can be oddly forthcoming when coin and drink flow and their own misdemeanours are not the subject under discussion. From them, I learned of three brothers, not long arrived in Damisk as refugees from Equinox. They were poorly suited to a life of crime, and swiftly acquired the nickname of the Lost Lambs. According to my sources, the Lambs were eking out a living working tables in one of the less savage dockside inns when a passing stranger commented that he had seen a rich merchant drunk on the street a little distance away. The more experienced patrons recognised the bait for what it was, but the Lambs gambolled straight into the trap, if you'll pardon my somewhat whimsical metaphor."

"They went to rob the 'merchant', I presume," said Derelar, beginning to see how the thing was done.

"Indeed. According to my discussions with the men of the City Guard, with whom I have a fair working relationship, at roughly the same time a robed woman accosted a passing patrol, claiming to have been robbed by a pack of thugs. She showed the men the direction in which her attackers had fled, which as I am sure you have already deduced led them to stumble onto the Lost Lambs as they stood over the corpse of the Ambassador. There was a fight, in which our Lambs showed more fang than their docile nickname might imply, but though their knives claimed two Guards the patrol consisted of five. My suggestion that taking at least one of the miscreants alive might have been advantageous was received poorly, and necessitated the purchase of several rounds of drinks to restore my standing."

"Guards are, in general, ill-disposed towards those who kill their fellows," observed Derelar. "Precious few of those who previously served the Royalists have managed to return to the Volumes without suffering reprisal. So, your theory is that the Ambassador was killed elsewhere, dumped in Damisk, and then deliberately set up to be discovered in such a way that would destroy the evidence?"

"It is no theory, Arch-Chancellor," said Julius, a little primly. "The deduction is unassailable, and there can be no other conclusion. And further, I have not yet presented you with the pearl within the oyster of this case."

"Then please do so," said Derelar, standing and heading over to the sideboard. The coffee-pot was barely lukewarm, but a quick jolt of Aether soon solved that, though the flavour would suffer. "Are you sure you will not..?"

"My thanks, Arch-Chancellor, but the work is all the stimulation I require this night. Having established that the Ambassador did not die where he was believed to have, I turned my attention to discovering where this infamous event in fact took place. A visit to the Daxalai Embassy confirmed that the Ambassador had left early on the morning of his death, accompanied, as he always was, by a bodyguard, a well-regarded Daxalai Initiate known as Wen Lian-Shi, or Willow-Sigh Wen. It appears that the Ambassador had had a meeting with Master Yukan of the Academy, and correctly deduced that he was a target for the Midnight Tiger."

"So he fled," said Derelar.

"Officially, he chose to return to Shan'Xi'Sho to deliver a vital report in person," said Julius with a thin smile. "So vital was it, in fact, that instead of taking a berth on a relatively slow Daxalai vessel, of which several were available, he discreetly took passage on a civilian trading ship, the *Flying Wight*."

Derelar remembered the name, and suddenly understood what had happened. Of course, he couldn't reveal his knowledge to Julius- at least, not yet. "I recall hearing of the loss of that vessel."

"Indeed, Arch-Chancellor. It was destroyed by the Blue Council and lost with all hands. Weapons that later washed up on the Gold Coast suggested that the *Wight* was involved in smuggling arms to Daxalai rebels, which would explain the involvement of the Blue. But this also raises a perplexing question."

"If Ambassador Yue were on that ship, how did he come to be found dead in an alley in Damisk later that day?" said Derelar.

"Quite so, Arch-Chancellor," agreed Julius. "That is the most singular mystery of all, and one to which I so far have no answer. However, I may yet have one final lead to investigate."

"And this is why you have come to me?" said Derelar.

"Again, you deduce correctly. There is, of course, the slim possibility that this plot was contrived at your direction, but I can conceive no way in which it might have worked to your advantage. Regardless, whilst no further sightings of Ambassador Yue have come to light, I did overhear a tale in the dockside inn of Damisk which the Lost Lambs frequented that seems, on reflection, to have relevance to the case. According to a patron- who confessed that his recitation of the tale was at least third-hand and might well have been more- a Toskan captain visited the establishment some days previously, claiming to have helped rescue two beautiful warrior women from the clutches of an evil sorceress. According to the story, and I apologise for the language but I am quoting, one was 'a red-head so fierce she'd have torn Naxxia's hair out at the roots and shat in her mouth when she screamed.'"

"Charming," commented Derelar, dryly.

"Again, my apologies, but the perils of Har'ii Murmurs must be avoided in the art of investigation. The other-"

"Har'ii what?" said Derelar, never having heard the phrase.

"Ah, a vernacular idiom, Arch-Chancellor. The etymology is too convoluted to explain quickly, but it refers to that situation where a tale changes in the telling from one mouth to another's ears. Being certain to quote verbatim is the only true defence. To continue, the other was 'coal-black of skin and bald as a seal, but with the eyes of a Dragon and fists like thunder on the open seas'. I am unsure as to who the red-head might be, but I believe the latter to be an accurate, if colourful, description of the appearance and abilities of a Daxalai Initiate."

"You believe it to be this Willow-Sigh Wen?" said Derelar. He had a horrible feeling, if Julius was right, that he knew who the red-head was as well, and by extension who the 'evil sorceress' might be. Once again, though, these were not thoughts he could yet share. He found himself wishing Magister Ollan were present.

"I do, Arch-Chancellor. According to the tale, the two warriors took ship with the Toskan, a man named Blue Kjôr, to Freeport. I propose to track them down, and see what light I can shed on the matter."

"Very well," said Derelar. "You will make no report of this in any way, official, or unofficial. I will give you documents allowing you to requisition a ship at Damisk to take you to Freeport, and to take a small stipend from the Treasury, but after that you will be on your own. I advise you to be extremely careful who you trust with this, Magister Julius."

"I will indeed, Arch-Chancellor," said Julius. "But I also have a capable man to watch my back."

Some minutes later, the door to the High Apartments opened and Julius stepped out. "We have our authorisation, Captain. We shall sail for Freeport within the week."

"Oh good, Learned Magister," said Captain Jerik, not meaning it for a moment.

33

*A*fter several futile minutes of trying to control the Moot through other methods, Mighty Tyrona finally resorted to the Speaker's Staff. Like the Thinking Seats, it was new, its predecessor having been lost in the Halls with Mighty Thror, but due to its nature this hardly mattered. Unlike the staffs borne by the Deluded Magisters or even the other Mighty Ones, the Speaker's Staff was attuned not only to the Ritemaster, but also to the Thinking Seats themselves. It was adorned with a trophy from each Seat- topped with a piece of Stonesinger rock and wound with a leafy vine from the Tree-Searchers, which bound in place a finger-bone from the Blackbloods and had a gold ring from the Heart-Eaters threaded through it. Shorewalker shells gave it its rattle, and its grip was wrapped in the tough skin of the Hearth-Tenders' gourd. All this, and the submission of all attending Mighty Ones when the Moot was convened, gave the Speaker's Staff the power to silence the occupant of any of the Seats at will. It was a power that had been used but nine times before in recorded history, and Tyrona used it on all six Seats before order was restored.

Even then, it almost didn't work. Second watched with bated breath as Xaraya began to rise from her Seat. To leave a Thinking Seat during a Moot was considered an unpardonable sin amongst the Mighty, and the leader of the Heart-Eaters locked eyes with Tyrona for almost a full minute before relenting and flopping back into her chair with an exasperated, if silent, sigh.

Satisfied that an assemblage of powerful warlocks with a combined age some twelve times her own had finally stopped squabbling like children, Tyrona pointedly thumped the Speaker's Staff on the ground, releasing the spell. "Thank you, my Mighty Peers."

"You are no peer of mine, whelp," muttered Xaraya, earning herself a fresh shake of the staff.

"I am Ritemaster, Mighty Xaraya," Tyrona reminded her. "Test me again on a night in which this staff has already seen unprecedented use, and I will familiarise you with some of its more painful abilities. Now, I see that the Blackbloods have brought us their prisoner. Mighty Black Skull, I recognise you."

A pair of Blackbloods dragged a white-robed man into the soft light of the Moot. Like all of their tribe, even their Mighty, the man and woman- a married couple, judging by the face-paint- bore the Hissing Serpent tattoo amongst their others. Receiving this tattoo was a rite of passage within the tribe, and turned both their blood and their saliva into a deadly poison that could kill a man in minutes. Amongst the other Free Tribes, to 'kiss a Blackblood' was a euphemism for self-inflicted death. The prisoner was an entirely different manner of man. Dressed in a torn, dirty white robe, he was grotesquely fat- it seemed the warriors were dragging him not because he was resisting, but because he was unable to walk.

Second's hackles rose. The man's eyes rolled in his head and his tongue lolled, and there was a scent... she concentrated, calling the Stalking Wolf to give her the senses of the beast without the form. Yes, there it was, that sickly-sweet smell she had sensed only once before. "Mighty Dokan!" she hissed, but the Mighty One was too intent on the newcomers to hear her. She tried to attract the attention of the First, but he, too, was distracted.

"This one was taken by one of our war-bands in the far east of the Forest Home, near the Shriven Marshes," said Black Skull, still speaking slowly and softly. "He was with others, who were slain and their corpses nailed to the trees as a warning to those who might trespass."

His fellow Mighty Ones, even the gentle Taris, nodded their approval. Whatever else might be said of the Blackbloods, they took their duties seriously. Mighty Lelioko was even smiling, but it was not a smile of appreciation, Second realised. It was the smile of the hunter whose prey was about to blunder into the snare.

"Does it... speak?" said Xaraya, leaning forward in her Seat to get a better look at the intruder.

"I have... much to say.. oh Mighty Xaraya. Much to say... and so little... little time." The man spoke slowly, almost as if he were in some sort of trance.

"Who are you?" asked Mighty Taris. He too seemed unconcerned, even as Second fought down the urge to scream a warning.

"I... am called.. Ronald.." said the Dendaril. "A... humble.. oh, blessed hive! A humble... Pilgrim." The fat man closed his eyes for a moment, and a blissful shudder ran through him. "I... bring.. only peace... to your... your.... people."

"And peace is a fine thing indeed," said Taris, reasonably. "And yet Mighty Lelioko tells us your peace comes at a terrible price, the price of a rebirth that is as good as a death, and a lifetime in service to your Hegemony. Does she lie?"

The man sank to his knees, and Second expected the Blackbloods, savages that they were, to force him to stand and answer the Mighty One. They did no such thing- in fact, she suddenly realised, they were gazing at the fat so-called pilgrim with something approaching reverence.

Then she saw the dried blood that had trickled down from their ears.

She opened her mouth to shout a warning.

Ronald exploded.

Immediately, pandemonium broke out. A swarm of horrific, droning flies erupted from Ronald's remains, engulfing Mighty Tyrona and the two Blackbloods. If the insects expected an easy conquest, however, they had seriously misunderstood what it meant to be a Mighty One, if indeed they were capable of understanding anything. With a great shout, Tyrona bathed the creatures surrounding her with a sheet of flame, blasting a clear spot in the middle of the circle even as the swarm split and twisted in search of easier targets.

The sight of so many of the creatures being immolated seemed to drive the two Blackbloods into a frenzy. With a scream of outrage, they hurled themselves at the Ritemaster. Drained from her exertions, Tyrona could only bat the man away with the Speaker's staff before his wife crashed into her and they went down in a thrashing heap. Then, all protocol forgotten, Xaraya was there, her looted sword in hand and flashing through the torso of the Blackblood who had reeled back towards her, bisecting it neatly. The leader of the Heart-Eaters took a single step towards Tyrona before another, smaller mass of the insects emerged from the gory remains of her victim.

Elsewhere, a surreal battle erupted, the Mighty Ones seeking to protect their people and themselves with blasts of flame that incinerated the insects wherever they flew. Here and there, even so, a warrior lay on the ground, screaming in terror as one of the things burrowed into an ear, a nose, or even, horrifically, an eye-socket. The warriors, unsure of how to fight so small but so deadly a threat, instinctively clustered around their Mighty, inadvertently hampering their attempts to destroy the creatures.

Only Mighty Lelioko and her retinue stood unaffected and unbowed. She strode through the melee, her magic flaring, destroying the things wherever they flew. After a few more frantic minutes the Moot was clear, though several warriors lay whimpering on the ground. Tyrona, having finally subdued her attacker, picked herself up and dusted herself down, and Second dared to believe the worst was past.

"Is.. is it over?" asked Tyrona, unconsciously echoing Second's thought.

"Over?" laughed Lelioko. "This was a mere taste of what is to come, Guardian. It was a squall of rain before the thunderstorm, the faint scent of woodsmoke before the forest fire. This," she leaned in close to the younger woman, "was *nothing.*"

"Can anything be done?" asked Mighty Renjka to Mighty Taris, who was squatting next to one of the warriors who had been downed by the flies.

"For this one, I think so," said Taris. "The Little One's Spirit is still distinct from his, and with care, it can be removed. This other one," he continued, indicating the Blackblood woman that Mighty Tyrona had subdued "is.. seemingly unaffected."

"That is the second stage of the Woe, Mighty Taris," said Lelioko, stepping over to them. "The Little One has been completely absorbed into her, and even now a new brood begins to fester in her guts. There is only one recourse- destroy the body utterly with fire." Without further discussion, she immolated the Blackblood. The woman died so quickly she didn't have time to scream- a mercy, Second supposed.

"I saw that when I killed the other one," said Xaraya. "Another swarm of those things emerged. Mighty Black Skull, how long ago did you take that.. pilgrim?"

There was no immediate response. As one, the Mighty turned to look at the Blackbloods' Seat. The Black Skull had not moved, and still sat upon it. To Second's shock, wet tears glistened on the dark face-paint.

"I have made a grave error," said the Skull, softly. The threat was gone from his voice, replaced by a deep sorrow.

"The disaster may yet be controlled, Mighty Black Skull," said Dokan, gently. "But you must tell us- how long ago?"

"You do not understand, Tree-Searcher," said the Skull, beginning to step down from his Seat. "We knew. It was two weeks ago, and *we knew.*"

There was a dead silence. "Two weeks..." breathed Lelioko, though she was still smiling.

"You knew what?" shouted Xaraya, finally, levelling her sword at the giant. "What have you done?"

"We knew of the Woe, and we knew that.. man-thing carried it. You must remember, Mighty Xaraya, the Blackbloods are the only tribe of the Free to rove in the Shriven Marshes. We have seen the Great Waders before, and felt the bite of the Little Ones, but they did not harm us. The Hissing Serpent slays any living thing that dares feast on Blackblood flesh."

"You... you thought you were immune..." murmured Mighty Taris. The Black Skull nodded.

"Aye. We thought to come to this Moot, and show the Free that we, the oft-reviled, the marsh-delvers, the outcasts among outcasts, had a way to defeat the Woe that did not mean subjugation to the Enslaver. We knew the Pilgrim was ripe to burst, for we had seen it happen to one of his fellows."

Lelioko grinned. "Oh, Mighty Black Skull, your people's sacrifice may yet save the Free, if only by their example. The whole war-band must have been infected, or else someone would have noticed the change in the personality of those two. Even so, only the Pilgrim's cunning enabled the ruse. Where are the rest of them?"

Black Skull pointed into the forest. "Out there. Over twelve score of them." Already, torches gleamed in the night. The rest of the Blackbloods were coming.

"Will they all... be as these were?" asked Renjka, clutching her staff.

"It matters not," said Xaraya, hefting her blade. "Fire is the bane of the Woe. We should strike them now, burn every one of them before they spawn any more of these.. things."

"Twelve score?" said Taris. "Even were I prepared to lend my Spirit to such a.. massacre we have not the strength- to kill them, perhaps, but to destroy them utterly? No."

"He speaks truly," said Lelioko. "You must decide, people of the Free. Come with us now, to the Tithing, and throw yourselves upon the mercy of my Master, or be subsumed by the Woe. There is no other way."

"There is another way," said Dokan, softly. There were shouts coming from the outskirts of the camp now. "We flee to the west, to the Doors of Patros."

"What?" laughed Xaraya. "And throw ourselves on the mercy of the Deluded?"

"Or upon their blades," said the Black Skull. "I am undone, my honour forsaken. A quick death at the hands of the Great Knight and his soldiers is more than I deserve. I am with you, Dokan of the Tree-Searchers, I and every Black-blood still pure."

"Then you must all choose!" cried Lelioko, her voice raised to a great shout. "Either go with Dokan to the Deluded, or with me to Master Ixil. Do not let your tribe choose for you, for the Master will see your heart. Do not let your fear choose for you, for His flame will burn it from your soul."

The first few Blackbloods were emerging into the light of the ritual circle now. To the untutored eye they seemed normal, but Second could smell the taint in the air- and with them, they had another of the bloated Pilgrims. More were surely coming. Xaraya brandished her sword again, but Taris held out his staff to restrain her.

"Mighty Xaraya, hold! We have seen the frenzy you will drive them into if you slay that one. We must flee- I am for Ixildundal, for only there will the children be safe. Each of you must choose for yourself."

Xaraya slammed her blade back into the scabbard in disgust. "Heart-Eaters! What say you to one last, great Reclamation?"

Dokan made to reply, and Second guessed that he planned a more peaceful path, but the Heart-Eater warriors let out a great shout of support for their leader. "Then we march west!" cried Xaraya. "Gather all the kin you can find- we go to the Doors of Patros!"

"I don't know if we'll be going anywhere," said Mighty Renjka, softly, pointing toward the west. "There are more of them out there, coming this way. We are surrounded."

"Then it is settled," said Black Skull, retrieving his staff from one of his warriors and pointing it at the Pilgrim. "My people! Follow whichever path you choose, for I free you from my flawed guidance. You, fly-lord, host of corruption, bringer of calamity to my kin! I am Mighty Black Skull, named Stone Falling from Winter Skies, son of Knife in the Dark and Blood in Secret Places, and I defy you!"

Before anyone could stop him, Black Skull hurled himself towards the Pilgrim, even as the man's bloated gut began to rupture. With a roar of defiance, he wreathed himself in a cloak of flame, burning the emerging flies. Just as their fellows had attacked Tyrona before, the Blackbloods guarding the Dendaril charged at him in fury.

"What in Nak's black heart is that oaf doing?" shouted Xaraya, putting her hand on her sword.

"Saving you, fool!" cried Lelioko. "They will only attack those who slay the Little Ones. Flee, now, while Black Skull sells his life for your freedom!"

Xaraya drew the sword, even as the other Free began to scatter into the night. "Know this, witch- I will never serve your Master. This is not over!"

Lelioko simply laughed. "As long as you remain free of the Woe, Mighty Xaraya, there is hope for you to one day find wisdom, and on that day I shall embrace you as a sister. May it be soon in coming!" She turned, and stalked off into the night, followed by Mighty Taris, Mighty Renjka, and many others. To Second's shock, even Mighty Tyrona and the Guardians went with her.

The rest, the Tree-Searchers, Heart-Eaters, and a few surviving Blackbloods who had not been taken, fled west. As they ran, Second shouted to Dokan.

"How is it possible, Mighty One? How could even Mighty Tyrona betray us?"

The First shook his head. "She has not betrayed us, Second, none of them have. The sworn duty of the Guardians is to protect the Mountain Halls, and Mighty Tyrona cannot do that if the Woe threatens her, nor can she from the lands of the Deluded."

Dokan nodded. "Aye. Both she and Mighty Taris made their choice to protect those in their charge. The Hearth-Tenders must care for the children, and they too cannot do that and follow us."

"Then what are we to do?" asked Second. "Are we to fight those who serve Ixili-nath for our home? Flee into exile in the lands of the Deluded? Or simply die on their blades, as Mighty Black Skull wished? None of these is the end I would have chosen for myself, Mighty One."

From the mountainside behind them came a sudden, blood-curdling roar, cut off a moment later by an ear-splitting detonation. A bright flash of flame lit the night sky, and several of the trees were set ablaze. Dokan held up a hand to halt the group.

"It would seem Mighty Black Skull has chosen his end, at least, and the Fly Lords have learned to rue it. Second, we shall use this respite to find the nearest Stone Path, I think. Meanwhile, the rest of you shall go to our people and tell them what has happened here. If you see any of these.. Dendaril, do not antagonise them! We must try to make the Doors of Patros before they do, and before Mighty Xaraya and the Heart-Eaters do anything.. regrettable."

With a quick nod, Second assumed the Stalking Wolf, the First hurrying forwards to collect her war-gear. If this was to be the last day of the Free Tribes, it would not be because she had shirked her duty.

34

*M*agister Thalia Daran stood by the window of the suite and stared out into the moonlit night. She had changed into a night-dress that Lady Alizabeth had insisted on giving her, made of fine blue silk. Though whoever had laid out the suites had clearly not been overly concerned with modesty, they were at least provided with a changing screen, so she hadn't had to worry too much about Athas still being in the room. After checking the balcony and deciding it was too high up for any but the most intrepid invader, the big Guard had carried a chaise-lounge over to the door and placed it to block the entrance before settling down on it, leaving the entire bed for her. Despite the lateness of the hour, though, she didn't really feel like sleeping yet.

She pushed open the window, and stepped out onto the balcony. The docks far below were still busy even at this time of night, sailors, merchants and other tradesmen hurrying back and forth and light blazing from the windows and doors of a dizzying variety of trading posts, taverns and inns. She felt filled with energy, as if she should be down there doing... *something* rather than cooped up in this luxurious prison for the night. It was probably just nerves, she told herself. By this time tomorrow she would have arrived in Abellan and met Queen Tondarin. For that matter, by this time tomorrow she might even be dead.

By this time tomorrow, I could be dead. It was hardly the first time such a thought had crossed her mind- in fact, at some points recently it had been practically a daily occurrence. But this time it seemed more troubling for some reason- perhaps simply due to the apparent safety and comfort of her surroundings. It was like a knife wrapped in velvet, as she remembered her father once describing the Abelians- outwardly beautiful and soft to the touch, but with a cold, sharp, deadly core.

There was a faint rattle behind her as Athas stepped out onto the balcony. "Oh, it's you, Learned Magister. I heard something from out here and I thought I'd better look into it."

She turned to look at him, almost silhouetted in the dim light from the room, but with moonlight glinting from the plates of his armour. "Sergeant," she asked, "have you been sleeping in that, or did you change into it again before you came out here?"

"Didn't take it off, Learned Magister," said Athas. "You said not to, after all, and I don't want any of the... ladies getting any funny ideas."

In spite of her fears, Thalia laughed, softly. "Athas, you can take it off to *sleep*, for Thelen's sake! What use are you going to be as my bodyguard in the Queen's court tomorrow if you're yawning every few minutes?"

"I suppose so, Learned Magister," said Athas. "It's not the most comfortable thing to doze in, after all, especially- ow!"

"What's the matter?" asked Thalia, suddenly concerned. The big man had abruptly clapped his hand to the back of his neck.

"Oh, it's.. ow.. nothing, Learned Magister. Must've ricked it when I got up off that silly sofa-chair thing. Honestly, who makes a piece of furniture that's not quite either- ouch!" He froze. "Owowow! Sorry, Learned Magister, I can't turn my bloody head, pardon me talking like an Expelled. Agh!"

Thalia sighed, and steered Athas back into the suite. "Sit on the bed, you great lummox, and let me- what?"

Even as he sat carefully on the side of the bed, Athas chuckled. "Sorry, Learned Magister, it's just that the last person to call me a 'lummox' was Healer Katria and now here you are trying to heal me and- gah!"

"Laughing isn't helping matters!" snapped Thalia, clambering onto the bed to kneel behind him. "You need to keep still.. hmm, the muscles in the side of your neck are badly inflamed."

"Can... can you fix them, Learned-?" began Athas. Thalia laid a hand gently on his neck.

"Athas, there's only the two of us here. If you call me 'Learned Magister' one more time tonight I will make you wish you'd never heard either word in your life. And the answer is yes, if you will just hold still!"

"But.. what should I call you then, Le-.. er..?" murmured Athas, as Thalia poked gently at the muscles, using her Aethersight to see where the inflammation was at its worst.

"My *name* is Thalia, Athas," she reminded him, quietly. "Now, since you were going to be removing this armour anyway, please release the fasteners on your breastplate and gorget. I can't get any Aether into those muscles with all that enchanted silver and steel in the way."

There was a dull click, and Athas' upper body armour unfastened, its design meaning the whole thing came loose. The heavy plates were designed to overlap, so by the time Thalia had finished carefully removing them Athas wore only his padded leather under-shirt above the waist. She began to work her Aether into the damaged muscles, and Athas let out a soft hiss of pain.

"Sorry Athas, but this is delicate work. It'd be a lot easier to fix a knife-wound in the gut- if I get this wrong I could paralyse your neck." That was only the half of it. Athas' muscles, powerful though they were, were twisted into a mass of knots. After a few more moments, Thalia growled in annoyance. "Sergeant, how long have you had this back pain?"

"Back pain, Learn- Thalia? What do you- agh!"

136

"I mean the fact that every muscle in your upper back is twisted and torn!" snapped Thalia, removing the finger she had poked him with. "This must hurt like a Jandallan ape-trap, why didn't you say anything? Take off the tunic, I need to get a better look and see if there's any chance you'll be able to walk tomorrow."

It took both of them to manoeuvre Athas out of the padded shirt, the big Guard at first trying to suppress the little gasps of pain until Thalia warned him that she needed to know what hurt and what didn't. Once the task was accomplished, she took a better look at the damage.

"That's better, and I'll be using your Seal for this since it's exposed anyway. Now the dog can see the rabbit, as my mother used to say. Keep still, damn it!"

Finally able to see what was wrong, Thalia worked quickly, using Athas' own Aether through his Seal to soothe and loosen the overtaxed muscles. As she had ordered, the big man dutifully gasped and groaned whenever she hurt him, and within the space of a few minutes, she was satisfied.

"That seems to have got the worst of it," she said. "Now lie down on your front so I can see what happens when you move."

Athas did as he was bid, letting out another soft hiss of pain as he did so. *There you are.* There was a muscle near the base of his spine that seemed to be the root of the problem. "I see what caused all this trouble." she said, poking the spot more gently. Athas hissed again.

"You'd better take off the rest of the armour- no, don't move, just release the fastenings and let me do it," she said, carefully lifting the remaining plates free when he complied. There was so much of it, the heavy fauld, greaves, upper thigh-plates and the.. "Oh!" she gasped, flushing as she realised what the round piece she was holding was for.

"What's wrong, Thalia?"

"N-nothing!" she snapped. "Just lie still and stop talking! I could still do some real damage if I get this wrong." She looked down at her work to focus her mind, and realised that her work was an extremely muscular young man now clad only in a pair of soft leather breeches. That didn't exactly help, nor did the fact that it was getting rather warm in the room, apparently. She pushed a slightly sweaty lock of hair out of her eyes, and concentrated, sending a final surge of Aether into the offending muscle and kneading both Athas' physical form, and his Pattern, at the same time.

"There," she said, finally. "That should do it."

Athas gave a slow, experimental stretch, and then rolled carefully onto his back before slowly turning his head from side to side. "Yes, that seems to have fixed it, thank you, Learned- I mean, thank you, Thalia." He made to sit up, but Thalia quickly laid a hand on his chest to stop him.

"What do you think you're doing?" she snapped.

"Er... getting up to go back to my post?" he said.

"You aren't going anywhere after all the trouble I took to fix you," said Thalia. "I want you to rest those muscles tonight, not immediately go straining them again." Gently, she pushed him back down.

"But.. but what about you?" asked Athas, staring up at her. She stared back, her eyes going from the open, earnest face, down the muscular chest, taking in the occasional scar and the wooden bead that nestled in his navel.

By this time tomorrow I might be dead.

Before the conscious thought had reached the part of her mind that might have stopped her, she leant down and kissed him. His eyes widened in shock, but not for long.

"I thought you said I shouldn't strain myself..?" he murmured when she finally let him breathe.

"Don't worry, Sergeant," she said. "Tonight I'll be doing all the work."

35

$\mathcal{I}$n the bathroom of the suite, Amanda Devereux ducked another splash as Delys paddled past. The little Swordmaster had been almost ridiculously eager to try out the massive bath, which was practically a swimming pool, but the depth meant that Devereux had initially been content to just sit on the side and watch. One downside of her augmented body was that without mission-specific modifications it had somewhat negative buoyancy, meaning that whilst she could swim or tread water if necessary she couldn't simply float as Delys had spent some time happily doing. The Swordmaster had untied the long, complex braid that normally kept her blonde hair in check, and now it trailed behind her head in the water, looking like a particularly opulent jellyfish.

The Operative had spent the majority of the time watching her- for Delys Amaranth certainly had a body that was well worth watching, even in less alluring circumstances- but there were also other things to consider. She kept replaying the footage Daniel had captured of the Siege Golems at the Farspan, trying to work out what it was about them and the Stickmen that unnerved her. There was also a low-priority alert from the medical suite awaiting attention, but it was probably just complaining about her blood alcohol level again- whilst the system was fully capable of completely sobering her up at a moment's notice, it wouldn't do it except on command or in an emergency. For now she was enjoying a pleasant buzz and planned to stay that way while she could get away with it.

She watched the footage again. There it was, a seemingly minor detail but the only thing that stood out. When the constructs had watched Thalia's little group walk past, each had turned its head to track them, but only so far. And yet, the design of the neck-joints should have allowed their heads to turn all the way around, just like the sensor mounts of a modern battle-mech. Perhaps if the things were mechanical there might be a cable or power connection that prevented the motion, but surely such things didn't apply to a magical construct? Then again, of course, Thalia had said that the College wasn't sure what powered the things, so maybe someone in Abelia had access to advanced technology.

The Stickmen were even more perplexing. They moved in perfect synchronisation when commanded to, but the rest of the time their movement was... eerie. Even the most advanced human-form robots she had seen, from high-end domestic servants to black-market sex-bots covered with the same TruHuman® synthetic skin substitute that disguised her own body, had a certain artificiality to their movements- either the unnaturally precise neural-net derived actions of one, or the oddly stilted motion-captured movements of the other. But the Stickmen moved with an easy grace that defied their artificial nature. Given that no particular attempt had been made to make them look like living things, the effect was every bit as unnerving as the dead-eyed early synthetics of the 21st century had been.

Delys splashed her again, this time deliberately, shaking her out of her reverie. The Swordmaster took hold of her arm, and started to gently pull her away from the side of the bath where she was sitting. Devereux resisted, shaking her head and pulling her arm back.

"No, Del, I can't float in that. I'm too.. heavy."

Delys backed up a little, and signed. *Can't swim? You'll drown?*

Devereux shook her head again. "No, I can swim, and I can breathe under there- remember back at Equinox? I just can't float like you can, because of all... well, everything inside me."

Delys signed again. *Sword.* She reached out her hand once more.

"What do you mean, 'sword'? Oh!" As Delys' hand grasped hers, Devereux felt a tiny electrical tingle flow through her.

++Operative Alert: Operative structural density reduced to 0.96g/cm³ by Aetheric infusion. 1 additional minor alert pending++

She didn't really need Daniel to tell her, because as Delys pulled her slowly into the water it became clear. She was floating. It wasn't a new sensation, exactly- if an Operative was required to float for a mission a buoyancy module could be installed- but to have it happen so spontaneously felt incredible. Of course, there was also the feeling of Delys' power running through her, which was having the usual effect. The Swordmaster enfolded her into her arms, and locked together they drifted into the deeper waters, Delys' hair surrounding them in a golden corona. Devereux felt herself losing control, but tonight, for once, she simply didn't care.

"Just.. just don't let go of me, OK?" she whispered. There was no need for Delys to reply with words, and besides, her hands were busy. Very busy.

Afterwards, once she had dried off and returned to the half of the suite she shared with the Swordmaster, Devereux remembered the other alert. Since the Hercules suite would keep appending the notification to every report until she at least read and dismissed it, she called it up.

A moment later she was hurrying back into the bathroom, heading for the door into Thalia and Athas' room, hoping.... hoping what? That she wasn't too late, or that she was? A quick check on thermal made it abundantly clear that there was nothing she could do, and with a small smile she turned back. This was going to be interesting in the morning.

++Operative Alert: Toxicology report, retrieved from archive at 00:54 ELT: Ingested foodstuff at 19:48 Estimated Local Time contains high level of naturally- occurring aphrodisiac. Estimated tactical threat negligible, estimated social impact on Operative negligible. Alert filed as advisory.++

36

*D*awn saw the men and women of the Second Volume already on the road, their Magisters eager to make up for lost time. Behind them, having arrived in the night, were the repaired wagons bearing the Petard Engines, but reorganising the column to guard them had slowed them down. Then, of course, there was the urgent message that had come in the early hours of the morning.

"An explosion?" said Ollan, as he rode next to Magister Haran. "I had wondered why you were up so late last night and then so early this morning."

Haran nodded. "Aye. According to the watchers at the Vigil, there was a large blast of fire in the depths of the forest, close to the location where Magister Thalia reported discovering Xodan."

"Surely that would be far further than they could see or hear?" objected Ollan. "That would be a distance of, what, four hundred miles?"

"And change," agreed Haran. "Apparently they have a very talented Scout who had been keeping an eye on the Expelled leadership."

"The same one mentioned in Thalia's report? The one the Expelled threatened with painful death if they ever caught him again?"

Haran shrugged. "I do not know. Judging by the depth they must have penetrated into Expelled territory, it seems likely. Clearly Alben Koont is not a man easily deterred. However, it is the latter part of the report that concerns me."

"A mass migration of the Expelled towards the Vigil," said Ollan, stroking his beard. "The timing of both events hardly seems to be a coincidence. It would appear the Dendaril are making their move."

"Agreed," said Haran. "And we are not yet in position, Thelen damn it. Magister Thalia is only due to meet the Abelian Queen today, and even if negotiations go well it will take them some time to mobilise."

"Ambassador Thalia Daran," said Ollan with a smile. "Now there is an appointment to make the diplomatic service turn cartwheels with delight. Oh, to be a cat under the table when she meets Tondarin!"

Haran glared at him. "How can you be so... flippant at a time like this? If we do not secure the Vigil before the Dendaril overrun it, it could be the end of.. of everything!"

"Indeed!" agreed Ollan. "But I have always found that to laugh in the face of peril at the very least causes one's enemies consternation, as well as doing wonders for my own morale."

"It also greatly irritates your allies," pointed out Haran. "Not to mention that in this case, our 'enemies' are time and a swarm of unthinking parasitic flies, neither of whom you are likely to dishearten with your bravado."

"Symbiotic," said Ollan. "Not parasitic. The creature and the host enter into a relationship that is mutually beneficial, for the most part."

"They destroy the minds of their victims and replace them with a new personality!" snapped Haran. "How is that mutually beneficial?"

Ollan shrugged. "It depends on the personality they destroy, I'd imagine. In the case of the Vice-Chancellor, I think people would want to give the insect responsible some sort of medal."

Haran threw his hands up in the air in exasperation, a feat made possible only by his skilled horsemanship. "You, Learned Magister, are an impossible, insufferable old man. I honestly do not know why I am putting up with you."

"Ah, Haran, that is because however much I might irritate my friends, you know I will do far, far worse to my enemies."

Haran gave a grim smile. That much, at least, was certainly true.

"Now," said Ollan. "Let us press on, and see how well the modifications Jarton suggested hold up. I should like to make Fort Tarim before noon, and in view of our dire circumstances I will even refrain from stopping off to test the quality of the local cuisine. Though having said that, I have it on good authority that the Sixth have terrible cooks, so it is no great sacrifice."

He rode off towards the head of the column as Haran had seen him do so many times before. Despite his words, he had to admit he was glad the old man had decided to come along, especially now that it seemed like the situation at the Vigil might be deteriorating. It would be useful to have an active Symposium Magister to hand if things got complicated with the Vigilants. There was also the matter of the letter Haran had been tasked with delivering to Sir Matthew, the contents of which would probably not be particularly well-received.

Yes, all things considered it would be very useful to have Magister Ollan Dane around.

37

*W*hen Captain Ariel Marigold entered the Vice-Chancellor's study at the Belus Manse, she was relieved to see that her mood seemed greatly improved since her last visit. When Anneke had awoken to find that Willow-Sigh Wen and Maike Dain had somehow escaped, she had been displeased, to put it mildly. Ariel supposed she didn't really blame Eri for deciding, when she recovered consciousness, to make good her own escape before the Matriarch of House Belus got hold of her. After all, she had been left in charge of the estate in Ariel's absence.

"Is there still no news on where Eri might have got to, Ariel?" asked Anneke, in a much milder tone than the Captain of the House Belus Guard had dared hope for. The loss of the prisoners had been a blow to the Vice-Chancellor's plans that the most powerful woman in the Empire had not been prepared for, and Anneke Belus was one who prided herself on being prepared for anything.

"Er, no, Learned Magister," said Ariel. "We know she slipped out a couple of nights after the escape, when we thought she was still unconscious. Whatever Maike and that Daxalai wench did to her clearly didn't do as much damage as it seemed. She must have pretended to still be out of it until no-one was looking, and there's been no sign of her since. I'm guessing she's probably gone to ground for fear of what you'll do to her when you catch her."

She had nearly said "*if* you catch her" but saw that misstep coming just in time. Anneke would not like the suggestion that failing to hunt down Eri was even a possibility.

The Vice-Chancellor sighed. "Ariel, my dear, when have I ever given you or any of my girls the impression that I was the sort of employer who looks for scapegoats? If I were going to punish anyone, it'd be that damnable Weaver who insisted that the wall illusion made the prison level escape-proof."

"You had him killed anyway, Learned Magister," Ariel reminded her. Anneke waved a hand in the air dismissively.

"Well, yes, but that was a purely practical precaution, not some sort of pointless vengeance. We could hardly have someone who knew not only that the prison existed, but also how to get into it, running around out there, could we? Which, of course, leads us back to the present problem." She took up the wine carafe from her desk. "Drink?"

"No thank you, Learned Magister," said Ariel. She'd seen the effect Anneke's personal cellar of wines had on most people, and certainly didn't want any part of it when the Vice-Chancellor was in such an enigmatic mood. Of course there was also the fact that it was still Dawn Watch, but that rarely stopped her.

Anneke sniffed, and poured herself a large measure. "Your loss, my dear. So, we have not one, not two, but three people out there who know secrets that could be exceptionally dangerous in the wrong hands- to whit, any but mine. Willow-Sigh Wen and Maike Dain remain the most serious problem, of course, but I want Eri found too."

"What if she's just trying to get the other two back? She had a bit of a.. connection with Little Red," said Ariel, using the nickname reflexively.

"Then if she succeeds before Jonas' crew find her, or them, she will be forgiven, of course," said Anneke. "If not... well, you know how efficient they are. See to it that he knows that the Daxalai is the priority target- her I want alive if possible, dead if not. As for Maike Dain- that girl has outlived her usefulness, I think. If I pay more for her alive it will only be so I can have the pleasure of watching that ungrateful vixen die in front of me."

Ariel felt at her throat, as she often did when Maike was mentioned. On that point, she and Anneke were in total agreement. "As you command, Learned Magister. But Jonas is going to need to know where to start looking, and the escape was two weeks ago. It would take a master investigator to track Maike down now."

Anneke laughed. "There, Ariel dear, we have had some luck. A master investigator is already on her trail, though he doesn't know it yet. Tell Jonas to head for Freeport and if he finds no more leads, to shadow Magister Julius Thule. If possible, he is to find the targets before Julius does, and make sure he never meets them."

"And if he does meet them?"

Anneke shrugged. "Then he is to make sure that neither Julius, nor anyone he is working with, leaves that island alive."

Ariel swallowed, hard. Magister or no, she would not like to be in the boots of Julius Thule right now, nor of any poor fools with him.

38

*T*halia was just becoming aware of the fact that dawn light was beginning to filter through the heavy drapes when a gentle tapping at the door of the suite snapped her fully awake. With that wakefulness came several other realisations in quick succession.

Firstly, she was completely naked. That wasn't in and of itself particularly alarming, except for the fact that there was someone else in the same bed as her in a very similar state of undress. A male someone.. *very* male, who was snoring softly. Then the full memory of the previous night hit her like a Demolition of War Golems. Athas.

"Blood, Ice and Fire!" she hissed, sitting bolt upright in the bed. "What in Thelen's name was I thinking?"

The knocking came again. "Learned Magister? Your carriage is waiting outside, but we have brought breakfast if you would care for it before leaving?"

Mind whirling, Thalia looked around the room wildly. There was no immediate sign of her nightdress and her spare clothes were still packed in one of the cases Athas had used to barricade the door. She knew she was going to have to use her magic to bring the cases over to the bed, but her mind was still full of fragmented images of the previous night and refused to focus. Just as she was about to throw caution to the wind and get out of the bed, naked or not, the connecting door opened and Amanda Devereux breezed in, fully-clothed and seeming totally unconcerned by the scene in front of her.

"Just a moment, please," said the Operative, striding over to the door and shoving Athas' simple barricade gently aside so she could poke her head out of the room. "The Magister is not yet awake- please leave the food there and we'll take it in when we are ready." She closed the door, and turned back to Thalia.

"Th-thank you, Amanda," said the Magister, trying not to look as flustered as she felt.

"No problem, Learned Magister," said Devereux with an altogether too knowing smile. "Good night?"

"I-" began Thalia, but Athas, showing impeccable timing, chose that moment to wake up. Where the Magister had woken slowly and cautiously, the big Guard came to his senses in a rush, throwing back the bedsheets and bounding to his feet almost before his eyes were open. Given his total lack of even a stitch of clothing, the effect was dramatic.

"Yeah, looks like it was," laughed the Operative, as Athas began to realise where he was and what was happening. Reflexively, the big Guard's hands shot down in a largely futile, and altogether belated, attempt to preserve his modesty.

"Oh! Ah.. Amanda- Learned.. I mean.. Thalia.. I... um.."

"Don't worry, Athas, it's nothing I haven't seen before," said the Operative, as Delys walked into the room grinning. "Look, why don't you go and have a quick wash whilst we find you some clothes?"

Grateful to have been given some orders to follow, Athas hurried through the connecting door, flushing bright red to the tips of his ears. As soon as the big man had left the room, Devereux brought Thalia's case over to the bed, as Delys retrieved the floating table with their breakfast on it. Using the bedsheets as an improvised robe, Thalia scurried behind the changing screen to dress.

"There's something you should probably know, Thalia," said Devereux, in a more serious tone, as the Magister emerged from behind the screen dressed in a spare nightdress. "The food in this place, or at least.." she took an experimental bite of a pastry "..the food we had last night, was dosed with a pretty potent-"

"-aphrodisiac?" finished Thalia. "I guessed that must have been it. Probably Indal's Ruin, the Abelians are famous for brewing it. Thelen's breath, last night.... we must have been going for..." she tailed off, blushing at least as fiercely as Athas had. She couldn't believe she was even daring to admit what she'd done, but there hardly seemed to be any point denying the overwhelming evidence.

"Yeah, I didn't notice it until it was too... late..." said Devereux, suddenly looking up. "Why is your nightdress hanging from the chandelier?"

"Oh, great Thelen," groaned Thalia, burying her head in her hands. "Is this food safe at least?"

"Seems like it," said Devereux. "I'm not getting any toxicology reports, but you might want to check it your way too, just to be sure."

"Wait.." said Thalia "are you telling me you could... taste that there was something in the food? Why didn't you say anything?"

"It's not quite that simple," said Devereux. "Yes, anything I eat is checked for poisons, sedatives or intoxicants, but I only get direct warnings if it's actually dangerous. Most food has some sort of effect on your mood or health one way or another, and it's pretty annoying to get a breakdown of every last detail of it, so I only got a low-priority advisory. After all, it wasn't going to do any real harm."

"No real harm?" snapped Thalia. "Amanda, I.. I slept with.. with.. *Athas!*"

Devereux took a sip of coffee. "You could've done a lot worse. So could he, at that. The important thing is what you do next."

Thalia frowned at her. "I don't follow you."

The Operative sighed. "Look, Thalia, Athas is a good guy. With the way he looks, and how gentle he is for a man his size, he's someone a lot of women want to get a piece of. Ariel, Melisa- hell, he was practically fighting them off at the Expelled's camp."

Thalia poured herself a cup of tea. "And?"

"And so far, most of the women he's... known.. have treated him pretty much like a piece of meat. He keeps going back to Ariel, but that woman's a stone-cold bitch who works for a ruthless alpha-bitch and we both know she's stringing him along- maybe even under Anneke's orders. So you need to decide if what happened here was an accident that'll never be repeated or the start of something else- and you need to make damn sure that Athas sees it the same way, or we're going to have a problem."

Thalia stared at her. "I.. I am a Magister, Amanda. I can't just... marry a Guard. The scandal..."

"Who said anything about marrying anyone?" said Devereux, quietly. "You think Anneke's heading down the aisle any time soon? Or Magister Kaine?"

"I'm not sure either example makes me feel any better," groused Thalia.

"The point is, where this goes from here is up to you and Athas, but you need to figure it out," said Devereux. "I don't think this was an accident- if the Abelians have spies that are half as good as Anneke's they'd know that you and Athas are pretty close, and you're about to enter into some very delicate negotiations. Using this to throw you off-balance is just the sort of thing Anneke would do, from what I've seen of her."

"Do you think that she...?" began Thalia.

"Anneke? No," said Devereux, shaking her head. "She's got no reason I can think of to want you to fail, even if she doesn't seem to like you much. No, I'm betting this was some home-grown Abelian skulduggery. It wouldn't even take that much setting up- I imagine everyone who stays here gets the same treatment as standard."

Athas emerged from the bathroom, now dressed in a tunic and breeches that Delys had thrown in to him. "I'm all done in there, L-" he paused, searching Thalia's face for a reaction. She gave him as subtle a nod as she thought he'd notice. "Learned Magister," he continued. "Is there any food left?"

Laughing, Delys tossed a hard-boiled egg at him, and the big man caught it deftly, popping it into his mouth whole. Thalia took a deep breath, and made for the bathroom. "Once you've eaten, Sergeant, I'd like you back in full armour, please. We have to make a good impression at the Court today."

"Yes, Learned Magister," said Athas, swallowing the egg. "Any.. other orders?"

Thalia stopped, and took a deep, steadying breath. "Sergeant, at least for now, as far as anyone outside this room is concerned what happened last night... didn't." She turned to face him. "I am sorry if that isn't what you wanted to hear. Truthfully, it isn't what part of me wanted to say. But we all know how important our task in this Thelen-damned country is, and we cannot allow our.. feelings to get in the way or distract us. Do you understand me?"

"Y-yes, Learned Magister," said Athas, softly.

Without saying another word, Thalia fled into the bathroom. For the most part, the steam disguised her tears.

39

ot since the last Reclamation had so many of the Free Tribes moved at
once. To the Second of the Tree-Searchers, it seemed as if every rock
and tree had given birth to a family or a small band of warriors. They moved as
swiftly as they could, having snatched the bare minimum of sleep, but even so the
sheer mass of people was slowing them down.

A small war-band of Blackbloods had insisted on forming a rearguard,
protecting the march west from the advance of the Fly Lords. They were led by a
new Black Skull, who had already taken on many of the mannerisms of his predecessor, even though he was clearly several years younger and almost a foot shorter.
Even now, the other Free, particularly the Heart-Eaters, regarded the Blackbloods
with some suspicion, the stigma that the tribe had already borne for their habit of
roving in forbidden lands exacerbated by the consequences of their recent actions.
And yet, Second thought such prejudice to be largely unfair, for even without the
mistakes of the Black Skull the Fly Lords had been coming. By showing the depth
of the danger, albeit unwittingly, the Blackbloods may well have saved the Free,
even as Mighty Lelioko had said.

To the north and south of the main mass of Free roved the Heart-Eaters,
fiercest and most numerous of the warrior tribes. Mighty Xaraya had argued
loudly for the right to lead what she still considered to be a final great Reclamation, but Mighty Dokan, supported by the other Mighty Ones of his tribe, had
pointed out that whilst in Tree-Searcher territory, the Free should be led by those
of that tribe. Since the forest to the south was the domain of the Heart-Eaters and
the north belonged to the treacherous Shorewalkers, Xaraya divided her forces in
order to protect and escort her own people from one direction, and repel any
attack from the other. Of course, once they reached the edge of the forest, the
territory of the Free would come to an end and Xaraya's demands would be far
harder to resist- and she commanded some twenty thousand warriors.

The First was shouting at several of his scouts when Second found him.

149

"Not one sign!" he growled. "We stand at our moment of greatest peril and none of you can show me a single trace of the Green Shadow!"

"Not for nothing is he so named, First," replied the lead scout, who like the Second bore the Stalking Wolf. "Few among the Deluded know our ways as the Green Shadow does. In truth, we have no way of knowing if he is even here at all."

"He is here," said the First. "I can feel it in my bones. I can taste his spoor in the air- he is here, and close."

"Then perhaps we should continue to chase our tails like fools searching for him as doom devours the Forest Home in our wake!" snapped the scout. "Perhaps then his laughter at our folly will give him away."

"Do you challenge my commands?" said the First, his voice low and dangerous. The scout bowed his head.

"No, First. If you order that we search, then my scouts and I will search. But the Green Shadow was only found before when he fell into our laps, and I doubt we shall be so fortunate a second time."

"And what say you, Second?" said the First, turning to her. "Are we to let the Green Shadow bite his thumb at us once more?"

Second took a deep breath. "Were it a decision to make only for myself, First, I would hunt him until the end of the world. I would chase him down- when he fled, I would hunt, when he slept, I would stalk, and when he woke, I would have my teeth at his throat. But for now, we are mere squirrels running before the wolves, and should we turn to bare our fangs we shall surely be torn asunder. No, First, for now I would not hunt the Green Shadow. If he is wise, he is going to the same place as us in any case."

"And if he is not wise?" said the First.

"Then he shall soon know the Woe and be the Green Shadow no longer," said Second. "A fate for which I shall shed no tears, from the eyes of woman or wolf."

"Well spoken, Second!" boomed Mighty Dokan, appearing from behind a tree. "First, I have taken counsel with the hawks of the dawn and the owls of the dusk, and they tell me that the Fly Lords continue their advance. They are slow, but they do not stop to sleep nor to bicker amongst themselves."

First bowed his head. "I am sorry, Mighty One, my desire to take the life of the Green Shadow has clouded my mind. My scouts shall concentrate on guiding the stragglers to the Stone Paths from now on."

The lead scout nodded. "It shall be done, First- but we shall run with eyes open and noses sharp, and should the Green Shadow cross our path it shall go ill for him. On this, you have my blood's promise."

Without another word, the scouts turned and headed into the forest, the young warriors serving as their apprentices coming forward to take their war-gear before they returned to the wolf-shape. The First watched them go, silently. "I do not like this, Mighty One," he said finally, once the last warrior had vanished. "We flee our native lands, deny our birthright. We allow one who has pulled our tails to go unchallenged in our lands, and we go to throw ourselves on the mercy of the Deluded. Truly has Woe come to us."

"Aye, that it has, First," agreed Dokan. "Second, what news of your errand?"

The Second swallowed. The First was not going to like this any more than he had anything else. "It is done, Mighty One. The children of the Tree-Searchers, Heart-Eaters and Blackbloods are delivered to the Hearth-Tenders."

First whirled. "What!? But the Hearth-Tenders-"

"-have taken Ixilinath's bargain, aye," finished Dokan, pointedly stepping forwards to stand between the two warriors. "But you know as well as I that we may have to fight our way past the Doors of Patros. There will be no hidden camp to fall back to, not in these times. Would you send the children to the rear, there to be taken by the Fly Lords? Would you place them in the fore, and hope that the arrows of the Deluded fly wide out of pity? Mighty Lelioko tells us that only those of fifty seasons or more can take the Firebrand, so for now, at least, they will remain safe and untainted."

"And you simply believed her?" shouted First, daring to brandish his spear at Dokan in his fury. "Even if we should save ourselves without taking the brand, you have placed our future in the hands of the Enslaver!"

"Better in his hands than rotting in the ground," said Dokan, ignoring the spear-point that hovered inches from his bare chest. "Mighty Lelioko may be a thrall of Ixil, but I do not believe she has lied to us- about anything. We will see to it first that the Free survive, and once that is achieved, we shall deal with the Enslaver."

"I would sooner die than live as a slave- to Ixil, to the Fly Lords, or to the Deluded," added Second. "But a corpse is no more free than a rock. We must endure, First, both in body and in spirit."

The First glared from one to the other, then turned away with an angry grunt. "Bah! These times are too complicated for a simple warrior. Give me a problem I can slay with a spear-thrust!"

"I hope it will not come to that, First," said Dokan, softly. The warrior laughed bitterly.

"I do not. I am a warrior, Mighty One. When we reach the Doors, I hope the Deluded close them to us, that we might finally cast that cursed fortress down stone-by-stone upon their heads!" The Defiant Boar and Great Ox tattoos on his skin flared brightly, and he struck the nearest tree repeatedly with his fist. "Damn these flies, damn the Woe, damn the Deluded and damn the wisdom of the Mighty!" The tree shuddered with each blow, and finally gave way, crashing to the earth in a shower of leaves and sending birds clamouring into the air in alarm.

Without another word, the First stalked off into the forest. Dokan and Second exchanged a worried glance.

"I hope others do not think the way the First does," said Dokan. "Or when we reach the Doors, there could be a bloodbath."

Second didn't dare tell him that every word the First had spoken could have come from her own heart.

151

40

$\mathcal{T}$he Wardens made it to the Wake well before noon, in the event, and the sight which met Haran's eyes was certainly impressive. What had been a mere muddy crater when last he saw it was now a sparkling lake, and within it lay a large artificial island, topped by a substantial wooden stockade. More usefully, a new and reassuringly sturdy-looking bridge now connected the end of the Road to the fortification.

"Well, this will certainly speed our journey, eh Haran?" said Magister Ollan. "I'll say this for your cousin- when she decides something needs to be built, it certainly gets built. Ah, and speak of the Magister, and the staff appears!"

Kandira Dar was indeed riding across the bridge to meet them. "Ho Ollan, Haran! You made good time!"

Haran smiled. Kandira Dar was one of those people who could drive ordinary men and women to extraordinary feats through sheer force of personality. "It is good to see you again, Kandira. I apologise for supplanting you on this mission."

Kandira laughed. "Nonsense! You're the man for the job, Haran, even those stone-deaf half-blind fossils in the Symposium can see that."

"It is certainly fortunate that no Symposium Magisters are present, then," said Ollan with a chuckle, "or they might take offence at such a comment."

"Oh, you're no fossil yet, Ollan," laughed Kandira. "Anyway, Haran, you needn't worry about me. After all, I'm coming with you."

"You're what?" said Haran reflexively.

"Coming with you, you ninny," said Kandira. "The interesting part here's done now anyway- do you know the Symposium has given this place to Jakob Adaran? Decided to call it 'Fort Tarim', too, as if the people who built the damn place shouldn't have a say in it."

"A ploy to get some of the Quoits out of House Adaran's musty coffers, I'd imagine," said Ollan. "Probably not a bad idea in the long run, but I agree not consulting you was a trifle rude. Which reminds me- where can we get a spot of lunch?"

"There's no time for that, Learned Magister, as you yourself pointed out." admonished Haran. "Much as I'd like to see what you've accomplished here, Kandira, I want to make the Vigil before nightfall. And there really is no reason for you to-"

"There're at least three reasons for me to come along," said Kandira, cutting him off. "And they're rattling their chains on those wagons of yours. I know you're planning to install those Engines at the Vigil. Well let me tell you, that's a job for someone who knows what they're doing, and unless you've dragged Jarton out here with you, that means you need me."

"I'm sure that the Choirmaster can-" began Ollan.

"A Choirmaster? Hah!" snorted Kandira. "I'll grant you, they train the crews of the Engines to set them up and shoot them, but you're talking about installing these things on an ancient pre-College fortress. The walls are almost two hundred feet high at the eastern side, and that's the smaller drop. Then you've got the upper battlement, which isn't anywhere near wide enough to fit the damn things on, even if the superstructure can take that much extra weight and strain. Let some idiot bodge together some sort of platform on the battlements instead of using a proper casemate and embrasure and you'll be lucky if the damn thing stays together long enough to collapse when you fire."

The other two Magisters exchanged a glance. "Did you understand any of that, Haran?" said Ollan, finally.

"Barely enough to understand why no-one has tried to mount Petard Engines on city walls before," admitted Haran. "Very well, Kandira, I accept your offer of assistance."

The older woman snorted. "As if you had any choice in the matter, Haran. If you'd said no I'd just have followed you there anyway. This place isn't ready to be attacked by hordes of screaming savages yet so I can't have you two accidentally knocking the Vigil over, can I? Now, let's get your lot moving and then we'll see about Ollan's spot of lunch, eh?"

"We really don't have time to-" Haran began to protest. Kandira, who had begun to ride off, turned in the saddle to give him an exasperated look.

"Haran, you nit, it's going to take the best part of an hour to get all that lot through Fort Tarim, which gives you plenty of time to get some food. And we both know that Ollan's no use to anybody once he gets hungry."

"There are many who question my usefulness when sated, Kandira," said Ollan with a sigh. "But we shall defer to your judgement, of course, eh Haran?"

Haran's shoulders sagged. "Oh very well. I can see that arguing with either of you would waste time I do not have. I shall instruct Captain Render to take charge of the column and join you shortly."

Even as he rode away to find his command staff, Haran couldn't completely suppress a smile.

41

The road from Dalliance to Abellan ran along the cliff-tops and presented an excellent view of the sea, for which Amanda Devereux was deeply grateful. For one thing, it gave Thalia something to talk about other than the very obvious elephant in the room. Not that anyone here would call it that- you'd have to start by explaining what an elephant was. It wasn't so much that Thalia and Athas weren't talking, it was more that they were taking such pains to make sure everything they said was innocuous and proper that all the easy camaraderie that they had built up had completely evaporated. On balance, thought the Operative, it probably would have been better if she'd warned Thalia in time.

For now, though, the Magister was keeping herself busy pointing out a ship out to sea. "There, Amanda, something you won't have seen before. An Abelian warship."

"A what? I thought the Whales sank any ship that took to sea with weapons on board."

"They do," agreed Thalia. "But the sea off Abelia's south-east coast is shallow and treacherous, and the Whales prefer not to go there. That's why they call it the Warrior's Sea. It's that way almost as far as Har'ii, and it's the reason why some companies of armed mercenary Lancers manage to make it off the island. You need a good navigator, though, or there's a very real danger that you'll hit a reef."

"Har'ii? That's where Sir Matthew got those instruments, isn't it?" asked Devereux. Thalia nodded.

"Yes, and it's where that Chime-Mage we saw at the Star of Gold came from, too. You remember the man with the floating silver bells? The entire island sits on top of a massive coral reef, and according to legend that itself grew on the remains of some giant sea-creature. I'm not surprised to have seen a Chime-Mage at a place like that, actually."

"Why's that?"

"Har'ii is heavily populated for its small size," said Thalia. "When a family has a new child, a member of the same family must be either put to death or exiled, by law, to control the population- mostly the latter," she added hurriedly, seeing Devereux's shocked expression. "Of course, human nature being what it is, wealthy families often 'buy' the right to a child from poor ones, so a peasant is exiled when a new lordling is born. Many young Har'ii men end up in the mercenary companies that way."

"They have almost the reverse problem to the Abelians, don't they, Learned Magister?" observed Athas, who was watching the ship intently. Like Imperial vessels, it was propelled by multiple banks of oars, but unlike them it sported a large ram and several serious-looking ballistae on the decks. It also seemed to have a sizeable number of sharks following in its wake.

"I suppose so, yes, Sergeant," agreed Thalia. "Few people from the Empire have ever visited Har'ii, but as I understand it they saw the overpopulation problem coming before it got too serious, so perhaps they are comfortable enough that they don't see trying to colonise Abelia as a risk worth taking. Then there's the twenty-sixth axiom of the Third Book of Thelen."

"*For every problem, there is a solution that is simple, neat, and utterly wrong,*" supplied Devereux. Thalia gave her a surprised look.

"Very good! I had no idea you were a scholar."

"I'm not," admitted Devereux. "Magister Julius quoted that one at us just before the Daxalai turned up the first time."

"Yes, well," said Thalia, looking a little put out. "The point being, there might be all sorts of reasons why the Har'ii couldn't or wouldn't help repopulate Abelia. It'd probably be a political nightmare, for one thing."

"I bet they haven't even asked," said Athas. "That's the problem, everyone being so bloody clever and 'thinking everything through' instead of just *doing* something."

Devereux suddenly realised they were veering into dangerous territory and changed the subject quickly. "That's the second time I've seen those Abelian ballistae. The College doesn't seem to use anything like them."

Thalia snorted. "That's because they're not much use against Magisters. Oh, they're dangerous if you don't see them coming and a direct shot from one is powerful enough to punch through most shielding spells, but once you've got direct sight on them it's trivially easy to stymie the mechanism. That's why the ballistae on the Farspan are hidden inside warded towers. Once you add in the need to carry bolts or stones for them to fire, the Petard Engine is a far superior device."

Devereux wondered how much of that was really true. She'd seen Magisters work their magic at quite impressive range- most notably when Ollan and Haran had saved them from crash-landing as they escaped from the collapsing Royal Keep- but the weapons on the Abelian ship looked like they would be able to shoot a long way. And that was ignoring any magical enhancements. Thalia seemed to read her mind.

"Of course, those things can shoot much further than we can usually reach," she said. "But once they get that far away, there's enough time to deflect the shot, rather than try to directly stop it. Generally, if a Magister has enough time to see a bolt coming, they can defend themselves against it, though obviously it's harder to protect something the size of a ship. That's part of the reason why those guns of yours work so well."

"Assuming that the Magister doesn't just break them," said Devereux, who had had exactly that happen more often than she'd care to remember.

"Magisters are good at breaking things," agreed Athas. Thalia opened her mouth to retort, but a shout from the driver brought her up short.

"*Viava Regiana!*"

"What in Thelen's name-" began Thalia.

"I heard about this at Castle Orsinio," said Devereux. "It's a traditional thing, it means 'Long live the Queen' or something like that. Coach drivers and couriers do it when the capital comes into sight."

Athas and Delys were already poking their heads out of the coach windows, the coach's shielding spell protecting them from the worst of the wind. "Oh... wow..." gasped Athas. "Amanda, Learned Magister, you should see this!"

The city that rose on the horizon looked every bit the capital of a great kingdom. The walls, perhaps, were not as massive or solid-looking as those of most of the Imperial cities Devereux had seen before, but the buildings that rose beyond them were breathtaking. Soaring spires and massive domes of every possible shape, size, design and colour rose high into the sky, no two alike and yet all serving as pieces of a coherent whole. Many of the taller towers were connected at various levels by narrow bridges. To the Operative, it looked like a cross between a fairytale castle and some late 20th century artist's idea of what the 'city of the future' would look like- except without the flying cars.

"It's certainly impressive," admitted Devereux, as the carriage passed some grazing pastures and fields of haystacks. "I wonder how many people there are to fill it."

"Well, Dalliance was pretty busy," said Thalia "but I suppose that quite a few of them were foreigners. This is the capital, though, so-"

"Something's up," interrupted Devereux, suddenly. "We're braking, hard."

"Well, we're nearly at the capital, so-"

"We're still at least half an hour away, but we're stopping," insisted the Operative. Athas stuck his head out of the window again.

"Hey, what's going on?"

"Straw cart in the road," shouted down the driver. "Looks like his axle's bust. We're going to have to stop and help move it out of the way, at least."

Athas sighed. "I'll get out and help, Learned Magister," he said, pulling his head back in and getting ready to open the door. "Shouldn't take too long to get it shifted."

"I'll come too," said Thalia. "It should be a simple matter to repair the damaged part, and then we can be on our way."

Devereux frowned. The last few fields had shown clear signs that straw had recently been cut in them, but there had been no haystacks. The field next to the place where the cart had broken down, however, boasted four, and all of them right next to the wooden fence at the side of the road. That might just be because the cart had come to load up, but her instincts and training were screaming at her.

"Del, come on, let's stretch our legs," she said, opening the opposite door to the one Athas and Thalia were getting out of and walking towards the haystacks, keeping her manner casual even as she switched her vision mode to thermal. Sure enough, though the haystacks themselves had been warmed by the late-morning sun, several heat signatures showed hiding behind them- three behind each.

++*Tactical mode activated. Designate detected targets as hostile?*++

Yes, but wait for my mark.

++*Targets designated. Operative advisory: Total available ammunition 14 rounds. Total designated targets 12.*++

So assuming that each target went down in one shot, that would leave just two more rounds in her guns and the last few reloads were in her case. Not ideal. Still giving no indication that she was aware of any danger, she turned to look down the road to where Athas and Thalia were approaching what she was now thinking of as a road-block. Three burly-looking men were standing by the broken axle, seemingly at a loss for what to do. She checked the straw in the cart with thermal and was alarmed, though not surprised, to see four more people hiding in it.

This was a delicate situation. If she simply opened fire, the Abelians might well consider it an unprovoked attack. If she shouted a warning to Thalia there was no telling who would react first, or how. Meanwhile, Athas was walking straight into a trap, though at least he had his armour and sword. It was just possible that the attackers would see those, and his impressive size, and decide to call the whole thing off. Possible, but very unlikely.

"Broken down, have we lads?" said the big Guard cheerfully as he approached the cart. "Well, we can't have you blocking up the road all day, can we? Let's see if we can't lift this thing between us, eh?"

"S'full o' wet straw," muttered the largest of the three men. "Might be able t'shift 'er wi' a biggun' like ye elpin', but t'bugger'll shiver t'bits if'n we drags 'er."

"An' fuck up t'road in't bargain," put in another of the men.

The driver and guard of the coach had taken the opportunity to snatch a crafty smoke. To Devereux's surprise, Delys sauntered over and pilfered a cigarette. The guard was taken aback as well, but shrugged and lit it for her. The Operative turned her attention back to the wagon. What were they waiting for?

"Maybe if we lift it together, Magister Thalia can fix your axle with her magic and you can get the wheel back on?" suggested Athas. "If that's OK with you, of course, Learned Magister."

"It should be no problem," said Thalia, a little stiffly. "After all, Magisters don't just break things."

Even as she winced at the resumption of Athas' and Thalia's sniping, Devereux saw what was going to happen. The ambushers planned to wait until the big Guard had his hands full with the cart before attacking. They might even hope to catch Thalia off-guard if she was busy with the repairs at the same time. She was just about to shout a warning when Delys burst into a fit of coughing.

"Too much for ye, eh lass?" chuckled the coach guard. "Not like whatever feeble weed they grow up north, eh?"

The little Swordmaster coughed again, made a face at the man, and flicked the still-burning cigarette away dismissively. It spiralled through the air, and landed smack in the middle of the nearest haystack. Whatever the men staring in alarm from beside the broken-down cart might have claimed, the straw was tinder-dry and dusty and caught light almost immediately.

"Del, no!" shouted Athas, who had been raised in the farmlands of Sommerlan and knew well the dangers of a straw fire. "That's a year's worth of- hey!"

157

The armed men and women hiding behind the hay were less concerned than the big Guard about the coming season's supply of straw, but were extremely concerned by their close proximity to what was rapidly becoming an inferno. Realising that their ruse had been uncovered, they broke from their cover and leapt to the attack. Though Delys had exposed their trap in a typically cunning fashion, she had also unwittingly presented Devereux with a problem- the Hercules suite had been maintaining its lock on the hidden ambushers with passive thermal sensors which the sudden burst of heat had all but blinded. Nonetheless, her right gun spoke six times, and the attackers still emerging from behind the furthest two haystacks were sent reeling. Reeling, but not dead, for most of them were wearing at least the breastplate of the same sort of armour that the Stickmen that had escorted Thalia to Naxxiamor had worn, and the targeting system had shot for centre body mass. Devereux had found that even armour-piercing rounds struggled to penetrate enchanted silver battle-plate, so now her guns were loaded with hollow-points. Those didn't go through either, but they hit with enough force to knock the victims sprawling.

Fortunately, the other group of attackers had Delys Amaranth to deal with. Emerging from the rapidly-growing cloud of smoke, blinking back tears and spluttering, they were met with a great-sword that danced like a rapier. Two went down before they even realised what was happening, and the remaining four abandoned their attempt to rush to the barricade and began to circle the blonde Swordmaster warily. Their own blades, hand-and-a-half swords very similar in size and shape to Devereux's own, were of the same high quality as their armour, though they seemed to have seen better days.

At the barricade, Athas made short work of the three men he had initially offered to help. Not bothering to draw his sword, he took the knife-thrust of the first on the side of his breastplate, trusting the heavy armour to repel the small weapon. Before the attacker could recover his balance, the big Guard seized the extended arm and jerked it savagely forwards, even as his right fist pistoned into the man's face. His victim's initial scream of anguish as his arm was popped out of its socket was abruptly choked off as the armoured gauntlet smashed his nose into bloody ruin. The other two turned to flee, but they had underestimated the length of the big man's stride, and he stepped between them, one massive arm encircling each grimy neck and squeezing.

"If I know the Learned Magister, she's going to want to talk to you, lads," said Athas as his victims gurgled for breath. "Which is good news for you, because otherwise I'd pull your heads off like you were fucking chickens. Drop the knives!"

The two weapons clattered to the floor, though whether it was because their owners had heard Athas' demand or because they were half-strangled wasn't clear. With the big Guard distracted, however, and Thalia's view obscured by his bulk, neither noticed four figures emerging from the straw in the cart. Three bore a sword in each hand, one of which they had probably planned to toss to their comrades, but the fourth held a nocked bow. Before anyone could react, she had loosed, and the blazing silver shaft buried itself in Athas' gut. The magic of the arrow proved far more effective at penetrating the enchanted silver plate than any bullet would have.

"Guh-" gasped the big man, falling to his knees with a crash before pitching onto his face. Fortunately for Thalia, his collapse also slammed both of the men he was holding face-first into the unyielding stone of the road, removing them both from the fight and from the realm of consciousness for the foreseeable future.

"Athas!" shouted Thalia in shock. Devereux, already sprinting towards her, saw the Magister raise a flame-wreathed hand towards the cart. At the last moment, even as the first swordsman bore down on her, she seemed to change her mind. The fire winked out, and the bandit was sent hurtling through the air by a blast of pure force that also shattered the cart into matchwood.

The Magister stepped forwards past Athas as the archer and the two swordsmen picked themselves out of the wreckage, her staff raised. Desperately, Devereux shouted to her.

"Thalia, no! Athas' vitals are fading, let me handle them!"

"Athas?" said Thalia, seeming to remember where she was. As Devereux ran past, her still-loaded left gun and *Liberty* at the ready, the Magister dropped to her knees in what was by now a rapidly-spreading pool of blood.

The two swordsmen closed ranks, protecting the archer. Devereux soon found out why- the young woman proved to be exceptionally skilled. Two arrows flashed across the ten metres separating her from the Operative, the first nicking her ear as she dodged whilst the second was blasted apart by a gunshot less than two inches from her heart. A third shattered almost as it left the bow, making the archer drop the weapon with a startled curse. Still seeming unwilling to retreat, the young woman took one of the swords from the man on her right, whilst the other swordsman hurled his own spare blade at Devereux's head. She batted it easily away with her own sword. The first swordsman used the distraction to lunge in, but by now the Hercules suite had recalibrated its targeting and a bullet practically took the man's unarmoured head off at point-blank range.

"Alek!" screamed the woman, raising her own sword ready to attack. Devereux levelled the gun at her, commanding the targeting laser to switch to a visible red spectrum for added effect.

"Stand down!" she shouted, as the red dot settled on the bridge of the woman's nose. "You can't win this. There's no need for anyone else to get hurt."

A scream from near the coach rather spoiled the effect of her statement. The archer glared at her defiantly, as the surviving swordsman started to try to circle around. "We still have you outnumbered, Orsinio bitch. We will take back what is ours!"

"Orsinio?" said Devereux, confused. "You've got the wrong people, and if you don't call yours off soon you won't 'outnumber' us for long. Del! Try not to kill any more of them!"

"Why shouldn't she?" growled Thalia. "Amanda, I'm doing all I can but Athas is slipping away from me!"

"Last chance," said Devereux. "Tell your side to drop their weapons right now, or we finish the rest of you off. I don't have any more time to waste on you."

The archer flicked her eyes quickly towards the coach. There was only one of the ambushers near it left standing, and the guard was methodically moving from one fallen figure to another and knocking any who moved back into the dirt with the butt of a stout spear. The driver, occupied as he was with preventing the team from bolting from the fire and sounds of battle, stayed in his seat.

"Very well," the young woman sighed, dropping her sword. "We surrender."

"Ilia?" said the swordsman in disbelief. "We-"

"Do they look like Orsinio nobles to you, Derik?" snapped the archer. "There's barely a mark on that blonde bitch and she's playing with Temis like a cat with a mouse. Give it up."

"Smart decision," said Devereux, as Derik's sword joined Ilia's in the dirt. Before anyone could tell Temis what was happening, Delys dodged a last lunge and swept the man's leg out from under him, sending him crashing to the ground.

"Now," said Devereux, once she was satisfied that the Swordmaster had the situation by the coach under control. "I'm betting you and your friends have Seals, yeah?"

"Of course." replied Ilia, looking confused.

"Well then get over there and let Thalia drain them," said the Operative "because if Athas dies you're going to wish you had too."

42

The Arch-Chancellor had finished his lunch and made a start on the afternoon reports by the time Anneke arrived. Her lateness was unusual, though not unprecedented, and Derelar wondered what had delayed her. It was also not unusual, at least in recent times, that he also wondered whether whatever explanation she gave him would be the truth. Well, let her keep her secrets for now- Magister Julius would be on his way to Freeport by tomorrow morning, and it was quite likely he would discover evidence that would blow the woman's schemes wide open.

What surprised Derelar, as the Vice-Chancellor poured herself a glass of wine, was how much that prospect concerned him. He certainly hoped Julius would be discreet enough that anything he did discover could be safely kept secret until the time was right. The last thing the College, or the Arch-Chancellor, needed right now was another urgent problem to deal with. There was still no word from Abelia on the success or otherwise of Magister- no, Ambassador- Thalia's mission and the College reinforcements were only now approaching the Eastern Vigil. If it turned out that Anneke's schemes required an urgent reaction, Derelar was going to be forced to employ.. distasteful measures.

"I apologise for my lateness today, Arch-Chancellor," said Anneke finally, sitting opposite him. "I was waiting in the hope that I might have some fresh news to give you."

"And do you?"

"Not really," replied Anneke with a sigh. "My people report that the Expelled haven't yet reached the Vigil, and Haran's Wardens are nearly there. Magister Kandira has also attached herself to the column, which is an unexpected bonus. She's sceptical about Jakob's plan to mount the Petard Engines at the fortress, but she seems to think that she can make it work."

"And the Abelian mission?"

"We know that Thalia should be almost at Abellan," said Anneke. "Though why the Abelians insist on conducting everything face-to-face in such a dire situation is beyond me."

"It is less dire for the Abelians," pointed out Derelar. "The Farspan is easier to secure than the passes through the Eastern Abelian Mountains- that, after all, is why the Vigil was rebuilt in the first place. When you also consider that the Abelians possess an army that is largely immune to the effects of the Shrive-Ticks..."

"..we need them far more than they need us," agreed Anneke with a sour expression. "Thelen's teeth, I'd like to go over there and give those preening idiots a lesson in basic arithmetic. If the Expelled are overrun, then the Empire is next, and after that the Abelians will have well over a thousand miles of border to secure against a threat the size of a small fly that numbers in the tens of millions. Those Golems of theirs might be impressive, but before long they'd be the only thing left."

Derelar nodded. "Indeed. In light of the danger, I have had Magister Stalis make initial enquiries with the new Daxalai Ambassador."

Anneke gave him a look of what seemed like genuine surprise, although the Arch-Chancellor couldn't believe she didn't know what the Chair of Mendarant had been doing. "Oh? Concerning what? You know the Symposium would never accept military assistance from the Daxalai, even if they somehow offered it."

"It was not military assistance that was discussed," said Derelar. "It was the possibility of establishing an Imperial colony in the Harmony. Should the Vigil fail and the Dendaril begin to spread across the Empire, I want us to have somewhere to fall back to."

Anneke had gone pale. "Flee to Daxalai? Derelar, you realise what that would mean- our entire way of life would be destroyed! The Daxalai permit no alien religion or power to operate within the Harmony outside of Gwai'Xi, the City of Foreigners- and for that matter, they consider the practice of Sealing to be comparable to mutilation."

"As was communicated to Stalis by their Ambassador, yes, though in more.. colourful terms," agreed the Arch-Chancellor. "I was informed that the only way in which we might be tolerated would be if we were to settle the uninhabited northern islands of the Harmony."

"The Realm of Yoshan'Ru?" breathed Anneke. "Arch-Chancellor, those islands are uninhabited for good reason! After the Yellow Curse War that took place when the Celestial Dragons founded the Harmony, every living thing there was killed and the land razed by dragon-fire. Nothing has lived or grown there since!"

"Quite so," agreed Derelar. "Nevertheless, settling there might be possible and the attempt is preferable to having one's mind erased by an invasive parasite."

"That's certainly true," agreed Anneke, grimly. "Better to freeze and starve to death than... that. But we have several million citizens, Arch-Chancellor- how would we get them there?"

"We would not," admitted Derelar. "Even using every available fishing and trading vessel and what Daxalai ships could make the trip at short notice, we would be fortunate to save more than ten thousand. We would start, of course, with Damisk, Lore, Phyre and Mernas, since those cities are on or close to the coast, and prioritise Faculty and other Magisters. After that... we would do all we could. But it would not be enough."

"Overall," said Anneke after a thoughtful pause, "I doubt the Symposium would like that any more than they'd like a Daxalai army."

"Then they could always choose to stay here," said Derelar. "I doubt many would exercise such an option."

"Hah! Probably not," agreed Anneke with a grim laugh. "It's just as well you never went through with that plan of yours, too."

"Indeed." said Derelar. "Your counsel on the matter was wise."

"Prepare both for the most advantageous and the most dire of circumstances, for to fail to exploit an opportunity is as fatal as to fail to anticipate a threat," quoted Anneke. "First book of Thelen. We need to handle this right, Arch-Chancellor. If we do, we secure the future of the Empire for generations."

"The threat is obvious," observed Derelar. "The opportunity less so. To what are you alluding?"

"Simply to the fact that if Thalia does her job right, the vast majority of the Abelian military will soon be in the Expelled Territories," said Anneke. "Meaning that they won't be in Abelia."

In spite of himself, Derelar was intrigued. "Go on, Vice-Chancellor," he said.

He really hoped Julius took his time.

43

he small quarters in the guard-house at the docks of Damisk would have seemed cramped to Captain Jerik Dale even if he had been the only one using them. If pressed, he would have admitted that recently his post as Captain of the Daran House Guard had led to him growing more than a little soft, but that, after all, had been the point. After his experiences at the Royal Keep of Equinox and at the Wake, the last thing he wanted was more danger and adventure. But somehow, he'd managed to inadvertently impress Magister Julius Thule, and the man had taken it upon himself to request that Magister Isadora lend him Jerik's services. Isadora had been badly distracted by the upcoming anniversary of the death of her husband, as well as worry about Thalia, and had agreed seemingly without really listening. Jerik was fiercely loyal to the family of Magister Thalia, who had saved his life on more occasions than he could easily count or cared to remember, but at that particular moment he'd have quit on the spot if he'd dared.

Instead, it had been 'yes Learned Magister' and 'right away, Learned Magister' and before he knew it he was sharing a sweaty room in Damisk with a man who seemed determined to get into trouble even if he had to go personally looking for it, an approach so fundamentally different to that which had got Jerik within touching distance of his fortieth birthday that he half-suspected that the Magister was insane. Then again, he had to admit that trying to stay out of trouble had spectacularly failed recently. The fact that he was still alive at all was nothing short of a miracle.

He gave the luggage a sour look. At least Julius travelled light, though that probably had more to do with the fact that he had tried sneaking into the Daran Manse to test one of his wilder theories than anything else. For Jerik's part, he had his sword, a couple of changes of clothes, and that was about it, other than the talking box. He didn't even know why he was carrying the thing, because according to Julius its power was almost completely exhausted, but it was a link to

Thalia, however tenuous, and he'd lost enough friends and comrades that he was loathe to leave the gadget behind.

"Ah, Captain, all packed? Capital!" said Julius, bustling into the room. "I apologise for the short notice, but this investigation is of the utmost importance and I was able to secure us a berth on a fishing vessel that leaves for Freeport within the hour. A most fortuitous development."

"Yes, Learned Magister," said Jerik, doing his best to keep his lack of enthusiasm out of his voice. "I'd be happier if I could have brought a shield or my armour with me, though."

"You'd stick out like a Daxalai at a Toskan fish-market," said Julius. "Only College infantry carry those large shields and no ship captain will let one on board for fear of angering the Whales. As it is we can only get away with the sword because we're staying so close to the shore. Anyway, we're not going to Freeport to fight anyone- after all, our quarry have already escaped from their captor and we're hardly going to try to imprison them again."

"They might not see it that way, Learned Magister," pointed out Jerik. "You escape from one Magister, you might well start seeing all of them as a threat."

"Which is much of the reason I asked Lady Isadora for your help, Captain," said Julius triumphantly. "You know the mind of the common man far better than I, and I fully intend to let you make the initial approach. Think of your role more as that of an interpreter and advisor, rather than a warrior."

"They're both women, though, Learned Magister," pointed out Jerik, as he picked up the bags and followed the Magister out of the door. "Any man thinks a woman is going to think the same way he does, he's in for nasty shock at best or a knee in the bollocks at worst- and that's assuming you don't *really* piss them off."

"Ah, about that," said Julius, quietly. "You might do well to consider that one of our would-be witnesses is a Daxalai Initiate. If such a worthy were to decide to introduce her patella to your testicular region in an aggressive manner, you would be fortunate to live long enough to see the remains of your scrotum disappear over the horizon. Or, to use a more succinct vernacular- I strongly suggest that you do not 'piss her off.'"

Jerik swallowed. "Er, yes, Learned Magister. Are Initiates really that powerful, then?"

"They vary, as do those who bear any Role," said Julius, as he led the way to the quayside. "Broadly though, it is enough to think of an Initiate as a Magister who uses their fists and feet to work their magic, rather than a staff. Anything one might expect a competent Magister to be able to destroy with a blast of flame or bolt of lightning, an Initiate could similarly annihilate with a blow, should he or she so wish."

They carried on through the busy docks, past net-menders, sail-wrights and itinerant sailors looking for a new ship. "Why bother hitting things, though?" asked Jerik. "I mean, if a Magister can do the same thing at a distance, why risk getting closer?"

"Efficiency and culture," said Julius. "The Daxalai consider the working of magic to be a very dangerous thing, that should only be attempted by the wisest of Sages- a not unreasonable position. Their warriors, however, are trained to manipulate their Aether, or as they call it, *ki,* into purely physical force rather than being subjected to Sealing- and when the range of an attack is reduced, the Aether required to perform it is correspondingly less."

"Wait.. so any Daxalai warrior could work magic if they were taught to?" said Jerik. They seemed to be heading to the shabbier end of the docks, he noticed.

"Indeed, just as you could speak Daxalai if correctly instructed," said Julius. "But to learn to do so fluently would take many years and the language has subtleties that might give grave offence if incorrectly observed, just as working magic inexpertly is fraught with danger. Thus, we teach the language only to those who truly need to learn it, just as only the truly talented are taught magic. In this, we and the Daxalai are not so different."

"You speak Daxalai, though, don't you Learned Magister?"

"*Nao*," admitted Julius. "But in my case I am self-taught due to a couple of months of boredom when I was twelve. I would certainly not dare to put my poor understanding of the tongue to the test in the Divine Pavilion. Ah, here we are."

They had stopped next to the most run-down, leaking mass of rotten wood Jerik had ever seen purporting to be a boat. It sat so low in the water that he half expected the next wave to wash straight over the deck and sink the thing.

"Er... Learned Magister, are you sure this is safe?" he asked nervously as they carefully negotiated the rickety gangplank.

"Fear not, Captain," said Julius. "I am reliably informed that the *Flotsam Queen* has been fishing the waters off Sigil for years without incident."

"Aye, that she has!" agreed a burly woman standing on the deck of the boat. "She may look like shit nailed together, but she's got it where it counts, you'll soon see."

"Ah, Captain Reka!" said Julius. "May I present Captain Jerik, of the Daran House Guard. Captain Jerik, Captain Reka."

Reka stood nearly six feet tall and wore her long, brown hair in dreadlocks that made her look halfway to being a Toskan pirate. The effect was not improved by a nose that looked to have been broken at least twice, a livid scar on her cheek, and a wide-brimmed Jandallan hat. Like most sailors in summertime, she wore only leather shorts and a brassiere of similar material to preserve her modesty. Her hands and bare feet were callused and battered, and the joints were wrapped in some sort of grubby tape for protection. For all this, though, she stood on the deck with an easy, relaxed confidence. "Stow yer gear in the cabin at the back, and we'll be off." she told Jerik, flashing a gap-toothed grin.

"How about the hold?" said Jerik, eyeing the small cabin doubtfully. "There's not much space in that cabin."

"Not much space in the fucking hold, less'n yer a fish," laughed Reka. "S'mostly flooded, I just pumps it out afore I sails."

Jerik put the bags in the cabin without further argument before he lost his nerve completely. There was little else in the small room except a single worn hammock.

"So.. where do we sleep?" he asked, as he emerged back into the sunlight.

"Y'don't," laughed Reka. "This here's a one-woman boat and I'll have you to Freeport well afore nightfall or my name ain't Captain Reka Mot. Now, y'might want to get on that there bilge and start putting them big Guard muscles to use, eh?"

"What?"

"Look, you land-grubbing numpty, this boat normally takes one person- me- and a bunch of fish. Right now it's got three people on it and it rides low when it's empty. So either you start pumping, or we all swim to Freeport, got it?"

"Got it," sighed Jerik, starting to work the bilge. Perhaps staying in the Eighth might have been a better idea after all.

44

The borrowed coach hurtled towards Abellan, going as fast as the driver dared. Within, Thalia fought with everything she had and had been able to borrow to save Athas' life. Had she been thinking about anything other than the grim task in front of her, she might have given thanks for the fact that the Abelian Roads were every bit as smooth and the suspension of their coaches every bit as effective as their Imperial counterparts, meaning that at least she was working on a stable platform. Such niceties, however, were the furthest thing from her mind. Her mission, the reason for the ambush- none of them mattered to her now. Only the guttering spark of life she was struggling to nurture held any importance.

Discussion of what to do with the surviving bandits had been necessarily brief. Most had lived- those Devereux had rendered *hors de combat* in the initial moments of the attack had massive bruises and some broken ribs and had then received further punishment at the hands of the coach guard, but would survive. Delys had killed the first two men to reach her before Devereux had shouted to her to spare the rest, and the man Athas had punched had suffocated on his own blood during the fight. Reluctant to simply let the survivors go, the coach guard had volunteered to take charge of them until reinforcements from Abellan could be summoned. They had left him methodically tying those not too injured to move to the fences.

Before leaving, Thalia had been forced to expend more Aether than she would have liked putting out the hay-fire. Already it had begun to spread to the dry fields behind the stacks, and left unattended could have inflicted untold damage. Ice magic was not the young Magister's forte, but she knew enough to chill the moisture out of the air above the fields and damp down the flames as those few bandits still able-bodied enough to do so helped to beat them out. This task done, Thalia had drained every mote of the remaining Aether from the lot of them, both replenishing her own reserves and also preventing them from summoning the strength to break their bonds before the Abelian authorities arrived.

The young woman, Ilia, who appeared to be the leader of the ambushers, rode with them in the coach, having volunteered herself as a hostage. That had several advantages, for as well as the fact that the rest of the group genuinely seemed to care about her, as an Archer she was less dangerous to have around without draining her personal Aether. Since the Seal of the Bow was a physical Seal, like the Seal of the Soldier, it was more efficient to tap her reserves to heal Athas directly. Meanwhile Devereux and Delys kept a close eye on the woman, and the Operative took charge of her interrogation, allowing Thalia to concentrate on her own work.

The wound to Athas' stomach was among the most serious the young Magister had ever dealt with, even including the near-mortal injury Amanda Devereux had dealt Delys at their first meeting. In that case, the Operative's stolen blade had penetrated the Swordmaster's chest and gone out the other side, but it had missed everything vital except her lungs. This injury, whilst smaller in overall size, was massively more complex. The silver-tipped military arrows fired by dedicated Archers in the armies of both Abelia and the Empire were made very differently to a simple hunting arrow, and had a far more deadly effect. Whereas a mundane arrow might have various different designs of tip such as broad-heads and barbs, military arrows featured nothing more physically complex than a simple cone of enchanted silver. Upon this cone were carefully-etched sigils that, when charged with the Aether of the firing Archer through a suitable bow, turned the mass of metal into a bolt of pure kinetic force.

It was a common misconception amongst civilians that such arrows were on fire, but the silver blaze that accompanied their flight was simply a visual side-effect of the magic. Instead, the attack the arrow delivered was a physical blow delivered at a point no larger than that of a very sharp pin. Once the arrow stopped moving, usually because the wooden shaft had also entered the unfortunate target, the remaining energy in the head was expelled outwards in an explosive, fiery blast. This detonation shattered the cone of silver into tiny shards of shrapnel, making such arrows strictly single-use in nature but exceptionally dangerous. Though the pieces of the head were not particularly large or sharp and were not greatly damaging if a missed shot should cause them to fly in the open, should an arrow manage to detonate within soft tissue the effects were dramatic. And, most usually, lethal.

This, then, was the task that faced Magister Thalia Daran as she worked on Athas' recumbent form in the suddenly-cramped confines of their borrowed coach. Whereas a blow from a blade might have cut and sliced the damaged tissue, leaving wounds that could be interpreted and effectively reversed, the arrow-blast had simply annihilated the flesh of Athas' gut. His armour, mercifully, had helped, reducing the power of the magic and causing the arrow to detonate well short of the big man's kidneys and spine, but there was still a sizeable volume of flesh, along with the attendant blood vessels, simply missing, not to mention the damage the shards of silver had caused to the surrounding tissue. In short, the damage was too severe for any but the most skilled and knowledgeable of Chirurgeon-Magisters to repair, and Thalia Daran was no such specialist. Instead, she retreated from the field of a battle she could not win, and made her stand on surer ground.

Plugging the gap in Athas' stomach with a globe of pure force that stemmed the worst of the bleeding, she turned her attention to the most vital strategic points in the big Guard's battle against the advancing armies of Death Herself. The most simple rule of Magister field medicine, as taught in the first Book of Sherenith, was simply to keep the heart of the patient beating at all costs, and their brain functioning. As with any simple solution to a complex problem, this was far more difficult on a living, or in most cases dying, subject than the pages of any textbook could ever truly explain, but it came down to using her magic to simply force Athas' organs to function. Though the art had never been seen in the Empire of the Thelenic Curriculum for Thalia to make the comparison, it was an endeavour with many similarities to spinning plates. As it was, though they were barely halfway from the site of the attack to the capital, Ilia's Seal was glowing so brightly that it must be nearly exhausted.

"How're we doing, Thalia?" asked Devereux, not taking her eyes off the Archer.

"Not well," admitted the Magister. "I'll need help from a proper Healer soon, or we're going to lose him."

"The best Surgeon-Wizards in the kingdom are in Abellan," said Ilia, quietly. "If we can get there in time..."

"You'd better hope we do," said Devereux, her own voice similarly quiet but carrying a deep undertone of menace. "Not that I'd expect the person who nearly killed him to care. Why did you attack us?"

"We.. we didn't really mean to," said the young woman nervously. Her long, black hair was tied back in an elaborate braided horsetail which had started to loosen in the fight, and she fussed at it distractedly. "We thought you were Orsinios, on the way to Court."

"And why would you attack *them?*" pressed the Operative. "Does it have something to do with your accent?"

"With my.. accent?"

"You talk like an Abelian noble," pointed out Devereux. "The rest of your unit had pretty thick provincial accents, but you and the man you were with speak much more like the Great Families."

Ilia sighed. "That's true. How much do you know about the Great Families?"

"Not much," admitted Devereux with a shrug. "Rich, powerful, what we used to call one-percenters back.. home. They train up as Royal Knights and lead the Abelian armies. What am I missing?"

"You've got it about right," said Ilia. "But you might not really understand what it means. Even before the Winnowing Ague, the Great Families controlled everything in Abelia. If you were a merchant, you worked for a Great Family and they took the dragon's share of the profits. If you were a farmer, you farmed for the Great Families and they took the dragon's share of the food. The Kingdom is carved up between them and then each Family owes allegiance ultimately to the throne."

"So it's basically a feudal system," said Devereux. "The Queen gives lands to the Families, the Families give lands to the Royal Knights, and the Knights give lands to the peasants. So what are you, republican revolutionaries?"

Ilia snorted, then caught herself, remembering her precarious position. "Hardly. Even before the Ague hit people put up with the injustices out of fear. For one thing, the Decree of Fire Thelen signed with the Dragons so long ago was tied to the blood of the ruling classes that became the Magister Houses and the Great Families. As far as anyone knows, if that system was overthrown by the people the

Decree would become void, and the Dragons would be free to prey on humans again."

"And you'd need the Magisters, Wizards and Royal Knights to have any chance of defeating them," mused Devereux. "All right, so that wasn't an option and then the Ague came along and killed most of the peasantry anyway. That doesn't even begin to explain why you'd be attacking an Orsinio coach."

"My name," said Ilia with a hint of self-importance, "is Lady Ilia Satisse Savalan."

This revelation did not have the impact that Lady Ilia was clearly expecting it to. In Thalia's case, this was due in part to the fact that having seen the Abelian's Pattern, she already knew her name. The title was new, but neither name nor rank caused any great reaction amongst the other passengers in the coach.

"That's great for you, your ladyship," said Devereux, "but it still doesn't answer the question."

"Of course it fuc- it does!" snapped the Abelian. "The lands west of the Orsinio Vineyards, from the River Bylan to the eastern bank of the River Distal, are the ancestral lands of the Savalan family, or at least they were."

"So that would make you a Royal Knight?" said Devereux.

"Do I look like a Knight to you?" said Ilia, pointing at her Seal. As she spoke, Thalia finally drained the last of the young Archer's Aether and the sigil winked out and began to turn black. The Abelian gave a gasp of pain.

"Thalia, stop! You're going to kill her!" cried Devereux.

"So?" said Thalia, hotly. "If I don't keep this up, Athas is going to die. That's not a hard choice to make."

Before Devereux could argue, Delys scooted across her lap to land on the seat opposite Thalia, pulling down the shoulder of her blouse to expose her Seal.

My turn.

Thalia opened her mouth to reply, but thought better of it. Much as she wanted Ilia to suffer, there was no time to discuss the matter and Delys would be a far better source of Aether. Without a word, she released the Abelian and returned to her work, drawing power from the little Swordmaster's faintly-glowing Seal.

"So, you're a member of a Great Family, but you're Sealed," said Devereux, after watching to make sure Thalia's treatment was still working. "I'm guessing the Orsinios are in some way responsible for that?"

"Them, the D'Honeurs, most of the other Great Families," said Ilia, bitterly. "You see, when the Ague struck, our Family did something no other dared to- we gave a damn about our people. That's how things are supposed to work!" Her voice was getting louder and faster, a demagogue's passion inflaming her words. "The peasants work for the Families, and in return we protect them. If raiders or invaders come, we offer the walls of our castle and the protection of our armies."

"And the other Families didn't?"

"Oh, they did *that*," said Ilia. "But when the Ague came, they did nothing. The Healers did what they could, of course, and every now and then a Wizard would think that they'd come up with a cure and go to some 'lucky' village to try it, but pretty soon they started to get the Ague themselves and retreated. Baron Rondal Savalan, my great-grandfather, refused to abandon his duty to the people. At the time, most of the peasants who worked our lands lived in scattered towns, farms and hamlets, with the town of Whist on the shores of Lake Distal as the largest single settlement. Lord Rondal chose to treat the Ague as he would any other attack on his people, and ordered them to evacuate to Castle Savalan."

"That's a terrible idea, surely," pointed out Devereux. "If you've got a contagious disease, the last thing you want to do is clump everyone together. All you're doing is helping it to spread."

"Several of Baron Rondal's advisors made the same case." said Ilia. "But the Ague was not a contagious disease- it seemed to strike at random and didn't spread from one person to another. The only treatment that was ever effective was to keep the victim alive with a constant flow of Spirit until the Ague passed, and by concentrating his people Baron Rondal allowed his family and their attendant Wizards quick access to the sick. Acting in concert, they were able to save almost every one of their people from the Ague and to this day more living humans survive in the former lands of the Savalan than anywhere else in the Kingdom outside of the major cities."

"This Ague is one strange disease," said Devereux. "So, I'm guessing that for some reason the other Families didn't like what Baron Rondal had done?"

"At first they didn't care," said Ilia. "But after about thirty years, when the Ague had largely blown over, almost every other Family was using Stickmen to till their fields and serve in their armies. The Savalans were still doing things the old way. Even with the sizeable tithe that the other Families had to pay to the High Wizards for their Golems, they had so few mouths to feed that they rapidly became far wealthier than us. Eventually the poorest Family in the Kingdom was that which controlled some of the most lucrative and fertile land in it. Many of our best and brightest sons and daughters chose to marry into other Families, particularly the Orsinios, who had been hit particularly hard by the Ague. Then the High Wizards, citing increasing costs, started to dramatically increase the tithe that they demanded for the Stickmen. Several Families found themselves staring at destitution unless they could find a new source of income- one that did not require more of the Golems to generate it."

"Wait.. so you're saying that the High Wizards make people.. rent the Stickmen out? Surely that makes them very powerful?" said Devereux.

"It did and it does," said Ilia. "In any case, the Orsinios finally claimed to have uncovered evidence that the Savalan were conspiring against the throne, and managed to have them blamed for the failure of a key campaign in the Fifth Thelenic War."

"The what?"

"The Thelenics call them the Abelian Wars," explained Ilia. "In the Fifth War, the new Siege Golems broke through the Pentus Line and the Royal Army got as far as Sommerlan. No-one is quite sure why, but suddenly some of the Golems went mad and attacked their own side. Maybe the Lily Magisters managed to cause it, maybe it was something else, but as the only Family still providing a traditional human army the Savalans got the blame. Less than a month later, the Orsinios led an attack on Castle Savalan. By that time the town of New Whist had grown up around the bailey of the castle and the money had never been available to redesign the defences, so there was no hope of holding off the attack."

"What happened to your family?"

"Most of the Savalans were killed, including Baron Rondal, who was well into his eighties at that point but insisted on taking the field. Several of the younger

Knights, including my own grandfather, escaped into hiding in the Wild Bocage. The armour of a Royal Knight is designed only for them, and when they die it discorporates, so within a generation there were no more Savalan Knights left."

"So the Orsinios control your family lands now? That's why you attack them?"

"No-one controls our lands now," said Ilia, bitterly. "Not long after the attack, the High Wizards reduced the tithe again. With the Ague having largely ended, they didn't need to make as many Golems any more and by then Wizards were beginning to marry into the Great Families anyway. Once that happened, the Savalan lands became less desirable, so the other Families declared 'justice' done, reduced Castle Savalan, and left. We've been picking up the pieces ever since. The plan today was to take a few Orsinios hostage as leverage towards the restoration of the Family."

"So is this the first time you've tried it?" asked Devereux. "We certainly hadn't heard anything about this road not being safe."

"It was the first time a coach had come past unescorted," said Ilia. "We aren't stupid enough to try to ambush a Royal Knight, and there's usually one riding behind the coach. We were expecting a couple of Wizards, maybe one of the younger nobles who haven't earned their armour yet."

"So you wanted to pick on an easy target?" growled Thalia. Athas was stable for now, but even with access to Delys' power she was worried that they wouldn't make it to Abellan in time. "Thelen curse this thing, can't it go any faster?"

"To be fair, Learned Magister, only picking a target you can handle is basic strategy," pointed out Devereux. "People who call their enemies' tactics 'cowardly' are usually just trying to cover up the fact that they can't figure out how to deal with them."

"Not that it did us much good in this case," said Ilia with some heat, glaring back at the Magister. "Your.. friend might be badly injured, but several of mine are lying dead in the dirt back there."

"Well whose fault is that?" snapped Thalia. "We didn't ask you to attack us, and you hardly gave us much chance to explain who we were!"

"I think we can agree that no-one has come out of this whole thing particularly well and leave it at that," said Devereux, gently. Her tone hardened. "Of course, a lot of that depends on whether Athas survives, because if he doesn't I'm going to be every bit as pissed off as Thalia is and professional detachment can go fuck itself."

Ilia blanched, seeming to remember the jeopardy of her situation. Even though Delys' Seal was starting to glow brightly with exertion and Thalia had clearly also taxed her own reserves, in her own weakened and unarmed state the Abelian had to realise that she was at the mercy of the Magister and her companions.

Devereux leaned out of the window. "We're approaching the main gate, Thalia. We need to decide what to do with Ilia here."

"What?" gasped the Archer. "I surrendered!"

"Yes, you did," said Thalia. "Which is why you're not dead, and may even be why Athas isn't.. at least not yet. Can you give me a good reason not to just hand you over to the Royal Army?"

"And remember," pointed out Devereux even as Ilia drew breath to answer, "the coach crew saw everything that happened, so pretending it was all some harmless misunderstanding isn't going to fly."

"Fly?" said Ilia, gaping in confusion. "Ah.. well.. you must realise that if Queen Tondarin learns a scion of the Savalan family attacked her guests I'll be lucky if all she does is kill me. More likely, I'll be tortured until they find the rest of my people, and I doubt they'll care how many innocents get caught up in the slaughter that follows."

"In your case, I don't care," said Thalia, coldly. "But I will not have the lives of innocent peasants on my conscience- assuming you're telling the truth."

"She is as far as I can tell, Learned Magister," said Devereux. "Unless she's been trained to be a damn good liar, that is. All the physiological and voice-stress data suggests she's been mostly straight with us."

Thalia took a quick glance out of the window. "Fair enough. Lady Ilia, you are sure you're of the bloodline of a Great Family?"

"My life upon it, Wizard," said Ilia, her jaw set defiantly.

"Good," said Thalia, her hand thrusting out to seize Ilia by the throat. "Then you will hopefully survive this."

"What-?" began Devereux, but before she could finish the question Thalia had kicked the door of the speeding coach open and flung the Abelian out into the hedgerow that was flashing past them.

"Shit," said the Operative after a pause. "I hope you didn't just do what I think you just did."

"I gave Ilia a fraction of her Aether back," said Thalia quietly, returning her full attention to keeping Athas alive. "With luck, her Seal will protect her and she can make her escape."

"But as far as the Abelians are concerned?" prompted Devereux.

"We took one of the ambushers prisoner so I could drain her Aether dry to save Athas," said Thalia. "She refused to talk, and once she was dead I disposed of her remains with no more care than the murderous bitch deserved."

"What if someone realises that she survived?" said the Operative. "Assuming she does, of course. This thing's slowing down, but we're still doing over forty miles an hour."

"If she dies, I'll not be that sorry," said Thalia, coldly. "I meant the 'murderous bitch' part. But should she survive and someone realise who she was, I will simply claim that I underestimated the resilience of those of noble blood."

The carriage rattled to a halt, and from outside came the sound of a hurried challenge and breathless explanations from the coach driver in response. A moment later, accompanied by several liveried guards, the man tore open the door of the carriage.

"We've arrived, Your Excellency," said the man, quickly. "A runner has already been sent to the Surgeon-Wizards of the Royal Hospital. In the meantime, these men stand ready to give their Spirit to aid you in keeping your man alive."

"Then step forwards, quickly!" snapped Thalia. Even as the first man did so, the coachman, gazing in awe at the bloodstained interior of the vehicle, seemed to remember something important.

"Ah.. Your Excellency, I apologise for the distraction, but did you... hurl the prisoner from the coach a little way back?"

"Yes," said Thalia shortly. "Her usefulness to me was at an end."

The man swallowed, hard. "Was she... is she dead?"

"She was completely drained and tossed out of a speeding coach," said

Devereux, fixing the coachman with a level stare. "What the fuck do you think happened to her?"

Before the visibly terrified man could fully process the answers he had received, a small group of Healers arrived at a dead run, bringing a floating litter with them. "Your Excellency Ambassador Thalia! I am Healer Alana Matisse, of the Royal Guard. The Surgeon-Wizards are preparing to treat Sergeant Athas, and my Healers and I have been tasked with conveying him to them... Queen's Grace, what a mess!"

"Tell me.. about it.." grunted Thalia through gritted teeth. Though Athas was still alive, she was having trouble maintaining the makeshift seal on his wound.

"I will take over from here, Your Excellency," said Alana, and Thalia could already see delicate tendrils of the Healer's Aether moving into the injury. With a sob of relief, she finally stopped pouring her power into the big Guard. The abrupt sensation of detachment was followed almost immediately by a crushing wave of fatigue, and she sagged against her staff before Devereux and Delys leapt to steady her.

"Easy, Thalia, you did it," said the Operative, gently. "He's going to make it."

Watching as the Healers prepared to move Athas, Thalia could only hope she was right.

"I'm going to go with Athas," announced Devereux, suddenly. "He should have someone he knows with him if.. when he wakes up." Delys moved to follow her, but the Operative waved her back. "No, Del, not this time. Someone needs to stay with Thalia until she's had a chance to recover, and anyway you need to rest yourself."

I'm fine! The little Swordmaster signed the words with almost savage speed.

"I know you are, but Thalia's going to need you. She still needs a bodyguard, and right now Athas needs someone too." *I don't trust them.* Her fingers flicked the message so subtly that Thalia barely caught it, but Delys clearly did. Her eyes narrowed, but when Devereux hurried away she made no move to follow.

"Your Excellency!" boomed a large, armoured man, striding forward before dropping to one knee. "I am Sir Terence Egret of Abellan, Custodian of the West Gate. On behalf of Her Exceptional Majesty, Queen Tondarin II, I welcome you to the great city of Abellan, and extend my own personal condolences and apologies for the attack on your person. Can you tell me exactly what happened?"

"I-" began Thalia, but the world had started to spin and for a moment neither thoughts, nor words, would form. With a startled oath, Sir Terence stepped forwards, producing a silver hip-flask.

"Queen's Grace! Where are my damn manners! You have come through a trying ordeal with the fortitude of the mightiest of Knights- I saw that stopper you had maintained in your man and I cannot begin to imagine how long you kept it in place! Please, drink this- slowly now, it has some kick."

Thalia took the proffered flask, which smelled strongly of khile-fruit, and took an experimental sip. The liquor burned her mouth and was so strong she dared not take a second draught, but it carried with it a potent jolt of Aether. Even as she tried to process what she was tasting, she was hit by a bout of coughing. Delys, taking her bodyguard duties seriously, patted her gently on the back until she recovered.

"Thelen's breath! What is that stuff?"

"Good, eh?" beamed Sir Terence, his forked brown beard bristling. "Aged khile brandy from my personal reserves. A potent restorative which would present a pretty major advantage if it didn't take almost a century to mature a barrel."

"Well," gasped Thalia, finding that although the world still seemed to be squirming about a little she at least now felt like she had strength to stand. "It certainly seems to have done the- Delys! Give that back to Sir Terence at once!"

With a grin, the little Swordmaster returned the flask to Sir Terence. The Royal Knight took it, and gave it an experimental shake. "By my father's sword, how much of this did you drink? That much would put my horse under the table!"

Yellow bucket, signed Delys, carefully, before sitting down in the middle of the road and immediately falling asleep.

45

*B*y late afternoon, the column of infantry was finally winding its way up the narrow approach to the Eastern Vigil. Pulling her horse up alongside Haran's, Kandira eyed the path and gave a low whistle.

"Hmph," she finally commented after a long pause. "It's just as well you brought me along, Haran. Just getting the Engines up that is going to be tricky enough without trying to mount the damnable things. The wagons are out of the question, for one thing. I'm beginning to wish we'd dragged Jarton out here as well."

"Is it really that much of a problem?" said Haran, looking at the path with renewed interest.

"The thing you have to remember is that the Vigil, or at least whatever pre-Imperial bastion it's built out of, was probably made to defend the old Eastern Empire from the West." pointed out Kandira. "I think I remember that insufferable bore Stalis telling me that one of the Warlocks threw it up during the Foundation Wars, though I wasn't paying much attention."

"Did someone mention an insufferable bore?" boomed Magister Ollan, cheerily, as he rode to join them from the rear of the column.

"Yes, and for once I didn't mean you, Learned Magister," said Kandira, sweetly. "It's a shame you missed such a rare event, really. As I was saying, the defences of the Vigil were designed to face in the opposite direction to the way they're now being used, so this approach is considerably more treacherous than that from the Territories. I think the whole damn path is a dead loss, Haran. If you'll give your permission, I'll get the Weavers to work on rigging a temporary bridge so we can wheel the Engines right up to the gates."

Haran blinked. "My permission?"

Ollan chuckled. "Aye, Haran. Whatever the Leaves may say, the Symposium put you in charge of this expedition and that means we are at your disposal."

Kandira nodded. "The old man is quite right, which makes two things I never thought I'd live to see in one day, much less say. You could even tell him to bugger off back to Lore and leave us in peace, if you'd like."

Ollan gave a solemn nod. "True, that he could. Of course, once I left the Dispensation I would cease to be under his command and could, therefore, turn around and come straight back again."

Kandira snorted in disgust. "They do say there's no fool like an old fool, but in your case, Ollan, they truly broke the mould. Haran?"

Haran, who had been watching the two bickering Magisters with a certain level of awe, remembered what he was supposed to be doing and nodded, quickly. "Of course, Magister Kandira, you have my full permission. I'll have Captain Render see to it that you have all the manpower you need and Magritte will liaise with the Weavers."

Kandira smiled. "Cheer up Haran, it could be worse. At least they have a lifting disc in there that can take the Engines up from the gatehouse- I'd hate to try and winch them up a four-hundred foot wall."

Ollan watched Kandira ride off towards the Petard Engine wagons, which had almost reached the foot of the slope and were starting to mill around in some confusion. "She's worried, Haran," he said, quietly. "Kandira always gets abrasive when she's concerned."

"She has good reason to be," pointed out Haran.

"Which?" said Ollan with a mirthless chuckle. "Abrasive, or concerned?"

"Both."

Ollan smiled. "Ah, Haran, you wound me. As did Kandira on one occasion, though that, I think, is a story for another, happier time. Ah, but the pride of Abelia approaches!"

Haran looked up the slope. Picking its way carefully down the path was a massive, silver-armoured figure riding an equally enormous armoured horse. Ollan gave a theatrical shudder.

"I know we're not presently at war with them, but the sight of a Royal Knight arrayed in his full panoply still brings a certain chill to the heart, eh? Still, I'd have preferred to have him around when the silver starts flying rather than packed off back to Lore. Best you be.. diplomatic in your dealings with him, Haran."

Haran swallowed, feeling the weight of the message cylinder in the pocket of his robes as if it were made of solid lead. He really hoped his gambit was going to work.

The Abelian made his way around the final bend of the path, and dismounted, slipping easily to the ground with a smoothness that belied the colossal weight of his armour. He strode over to the two Magisters, and when he had almost reached comfortable speaking distance, stepped straight out of the armour without breaking stride. The suit, somewhat disconcertingly, followed along behind him after taking a moment to reassemble itself.

"Ambassador Sir Matthew, I presume?" said Haran, formally. "I am Magister Haran Dar of the Lily College, and I relieve you, Sir."

"I stand relieved, Sir," replied the Abelian, with a similarly formal tone. "How-ever, with the permission of the new Gifted in Residence, I should like to remain present at the Vigil as an observer for the duration of the present crisis."

"Ah," said Ollan, quietly. "That may be.."

"A moment, please, Your Excellency." put in Haran, swiftly. "I also have a message cylinder for you from the Symposium which I was asked to convey." He reached into his robe, and handed the offending article over. With a grunt of annoyance, the Abelian took it, and swiftly ripped the lid off. There was a small flash of silver fire, and he dropped it with an oath.

"Queen's Grace! What foolishness is this?"

Haran gave an apologetic bow. "My apologies, your Excellency. The cylinder was warded so that only the intended recipient could open it without destroying the message within, but it appears an error was made in the calibration. I will, of course, request that the Symposium sends a replacement with all due haste."

The Abelian glanced from one Magister to the other. Haran kept his expression carefully neutral, though he sensed Ollan was trying very hard not to laugh. Finally Sir Matthew shrugged.

"Bah. Wizard politics, no doubt. If there is nothing further, Magister Haran, I will return to the rampart. The Dendaril are abroad, and they drive the hide-wearers before them."

"Of course, your Excellency. Please do not allow me to delay you," replied Haran. With a curt nod, the Ambassador turned on his heel and strode back to his horse, his armour once again enveloping him as he went. One the Royal Knight was safely on his way, Ollan bent down to pick up the discarded cylinder.

"Hmm. Most curious."

"What is?" asked Haran, innocently.

"This cylinder is certainly correctly calibrated. The ward was set so that only the Gifted in Residence of the Eastern Vigil could... oh. Oh, Haran. There may be hope for you yet, my friend!"

"I'm afraid I really don't know what you mean, Learned Magister," said Haran, blandly. "I simply carried out my orders to the letter, which as you well know were to relieve Sir Matthew and convey that Message Cylinder to him. Now, I believe you and I have more important things to attend to than such trivialities, do we not?"

"Oh, of course, Magister Haran," replied Ollan, as seriously as he could manage. "There is just one small detail I'd like to ask you about, though."

"Which is?"

"What would you have done if that had been a Perdition-level ward?"

Haran blinked at him. The idea had come to him so late that he hadn't had an opportunity to check.

46

In the end, Sir Terence ended up carrying Delys to the Ambassadorial quarters. The weight of her sword elected another surprised oath from the Abelian, and after a moment's consideration he stepped out of his armour, allowing the empty suit to bear the punishing burden of the blade whilst he carried its owner.

"Queen's Grace!" the Knight muttered, as the ambulatory suit hefted the weapon onto its shoulder with some difficulty. "How does so dainty a thing wield so dolorous a sword?"

"It's an instinctive reaction, I'm afraid," said Thalia. "A Swordmaster can vary the weight of their blade to suit the circumstances, and often if they lose consciousness the last thing they do is make it as hard to move as possible. Since Delys is a Swordmaster of rare ability... well, the effect is particularly dramatic."

"Were the words to be etched in the slabs of the King's Font, they could be no more true," agreed Sir Terence. "I for one am grateful that the Queen saw fit to move the Ambassadorial Residence into the Green Palace, for it lies a mere stone's throw from the West Gate."

Given that they had been walking for some ten minutes and had negotiated several flights of steps, Thalia considered that the stone in question was probably hurled by a Siege Golem. Finally, they came to a stop in front of an imposing silver-bound wooden door, which was set in a wall made entirely of green marble. There certainly wasn't any need to ask how the building had got its name.

"This is the Green Palace, your Excellency." said Sir Terence, somewhat redundantly. "Construction began in 1597, a year after General Sebastian Vox of the College was slain here in the Second Battle of Abellan. The fine marble was quarried in Abelian Jandalla, and the wood is from Takalla trees of the same clime."

"So this palace is built on the site of the most infamous defeat in the College's military history?" asked Thalia, slightly sharply. At the time, the College military had been considerably more independent of the Magisters, and General Vox's failure to anticipate an Abelian ambush had been part of the reason why the system had changed. Indeed, the rank of General had been completely abolished as a direct result. Most Magisters considered the fact that no subsequent campaign against the Abelians had achieved even the same level of success to be an irrelevant detail.

Sir Terence gave a slightly embarrassed laugh. "Aye, Your Excellency. In fact, in the Great East Hall you will find a plaque that marks the exact spot where General Vox.. but I am being impolitic again. If I might be so bold as to make the observation, whatever the... historical resonance of Her Most Exceptional Majesty's choice, the accommodations are of vastly superior quality to those the previous Embassy occupied. Now, if you will please follow me.. ah."

The great door swung open, to reveal a scene of some disarray. The interior of the Palace had clearly been decorated by the previous Ambassador to reflect its status as an outpost of the Lily College, but the premises had obviously been recently subjected to a rather enthusiastic search. Or, thought Thalia, looking around at the shattered furniture, slashed paintings and rumpled carpets, a particularly malevolent hurricane. She turned to glare at Sir Terence, who had the good grace to look somewhat embarrassed.

"What is the meaning of this?" she snapped.

"Ah, you must understand, Your Excellency, that your.. predecessor was implicated in a plot to murder the Queen. The Royal Guard were most determined to discover evidence that might uncover any co-conspirators."

"This Embassy is sovereign territory of the Lily College!" said Thalia, feeling annoyed that the office of the Ambassador had been slighted despite having never really wanted the job in the first place.

"Indeed it is," agreed Sir Terence. "But when the College learned of the assault on the Queen and saw the evidence against the.. previous incumbent, your Magister Stalis gave the Royal Guard *carte blanche* to investigate the Embassy, that they might satisfy themselves that the plot was not officially sanctioned. I regret, however, that the housekeeping spells are only capable of dealing with simple dusting and cleaning, rather than reconstructing smashed side-boards. Your own staff will need to attend to such work, and given that the Palace contains several hundred rooms they might be forgiven for being... overstretched."

As if on cue, a head poked out of a doorway that opened onto the upper balcony, only to be immediately retracted with a startled gasp. A moment later, a prim, thin man in a green silk liveried uniform came bustling out of the door and down the stairs.

"Learned Magister! I am Herenford While, adjutant to the Ambassador- that is to say, your adjutant. I apologise for the, er, condition in which you find us, but as I am sure Sir Terence has explained, we find ourselves faced by something of a crisis *vis-a-vis* the availability of furniture that is... well, that is even capable of remaining upright by its own virtues, if I might be frank. I have begun making arrangements to purchase replacements, but finding fittings of appropriate quality is challenging and the Abel- our generous hosts have impounded the contents of the Treasury as.. evidence."

Thalia swivelled her gaze back to Sir Terence, who was by now blushing bright red. "An.. oversight, I am sure, Your Excellency. The funds should have been released when the investigation was concluded. I will see to the matter personally."

"Very well," said Thalia, coldly. "Herenford, is there at least a functional bedroom we can use and somewhere I can wash and change?" She gestured at her robes, which still had a fair portion of Athas' blood on them. The man had been studiously avoiding staring at her, and his eyes widened when he saw the gory evidence of her recent travails.

"Of.. of course, Learn- Your Excellency. The staff have been engaged in searching the Palace top-to-bottom for what can be salvaged since the... incident. You will find the Master Bedroom fully-furnished, if regrettably uncoordinated." He looked at the recumbent form of Delys in Sir Terence's arms. "Your Excellency, if I might inquire- where is the rest of your party? Are they...?"

Thalia sighed, feeling another wave of weariness wash over her. "There are two more, Herenford, and despite.. this.. both of them are still alive. Thelen willing, Sergeant Athas will stay that way. For now, I require simply a wash and a change of clothes, and somewhere for Delys to recover from her.. recent exertions."

Herenford led the way into the Master Bedroom, which proved to be spacious and almost embarrassingly opulent, even though one of the windows was boarded up and the wallpaper had been ripped loose in several places. As in most of the other parts of the palace Thalia had seen, the remaining décor was almost over-whelmingly green.

"I will see to the rest of your luggage, Your Excellency," announced Sir Terence, once Delys had been safely settled in a comfortable-looking, if battered, armchair inevitably trimmed in crushed green velvet. "The Wood Golems should be arriving with it directly. Under the circumstances, I am instructed to tell you that the Queen will grant an audience tomorrow morning, once you have had a chance to recover from your ordeal." He bowed, and hurried out, his armour following after carefully propping Delys' sword up against the wall.

Herenford fussed about, directing a small gaggle of maids and footmen as they scampered around putting the guest rooms into some sort of order. All of them, Thalia noticed, bore the Seal of the Operator. The observation brought a question to mind.

"Herenford," she asked, as the adjutant passed the Master Bedroom carrying a chair which clearly had at least one leg cannibalised from an entirely different piece of furniture. "Do we have a Messaging Crystal in the Embassy?"

"Ah, yes and no, your Excellency," said the adjutant, carefully. Thalia simply arched an eyebrow at him until he volunteered the rest. "We have a Messaging Chamber, but the Crystal was... erm.."

"..confiscated as 'evidence'?" suggested Thalia.

"Just so, your Excellency," replied Herenford. "I, of course, protested, but the Royal Guard were in no mood to negotiate. The spares, similarly, were either removed for investigation or succumbed to rough handling. Needless to say I have registered an official complaint, but..." he spread his hands in exasperation. "I do apologise, your Excellency."

"There's a lot of that going around, Herenford," said Thalia. "Ever since I crossed that ludicrously overblown excuse for a bridge the Abelians have been throwing obstacles at me with one hand and apologies with the other. We can ill-afford this delay." She gave a mirthless snort of laughter. "Do you know the one reason I'm looking forward to meeting with the Queen tomorrow?"

"The, er, privilege of making Her Exceptional Acquaintance?" suggested

Herenford, hopefully. Thalia gave him the sort of smile Delys usually reserved for an interesting opponent.

"Hardly. She's the one person in this twisted carnival mirror reflection of a country who's probably going to be honest about hating me. I think I'm going to find it.. damned refreshing, as Sir Jeremiah might say."

"As, er, you say, Your Excellency," said Herenford. "If I might request, though- could you possibly attempt to refrain from provoking the Queen into, well, killing you? Two such dramatic changes of Ambassador in less than a month might be more than we can take."

Thalia gave him a level stare. "With the mood I'm in, Herenford? I'm almost hoping she tries it."

"If I might be permitted to move the conversation to less terrifying matters," said the adjutant, clearly deciding not to push the topic further, "the cook is preparing a meal for you which will be served at your convenience. Will any other members of your, er, party be joining us?"

"I.. doubt that very much, Herenford," said Thalia, slowly.

She could only hope that Athas would pull through, and that Devereux could keep him safe. There was too much between them that was still unsaid.

*a*manda Devereux, as an Operative of the Office of Special Operations, was trained to function primarily as a lone infiltrator. Such 'Desdemona-class' Operatives were rarely used in hot-combat situations where they might be expected to witness the horrors of war first-hand. Nevertheless, she had been through enough contested extractions or blown operations that the experience of accompanying a seriously injured comrade into the care of a team of medics was nothing new to her. In fact, possibly the strangest thing about it was how familiar the whole thing felt.

The jargon was different, of course- the white-robed Healers and the Surgeon-Wizards who met them at the gates of the Royal Hospital talking about 'disruptions in the thaumic layer of the morphic field' rather than more familiar phrases-but much else was very similar. There was the air of unhurried urgency, the cool confidence in the face of a crisis, and the hollow feeling of helplessness that came with being a relatively unskilled bystander when a friend or colleague was in mortal danger. And so Amanda Devereux had stood, and paced, and sat, outside of the room in which some of the most skilled medical practitioners in the Kingdom of Abelia fought to save Athas' life, just as countless friends, relatives and lovers had done since the very invention of medicine.

It didn't help that she also felt dangerously lightly-equipped. Though the coach crew had had some opportunity to see her in action during Ilia's abortive ambush, they had returned with their vehicle to the Orsinio estates almost immediately, and so the Operative had left her guns concealed in the luggage and reverted to the cover of being simply a College Swordmaster. Perhaps, if the Surgeon-Wizards had subjected her to close scrutiny, Anneke's false Seal might not have gone unnoticed, but seeing as she was uninjured and Athas' own wounds were both extensive and potentially fatal, she had been largely ignored.

She stood, with her back to the huge, silver-bound doors that led into the operating theatre. They had been at it in there for over an hour now, and she resisted the temptation to use her enhanced senses to try to find out what was going on. It wasn't as if the knowledge would do her much good- for one thing, one of the few sounds that she had heard coming from the room with her own natural hearing had sounded, incongruously, like the bleating of a sheep. Instead, she stared out of the lead-lined window into the heart of Abellan.

The Abelian capital was as different to Lore as it was possible to be- where the capital of the Empire was laid out according to a strict plan, Abellan seemed to have grown up almost entirely organically. It reminded her of one of her missions in London, with some buildings that had clearly been built many centuries ago nestling up against others of more modern construction. Like the English capital, Abellan showed signs that at some point in its history entire neighbourhoods had been completely levelled by war or some other disaster before being rebuilt with varying levels of respect for their surroundings. Over to the north-west, towards the gate through which they had entered the city, the Green Palace in which she had been told Thalia would be staying rose up from the urban sprawl. It was a sizeable building, at least as large as most in Lore, but it was utterly dwarfed by the Alabaster Durance, the enormous white castle that dominated the centre of the city. Devereux had picked up the name from listening to Thalia's conversations with the Orsinios, but had learned precious little else about it other than that it was the residence of the Queen. For one thing, she had no idea why it had a name that implied that it was more prison than palace. Notably, and in common with the Green Palace, the building lacked the high bridges that connected most of the other large structures to each other.

Those bridges, along with the many multi-coloured domes and tower roofs, were one of the most distinctive and interesting features of the city. They varied immensely in size and shape, some so slender that two people could scarcely walk abreast across them, others so large that small villages existed entirely within their span. Between the seemingly random arrangements of the bridges and the equally esoteric layout of the streets far below them, it was clear that Abellan would be an utter nightmare of a city to attempt to storm by force. For that matter, conversely, it would be extremely difficult to defend. Securing all but the very smallest area without there being some way an enemy could slip past would be all but impossible, and the Hercules suite had already noted several thousand excellent positions for snipers.

And yet, for all the city's size and magnificence, for all its bustling, chaotic vitality, there was something clearly wrong with the city of Abellan. Yes, everywhere she had gone so far in the city there had been people, but from the vantage point of the Royal Hospital, which stood on a small hill in the south of the city, she could see that a distinct stillness lay over it. Entire neighbourhoods seemed to be entirely deserted or populated only by the stiff-limbed Stickmen, and Devereux would be willing to bet that when the day drew to a close, few of the windows she could see would have lights burning in them.

She was prevented from any further study of the view by the sound of the door opening behind her. The figure of the Healer, Alana Matisse, emerged a moment later.

"Ah, Master Devereux. The Surgeon-Wizards are finished with their ministrations to your friend- would you care to see him before we take him to the recovery ward?"

"Yes!" said Devereux, a little too quickly. "I mean, yes, please. Is he awake?"

"Not yet, I'm afraid," said Alana, leading the way into the operating theatre. She was a slight woman, the hood of her white robe now down to reveal that her platinum-blonde hair was pulled back into a tight bob. As they entered the room, two more Healers were wheeling a trolley out through another door. The sight of what was on it stopped Devereux dead.

"Healer Alana," she asked, quietly. "Why is there a... dead sheep on that thing?"

The Healer gave her the sort of look doctors across all of time and space reserved for the truly, tragically ignorant. "That was the donor beast, of course. It's a little inefficient to use a whole one for only one case, but the porters shall dine on mutton this evening if I'm any judge."

Though concerned that she might be revealing too much of her feelings, Devereux couldn't stop herself blinking in surprise. "Donor... donor beast?"

Alana laughed, softly. "I forget sometimes that you Thelenics can be a little behind the times. Look, here." She walked over to Athas' sleeping form, and Devereux was relieved to see that he seemed to be sleeping peacefully and some colour had returned to his cheeks. Without any particular ceremony, Alana moved the bedclothes aside to reveal the flesh where he had been wounded. Incredibly, it was completely whole, without even so much as a scar to show where the injury had been.

"That's... impressive work," admitted Devereux. She knew she shouldn't be that surprised- Thalia had practically brought Delys back from the dead and even a Sealed Healer could apparently cure cancer- but given the amount of trauma Athas had suffered she was still somewhat amazed.

"As you can see, we had to replace a sizeable amount of Sergeant Athas' flesh," said Alana. "With so severe an injury, simply stemming the bleeding and allowing the natural healing process to take its course was obviously not an option, so stronger measures were required."

"I get that," said Devereux, somewhat stubbornly. "But a sheep?"

Alana sighed. "The principle is simple enough that I'd have thought even a Thelenic sword-polisher could-" she snapped, but brought herself up short. "My apologies, Master Devereux, this has been a long day. Simply put, then, the easiest way to replace living flesh is with more living flesh. It is reduced to Spirit, or Aether as the College prefers to call it, and then reconstituted at the site of the injury. This, of course, is the simple part, for then the Surgeon-Wizards must adapt and meld the new material to exactly match that which was there before. If this process is not performed to the very highest standard, rejection can occur and the consequences can be.. most unpleasant."

Once again, Devereux was struck by how things could be so different in this world, and yet so similar. What Alana was describing sounded very similar to some of the work that had been done in transplanting animal organs into humans, before the advent of bio-printing and nano-cultured cells- and even those procedures often used raw molecules sourced from animals. Outwardly, though, she stuck to the character of the 'Thelenic sword-polisher' that the Healer was expecting.

"Fair enough, I don't understand it but it looks like it worked, and that's enough for me," she said. "When's he going to wake up?"

"He will sleep at least until tomorrow morning," said the Healer, a little stiffly.

"With such extensive surgery, it is best to allow the subject's morphic field time to adapt before the conscious mind has to come to terms with what's happened."

Devereux, still staying in character, gave her a blank look. "Eh?"

"I mean we don't want him realising too early that we had to stuff sheep bits into his guts!" said Alana in an exasperated tone.

"Oh, right. Yeah, that'd probably mess me up a bit, too."

"That would certainly be a terrible shame," said the Healer with mock sincerity. "Now, I assume you will be travelling to the Green Palace to rejoin the Ambassador. Would you like an escort to show you the way?"

"Tha- the Ambassador told me to stay with Sergeant Athas until he was fully recovered," said Devereux, embellishing the truth more than a little. "Until he's ready to travel, I'm not going anywhere."

Alana threw up her hands in annoyance. "Fine, fine. It's not like we have all that many patients at the moment anyway, what with- ah, I mean, you can have a bed next to his so you can wait in comfort, if you'd like? And I'm, er, sure we can arrange for some simple food."

Careful not to show that she'd noticed Alana's slight slip, Devereux made a point of brightening at the mention of a meal. "That'd be great, thank you!"

"Very well," said Alana. "I'll see to it once the porters have taken Sergeant Athas to recovery." She suddenly gave a crooked smile. "I should warn you, though- you'll probably just get some of the mutton."

48

*S*taff jangling softly in his hand, Smiling Snake walked carefully among the corpse-piles that the slave labourers were slowly building. Around him lay the mortal shells of some hundred thousand warriors, all that remained of the White Turban rebels. Any observer might have expected the sight to bring him if not joy, then at least satisfaction, for it was at the hands of the army of the Hono clan that the traitors had at last been brought to battle and destroyed. The victory had greatly restored the standing of the Clan in the Divine Pavilion, going a long way to mitigate, if not erase, their failure to successfully conquer the Chaotic East. And yet, whilst some quiet appreciation of the success of his plans found a home in his heart, it was tempered by both a deep sadness and a feeling of utter waste. The White Turbans, after all, had been one of his most useful creations.

It was in hope of salvaging part of that creation that he had come to this place, which already was starting to stink in the heat of the afternoon sun. Few of those mighty warriors who wrote epic poetry about the glory of battle had to deal with its aftermath- the rot, the excreta, the pooling blood and buzzing flies. The last of these in particular, given his recent experience with the Tapestry, came perilously close to disturbing the Sage's veneer of calm on several occasions. No, there were no Generals to be found here, no valiant heroes, and it was rare for a Sage to be seen in such a charnel pit. Indeed, if anyone did see him there it would almost certainly elect some uncomfortable questions, but the task of heaping up the dishonoured dead for disposal fell entirely to the slaves, each of them a convicted criminal, branded with the fox-tail mark and with their tongues cut out. Only such creatures, considered barely human, might be expected to handle the flesh of corpses in so doleful a place. Those few who passed him, naked but for a rough linen loincloth, kept their eyes carefully averted and would not have been able to answer questions even if anyone had thought to ask them.

Along with the lacerated remains of the slain, the slaves also bore their equipment. Metals, in particular the iron that was so irritatingly common in the Chaotic

East, were comparatively rare in the lands of the Harmony and so the weapons and armour of the fallen foe were carefully gathered to be broken down into their component parts and forged anew. Military arrows, by their nature therefore unfired and not marred by dishonour, were similarly recovered and tithed to the Imperial Arsenal. Though those used by the armed forces of the Harmony were typically tipped with jade or onyx, which were mined in plentiful quantity from the mountainous Imperial heartlands, many of those recovered from the rebels were instead made from silver. These had most certainly been smuggled over from the East- Rya-Ki even knew which ships had been involved. For that matter, he had indirectly arranged some of the shipments. If *gwai-sen* were willing to risk the wrath of the Blue Council for mere money, he was more than willing to take advantage of their greed.

Hearing a sound from behind the nearest pile of corpses, he raised his staff and blocked the blow of a *baoha* that flashed out from around it. The wooden fighting staff proved to be held by a slender, bald young man wearing a simple green robe that was heavily bloodstained. On seeing who he had attempted to strike, the man fell to his knees, dropping the weapon to the muddy ground.

"Sage Rya-Ki! A thousand apologies!"

"For your attack, or for the ineptness with with it was delivered?" said Smiling Snake, stilling the staff's chimes with a thought.

"My poor skills have proved sufficient to deal with those few witnesses I have had to... remove," said the young man, still staring down at the ground. "I would never presume to match them against those of a Great Sage."

"Stand up, before I strain my neck from craning it at the top of your head," said Rya-Ki. "Have you had to.. remove many?"

"A few wretched battlefield looters, nothing more," replied the other, standing and retrieving the *baoha*. The simple wooden staff, some five feet in length, was often carried by apprentice Sages as well as being the first weapon studied by all Generals. "Their bodies now lie with the other scum of this place."

"Have a care, White Crocus," admonished Smiling Snake. "The extinguishing of a life, even such as these, should never be a thing lightly undertaken."

White Crocus swept out an arm to encompass their surroundings. "In that case, O Great Sage, your burden must be heavy indeed."

Some Sages might have considered the comment disrespectful, but Rya-Ki merely nodded. "In this you speak truly, Bai Faoha. I must balance these lives against those I preserve, but when the weight is so great, the arms of the scales must be mighty. Some day, it is a load you yourself might also bear." He passed the bundle he had been carrying to the other man. "Here, clothe yourself in fresh robes that we might be away from this place."

Bai Faoha bowed, and took the offered clothing. Swiftly he stripped, burning away the worst of the blood and dirt on his naked body with a surge of *ki*, and dressed in the pale golden robe of a Sage of the Hono clan. Soon, there was little sign that he had spent the last few hours apparently lying dead on the field of battle.

"Your strategy on the final day is to be commended," said Smiling Snake as White Crocus put the finishing touches to his appearance. "Brother Tekkan-Cho and General Pao-Sho of the Doha were confounded by the sudden appearance of the Threefold Loom in so unexpected a location."

Bai Faoha bowed again. "I took inspiration from the fourth campaign of the Chrysanthemum War. For a moment, I feared it might have been too effective."

Rya-Ki nodded. "It might have been, had I not caused the deployment orders of the Third Army to be inexplicably mislaid. As it was, the reserves of the Hono clan arrived too late to be caught in the trap and unravelled the Loom from behind."

"And thus was my strategy countered without the honourable Generals being aware of your hand in it," mused White Crocus. "Truly is this the pinnacle of the Sage's art, to employ wisdom in a guise so invisible that it appears to be another's foolishness. Still, it is regrettable that the White Turbans are no more- I had assumed that your plans for them ran to a longer term."

"And they did," admitted Rya-Ki, as they began to walk back to the Hono war-camp. "But in His Immortal Wisdom, the Son of Heaven stripped the wings from my Dragon when he granted Brother Tekkan-Cho the fatal honour of his title. Despite all my efforts, the Chaotic East still stands almost untouched by Harmony, and had I not been able to provide this victory, the long tale of the Hono might have come to a most abrupt end."

"And yet, now?" asked White Crocus. "The Empire of the Devil Thelen still stands and there is no time to manufacture another convenient insurgency for General Tekkan-Cho to crush. What, then, is to be our course? Perhaps the worm-riders of Jandalla or the Har'ii coral-singers might provide a more easily-gained toe-hold on the treacherous slopes of this mountain?"

Smiling Snake nodded. "These things and more have I considered. However, you need not concern yourself with them. Instead, I have another, more pressing task for you."

"More pressing than keeping the heads on the shoulders of the Hono brothers?" said Bai Faoha. "What great cause might be of more import than that to our clan?"

"Its future," replied Smiling Snake, quietly. "Should I fail- should Brother Tekkan-Cho and I find ourselves gazing upon the Imperial Gardens from the vantage of a spike- the Hono clan must continue."

"It is well known that Swan-neck Tsue is the successor in waiting to Tekkan-Cho," pointed out Bai Faoha. "Hers are hands both assured and skilled, and as General Who Pacifies the North her honour is untouched. What fear, then, can there be for the clan's future?"

Rya-Ki looked the young man up and down. In terms of his skill and knowledge, Bai Faoha was a Sage of at least four Rings, though only two of them had been formally ratified before the strategist had taken on the guise of Green Dragon Tsaoh, the mysterious demagogue of the White Turbans. The carefully-crafted prosthetics that had facilitated that persona now lay buried deep within the funeral pyres of the fools who had flocked to the banner of his fraudulent rebellion. He had performed the task, distasteful as it was, flawlessly, even to the extent of trying with all his strategic might to defeat the combined armies of the Doha and Hono clans in battle despite being outnumbered more than six to one. He had come closer to achieving this goal than even Smiling Snake would care to admit, but there had been no other way to make the fall of the White Turbans convincing. He had simply had to trust that his own experience and brilliance would be superior to those of his protégé. That this had only just proved true was simultaneously reassuring, and deeply troubling. Nonetheless, he was fast running out of options.

"Sage Bai Faoha," he said, slowly. "You are correct that the heart and soul of the Hono clan will be in the finest of hands should Brother Tekkan-Cho be taken from us. But it is the mind that is the concern of the Sage, and amongst my present apprentices and attendants, there is... no truly suitable candidate to replace me."

White Crocus gasped, and fell a full pace back in shock. "But.. how can this be? The Hono clan is well known for the wisdom and knowledge of its Sages! Is there truly none among us with the qualities to succeed you?"

"The role of Great Sage requires more than mere knowledge and wisdom," said Smiling Snake. "Wise, educated, honourable- A Sage may be only these and be content. A Great Sage, though, must know the darkness, must understand that shadow is the inevitable consequence of light. He must understand, he must truly *believe*, that sometimes dishonourable acts and evil deeds are needed to serve the causes of honour and justice. He must walk the shores of the island of Paradise with his bare feet lapped by the tide of Damnation, and yet never allow himself to wade in the shallows or to flee inland. He must know balance- he must *be* balance, for it is that most elusive of qualities that lies at the heart of true Harmony. The Sages of Hono, wise though they may be, have been too long shielded from the shadows and no longer realise that they dwell in the light."

"And yet I have dwelt in shadow," said White Crocus. "I have seen the light from within the darkness, this is true. But *Shansenshao*, I am not yet prepared for such a task. I am a blade that has been tempered, but not yet sharpened nor supplied with a hilt."

"And I am not yet dead," pointed out Smiling Snake. "Nor do I intend to become so for many years, but intention and result are rarely the same, no matter how peerless the strategist. There are secrets and mysteries you must learn, even as we see to it that your skills as a Sage are formally recognised."

"Truly is it said that a mirror is no more wise than he which it reflects," said White Crocus. "But any mirror with the good fortune to stand in the presence of the Smiling Snake of Hono is wise indeed."

Rya-Ki grimaced. "Do not speak to me of mirrors-" The rest of his reply was cut off as he saw Tekkan-Cho approaching, still in his full armour though with his helmet under his arm.

"Brother!" boomed the General, paying absolutely no attention to the minor underling attending the Great Sage, as was proper. "The victory is ours! You were missed at the ceremony giving thanks to the Son of Heaven."

"I gave my thanks on my own, Brother Tekkan-Cho," said Smiling Snake. "I felt the need to survey the field of battle one final time as I did so. We must never forget the terrible cost of war and rebellion, even as we glory in our triumphs."

Together the brothers looked out across the battle-ravaged plains. By now, the slaves had finished assembling the pyres and digging the ditches that would first serve as fire-breaks, and then as the last resting place of the ashen remains.

"You speak words of wisdom as always, Brother," said Tekkan-Cho after a moment. "And this was but an insignificant band of rebels, fierce though they were and tactically astute as they proved. What great piles of the dead might we have to raise should we succeed in bringing Harmony to the Chaotic East?"

191

Smiling Snake looked at him with some surprise. "Are you concerned at the cost of doing your duty to the Son of Heaven?"

"Never!" said Tekkan-Cho, stoutly. "And yet I find myself thinking, in quiet moments, of your words at our prior meeting. That perhaps there might be some way to bring Harmony to the Eastern Devils without such... wholesale slaughter."

"And what conclusions have you drawn?" said his brother, softly. Standing a respectful distance behind them, White Crocus was nonetheless listening carefully. Good.

"None!" laughed Frowning Iron, breaking the tension. "In war, quiet moments are few and far between, like diamonds in the coal mines of Tianloan. And yet, we must devise our new strategy soon. I am summoned to the presence of the Son of Heaven tomorrow to report on this campaign, and from then it is only a question of time before results in the Chaotic East are once again expected."

"The matter occupies my every waking thought, and stalks me in my dreams," said Smiling Snake. "We will prevail yet, Brother. We must."

"And necessity is the father of victory!" said Tekkan-Cho, firmly. "Now, General Pao-Sho invites us to take tea, and it will not do to keep him waiting. Come!"

Tekkan-Cho turned on his heel, and led the way back to the command pavilion. Smiling Snake didn't need to turn around to know that White Crocus had gone. Enough had been said for the young man to understand what he must do. As the brothers began to walk, a massive, sinuous shape flew overhead, followed by another and yet another. The Celestial Dragons had come, roused from their nests in the Divine Pavilion to cleanse the field in fire and sate their hunger on the flesh of traitors.

Of course, with their might the Dragons could have ended the battle in moments. But the ways of Heaven were not for men to question.

49

"*Watch* that bloody hawser!"

Magister Kandira Dar had the sort of voice that Chania Steine rather guessed would even make a Dragon sit up and take notice. As she watched the sweating teams of Guardsmen heaving on ropes so thick that they looked almost like bundles of tree branches she marvelled at the old woman's energy. She seemed to be everywhere at once, checking a shackle here, moving a pulling team there and storming up and down the twisting, treacherous path that led from the temporary camp the Wardens of Phyre had thrown up to the western gate of the Vigil. Trailing along behind her came another Magister, this one an even older man who at this distance seemed to be composed almost entirely of a long white beard. Since Magister Haran Dar, the new Gifted in Residence, was already in closed session with High Vigilant Wilhelmina and Sir Matthew, the other one must be the infamous Magister Ollan Dane.

The difference in styles between the two Magisters was almost amusing, despite the dire situation. Where Kandira bustled about, seeming to get things done by nothing more than sheer determination, Ollan would sidle up to an unsuspecting work-gang, seemingly just take a few puffs of his pipe and amble away again- which was usually followed by a sudden frenzy of activity as soon as the Guards thought he wasn't looking. With the western wall of the Vigil commanding a height of almost four hundred feet before it met the twisting path, which was itself narrow and bordered by a sheer drop, it had taken a fair amount of engineering to find a way to get the Petard Engines even as far as the gatehouse. Between them the two Magisters, along with the Weavers who were responsible for overseeing the Petard Engines, had swiftly arranged the construction of a sturdy wooden bridge, built from felled trees and- much to the apparent aggravation of some of their crews- the remains of two of the three wagons the siege engines had been transported on. This structure was supported by the existing path and lay flat upon it, spreading the load as evenly as possible.

The bridge was a little wider than the wagons, and once it was completed the third wagon was driven up to the bottom of it. The slope was steep enough to give horses pause even when they were being ridden up the winding path with no burden other than their master, and with the straight bridge taking the most direct route it was steeper still. So the horses were unhitched, and thick ropes were attached in their place. These had been requisitioned from barges docked at the town of Tearlight almost a hundred miles down the River Travail, which had been used as part of some sort of herb-gathering operation. In her younger days, Magister Kandira had saved the town from certain destruction at the hands of the Expelled, and her name still carried enough weight that the barge captains had been happy to help out when Outriders had arrived with her plea for assistance.

From her vantage point on top of the battlements, Chania watched the whole process play out. With the grudging agreement of the High Vigilant, the Magisters had disconnected the great chains that lifted the drawbridge that protected the first of the three gates and wound the long ropes around the winch instead, allowing the mighty windlass to do the job of hauling the wagon up the slope. Once the wagon reached the foot of the drawbridge, it would finally be on level ground and could be manually pushed the rest of the way comparatively easily. Of course, the Patrons were not so kind as for the process to be that simple, and it soon became clear that whilst the windlass was strong enough for the task, a drum designed to bear some twenty feet of chain was hopelessly small to accommodate roughly ten times that length of thick rope. So the ropes were wound around the mechanism and then back out, to be hauled down the bridge by more groaning Guardsmen even as the wagon inched its way up it. Magister Ollan had suggested simply attaching heavy weights to the ropes and kicking them off the edge, but Kandira's vehement reply had practically taken his eyebrows off.

For now, Wilhelmina had explained to Chania as she was getting ready to meet with Magister Haran, the gatehouse was as far as the Engine would go. Though the Vigil had been equipped with a system of internal Lifting Discs that could take heavy loads up as far as the battlements, there were serious concerns about the safety of mounting something so massive so high on the walls. Instead, Magister Kandira had proposed building something she called a 'casemate', a fortified opening in the eastern wall in which the Petard Engine could be both protected, and more sturdily supported. It would apparently involve partially dismantling a large section of a rampart that had stood largely inviolate for centuries, and Wilhelmina, among others, was less than enthusiastic about the idea, especially with a large force of Expelled apparently bearing down on them from the forest. The foul-smelling but undeniably skilled Scout, Alben Koont, had arrived that very morning warning that the 'Skinnies' were less than a day's march away and moving quickly.

Chania was too young to have ever witnessed an Incursion, but all the stories she had heard and songs she hard learned about them suggested that weakening their defences would be an extremely foolish thing to do. The High Vigilant had been of similar mind, and flat-out refused to allow any work to begin on the walls, but Sir Matthew and the Magisters seemed convinced that something far more dangerous was following on the heels of the Expelled warriors. Since the role of Gifted in Residence was technically only an advisory position and the authority of the High Vigilant was absolute when it came to the physical defence of the Vigil, it fell to the Magister and Ambassador to convince the sceptical Wilhelmina of the merits of their plan. It didn't seem to have helped that the Abelian had only learned of it at the same time she had.

A shout from the watchmen distracted everyone's gaze to the skies. Not for the first time in recent days, the great Dragon, Antorathes, had taken wing, and now she was returning from the Territories to her lair somewhere in the mountains north of the Vigil, flying so low that it almost seemed Chania could have reached out and touched her. People often forgot that the fortress did not guard the only route through the mountains, merely what would otherwise be the easiest and safest one. The presence of the Dragon, though, was one of the reasons why the Expelled rarely tried to take any of the narrow northern passes- although the creature herself rarely attacked humans unless they violated the Decree of Fire by straying into her domain, her passage near an unstable rock-face or loose snow could have fatal consequences for anyone caught in the wrong place. And she was not the only Dragon to make her home in the Abelian Mountains, merely the one who was currently most obviously awake and active.

Several of the Wardens, who despite their reputation as stoic killers had mostly not seen such a creature so close before, stood in slack-jawed awe as Antorathes swept low over the Vigil, whilst others ran for cover or reached for their bows, before roaring Sergeants put paid to any thoughts of shooting. Chania had seen the effect before, and more than one freshly-recruited Vigilant had had to be plucked to safety after overbalancing on the battlements whilst trying to follow the beast's flight. In this case, though, the effect was if anything more dramatic. Ten of the burliest Wardens were heaving on the rope, their strength and the assistance of the windlass only just sufficient to counteract the massive weight of the Petard Engine. As the Dragon passed overhead, they were no less affected than their fellows, and those few members of the team who managed to maintain their concentration were unable to also maintain their grip on the hawser. Startled oaths rose up from the gatehouse as the Vigilant manning the windlass abruptly found the handle torn from his grasp by the suddenly-unopposed weight of its load, and before anyone could do more than shout the wagon was rolling back down the steeply-sloping bridge, picking up speed as it went.

Everything seemed to snap into slow motion. Where most of the Wardens and Vigilants could do little more than hurl themselves out of the way or make desperate grabs for the rope that was blurring past them, the Magisters reacted with the speed of veteran magical duellists. Magister Ollan was closest, and flung his hand out towards the speeding wagon, chanting loudly. Even as Magister Kandira hurried over to assist, the air around the wagon froze solid, attaching the whole mass solidly to the bridge and stopping the careening vehicle dead in its tracks. The same could not be said for the loose end of the rope. Speeding towards the gatehouse of the Vigil, the massive hawser reacted to the sudden removal of the source of its acceleration in the only way it could- too thick to simply bend in on itself, it instead flew into the air. And it was heading straight for the section of the battlements on which Chania Steine was standing.

Though she had seen her share of action in the desperate last days in Phyre, Chania was no warrior, and lacked the instinctive reflexes that might have saved her from the oncoming danger. Fortunately for her, she was not the only person to have been watching the Wardens work from the battlements.

"Chani!"

Even as she heard a familiar voice shout her name and tried to think where she knew it from, the Bard was knocked sprawling by a tall, dark-haired woman wearing the leather armour of a Swordmaster of the Second Volume. The two of them rolled clear in a tangle of limbs as the thick rope slammed into the stonework where Chania had been standing with enough force to crack it slightly.

For a moment, everything was terribly still. Then pandemonium broke loose. Guardsmen ran in all directions, some rushing to get the hawser under control as its weight began to drag it back off the wall, others going to the aid of comrades who had flung themselves over the edge of the bridge to avoid the wagon and were now clinging to the sides. From far below, Chania could already hear Magister Kandira shouting curses at the men and women who had lost control of the wagon. On balance, her own near-death experience notwithstanding, she decided she wouldn't want to be in their boots. Next to her, the Swordmaster sprang lightly to her feet, and the Bard noticed that she had rank insignia on the breast of her armour. The tall woman offered a hand to help her rise.

"Th.. thank you.. Captain..?" said Chania as she was hauled to her feet. Feeling a warm wetness at her brow, she carefully probed her hairline and was relieved to find only a shallow cut.

"Chania, it's.. ah, Captain Damia Render, Second Volume," said the woman, her tone suddenly becoming more formal as if she had changed her mind about something. Chania didn't mind. Still, she would have been a poor Bard if she hadn't realised by now.

"Thank you, Captain Render," she said, with a smile, not mentioning that she hadn't introduced herself. "It was certainly lucky for me that you were here. Amaran must have been watching over me."

"I.. was keeping an eye on what my troops were doing," said Captain Render, slowly. "Turns out I was in the wrong place to help them, but..."

"Well, they certainly need your help now," replied Chania quietly. "The way they're running around down there, they look like they'd struggle to put out a fire in a boat, as my old friend Jonas would say."

Captain Render shot her a confused look. "They aren't that... ah.." A moment later, she carried on, more quietly. "We.. shouldn't be seen together.."

Without saying another word, the Swordmaster turned on her heel and strode off, already shouting orders. Chania smiled to herself. Even if neither of them could publicly acknowledge the other, it was good to know her sister was still alive. The Boss had done an excellent job disguising her, but no Bard ever forgot so familiar a voice.

50

*M*agister Haran looked up as the High Vigilant came back into the room. "Is everything all right out there?"

The armoured woman gave an exasperated snort. "Mostly, Learned Magister. Your two Learned Friends just came perilously close to knocking down my western gatehouse and killing a friend of mine, but it seems they have the situation under control now."

Haran's eyebrows shot up. "I apologise, High Vigilant. I would not have expected so veteran a pair as Magisters Kandira and Ollan to make such a dangerous mistake."

Wilhelmina sat down, her armour creaking with the movement. "To be honest, Learned Magister, it was that mischievous overgrown bat Antorathes' fault, mostly. She seems to take delight in flying as low over the Vigil as she can get away with, and she distracted the work-crews at what appears to have been an inopportune moment."

Sir Matthew leaned forwards in concern. "High Vigilant, though the question might seem insensitive I must ask it- was any of the.. equipment damaged?"

Wilhelmina shook her head. "No, Your Excellency. The Petard Engine was unscathed though I understand the wagon it was being transported on buckled under the strain of being halted so... abruptly."

"Don't tell me," groaned Haran. "Magister Ollan froze it solid, didn't he?"

Sir Matthew gave a short bark of laughter as the woman nodded. "Hah! You know your friend well, Magister Haran!"

"Thelen help me, but I do, Your Excellency. Now, we must return to the matter at hand whilst there is yet time." He turned to Magritte, who was in charge of a thick dossier of papers, accepting the sheet she handed him. "These are the preliminary plans for Magister Kandira's casemate."

Wilhelmina took the blueprint, and peered at it. "This is... a fairly major piece of construction, Learned Magister. The Vigil has stood for centuries without needing any such thing, and with an army of Expelled a day away-"

"'Bout half a day now, beggin' yer pardon," put in Alben Koont. The foul-smelling man was lurking in a corner, but Haran had still found it necessary to suppress his senses to put up with him. "Buggers'll be on us by nightfall, if they're minded t'be."

"Why would they not be, Scout Koont?" asked Sir Matthew, who was using an enchanted pomander to mask the man's stench.

"Don't y'get me wrong, y'worship- I hates the Skinnies much's the next man and prob'ly more," said Koont, with a look of some venom. "But this'n ain't no raid an' it sure's shit ain't yer bog-standard Incursion. There's Blackbloods with 'em, f'starters."

"And why would the presence of these.. Blackbloods.. make an attack less likely?" said Haran, shooting a glance at Magritte, who leafed quickly through her papers and shook her head.

"The Blackbloods are the tribe who control the far eastern part of the Expelled Territories, Learned Magister," supplied Wilhelmina, earning a nod from Koont. "They rarely mix with the other clans of the Expelled and they've never before been known to take part in an Incursion. If they're going west...."

"Then this is a migration, not an invasion," said Haran.

"Aye, but then no," objected the Scout. "See, there's no kids, and not all've the Skinny tribes're there. No Hearth-Tenders, no Stonesingers, no Shorewalkers. Plenty 'o fuckin' Heart-Eaters though, and those shit-fingered murderers'll kill yer soon as see yer."

"How many are there?" asked Haran, quietly.

"More'n I can count, even if'n I takes me boots off," laughed the Scout. "I'd reckon it's getting on f'r half of all o' the Skinnies in that stinkin' forest."

"And do you think the Vigil could hold against that many?" said Haran, turning his gaze back to Wilhelmina.

"If they were all warriors, no," said the High Vigilant. "But from what Scout Koont tells me, most of them aren't. They've got elderly with them, hunters, smiths, craftsmen. The problem's never been them storming the place, though- what usually happens is one force attacks, and another uses the distraction to work its way around through the mountains. That's another thing that's unusual about this, if it's an Incursion- they rarely try it whilst any of the local Dragons are awake. Makes the mountain passes way too dangerous."

Haran considered. Like most border fortresses, the Eastern Vigil didn't exist so much to completely stop invaders as to slow them down and give warning of their approach, as well as making it hard for them to get any loot back to their own territory. From what he had learned about the Dendaril, it wasn't going to be enough.

"Your Excellency," he said, deciding to change tack. "Perhaps you could tell us why you responded to the man in the forest in the way that you did?"

Sir Matthew blinked. "Magister Haran, did you not begin this meeting by explaining the threat of the Dendaril to the High Vigilant?"

Haran nodded. "I did. But I would like to hear the Abelian perspective."

The Ambassador sighed. "Very well. Knowledge of the Dendaril has been passed down through the Great Families for centuries, much as it has in your

College. Most of the more... complicated details have long since been forgotten, but it is believed that the original source of the lore is the Har'ii."

"The Har'ii?" snorted Wilhelmina. "What do those shell-polishers know about anything?"

Sir Matthew gave her a strange look. "It must be liberating, High Vigilant, to know so little of the world beyond your walls. Magister Haran, does your most capable adjutant there possibly have an atlas amongst her papers?"

Magritte did, and the Abelian swiftly unrolled the map on the conference table. "So, see here. The Hegemony occupies a vast tract of land- not the size of Jandalla and certainly not the equal of Daxalai, but massive, nonetheless. And it extends south to within a few hundred miles of the island of Har'ii. The waters between are not as shallow as those of the Warrior's Sea, but they are shallow nonetheless, and dotted with many small islands. On several occasions in the past, the Pilgrims of the Dendaril have attempted to cross to the Coral Kingdom, using small boats or even swimming and wading."

"I had wondered, when we were briefed on the Dendaril threat, why they did not simply come to us in ships," mused Haran.

"A fair question." said Sir Matthew. "In the Warrior's Sea, the Royal Abelian Navy sink any ship the Dendaril send our way with their ballistae. Fortunately, though they are far from stupid the Hegemony seems to have little interest in developing military technology and no such vessel has been sighted in several decades."

"Then in the northern sea- the Whales....?" said Haran.

Sir Matthew shook his head. "The Blue Council do not concern themselves with the Dendaril, for reasons only they know. But the Toskan pirates certainly know of them, having suffered losses to them in the past at the dawn of their kind."

"I do not like the idea of owing those villains anything," grumbled Haran.

"Nor would I," agreed Sir Matthew. "But even if the Dendaril could avoid them or the Toskans chose to let them pass, the northern coast of your Empire is treacherous, with many a submerged rock and sheer cliff. They would have to land at one of your ports, and they tend to avoid large settlements until they have grown strong."

"This still isn't telling me why I should let you knock holes in my walls, Learned Magister," pointed out Wilhelmina.

"Then think on this," said the Abelian. "It was the Har'ii that taught us to fear the Dendaril, and how to repel them. Ever since the first attempt to infiltrate their island was repelled, the Har'ii have maintained a network of lenses and mirrors in the lighthouses that surround the Coral Kingdom. At a moment's notice, the light of those innocent guides for travellers can be focussed into a beam of pure incandescence that can burn a ship to ash in seconds. They demonstrated it on the second attempt to attack them. There was never a third."

"High Vigilant," said Haran as the woman sat with her chin resting on her gauntleted hands. "This is not a question of trying to stop a single ship. If the Dendaril are allowed to infest the Expelled, within the course of a few years we could be looking at untold millions of them. I do not know if the Har'ii learned of their fear of destructive magic and exploited it, or if their defence was simply a logical tactic, but regardless, without that Petard Engine in position and charged, when they arrive the Dendaril will sweep over us like a tidal wave hitting a sand-castle. Now, do we have your permission?"

The High Vigilant slammed her hands down on the table. "Damn it all! Very well, Learned Magister, assuming you can even get those things into position, Magister Kandira may build her 'casemates'. But I still want to know what you plan to do about the Expelled in the meantime. They're hardly going to just stand there and let us work, especially with these Dendaril breathing down their necks."

"Let me worry about that, High Vigilant," replied Haran. He meant every word, because worrying about it was exactly what he was going to do.

51

*D*usk was beginning to fall by the time the combined forces of the Free Tribes came to the edge of the forest. Before them stood the Doors of Patros, an obstacle that had frustrated the Free since the Great Exodus.

"A sad irony, is it not, First?" said Mighty Dokan, as the vanguard of the Tree-Searchers halted. "Patros the Defender, most mighty and wise of the Ancestors, built this place to protect the Free from the Deluded, and yet through the failings of lesser men and the pride of fools it was lost to us." He threw back his head and sang.

> *"No more need we walls of stone when the trees are our home*
> *And no more need we war and fight when peace has come*
> *Let mantle crumble, stone decay*
> *Knife and spear in slumber lay*
> *Our chains lie sundered and never again shall we*
> *Stand guard on the Doors, for we are Free"*

"It does not sound like foolishness to me, Mighty One," said Second, sadly. "It sounds like the words of one who was tired of war."

"Perhaps," said Dokan. "But the fact remains that the Free left this place in ruins, thinking themselves safe in the Forest Home, and then the Deluded turned it to their own purposes. Had we remained..."

"Had we remained, things would have been very different, aye," said Mighty Xaraya, stalking out of the trees. "But the hardships of the Reclamations have made us strong. We should thank the Deluded for making us work for our plunder. Look there!"

They looked where the red-haired warrior pointed. For some reason, a hole gaped high in the wall next to the main gate, and a host of Deluded were gathered around it, some obviously labourers, others dressed in the ridiculous silver armour they insisted on wearing. These latter warriors were stood outside the wall at its foot, and they were joined by a pair of robed figures. "See how fat that one is! That is what passes for a Mighty One amongst the Deluded!"

"Ancestors be praised he doesn't dress like one," quipped one of the other women. "As it is the image is one I will struggle to purge from my mind's eye. Even Mighty Thror, Ancestors honour him, would put that one to shame!"

"The Green Shadow is there, Mighty Ones," muttered the First of the Tree-Searchers. "I can taste his spoor on the wind."

"Perhaps, First, perhaps," said Dokan. "But even if he is, he stands on the soil of the Deluded. Unless war should be our fate, his life is not forfeit in this place."

"What else might our fate be?" laughed Mighty Xaraya. "Look upon them, Dokan, the fools knock down their own defences! With the aid of the Dashing Elk, our warriors might even be able to leap straight into the fortress! We should attack now, before whatever foolishness they are engaged in comes to bear its rotten fruit!" Her face was flushed, and Second didn't need the wolf-senses to smell her excitement. As was often the way with the Heart-Eaters, her passion was infectious- many of the warriors were already loosening their weapons and Second felt the beast stirring within her.

"Hold!" roared Dokan, even his own composure almost slipping in the face of Xaraya's ardour. "We will not make war on one enemy with another at our backs, not if there is another way. Not whilst I speak for the Tree-Searchers."

"He speaks wisdom, Mighty Xaraya," rumbled Black Skull, seeming to melt out of the deepening gloom of the forest. "I am for words with the Deluded, before we bare our blades."

"*You?*" laughed Xaraya. "When did the feared Blackbloods speak the counsel of peace and the tongue of the coward? Has travelling so far west cooled your poison blood?"

"My... predecessor thought himself wise, and believed he knew all there was to know about his foe," said Black Skull, simply. "In this, the trees know, he was wrong. I will not make his mistake- I will know my enemy's mind before I try to put my spear in his heart."

"Then come, Mighty Black Skull, Mighty Xaraya," said Dokan. "Mighty Thalia proved to me that the Deluded can be people of reason. Let us see what the fat one and his friend will do when approached by foes with empty hands."

The Mighty Ones began to advance, their weapons sheathed. The Firsts of the Blackbloods and Heart-Eaters followed them, but Dokan motioned Second forward. "First, you will remain here. Tell the other Mighty Ones what happened if we do not return."

"But Mighty One-" began the First of the Tree-Searchers.

"You have sworn a blood oath to slay the Green Shadow," said Dokan, sadly, "and you are an honourable warrior. I will not force you to choose between the fate of your people, and your honour. Stay. The Second will attend me capably."

"Very well," said the First, his eyes darkening. "I will not wish you success, Mighty One, for you know my spear aches to taste Deluded blood. But I will wish you safety."

"He is too honest and honourable for politics, that one," said Dokan, quietly, as they walked towards the silver-armoured warriors.

"He is a good First, Dokan," said Xaraya, fussing at her diadem. "You may well need him this day."

They had covered about half the distance to the wall unchallenged, though watched, when the huge drawbridge of the fortress suddenly slammed down. There was only one figure on it, but it commanded the attention of all who watched.

"The Great Knight!" exclaimed Second. "Umba's teeth, look at the size of that horse!"

"It is impressive indeed, Second," said Dokan. "Still, I take this to be a good sign."

"So do I!" laughed Xaraya. "I have been looking forward to killing that one. Do you think his heart is made of silver like the rest of him?"

"Fool," said Black Skull, flatly. "Mighty Dokan means that the Great Knight usually slays intruders with his burning bow. If he approaches us on his horse, it means he is here for parley."

"I... knew that, of course!" snapped Xaraya. Turning to Dokan, she whispered. "How did *he* know that?"

"This Black Skull is very different," said Dokan, with a small smile. "See, though, he speaks truth. The Great Knight goes to join his fellows. His sword and lance sleep."

A few more minutes of walking brought the small party into earshot of the Deluded. As they approached, the slimmer of the two robed figures slammed his staff into the ground with a thunderous boom.

"Expelled! I am Magister Haran Dar, Commander of the Second Volume of the College Guard and Gifted in Residence of the Eastern Vigil. In the name of the Symposium and in accordance with its edicts, I demand to know who you are, and why your people have come to this place."

"I am Mighty Dokan of the Tree-Searchers, and you know why, Mighty Haran," replied Dokan. "The Fly Lords follow on our tails, and we, the Free Tribes, seek passage through the Doors of Patros. Deny us this, and there will be blood and fire. Turn us back, and within a week our bloated bodies will be back at your walls, but this time as harbingers of the Woe."

"I cannot grant you passage, Mighty Dokan, you or your people," said Haran, carefully. "The law of the College is clear- the Expelled- my apologies, the Free Tribes- may not enter our lands until any Warlocks amongst you have been either Sealed, or accepted for formal training as Magisters."

The Mighty Ones exchanged glances. "Who among us are those you call 'Warlocks?'" asked Dokan.

"Er, just about all of you, unfortunately," said the fatter man. "Magister Ollan Dane, of the Symposium, pleased to meet you and all."

"Then hear my words, Magister Ollan Dane, Mighty Haran-"

"Why do you get to be 'Mighty' and I'm still stuck with 'Magister'?" complained the fat man to his colleague with such a complete lack of rancour that Dokan was briefly thrown off his stride. Xaraya took advantage of the distraction to step forward, drawing her sword.

"Listen, you fat, soft fools!" she shouted. "Either you open your doors, or we will storm your gates! I have twenty thousand warriors at my back and you a score and a wall with a hole in it. Yield!"

"Does she remind you of anyone, Haran?" asked the old man, lighting a pipe.

Second goggled at him. Xaraya's fury was so palpable that the hairs on the back of her neck were starting to rise, and yet this fool seemed more interested in blowing smoke rings. Then, suddenly, the wolf-mind screamed a warning at her. *Danger!*

For a moment she couldn't tell what it was. The warriors behind the two fat men- the Magisters, they called themselves- had readied themselves to fight, of course, but they were just men and women in foolish silver armour. One of them, she noticed, carried a sword much like the Silent Blade's, but still there was no reason for-

Then she saw their eyes, and a lance of cold fear pierced her heart.

Before she could find a voice for her fears, Black Skull spoke. "Xaraya, Dokan. Stop. Look."

Xaraya, who was still in full flow hurling curses at the Deluded, whirled. "What? What are you babbling about, you-"

Mighty Dokan suddenly let out a strangled gasp. "M-Mighty Xaraya, do as the Black Skull says. Look upon these warriors with the Eye."

The Heart-Eater rolled her eyes. "Very well, if it will make you... make you... great Ancestors!" She took a full step back, almost dropping her sword. "How? How do they even stand?"

The First of the Heart-Eaters looked around him, wild-eyed. "Mighty One, what is wrong? What do you see?"

Dokan exchanged a glance with the other Mighty Ones. "We must show you. Prepare yourselves!"

Each Mighty One reached out to their attendant, placing one hand lightly on their temple. Second had seen this done before, a simple trick that allowed a warrior to share the sight of the Third Eye. Usually it simply rendered the world into a confusing mass of shifting colours that the untrained could not comprehend, but today it was all she could do not to shrink away from Dokan's touch. Somehow she already knew what she was going to see. Then the Mighty One's hand reached her, and the world exploded into madness.

"Now, Second," came Dokan's voice into her mind. "Look upon these warriors, and mark well what you see. Others must know, and believe as we do."

And she looked, and she saw.

Standing before the wall were no longer merely a score of hard-bitten soldiers. Now a mass of grey, snarling shapes swarmed and writhed about them, formless fangs bared and sharp, incorporeal claws tearing. There were thousands of them, some as small as children, others the size of large warriors. Soundlessly, they screamed their hatred at the men and women of the Second Volume. Again and again they struck savage, harmless blows, and yet the lack of effect did nothing to dispel their rage. Again and again they attacked with such terrible violence that it seemed incredible that anything could withstand their wrath. And none was the focus of more malice, of more furious, impotent vengeance, than Magister Haran Dar.

Second's eyes were streaming with tears and her breath was coming in short gasps when Dokan released her. Next to her, the First of the Heart-Eaters was on his knees, vomiting into the dirt. Even the First of the Blackbloods had been affected, and now stood stock-still with her eyes screwed shut as Black Skull whispered urgent words of reassurance into her ear.

The two Magisters looked on in bewilderment. "Did I do that, or did you?" said Ollan.

"It was no work of mine, Learned Magister," replied his companion. But Second could see his eyes, hard, cold and grey, and in their depths she could still make out the vengeful ghosts. Deluded, the Free called them. Well perhaps that was so. But these warriors were tortured by spirits that tore constantly at their souls, and yet they stood firm. These were men and women who knew death so intimately that should the Free give them a reason, they would slay everything in front of them without pity or remorse. Perhaps they would still fall, but there would be no glory in such a fight and the price would be the very souls of their conquerors.

"This is all very... interesting," said Magister Ollan, after a moment. "But I think, perhaps, that we need to get on with things, eh Haran?"

"I agree, Learned Magister," said Haran, turning those terrible eyes on the Free. "Mighty Dokan, as I have said, we cannot allow you to pass the Vigil. I also do not recommend that you attempt to go around us. At least one Dragon is abroad and the Decree of Fire does not explicitly protect those who trespass in their mountains."

"And yet," said Dokan, recovering his composure, "we cannot go back to the Forest Home. What, then, would you have us do?"

The Great Knight finally spoke, his helm flaring with silver light. "Help us with our work. We have a way to stop the Dendaril, but we need time to prepare it. Until then, you may camp at the foot of the walls."

"At the foot of the walls?" said Xaraya, her attempted laugh of derision coming out more like a sob. "What defence is a fortress to those standing outside it?"

"No castle is proof against the Dendaril in any case," pointed out Magister Haran. "The flies can penetrate any fortress. The Vigil's benefit is that it offers our Archers range to safely strike down the Pilgrims and their thralls, and with our Magisters, the Mighty Ones and Sir Matthew working in concert we should be able to repel any of the parasites that get too close."

"Symbionts," corrected Magister Ollan.

"Our own bows will still be better employed from the top of your walls." pointed out Black Skull.

"Absolutely not!" snapped a woman in heavy silver armour. "Learned Magister, if you think I'm letting any of them inside the Vigil then you've got-"

Haran turned and glared at her. The woman managed to stand her ground for almost five heartbeats, which impressed Second despite the fact that hers were definitely coming considerably faster than usual.

"High Vigilant," said Haran, coldly. "I have respected your autonomy as far as I possibly can, but on this day the Free Tribes are not my enemy. So you must choose whether you wish to become my enemy in their place. Do so quickly."

"I-" began the woman, but the Magister's glare proved too much for her. "Y-yes, I mean no, Learned Magister. May I request that the Expe- the Free Tribes are dispersed across the wall and kept under observation?"

"A sensible precaution, eh Haran?" prompted Ollan, hopefully.

"Very well. But the integrity of the defence must be our first priority," said

Haran. "Mighty Ones of the Free Tribes, hear me now and hear me well. Whatever your beliefs about the balance of power, know that in this alliance my authority will be absolute. Your warriors will serve where I order, they will kill when I order and if necessary, they will die when I order. Do you understand?"

This was too much for Xaraya, even after the shock she had just endured. "What? You think I will let you send my kin to their deaths on a whim? I-"

The Magister whirled, fixing her with his gaze. "I do not know what you saw when you looked at me, Mighty One, but heed my words. No-one living knows the terrible cost of war as well as I. The lives of good, brave men and women are the most dire coin to spend, but if it must be done, believe me when I tell you I will do so without hesitation or prejudice. Even if that life should be my own- Thelen knows, it would be about time. Now, we must make haste to bring your people into the shelter of the walls and make our preparations for the arrival of the Dendaril, unless anyone else would prefer to waste time arguing."

Without bothering to wait for a response, he turned on his heel and marched off towards the fortress. Magister Ollan made as if to follow him, but then turned back.

"I do wish you hadn't pushed him quite so far. Haran is a good man at heart, but sometimes I think he's all too willing to make the hard decisions, even when an easier one would do. For all our sakes, I'd suggest you avoid provoking him."

"We will bear that in mind... Mighty Ollan," said Dokan with a faint smile. The old man puffed out his chest, and began to walk away.

"Oh, there was one more thing I wanted to ask you," he said, turning back.

"And what might that be, Mighty One?" replied Dokan.

"Did Thalia really end up dressing like... that... when she was visiting with your people?" asked the old man, gesturing at Xaraya.

"She did, aye," said Dokan. "As we would expect of any of your rank, Mighty One."

Ollan looked from one Free to another, taking in the hard, lean muscles, tattooed skin, and simple buckskin loincloths.

"That's Magister Ollan to you," he chuckled, and ambled off.

52

It was just about dark by the time the *Flotsam Queen* tied up at Freeport, but Jerik decided it probably wouldn't be wise to quibble over whether Captain Reka had made good on her boasts. From her Seal, and the way she handled her long-handled boat-hook, he was fairly sure she was a veteran of the Seventh Volume, and members of the Sea Guard were notoriously prickly about their seamanship. Besides, he was far too tired. He released the handle of the bilge pump with a groan of relief, just in time for the burly woman to clap him on the back so hard that he nearly went overboard.

"Good job there, ground-pounder! We could've made a sailor of yer, were ye minded."

"I don't think I even want to see a boat again, leave alone crew one," grumbled Jerik. His hands were raw and blistered from the rough handle of the pump, and the silver glow of his taxed Seal threw the deck into ghostly relief.

Reka looked at the way he was clenching and unclenching his hands, and without preamble grabbed him by the wrist. "Ah, looks like ye've got yerself a good set of sea-scars coming in there. How's it feel?"

"Honestly?" said Jerik, too tired to care about machismo, "It hurts like a Dragon chewed it. I felt better when I sliced my own hand open."

Reka was looking at the long scar on his left hand. "Aye, this'n? Sword-cut's clean, they bleed like it's their time of the month but that's all. These bastards are all ragged and manky with muck. Here, plunge 'em in this bucket."

Not stopping to think, his mind dulled with fatigue, Jerik did as he was bid. The water was incredibly cold, and for a moment his hands felt almost numb. Then the pain came roaring back twice as fiercely as before, and he hissed.

"Thelen's fucking balls, woman! What's in this thing?"

"Just cold sea-water, mixed with a bit of healin' gunge that Jandi Gundala makes. Thing with yer Jandallan herbalists, they might not be as gentle as a

College Healer but ye can keep one of their potions in yer pocket in case it all goes to shit on the seas. Can't do that with some white-robed bed-botherer."

"It feels like my hands are on fucking fire!" growled Jerik.

"Yeah, but y'can feel it working, can't ye?" said Reka. "Else ye'd've yanked yer hands out by now, eh? Knew a bloke once, got his arm bit off by a shark. He put one of Gundala's poultices on the stump and it stopped the bleedin' right then and there."

"And he survived?" said Jerik, impressed in spite of himself.

"Well, nah. He were in a row-boat and he couldn't get back to port on just one oar. Starved ter death. But that weren't the medicine's fault."

Jerik stared at her, wondering if he should bring up the obvious flaws in her story. Before he could make a potentially fatal decision, Magister Julius emerged from the rear cabin with the bags.

"Ah, Captain Reka, Captain Jerik, I trust we are ready to head ashore? I am eager to begin our search!"

"Y'don't want ter be beginning anything at night in Freeport, yer Learnedness," said Reka with a grin. "And you, ground-pounder, y'want to be covering up that blade while yer here. Ye'd attract less attention walking about with yer cock out."

"Leaving aside any possible discussions regarding the size of Captain Jerik's manhood, Captain Reka, I think you will find this ample payment for your services." said Julius, handing over a bag of silver Quoits.

"Er, I don't think that was what she meant, Learned Magister..." said Jerik, taking his hands out of the water. They were stiff with cold, but the bleeding had stopped and the raw flesh was healed.

"Don't ye worry little man, I know yer not packin' a minnow in yer cod-piece," said Reka with a wink. "Still, if ye feel the need to prove it, I'll be stayin' at the Last Anchor for a spell. Cheaper'n me payin' for it, which's how it usually shakes out these days."

"Are you not concerned that someone might make off with your boat?" said Julius, as Jerik goggled at the directness of Reka's offer.

"The *Queen*? Nah. Any bastard wants to try sailin' this bitch without me's welcome to try it. If ye can sail and ye're in Freeport, ye've got one of yer own anyways and most're better than this heap. Anyways, ye'll be wanting the High Cliffs if yer need lodgings. Much safer for ground-pounders than this neck o' the woods." She picked up the simple pack that held her few belongings, tossed the bag of Quoits in the air, and caught it, before strolling off, singing to herself.

"Give me a raft, give me a boat
Give me anything long as it floats
I'll sail it any place y'please
And drink to life lived on the seas!"

Julius watched her leave with a fascinated gaze. "Who would have thought that so... brusque an exterior contained so fine a voice? I may have to have a word with my friends at the Lipwig Memorial Theatre in Gyre..."

"You aren't serious," said Jerik. "I mean er, you aren't serious, Learned Magister."

"Perhaps we should stand less on ceremony whilst we are here, Cap- Jerik," said

Julius, who Jerik now noticed had changed into a coarse linen robe. "It would not do to draw undue attention to ourselves. You will address me merely as Julius whilst we are here."

"Why not use an alias, Lear- Julius?" said Jerik.

"Much though it would flatter me to think otherwise, my fame is not so widespread nor my face so well-known as to make such a subterfuge necessary." said Julius. "Besides which, as we have both amply demonstrated already, remembering to drop titles is quite hard enough on the instincts without also trying to remember false identities. So we are Julius and Jerik, I a Healer and you a veteran of the College Guard, and we will provide no more detail than that."

"The staff might be a bit of a giveaway though.. Julius," pointed out Jerik.

"Ah, quite so." agreed the Magister. "Sometimes, proud though we are of them, we Magisters tend to forget they are even there. A moment." He ran his hand along the length of the staff, and in its wake the carved wood blurred briefly before taking on a new form. When he was done, he no longer held an elaborately-decorated symbol of office, but instead a simple, gnarled walking staff.

"I've never seen anyone do that before," confessed Jerik. "Does it still... work?"

"Of course," said Julius. "This is merely a glamour- any competent Aetherwielder will see through it should they care to look. We should take pains to see to it that they do not have reason to. Now, the High Cliffs await!"

"I was wondering about that," said Jerik, picking up the bags as they started walking. "I was thinking we should head over to that Last Anchor place."

"Oh really?" laughed Julius. "Thinking of taking the good Captain up on her offer, were you? I can't say I entirely blame you- she might be more robust than resplendent but there is a certain allure to such unvarnished physicality, in my experience. Not that my own tastes have ever really leaned towards the fairer sex."

"In her case I'm not sure that fairer- wait, you mean you're...?"

"Indeed," said Julius. "Is that a problem?"

"Eh, n-no!" said Jerik, flushing slightly. "It's just I didn't... well, you didn't say that you..."

"Would it have mattered if I had?" asked the Magister with a slightly mischievous grin. It suddenly struck Jerik that far from being offended, Julius was quite enjoying his discomfort.

"Er, look, we've got a little distracted," said Jerik, rallying slightly. "That wasn't the reason I thought we should go to the Last Anchor... well, it sort of was, but not like *that*.."

Julius raised an eyebrow. "You are suggesting that as a place to which someone like Captain Reka might head on first coming into port, and an establishment in which services of an.. intimate nature might be negotiated, the Last Anchor might be a good source of information on our quarry?"

"Er.. yes?" said Jerik, after taking a moment to decipher the sentence.

"I concur entirely," said Julius. "However, I also take Captain Reka's point that we should have a care in the less.. salubrious districts of Freeport at night. So we shall firstly see to finding lodgings for the next few days, and acquaint ourselves with the surrounding area, before we attempt to pursue our investigation in earnest."

"Oh," said Jerik, feeling foolish. "Yeah, of course that makes sense. Sorry, Le-Julius."

The Magister stopped and turned back to look him in the eye. "Do not apologise, Jerik, your instincts in this case were excellent. We may well acquire more promising leads over the course of this expedition, but the Last Anchor will provide a fine starting point."

"Oh, right, good!" replied Jerik, relieved.

"On the other hand, if you accidentally start to refer to me as 'Learned Magister' again whilst we are on this island, I may be forced to cut your tongue out to preserve our cover," said the Magister, mildly.

Jerik stared at him. If the man was joking, he showed no sign of it.

53

Moon Behind Dark Clouds led the war-party as they stole through the night of the forest. It was amazing, thought the First of the Shore-walkers, how quickly the place had ceased to truly feel like home. Not long ago, the very idea of hunting an enemy so close to the Mountain Halls would have felt ludicrous, but now, with a great column of the Free fleeing towards the Tithing, the dark trees felt like they might hide a foe behind every shadowed bough.

On the mountainside high to the south-west, the woods still burned with the aftermath of the Black Skull's sacrifice. Moon had only heard part of the story, relayed in quick shouts as Mighty Lelioko's war-band passed, but he knew the Blackbloods had made a fatal error in believing their venom would protect them from the Woe, and the Black Skull had paid the ultimate price to save what was left of his people. The First was torn between respect for the Mighty One's courage, and contempt for the foolish decision his tribe had made. That almost half the Free had chosen to rush into the arms of the Deluded rather than accept the Master's gift was inexcusable.

And yet, even as the thought crossed his mind, something in the very deepest core of his being rebelled against it. He knew that, whatever they might tell themselves, those of the Free who gave themselves over to the service of Ixilinath forever forfeited the right to the name. Despite anything they might tell the newcomers, despite the fine speeches Mighty Lelioko and the other Mighty Ones might make, they were Thralls of Ixil now. They had only the Master's promise that He would not use the unbreakable hold He had on their souls to compel them to the most monstrous of acts. It was said that as one of the Ancestors, those who had originally slipped the chains of the Deluded and escaped the realm of the scions of Thelen, Ixilinath's word was absolute and inviolate. "Only a fool lies, for to lie is to try to make the world what it is not," was the first thing young warriors were taught by the Mighty Ones, and there was much wisdom in it. But the

Master's promise could never be proven to be unbreakable, and were it proved false even once it could never be redeemed.

He was prevented from further dark thoughts by a signal from his Third. His wife, the Second, had remained at the Tithing to receive the newcomers and cast the Stepping Stones, for the Third, young though he was, bore the Stalking Wolf and was of more help in their mission. Now the young warrior, naked from his shape-shifting, was using the Lark's Tongue to give a call to war. Many warriors bore this simple tattoo, which allowed them to mimic birdsong so perfectly that only a Mighty One might tell that the sound came from no avian throat. Them, and those who knew that a green-crested gull would not usually be heard so far south.

In this case, the gull's cry could mean only one thing- the minions of the Fly Lords were abroad. It fell to Moon's war-party, and to the others also racing through the Forest Home, to see to it that none got close enough to spread the Woe to the great mass of Free who were travelling by Stone Path to the Tithing. He pulled his war-cloak close to him, concealing the glow of his tattoos. They would be less effective in this state, hidden rather than displayed proudly, but he needed to get a closer look at the enemy before he ordered the attack.

The cry of a lakibird from further south brought him up short. The creature would often be seen in this part of the forest, but this had been their mating call which was heard only during the daytime. Another scout had sighted the enemy, but unlike the gull-call this one was as much a warning as anything else. Then another call, this time from the north. The foe were present in great numbers, and at least some of them were armed for war.

Sliding aside his cloak to reveal the Roaring Toad, Moon concentrated. The Toad was usually employed to simply amplify the voice of a commander, but in this case more subtlety was required. He gave a long, deep grunt, so low in pitch that it barely registered as sound to human ears. But to the bearers of the Hare's Ear, who accompanied each war-party, the command was clear. Strike from concealment. Those warriors who carried the Stalking Wolf would hunt down isolated enemies and take them if it were safe, whereas the hunters with the Soaring Eagle would use their exceptional vision and powerful khile-wood bows to eliminate targets of opportunity from the concealed safety of the highest trees.

Ordinarily, of course, the Free would simply retreat into the depths of the Forest Home when faced with such a numerous enemy, there to link up with enough warriors to strike with overwhelming force. But that was not an option on this night. Until the long column of refugees had reached the Tithing, or at least attained a safer distance, the Fly Lords could not be permitted to advance. Moon hunkered down as low as he could in the shadows of his tree, barely even allowing himself to breathe, and listened as Death whispered through the leaves. Here and there he heard a strangled gasp or gurgle from the distant forest as the blade-glass tipped arrows struck home. The Eagle slay-teams would work together in groups of three, one picking a target and the others watching to eliminate any bystanders who might see the death of the first and try to raise the alarm. It took skill and exceptional coordination, and many slay-teams were comprised of siblings or spouses who knew how each other thought. Even so, there were only so many opportunities to strike before the enemy realised that they were under attack.

A moment later, a great shout and flash of light from the forest ahead told him that they had run out of time. Mighty Lelioko had warned him that the Pilgrims of the Fly Lords were Spirit-wielders and many of them had the Third Eye, and so Moon knew he could not hesitate any longer. He cast off his cloak and this time put the Roaring Toad to its more typical use, issuing a shattering bellow that could be heard for miles around. Answering war-whoops, lacking the power of his own cry but not the purpose, rose from all sides. From the sound of it, several other war-parties had linked up with his own. Good. There were enough foes for everyone.

As he ran, seeing and hearing the sounds of battle from up ahead, the First remembered the gift the Master had given him before sending him on his mission. He looked about hurriedly, searching for a fallen warrior, and his eyes alighted on the corpse of a Fly Lord. The woman wore simple leather armour and was sitting with her back to a tree, blood staining the front of her clothing from where an arrow had torn her throat out. As he withdrew the gem from its pouch, Moon grunted in approval- the kill had been clean and silent. The enemy had not been alerted by this one, nor had the prey suffered unduly. Be the target a beast for the roasting spit or an enemy in battle, the Eagle Hunters held their kill-shots to the same exacting standard, at least until the chaos of battle made such niceties impossible.

Putting such thoughts aside, and mindful of the growing clamour around him, Moon placed the sharp point of the gemstone on the forehead of the warrior, and then rapped it sharply on its flat top with the heel of his hand, driving the tip into the bone. For a brief moment nothing happened, and he had just enough time to worry that he had misunderstood his instructions before the gem burst into life with a blaze of fire. In a heartbeat the flames spread from the gem to wash over the corpse, and Moon leapt back with an oath, wrinkling his nose against the expected stench of burning flesh. And yet there was none, nor did the fire spread to the tree or the dry undergrowth. Instead, there was just a clean-picked skeleton, flesh, sinew and clothing all consumed, which rose smoothly to its feet as if it were a fresh-faced young warrior.

"*THEY COME, THEN,*" Ixilinath's voice seemed to come from far away, even though Moon knew it must be coming from the skeleton. The small part of his mind that was not paralysed with fear noted that the gem had gone, but the eye-sockets of the skull still glowed with a familiar fire.

"Y-yes, Master," he replied, simply. "There are many. We may not have enough warriors to-"

"*IT WILL SUFFICE,*" The skeleton looked down at the simple sword that the Fly Lord had been carrying. "*A POOR TOOL, BUT IT, TOO, SHALL SERVE. MARK WELL MY WORDS, MY THRALL. THIS VESSEL SHALL AID IN YOUR FIGHT, BUT ITS TIME IS SHORT. WHEN THE LIGHT IN ITS EYES FADES, FLEE WITH ALL THE SPEED YOU CAN SUMMON.*"

Without any further word of explanation, the Vessel turned, and charged into the fray. Despite the disquiet in his heart, Moon followed.

54

*N*ever in his life had Joniah felt such abject terror. When the Pilgrims had come to his village from the east a few days after Ronald had left, he had thought it a great honour to have been chosen as a Porter. The Pilgrims told of a great land to the west that had been denied the Blessing through evil sorcery but which was now ready to accept the gifts of the Dendaril. Even so, they said, there were some in that land who were afraid of the Blessing and who might resist with force, and so it was that some of the greatest among the Pilgrims had been mustered at the border city of Sylastine, along with a Crusade.

No-one in the village had even heard of such a thing, but the Pilgrims explained that among the Other, disputes were often settled violently through something they called 'war'. The Dendaril, of course, had no need of something so crude thanks to the Blessing, but patrols of armed soldiers were stationed in most towns and cities as a defence against the occasional pack of wild animals. Joniah had even heard rumours that the fearsome pirates known as the Toskans occasionally raided the coastal settlements, though why anyone should choose to do such a thing was beyond his comprehension.

At the time, Joniah had felt himself quite fortunate to have reached a level of ripeness that meant his belly was too fat to wear the armour of a soldier, and had been ecstatic to be given the role of helping to carry one of the Elucidated Pilgrims to the west. The Elucidated Pilgrims lived only in the great cities like Sylastine, and had nobly chosen to delay their Time in order to pass on their great wisdom and knowledge to the Blessed. Most of them were so incredibly swollen with Bearers that they could barely move at all under their own power, and so were carried on the rare occasions where it was necessary on huge, ornate palanquins. Such was the strength granted by the Blessing that any one of the four Porters who carried Pilgrim Toroth could have borne his great weight alone if needed, but with four the effort was so minimal that it had barely felt like any effort at all.

All that, of course, had changed when they reached the Border Marshes. The terrain was soft and boggy, and more than one Porter stumbled and nearly fell, but each time their fellows and the powerful magic of the Elucidated Pilgrims saw them through the crisis. Still, the journey was hard and the food was mostly the roasted meat of the mighty wading beasts who were compelled by their own, lesser version of the Blessing to wait meekly for the slaughter. It was filling, but hardly pleasant. But if the Blessed had thought the journey through the swamp to be difficult, it was as nothing to what awaited them in the forest beyond. On the edge of the idyllic-seeming wood, they had found the bodies of Ronald's escort nailed to the trees. From the state of the corpses it was clear that the Bearers had spread the Blessing to their killers, so there was much rejoicing at this early success, but at the same time Joniah had been shocked at the savagery that the Dendaril had been subjected to. On top of that, the forest had soon proved to be home to venomous beasts, snakes and spiders that showed scant respect for the Blessed.

He had thought, then, that he had seen the worst the forest had to offer. Now, as a mob of screaming, roaring savages erupted out of the darkness, he realised that he had seen nothing. The Crusade numbered in the hundreds of thousands, a long, ragged mass that stretched so far back that some stragglers were still leaving Sylastine even though that city lay almost six hundred miles to the east. Even with this dispersion there were over ten thousand in the host that accompanied Elucidated Pilgrim Toroth, opposed by maybe five hundred. Yet those five hundred, attacking as they were in a sudden, tightly-coordinated rush, seemed to Joniah to be far, far too many. Caught in the process of setting up an encampment in a forest clearing lit only by torches and the light of the Pilgrims' staffs, the Crusade was slow to respond coherently.

Even greater horror was to come. As the first line of attacking warriors struck home, the Dendaril soldiers attempting to halt them fell in droves, their simple leather armour, wooden shields and steel swords proving a poor match for the barbarians who danced among them, black-tipped spears stabbing and long, curved knives slashing. Even so, no great sense of panic gripped the Dendaril throng, for as each soldier fell, a small cloud of Bearers erupted from their dying bodies, swarming about for a few seconds before throwing themselves at the nearest attacker. In mere moments, this distasteful spectacle would be over, and the Crusade would have new, capable warriors to help defend it. But as the lead attacker was engulfed by the dark clouds there was a sudden, terrible burst of fire before the surviving insects were sent spiralling away, many of them being consumed by the flame as they went.

A low moan of dismay erupted from the host of Dendaril. Never before had anyone present seen the Gift so brutally, viciously rejected. Never had the life of a Blessed been lost only for the Bearers to also be wasted. For a moment, the entire Crusade wavered, the psychic shock resonating down the Communion as far as the border even though most common folk were only dimly aware of its existence. Then, with a terrible, atavistic rush, resolve came surging back. These things in human shape spurned the Gift and were unworthy of life, and the Blessed would take it from them. A Pilgrim rose into the air above the throng, flame leaping from her staff to consume the nearest savage. Seconds later, three black-flecked arrows appeared in her breast and she fell back, mortally wounded, but the fact remained- deadly they may be, but these creatures could die. And die they would.

215

With a roar every bit as primal as that which had heralded the initial attack, the Crusade surged forward, and somehow Joniah sensed that even those far to the east had drawn their blades, bared their teeth, and begun to charge. The mass of bodies slammed into the thin line of barbarians and bore them back, though ten Dendaril died for every savage corpse that was bludgeoned, hacked and stabbed into the dirt. More arrows hissed from the forest, each aimed with deadly intent at the Pilgrims, but the Dendaril leaders had their measure now and shields of shimmering magic repelled every dark shaft. The battle raged for a few more brutal moments, the savages giving ground only grudgingly, each killing a man or woman with every stroke. Then something emerged from the treeline.

It had eyes that blazed with malice, and Joniah thought that even at a distance of several hundred feet it was gazing straight into his soul. He felt the Bearers in his gut suddenly stir, as if they might try to force their way out of his body to flee. It was a naked, skeletal figure, armed only with a simple sword, but it was attended by surging flames that seemed to serve as crown and robe both. Even the savages seemed stunned by the thing's arrival, but as it stormed into battle their rank opened to let it through before surging forwards in its wake.

Joniah had heard fireside stories of the risen dead, of course, from the dark times before the Blessing. Always these things shambled or lurched, their terrible deathless resilience easily outmatched by the cunning hero or wise man. They did not fight with the grace of a master swordsman, as this creature did. They did not shrug off blasts of fire and lightning from desperate Pilgrims, as this creature did. And they did not speak, as this creature did.

"FLY-RIDDEN SCUM! KNOW THAT I AM IXILINATH, AND THESE THRALLS ARE MINE! GO BACK TO YOUR FESTERING HOME AND DREAM OF THE WEST, FOR NEVER SHALL YOUR KIND SET FOOT THERE WHILE THE FLAMES OF IXILDUNDAL BURN!"

The three Elucidated Pilgrims that accompanied the vanguard of the Crusade, Toroth among them, replied with a colossal bolt of lightning that streaked from each of their corpulent bodies to strike the skeletal thing, before another blast slammed down from the clear skies. Bodies, both Dendaril and barbarian, were blasted to atoms and flung in all directions by the impact, but when the smoke cleared the skeleton had merely been knocked to one knee. It stood like a man who had just finished tying a loose bootlace, and gave a mocking bow.

"A FAIR EFFORT. YOU HAVE EARNED YOUR PASSAGE FOR NOW, BUT VENTURE NOT INTO MY DOMAIN, OR THIS SHALL BE BUT A PALE SHADE OF THE DOOM YOU SHALL SUFFER. FAREWELL."

As the thing spoke its last word, the lights in its skull suddenly winked out and it collapsed into a pile of bones. Immediately the barbarians disengaged, some leaping back to the trees in a single bound, others simply turning and sprinting away. Joniah dared let out a sigh of relief.

Then the bones exploded.

The detonation was incredible, reaching far enough to knock some of the closest trees over and sending the slower of the barbarians sprawling. Closer to the epicentre, the nearest Dendaril soldiers were reduced to ash on the spot, and even as far back as the Elucidated Pilgrims a shock-wave slammed up against their Vrae-shields. But at last, for now at least, it was over.

"A..... satisfactory.... outcome..." said Toroth, slowly, his voice coming as little more than a series of whispered gasps.

"Begging your pardon, Elucidated One, but we have lost thousands simply to slay that one creature!" gasped Joniah. "If there are any more of them..."

"We... did not... slay... Him..." corrected the Elucidated Pilgrim. "He is... of the ... old blood... and... will not... die... easily. But.... His Vrae... is... taxed... for now.... and we... have untold.... millions. Now... we move.... west...."

Joniah swallowed, and shifted his burden on his shoulder. It seemed this nightmare was only just beginning.

55

*A*manda Devereux lay in the darkness of the silent hospital ward, and stared at the ceiling. She could have commanded the medical suite to release a sedative to send her off to sleep, but something about the city of Abellan put her nerves on edge. In the next bed over, Athas was sleeping peacefully, and it took her a moment to realise why that, too, worried her.

Suddenly the realisation hit her- Athas was a snorer. Perhaps not in the sense that he kept people awake, but usually when the big man was asleep in a room someone standing outside could certainly hear him if they chose to listen. But right now, he was sleeping without the slightest hint of anything other than normal breathing. Of course, there were several entirely innocent explanations- maybe the magic the Abelians had used to sedate him had a side-effect. For that matter, since snoring was sometimes the harbinger of a more serious respiratory condition, the Healers might have chosen to deal with it out of professional thoroughness. If so, though, they certainly hadn't mentioned it to her.

As concerns went, it was hardly a major one. If Athas woke up the next morning as if nothing had happened, then Devereux would happily take it as a win and head to the Green Palace to rejoin Thalia without a backward glance. And yet she couldn't shake the feeling that she didn't expect it to happen. For one thing, there was something distinctly eerie about the Royal Hospital. This ward alone had beds for thirty patients but she and Athas were the only ones in it. She lay back, closing her eyes, and set the Hercules suite to make a full-spectrum active sweep. Doing so required bypassing several security protocols since most of her augmentations were in stealth mode, but it seemed very unlikely anyone with the ability to detect them would be nearby.

The results were largely as she expected. Thermal and ultrasound scans revealed that other than a Healer who was stationed in a nearby office in case of any complications in Athas' recovery, the Hospital was largely deserted. At extreme range, though, some three floors below the level she was on, there were a couple of heat signatures and something that the analysis software was fairly confident was a conversation. Ordinarily at such a distance and through several solid walls and floors, there would be so much interference from external sources that even the Hercules suite would struggle to filter them out, but so quiet was the city of Abellan that it seemed it might be possible.

++Two subjects detected. Subject designated Alpha: 78.3% voice-pattern match for Healer Alana Matisse. Subject designated Beta: Voice-pattern unknown and filed.++

"-again for your visit, Esteemed Sir. I hope you found everything in order?" That was Alana, according to the analysis, though the voice was greatly distorted.

"It was, thank you," replied the other, subject Beta. "The equipment stored here is extremely delicate and must not be disturbed."

"There is little chance-" here the words briefly devolved into digital mush for a moment. "-all, you have the only key."

"A simple precaution, nothing mo-" another burst of interference. Devereux frowned in annoyance. Whoever they were, they were moving out of range and even as stealthy as she was, trying to get closer would louse up the calibration.

"-in three days ti-"

++Operative advisory: Signal degradation at 86.9%. Further monitoring impossible.++

Devereux closed her eyes and sighed. So someone 'esteemed' had something important stored in the Royal Hospital, and from the logs she had a fairly good idea where it might be. Her training told her this was something she should report to her handler and continue to monitor- trying to investigate without backup or any reconnaissance would not only be extremely dangerous, but might also jeopardise both Athas' treatment, and Thalia's mission. But her handler was in another plane of reality altogether and probably thought she was either dead or a defector, the strange words Magister Fredus had muttered at his self-committal notwithstanding.

If anything happened to make her think Athas was in danger, she was damn well going to uncover this secret, whatever it was. It might put Thalia at risk, but if she let the big Guard die the Magister probably wouldn't forgive her anyway.

Begin condition monitoring.

++Monitoring enabled. Subject: Athas Elmflower. Rank: Sergeant. Affiliation: College Guard, 8th Volume. Status: Blood pressure 110 over 70. Heart rate 41 BPM. Vital signs stable.++

The Hercules suite would alert her if anything significant changed. Satisfied that she had done all she could for now, Devereux let sleep take her.

56

*A*rch-Chancellor Derelar Thane massaged his temples and tried to concentrate on the papers in front of him. Midnight had come and gone some time ago, and he knew that if he tried to persevere much longer his customary early start was likely to prove challenging. The day's meetings had gone on much longer than expected, with Magister Jakob in particular proving troublesome. The Chair of Yar had demanded to know why the White Riders and several Volumes of the Guard were being quietly redeployed to the west of the Empire when the Expelled and Dendaril both threatened from the east, and Derelar rather suspected that he had already deduced the reason. After all, the man had hardly gained his position as head of the College military through nepotism. Quite the reverse, in fact.

In the end, the Vice-Chancellor had suggested that as well as giving Jakob responsibility for the new settlement at Fort Tarim, he should take over operational command of the Sixth Volume, who were already based out of the new settlement as much as they were their traditional home of Kathis. There, he was to oversee the precautions against invasion should the Eastern Vigil fail to contain the Expelled, the Dendaril, or both, as well as making preparations to raise a new Ninth Volume to replace that which had been annihilated at Manadar. Grudgingly, the veteran Magister had agreed. He had also, somewhat to Derelar's surprise, pointed out that his new posting would make it difficult to serve as the Chair of Yar for either Lore, or the High Seminar, and made some suggestions as to a possible successor. Anneke, of course, had insisted on supplying detailed dossiers on each of the candidates and the resulting paperwork was largely responsible for the Arch-Chancellor missing his preferred bedtime by some hours.

There was a sudden disturbance of air in the room, and Derelar closed his eyes and sighed. Now, of all times. At least he wasn't in bed.

"Ambassador," he said out loud. "How may I help you?"

"You may not," replied the robed figure, seemingly not at all surprised that the

Arch-Chancellor had known it was there without looking. "I come bearing intelligence of note for your attention."

Derelar levered himself to his feet, strode over to his sideboard with forced nonchalance, and poured himself a lukewarm coffee. If he saw the next dawn break now it would be because he didn't bother going to bed. "I was unaware that the Parliament employed you as a scout, Ambassador."

"That is because they do not," said the Ambassador, not rising to the bait. "This information comes from Mighty Lady Antorathes, third Seneschal of the Spine of Rôl."

Derelar's eyebrows shot up. He remembered Magister Fredus saying that Antorathes seemed to take more interest in human affairs than her fellows, but he couldn't remember any record of her ever choosing to relay a message. "Indeed? And what might that information be?"

"The Dendaril are moving, Arch-Chancellor. They have been sighted in the Field of Thranaluin's Wing, that place which you call the Expelled Territories."

Mentally filing away the unfamiliar place-name for future investigation, Derelar nodded. "We were aware that they were coming, Ambassador. What of the Expelled?"

"The Fallen Children have shown uncharacteristic wisdom," replied the Ambassador. "They retreat before the Dendaril, fleeing to the Doors of Patros. Some half of their number, however, have disappeared into the forest, and Mighty Lady Antorathes does not know where they have gone. Among the missing are their young."

"Half of the Expelled have just vanished?" said Derelar. In truth, Anneke had told him that according to her agents only half of the Expelled tribes had been sighted at the Vigil, but the Ambassador didn't need to know that. "Couldn't she find out where they were?"

"It is perilous in the extreme for any Dragon to approach the Dendaril closely," admitted the Ambassador. "They must fly higher than the little beasts can reach, lest they be lost. Such height does not lend itself to seeing beneath the thick trees."

"A *Dragon*?" gasped Derelar, genuinely shocked. He would never have believed something so powerful might be at direct risk from the Shrive-Ticks. Suddenly the Vice-Chancellor's reaction to his earlier gambit began to make more sense.

"Are you telling me that the Parliament is concerned about the spread of the Dendaril because they themselves might be threatened?" he said, when the Ambassador remained silent.

"Those are not words that I have spoken," replied the robed figure.

"And yet you have not denied it."

"I have not."

"What of the woman who threatens you?" said Derelar, suddenly. "When last we spoke, you considered that to be a matter of the utmost urgency and yet now you do not even mention her."

"That matter is urgent as Dragons reckon time," said the Ambassador. "This matter is urgent as humans measure it. To the Dragons, mere eye-blinks remain to avert disaster. Had the Daxalai- gnh."

The Ambassador abruptly stopped speaking. "Had the Daxalai what?" prompted Derelar.

"I did not speak of the Daxalai," said the Ambassador, nothing in his tone suggesting that there might be any doubt in the matter. The Arch-Chancellor knew it would be pointless to pursue that line of inquiry. The Parliament kept their emissary on a tight leash, and they had given it a tug. "Have you any news regarding the Mother of Calamities?"

"I have learned nothing further of anyone by that name." said Derelar, carefully, though it rang a faint bell. He had his suspicions, but they were barely ready to be shared with anyone, least of all the Dragons. The Ambassador gave him a long look, or at least pointed its darkened hood at him in a way that suggested one.

"I depart," it said, finally. Derelar turned his back as was customary, and with another sudden rush of air he was once more alone in the High Apartment. He returned to his desk, drained the coffee, and sat down. That the Dendaril were on the move, he already knew. That the Expelled had been driven before them, he had been told. But that the Dragons themselves were concerned- that was new information. New, and potentially useful. He took up a fresh sheet of paper, dipped his pen, and began to write.

57

*T*he secret chamber was quiet and still, and there was no other living soul in his laboratory save one. And yet Smiling Snake still felt that he dare not raise his voice above a whisper, such was the importance of the secret he had to impart. On their return to Shan'Xi'Sho, he had convened a meeting of the most senior Sages of the clan, and made sure that White Crocus was recognised as a full Sage in his own right. The young man now carried a *shansenbao* of his own, though his so far only bore four rings.

Bai Faoha looked at the Tapestry, and gave a non-committal shrug. "It is.. a fine piece in its way, Great Sage. The execution is perhaps not as perfect as some other works in the Imperial Galleries."

"This is no work of art, Bai Faoha, not in that sense. Those that hang in the Galleries express Harmony through their fine weaving and rich colours, and as such are great and worthy things. This is no such work. The only art here is the art of subterfuge, and it serves the Harmony in a very different way. Look upon it with the eye of the Dragon."

He watched carefully as the young Sage did as he was bid. "It... it is incredible," whispered White Crocus after a full five minutes of contemplation. "What does it mean?"

"Everything," said Rya-Ki. "And yet to the eye, nothing. To truly understand the Tapestry, you must listen, not look."

"Then why did you tell me to do so?" asked the Sage, his tone still soft and reverent and his eyes still staring into space.

"To fully appreciate the power and complexity of the device," said Smiling Snake. "Without first contemplating it in a safe manner, opening oneself to it can be.. perilous." And even then, he thought, thinking back to his previous experience, there were risks.

White Crocus snapped back to reality. "I do not understand, Great Sage, but I will obey. What must I do?"

"Step close to the Tapestry, close your eyes, and listen with the very core of your being. You may hear many voices- do not attempt to focus on them. They will come to you."

Bai Faoha did as he was bid, closing his eyes tightly and reaching out to the artefact. "I hear... voices. They speak.... their words are alien to my ears..."

Smiling Snake nodded. Another thing White Crocus would need instruction in was the languages of the Chaotic East, but any Sage could do that. Suddenly the young man's eyes snapped open with shock. "What!? Such... immodesty!"

Rya-Ki laughed softly. "Ah, and now I know you have achieved success, my student."

Bai Faoha turned to him, his face hot with shame. "Great Sage, what is the meaning of this? The last voice was a woman of Daxalai, but she was.... was..."

"Engaged in lovemaking with the enthusiasm of a mountain hare?" suggested Smiling Snake.

"Ah.. so it would seem, yes."

"That would be Kiysu Taokoa, the Flying Fox," said the Great Sage. "She wears an *oba-sie* cut from the robes of a Sage of the Toha clan, and when the mood takes her, which is often, she rarely cares to remove it completely. I would snip out that thread, but the Tapestry does not take kindly to meddling unless a strand has gone silent, and that one is anything but." It was also quite stimulating to listen in occasionally, not that he would admit it.

White Crocus stared at him in confusion. "I am lost like the snake who tries to hide in the corner of a bucket, Great Sage," he confessed.

"Then perhaps we should look at this puzzle from a different angle," said Smiling Snake. "Pass me the small sandalwood case that rests on the mantle."

The younger man did so. Rya-Ki made to open the case, but gave a final word of warning. "What I am about to show you is both valuable, and fragile. Whilst this box is open, you shall neither move, nor breathe. Are you prepared?"

Bai Faoha took a deep breath, and nodded. The Great Sage opened the case, showed him the contents, and then carefully shut it again. "What did you see?"

"A single strand of silk, Great Sage," said White Crocus. "I confess understanding still eludes me as the monkey does the tiger."

"That strand is taken from a bolt of silk that was shipped some months ago to the Kingdom of Abelia, in the Chaotic East. While the *gwai-sen* are largely ignorant of our ways, all know that the Hono clan provides the very finest silks for the very lowest of prices."

"Are we merchants now, Great Sage?" said Bai Faoha. "Is is not said that he who lives for coin surrenders warm life for cold metal?"

"That is said, yes," replied Smiling Snake. "Though mostly by wise men who have never known the ache of an empty belly or tried to coax living rice from a dead field. But in this case, it is not mere money that is the goal of the trade. By now, the bolt that this thread came from has been made into a fine robe, or a dress for a noble lady."

"Or a bandit's small-clothes," pointed out Bai Faoha with a smile.

"Perhaps. Let us see what happens if we introduce this thread to our Tapestry. Firstly, we must spend an hour in meditation. Use this time to allow your senses to feel the presence of both thread, and weave."

They sat in silence for the hour, accompanied only by the light of a single candle. Smiling Snake often found it aided his focus to watch the small flame dance, darting back and forth in response to tiny draughts too small for any but the most highly-trained Initiate to sense. Instead of concentrating on the thread, he turned his attention to White Crocus. The young man had done well so far, even if Flying Fox had discomforted him with her antics. It was always wise to remember that even in the most serious of circumstances, the Heavens could be as whimsical as the wind. Now, however, Bai Faoha had regained focus and peace of mind. He was ready.

They stood, and Smiling Snake brought the chamber's lights up to their full brightness- it would not do to be squinting at shadows during the process. He held the box out to White Crocus.

"Now, Bai Faoha, it is your time. Open the box, remove the thread, and put it in its place in the Tapestry."

"How will I know where that place might be?" asked the young Sage.

"If it has a place, that place will become known to you. If it does not, if the thread is inert, then even the Son of Heaven could not compel it otherwise. Trust in the Tapestry, and in your own instincts. And do not breathe again until the process is complete."

White Crocus nodded. The meditation had done much to prepare him for the unexpected. Without further discussion, he took a deep, slow breath to centre himself, and carefully opened the box, lifting the thread out gently with his *ki*. Though he showed no outward sign, Smiling Snake was stunned. Never in the many years that he had tended the artefact had he considered placing a thread without physically touching it. To do so would require the most exacting control, and yet Bai Faoha was doing it without any apparent effort. Even as he wondered if such a thing would even work, he found himself slightly in awe of the young man.

Moments later, White Crocus surprised him again. The Great Sage had always placed threads by carefully moving them across the surface of the Tapestry until he felt them begin to bond. Bai Faoha simply allowed the thread to drift close to the centre of the artefact, and then released his hold on it. It was all Rya-Ki could do to prevent himself from leaping forwards to try to grab the precious strand of silk before it struck the floor. And yet there was no need- the thread drifted in the air for a moment, suspended on the same tiny draughts that had buffeted the candle, and then slid gracefully into place in the design. As one, Sage and Great Sage exhaled gratefully.

"Now, let us see what tale our new thread can tell us," said Smiling Snake. "You have not yet mastered the Eastern tongues, so this time I shall share my under-standing with you. Are you prepared?"

Bai Faoha nodded. "I am."

Rya-Ki reached out to the Tapestry, listening carefully, at the same time opening his awareness to White Crocus. After a moment, a voice drifted into their minds.

"I am very sorry, Mama. The Healers say the seed did not take."

A young woman, and certainly Abelian nobility from the accent.

"But I did everything I was supposed to! I took the Mother's Root and made sure to open myself to his Spirit. Perhaps there was something wrong with him?"

One disadvantage of the Tapestry was that it only usually conveyed half of most conversations. In this case, the context was certainly not entirely clear.

"No, Mama. If need be, we still have the ripped dress and I made sure to get a little of my blood on it afterwards. The Ambassador is unlikely to want to make an incident out of it, considering the situation."

Smiling Snake made careful note of this. If it concerned who he thought it did, it could prove extremely useful.

"Very well, Mama. I will get ready to travel to Dalliance tomorrow. I only hope I find another as gentle as he was."

They waited for a few minutes, but the Tapestry was silent.

"Do you understand now, Bai Faoha?" asked Smiling Snake. The young man shook his head slowly.

"I understand only that there is much I do not understand, Great Sage. But light glimmers on the horizon as a prelude to dawn."

"Then share with me your first rays," prompted Rya-Ki, gently. White Crocus settled into a cross-legged position and closed his eyes.

"The young woman- she attempted to conceive a child. The father was coerced by trickery, and is either an Ambassador himself, or is a close attendant to one. Dalliance I know to be a port city of the Kingdom, though its significance in this tale is unclear to me."

"And what of the Tapestry itself?" asked the Great Sage.

"The key is the silk it is woven from, that much is clear," said the younger man. "The silk-farms of the Hono provide materials that become the robes of the rich and powerful from Shan'Xi'Sho to Torak, worn by Sage and Magister, Chime-Mage and Wizard. All those who possess mastery of *ki* use it to add colour to their clothing, their life-energy both beautifying, and reinforcing the fabric that it might protect against heat and cold."

"This is so," said Rya-Ki. "Indeed, during their civil war the *gwai-sen* of the Lily College who supported the mad royal siblings even changed the colour of their robes from green to purple to signify their rebellion."

"Then I would suggest that there is some... connection still between these threads, and those woven into the robes of those powerful *gwai-sen*. When they invest their *ki* in the clothing, it reinforces that link, and allows he who possesses the Tapestry to listen in to their conversations. Truly is this a device of great power, and limitless possibility!"

"And yet you have also witnessed its limits," pointed out Smiling Snake. "You have seen that the Tapestry can be fickle, even mischievous, and that one can only hear one side of the conversation. In truth, I believe one hears only what the wearer intends to say before he or she says it. One should be informed by it, but never trust it."

White Crocus was staring at the device again. "Is... is the robe of the Son of Heaven-"

"No!" gasped Smiling Snake. "Do not even consider such a thing! The Imperial Court wear robes woven from the silk of their own gardens, and even if such threads could somehow be obtained the risk of introducing them to the Tapestry would be extreme."

White Crocus cast his eyes to the floor. "I am sorry, *Shansenshao*. I have disappointed you with my foolishness."

Rya-Ki gave him a moment to compose himself, then sat down opposite him. "Not so, White Crocus. I presented you with a great wonder, and your only fault was to consider it, and to ask how far that wonder might reach." He laughed. "Know that you approached the task of adding the new thread to the Tapestry completely differently to me."

"Did I?"

"Yes. And yet you were successful. Only now has it occurred to me that my own master, when she taught me the ways of the Tapestry many years ago, also allowed me to find my own way. Perhaps she was as surprised by my approach as I was by yours."

"Many birds fly from one tree to another, yet few follow the same path," observed White Crocus.

"This is true. Now, tomorrow you will start your instruction with Six-Tongue Yao. The language of the Chaotic East cannot be a mystery to a Great Sage."

"And what of you, *Shansenshao?*"

"Me?" said Smiling Snake. "I shall be endeavouring to make sure that your promotion is long-delayed."

58

*O*rdinarily, the sight of Night's First Raven in the early hours of daylight was something to gladden Moon Behind Dark Clouds' heart. This morning, however, as he led his battered, bloody war-party through the outer gates of Ixil-dundal, he could tell from the look on her face that something was wrong.

Though his limbs ached with fatigue and his heavy eyes itched with the desire for sleep, Moon had been feeling proud of the Shorewalkers' sortie against the Fly Lords. Any who had doubted that the power of the Master could protect the Free against the Woe could have no such doubts now. His Third was still talking about the experience of the tiny insects trying to burrow into his skin, only to be destroyed by Ixil's flame. And then, when the attack had seemed to be bogged down and the war-parties were in danger of being enveloped, had come the terrifying Vessel into the fray. Perhaps other, more 'civilised' peoples might have balked at fighting alongside a skeleton that stood and fought like a man, but the Eternals had guarded the Mountain Halls for as long as any Free living could remember.

Moon was just glad that the Master was on their side- or more accurately, that they were on His. As it was, they had taken some casualties and few of the warriors other than the Eagle Hunters had come back unwounded, but without the Master's power things would have been far worse.

"Greetings, husband," said Night's First Raven, the genuine relief in her voice matched by a softening of her expression. "The Seneschal tells us your raid went well."

"Aye," said Mighty Taris, who had been waiting with her. "None of the Fly Lords broke through to threaten the Free. All are now... safely within the walls of Ixildundal."

Moon noticed the Mighty One's hesitation. "Thank you, Mighty One. And yet, you seem troubled."

The Hearth-Tender fussed at his long, wispy grey beard in agitation. "I am,

First of the Shorewalkers. I fear that faced with an impossible decision and little time I have made a terrible mistake."

Moon struggled to control an enormous yawn, and largely failed. "A mistake?" he said, once he had recovered. "You and the rest of your tribe still draw breath and you are beyond the reach of the Fly Lords. In so choosing, you saved not only your own, but also the young of all the Free, even those who were so unwise as to spurn the Master's offer. How could such a deed be a mistake?"

His Third came up to him, dressed once again in war-cloak and harness. "Is there a problem, First?"

"No," replied Moon. "Go and take the wounded to the Healers, and then get yourself and the other warriors food and rest. You fought well this day, Third."

"As did you, First," said the young warrior, eyes shining. "With the power of the Master and the wisdom of the Mighty Ones, the Free shall drive all foes before them!"

"That is what worries me," said Mighty Taris, softly, as the warriors of the war-parties drifted off in search of food and rest.

"You fear the Master dreams not only of defending the Free, but of conquest?" asked Moon. "Be aware that anything you say to a bearer of the Brand might as well be spoken into His own ear."

Taris gave a thin smile. "Your warning is kindly given, First, but unnecessary. I am aware of my position. Know that your Master need have no fear of betrayal from the Hearth-Tenders, even were it within my poor power to threaten him."

"And yet?" prompted Night's First Raven. "You told me you had a matter of urgency to discuss, Mighty One, and my husband is eager for his bed. As am I."

In spite of the circumstances, the way his wife looked at him when she spoke the words set Moon's heart to racing. At least he suddenly didn't feel so tired.

"You speak truly, Second of the Shorewalkers," said Taris. "I shall be direct, then. I fear the Heath-Tenders cannot accept the Master's bargain."

All thoughts of the pleasures of his bed fled from Moon's mind like wolves before a forest fire. "What? Mighty One, you stand within the Master's very walls! To reject the Brand once you have been allowed to enter this place is to invite the most terrible of doom."

"I know this," said Mighty Taris, sadly. "But First, you know the oath of the Hearth-Tenders. We long ago forswore violence in all its forms. We eat only the food the Forest Home gives us- our meat is only what carrion we find. We bear no weapons, not even hunting knives, and our spirit-tattoos are never bared for battle. Should we take the Brand, your Master could compel us to break that oath. Not only would that invite the gravest of dishonour, it would jeopardise our role as guardians of the life of the Free."

Moon knew what he meant. Traditionally, on the rare occasions where the tribes of the Free fought amongst themselves, the Hearth-Tenders looked after the children of both sides until the dispute was resolved. In exchange for a strict vow of non-violence, no Free would raise a hand against them. Both the Stonesingers and Blackbloods had been saved from virtual extinction by this arrangement, which had been made at the first, and greatest, Moot of Kings. Nevertheless, he raised the most obvious objection to the Mighty One's argument.

"Once all the Free are sworn to the Master's service, there will be no more conflict between them," he pointed out. "The Hearth-Tenders will no longer need to protect us from ourselves."

"And what of the Tree-Searchers, Blackbloods and Heart-Eaters?" said Taris. "They may have turned to the Deluded, but their children are entrusted to my care. Once the Fly Lords are vanquished by the Master's power, what happens if they choose to return to the Forest Home?"

"They have deserted the Forest Home!" snapped Night's First Raven. "They have no right to call themselves Free!"

"And yet they do not call any 'Master,'" replied Taris, simply. "They are more Free than either of you."

The Second was practically quivering with rage. "Have a care, Hearth-Tender, lest I make an oath-breaker of myself! You shall not speak such of my tribe, Mighty One or no."

Moon laid his hand gently on his wife's shoulder, feeling the tension vibrating through her muscles. Gradually she responded to his touch, her anger cooling.

"I regret my words, Night's First Raven," said the Mighty One. "They were poorly chosen. But I beg that you understand my dilemma. I have heard what happened to Fire in Deep Woods from his own mouth. If any Hearth-Tender pledges themselves to your Master and has even the slightest doubt in their heart, his fire will consume them. And believe me when I tell you, Shorewalkers, there will be doubt in many hearts."

Moon felt a deep pit yawning in his stomach. Not only was Mighty Taris right, but the problem was possibly even worse than the Hearth-Tender realised. Mighty Lelioko had already warned him that the ritual Ixilinath planned to use to Brand hundreds at a time required nothing less than total commitment from all present-almost seven hundred of them at least. The magic, she had confessed, was too powerful and ancient for her to truly comprehend, but there was every chance that if the ritual were thwarted the Master's fire would consume not only the doubters, but every participant.

"I-" he began, but trailed off, not knowing what to say. Mercifully, the decision was taken out of his hands as a familiar, masked figure drifted into view.

"The Master wishes to speak with you, Mighty Taris," announced the Seneschal.

59

*M*agister Haran Dar held a strategy meeting at dawn. All the senior staff of the Vigilants and the Wardens were present, though Kandira sent one of the Weavers, a skinny, bookish young two-Leaf Magister called Hendrik Dar, in her place. He was a sallow-faced man, his plain green robe worked with white thread and stained with ground-in masonry dust.

"Magister Kandira sends her.. regrets, Learned Magister," said Hendrik as they assembled around the strategy table. "In her words: 'As soon as we can see, we're working, and if we're working I have to be there or someone will bugger it all up.' If you'll pardon my talking like an Exp- ah, like someone with an inappropriately coarse tongue, Learned Magister."

"Are you suggesting Magister Kandira has a potty mouth, Magister Hendrik?" asked Ollan, ambling in behind him carrying a plate of sandwiches. The younger Magister went pale.

"Ah, no, of course not, Learned Magister! I meant only that... ah..."

"Don't worry, man!" chuckled Ollan, pointedly pulling up a chair next to him. "You're quite right, except that usually her coarse language is entirely warranted by the circumstances. If Kandira Dar ever reacts to dire circumstances with a chaste 'oh dear me, whatever shall we do' then we shall surely be done for. Sausage sandwich?"

Haran eyed the plate of food, and the steaming pots of tea and coffee Magritte was bringing in to accompany it. "I wasn't aware I had scheduled a working breakfast, Learned Magister."

"You didn't," agreed Ollan. "But you also didn't expressly forbid it and I for one do not plan on dying on an empty stomach. Not that I plan on doing it at all today anyway, that is."

Magister Hendrik looked from one of the senior Magisters to the other, and gingerly took a sandwich. Taking her place opposite Haran as was traditional, the

High Vigilant looked around. "That's unusual. Isn't Chania coming to the meeting?"

"Your Bard?" said Haran. "Why would she be? This is an emergency council-of-war, not a recital."

Wilhelmina shrugged with a slight rattle of armour. "It's just she usually just.. turns up. Says it helps her to write inspirational songs if she knows what's going on. We've just got used to it, really."

Sir Matthew nodded. "True enough, and her wit is a pleasant distraction in dire times. Though based on what I've seen so far, we do not lack for that.. nor for her beauty." The last remark was addressed to Captain Render, who was helping Magritte arrange food and paperwork in such a way that the twain did not meet in disastrous fashion. The Swordmaster gave him a hard look, but did not respond.

There was a brief commotion at the door. "We will enter!" boomed a voice that Haran recognised. The Vigilants on guard duty didn't seem to agree, and at his gesture Magritte moved to intervene. After a few moments of soft-voiced discussion and some fairly violent swearing, the two Mighty Ones stalked in. To Haran's great surprise, both Mighty Dokan and Mighty Xaraya were wearing simple cloth robes over their leather and buckskin harnesses, though Xaraya looked distinctly ill-at-ease in hers.

"The greetings of the dawn to you all," said Mighty Dokan, as Magritte showed the two Expelled to their seats.

"And to you, of course, Mighty Dokan," said Haran, wondering if he should address the dragon in the courtyard.

"New tailor?" said Ollan, charging in and damning the dragon-fire as usual.

Dokan chuckled. "When Mighty.. ah, Magister Thalia came to our lands, she did us the honour of adopting the dress of a Mighty One, Magister Ollan. Now we come into your halls, and so we do the same. I understand that by your traditions the right to wear 'Leaves' must be earned and so we do not bear them, nor do we adopt the green of your College-"

"-and we never will!" snapped Xaraya, casting a challenging glare around the room.

"-but I hope this goes some way to showing how seriously the Free Tribes take this situation."

"You didn't need to go to all that trouble on my account, my dear," said Ollan with a sidelong glance at Xaraya.

"I have thrown away things stuck in my boot whose opinion I cared about more than yours.. Learned Magister," responded the Mighty One, though she couldn't quite keep a smile from twitching the corner of her mouth.

"Perhaps we could get on?" said Wilhelmina, stiffly. "I am sure the Ski- the Mighty Ones would like to get back to their people, and I have other responsibilities to attend to this morning."

"Very well," said Haran. "The first order of business is that I am greatly concerned as to our lack of intelligence." He shot a warning glance at Ollan before he could crack another joke. "I received word this morning from the Arch-Chancellor that the Dendaril are moving through the Expelled Territories- no, the Forest Home-" he corrected, seeing the Mighty Ones' narrowed eyes "-in some force."

"And where came he by this news?" asked Dokan. "Certainly none of the Free would have sent such a message so far west."

"It came from the Ambassador," said Haran, simply. Sir Matthew started. "What? Not as far as I know, it didn't!"

"Not you, Your Excellency," said Ollan, quietly and now deadly serious. "The only Ambassador who is known simply by that name."

"Queen's Grace!" gasped the Abelian, so surprised that his armour, which was standing behind his chair, took an involuntary step backwards. "The Dragons?"

"Indeed," said Haran. "It was made clear to the Arch-Chancellor, however, that more such information was unlikely to be forthcoming due to the risks involved in gathering it."

"I'll say," said Ollan. "The idea of a Dragon getting infected with those things doesn't bear thinking about."

"Lies!" snorted Xaraya. "All know that the Dragons see through the eyes of their enthralled black eagles! The Little Ones could never catch such a creature!"

"*Did* we know that?" mused Ollan. "I'm not sure we did."

Dokan gave Xaraya a somewhat embarrassed look. "Ah, Mighty Xaraya, did you have occasion to meet Magister Thalia during her visit?"

Xaraya shot him a sharp look. "Briefly. We did not.... see eye-to-eye so chose to stay apart in the interests of.. peace," she spoke the last word as if getting something unpleasant out of her mouth.

"Did you happen to notice the black eagle feathers that adorned her harness?"

Xaraya laughed, suddenly. "Umba's teeth! She downed a Doom Eye? It is rare that they can even be seen, much less struck!"

"That would be Amanda's doing, if I'm any judge," said Ollan. "In her.. line of work she tends not to take kindly to things or people trying to spy on her."

Dokan shrugged. "Whatever the reason, it is believed that the black eagles are very rare, no more alike to a common bird as a Red Bear is to a rabbit. If Magister Thalia or Steel Heart did indeed down one, they may have blinded the Dragons over the Forest Home for a time."

"At the one time when that is most inconvenient," said Haran, grimly. "I have never believed in any sort of gods, but if I did I would think Amanda Devereux a punishment from a particularly devious one."

"I would hesitate to trust information from that source anyway, Learned Magister," said Captain Render. "We have to assume that anything the Dragons tell us furthers their own ends before anything else."

"She speaks truly, Magister Haran," agreed Mighty Dokan. "There are many whose word I would trust implicitly, but the Dragons and their minions are not among them."

"Agreed," said Haran. "Therefore, I propose that we send a scouting party into the Forest Home to assess how far the Dendaril have come and give us a better idea of how much time is left to prepare."

"That task can be safely left to the Free," said Dokan. "There are none who know the Forest Home as we do."

The High Vigilant snorted. "Hah. That's not entirely true and you know it."

"Regardless," Haran said quickly, before an argument could break out, "based on what we have just discussed a party composed only of one... partner in this alliance is unacceptable. We need a unit drawn from the Free Tribes, the Vigilants, and the Wardens. Captain Render, you will select two Wardens to accompany you, with scouts from both the Vigilants and the Free Tribes."

Captain Render nodded. "Yes, Learned Magister. I'll take Sergeant Tika and Guardswoman Dani. Even with the prosthetics she's the best shot in the Volume."

Xaraya bridled. "You cannot expect us to place one of the Free under the command of.. of a city-dweller, much less allow them free reign in the Forest Home."

Haran gave her a level look. "Mighty Xaraya, in case I did not make myself clear yesterday I do, in fact, expect the Free to place themselves under my orders, just as I have placed them under my protection. Nonetheless, if it makes you feel any better, consider that your scout will be present as an advisor and observer to Captain Render's mission."

"I wouldn't expect to tell one of your people how to scout in their own territory anyway, Mighty One," said Render, diplomatically.

"Nevertheless, there is more than one Tribe of the Free present," pointed out Dokan. "We should therefore send two representatives. I will offer my Second, who was the first to sniff out the Fly Lords and bears the Stalking Wolf, making her well-suited to the task. Moreover, unlike your Scouts, she is a warrior of some renown."

Xaraya, seeming to realise she was in danger of being outdone, swiftly changed track. "Then I shall offer... Red Trace in White Snow." Dokan laughed.

"A shrewd decision, Mighty Xaraya. Magister Haran, Red Trace in White Snow is one of the most fierce warriors of the Heart-Eaters, and one of the few to carry the Enraged Bear. He carries little love for his fellow man in his heart, and none whatsoever for the Deluded."

"The who?" said Ollan. "Ah, on reflection I can see who you might be referring to. Are you suggesting, then, that it might be best if this hot-tempered fellow were not kept in close proximity to people whose internal organs he would quite like to turn into a tasty snack? On which subject, by the way, you really should try the sausages."

Haran gave Xaraya another hard look. "Mighty Xaraya, I respect your judgement in this matter, but can you assure me that this.. Red Trace in White Snow will not jeopardise the mission in a flash of temper?"

"He will not," said Xaraya, firmly, though she still could not hold the Magister's eye for long. "His wife, Fleeting Deer, serves as my Third and he will do nothing to disappoint her."

"The Ancestors were most wise," said Dokan, approvingly. "Fleeting Deer has done much to cool that one's hot head, and knowing he has her to return to has taught him caution."

The Magisters exchanged glances. "I am very glad that Scout explained the.. Free Tribes' naming and mating customs to us, or that conversation would have been extremely confusing," confessed Ollan. "Speaking of which, I assume the Vigilants' contribution to this party will be..?"

"Alben Koont," confirmed Wilhelmina, with a look of barely-concealed malevolence at the two Mighty Ones. Much to her evident disappointment, Dokan gave a grave nod of acceptance.

"Ah, the Green Shadow. I had expected as much, and it is well."

Wilhelmina's eyebrows shot up. "What? I thought you hated him?"

"We do not honour those we hate with a Name," replied Dokan. "The Green Shadow is an enemy of the Free, aye, and my First has sworn to hunt him down and slay him for his trespasses, but he is an honourable foe."

"Honourable!" laughed Wilhelmina. "He sneaks up on people and stabs them in the back!"

"Of course," agreed Dokan. "The snake slithers through the grass and bites the unwary hunter, because he is a snake. No warrior could expect a snake to face him breast-to-breast on the field of battle, spear in hand, for the snake has neither breast nor spear."

"Are you calling my best Scout a snake?" growled the High Vigilant.

"Yes," said Dokan. "But there is no shame in it. Were he to pretend to be otherwise, then perhaps. But when there is long grass to be slithered through, there is no better for the task than a snake."

Haran looked around the table. "Very well, then. Unless anyone wishes to propose an addition to the party, it shall consist of Captain Render, Sergeant Tika and Guardswoman Dani of the Second Volume, the Second of the Tree-Searchers, Red Trace in White Snow of the Heart-Eaters, and Scout Alben Koont of the Vigilants. Agreed?"

There was a general mutter of assent around the table. Sir Matthew spoke up. "I am content, Magister Haran, though I suppose I could insist on an Abelian contingent. However since that contingent would have to be me and I am ill-suited to tree-climbing, I will forgo that honour. But do we not have three tribes of the.. Free.. enjoying our hospitality?"

Dokan nodded. "Aye. The Black Skull, though, is new to his position and many Blackbloods have already been lost to the Woe. Their knowledge is also mostly of the far eastern forest and the marshes beyond, a place our scouting party will be unlikely to reach."

Captain Render gave a short laugh. "That's true enough. If we come out the other side and haven't found any Dendaril by then, we've got nothing much to worry about anyway or it's too late."

"Nevertheless, please extend my compliments to the.. Black Skull, and be sure he does not wish to send a representative," said Haran. "I do not desire for this already tense situation to be inflamed any further. Now, Magister Hendrick, I believe the next item on the agenda is your report on progress made towards mounting the first Petard Engine?"

Hendrick, who had been listening to the discussion wide-eyed, shook himself back into focus. "Ah, yes, Learned Magister. As you are no doubt aware, parts of the Eastern Vigil are almost a thousand years old. Moreover, the structural magic..."

Almost an hour later, after a detailed and largely inconsequential report from the Weaver that did at least confirm that Kandira expected to have the Engine mounted, if not fully entrenched, by the end of the following day, Haran was left alone with Ollan in the war-room. When it had become clear that they were not needed for anything else, the Mighty Ones and Captain Render had excused themselves to make arrangements for the patrol, whereas Wilhelmina had sent a runner to find Alben Koont. She and Sir Matthew, being more familiar with the fortress than anyone else in the room, had peppered the Weaver with questions but had largely found the answers to be to their satisfaction.

"A productive meeting I think, eh Haran?" said Ollan, fishing out his pipe. "Interesting to see everyone playing the old two-tile gambit with that patrol of yours, too."

Haran looked at him quizzically. The two-tile was a common move in Impose that both used a piece to attack, and simultaneously got it out of the way of another piece's movement. "How do you mean, Learned Magister?"

Ollan pointed at him with the pipe stem. "You must have spotted it. Did you notice who Render picked?"

"Sergeant Tika and Dani... hmmm. Now that you mention it, they were two of the Guards caught up in that business at Equinox, were they not? The piece of marble that as we speak is being carved into a memorial for the fallen of the War of Rule?"

Ollan nodded. "That's them. But more importantly, they're two of the more prominent Breathers in the Second Volume, and you know that's been causing friction. Render's using this patrol to get them out of the way for a while, and it helps that they're also two competent veterans- though in your Volume it's hard to find someone who isn't."

"Are the Breathers really that much of a problem?" asked Haran. "The religion has been a part of College life almost since its inception."

"They're becoming increasingly vocal, and associated with several anti-College movements, most notably in Kathis," said Ollan, sadly. "It doesn't help that Oberon Thane has been trying to stamp them out and just inflaming the situation. Though I hate to say it, if it weren't for some of Anneke's evil little tricks we might even be looking at a revolution by now."

"To return to the patrol, by the same token, it's obvious why Xaraya is sending this Red Trace," said Haran, realising they were straying from the point. "Clearly she is concerned that, his wife's influence notwithstanding, he might get out of control when surrounded with so many he would usually regard as enemies. As for Alben Koont.."

"A singularly unpleasant individual," said Ollan, wrinkling his nose. "I'm not sure I buy that story about his Seal, but he truly hates the Free Tribes and he certainly knows how to get around their territory."

"Should we be concerned that he might take the opportunity to murder the others and slip away?" mused Haran.

"I'm sure the thought will cross his mind, at least with regard to the Expelled. I took Wilhelmina aside and made sure she impresses upon him that if he gets back to the Vigil without the rest of the patrol, whatever excuse he makes, we'll give him to the Heart-Eaters. I'm sure Fleeting Deer in particular would have some inventive meal suggestions for him, however bad he might smell. Other than that, we'll just have to trust that Captain Render can keep him in line."

"So that only leaves the Second of the Tree-Searchers," said Haran. "Mighty Dokan gave several compelling reasons why she should be chosen, and I know of no reason why he might want rid of her. Which, in light of the other selections, raises some interesting questions."

"Quite so," agreed Ollan. "Is Dokan playing the same game as everyone else, but far more subtly, or is he playing a different game altogether?"

"He may simply not be playing a game at all, Learned Magister," pointed out Haran.

"Ah, Haran. Everyone is playing the game. The only difference is what they think the rules are."

60

*M*agister Thalia Daran had left strict instructions that she should be knocked awake at dawn if she had not already risen, so when she heard the first thump, she assumed that was what it was. When she levered her eyes open, however, the room was still almost completely dark. She padded barefoot over to the window and peeked past the curtain, to see that whilst the sky was certainly getting lighter, dawn had not yet broken.

Thump.

Now mostly awake, she could tell the sound was coming from the room next door, which had been prepared for Delys and Amanda Devereux. When the drunken Swordmaster had shown no signs of waking, she and one of the maids had seen to the task of settling her into the hastily-repaired double bed, though her sword had been too heavy to lift and had stayed firmly where it was. Briefly she wondered if the Operative had arrived at the Green Palace late at night and she and Delys were renewing their relationship in enthusiastic fashion, but that seemed unlikely. After a moment's consideration, she summoned her staff into her hand and headed out to see what was going on. Stepping out onto the landing, she surprised Herenford, who was approaching her door with a breakfast tray. He took in her night-dress, bare feet and staff with a quick glance.

"Your Excellency! I was just coming to give you your wake-up call- is something the matter?"

"That's what I'm-" began Thalia, but she was immediately interrupted by another thud from Delys' room. "That's it, I'm going in!"

She pushed open the door, not bothering to knock, and took in the scene just in time to throw out her staff sideways to block the adjutant from following her. "Wait outside, please, Herenford, I will be fine."

She stepped in, closing the door pointedly behind her. Delys was standing by the bed, stark naked, banging her head slowly on the window.

"Delys! What in Thelen's name are you doing?"

The little blonde Swordmaster turned to look at her, her usually tightly braided hair half-loosened and dishevelled. In the half-light Thalia could see that she was crying, but she couldn't see any reason why.

Hurts. Delys signed the world slowly, as if even moving was causing her pain.

Thalia sighed inwardly. With Devereux still keeping an eye on Athas, she had been depending on Delys to accompany her to the Alabaster Durance that morning. The last thing she needed was for her to have some kind of nervous breakdown. After a moment, though, the look of utter misery on the younger woman's face drove such selfish thoughts from her mind.

"What hurts? Your head? If you keep banging it on the window I'm not surprised!"

Delys shook her head firmly, and from the expression of pure agony that followed it immediately regretted it. *No. Head hurts inside.*

"You've got a headache?" said Thalia, trying not to laugh in relief as she began to study the Swordmaster with her Aethersight. "Let me see.... oh. Blood, ice and fire, but that looks to be a particularly monstrous hangover."

Delys gave her a desperate look, and sat down on the edge of the bed, her head clutched in her hands. She was sobbing with pain. Not wishing to prolong the girl's suffering any longer, Thalia reached out with a little Aether and soothed the headache- it was certainly much easier to fix someone else's than your own.

"Herenford?" she called softly. "Put the breakfast tray in my room, and bring us some ice-water please, as quickly as you can." She turned back to Delys. "Come on, let's get you dressed before he comes back. You'll give the poor man a heart attack."

Delys grinned at her, the pain already mostly gone. Within ten minutes she was drinking copious amounts of water and tucking into a plate of bacon and eggs. Thalia, addressing her own bowl of grains and sliced fruit, eyed her curiously through the steam of her tea- she had given Herenford a little of the Daxalai leaves from Sir Matthew, and the man had made an excellent job of preparing it. Something about this was bothering her, and it took her a moment to realise what it was. In all the time she had known Delys, the Swordmaster had never been ill. Mortally wounded, yes, on one occasion, and lightly injured on several others, but such was the lot of the warrior. But never could she remember her having a headache, or a cold, or being sick.

The obvious explanation was something in the khile brandy she had drunk the day before. Well, yes, said a sour little voice in her head, they call it alcohol, but though the amount Delys had downed had stunned Sir Terence Thalia had seen her intoxicated before. The cider-like drink the Expelled brewed, for one thing, had a kick like an Abelian war-horse, but the next morning Delys had awoken as aggravatingly fresh as usual. Were this an experiment being carried out in a Manse laboratory, the next step would be to expose the subject to various intoxicants and pathogens in the hope of finding which ones had an effect on her, but even ignoring the obvious ethical concerns- and some Magisters would- she had no basis for a comparison.

Had something about Delys simply changed? She remembered when Amanda Devereux had sneezed on the way to Ratheram Forest, which for her had been the harbinger of a total failure of the arcane technology that apparently kept her alive. But for all that the two women had in common, their physiology certainly couldn't be more different, so there was unlikely to be a common cause. She decided to see if she could get some answers from the horse's mouth.

"Delys, are you feeling better now?"

Delys, her mouth full of bacon, nodded.

"Have you ever had a hangover before? I mean, had a headache and felt really sick when you woke up after drinking some alcohol?"

The little Swordmaster cocked her head to one side and give her a puzzled look. *No.*

"Have you ever been sick at all? Had a cold, a... sore throat, a cough, anything like that?"

No. Delys had stopped eating now, and was staring at Thalia intently. *Hungry dream.*

Thalia was thunderstruck. With everything else that had happened with Athas, the ambush and the ransacked Green Palace, she had almost forgotten about the strange incident on the way to Dalliance. Perhaps Delys had been subjected to some sort of attack- or perhaps Athas had been right after all, and it had been the Winnowing Ague, however unlikely that seemed. Certainly 'hungry dream' seemed to fit what she knew of the disease. Quickly she looked the Swordmaster's Pattern over again, but she was no expert in the art of healing and Delys' Pattern had been so extensively Folded that she barely knew what it was supposed to look like, much less whether anything significant had changed.

"Well, I can't see anything wrong with you now, so that's something. Are you sure you're fit to accompany me to the Alabaster Durance today?"

Delys nodded again, very firmly. Amanda had entrusted Thalia's safety to her, and it was clear the little Swordmaster intended to take her duty seriously. At least, thought Thalia with a smile, as seriously as she took anything.

"Very well then. Finish your breakfast and make sure you have a thorough wash, and we'll unpack your battle armour. I want you looking suitably intimidating today."

Delys grinned at her again, and suddenly hooked her hands into claws, baring her teeth with a theatrical growl. The effect was rather spoilt by the fact that she had bits of bacon stuck in them.

In spite of herself, Thalia laughed. Perhaps she had been worried about nothing after all.

61

++ *Operative returning to full cognition. Subject status report: Blood pressure 108 over 70. Heart rate 39 BPM. Vital signs show minor negative fluctuation.*++

And good morning to you too, Daniel, thought Devereux, grumpily. Since she and Delys had begun... whatever exactly their relationship was, she never felt properly rested if she slept apart from her. There were more important things to think about right now, though. Athas' vitals still didn't exactly look bad, but they were definitely slightly weaker than they had been the night before. She hopped off the bed, and went to take a look at him. The big man was still apparently sleeping peacefully, though his breathing was slower and less deep than she might have expected.

She gave him an experimental poke. "Athas? Athas, wake up, damn it!"

There was no response. She tried giving him a firmer shake, but the big Guard wasn't stirring. Thinking to check the site of the surgery, she lifted up the tightly-tucked bed-sheet, and was surprised to see a faint, silver glow. Athas' Seal was active. It was only glowing very dimly, but nevertheless it was certainly doing.. something.

Healer Alana chose that moment to make an appearance, carrying a breakfast tray. "Good morning, Master Devereux," she said with a smile. "Is our patient hungry?"

"Something is," growled Devereux, pointing at the Seal. "What the fuck is going on here?"

The Healer's face fell. "Oh. Oh no."

"Oh no? Oh no what? What's the matter with him now? You said he'd wake up this morning!"

"I..." began Alana. "I am sorry, Master Devereux, but I think your friend has contracted the Ague. His Seal is glowing because of the drain on his Spirit."

Devereux felt cold in her gut. "Y-yeah, but he's in the best hospital in Abelia, isn't he? You can help him, right?" She thought of mentioning how the Savalans

241

had treated their people, but as far as the Abelians were concerned Thalia's party didn't know anything about who had ambushed them.

"I.. cannot," said Alana, setting down the tray and backing towards the door. "There is no known cure for the Ague. If he is strong, he'll survive. If not..."

Devereux took a menacing step forward. "Listen to me very carefully. Athas is my friend, and if he dies, I will see to it personally that you do not live to fail anyone else. And then I'm going to find every one of those jumped-up quacks who treated him and do the same to them. *Do you fucking understand me?*"

"L-look," said the Healer, holding up her hands in a placating gesture. "I'm just telling you what I've been taught. It's not the fault of anyone who treated him- you can see for yourself that his injuries are completely healed. The Ague.. it seems to strike completely at random and can only be detected through its symptoms. He might even have already had it when we healed him."

Devereux's anger cooled. Biting the heads off the people who might be able to help wasn't going to get her anywhere, though her threats did at least seem to drawn more information out of the Healer. "So you're saying you can't.. see the Ague at all, even if it's killing someone?"

Alana sighed. "No. Other than a small, steady and persistent drain on the subject's Spirit, there is nothing in their Pattern to suggest that anything is wrong."

Devereux saw her opening. "Wait a minute.. so it's the drain on their Aether- their Spirit, that kills them? So what if we just give him some of ours? Won't that help keep him alive?"

The Healer blanched. "That would mean making a direct link between yourself and someone suffering the Ague! It would be far too risky to attempt."

"But didn't you already do that yesterday when you were treating him?" pressed Devereux.

"That- that's not the same thing!" gasped Alana. "It's.. not easy to explain to a.. to someone who isn't trained in chirurgia. I'm sorry, but I really must go back to my other duties. I hope your friend recovers soon- I'll have someone see to setting up a feeding tube so he doesn't starve while he sleeps."

She hurried away, and Devereux let her go. It was clear that the Healer was going to be little help. At least one of her concerns had been addressed- she had been worrying about keeping Athas fed. But that still left two very serious problems to deal with. The first, and most immediate, was what to tell Thalia, and for that matter how. She could probably find someone to send a message, but the Magister was due to meet the Queen that morning and that mission was possibly critical to the survival of the College, the Abelians, and the Free Tribes. If she knew Athas' condition, Thalia would be forced to make a terrible decision and even if she went through with the audience, she might be dangerously distracted.

No, sending Thalia a message was out of the question for now. It was a harsh decision to make, possibly, and one the Magister might not forgive her for, but it had to be made. That didn't mean, though, that she was just going to let Athas die. She brought the Hercules suite up to full tactical alert, making sure she'd have ample warning if anyone approached, and then reached out to touch the big Guard's Seal. She didn't want anyone seeing what she was doing in case they realised her own was a fake.

She'd never done anything like this before- at least, not willingly- but in theory since she was capable of basic magic, she should be able to give Athas' some of her

Aether- a transfusion, in effect. She almost expected to feel something from the Seal, like the faint electrical tingle that happened whenever Thalia borrowed some power from her, but there was nothing.

Will, that was the thing. *The causation of change under will,* as the Crowley quote the Hercules suite had supplied when she first encountered magic went. She wondered if there was anything to the effect in one of the Books of Thelen. Suddenly, she realised she had done something similar to this before- at Equinox, when Delys had been lost to a berserker rage, she had managed to calm the little Swordmaster by touching her and willing her to come back.

Come back to me, Athas.

Nothing happened. Of course, this situation was different. Even the most powerful of the Savalan Wizards hadn't been able to actually heal the Ague, only to keep the sufferer alive while they fought it. She needed to find another way to-

++Operative Alert: Two inbound contacts closing at approx. 1.5 m/s. Range 200 metres. ETTC 2 minutes 25 seconds allowing for topography.++

That didn't help matters. She felt an impotent fury rising, and savagely countermanded her medical suite's attempt to release a mood stabiliser. She grabbed Athas roughly by the shoulder where his Seal was and tried to imagine him getting stronger, getting healthier. Still nothing.

++ETTC 2 minutes.++

She thought back, desperately, trying to recall everything she had been told about magic and healing. Magister Haran had told her that fire was the most primal expression of magic, lightning the most controlled, and ice the most unnatural. Not much help there. *The more a man knows, the less he understands.* That was from one of the Books of Thelen, but it was of no more use. Or was it? Master Yukan had told her that a warrior fought without thinking, because their instincts were faster and more reliable than conscious thought. He had been appalled by the Hercules suite, the SUCS system's physical overrides in particular. Perhaps control was the answer here- at the moment, there were effectively two minds in charge of her body, rather than one.

Disable all non-critical Hercules functions.

++Operative alert: Procedure is not advised. Condition and tactical monitoring will be unavailable. ETTC to contacts 1 minute 20 seconds. Confirm system shutdown?++

Confirm, damn it!

++Hercules suite shutting down. Immediate reboot will be available on request. SUCS offline.++

That was it, then. No sensors, no combat enhancements, no boosted muscles or enhanced cognition. Just her, and the few pieces of meat that genuinely had the right to be called Amanda Devereux. Or which would have, were that actually her name.

Athas! Athas, take what you need, damn you!

For a moment, there was still no response. She felt tears pricking at the corners of her eyes, felt herself flushing red, her heart racing. The medical suite had taken over so many of the basic functions of her body that without its help, it was hard to keep her emotions in check. But of course that was probably part of the problem anyway. Unable to hold back her misery any longer, she let the tears flow, felt a hollow pit of despair open up in her gut.

"Athas! Don't you dare die on me you fucking-"

And then, suddenly, she felt something open up inside of her. A rush of energy seemed to flow from the very core of her being and down her arm, pouring into the big Guard. It seemed to last for a sob-wracked eternity, her desperate fury at the unfairness of the young man's fate finding expression in both body and soul.

"Hey! Hey, come on now, don't cry. We're here to help."

She suddenly became aware that someone was gently lifting her away from Athas. Though she hadn't even realised that she'd closed them, her eyes were screwed tight shut, and when she forced them open the last of her trapped tears gushed out onto her cheeks.

++Operative Alert: Operative vital signs fluctuating. Medical suite re-initialising in one second unless countermanded. Addendum: Aether reserves at 53.2%++

Even as she gently pried herself from the grasp of the man holding her, who turned out to be a burly but kindly-looking hospital Porter, she felt her mood stabilising. She let the Hercules suite reboot.

"There now," said the Porter, softly. "I know it looks bad, but people come around from the Ague all the time. Healer Alana sent us to set up a feeding tube, and since your friend here is with the Ambassador, we've broken out the good stuff."

"Aye," said his companion, a Healer. "This here gunge's got mulched-up khile fruit in it. Give's it a bit 'o fizz, if y'get my meaning."

++Subject status update: Blood pressure 109 over 70. Heart rate 41 BPM. Vital signs stable.++

Devereux gave the men a smile of genuine relief. "Thank you. I'm sure that'll be very helpful."

"Now then, this bit can get a tiny bit messy," said the Healer, starting to unspool a length of tube from a trolley the two men had brought with them. "I reckon you'd best go take a little walk while we get 'im hooked up, eh?"

"Probably best take one of them bacon sarnies with you too," said the Porter, with a pointed glance at the tray Alana had brought in. "Smell of those beauties cooking's been driving me mad. I'm not saying they won't be here when you get back, but.."

"..but yes, that's exactly what 'e's sayin'," put in his colleague. "Anyway, t'would be a crime to let 'em get cold."

Devereux took the hint- and a couple of the sandwiches- and took her leave. She had somewhere important to go, in any case.

62

*a*rch-Chancellor Derelar Thane had to read the report three times before he entirely believed it. He was so engrossed in the third reading that he didn't even notice Anneke knocking. After a couple of attempts, the Vice-Chancellor bustled in anyway, shrugging off a blast from the defensive ward that would have reduced most Magisters to a gibbering wreck on the carpet. That, at least, got Derelar's attention.

"Vice-Chancellor?" he said, mildly. "I hope the defensive enchantments did not inconvenience you unduly? It is usually advisable to wait until given permission to enter."

"There's no time to worry about that right now, Arch-Chancellor," said Anneke, otherwise completely ignoring the question. "I assume you've read the reports from the Vigil?"

Derelar took a sip of his coffee, which turned out to have gone stone-cold whilst he was reading, and grimaced. "I have done little else since I awoke. It makes for.. interesting reading, to say the least."

"That's putting it mildly," said Anneke. "I wouldn't have thought three experienced Magisters like Haran, Kandira and Ollan would go as far as letting Expelled into the Vigil. The damn thing was rebuilt specifically to keep those savage idiots out!"

"I would contend that that very experience is the reason we entrusted Haran with the task of defending the Vigil in the first place," said Derelar. "And in point of fact, the purpose of the fortress is to defend the Empire from threats from the east, not specifically to stop the Expelled. Magister Haran has clearly concluded that the danger from the Dendaril is an order of magnitude greater than that from these... Free Tribes. I would think that given your own opinions on the Shrive-Ticks, you would be in complete agreement with him."

"Hmph," grunted Anneke, pouring herself a large measure of wine. "There you

245

have me, Arch-Chancellor. I still can't say I'm overly fond of the idea of the Expelled running about unchecked like that."

"The majority are still encamped at the foot of the Vigil's walls," pointed out Derelar. "Though admittedly, their Warlocks- the Mighty Ones, as they call them- seem to be allowed in and they are probably the most dangerous."

"Then there's the 'unfortunate error' with the recall orders for Sir Matthew," said Anneke, although this time she was grinning. "I wouldn't have thought Haran capable of pulling a trick like that, but it works to our advantage."

"How so?" said Derelar. He considered re-heating the coffee, but decided it was too far gone, and so made his way over to the sideboard for a fresh cup.

"The Expelled know Sir Matthew by reputation and they've seen him in action," said Anneke. "Him staying at the Vigil will be very useful to help keep them in line."

"Agreed," said Derelar. "The Symposium will, of course, find out what happened, but I am sure we can impress upon them that things in that regard are better left as they are- by the virtue of our arguments, not by other methods, of course."

"Of course, Arch-Chancellor," said Anneke, giving him her most innocent look. "I have some other news from my own sources that you may find interesting, though. Ambassador Thalia is due to meet Queen Tondarin this morning. Her party was apparently attacked on the road yesterday and suffered casualties, but no-one of note or name."

"Has the Ambassador reported in officially yet?" asked Derelar.

"I'm afraid not. According to my sources in Abellan, when Stalis let them investigate the Embassy the Royal Guard were.. shall we say, enthusiastically thorough. Thalia is currently without a secure Messaging Crystal until the Abelians return those they confiscated, and even when we do get them back I'd still prefer to ship over new ones that we can trust haven't been tampered with."

Derelar gave her a level look. "Your agent could, of course, offer our Ambassador the use of whatever channel they are currently using to relay messages back."

"That's effectively what they *are* doing, Arch-Chancellor," said Anneke, smugly. "The only thing is she doesn't know about it, and neither do the Abelians, which is the way I'd prefer to keep it."

The Arch-Chancellor considered this for a moment. While he would certainly prefer that Thalia could communicate with the College directly, risking compromising Anneke's own secret channel by exposing it to the Ambassador left open the prospect of losing contact altogether. "Very well, Vice-Chancellor, but you will make getting a secure replacement Crystal installed in the Green Palace a high priority, is that clear?"

"Crystal clear, Arch-Chancellor," said Anneke with a soft chuckle at the pun. "I'll have a shipment added to Magister Elsabeth's baggage train when she leaves to take over from Thalia."

Derelar gave a small nod of satisfaction. He had fully expected Anneke to press for a Belus or a Thane to be the new Ambassador to Abelia, but to his surprise the Vice-Chancellor had agreed with his and Stalis' choice of Elsabeth Thule, the current Chair of Mendarant in Sommerlan. Elsabeth was known for a flamboyant dress-sense and distinctive personal style, but was shrewd and had a true flair for negotiation. She also had no current personal attachments, making her both available for the move and difficult to manipulate. Young and ambitious for a Chair, being barely into her thirties, her rapid rise had been worrying the city's current Chancellor who would be quite relieved to be rid of her.

"Now there is one other thing, which I have left until last because it raises some intriguing questions," Anneke continued.

"More of them? Mysteries are one thing we do not lack for, Vice-Chancellor."

"And this one is a real beauty. You'll recall that only roughly half of the Expelled tribes have been sighted at the Vigil?"

Derelar flicked his eyes down to the report. "The Heart-Eaters, Tree-Searchers and Blackbloods, yes? Leaving the Stonesingers, Hearth-Tenders and Shore-walkers unaccounted for?"

Anneke nodded. "Just so. Add to that the tribe responsible for guarding the now-destroyed ruins of Xodan- a tribe who would have saved us all a lot of trouble if they'd made a better job of it, I might add- and all their children."

"All their children?" said Derelar, keeping his expression unreadable. "That detail seems to have been omitted from the official report."

"It's more like the children simply aren't mentioned," said Anneke. "The report just doesn't say anything about them at all, but my people have overheard a few conversations among the Expelled. It seems that whenever war breaks out, all the children are entrusted to one tribe, the Hearth-Tenders, who are sworn to complete non-violence."

"And since the Hearth-Tenders are missing..." mused Derelar. Anneke nodded.

"Mhm. The Expelled weren't sure if they were heading into a fight, so they sent the children away. But away where, was the question. Any safe refuge they could have fled to would seem to be somewhere they could have all gone. Well, it turns out that the other tribes have struck some kind of bargain with someone or something called 'Ixil.' Whoever this Ixil is, they promised protection from the Shrive-Ticks, in fact actual immunity, but the price was their allegiance."

"And not wishing to pledge allegiance to the College was the very reason the ancestors of the Expelled were driven out in the first place," said Derelar. "Ironic that in order to preserve their tradition of independence, the Expelled have come to us."

"It's a shame they didn't go to Abelia," said Anneke, sourly. "But the route to the Farspan probably went too close to the Dendaril advance, and the Abelians tend to shoot first and ask questions later if anyone unauthorised tries to cross it."

"Is there any evidence of the Dendaril themselves trying to cross the Farspan?" asked Derelar.

"No, and that's interesting as well. But I'm most intrigued by this Ixil, whoever or whatever it is."

"Was not the Garnet Keep at Phyre built by a Warlock called Ixilinath, the same that the flame-wreath is named for?" said Derelar. "Could there be a connection?"

"Not unless he's pushing a thousand years old!" laughed Anneke.

"Could he be a Dragon, or one disguised as a human?" said Derelar, interested to see how Anneke would respond to the suggestion.

"I doubt it. They do live for a ridiculous amount of time, but I can't see why a Dragon would bother building a castle, much less go recruiting an army of Expelled barbarians. No, I think the most likely explanation is a descendant, possibly a very powerful Mighty One with delusions of grandeur. Still, the claim of a method to protect against the Shrive-Ticks bears investigating."

"Agreed," said Derelar. "We will raise the matter of this Ixil at the Symposium and see if anyone can throw more light upon it."

"I'll look into where these other Expelled might have gone, as well," said Anneke. "If we can get hold of one of them and work out how this protection of theirs works, assuming it's even genuine, it could be extremely useful."

"Vice-Chancellor, I must stress that I want no hostile action taken against this Ixil without my direct approval. We have quite enough enemies and threats at the moment without aggravating a fresh one."

Anneke nodded. "On that subject, I have some documents for the Imperial Games for your approval."

Derelar was momentarily nonplussed. The Imperial Games were a series of sporting events that saw champions from each Volume compete in a variety of tests of strength, speed and skill, but the most recent Games had been cancelled due to the War of Rule. He took a moment to gather his wits before responding.

"Am I to take it that this is connected to the redeployed Volumes of the Guard?"

Anneke nodded, a broad grin splitting her face. "Astute as always, Arch-Chancellor! Yes, we've been meaning to arrange a date for the reinstated Games since the end of the War of Rule. Since the tournament fields are traditionally just south of the Silverun, it gives us a convenient and very public reason for plenty of burly Guardsmen to be milling about within striking distance of Abelia. It's been a little more than the usual three years since the last Games, after all, so the fields are pretty overgrown. Even the Volumes that are committed in other places will still be able to spare a champion or two."

"The Eighth Volume will be aggrieved," pointed out Derelar. "Their finest Swordmaster and one of their strongest Guardsmen are currently stuck in Abellan."

"Ah, yes, that is unfortunate," said Anneke, pointedly failing to mention that the Guardsman Derelar was referring to was currently lying injured in an Abelian hospital bed, a fact Derelar's own sources had appraised him of. "However, we may well turn even that to our advantage."

Derelar steepled his hands on his desk. Despite all his doubts about Anneke, it was still genuinely a pleasure to watch her play the game.

"We're already making sure the news-sheets tell everyone that the Wardens are visiting the Eastern Vigil as part of a goodwill tour." said the Vice-Chancellor. "We just need to expand that concept. News that the Expelled are clustering around the fortress is already coming out, so we invite a contingent to the games."

Derelar could see where this was going. "And if we invite the Expelled, traditionally our enemies, why not the Abelians?"

Anneke smiled. "I do sometimes wonder if you can read my mind, Arch-Chancellor. If the Abelians do send a delegation, the champions of the Eighth can travel with them. Of course it will delay the start of the event, but so much the better."

Derelar was looking at the documents that Anneke had placed on his desk, which were mostly orders for supplies, construction and redeployment. "It is a good idea, Vice-Chancellor, but I feel it does not go far enough."

Anneke, completely unconcerned, raised an eyebrow. "No?"

"No. I think that if we are going to invite the Abelians and Expelled, we should cast our net still further. We should invite competitors from Daxalai, Jandalla, Har'ii and the Toskan Federation. Wild-card competitors, too, in the initial rounds. For too long we have had only vague ideas of the abilities of the rival powers of the world- I think it high time that changed. Let these Games become a truly international affair, and we will reap a fine harvest of both silver and intelligence, I think."

Anneke put a hand on her chin thoughtfully. "It could be done. The barracks at Rally are largely disused and could be converted into accommodation for the champions. That would also give us an excuse to have a Volume less than a day's march from the Pentus Line. We'd need to press the Symposium for an exemption to the Warlock Laws, but if we're going to invite the Free Tribes then we'd need to do that anyway."

"Free Tribes?"

"It's what the Expelled call themselves," said Anneke. "If we're going to have some as guests we need to watch that, they get very prickly about it. There's also some quite important information about their naming and, er, mating practices that would need to be made clear to anyone dealing with them. Still!" she clapped her hands together delightedly, "This will be quite the undertaking, and a great opportunity!"

"I am pleased that you are so enthused, Vice-Chancellor," said Derelar, and largely meant it. "Just do not lose sight of the deeper goal, and let us remember that if the Dendaril break through in the east, we will have far more important things to worry about."

Anneke made a sour face. "Oh, definitely, Arch-Chancellor. For a moment I almost thought you were thinking of inviting some of them, too."

63

*W*hen Jerik woke up in the grubby, but comfortable, room Julius had rented for them in the Billowing Jib, one of the more basic inns in the Upper Tier of Freeport, he found that the Magister was already awake, and staring at the talking box.

"Ah, good morning, Jerik," said the Magister, indicating a steaming bowl on the small table. "Breakfast this morning is some sort of spiced porridge. I'm not sure what the spice is, exactly, but it has the distinct merit of not being fish."

Splashing some water from the bucket by his bed on his face, Jerik offered a silent prayer of thanks for that. When they had arrived late the previous night in search of a hot meal, the entire menu had been fish of some sort. Given the lack of arable land of any quality on the island, that wasn't all that surprising. He took up a spoon, and had an experimental taste.

"Hm, you're right. Not bad at all. What are you doing with that thing?"

"This? I found myself unable to sleep last night and whilst going through the bags for some reading material, I came across it. It provided a suitable distraction."

Jerik took a larger spoonful of the porridge, enjoying the warmth. "I dunno what's so distracting about it, Julius," he said, once his mouth was clear. "It's buggered."

"Even were that true, it remains a most singular device," said Julius. "However, it is not, in point of fact, buggered, or any other colourful euphemism for being rendered non-functional for that matter. Within this device lies a tiny cell, comprised of a metallic compound with which I am unfamiliar- indeed, since it was created by Amanda Devereux, it may even not naturally exist in this world. It maintains a tiny charge of energy, very similar to lightning."

"Yeah, you said that before," said Jerik. "But it ran out of... lightning, didn't it?"

"Not completely," replied Julius. "As it turns out, even after we lost contact with Operative Devereux a tiny charge remained. When I moved the box out of the bag last night, I noted that part of its Pattern had entered a state of high excitation."

"It was supposed to help Amanda find Maike Dain, I think," mused Jerik. "Not that she's got any chance to go chasing after her right now, what with Magister Thalia getting packed off to Abelia as the Ambassador." Hearing that particular piece of inn gossip had nearly made Jerik fall off his chair.

"Indeed," said Julius. "So we are left with some interesting data. When last heard of, Maike Dain was in the custody of the Vice-Chancellor. The Toskan sailor whose story brings us here in pursuit of Willow-Sigh Wen mentioned a red-headed woman accompanying her who was possessed of a violent temper and a foul mouth."

"That seems to fit that little harridan," agreed Jerik.

"Additionally, the Toskan mentioned that both women had recently escaped from an 'evil sorceress'. Whilst I would not presume to make such a value judgement without much more extensive evidence, there are many who would ascribe such a description to Anneke Belus. We should certainly entertain the notion, then, that Maike Dain and Willow-Sigh Wen escaped from House Belus together, and that this device is reacting to Miss Dain's proximity."

"Oh great," said Jerik, flatly. Maike Dain was not someone he relished the idea of crossing paths with again. "It's a shame we can't.. put some more lightning in it, I suppose."

"Actually," said Julius with a smile, "I rather think we can. The Pattern of most of the device is indescribably complex, but that of the energy cell is fairly simple. I believe I have identified the part of it in which the lightning is stored. With your permission, I will attempt to.. rejuvenate it."

"My permission?" said Jerik, surprised. "If that's because of the whole 'just Jerik and Julius' thing, it's taking it a bit far. You're still in charge."

"Not a bit of it," replied Julius. "It is merely that the device is your property, not mine, and I cannot be absolutely certain that this attempt will not irredeemably damage it."

Jerik shrugged. "Fair enough. It's already buggered, so you might as well try to fix it."

Julius gave him a sharp look. "As I said, it is most definitely *not*- oh, why in Mendarant's inkwell do I bother? Please stand back, Jerik."

"Why? Is it dangerous?"

"If I read the Pattern correctly, too *much* lightning may cause the device to, ahem, explode. Or merely catch fire."

"You can say that about anything, really," pointed out Jerik. Julius gave him a level stare, then laughed.

"Ahah, yes, I suppose that is true. Onward in the pursuit of knowledge, then!"

He extended a hand carefully towards the box, and Jerik thought that maybe for a moment he saw the air around the device shimmer. Then the Magister sagged, as if he had just made a great effort.

"Was that it?" asked Jerik.

"*Was that it?*" snapped Julius. "I would have you know that I just performed a feat of extremely exacting high-precision thaumaturgy!"

"It's just that I was expecting, you know, lightning."

Julius glowered at him. "Were I a man given to idle threats, I would say you are proceeding in a manner likely to cause you to witness more lightning than you would find tolerable, and at extremely close-quarters. However, since I am not such a man, I will merely suggest that you see if the device is no longer, to use your preferred idiom, buggered."

Jerik reached for the button on the box, but then stopped. "Are you sure it's not going to blow up?"

"I am beginning to wish that it had," said Julius, slightly grumpily. "But no, the device appears stable, at least for now."

Approaching much as he might a particularly angry dog, Jerik carefully pressed down the button. After a moment, Amanda Devereux's synthesised voice filled the room.

"Jerik? What the hell is going on? Your tracker just downloaded a whole mass of diagnostics to me. I thought it was out of charge!"

"Operative Devereux, this is Magister Julius Thule," said Julius, leaning close to the box. "Am I to take it that my attempts to repair this device were successful?"

"I'm here too, Amanda," put in Jerik, quickly.

"Well, you're half right, Learned Magister," replied the box. *"You've managed to restore about a third of its charge, but whatever you did has damaged the power cell. It's discharging unevenly- the circuits will burn out any minute."*

"Unfortunate," said Julius, sadly. "Nevertheless, a partial success is better than no success at all."

"Hey, I'm impressed," said the box. *"Look, there's a couple of things you should know. Jerik, Athas is sick. He's got the Winnowing Ague, but I'm doing all I can. Del's looking after Thalia."*

"You keep him alive, you hear me?" growled Jerik. "Athas is a good lad!"

"Yes, he is," agreed the box. *"The other thing is that you're very close to Maike Dain. The tracker puts you less than half a click away."*

"Half a what?" asked Jerik, confused.

"Er, under two thousand feet? I've got to go- and don't try to use the communicator again. I think if you close the circuit once more it might overload catastrophically."

Jerik released the button and hopped back in alarm. "You said it was stable!"

"I said stable *for now*," pointed out Julius. "Which proved accurate. I must declare myself quite satisfied with the outcome of this experiment, Jerik. Not only was I able to partially restore this device, but we have gained valuable data. For Maike Dain's presence in Freeport to be a coincidence seems staggeringly unlikely."

Jerik was still eyeing the box doubtfully. "I'm not sure I like the idea of carrying this thing around after that."

"I dislike the idea of leaving it for an innocent bystander to stumble upon even more," said Julius. "Put it in the top of your pack for now until we have an opportunity to safely dispose of it. Now, I think it time we paid a visit to the Last Anchor."

"You want to visit a flea-pit pub at this time in the morning?" asked Jerik, incredulously.

"Indeed. The establishment will be less busy, and we will have a better chance to differentiate long-term tenants from the regular clientele. Now do come along!"

They headed downstairs, through the main dining area of the inn which was inevitably decorated with fishing nets, floats, and a large, sea-scarred ship's wheel. The cook was serving up more bowls of the hot porridge to early customers, as well as to a few who looked like they had never got around to leaving.

"A fine breakfast repast, my good man," said Julius amiably as they passed. "It certainly made a welcome change from the fish!"

"Nah," chuckled the cook. "S'seaweed porridge spiced wi' ground lobster-shell. Anyfing 'round 'ere y' eat that didn't come outta the sea, y' prob'ly shouldn't be eatin' it."

Exchanging a resigned glance, Julius and Jerik stepped out into the morning sunlight. At least this part of Freeport didn't smell of fish, thought Jerik. He had taken a few more strides before he noticed the Magister wasn't behind him. Turning, he saw Julius picking up something from the ground near the inn door.

"What's that? Feh, a roll-up? I didn't even know you were a smoker, let alone a desperate one."

Julius took an experimental sniff. "I am not, but the study of aroma is often key to the art of investigation, and this particular one tells a most singular story."

"I don't see how. It's just a cheap dog-end. All sorts of people smoke them." Like Yrena, thought Jerik, suddenly. How long had it been since he'd thought about her?

"This one, however, is a curious beast," insisted Julius. "The wrapping paper is indeed cheap, but the tobacco is of excellent quality- Chancellor's Silver Leaf, if I am not mistaken."

"Shit, that's the good stuff, all right!" exclaimed Jerik. "A pouch of that'll set you back ten Quoits, if you can even find it."

"Indeed," agreed Julius. "In point of fact, this particular vintage has not been available in the Empire since the beginning of the War of Rule- the plantation in Imperial Jandalla was destroyed in the civil strife that gripped that territory when the leadership of the College was in doubt. I believe one of the last shipments was issued to the officers of the Verge City Guard shortly before the Howling Plague."

"Fuck me," pronounced Jerik, with feeling. "How do you know things like that?"

"I listen, I observe, and I remember," said Julius, simply. "But the unusual provenance of the hindquarters of this particular canine is not the most singular fact in the matter."

"It isn't?" said Jerik, after a moment to decipher Julius' phrase back to 'dog-end'.

"It is not. What is most singular about it is that I found the exact twin of it near the docks when we arrived last night. The smoker of these expensive, yet ill-cultured, narcotics has now been present at two locations we have visited, and on both occasions the cigarette had been only recently extinguished."

Jerik felt ice run down his spine. Somebody was following them.

64

*A*manda Devereux stepped silently out of the shadowed alcove she had hidden in when the Hercules suite had suddenly received the unexpected transmission from Jerik's tracker. It wasn't that she was incapable of carrying on a discussion on her communication system at the same time as she was sneaking around the Royal Hospital- she had used it during an operation many times before, after all- but it was considered good practice to avoid multi-tasking when it was unnecessary. In particular, if she had unexpectedly needed to talk her way out of trouble things could have got complicated.

Investigating the quiet hallways of the building felt at once reassuringly familiar, and worryingly alien. Certainly, it was hardly the first time that she had infiltrated a facility undercover in order to find out what was going on there- for that matter it wasn't even her first hospital. Unbidden, memories of an underground laboratory in Chechnya came to her mind. A bio-mafia organisation had dissected abducted civilians and sold on their harvested organs, passing off the sterilised merchandise as the latest lab-grown replacements. The corrupt doctors operating the place had been terrifyingly resourceful at keeping the unwilling 'donors' alive even when most of their vital organs had been removed. She was glad that the video recordings of the mission had been purged from her system afterwards. The Office could have done the same for her biological memory, but such memory gaps tended to have more adverse effects than the trauma they obfuscated.

What made this mission unfamiliar was exactly the fact that it wasn't really a mission at all. There was no support team quarterbacking from the local Office, no calm voice in her ear guiding her to the next objective and no set of detailed blueprints of the building. Even with the Hercules suite on full tactical alert she felt like she was working blindfolded and with one hand behind her back. Nevertheless, Operatives were trained to think on their feet in an emergency, even if the vast majority of the time all they were supposed to do was get themselves out of trouble as fast as possible and go to ground.

Today, though, that simply wasn't an option. It wasn't even as if she was in any real danger, though if she was found too far from the recovery ward some questions were likely to be asked. Still, Athas was depending on her to either find a way to cure him, or to keep him alive until he fought off the Ague himself, and she didn't plan on failing him. If that meant going places the Abelians would rather she didn't, so be it. She had to admit, though, that all she was really working on was a hunch- that whatever the mysterious visitor to the hospital the previous night was doing here had something to do with the big Guard's condition.

For the most part, getting to the place the Hercules suite estimated the conversation she had heard to have come from was disconcertingly easy. The Royal Hospital was a huge building, every bit as large as an equivalent facility back home might have been, and was kept scrupulously clean, presumably by housekeeping spells since there seemed to be precious few staff. It was that sheer emptiness that was most unnerving, especially when coupled with the fact that the wards and operating theatres she passed were in such a state of readiness that it seemed the doctors and nurses must simply have stepped outside for a moment. And yet, other than a handful of Porters walking the halls and dealing with some of the more involved pieces of maintenance, who she easily avoided, the place was practically deserted.

She worked her way down several floors, the décor gradually shifting from the welcoming white-and-blue of the treatment levels to the dull brown of the utility corridors. Down here the rooms were given over almost entirely to storage, and most were firmly locked. She slowed her pace, knowing that she was within the search area, though in the warren of rooms and corridors an exact location was impossible to determine from the sounds alone. There were other methods, however, and in some respects they hadn't changed since the dawn of espionage. As lower-priority and non-sterile areas, the store-rooms were less rigorously maintained and clearly not supplied with housekeeping spells, because a fairly thick layer of dust covered the floor. And that dust told a story.

There were several sets of tracks, though most of them were clearly not particularly fresh. One which was, however, came from two people, one of whom had small feet clad in soft boots, which the Hercules suite matched by stride length and size to Healer Alana with a 96% probability. The other person was taller, with larger feet, and wearing hard-soled riding boots. The analysis software estimated them to be a male of 5'10" to 6'2" tall by stride length. Furthermore, a slight disturbance to the surrounding dust suggested that the person in question wore either a long skirt, or a robe. Far more importantly, however- and far easier to discern, even without Daniel's help- was the fact that the tracks led to a door that was in most respects identical to the rest. The smaller set stopped outside, but the larger crossed the threshold into the room.

Devereux cast a quick glance behind her to confirm that her nanite swarm was rearranging the disturbed dust and covering her tracks. It suddenly struck her that if the person she was tracking had been, as she suspected, a Wizard or some other type of magic-user, they could almost certainly have used their powers to do much the same thing. Fortunately, with the storage area being so far from anywhere people usually had any cause to visit, they clearly hadn't seen any reason for such a precaution. Unless, of course, they had been paranoid enough to leave a false trail.

A moment of terrible doubt seized her, and she quickly replayed the recorded conversation. There was nothing in it to suggest that Alana regarded what was happening as at all illicit, and had her important visitor started magically altering their tracks she would probably have made some sort of comment. Of course, even that could have been staged for a listener's benefit, but that sort of second-guessing rarely led anywhere useful.

Slowly, carefully, she reached for the door-handle, finding it locked. This was hardly surprising. The door was made of simple wood and didn't look particularly sturdy, but Devereux had learned the hard way that just as a wooden door in a fugitive oligarch's bolt-hole might conceal steel reinforcement and light armour plating, so a door such as this in this world might be bolstered with all sorts of powerful magic. She didn't really want to break the thing down anyway, since there was still every possibility that the whole situation was entirely innocent and even if it wasn't, she didn't plan on leaving any evidence of her visit.

She squatted down slightly, bringing herself to eye level with the lock and allowing the Hercules suite to perform a detailed full-spectrum analysis. As was often the case with magically-reinforced materials, most of the more direct scans simply failed to penetrate the wood, but the keyhole proved more susceptible to investigation.

++Analysis complete. Target mechanism analogous to mortise-lock, eight-tumbler mechanism. Covert penetration options: Manual tumbler operation by nanite manipulation, or fabrication of compatible key from locally-sourced materials.++

Devereux, who had been expecting this, reached into one of her subcutaneous storage pouches and produced a steel butter-knife she had pilfered from the breakfast tray.

Commence fabrication.

Before her eyes, the metal seemed almost to melt, shimmering as the microscopic machines worked. Within the space of a few seconds, she held a steel key, albeit one with a knife-handle. Reaching out, she carefully tried the key in the lock, which clicked smoothly open.

++Penetration successful. Schematic filed for future reference.++

There was still one other thing to consider, and it was by far the most worrying. Since she strongly suspected that the door had been locked by a Wizard, there was certainly a possibility that there was some sort of defence or alarm magic on the door. Thalia had explained that most Chancellors, for example, put spells called 'wards' on the doors to their studies that could stun or kill the unwary intruder, or simply trigger a silent alarm. There wasn't much she could do about an alarm other than keep her perimeter monitoring up and make herself scarce if anyone came to investigate, but from what she had learned of warding spells, most reacted to organic tissue entering their perimeter. The part of the spell that determined whether or not the ward should trigger had to be very simple in order to make it hard to detect, and simple meant stupid.

From another pouch she removed a somewhat dishevelled-looking bacon sandwich. Pulling the door open carefully and doing her best to follow in the dusty footsteps of her predecessor, she advanced slowly into the dark room, sweeping the food in front of her like some sort of scanner. Feeling deeply foolish, she was about to put it away when the end of the bread started to smoulder.

++Operative Alert: Temperature of improvised probe increasing beyond 400 degrees Fahrenheit.++

That, mused the Operative to herself as she withdrew a little, was one seriously overcooked piece of toast. The footprints carried on past the ward, so obviously whoever set it either did so when they left, or was immune to it. Carefully she checked from one wall to the other, but found no gap.

Shit. Level Ten Operative or not, around here I'm out of my depth.

Depth. That was a thought. The ward clearly extended from the floor upwards, but how far? Reaching as high as she could, she tested again, and discovered to her relief that the magical barrier only extended about seven feet upwards. There were another three feet until the ceiling, which was helpfully made of wooden beams. A quick leap took her up to it, and she soon clambered past the threshold of the ward, going as far past it as she could towards the back of the room. Even so, before dropping down she latched on with both legs and one hand, lowering the last remains of the sandwich before her to be certain she was in the clear. Finally, after landing silently on the floor, she turned back to the barrier and advanced on it until she found its edge.

++Perimeter of counter-intrusion kill-field determined and marked.++

Now that she knew where it was, the Hercules suite added a simple overlay to her vision, outlining the estimated area of the ward. Devereux gave silent thanks for the fact that Thalia liked to talk about magic when she was bored- the time spent at the Expelled's Moot and then cooped up in various carriages had proved very useful in that respect. Now, though, it was time for the main event.

I'm going to be pretty pissed off if all that was to protect some Wizard's wine cellar.

Her low-light vision operating at near-maximum in the dark store-room, Devereux took a look around. Well, it certainly wasn't wine. In one corner loomed a humanoid figure that almost had her reflexively reaching for her sword before she realised it wasn't moving. Given that she had left the weapon with her other possessions to allay suspicion, that was probably just as well. Closer inspection revealed the thing to be a Stickman, but unlike the others she had seen this one stood stiff and still. Was it broken, or incomplete? It seemed a strange thing to find in such a place, and given how robust the automata had proved it certainly didn't fit the bill of 'delicate equipment'.

Something that possibly did rested on a workbench at the back of the room. It was blocked from view from the door by a medical privacy screen, and Devereux, her caution now bordering on paranoia, stepped around the barrier with her improvised ward-detector thrust out in front of her. What she found was a completely baffling contraption. On the bench rested a large glass cylinder, containing what seemed to be some sort of fluid. At the top of the cylinder a silver lid was screwed on, and to that was attached an impossibly thin length of wire made of the same material. This led to an ornately-carved wooden stand, on which rested a large, green gemstone, which was glowing faintly.

What in the flying fuck is all this supposed to be?

++Operative advisory: Visual analysis of gemstone gives 92% probability of match for material designated Abelian Aether-Emerald.++

Analysis of the cylinder? Devereux issued the request without much optimism. Like most other magical devices, it would almost certainly prove impenetrable to her nanites and sensors.

++Working.... complete. Cylinder: Composed of soda-lime glass, primarily SiO_2. Contents:62% H_2O, 38% Organic compounds including miscellaneous lipids, proteins,

carbohydrates and glucose. Operative Advisory: DNA sequence detected. Species unknown. Sequence filed.++

Devereux's mind reeled. The Hercules read-out was displaying a more verbose breakdown of the fluid's composition, but it meant little to her. Whatever was in this apparently non-magical container, though, was organic, if not exactly alive. And yet somehow, unless she completely misinterpreted the glow of the gemstone, Aether was being fed into the cylinder.

She stepped back from the workbench, hands on her hips in frustration. This certainly wasn't any sort of smoking gun, certainly nothing she could confront the Abelians with and demand answers. It certainly did look delicate, and for all she knew this was some sort of ongoing magical or medical experiment. The tube could be part of some unfathomably evil scheme, or it could be part of an incredibly important clinical trial. The location seemed to make the latter unlikely, but it was always possible that whoever made the breakthrough stood to make a lot of money out of it and so had chosen to work in secret. Without understanding what it was, she certainly wasn't going to tinker with it.

There seemed to be little else of note in the store-room, and a few minutes later she was retracing her steps, once again clinging to the roof-beams to bypass the ward before silently leaving the room and locking the door behind her. Finally, with the door secured, she reversed the fabrication routine, returning the butter-knife to its original form. Even if someone realised that an intruder had been in the room, there would be precious little evidence to prove who, other than a faint odour of burnt toast.

She walked briskly but quietly back to the recovery ward, her mind working. "In three days time.." the visitor had said. Devereux would be making regular visits to their little experiment until then, and when the man returned, she planned to be there.

If Athas lived that long, of course.

65

*M*uch to Second's surprise, she found herself quite liking Captain Damia Render. Perhaps it was in part that the large sword she carried reminded her of Silent Blade, but there was also a directness to her manner that was refreshing. When Second explained the capabilities of the Stalking Wolf to her, the tall woman barely batted an eyelid. It also helped that compared to the rest of the grim-faced troops under her command, those eyes were kind. They were eyes that had seen pain, yes, but not to the extent of the other warriors, who Mighty Dokan had told her were called Wardens.

"Do not ask them why, nor enquire about the calluses on their hands, Second," warned the Mighty one. "To do so may cause the gravest of offence. It is a tale told only in whispered songs, among the most private of company."

The other two Wardens were less pleasant company, but at least they were quiet. Sergeant Tika, the woman who served as Second of the small patrol, was slightly shorter than the Captain, and had shoulder-length curly red hair and freckles. Often a woman of her age in possession of such features, as well as a slender, almost boyish figure, would be considered less than intimidating, but one look at the soldier's expression would kill such infant thoughts in their crib. Her colleague, the archer called Dani, was even shorter and darker, but she bore one of the coveted silver-inlaid bows that made the Archers of the Deluded so deadly. Second knew a few Eagle Hunters who had managed to acquire such weapons, and all considered them superior to the khile-wood and horn composite bows made by the Free Tribes, wickedly effective though those weapons were.

Dani caught Second looking at her, and glowered back. "What're you staring at, wolf-girl?"

Caught off-guard, Second said the first thing that came into her head. "I- I was wondering what happened to your hand."

For a horrible moment she thought she had strayed into dangerous territory, but Dani, who had several fingers on her right hand replaced with khile-wood, held it up to her face with disinterest. "This? Pissed off the wrong bitch. Thought I was pretty good until I saw what Devereux could do with those 'guns' of hers."

"The weapons of Steel Heart are indeed formidable," agreed Second, still entranced by how much like living fingers the prosthetics moved. "Mighty Dokan mishandled one, and was fortunate to retain his head when the entrapped fire-demons showed their displeasure."

"Hah!" laughed Red Trace in White Snow, who was bringing up the rear of the group. "I need only this axe, and my fangs and claws. Bows and 'guns' are the weapons of little girls playing at being warriors."

United in disdain, Second and the Wardens looked him up and down. Alone among them, Second knew that the Heart-Eater's words were not entirely mere bombast. Red Trace held no rank in the Tree-Searchers, for he was too unstable, but his prowess as a warrior was almost without peer. Unlike the Stalking Wolf, the Enraged Bear tattooed on his chest could only be triggered when the bearer was worked up to a killing fury, and even then the resulting change of form might only be partial. Depending on his state of mind, the Heart-Eater might become a mighty bear, or a twisted amalgam of man and beast. The latter, still being able to wield Skull-Hewer, his great, silver-headed battle-axe, was if anything even more dangerous. Second had heard that the weapon had been seized from the Great Knights, and it was heavier and more vicious than any blade of the Free.

"Well, ladies, it looks like we have nothing to worry about," said Captain Render, without much humour in her voice. "If we run into any Dendaril, our observer here will be volunteering to hold them up while we run away, since we so obviously need protecting."

Red Trace in White Snow puffed out his chest, muscles rippling. "Mock me if you wish, Deluded warrior-wench. Words are not spears, and they cannot draw my blood. But know that words can also be chains, and by mine am I bound to keep all of you safe from the Fly Lords. So I have sworn to Fleeting Deer and Mighty Xaraya, and so shall I do."

"I feel safer already," muttered Sergeant Tika. Second was just grateful that the warrior had managed to keep his temper, at least for now. A disagreeable scent came to her nostrils, making her glad she had not yet shifted to her wolf-shape, and the Green Shadow melted into view out of the forest. Dani saw him a second later, and was so shocked she had her nocked bow pointed at him before she realised who he was.

"Shit! You nearly got yourself turned into *Kallouris*, you stupid bastard!"

"Nah, you're too good for that, girl," said the Scout, grinning. "And anyhows, I know ye'd never shoot a handsome cunt like me." He turned to Captain Render. "No sign of these white-robed wankers so far, Cap'n. They've never been in these parts before and they don't know shit about wood-craft, so if'n they were about, I'd know."

"We need to find them before they get too close to the Vigil," said Captain Render, flatly. "Second, is there a good vantage point we could head to to get the lie of the land?"

"What sort of bloody name is 'Second' anyway?" groused Tika. "Second what?"

"I am Second of the Tree-Searchers, Sergeant," explained Second. "But I am the First of Green Water Falling, who bore me. Some day, if the Ancestors will it, I shall learn my True Name."

"Well, that clears that up," muttered the Sergeant, but Captain Render silenced her with a glare.

"For your question, First- I mean, Captain, the Mountain Halls stood at the highest point of the Forest Home, and near to its heart," continued Second. "From there we will have the best chance of finding the Fly Lords."

"Nak's Skull!" growled Red Trace. "You cannot take outsiders there, Tree-Searcher! Those grounds are only for the Free!"

"The Fly Lords have already defiled them once, the Guardians have fled into the arms of dread Ixil and the Halls are a pile of melted rubble," Second snapped back. "I think the Harbinger Skulls have already seen enough shameful acts that one more is unlikely to stir their wrath further. You heard the words of the Mighty Ones- either we stand together with the Deluded, or we fall to the Woe."

"Bah," rumbled Red Trace, his anger cooling as fast as it had heated. "Next time come at me with your knife, girl. I cannot wrestle with your tongue. Do what you think you must."

"How do we get there?" asked Captain Render. "If it's in the heart of the forest, that's got to be a hundred miles away at least. We don't have that sort of time."

"I shall take you to the Stone Paths," said Second. "Those of your tribe who came before were able to draw strength from them much as the Free do, and with it we shall run."

Captain Render considered. "Yeah, but we might have a problem there. Magister Thalia's retinue had, what, Sergeant Athas, Delys Amaranth, and the Devereux woman, but we've got a Scout."

Second blinked in confusion. "So? The Shield That Strikes was weak in Spirit, but his Silver Shackle still aided him. So it is with all the Free."

Alben Koont chuckled, pointing a grubby finger at his Seal. "Yeah, you Skin-nies're all Warlocks, though. This beautiful burning bastard on my shoulder's not a physical Seal, so it don't make me stronger like the ones these girls have. Your Stone Path'll be fuck all use to me."

"We could just send him back," suggested Dani, hopefully.

"Fuck that," said the Scout, with feeling, jerking a thumb back at Red Trace. "I go back there without you lot, his wife gets me bollocks on toast. Not fucking happening."

The big warrior gave a heavy, rumbling sigh. "I will carry the Green Shadow. Let us be off!"

As one, the rest of the scouting party stared at him. "You'll do what?" said Tika, finally.

"I. Will. Carry. Him," said Red Trace, leaning down towards her and speaking slowly, as if to a child. "I am among the mightiest of the Free, and he is as much a twig as he is a man, though he might smell like one rolled in dung. Skull-Hewer is a heavier burden than he, and a more worthy one."

Without further preamble, he strode over to the surprised Scout, and presented his back. "Take up the Second's spear and war-cloak, Green Shadow, for she shall soon have no arms of her own to carry them."

Wordlessly, Alben Koont took the weapon and cloak from Second, and clambered with surprising grace onto the big warrior's back. Suddenly Red Trace laughed.

"When we return, it will give me great pleasure to tell the First of the Tree-

Searchers that I laid my hands upon the Green Shadow within the Forest Home, and yet let him live. His wails and lamentations will be heard as far as the land of the Black Devils."

"You won't need to tell him," pointed out Sergeant Tika. "He'll be able to smell the dirty bastard."

The big warrior laughed again. "I like you, little sister, in spite of your people's evil ways. If ever I have to kill you, know that I shall make it quick, and painless."

"Thanks," muttered the Sergeant.

Second smiled. "O great Red Trace in White Snow, perhaps if you practice enough, the Shield That Strikes shall not defeat you the next time you run the Burdened Race."

"He did not win fairly!" roared Red Trace, whirling so fast that Alben was nearly hurled off into the forest. "His... meek heart attracted tiny girls to his back, and I was left with fat strumpets and frail old men!"

"Might be a lesson in there for you somewhere," said Captain Render, quietly. "What do we need to do, Second?"

"I do not *know* what you must do," replied Second, truthfully. "First, I must become the wolf and lead you to the Stone Paths. There, you must learn to draw strength from them, and we shall run. How the warriors of the Deluded do this thing, I know not, but I have seen it done."

"I hope we don't need a Magister for this, or we're fucked," said Dani, slinging her bow.

"I shall avert my gaze for your Change, Second of the Tree-Searchers," announced Red Trace in White Snow. "You shall do the same, Green Shadow, or you shall find the journey irksome on account of making it with your heels above your head."

Once the men were looking away, Second slipped quickly out of her battle-harness, passing the leather straps to Captain Render, who delegated the task of carrying them to her Sergeant. Then she dropped to all fours, and her senses sharpened as the wolf-shape took over.

"Fuck me," said Dani.

"Yeah," agreed Sergeant Tika, who had missed the change and was holding Second's harness in front of her incredulously. "How the fuck does she even get into this thing?"

The wolf's mouth fell open, and she turned to lead them into the forest.

66

*T*halia arrived at the reception hall of the Green Palace in time to see Sir Terence enter, accompanied by a troop of Stickmen bearing a stack of wooden chests.

"Good morning, Your Excellency," said the Abelian with an elaborate bow. "As promised, I have brought the items removed for investigation by the Royal Guard. Among them you will find the contents of your treasury, your Messaging Crystals, and sundry documents."

"And, one would hope, the good silverware and the coffee pot," snapped Herenford. "Not to mention every tapestry in the East Wing and four sets of monogrammed cufflinks that date back to the rule of King Tomsk. And six pairs of guest-room curtains."

The Royal Knight flushed. "I, er, am sure I had an itemised list somewhere..."

"It can wait," said Thalia, briskly. "Herenford, see to the.. repatriation of our goods. If there is anything else missing, prepare a manifest for my inspection when I return. Sir Terence, I must attend my audience with the Queen. Do we have horses?"

"With respect, Your Excellency, the sort of horses bred in Abelia are not suited for domestic riding," replied Sir Terence. "They are intended to carry the Royal Knights to war and little else. The second-string, however, do pull our carriages and such a vehicle awaits your pleasure outside."

And it's so much easier to control where I go if I have to use a carriage to get about.

Thalia dismissed the thought crossly. Like it or not, she was entirely in the Abelians' power and being angry about it wasn't likely to help. Delys, on the other hand, might have something to say about it, through actions if not words. The little Swordmaster was dressed in her full battle-armour, not as heavy as that of a line Guardsman but still impressive. She had even, for the first time Thalia could remember, put the helm on, though hers was fully open at the face and adapted at the back to let her braided hair spill out.

263

Next to one of the Royal Knights in their own armour, she still looked like a small child playing at being a soldier, of course, but not a poorly-equipped one. Even so, more than one foe had made the mistake of underestimating her. Few had lived to regret it.

"Well, we should probably be off, then," Thalia said, brightly. She realised that her heart was pounding and there were butterflies in her stomach. The feeling from mere days ago that she could face anything the world could throw at her had completely evaporated, but that was hardly surprising. Then, she had had not only Delys, but Athas and Amanda Devereux at her side. Now, the only person she felt she could truly trust couldn't even talk back to her. She had already asked Herenford to send messengers to check how the big Guard's recovery was going, but as of yet they hadn't returned.

"I have some documents for you as well, Your Excellency," said Sir Terence, as he led the way out to the coach. "They are a communique from your government."

"Which you, of course, have not read," said Thalia, pointedly.

"*I* most certainly have not," replied the Royal Knight, "but since they were received on our own Messaging Crystals and transcribed by the diplomatic service, I would say that little which they contain will come as a surprise to the Court."

Thalia had to concede the point. Even when the Messaging Chamber at the Green Palace was back in action, she was going to be treating it with a healthy dose of caution. If at least one member of the Embassy staff didn't report to an Abelian version of Anneke Belus, she'd eat one of her boots. For that matter, if another didn't report to Anneke herself she'd eat the other one.

The Stickmen were already marching off down the street when they left the building, but Thalia paid them little attention. Her eyes were on the coach, which proved to be even more magnificent than the one the Orsinios had provided, and made the D'Honeurs' vehicle look like a village honey-cart. It was pulled by a team of no less than six horses, each a massive beast that stood almost seven feet high. It was painted in exquisite purple lacquer with silver and gold trim, and crewed by a team of liveried footmen who were busily putting the large luggage-rack on the roof into order. Standing behind the vehicle was an even larger horse, this one plated in battle-armour, and Sir Terence strode boldly over to it.

"Your Excellency, may I present Lord Ambrosia Yellow Starling Grist, the Third."

"What?" said Thalia. "Are we travelling to the Durance with another dignitary?"

"I was referring to my mount, Your Excellency," said the Royal Knight, with a grin that suggested he had caused the misunderstanding deliberately, and not for the first time. "Though I call her 'Thunder' for short."

Thalia suddenly understood how Amanda Devereux had felt on being introduced to College society. Rather than ask how, exactly, a horse called Lord something was also female or why it had more names than most noblemen, she simply nodded. "I see. She is a fine mount, Sir Terence. I take it my documents are in the coach?"

"They are indeed, Your Excellency," replied the Royal Knight, looking a little put out.

"Then I see no further reason for delay. Out of the way, man!" She snapped the last at one of the footmen, who was fussing over the cabin of the coach.

"Ah, Your Excellency, I have not quite finished-"

"Blood, ice and fire!" exploded Thalia. "I am in danger of being late for an audience with your Queen! Do you want my first words at Court to be the name of the man who delayed me, Rutlin Dire? Do you?"

The footman's mouth fell open in shock. "N-no, Your Excellency!"

"Then move your pampered backside!"

Even though she knew she shouldn't have done it, it felt good to vent. The old name-reading trick rarely failed to put non-Magisters off balance. In less than a minute they were speeding through the streets, Thalia skimming through the documents as Delys pressed her face against the glass of the windows. The news wasn't good, though she had to confess it could be worse. The Dendaril had been sighted moving through the Expelled Territories, though their advance guard had been all but wiped out by the sacrifice of the leader of the Blackbloods. Thalia marvelled at that- the Blackbloods, much as Alben Koont had claimed, had not been popular with the other tribes at the Moot of Kings, and had played little to no part in the celebration that followed it. Even Mighty Xaraya, who Dokan had warned her not to provoke, had at least managed to be icily civil for the few moments they had spent together.

Now, apparently, the Free Tribes were sheltering at the Vigil. The fate of almost half of their people was presently unknown, including that of all their children. Thalia thought back to the grinning, fruit-spattered urchins who had been practically dragged away from the party to be washed, and tears pricked at the corners of her eyes. If these 'Dendaril' wished to conquer and rule the Expelled Territories that was understandable, but if the children had been harmed...

She set her jaw in determination. If she failed to convince the Queen, it would be more than just the children of the Expelled who would suffer. Every man, woman and child in the Empire and the Kingdom would be at risk, and that would be only the start. She could not, would not fail them.

67

*E*ri Trevalyn watched the morning's bouts with an air of professional appreciation. Though most Guards were no strangers to a good old fashioned bare-handed brawl, she had always had a particular aptitude for fist-fights. Cutting someone with a sword was all very well, and Yar knew, she was as good at that as the next woman, but when you won there were usually only a handful of seconds to enjoy it. Sometimes, if you got a really good strike in, the victim didn't even register that they'd lost before they died, which was amusing in its own way. But bare-handed, that was a different story. There was often that delicious moment when an opponent was still standing and still trying to fight back, but both fighters already knew who was going to come out on top. Occasionally, if the situation allowed, she'd give them a moment to get their wits back, let a little futile hope enter their eyes, and then beat them down again twice as hard.

Better yet, sometimes you could get a good choke-hold or sleeper on them, and feel them go from a breathing, fighting opponent to a helpless lump of quivering flesh. You had to watch you didn't accidentally kill them, though. That tended to get you into trouble, and anyway it was much more fun to let them live and maybe try again some other time. The moment when a returning challenger realised that just as they'd used the time since their last attempt to get stronger, so had their nemesis, was as exquisite as the finest wine. To see the confidence die in their eyes as the new trick failed, as the hard-learned lessons proved not to have been enough. It might be a cliché to call it better than sex, but as far as Eri was concerned it was pretty much true. Then again, working for the Vice-Chancellor you got a bit jaded about sex after a while.

Thinking about Anneke sent a cold shudder down her back, and she missed the end of the fight. Not for the first time, she queried whether to go through with her plans. Sure, Freeport was a salt-stained rocky shit-hole that reeked of fish, but she had escaped, and she was alive. Maybe there was no need to try to bring Maike

Dain back and make up for her failure. Maybe she could just hide out in Freeport, build a new life there.

It wasn't as if the idea of taking Maike in was without risk. For one thing, that bald Daxalai bitch was still hanging around with her. Eri had managed to track the pair as far as Sigil, but hadn't dared make a move whilst they were together. She'd assumed that once they escaped the College, the two would go their separate ways, but that happy event had not yet occurred. Still, every now and then Maike went off on her own, and it should be simple enough to jump the little tart. Maybe, once she took her back, they could use Maike as bait to lure the other one, if she actually did give a shit.

Eri had to admit, though, that it seemed the Dax had taught Little Red a few tricks. Maike had always been a tough little scrapper, but she lost her cool too easily and left too many openings. That, and unless someone was stupid enough to use magic on her, she didn't really have the strength or endurance to be much of a fighter- and then, of course, something had been done to her Seal and she'd lost even that advantage. But since arriving in Freeport a few days ago- she'd had to find a ship from Damisk, because none of Sigil's timid fishermen were as daring as Blue Kjôr- Eri had seen Maike fight a couple of times, and something had definitely changed. For one thing, she'd won both bouts. Then there'd been that weird outburst the other day, which had got the Dax briefly very excited. On balance, Eri was glad she hadn't gone with the first plan that had occurred to her on seeing Little Red in the ring, which had been to just call her out there and then. Even if Maike had been prepared to stake her freedom on the result, there'd be no guarantee that the Dax, or the pit's rough clientele, would have honoured the debt.

So for now, unsure of exactly how to proceed, she chose to watch and wait. Maike was up next that morning, and this time her opponent was the tough-looking Toskan woman from the other day. From what Eri had seen it was going to be a close one, which was strange, now that she thought about it. The Toskans used those burning rune things on their chests, which seemed to work a lot like a Seal even if they looked a bit more impressive, and without the protection of her own Seal a blow from someone that strong should be enough to practically knock Maike's little red head off. And yet she'd seen the girl if not shrugging off blows from Sealed fighters, then at least taking them as well as any Guard might. Something weird was definitely going on.

Suddenly, just as the pit's barker was getting the crowd whipped up for the fight, his two children scampering around to take bets, she saw something that turned her blood to ice and had her shrinking back into the press of bodies, pulling her hooded cloak tighter around her. Or more precisely, someone. Few people, on seeing the small, scruffy, dark-haired man smoking a roll-up on the balcony of the Last Anchor would have given him a second look. Bundled up in a robe every bit as concealing as Eri's own attire, the little man eyed the scene below him with an air of studied disinterest. But where the fugitive Guardswoman's cloak hid little more than her identity and a small fighting-dagger which was all the captain of her ship would allow her to bring for protection, the robes of the man known only as Gelt concealed far more. Eri knew that the freelance bounty-hunter carried an array of gadgets that ranged from the utilitarian to the horrifyingly lethal, and he was far from shy in using them.

If Gelt was here, that meant his two team-mates, Jonas and Erika, were sure to be nearby. The latter, a statuesque blonde bitch of a Swordmaster, was someone Eri had taken great pains to avoid. She knew that 'Erika' was no more the hired killer's real name than any of the other pseudonyms she had used in the past, but Gelt hadn't let that stop him from using the similarity to try to stir up trouble. Maybe if there had been any guarantee that the knives would stay out of it Eri might even have played along, but only the worst kind of idiot fucked with a Swordmaster armed with their chosen weapon. Even with a dozen witnesses, picking that fight would get your death written off as a suicide. So Eri put up with Gelt's taunts, laughed along with Erika's rebuttals, and kept her gaze firmly pointed in another direction if the glare of those ice-blue eyes fell on her.

If she had avoided Erika, she had positively fled in terror from Jonas. It wasn't as if the tall, dark-haired man was unattractive or even unfriendly, but people who got involved with him tended to be found dead, if at all. Maybe he and Erika had something going on and the Swordmaster was the jealous type, maybe it was something else, but Eri had taken great pains not to find out, which meant keeping a careful watch for them. And right now, she could only see one of the three.

Of course, they almost certainly weren't here for her- at least, not primarily- but Jonas' crew rarely went anywhere or did anything unless Anneke was paying them to. And Eri Trevalyn, dead or alive, was definitely on a list of things the Vice-Chancellor wanted to acquire at the moment. Still, it was far more likely that they were looking for Maike Dain and the Dax, and now they had them. Not that Eri expected either to go quietly. She carefully slipped to the back of the crowd as the fighters closed. Right now, it was likely to be very unhealthy for anyone to get between the hunters and their prey.

68

*J*erik followed Julius out of the rear door of the Last Anchor with a sense of more than a little trepidation. The barkeep had been a surly, intractable sort but Julius proved surprisingly good at ingratiating himself to the man, getting a grim smile out of him with a couple of ribald jokes that might have made Captain Reka blush. That, and a couple of rounds for the few hardy souls already well into their cups in the late morning, had led to a wide-ranging chat on the ills of society in general and Freeport in particular, and eventually to the subject of recent unusual arrivals in the town. Such as, for example, a certain bald-headed Daxalai who had humbled the local champion in the rough prizefighting arena at the back of that very inn, and of her red-headed protégé who would be in action there within the hour.

The shouts of the crowd, and occasional firm report of fist on flesh, were growing louder when Julius suddenly held up a hand to stop him.

"A moment, Jerik. Do you detect that aroma?" he murmured, quietly.

Jerik wrinkled his nose. "Which one? Stale sweat, even staler beer, or bloody fish?"

"None of those, pungent though they indeed are. No, I detect a strong waft of Chancellor's Silver Leaf."

"Shit," muttered Jerik. "Maybe we should come back later?"

Julius shook his head firmly. "I think not. Whoever has been following us has got here before us, and that can only mean that they, too, have an interest in our quarry. They may even have used us to find them."

"Yeah, so perhaps if we fuck off now they'll grab them and leave us alone," suggested Jerik, more in hope than expectation.

"More likely they would seize one prey, and then return for the other. Moreover, if we cannot interview Willow-Sigh Wen, we will have lost the most promising lead in our investigation."

"So what, we just press on? My old Sergeant used to say it's not a trap if you're expecting it to be a trap."

"An interesting supposition. Was it borne out by events?"

"Nah. She got killed in a Royalist ambush."

Forewarned, and hopefully forearmed, they moved out into the late-morning sunshine. The crowd was densely-packed, but through occasional gaps as people jostled back and forth Jerik could just see what looked like the closing moments of a pretty decent fight. The blue-haired Toskan girl seemed to be getting the better of it, the flaming brand on her chest blazing as she pressed forwards. Even so, Jerik could see a fair crop of welts on the pirate's tanned skin and as he watched she reeled back a step, wiping blood from her mouth before advancing again with a gap-toothed grin.

"Certainly a most.. stimulating display of pugilism, Jerik," said Julius, with an odd note to his voice.

"Looks like a good old Iken barn-stormer, as my Dad would say," agreed Jerik. "By the way, our friend with the expensive taste in dog-ends is on the balcony behind us."

"Well observed," murmured Julius. "Hmmm.. most singular.."

Jerik gave Julius a sidelong glance. The man seemed almost enraptured. He knew some people got a bit.. over-excited watching this sort of thing but he hadn't got the bookish Magister pegged as being among their number. A sudden scream from the fighting pit tore his attention away from his companion. It was a feminine cry, more of anger than of pain, and it was followed almost immediately by the bone-on-bone clack of a soundly-delivered punch. To his surprise, the Toskan's limp body slammed into the crowd just in front of where he and Julius were standing, accompanied by a mix of cheers and groans from the spectators.

"Red's done it again!" grumbled the man just in front of Jerik. "Little bitch always seems to be on the verge of going down and then pulls out a punch like a fucking avalanche. That's me down two Quoits and a Rubal."

"Yeah." agreed the woman next to him. Shit, looks like Hjëlga's not breathing."

"Move aside, please, thank you very much," said Julius, quickly. "I am a Healer, trained in the Gyre Infirmary."

Jerik did his best not to look surprised as Julius worked on the unconscious Toskan. Even though he knew the man was no Healer, he'd seen Thalia and other Magisters treat some fairly serious injuries before, so hopefully the girl was in good hands.

"Hm. Her jaw is broken in two places, several teeth are missing, but the pressing issue is the lack of respiration," muttered Julius, passing a hand lightly over the blue-haired woman's face. "Aha, there we are."

"What foolishness are you working, robe-wearer?" snapped a woman who had hurried over from the other side of the ring. Her skin was pure alabaster white, and a wide-brimmed hat with charms dangling from it shaded her pink eyes. A Jandallan, if Jerik was any judge.

"I am endeavouring to save this young woman's life, madam," Julius shot back. "Would you prefer I did nothing? Her breathing is already returning to normal."

"Don't worry, Learned Magister," said a voice Jerik recognised. "Gundala gets a bit territorial about her patients. Ow."

"I told you not to speak yet, foolish one! If you wish to chit-chat this soon after fights, refrain from letting people punch you in the mouth!" grumbled the Jandallan, who by now had elbowed Julius aside and was administering various evil-smelling herbal concoctions and lotions. The Magister watched in open fascination for a moment before his ears seemed to get the attention of his brain.

"Ah, young lady, you do me too much credit. I am a simple Healer, not some high-and-mighty Magister. More's the pity, eh?"

"Then why do you have one of their staffs?" said Maike, pointing at the offending article. She didn't seem to have noticed Jerik yet, but then they had only really met once and she'd spent most of that time tangling with Delys.

"This?" said Julius, with an air of complete nonchalance that impressed Jerik given the circumstances. "This is a simple walking staff, madam, certainly nothing as impressive as-"

"A shark ate that leg, pull the other fucking one," laughed Maike. "It's got a bloody great horse holding a crystal on it and there're lilies all over the thing."

As one, Julius and Jerik glanced at the plain-looking wooden staff, the true appearance of which the sweaty, battle-scarred red-head had just described with no apparent effort. "Are there really?" said Julius, mildly.

"Ah, who fucking cares?" said Maike with a shrug, before suddenly shooting a hard stare at Jerik despite the fact that one of her eyes was starting to swell. "Hey, don't I know you from somewhere?"

"I-" began Jerik, before all hell broke loose.

Ranlaou, Atoa! someone shouted from near the middle of the ring. At the same time, Jerik saw a dark-skinned figure leap into the air behind Maike, her bare foot flashing around in a kick that was almost too fast to see. Something small whizzed over his head from behind him, only to be intercepted by the Daxalai's kick and sent hurtling back almost precisely where it had come from. A started oath from the balcony was interrupted by a loud detonation.

"What the fu-" began Maike, whirling. "What just happened?"

The Daxalai, landing elegantly from her leap, said something Jerik didn't catch. A small, equally dark man at her side with a thin ponytail translated. "Master Wen says that the Dragon who is fooled once by a thief dines the next day on burglar."

Julius gave a careful, formal bow. "Willow-Sigh Wen, I presume. Madam, I am Magister Julius Thule of the Lily College, and-"

"And you will all be coming with us," supplied a new voice. A tall, dark-haired man emerged from the crowd, a blonde woman of almost equal height standing at his shoulder. Jerik couldn't help noticing that the latter was carrying a pair of extremely dangerous-looking knives and had an expression that suggested she knew how to use them.

Julius looked the pair up and down, apparently unconcerned. "My good man, you are clearly delusional. There are two of you, and.." he looked to his left and right, apparently trying to decide how many of those present might be counted on, "certainly rather more than that of us."

"Us?" said Maike, mildly.

"These people intend to take you, myself, Jerik, and Master Wen prisoner, Disruptor Dain," pointed out Julius. "Under the circumstances, I felt the collective noun justified."

"He's right, Miss Dain," agreed the tall man. "You do indeed have us at a disadvantage. Except I have, shall we say, deep pockets. Ladies and gentlemen, the

Daxalai, the red-head and the... Healer are worth fifty Quoits each to me, dead or alive!"

"Fuck off!" shouted a voice in the crowd. "Freeporters don't sell each other out fer a string o' silver!"

"Yeah, but they ain't Freeporters, is they? I'm fer the money!" countered another voice.

That was the last of the verbal discussion of the issue. Within seconds, the entire area was surrounded by struggling, brawling knots of people, though worryingly more of them seemed to be trying to get at the targets of the bounty than were objecting to it being claimed. Of course, human nature being what it is was, some were simply trying to stop the competition claiming the reward first.

"Perhaps a withdrawal to safer environs might be pertinent?" mused Julius, ducking a knife swing and riposting with a firm blow from his staff, the glamour disguising it dissolving into shards of light as he did so.

"Or we could just get the fuck out of here!" growled Jerik, struggling to get the sword out of his bag. Managing it just in time, he hurled the pack at the man who had been trying to charge him down. Quite a few of their possessions were in there, but that hardly seemed important right now.

"No!" shouted Maike Dain, charging forward. "Look!"

In the middle of what had been the ring, surrounded by brawling fighters and flashing knives, the barker and his two young children were huddled together. The Daxalai woman was already rushing to their aid, and Maike moved to follow her. Jerik made a grab for her arm.

"Are you fucking insane, girl? We need to get out of here!"

"Those people have been good to me," snarled Maike, wrenching the limb free with incredible strength. "I'm not letting them get hurt!"

"Well, she's changed," said Jerik, as he and Julius followed the two women.

"Indisputably," agreed Julius. "This situation is rapidly getting beyond all control, Jerik."

"You think?" shouted back the soldier, bashing a woman who lunged at him in the face with his pommel. "Someone is going to get fucking killed in a minute!"

"Oh, I certainly hope so," said the blonde woman, as they broke through the press into the blood-spattered area where Maike and Hjëlga had clashed mere minutes ago. She had one of her knives to the barker's throat, and the other to his daughter's.

"A deadly mistake in this business, girl," advised the tall man, who had produced a short oak stave. "Never let the enemy know what, or who, you value."

Willow-Sigh muttered something, her tone low and dangerous. Julius furrowed his brow. "Unless I miss my guess, Master Wen wishes to inform you that whilst both tigers and curs may hide in long grass, only the.. lowest dog preys on another's cub. I confess it may have lost some poetry in the translation."

"Here's some fucking poetry for you, you cowardly little bitch," snarled Maike, who stood a head shorter than the blonde. "Harm one hair on their heads and I will fucking kill you. Dead."

"It seems we have an impasse," said the tall man. "However, I am a reasonable man. Captain Jerik, Magister Julius- if you will deliver the other two fugitives to us and agree to give up on this investigation, we will allow not only you, but this lovely family here, to go free and unharmed."

Jerik swallowed nervously, acutely aware of how close to Maike he was standing, but Julius rapped his staff on the hard-packed earth firmly. "I think not. I have never before abandoned a case nor allowed a suspect to escape justice, and I do not intend to begin doing so now. In point of fact-"

Suddenly, Jerik realised that the crowd around them was starting to press in. Those bystanders who had objected to the bounty seemed to have been either subdued or driven off, and the rest were eager for their coin.

"Learned Magister, we're running out of time.." he hissed. Then, incredibly, Amanda Devereux's voice came out of the crowd. It was oddly distorted, with a strange crackle to it.

"Jerik! What the fuck are you doing? Get away from the-"

Something exploded in the direction the voice had come from with a dull boom, sending stunned figures flying in all directions. For a moment, the blonde woman was distracted, and that moment was all that was needed. Willow-Sigh Wen, who had been standing as if completely relaxed, hurtled forwards through the air, the side of her foot extended in front of her. Had the kick connected cleanly, it would probably have decapitated its target, but the blonde was clearly possessed of impressive reflexes of her own and threw herself back out of the way. Nevertheless, the deadlock was broken. Even as Wen landed from her attack, not unbalanced in the least, and the blonde rolled to her feet with her knives raised, the tall man cursed and reached into his pocket. He threw a handful of small, glowing objects onto the floor, and where they struck human figures appeared in a flash of light.

"Thelen's breath!" gasped Julius. "Glimmer-men! Ms Dain, Jerik, get those people to safety!"

Jerik stood for a slack-jawed second before he could respond. Each of the men who had suddenly appeared was armed as a College Guard, their silver plate armour and swords sparkling in the midday sun. But there was nothing human about their faces. He had heard whispers of the dark art around camp-fires, but such talk had always been shut down by the Magisters. Just as an inanimate object, including a corpse, could be converted to pure Aether, so it was possible, some said, to do the same to a living person. The mind of the victim was destroyed in the process, of course, but if performed correctly the magic could create a tiny gem, which would produce a warrior when smashed on the floor.

He had heard that such warriors were simply berserk killing machines, unable to determine friend from foe and prone to attacking the first thing they saw, and so it proved. Even as he and Maike ran to the aid of the barker and his daughter, Julius blasted the first figure full in the face with a bolt of lightning. The thing's head exploded, and it sank to its knees before dissolving into dust.

On the far side of the fighting pit, even as the crowd rushed in, Willow-Sigh Wen and the blonde woman duelled. The knives flashed out, almost too fast to see, and Jerik's heart leapt into his mouth. Surely, skilled as she may be, the Daxalai woman could not survive such an attack unarmed. But Julius had told him that an Initiate was a Magister who worked magic with their fists and feet, and so it proved. Before he lost track of the fight in the press of bodies, he could see that far from pressing her attack, and despite her opponent being surrounded on all sides by enemies who sought to seize her, the blonde was fighting desperately to stay alive.

"Get back, you mercenary fuckers!" he shouted, brandishing his weapon as people still rushed at him and Maike. "This blade ended the Red Witch and the next one of you bastards to try something gets it right in your favourite face!"

That got their attention. Whether or not anyone believed what he said about the weapon, on an island full of daggers the swordsman was king, and seeing the look on Jerik's face and the dangerous gleam in Maike Dain's eye most of the crowd rapidly lost all interest in the proceedings. Gundala, the Jandallan woman, came scurrying over to look after the barker, who had taken a few knocks during the rescue, but he and his crying daughter were largely unharmed. The herbalist had also found the man's son in the melee, and soon the three were reunited.

Jerik looked back towards the inn. Another blast of lighting split the air.

"Right, that's got them safely out of danger. Now to get back in there and drag the Magister out of the shit again. I'm supposed to be fucking retired."

"What happened back there?" said Maike, as they began to advance.

"Think someone stood on something in my pack," said Jerik. "I-"

With a soft, metallic tinkle, something landed at his feet. He looked down. "What the fuck is-"

Then there was a sudden flash of light, and everything went black.

69

*I*t was, thought Willow-Sigh Wen, the most chaotic battle she had ever fought. On all sides there were enemies, but most were fools lured by the hollow promise of wealth. Such a foe was to be pitied, not slain, and so each knife that slashed or stabbed at her was cleanly deflected with an open hand to the wrist or a precision strike to the inside of the elbow. At the same time, the blonde woman whose *ki* flowed with a dark, twisted malevolence came at her with lethal intent. There was evidence in her technique that someone involved in the killer's training had knowledge of the Path of Lightning, but no *Shansenshao* would ever have taught one with such chaos and hatred in their heart.

Nevertheless, just as darkness was required for light to be seen, so Chaos formed the perfect backcloth to Harmony, and as Wen fought she was as much ambassador as warrior. She deflected a blow from a man armed with a billhook, most likely one of the sailor-warriors of the Devil Thelen, and shoved him firmly back with a double-palm strike. The man glowered at her, and made to resume his attack when one of the silver-armoured beasts leapt at him, teeth bared and sword raised. Without breaking stride in her pursuit of the blonde killer, Wen hit the thing in its shoulder with a *Nao-Ken* strike, severing its sword-arm, before spinning into a leaping kick that smashed its head to ruin. The man she had repelled and then saved looked from her, to the weapon in his hands, and dropped it before beating a hasty retreat.

She drove on, combining deadly force where it was needed with restraint where that was more appropriate, but by now the blonde woman, responding to a shout from her companion, was in full flight and clear of the press of bodies. She was about to pursue, to leap onto the heads of the mob and simply run over them, when the sound of a dull explosion some way behind her drew her attention. She knew that sound- this was the second time this day she had heard it and the third in her life- and knew it could only herald trouble. Yet on turning, she found a more immediate problem. There were still several of the beast-men the tall *gwai-*

275

sen had somehow created rampaging through the crowd, most of whom were now simply trying to escape. But the things wore full armour and carried swords and shields, and moved with the speed of the desperately insane, and even as she watched a man contorted with agony as a silver blade was rammed through his back.

Muttering a curse against sorcery in general and the thralls of the Devil Thelen in particular, Wen moved to intervene, channelling her *ki* to scream a challenge.

"Murdering beasts! Things less than men, lower than worms! I am Willow-Sigh Wen of the First Chamber of Yoan-Shu! If you would drink blood and chew flesh this day, there is none worthier than mine. Come, then, and try to take it!"

The things did not understand her words, of course- few in that place could, even amongst those that were sane- but just as the Lullaby of Sun and Wind had charmed a Red Bear with its calm intent, so the fury of her challenge was clear to the beast-men. Turning aside from their other prey, they rushed at her, shrieking their hatred. Even as they did so, the hindmost was blasted to smithereens by the *gwai-sen* Sage who seemed to understand a little of her language, but then the rest were upon her. This was as it should be- the violence of Chaos meeting the stillness of Harmony in the battle that defined Creation itself. She slipped the first sword-blow, responding with a kick to the thing's upraised shield that shattered its arm and sent it sprawling backward into its fellows. Heedless, the rest still rushed in, no strategy or finesse polluting the purity of their aggression, and she responded in kind, a *Nao-Ken* severing the neck of the first and the motion flowing smoothly into a spinning knife-hand chop that smashed straight through the defences of the next to crush its ribcage. Even as she finished the move, her raised foot crashed down to pulp the face of the downed attacker. The last one, perhaps retaining a shred more cunning than the rest, tried to come at her from behind, but she pivoted forward, her right foot shooting out behind her and striking the creature in the groin so hard that it came out the other side. She retracted the kick rapidly, ignoring the disagreeable sensation of viscera around her toes and screaming her victory to the Heavens.

A blast of lightning flashed past her, annihilating the beast-man even as she realised that despite the horrific injury it had somehow remained standing. And then there was silence. The *gwai-sen* Sage walked towards her slowly, fatigue etched into his face, leaning on a staff for support which was carved with a prancing horse. The green crystal clutched in the animal's hooves glowed brightly.

"The last of them, that was," said the Sage, in passable Daxalai though his accent was oddly stilted.

"I thank you, Great Sage," replied Willow-Sigh, clutching her hands together in the customary bow of respect. "But I fear that a terrible fate may have overtaken my friend."

Rat-Tail Lao and Gundala hurried over. "Most esteemed Master Wen!" gasped the little merchant. "*Ranlaou* and the swordsman have been taken!"

"What happened?" asked Wen, though she thought she might have an idea.

"There was a woman- a blonde one, in a cloak, but not that she-dog that you fought," said Rat-Tail. "She threw a small device at the feet of *Ranlaou* and the swordsman and it exploded with the fury of Father Thunder. Then she gathered them up, and took them towards the docks with the help of a passing labourer."

"Then that is where I must go!" said Wen, but Rat-Tail shook his head.

"It is too late, Master Wen. Whilst you were engaged with those... things, she was already fleeing. You will never catch up with her!" He shouted the last at Wen's back.

Whether or not she could possibly succeed, she had to at least try to retrieve *Ranlaou*. There was too much at stake to do otherwise.

70

*T*he Last Anchor was close enough to the docks that Eri could still hear the sounds of fighting when she arrived and started looking for a boat. A casual observer might have thought it strange that someone as small and slender as the young warrior could carry Maike, a girl of about her own size, and still move at any speed, but the strength her Seal granted made it possible, if not easy.

She tossed the promised bag of Quoits to the man she'd bribed to carry the swordsman, who gave a curt nod, dumped the unconscious man on the jetty, and slouched off. It wasn't as if it had cost her anything- like the stun-bomb she had used, the money had been stolen from the robes of the unconscious Gelt. It was a bit of luck that during one of his many visits to the Belus Manse, the little man had shown off his new toy and the method of detonating the bombs it threw without using the Jandallan catapult that usually launched them. Despite the temptation, she'd left him in possession of the weapon, which he called *Myrka* after the former Crown Princess. She didn't want Jonas' crew to have any more reason to come after her and it was always possible there was a tracking spell on the damn thing.

Looking around the docks, she cursed under her breath. Those few ships that were in port were laid up to load or unload. Certainly none looked likely to be ready to depart at short notice. That only left the last resort. She ran down the jetty to where a grizzled old fisherman was preparing to put to sea in a small skiff.

"You!" she shouted, brandishing the sword she had looted from her captives. "Out. I'm taking this boat."

The old man looked from her, to the sword hovering by the tip of his nose, and hawked before spitting a large gob of chewing tobacco into the sea. "Like fuck y'are. You put t'sea in this tub without a man knows how t'sail 'er, y'may's well ram that fancy-pants sword in yer own guts."

For a split second, Eri dithered. Perhaps the man could be paid to sail her to the mainland, but the boat was so small that there was no way that she would be able to fit both of her prisoners in it along with him. She knew a bit about handling small boats- her father was a fisherman in Mernas- and there was no time to argue. Already she could hear that the battle at the back of the inn was over, and the winners, whoever they were, surely wouldn't take long to hear about her prisoners.

"Yeah?" she snapped, smashing the pommel of the sword into the man's face and knocking him reeling into the water. "Let's see."

She was just making sure the knots tying Maike and her friend together were sound when she looked up, and saw Willow-Sigh Wen running towards the docks. Her heart froze in her chest. She'd heard Gelt's tales of the fight on the beach before they'd captured the Initiate, the lethal power of her blows, and even at this rapidly decreasing distance she could see that both Wen's hands and feet were bloodstained. There was no question that if the Daxalai reached her, she was dead.

Quickly she pushed off, almost tripping over Maike's unconscious form as she tried to get into position to work the oars. Still, the childhood days helping her father paid off, and her Seal-enhanced strength saw the boat well clear of the dockside and accelerating by the time the black-skinned woman began to clatter across the boards of the jetty. Someone less scared and more cocky might have shipped their oars and stopped to revel in their victory, but Eri had heard enough heroic tales to know that people who did that sort of shit ended up dead. She kept rowing as if Death Herself pursued her. It didn't feel that far from the truth.

It suddenly struck her, even as the dock began to recede, that the Daxalai was going too fast to stop. Perhaps she planned to try to swim in pursuit, but Eri was sure that no-one living could swim faster than she could row. Still, she redoubled her efforts, and did well not to fumble the oars in shock when her pursuer ran off the end of the jetty and kept going.

Had Magister Julius been present, he might have explained that the terrified young woman was witnessing a superb demonstration of *Linyo-Shuyan*, the Calmed Waters. But he was not, and all Eri could tell was that the Daxalai had left the jetty and was now sprinting towards her across the waves. She fought down a thrill of panic and pulled at the oars again. Suddenly it seemed the boat wasn't moving as fast as she had imagined, and every beat of her hammering heart brought Death closer. The expression of perfect calm that Death bore made it all the worse.

"Shitshitshit...." she muttered, casting her eyes around for something, anything that could help. Her gaze fell briefly on the sword, but she put that thought out of her mind immediately. She'd seen enough of the Dax's skills to make fighting her seem like insanity. Then she saw what else rested in the boat, and a desperate plan began to form. Doing her best to look like she was panicking, which took little acting ability under the circumstances, she watched as the Initiate closed her down, picking her moment. She'd seen how the Dax handled Erika, and-

There it was! As she covered the last few strides separating her from the boat, the Daxalai leapt into the air, in a kick which even if it failed to connect would surely carry her into the tiny vessel. At the same instant, Eri ducked and swept up the heavy, barnacle-encrusted fishing net that had been nestling in the stern. The net, which was weighted at the edges, filled the air between warrior and boat and left nowhere for Wen to go. Giving a strangled gasp, her focus completely disrupted, the Daxalai woman hit the water with a ragged splash. Not even daring to look to see what her pursuer's fate might be, Eri bent to her oars again. She rowed as if possessed by nothing but the desire to row, as if rowing was the sum totality of her existence.

71

*S*miling Snake sat and watched the morning's proceedings with a sense of some foreboding. This day, Frowning Iron would deliver his final report on the defeat of the White Turbans, and there would be celebration and great honour. But then, the subject of the pacification of the Chaotic East would be raised. Once again, the Hono clan would be pressed to extend the Celestial Harmony's reach to the lands of the Devil Thelen or forfeit the head of its leader, his brother.

He had considered and rejected several strategies already. Swan-Neck Tsue, an ambitious and suitably distant cousin, was already positioned to inherit the leadership of the clan, and he had briefly entertained the notion of engineering the succession whilst his brother yet lived. Even allowing that such a thing could be done without heaping such dishonour on Tekkan-Cho that he was driven to suicide, there would be no guarantee that his title as General would be passed on at the same time. Frowning Iron could very well find himself with the same task, and reduced resources with which to accomplish it.

The Stepping Mirror, that ill-starred gift from the Purple Robes, seemed still to function. He had investigated the device further, and it seemed that there may yet be other places it could take him but he could not be sure where any of them might be, and to activate the device again to a new destination would cost more sacrificial vessels than the Hono clan could command. Even if such a thing could be done, he had nothing but the vaguest of ideas as to where the other portals might be, and without that knowledge the Mirror would remain silent.

Of course there was yet time, and even as he sat next to his brother Bai Faoha was deep in communion with the Tapestry, searching for any information that could be of use. It was certainly helpful to have another who knew how to use the device, though he always preferred knowledge to be gleaned first hand. Though he trusted White Crocus implicitly- the Heavens knew, the young Sage already knew enough secrets to destroy him were he traitorous- there was always the risk that information might be relayed imperfectly, or that a minor detail might be missed.

General Pao-Sho of the Doha was coming to the end of his speech, the Son Of Heaven fixing him intently with his terrible gaze. The veteran General Who Shields Cities kept his account short and to the point, neither embellishing nor downplaying his role, as was proper. Perhaps a later epic poem might allow for such liberties, but they withered in the face of Heaven's own representative. Nevertheless, he was fulsome in his praise of the Hono clan for their prompt assistance and the honourable manner of their conduct.

"Once, in Roan-Lin, a swallow was seen in winter," said the Son of Heaven when Pao-Sho had finished. "All marvelled at the sight, for the swallow flew east at the first sign of snow and returned only with the spring rains."

"The Son of Heaven considers that the timing of the Hono clan army's return was most fortuitous," translated the old man who was Echo of the Clouds for this morning's audience. "He asks what explanation you might have for this."

Pao-Sho stroked his beard thoughtfully. "I can only think of it as the beneficence of Heaven. The starving man does not ponder the miracle of rice when his supper is placed before him, he is merely grateful for it."

The Son of Heaven smiled and nodded, and closed his terrible eyes for a moment. The Mouth of the Day took the cue, and pronounced Pao-Sho's audience completed. Then came the words Smiling Snake had dreaded.

"Presenting to His Most Glorious Imperial Majesty, who Speaks with Thunder and Calms the Storm, Tekkan-Cho of Hono, General who Subdues the East."

Frowning Iron stepped boldly forwards and pressed his face to the floor at the foot of the throne, as his brother had seen him do so many times before. Fortunately, on this occasion Rya-Ki himself would not be called upon to speak, since the matter at hand was purely military.

"O great Son of Heaven, whose might is as boundless as the skies and whose power is as enduring as the greatest mountain, I, Tekkan-Cho of Hono, beg to report that the White Turban rebels have been defeated. Through the masterful strategy of Sage Rya-Ki and the valour of Pao-Sho Doha and the warriors of our two clans was this thing done. The facts of the campaign are exactly as the General Who Shields Cities related them."

"When the island of Wonloan sank beneath the waves, only the temple of Xu remained above the waters," said the Son of Heaven. "Yet all knew that the golden treasures of Emperor Tso still slumbered beneath."

"The Son of Heaven knows that there is more you wish to tell Him, General," said the Echo of Clouds.

Smiling Snake thought that to be one of the most unnecessary translations he had ever heard, and yet protocol must be observed. A tiny thrill of fear ran through him, however, and he had to focus to prevent the ring-chimes on his staff from jangling in sympathy. What had Tekkan-Cho left unsaid?

"The Son of Heaven is most wise, and his knowledge eclipses the brightness of Mother Sun," said Frowning Iron. "Upon the bloody field of victory, I came to a realisation. It is a matter of philosophy, not of fact, but I will share it if that is Heaven's will."

The Son of Heaven smiled, and nodded. Tekkan-Cho took a deep breath.

"It shall be as the Son of Heaven commands. I stood upon the field of Sool-Yan, that lies east of this blessed city, and watched the bodies of those who dared deny Harmony heaped in piles. And yet I confess that the sight, which should have brought me joy, instead filled me with a deep sorrow."

A low murmur of consternation rolled around the audience chamber. To admit to such thoughts whilst carrying out one's duty to the Harmony was a dangerous thing. The expression of the Son of Heaven, however, did not change.

"I am the General who Subdues the East, by title," continued Frowning Iron. "And I am the first to set foot in the lands of the Devil Thelen since the inception of the post. I have already related the tale of what I faced there, of savage warriors and of the wrathful *kami* who forced the Hono's retreat and closed the way to us. But as I looked upon the charnel fields of Sool-Yan, I wondered what might have been had our assault succeeded. I saw a man, a Sage among his people, who I had taken to be a Necromancer with no honour, sacrifice himself to halt my advance. I saw innocent women and children flee from a bared sword that sought only the blood of the guilty and corrupt."

"The cubs of the Great Lion of Hein-Xao feared not Waolan the Hunter," said the Son of Heaven. "The bow he bore was only for their man-eating father."

"None who are innocent need fear the blade of Justice," said the Echo of Clouds.

"The Son of Heaven is most wise and correct in all things," said Tekkan-Cho, sadly. "And yet fear me, they did. I am a General, and my tool is the sword. If a knotted rope bars my path, I take out my sword and cut it. It does not cross my mind to pause, remove my gauntlets, and seek to untie the knot, that the rope might be put to good use. But at Sool-Yan, I saw what lies at the end of such a path. Not honour, not glory, not Harmony. Merely death, misery and fear."

Slowly, making sure it could not be interpreted as an attack, Frowning Iron drew his sword. "This blade was forged for my father's father by his father. It is said that were it ever to taste the flesh of an innocent man, it would shatter into a million pieces. O great Son of Heaven, I fear that should I take this sword again into the lands of the Devil Thelen to impose Harmony upon their Chaos, it will break."

He slid the weapon carefully back into the sheath. "So I sheathe this blade. I shall draw it to strike the enemies of Harmony, and I shall draw it to strike those who wilfully deny the divine right of Heaven. But I shall not draw it to strike those whose only crime is to be ignorant of the true path. Such as they are in need of a guiding light, not a cutting blade."

He dropped again to his knees, pressing his face against the ground. "This, then, is the revelation that came to me on the field of victory. If my words are displeasing to the Son of Heaven, I offer my unworthy head in recompense. I ask only that my clan be spared, for these thoughts are mine, and mine alone."

There was silence. Smiling Snake had watched and listened with mounting horror as his brother's speech had continued. To think, after all his efforts to protect the clan and Tekkan-Cho's head, that an idle remark of his could have borne such perilous fruit! And yet to all outward appearances, the Great Sage bore an expression of complete calm. His clan head had spoken, and the Son of Heaven was yet to respond. To show any opinion of his own at this moment would be most improper.

Suddenly the Son of Heaven broke out in a bright, beaming smile. "The Yellow

Curse fell upon Yoshan'Ru, and great was the sadness of that people. But from that sadness was born the joy of Harmony, though it took two-hundred years."

"Great sorrow often leads to profound revelation," said the Echo of the Clouds. "Such it is with you, Frowning Iron of Hono."

Frowning Iron looked up in confusion. "I... I do not understand, O great Son of Heaven."

"And then was Waolan's divine bow burned for seven years in the fires of Wen-Shian," said the Son. "But great was the rejoicing, for his people's need was for warmth."

"Rise, General Who Brings Harmony to the East," translated the Echo. "Yours is a revelation that has been long in the coming."

72

he coach rolled smoothly through the twisting streets of Abellan, the clattering of hooves drowning out any other sounds. Within the confines of the city the vehicle was restricted to a far slower pace than they had travelled at previously, which at least gave Thalia a chance to admire the scenery. The streets were busy enough, but she noticed that many of the passers-by were dressed in the livery of the various Great Families.

"This is a charade, put on for visiting eyes, I think," she mused, as much to herself as to Delys. "I'd be willing to wager that if we left the main streets and took to the back roads, we'd be seeing deserted pavements and empty houses."

The little Swordmaster didn't reply, which was hardly surprising. She'd been distant all that morning, ever since they had left the Green Palace without word from the hospital.

"Don't worry, Delys," said Thalia, trying to be encouraging. "I'm sure Amanda and Athas are fine. Actually, with that link of yours, surely if Amanda was in danger you could tell?"

Delys nodded.

"Wait, do you think that she is?" Another nod. "Thelen's breath, why didn't you say.. I mean, why didn't you tell me?"

The Swordmaster shrugged. *Nothing to tell.*

"I suppose not. So you've got a.. feeling that something isn't right, but you can't tell what?"

Delys nodded again, more emphatically this time.

"Hmph. Me too. Listen, once I'm done meeting the Queen, we'll visit the hospital. If these idiots won't take us then we'll find another way, but we're going. Agreed?"

Yes.

Thalia watched as the view from the coach window climbed higher. Though Abellan showed no overall sign of having been built to a plan, there was

285

certainly a network of main streets that ran through the city, and this one was spiralling upwards and inwards, towards the summit of the hill that the Alabaster Durance was built on. There were almost certainly more direct routes, but this one gave a traveller a good look at the size and majesty of the Abelian capital. She had to admit that it was impressive, and even larger than Lore. Despite the fact that a mere fraction of the people it had been built to accommodate still lived there, the Stickmen were maintaining the city in excellent condition.

"That's one thing the Empire and the Abelians have in common at the moment," she said, wanting to fill the silence with something other than hoof-beats. "More places to put people than people to put in them. Mind you, we only lost a city or so worth- well, two if you count Manadar, but most of the civilians were evacuated."

Three. Delys signed the number with some force.

"Three? Blood, ice and fire, you're right. There was Phyre too. Our last civil war cost us almost the entire population of three cities and we're still better off than the Abelians! Do you know, Delys, I think that Athas was on to something."

Delys cocked a head to one side enquiringly.

"About the Har'ii, I mean. They have too many people, we and the Abelians don't have enough. If we can deal with this Dendaril problem, I'm going to be having words with anyone who'll listen about offering the Har'ii a place on the mainland."

As if it would be that easy, she thought, sourly. The Abelians seemed fairly happy with their nation of stick-puppets and she couldn't see many of the Magister Houses wanting to give up territory to the Har'ii, however much sense it would make. None of it would matter anyway if she couldn't convince Queen Tondarin, though. She needed to focus on that for now.

The coach swung around again, and the walls of the Alabaster Durance hove into view. They were close now, and making a final approach to the outer gates. Thalia studied the walls as they passed. She was sure they couldn't actually be made of alabaster, and a quick look confirmed that the pure white cladding covered walls of plain marble. Opinion among the Weavers differed on exactly why, but marble was a far easier material to reinforce with Aether than common stone, and even certain precious and semi-precious stones responded poorly to the process. The alabaster did look impressive, though, and the walls were both high and well-fortified.

They passed through the outer gates unchallenged; the coach presumably came with certain privileges, and Thalia had a nasty feeling that commandeering it for her trip to the hospital was going to be difficult. As the massive doors closed behind them, Sir Terence rode up alongside the coach window and gestured at the glass, which dissolved away. She did her best not to look impressed at the trick.

"We are now approaching Castle Valour, Your Excellency," said the Royal Knight.

"What?" said Thalia. "We're *approaching* the castle? What was that we just went through, then?"

"The Alabaster Durance was built to defend Castle Valour, Your Excellency," said Sir Terence, patiently. "But also, at times, to contain it. See here."

He pointed back the way they had come, and Thalia looked to see the inside of the huge, fortified wall that surrounded Castle Valour. It was every bit as well defended from this direction as from the other.

"The Alabaster Durance is unique among fortifications," said Sir Terence, his helm flaring with light as he spoke. "It is designed so that, in.. unusual circumstances, the city can be defended against the ruler, or the ruler against the city."

Thalia vaguely remembered being told something about this at school, but at the time Abelia had seemed a distant land not worthy of her attention. "Has it been.. used often?"

"Twice, in recorded history," replied the Knight. "But see, we have reached the main gate. Here I must leave you, Your Excellency, and wish you good fortune!"

Unable to bow on his horse, Sir Terence instead touched his hand to his helm in salute, and wheeled his horse to ride back the way he had come, the window shimmering back into place as he did so. Thalia took a quick look at Castle Valour as the coach slowed. In stark contrast to the Durance, it was built of glossy black marble, shot through with purple veins and accented with gold crests. And the flags! From every tower and battlement flew a multitude of flags, pennants and banners, in wildly clashing colours and designs. Some were clearly war trophies- she saw the old battle standard of the Third Volume, lost when Sebastian Vox had fallen- but she recognised few of the others.

The coach stopped, and one of the footmen opened the door for her. She stepped out, closely followed by Delys, and blinked in the late-morning sun. A vast, perfectly-manicured lawn stretched from the castle as far as the walls of the Durance, dotted with statues, tinkling ornamental fountains and flowerbeds and patrolled by tall, brightly-coloured flightless birds. Thalia noticed, however, that the space was entirely flat and few of the ornaments would provide any sort of cover to an attacker. This was a killing-ground, albeit an aesthetically-pleasing one.

The footmen led the way over a drawbridge that spanned a wide, clear moat. Looking over the side, Thalia could see all the way to the bottom, her view obscured only by shoals of fish if anything even more vivid than the birds.

"Have a care, please, Your Excellency," said the head footman, seeing her craning her neck to look. "These waters may look inviting, but some of those fish are man-eaters."

"Aye," nodded another. "The last fool to try to swim that moat was clean-picked in minutes. We had to use the Stickmen to get the bones out."

Thalia straightened up carefully. "I see. Thank you for the warning. Should I assume that those birds are equally dangerous?"

The head footman smiled. "Aye, Your Excellency. They are usually passive, but on the Queen's command they will attack, and a kick from one of them will dent a War Golem."

Thalia swallowed. Not for the first time in this place, it seemed beauty and danger went hand-in-hand. Of course, she thought with a sidelong glance at Delys, that also counted for her own company. They carried on walking, through a large entrance hall every bit as impressive as that in the Royal Keep in Equinox had been. It was finished in rose quartz, with a floor of white marble patterned with swirls of black and purple, surmounted by a wide gold carpet that led up a flight of stairs to a massive set of white-gold doors. As they reached them, the head footman dropped back a pace and murmured softly to Thalia.

287

"A word of caution, Your Excellency. The Queen is currently five months, two-and-a-half months, and five weeks pregnant. Her mood may be somewhat.. mercurial."

Before Thalia could ask for an explanation of this bizarre pronouncement, or even close her gaping mouth, the doors swung open and the footman advanced to announce her.

"Presenting to the Court Her Excellency Ambassador Thalia Daran, Daughter of Isadora and Talion Daran, the Mountainbreaker. Your Excellency, you stand in the presence of Her Exceptional Majesty Queen Tondarin II, Daughter of Her Refined Highness Lady Doras and His Most Exceptional Majesty King Tobias I, and Queen of Abelia, Abelian Jandalla, and the Islands of the Warriors' Sea."

Thalia, still open-mouthed in surprise, remembered to curtsy as Lady Ysabella had shown her just in time. Why the Orsinio hadn't mentioned the Queen's pregnancy, she could not understand, and nor could she reconcile what she had been told with what she was seeing. The Audience Chamber was huge, and lined with various noblemen, Royal Knights and Wizards. The walls positively dripped with fine paintings, tapestries, even more banners and all manner of other artworks. None of this was any great surprise to her, but the occupant of the throne that stood on a raised dais in the centre of the room certainly was.

The woman seated there looked every inch the regal Queen of Abelia Thalia might have expected. In her late thirties, she was tall, and possessed a cold, regal beauty. Her hair was raven-black and exquisitely coiffured, arranged in a much more elaborate version of the horsetail braid Ilia had worn. Her flawless skin was almost as white as the walls of the Alabaster Durance, and her lips were the red of fresh blood. Aristocratic eyes of deep brown topped by finely-plucked eyebrows stared at Thalia coldly as she began to come to her feet. Yet none of this, impressive as it was, was causing the Magister's shock.

The Queen wore a long, elaborate dress that plunged at the front in a manner no less daring, or indeed challenging, than that of any of the other Abelian noblewomen Thalia had met. It was made of rich purple silk trimmed in gold, black, and white lace, and cinched in tightly at the waist by a corset which the Orsinios had told her was armoured. Indeed, the woman's waist was no wider than Delys', and made Thalia's look decidedly plump. And yet this was a woman who was apparently, according to what she had been told, heavily pregnant. In triplicate, somehow.

If the Queen herself presented an impressive figure, those flanking her throne were no less so. To her left stood what Thalia presumed must be her personal armour. It was designed much like that of any other Royal Knight, though more richly-decorated, and the breastplate and general design left no doubt to any observer that the wearer was female. Thalia had seen the large, and probably optimistic, cod-pieces on the armour of several of the Knights, but this was the first time she had seen the concept taken to such an extreme, much less in such a feminine direction. To say that the Abelians placed great stock in fertility seemed to be an understatement.

To the right of the throne was an even more imposing figure. Where the Queen's armour was almost eight feet tall, this one stood nearer ten, and bore a massive, decorated shield on one arm. Though as large and heavy-looking as a War Golem, the automaton had fully articulated hands, and its sword, almost as large as Delys', rode in a scabbard at its hip rather then being built into its wrist. This, then, must be the Guardian. Looking at the three of them, Thalia could only conclude that the man who tried to assassinate the Queen under such circumstances must have been categorically insane.

"You are Thalia Daran?" said the Queen, her voice so commanding that Thalia almost felt the need to snap to attention.

"I am, Your Exceptional Majesty," she said, adding a second, smaller curtsy for good measure.

"Excellent," said the Queen. "Take her to the dungeons."

73

By the time Wen Lian-Shi had disentangled herself from the net and kicked back to the surface, her lungs were screaming in protest. She had to confess that she had not thought *Li-lan* to be so resourceful. Underestimating her had been a serious, and very nearly fatal, mistake. The boat was still in sight when she finally gasped a much-needed breath, but there was no point in attempting to pursue further. Her *ki* had already been sorely taxed by the fight, and the *Linyo-Shuyan* required a running start in any case. Resigning herself to the fact that once again the Heavens had seen fit to thwart her designs, she kicked powerfully for the shore. No Initiate needed to resort to their *ki* for mere swimming.

When the *gwai-sen* Sage found her, she was drying herself in the midday sun whilst meditating, her eyes staring out to sea. The man was sweating with the effort of the days' exertions, but he had clearly taken a moment to gather himself before following her. He had also taken the precaution of employing the services of Rat-Tail Lao.

"The *gwai-sen* asks if you were successful in your pursuit, Master Wen," said the little merchant.

"That is a question which needs no answer," replied Lian-Shi, softly, not taking her eyes from the sea.

"Regardless, The Most Learned Magister Julius wishes to convey his thanks for your assistance with the... Shining Men."

"They are neither necessary, nor wanted," said Wen. "I did only what any servant of Harmony must do when peril threatens the innocent."

"There are very few of those here," pointed out Rat-Tail.

"They were innocent of anything I knew of," replied Wen, but a slight smile twitched on her face and after a moment she stood and bowed to Julius. "Very well. If you will not leave me alone, Sage, then we shall speak."

"If the Heavens did not wish us to speak, they would not have gifted us tongues," replied Julius directly. "Better is my Daxalai when quoting Ton-Fan Rin."

Lian-Shi winced. "Your accent still hurts my ears, Sage. What of *Konto, Shimen* and *Daolin*?"

The Magister gave her an odd look, thought for a moment, and then spoke rapidly in his barbarous tongue for Rat-Tail to translate. "Magister Julius wonders where you found a trio of traditional Daxalai instruments, and why you ask about them now."

"They are the names by which I know those three dogs who attacked us," replied Wen. "Until now, I knew them only by the sounds of their voices."

Julius didn't wait for a translation this time. "Where?" he asked excitedly, using the most imperative form of the word in a manner so impertinent that Wen had to resist the urge to box his ears.

"It was when I was the guest of the Most Learned Vice-Chancellor," replied Wen. Julius' eyes went even wider than they already were, and he motioned urgently, muttering to Rat-Tail.

"The *gwai-sen* considers this a matter best addressed in private," said the merchant. "He suggests we reconvene in his room."

A brisk walk took them to the inn in the Upper Tier where Julius was staying. Ignoring the stares of the cook and clientele, the Magister led them up to his room, offering Wen a bucket of clean water to wash the salt from her skin. Swiftly she stripped off her clothing whilst the man secured the door, and she felt his *ki* surge.

"I have silence to this place brought," said Julius, turning back and almost dropping his staff in shock at the sight of Wen's nakedness. Rat-Tail laughed.

"Magister Julius' people still regard the naked form as taboo, Master Wen," he reminded her. "He was not expecting you to completely disrobe."

Wen shrugged. "My clothes are irksomely soaked through with salt water. Unless the Sage has any others, I will remain this way until they are washed."

Julius had turned his back, his skin flushing bright red in the same odd way *Ranlaou's* sometimes did when she was angry or embarrassed, and Rat-Tail chuckled again. "He says he will buy you fresh clothes once you have talked, and asks if you will cover yourself with the bed-sheet until then."

Rolling her eyes at the infantile nature of Eastern culture, Wen did as she was bid. Fortunately one sheet of cloth was much the same as another, and she was able to fashion a simple robe with a knot that she could release quickly in an emergency. As she finished tying it, Julius spoke again.

"Magister Julius says this would be easier if you would allow him to cast the spell," translated Rat-Tail with some reluctance. Wen shook her head. On the way to the inn Julius had suggested that he cast a spell that would allow her to speak and understand his language. Whilst she could understand the usefulness of such a thing, Lian-Shi had been taught that to speak such tongues was to invite Chaos into the mind, and she had no desire to do so. Her relationship with the Heavens seemed to be quite complicated enough already.

"Very well," said Julius, through Rat-Tail. "Then please, tell me how you came to be in the power of the Vice-Chancellor."

As quickly as she could whilst leaving nothing out, Willow-Sigh explained how she had been forced to escort the Daxalai Ambassador, Silver-Tongue Yue, as he fled death at the hands of the Midnight Tiger. How the ship that they had taken passage on, the *Flying Wight,* had been overtaken by Toskan pirates and sunk by a Whale after the battle, with the Ambassador borne away alive. And how she had found herself washed up on a lonely beach, before her encounter with a pack of scavengers had ended with them dead and her unconscious at the hands of a stun-bomb.

"So that was what you kicked back at the inn balcony!" exclaimed the Magister as Rat-Tail swiftly translated. "Regrettably, there was no trace of any of those three after the fight. I should dearly like to encounter them again."

"As would I," agreed Lian-Shi. "But to do so would mean to return to the Vice-Chancellor's lair, and that I will not do. *Do-Sou-Roh* is not one for a simple mortal to trifle with. I know not how, but that one commands the might of Heaven."

74

The scouting party arrived at the Mountain Halls a little after noon. The scene was as terrible as Second had imagined it would be. Hurriedly, she slipped behind a nearby tree and changed back to the woman-shape. The senses of the wolf were being overwhelmed by the stench.

"Shit," said Tika, after reuniting the Tree-Searcher with her harness. "I'd heard about what happened here, but... Thelen's breath."

Second nodded as she adjusted the fastenings of her clothing. "Aye. I have never seen anything like it."

"We have," said Dani, bluntly. "Doesn't get any better when you see it again."

Red Trace arrived, and set down Alben Koont, who wordlessly handed over the rest of Second's gear. For once, no-one really noticed the smell. Ahead of them lay the clearing in which the last Moot of Kings had been held. Before, it had been a pleasant, calming place, surrounded by proud, tall trees that had stood firm through the devastation of the Mountain Halls. Now, most of those trees lay in smouldering ruin, and fire-blackened corpses were strewn about as if hurled by some monstrous hand. Near the centre of the clearing, where Second had last seen the Black Skull, several bodies were huddled in a heap, though few of the charred cadavers retained all of their limbs.

Captain Render gave the pile an experimental poke with her sword. "Looks like what Sir Matthew told us was right, anyway. Burn the corpses quick enough, and those Tick things can't get out to infest anyone else."

The other two Wardens stared at her in horror. "Captain..." hissed Tika, jerking her head at Red Trace and Second.

"What? Oh, fuck me," gasped the Captain, retreating hurriedly. "Sorry, these were your people. I should have shown more respect."

"Why?" said Red Trace in White Snow, with a snort. "They are dead. They do not care."

He strode around the clearing, heedless to the crunching of charred bones beneath his boots. Reaching the Seat that had belonged to the Heart-Eaters, he gave a grunt of appreciation. "See here the power of a Mighty One, Deluded. So hot was the final fire of the Black Skull, that even the fine silver blades of your people could not withstand it."

Second could see what he meant. Alone among the Thinking Seats, that of the Stonesingers had largely survived, the magically-worked stone burned black but still whole. The others had been almost completely obliterated, and in the place where the Heart-Eaters' plundered armchair had stood were nothing but ash and a few pieces of melted metal.

"This is all very interesting, Second," said Captain Render, "but we need a vantage point and this doesn't look like one."

"We must go further up the mountainside," replied Second. "But this is as far as the Stone Paths could take us."

"This place is also where the Blackblood Woe-bearers were last seen," rumbled Red Trace. "We should not be so foolish as to think that Black Skull slew all of them in his final act, Mighty though he was."

Render nodded. "Aye to that. Alben, scout ahead, make sure our way is clear. Second, bring up the rear and watch our backs. Everyone make sure you have your oil flasks ready."

Second checked that the flask of foul-smelling black liquid was still in its place on her harness. The Mighty Ones and their robed counterparts seemed convinced that the method they had come up with to counter the Woe would work, but she wasn't so sure. After all, the Blackbloods had been certain that the Hissing Serpent would protect them, and the trees knew how that had turned out.

They moved on up the slope, travelling as fast as they dared. Second longed to shift again, to let the keen senses of the wolf take over once more, but stealthy as she was she had to admit that the Green Shadow was almost impossible to detect when he wanted to be. Were they to encounter a Woe-bearer, her spear would be of more use than her nose.

As if she had summoned him with her thoughts, Alben Koont suddenly appeared ahead of them. His fingers flicked a quick sign that Second couldn't understand, and Captain Render immediately held up a hand for them to halt. She motioned Second and Red Trace over to her and they hunkered down to listen.

"There's one of your people up ahead. Chances are he's become one of those Dendaril things, but we need to find out who he is and what he knows," she whispered. Red Trace nodded, and stood up.

"What are you doing?" hissed the Captain.

"You wish to know who he is? I shall ask him," said Red Trace, flatly, shouldering his axe and striding ahead.

Dani and Tika exchanged a glance. "Well, better him than me," muttered Dani.

"Shut it," whispered Render. "Dani, you know what to do."

The Archer nodded, and nocked an arrow. Ahead of them, they heard Red Trace call out a greeting.

"Ho, warrior of the Free! I am Red Trace in White Snow, of the Heart-Eaters. What brings a man of the Blackbloods so far from your lands?"

"The Blackbloods?" replied the other man. "I do not know what you mean, my friend. My name is Walter."

Red Trace's axe-head thudded into the earth as he rested his hands on the weapon's haft. "I think that unlikely. You bear the Hissing Serpent, mark of your tribe. No warrior of that tribe ever owned such a name, especially not one unmarried, as your face-paint tells you to be."

"What does being married have to do with my name?" laughed 'Walter'. "I think you are confused, my friend. Come with me to see the Pilgrims, and soon you will know the truth. My hand is open, as is my heart."

Unable to hold themselves back any longer, the rest of the scouting party, with the notable exception of Alben Koont, gathered behind Red Trace to see what was going on. Second gave a gasp of surprise.

"This one is known to me. He is a warrior of the Blackbloods, as you say, Red Trace in White Snow. He is the Second of Blood in Secret Places, and brother to Mighty Black Skull who sits now with the Ancestors. I saw him before the Moot."

"Black Skull who does what now?" said Dani, confused.

"I think she means the dead one," said Sergeant Tika. "You know, it's a title and it got passed on when this guy's brother blew himself up back there."

"Do you remember your brother, Second of Blood in Secret Places?" said Red Trace, with surprising gentleness. "Did you witness his fate?"

"Oh, I have many brothers and sisters, friend," said the man with a broad smile. "Though I do not know of whom you speak. Come, let us go to the Pilgrims."

"Where *are* the Pilgrims, Walter?" asked Render, suddenly, furiously gesturing for the rest of them to be quiet.

"Why... I..." said Walter, closing his eyes for a moment. "Ah, they are still far to the east. They are coming here, though. Perhaps it will be easier if we wait for them together? I have gathered some fruit, will you share some?"

Tika put her hands on her hips in bemusement. "Riiight. I don't know about anyone else, but I'm not getting that 'dangerous invader' feel from this guy."

"He looks the part, though," said Dani thoughtfully, still keeping her bow ready. "I mean look at him. Six foot of muscle if I'm any judge, all the usual battle-tattoos the Skinnies- shit, no offence- have. But he talks like a librarian in Lore."

"That's the fucking point," hissed Captain Render. "Those tick-things do this to a person- replace who they were with... with whatever this is. This bastard might seem harmless, but he doesn't even remember his own brother!"

"I tire of this," said Red Trace in White Snow. "Walter, was it? Do you bear the Little Ones in your gut?"

"I bear the Gift, yes," said Walter with a smile. "As do all the Blessed. With the Pilgrims we will carry it west and share it with everyone we meet. Such peace and contentment it brings, friends! Such happiness when the time comes for your Ending, and your eyes behold the Bearers emerging to bring a new birth!"

"To bring a new birth?" said Tika, slowly. "What do you mean?"

"Why, it is simple, sister-to-be," said Walter. "When a child is old enough for their Beginning, a Vessel is chosen, and from the throes of their Ending emerge the Bearers. The swiftest joins with the child, and a new brother or sister is born. Truly, it is a wondrous and most beautiful ceremony, though I am too young to have witnessed it yet."

"Too young?" said Second. "You are a man of some eighty seasons, Second of Blood in Secret Places!"

Walter laughed. "So the flesh-that-was may have been. But I am Walter, and I am as yet mere weeks old."

"Then how do you even know any of this?" asked Captain Render. Walter chuckled.

"Because I have the Gift, of course! These things are known to all the Blessed."

Second suddenly noticed that Dani's bow-string was taut, and her arms quivered with tension. "They... they do it to fucking kids, Sarge," she growled, her voice low and dangerous. "They put those things in *fucking kids!*"

"Easy, Dani," muttered Tika. "You know we can't point fingers after what we did..."

"Fuck that!" snapped Dani. "I'm not denying we did terrible shit, Sarge. Thelen knows, we'll answer for it when we go back to Him. But we never pretended we were doing anyone a fucking favour! Look at this grinning cunt- he thinks scooping kids' brains out and replacing them with a fucking *bug* is something to celebrate!"

There was a soft thump as Red Trace in White Snow leant his axe against a nearby tree. Smiling, he walked over to the man who called himself Walter, pointedly placing his bulk between him and Dani's bow.

"Friend Walter," he said, quietly. "You say that you will bring your gift to all of the Free? To our wives, mothers and children, who will be reborn as new in your great family?"

"Of course!" said Walter, beaming. "The Blessing is a gift to all, and it will be my honour one day to bear it forth!"

"But not today?" said Red Trace, draping his arm companionably around the shorter man's shoulders.

"Not for me, no," said Walter. "I am not ready to be a Vessel at my tender age, friend. Scarce few Bearers make their nests within me."

"Know that this gives me no pleasure, man who now calls himself Walter." said Red Trace, sadly. His enfolding arms suddenly tightened, locking the man in a choking grip.

"F-friend... I..." croaked the Dendaril, clawing at the iron-hard muscles constricting his neck.

"Woe upon this day," said Red Trace in White Snow, squeezing harder. "Woe upon the day that Red Trace in White Snow slew a man who in his dying breath named him friend."

There was a sudden, terrible crack, and the Dendaril went limp in the warrior's arms. He dropped the corpse and stepped back, a look of slack despair on his face.

"Don't just fucking stand there!" snapped Captain Render. "Sergeant! Oil!"

Shaking herself out of her shock, Sergeant Tika ran forwards, pulling the stopper on her oil flask and dousing the twitching corpse liberally with the contents. Even as she did so, something began to try to force its way out of the man's mouth. She leapt back, and the moment she was clear Dani loosed her arrow. The streak of silver fire struck the oil-drenched body, and immediately the entire corpse was engulfed in flame. One insect still somehow managed to take flight, its wings blazing, but Red Trace's massive hand slammed it into ruin against a tree.

They watched the thing burn to ash for a minute or two in silence. Then Captain Render turned to Red Trace.

"What the fuck was that?"

The big warrior shrugged. "What else would you have had me do? We could not take him with us, and these trees know we could not allow him to simply roam the Forest Home with those things gnawing through his gut! Umba's teeth!"

He stomped over to his axe and retrieved it. "Think you that I took pleasure in this? There was no glory in this act, there will be no song sung of it! But know this, First of the Wardens." He turned to glare at Render. "There is nothing I will not do, no grief I will not bear, to keep those things from taking Fleeting Deer and my daughters from me. Return to the Doors of Patros if you wish, but I will not yield."

Captain Render nodded. "Fair enough. Can't say any of this shit sits well with me but I can't argue with that."

"At least we know the oil works," said Tika. "I'm out, though. Maybe we could have got away with using less, but I didn't fucking fancy risking it."

"We've still got... six more flasks between us," said Render. "Still, this is a scouting mission so unless any others we see look important we'll try to avoid any more encounters with these.. things."

"*A WISE COURSE, CAPTAIN,*" came a deep, rumbling voice from the tree behind Red Trace. With an oath, the big warrior whirled, smashing a Harbinger Skull which had been hanging from the branches to pieces with his axe.

"*REFRAIN FROM DOING THAT AGAIN,*" said the same voice from another tree a little further away. "*PRECIOUS FEW HARBINGERS REMAIN.*"

"What.. the.. fuck..?" gasped Sergeant Tika, her sword hissing out of the scabbard.

"It is the work of dread Ixil!" roared Red Trace, advancing on the second Harbinger Skull. Second saw that the thing's eye-sockets were blazing with an unnatural fire.

"Stay back, Thelen damn it!" snapped Render, drawing her own sword and holding it out to block the big warrior's path, lodging its tip in the tree. "We're here for information, remember?"

"*YOUR MISTRESS CHOOSES HER SERVANTS WELL, AMILEA LEVELL,*" said the skull. "*I BEAR TIDINGS WHICH ALL MUST HEAR.*"

"Who?" said Tika, looking about, but Second was too angry to pay attention to her.

"Be silent, dread one!" she shouted. "The Forest Home is not yours to claim, and the Free are not your tools to use! Begone from this place, and never return!"

"*I WAS IN THIS PLACE LONG BEFORE YOU WERE BORN, WOLF,*" said the skull. "*AND DO NOT THINK YOUR TRUE NAME IS A SECRET TO ME.*"

"No!" gasped Second, clamping her hands to her ears desperately.

"I will smash you to powder, minion of evil!" roared Red Trace, trying to lever Render's sword out of the way with his axe and finding, to his evident surprise, that he could not.

"*ENOUGH BLUSTER, WARRIOR,*" said the skull. "*YOUR VALOUR IN DEALING WITH THE DENDARIL WAS WHAT MADE YOU WORTHY OF MY TIME. DO NOT SQUANDER THIS BOON.*"

"I.. What?" said Red Trace, confusion painted on his face as clearly as his marriage-marks.

"*KNOW, WARRIORS OF THELEN THE FOOL, THAT THE DENDARIL ADVANCE. MY THRALLS HAVE SLOWED THEM, AND YOUR WISER FELLOWS NOW PROSPER AT IXILDUNDAL. YET I WILL NOT ABANDON MY PEOPLE. KNOW THAT THE WOE-BEARERS ARE SIMPLE BEASTS, WHO*

SEEK TO DRIVE WEST SIMPLY BECAUSE THAT IS WHERE THE MOST PEOPLE MAY BE FOUND TO JOIN THEM. YOUR BASTION WILL NOT HOLD, BUT IT MAY DELAY THEM."

"How do you know all this?" said Captain Render, her tone still level though her eyes were wild.

"KNOW THAT THE ENGINES WILL FAIL," said the skull, ignoring the question. *"THEIR POWER CANNOT BE CONTAINED, ONLY RELEASED, AND THE WOE-BEARERS FEAR POTENTIAL, NOT ACTION. THE ONLY HOPE FOR YOUR PEOPLE IS TO COME TO ME. MY THRALLS WILL HOLD THE TITHING OPEN AS LONG AS THEY CAN."*

"The Free will never submit to you, Ixil," growled Red Trace, but the fire in the skull's eyes had faded and it did not respond.

"Well, that were all a bit fuckin' weird," said Alben Koont, appearing from behind the tree.

"If that was you pulling some kind of trick-" began Sergeant Tika, but the Scout shook his head.

"Nah, girl, I'm as shit up as y'are. Thought I'd stay outta t'way while you lot dealt with Walter there. Found a quick way up, too. Good vantage, Cap'n."

"Good work, Scout," said Render, sheathing her blade. "Sergeant, what the fuck are you doing?"

"Writing down exactly what that skull thing said," replied Tika, scribbling on a scrap of paper she'd fished out of her pack with a stub of pencil. "You know the Magisters are going to want to know about it."

"Let me see that," said Render, taking the note. Quickly, she tore part of it off. "Sergeant, that name it used- you will forget you ever heard it, is that clear?"

The two Wardens exchanged a quick glance. "What name's that, Captain?" said Dani, levelly. Red Trace shrugged.

"Bah. The names of the Deluded have no meaning to me. Whatever ramblings came from the mouth of dread Ixil are best forgotten. Come, let us see what the Green Shadow has found for us. I would be away from this place."

The rest of the patrol started to move off, following the Scout. Second made to follow, but a thought suddenly occurred to her. Sergeant Tika was right that the Mighty Ones would want to know what Ixil had said, but what if they could simply ask him themselves? She reached out, carefully, and unhooked the Harbinger Skull from the branch it hung from, attaching it to a carrying-loop on her belt. Not long ago, such an act would have felt like the most heinous of crimes.

Now, it wasn't even the most terrible thing to happen that day.

75

"*Y*ou're fucking lost, aren't you?"

The soldier growled the words at Eri from a parched throat, and she had to admit he had a point. At first, she'd been so determined to escape from the pursuing Daxalai that other than the fact that she'd been rowing away from Freeport she hadn't paid much attention to where she had been going. That shouldn't have been a problem, though- the docks being to the south of the island meant that must have been the way she was going. In theory, all she should have had to do was turn the boat to her right, and she'd be heading towards the mainland. Once it was in sight, it would be a simple matter to follow the coast north until she hit Sigil.

Only it hadn't worked out like that. She soon realised that she had no idea whether she'd been rowing straight, and when she turned it was hard to tell by how much. She had meant to turn whilst the island was still in sight, but not so close that anyone watching could see where she was going, but somehow she must have miscalculated. Her next idea had been the small travel compass she was carrying, part of a College-issue scouting and navigation kit she had stolen while escaping from the Belus Manse. That plan had lasted until the first swell had lifted the boat and set the needle bouncing all over the place just as it was starting to settle. The second swell had led to a desperate moment of indecision between controlling the tiny device and rescuing an oar. She chose the oar, and the compass fell into the depths of the boat. She didn't bother looking for it.

"Shut up, you," she said to the man, without heat. "I'm just.. waiting for the stars to come out."

That was pretty much all she had left. She was fairly sure she could use the stars to work out which way to go. Reasonably sure. As she looked at the soldier- Jerik, that was his name- she saw the sword she had stolen from him propped up by the rowing bench. There was no danger of him getting to it, of course, she had

299

tied him and Maike together back-to-back and she knew knots, but the sight of the weapon brought the words of the old fisherman back into her mind.

"You put t'sea in this tub without a man knows how t'sail 'er, y'may's well ram that fancy-pants sword in yer own guts."

Well fuck him, fuck Jerik, fuck Maike fucking Dain and fuck any passing Whales. She was going to get out of this, succeed where Jonas, Erika and Gelt had failed, and take back her place in the Belus Guard. She'd like to see what Ariel would have to say about that. Idly, trying to show that she wasn't worried, she picked up the sword and took a better look at it. It was a pretty nondescript one, the blade a little shorter than three feet and the hilt stamped with the mark of the Second Volume, which was odd.

"Hey, Jerik," she said, pointing at it. "Thought you were with the Eighth? What's all this about, then?"

The soldier glared at her, his hair plastered down on his head with sweat and sea-spray. "It's borrowed. Why the fuck do you care? What do you even want with me?"

"You?" laughed Eri. "You're a bonus. It's her I was after. And the Dax, but I'll take what I can get. I could always let you go, I suppose."

"What?" said Jerik in surprise.

"Yeah, but you'd have to get off my boat."

"Hah-fucking-hah," said Jerik. "I'll take my chances, thanks very much."

"You're welcome," said Eri, finding the banter was taking her mind off her predicament. "How about you, Little Red? How're you holding up?"

There was no response, and Eri suddenly felt cold in her gut. She'd heard people say that sometimes if you knocked someone out and didn't do it just right they might never wake up again. She'd never heard of it happening with one of Gelt's bombs, but the way her luck had run recently...

"Hey. Hey, Maike! Are you dead or something? Talk to me, you little bitch!"

"She's still warm," supplied Jerik, helpfully. "If she's dead, she hasn't been for-fuck me!"

"What?" said Eri, snatching up the sword again. "What's wrong?"

"She's warm all right- Yar's tits, she's burning up!"

"Shit," replied Eri. "You mean a fever? I think I've got some chewing-leaf in my pack, that sometimes brings it-"

"Nolmeanonfire!" said Jerik, running the words into each other in his haste. "Fuck fuck owowowow!!!"

"Wha-" began Eri, but before she could even frame a question Maike bounded to her feet with a scream, the ropes falling from her wrists in smouldering fragments and the boat rocking alarmingly. She turned, and fixed Eri with a look of pure malice.

"Hey, Eri. I've learned a few things since I last saw you. Want to see?"

"S-stay back!" gasped Eri, brandishing the pilfered blade. "I- I've got a sword!"

"That's nice," said Maike. "But I just don't fucking care."

The next second Maike was on her, one hand clutching at Eri's throat while the other seized the wrist of her sword-arm. There was no question of holding her off without the Seal this time, and even with it Eri found to her shock that she was struggling. Somehow the wiry red-head had become almost inhumanly strong. She saw spots before her eyes as the one-handed choke squeezed at her throat, and used her free hand to break the hold. However strong you were, strangling someone with only one hand was almost impossible without something to push against.

A moment later, and the lack of anything for Maike to push against was no longer an advantage. As Eri wrestled desperately with the girl, close enough to feel her hot breath on her face, she felt herself being pressed back into the prow of the boat. Desperately she braced her foot against the hull, but it was only delaying the inevitable. Thinking quickly, she changed tack, her left hand which was locked with Maike's right suddenly pulling instead of pushing as she ducked and twisted. It hurt like hell- the red-head held on far longer than she should have with the punishment both women's joints were enduring- but the move worked, and Maike suddenly found Eri standing behind her with one arm looped around her neck. The blonde had maybe a second to gasp a lungful of air in relief before Maike's head snapped back into her face, knocking her sprawling backwards and sending the sword spinning from her grasp. She fell over Jerik, who had finished freeing his own hands and lunged to grab the weapon, and Maike, consumed by rage, flung herself over the sprawling soldier in pursuit.

Eri had seen her coming, and managed to get up a booted foot to kick her in the face. She would have preferred to use both feet to shove the crazy bitch off the boat altogether, but the other was still tangled up with Jerik. Her foot glanced off Maike's jaw, but the blow wasn't enough to stop the red-head's momentum and she landed heavily on Eri, her hands clutching for the blonde's throat again. Eri pulled her foot free from under Jerik, losing the boot in the process, and wrapped her legs around Maike, trying to squeeze the fight out of her. Effective though the scissor-hold was, though, it was no match for the full-blooded choke Maike was applying, and once again colours danced in front of Eri's eyes.

"Kill you... bitch..." hissed Maike through bloodstained teeth. Her eyes were wild, and almost seemed to be lit by an inner fire.

Eri tried to pry Maike's hands away from her throat, but her position afforded her little leverage. She punched and slapped at the other's face, inflicting some damage and bloodying her nose, but it wasn't enough to break the hold. In desperation, she took hold of Maike's damp, sweaty hair and yanked at it savagely like a bar-room strumpet. That at least drew a satisfying gasp of pain from the girl who was trying to strangle her, but Maike clenched her teeth, screwed shut her eyes, and redoubled her efforts. The colours had gone, and Eri was starting to see shadows at the edge of her vision.

The boat was rocking dangerously now, and Eri had one last, desperate idea as she felt her strength start to fade. She started to time her yanks on Maike's hair to match the movement of the boat, trying to use the extra momentum to throw the other off.

"Fuck me...." she heard Jerik gasp. Typical man, even in this desperate situation he probably couldn't keep his eyes off the fight. At least he hadn't piled in to help Maike for some reason. A huge swell tipped the small vessel almost onto its side, and Eri took the opportunity to finally unbalance Maike and dump her into the sea with a startled, angry yelp. She took a ragged, grateful breath even as she tried to brace herself in the bottom of the boat, and then saw what Jerik had been looking at.

Looming over them, its vast mouth agape, was a massive Whale. For a moment there was nothing but darkness and the glint of enormous teeth.

Then there was just the darkness.

76

There was a stunned silence in the audience chamber. It seemed that the Queen's decision to have Thalia arrested had taken everyone present by surprise.

"Ah, forgive me, Your Exceptional Majesty," began a slender, grey-haired man standing near the throne. "But to detain the Ambassador might be taken as an act of-"

"We said throw her in the dungeon," said the Queen again. What worried Thalia most was how completely level and controlled her voice was. This was no temper tantrum- it was a premeditated, and deadly serious, act. Behind her, she sensed Delys tensing, and she held a hand out behind her to calm the little Swordmaster.

"Easy, Delys. We didn't come here to start a war." *At least, not this one.*

Seeing that there was no immediate chance of the Queen changing her mind, several of the ceremonial guards, led by one of the Royal Knights, began to slowly advance on Thalia and Delys.

"I apologise, Your Excellency, but the Queen's word is-" began the Knight, who at least hadn't thought it necessary to don her armour. Before she could finish the sentence, though, she was cut off by the sound of loud, thudding footsteps from next to the throne. Both Magister and Knight turned to look at the source of the sound, accompanied by most of the Court. The Guardian was advancing- and not slowly. Despite its size, or partially because of it, it took the stairs down from the dais two at a time, and when it reached the bottom it was practically running.

Almost everyone was looking at the automaton, open-mouthed amazement on their faces, but Thalia's gaze also took in the face of the Queen. At first, Tondarin simply looked surprised, but after the Guardian had taken a couple more paces that look turned to shock, and then briefly to something approaching panic. In a moment, however, that expression had gone, replaced by the impassive mask of a veteran Chasten player.

"That will do," she said, in clipped tones. "We were merely testing the resolve of the Court and the wisdom of our advisors. Ambassador Thalia is our honoured guest, and free to go as she pleases. Guards, you may stand down."

Looking hopelessly confused now, the guards and their commander ceased their advance, or rather those of them who hadn't done so already to watch the Guardian did. A moment later, the automaton stopped its own charge, and turned to walk steadily back to its place by the throne. Thalia had to admit she was more than a little grateful for that. The speed the thing had been going it wouldn't so much have arrested her as smeared her all over the walls.

The grey-haired man smiled, and clapped his hands together. "A most enlightening and instructive test, Your Exceptional Majesty. I trust you found the Court's response satisfactory?"

"We did not, Chamberlain Renholt," sniffed the Queen. "We expect our Royal Guards to obey our orders without hesitation, not dally so long that we are forced to send the Guardian to enforce our will."

"I most humbly apologise, Your Exceptional Majesty," said the Royal Knight who had led the guards. "I confess the.. alacrity of your Royal Pronouncement caught my men and I somewhat flat-footed. I shall endeavour to see that it does not happen again."

"See that it does not, Lady Annabelle," said the Queen, coldly.

Thalia could feel her temper rising, and took a deep breath to help keep it in check. Perhaps in front of a couple of minor nobles or liveried flunkies she could allow herself the luxury of an outburst, but in this place such a thing might have terrible consequences. Instead, as she had been warned she must do, she patiently waited to be summoned to approach the throne. As she did so, she noticed three noblewomen standing a little way behind it, along with a gaggle of butlers, footmen, maids-in-waiting and other functionaries. They stood out from the rest because one of them was fairly heavily pregnant and the other two were beginning to show. Five months, two-and-a-half months, and five weeks? It certainly seemed to be quite the coincidence.

"You may approach the throne, Your Excellency," said the Queen finally, with what seemed to Thalia to be some reluctance.

What in Thelen's name is going on here?

Motioning Delys to stay where she was, Thalia advanced on the throne, her staff thumping on the rich golden carpet as she went. The various assembled nobles, Knights and Wizards watched her intently as she passed. Well, let them see how a Magister comported herself. She kept her head held high and her gaze locked on the Queen the whole way. As she covered the last few steps, Tondarin rose and extended her right hand, clenched in a fist.

"You may kiss the Royal Ring,"

Thalia groaned inwardly, but again the Orsinios had warned her and her displeasure showed only in her eyes rather than on her face. As she had been instructed, she bent to kiss the large diamond ring on the Queen's hand, being careful not to touch her in any other way. Just as Thalia's pursed lips met the stone, Tondarin jerked her hand forwards slightly, causing the diamond to press painfully against Thalia's mouth. Summoning all her self-control, Thalia held her ground even as she tasted blood. So that was the game they were playing.

When the Queen drew back her hand, blood was flowing freely down Thalia's chin from her cut lip. She pointedly ignored it. "Thank you, Your Exceptional Majesty. I have been authorised by the Symposium to begin negotiations for our joint campaign against the Dendaril."

"Ah, Your Excellency, you are bleeding..." murmured Chamberlain Renholt, stepping quickly forward with a silk handkerchief. "With your permission?"

Thalia nodded, still not taking her eyes off the Queen, and the man dabbed gently at her lips for a moment before ducking away like a footsoldier under arrow fire.

"We seem to have somehow got a little blood on the Royal Ring, Chamberlain," said the Queen, far louder than she needed to. "If you would be so kind?"

The Chamberlain hurriedly did as he was bid before retreating again.

"The Dendaril have been sighted in the east of the Expelled Territories, Your Exceptional Majesty," said Thalia, deciding that getting straight down to business might possibly forestall any more pettiness from the Queen. "The Symposium suggests that the Abelian Army drives them out with their automata."

The Queen settled back onto her throne, crossing her legs with a look of sly superiority on her face. "And why should we? Our two nations have a long history of war, Your Excellency. Why should we not simply wait for the Dendaril to destroy you, and then move in to pick up the pieces?"

"We have as long a history of peace, Your Exceptional Majesty," pointed out Thalia. "And during such times we prosper far more than we do when we are at war. Moreover, however, it is in the interests of the Kingdom to act now, before the Dendaril gain a foothold."

"Explain," said the Queen, in a disinterested tone that suggested she didn't much care whether Thalia did or not.

"The Dendaril multiply quickly when they find a new source of hosts and food," said Thalia. "At the moment, though many thousands of them are advancing, their numbers are manageable. Should they overrun the Empire, however, you would be faced with holding them off in far greater numbers and over a far wider front."

"Hmm," said the Queen, still appearing bored. "Chamberlain Renholt, what forces are available for such an expedition?"

"The First through to Fifteenth Demolitions are already mustered as ordered, Your Exceptional Majesty," replied the tall man. "Supporting them are twenty Assemblages of Wood Golems with military sigil-engrams and equipment. The entire force, along with the Knights and Wizards required for command and control, will be ready to move by tomorrow, though advance elements are already posted at Naxxiamor."

Thalia almost collapsed in relief. "Your Exceptional Majesty, forgive my impertinence but am I to assume that you have already decided to intervene?"

Queen Tondarin laughed. "Of course. Our own advisors had already made much the same case to us. There is only one condition of this action."

Thalia saw the dangerous look in the Queen's eyes, but knew she had to ask. "If it is within my power, Your Exceptional Majesty, I shall see to it. What do you require?"

"You," said the Queen, curtly. "You and your.. retinue, assuming that your man survives the Ague."

Thalia fought with every ounce of her willpower not to show the shock she was feeling. Athas had the Winnowing Ague? She had been so concerned about the arrow-wound that she hadn't even considered such a thing. "You require us to serve as a liaison with the Free Tribes?" she said out loud.

"To keep them out of our way, yes," replied the Queen. "Once these Dendaril have been crushed beneath Abelia's shining silver heel, we will see to their fate."

"Their... fate, Your Exceptional Majesty?" said Thalia, her tone low and dangerous. She noticed that the Chamberlain had seemed surprised by the Queen's words and had very nearly dared to speak.

"Of course. If they cannot protect their own lands, we see no reason why they should simply be given them back. Perhaps the freedom they purport to cherish is less valuable than they thought it to be."

Thalia ground her teeth together in silent fury. The Free Tribes would never accept Abelian dominion any more than they would accept the rule of the Empire. Once the Dendaril had been driven back, it looked like there would be yet another war. Of course, many in the Symposium would probably consider that a war between two of their enemies could only benefit the College, but the idea of letting the Abelians conquer the Free almost made her feel sick. And yet the alternative was worse.

"If I may ask, Your Exceptional Majesty, if the Kingdom possesses the might to defeat the Free Tribes, why have you waited until now to do so?"

Tondarin laughed cruelly. "Is it not obvious? Before, those savages were in a position to stop us burning down that miserable forest. But now that the Dendaril have driven them out and we have you to convince them that we are no threat..."

By now, Thalia was clenching her first so hard that she felt her nails digging into her palm, but she knew that nothing she could say or do would help. So she simply smiled, and nodded, and imagined every possible terrible fate for Her Exceptional Majesty Queen Tondarin II.

"Well, we seem to have concluded our business for now, Your Excellency, wouldn't you agree?" said the Queen, brightly. "You will, of course, do us the honour of dining with us tonight. You, and all those of your party who are still... capable of attending."

"The honour is all mine, Your Exceptional Majesty," replied Thalia through gritted teeth. "On the subject, I should like to visit Sergeant Athas at the Royal Hospital, if that might be arranged?"

The Queen yawned with boredom, and Chamberlain Renholt stepped forward hurriedly. "That will be no problem, Your Excellency. The coach is at your disposal, and will convey you anywhere in the city that you wish to go."

Thalia essayed a deep, formal curtsy. "Then with your permission, Your Exceptional Majesty, I take my leave."

She waited until she and Delys were back in the coach and heading for the hospital before venting. "That blue-blooded, pin-headed, stuck-up inbred bitch of a woman! Blood, ice and fire, I'd sooner gargle molten lead than spend another minute in Her Insufferable Presence!"

Delys nodded. *Bad. Dinner?*

"What? Oh, yes, of course we'll go to the dinner. We'll have to or it'll risk another diplomatic incident and Thelen knows, we can't afford any more of those. I really hope Amanda can come with us, though. I'm not sure I can take another conversation like that without someone else to talk to. Not that you're not good company, Delys, but... well..."

The little Swordmaster just smiled. *I know.*

Before anything else, though, they needed to find out if Athas was all right. If the Queen had been telling the truth- and Thalia could believe Tondarin might have lied just to throw her off balance- then she couldn't think what she was going to do. But if Athas died, someone was going to pay.

77

*W*hen Jerik woke up from unconsciousness for the second time that day, the first thing he became aware of was almost total darkness. He blinked and rubbed at his eyes a couple of times to no avail, but fancied that maybe he could make out something of the shape of his hand in front of his face. The second thing was that wherever he was, it smelled atrocious. Come to think of it, the stench of rotting fish wasn't that different to how Freeport usually smelled, but this was considerably stronger and even more unpleasant.

The third thing was that he could hear the sounds of someone fighting. It wasn't the same as the noises he'd heard from the ring behind the Last Anchor, but he could certainly hear the sound of heavy, laboured breathing, gasps of pain and growls of anger, and the occasional slap of flesh-on-flesh. If the voices were anything to go by, that flesh was feminine to go with them, which meant he could be pretty certain who it belonged to unless a couple of passing mermaids had suddenly got into a violent disagreement. As he strained his eyes to look, he realised that the tiny bit of light must be coming from a Seal, which was being largely obscured by the two struggling forms he could just make out in the gloom.

"Maike? Are you there?" he croaked, finding it hard to get enough good air to breathe, let alone talk. The air in this place was warm and humid, as well as foul on the nose. More incoherent growls and grunts were the only response.

"For fuck's sake pack it in!" he gasped. "We've been swallowed by a damn Whale! This is no time to be trying to kill each other!"

There was no reaction, but a moment later he felt a cool, fresh sea-breeze enter.. wherever they were. Beside him a crack of light opened up, and gradually widened to reveal that they were in the mouth of the largest creature Jerik had ever seen. As the light flooded in, he found he was sitting on a pad of pink flesh, ringed by huge, conical teeth each almost as tall as a man. What made the sight doubly terrifying was that from what little he knew about whales, their mouths tended to be comparatively small.

There was a splash from the other side of the mouth as the two women, still locked together, pushed off from the tooth they had been wedged up against and rolled into the puddle of deeper water at the centre. The impact briefly pulled them apart, and Jerik, who had somehow managed to retain his grip on his sword throughout the whole thing, waded in between them to keep them separated. Perhaps without the blade they might have simply ignored his presence, but three feet of razor-sharp metal tended to make a compelling argument.

"Yar's tits, the state of you two," said Jerik, immediately regretting his choice of words. The blonde woman- he couldn't remember them being introduced, but he thought Maike had called her Eri- had got the worst of the exchange. Her face was bloody with scratches, and cuts and bruises dotted her exposed skin, which was more exposed than she might have preferred since the simple linen blouse she had been wearing was badly ripped. On the other hand Maike's eye had been halfway swollen shut from the damage sustained in her previous fight, and a bloody nose courtesy of Eri's boot hadn't improved matters.

The red-headed woman glared at him, her breath coming in ragged gasps, and for a moment Jerik thought she was going to rush him. Then the savage look left her face, and she glanced around in confusion. "What? What the fuck happened?"

"That's what I'd like to know," said Eri, sullenly. "She was more fun before."

"Oh, when I was a weakling, you mean?" snapped Maike. "Yeah, I bet that was fun for you, you and your necklace of my fucking teeth!"

"Her necklace of what?" said Jerik, turning to look at Eri incredulously. "No, never mind. Look, I don't know what's going on with you two-"

"I hate her fucking guts and I'm going to throttle her," supplied Maike, helpfully.

"-apart from that, but we're having this conversation in the mouth of a fucking Whale! Doesn't that worry anyone else?"

"Shit," said Eri suddenly, looking down into the shallow water they were knee-deep in. "Are we standing on its tongue? Do whales even have tongues?"

"How the fucking hell should I know?" snapped Jerik, starting to feel his already fragile composure slipping. "This is the first time I've been swallowed by one!"

"Swallowed you were not, Jerik-Captain," said a strange, deep voice from behind them. "The stomach of Great Sounds in Deep Places contains not the dry-air needed for your lives to continue."

As one, the three turned to see a large crab standing near the threshold of the Whale's mouth. Maike took a deep breath. "Right, you two heard that, yeah? I'm not going fucking insane?"

"This one is Tikaclikclak, Speaker of Great Sounds in Deep Places, Emissary of the Blue," said the crab, at least as far as Jerik could tell. "Apologies I bear for the destruction of your vessel."

As if everything else about the situation wasn't bizarre enough, Jerik had never once heard of the Whales saying sorry for sinking a ship, even when vessels with a crew of hundreds had been destroyed over a minor infraction. "You.. you're sorry?" he said. "Then why did you swallow.. er, I mean.. pick us up in the first place?"

"Unworthy of the great seas, your vessel was," replied the crab. "Inexpertly was it crewed, and distracted its occupants."

"Yeah, and whose fault was that?" growled Eri, glaring at Maike.

"Keep it up, and I'll distract you some more," snapped back the red-head.

"Yeah, okay, we were in a spot of bother." said Jerik, aware that if the College awarded prizes for understatement he had probably just won one. "But still, I've heard of dolphins saving sailors, and sharks eating them if the Blue destroy their ship, but I've never heard of a Whale rescuing anyone."

"Thelen's balls, I've just remembered where I heard that name!" gasped Eri. "This is the Whale that went to Mernas and delivered that message about mirrors! He's a pretty big deal in the Blue Council."

"Oh, really?" said Maike, gesturing at the enormous mouth surrounding them. "What gave it away, genius?"

"Great Sounds in Deep Places is the Emissary of the Blue," reiterated the crab. "To him falls the task of meeting with the children of Thelen-Conqueror when to them the Blue must speak."

"Yeah, but us?" said Eri. "You're not exactly talking to the Chair of Mendarant and a couple of his aides here, you know?"

"To you, the Blue need not speak," said the crab, flatly. "To Jerik-Captain, the Blue need not speak. But to the fire-bearer, the Blue must speak."

"Huh?" said Maike, after the three humans had exchanged glances and come to the same conclusion through a process of elimination. "Me?"

"Maybe they just like carrot-tops," said Eri.

"Unimportant is the head-fur of the fire-bearer," said the crab, waving its claws in the air with apparent irritation. "Important is the burden it carries. To the fire-bearer, the Blue must speak."

"Yeah, we heard you the first time," said Maike. "So I'm here, you're here and it's not like we're fucking going anywhere. What do you want to talk about?"

"It is not Great Sounds in Deep Places with whom the fire-bearer must speak." said the crab. "It is the Blue. It is all of the Blue."

Jerik's vision suddenly began to swim in front of his eyes. "What? I don't... I don't understand.."

"Sleep, the children of Thelen-Conqueror now must," said Tikaclikclak softly, as they collapsed. "For long and deep, the journey is."

78

*W*hen Amanda Devereux received the notification from the Hercules suite that someone was entering the Royal Hospital, she was sitting on her bed after giving Athas another jolt. The big Guard's vital signs had started to dip again, though it seemed the feeding-tube was helping. This time the process of donating her Aether to him had been considerably easier. She hoped that it was just because she was getting the hang of it, and not a repeat of the whole Delys situation- that might make things extremely complicated with Thalia. As if on cue, the Magister had duly arrived.

When she got to the ward a few minutes later, Thalia was practically running, with Delys following a pace behind her. "Amanda!" she gasped. "I came as soon as I heard! Is Athas..?"

"He's OK for now, Learned Magister," replied Devereux, noticing that the perimeter monitor was also tracking Alana following along at a slower pace. *Need to talk in private,* she signed, quickly. Thalia's eyes narrowed.

The Healer bustled in a moment later. "As I told you, Your Excellency, there was no need to hurry. Sergeant Athas seems to be stable now that we have the feeding-tube hooked up to him. Within a couple of days, I would expect him to make a full recovery."

Thalia gaped at her. "Really? That soon? I had heard that the Ague could take weeks to run its course!"

Alana nodded. "Yes, that is true. But Athas has barely weakened at all since we realised he had contracted it. Sometimes that means that the patient has had the Ague for some time, but has been fighting it so successfully that they were still able to function. Other times it simply means that it is a mild case. In either event, it is rare for someone who is resisting the affliction so effectively to take long to recover from it. I must admit," she said, with an admiring glance at Athas, "it is unusual for anyone so... physically impressive and apparently weak in Spirit to survive the Ague at all, much less so emphatically. Sergeant Athas is a remarkable man."

"Yes, he is," agreed Thalia, with a slightly cold tone and a hard stare at the Healer.

"I'm sure the excellent quality of the treatment here helped, too," said Devereux, hurriedly. "Healer Alana, I apologise for getting so angry with you earlier."

"Th-think nothing of it," said Alana, somewhat nervously. "It was completely understandable under the circumstances. Now, I am sure you would like some time alone with your comrade. I will be in the nurse's office down the hall if you should need anything."

She beat a hasty retreat. Thalia watched her go, and once she was satisfied Devereux felt the slight tingle of her magic.

"I have cast a silence spell," said Thalia. "Now, Amanda, what did you want to tell me?"

"There's something seriously strange going on here, Thalia." said Devereux. The Magister gave a bitter laugh.

"Oh, really? I can't say I'd noticed. Do you know, the Queen tried to have me arrested and then suddenly changed her mind for no reason? Also she's apparently pregnant, but in fact it's not her but three of her ladies-in-waiting who are. Oh, and she'd already decided to move against the Dendaril but she waited until she'd had an excuse to grind a fucking diamond ring on my face before she bothered to tell me. And she's planning to use the opportunity of driving back the Dendaril to conquer the Free Tribes by burning them out of their forest. And on top of all that-" she paused to add the final indignity "-we're all invited to dinner tonight. But I'm sorry, you were going to tell me about something strange."

"Feel better?" said Devereux, having watched the Magister practically deflate as the angry tirade poured out of her.

"Much, thank you," said Thalia.

"Did she really grind a ring into your face?"

Thalia pointed at the freshly-healed cut in her lip. "Well, I didn't get this from sparring with Delys, did I?"

"What a bitch," said Devereux. "Anyway, I'm not sure I can top your day, but this is still very weird and I think it might be connected to Athas' condition."

Quickly she related the tale of her trip to the locked store-room, and described the strange device she had found there, as well as her efforts to keep Athas alive. "Do you have any idea what it might mean?"

Thalia didn't immediately answer, instead turning to study Athas. "I'm glad you told me about giving him your Aether, Amanda, it explains a lot."

Devereux suddenly thought back to the last time Thalia had seen someone else's Aether in Athas' Pattern. "Shit! Thal- Learned Magister, I assure you that I-"

Thalia laughed softly, a welcome sound under the circumstances for many reasons. "Don't worry, Amanda, you did the right thing. You used Athas' Seal as a conduit for your magic, which makes the process far more efficient and looks very different to.. what that Abelian trollop did. It's impressive that you were able to do it at all, though. Perhaps Magister Kaine is a better teacher than I gave him credit for."

"It wasn't easy, I have to admit," said Devereux. "But anyway, we need to work out what's going on here. Alana might think that Athas' is fighting the Ague off, but she doesn't know what I've been doing. She thinks I'm Sealed, and she doesn't know about our little chat with Ilia, either."

"Good point," conceded Thalia. "Hmm. You said that you... examined the liquid in the cylinder and it seemed to be alive?"

"That's right."

"Could you do the same for the new flesh that the Abelians gave to Athas?"

"What?" said Devereux in surprise. "It doesn't even look the same, why would I do that?"

"Humour me."

Devereux shrugged. She turned the Hercules suite's analytical tools on the place where Athas had been wounded, and grunted in irritation as the medical fail-safes triggered.

++Operative Advisory: Medical suite nano-assist functions unavailable in any external living subject as per Helsinki Accords, ref 234635/ISA. Non-invasive analysis functions are permitted but all such actions will be logged and reported. Continue analysis?++

Acknowledged. Continue analysis. Check for tissue match with previously scanned sample.

++Working.. completed. DNA correlation negative. No statistically significant match found++

"Well, that was a bust," announced Devereux. "It's completely different."

"It was worth a try," said Thalia, thoughtfully. "I was thinking that you finding some sort of living tissue in that cylinder and the Abelians implanting living tissue in Athas might not be a coincidence. I think the next thing I should do is have a look at this device for myself."

"That might be a little tricky," said Devereux. "The Abelians don't know that I've been down there, and if we try to slip away now somebody's bound to notice."

"Not necessarily," said Thalia, looking at Delys. "After all, you said that usually only Healer Alana comes to check on Athas, yes?"

Devereux nodded. "That's right. If she's true to her usual routine she'll be back in less than an hour."

Thalia stroked her chin thoughtfully. "And we need to check in with her before we leave, so we can't just hope she'll assume we've already gone when she comes back and doesn't find us here. But what if she had.. some trouble getting out of her office?"

The Operative considered, bringing up the schematic that the Hercules software had gradually pieced together whilst she had been investigating the building. "Well, there's only one door out of that room, but if she can't get out of it you'd expect she'd start to try to attract attention. Still, I think I have an idea."

A few minutes later, they waited around the corner from the door as Delys walked ahead of them and knocked on it. Alana came up to the door and opened it.

"Yes? What do you want?"

Delys smiled at her, and enveloped the Healer in a big hug.

"Hey, what are you doing? Get off me!"

The Swordmaster didn't immediately respond until Alana started to try to lever herself out of her grasp. Once it was clear that the Healer wanted to be released, Delys let her go and stood there looking miserable.

"Oh!" said Alana. "I'm sorry, I... didn't realise you were mute. You can't understand what I'm saying either, can you?"

Delys gave her a big, friendly grin.

"Well, at least you seem happy. Why that Ambassador makes someone as.. afflicted as you follow her about I don't know."

Without warning, Delys gave the Healer a playful shove, sending her staggering back into her office, and shut the door firmly. As soon as she did so, Devereux's nanites swung into action, jamming the simple mechanism of the door, which as the Operative had suspected lacked the magical protection of the more secure locks.

Scowling in annoyance, Alana tried to open the door to remonstrate with the Swordmaster, but found it firmly stuck. "Why you little- hey! What did you do to the door?"

Delys smiled at her through the small window, her face a study in innocent incomprehension.

"Look, this door's jammed. Can you go and get help?"

Delys smiled at her again. Devereux touched Thalia on the shoulder. "If I know Del, she can keep this up for quite a while. Alana will think she's always on the verge of going for help but she'll never quite get there. Let's go."

They rushed off as fast as they dared, in search of the store-room, and possibly, some answers.

---

79

*T*halia watched in fascination as Devereux used a pilfered tea-spoon to fabricate a new key for the lock.

"It never ceases to amaze me to see the things that you can do without the use of Aether, Amanda."

"Trust me, Learned Magister, it's nothing compared to how surprised I am at the things *magic* can do," replied Devereux. Even with the logs the Hercules suite was constantly keeping, she had long suspected that if she ever did get back home, anyone she tried to tell her story to would think her to be hopelessly insane.

They had decided on the way that as far as possible, Thalia would avoid using her magic. Clearly, the Abelians had not detected Devereux's previous intrusion, which was most likely due to it being achieved through technology and cunning. Both Operative and Magister agreed it was best to keep it that way. Still, Thalia used her Aethersight to check the door for wards before they opened it, and once they did so she gave a low gasp.

"Amanda, there is a fire ward in this room, as you said. You found it with.. with a sandwich?"

"Yeah," said Devereux. She had to admit, it sounded foolish when Thalia put it like that.

"It's a good thing you did," said the Magister, quietly. "That ward is one of the most powerful I have ever seen. I doubt even your remarkably durable body could survive it."

"Right now it's more your body I'm worried about, Learned Magister," said Devereux. "I got past it by climbing in the ceiling, but.."

"Certainly not an option for me," said Thalia. "I think it's probably easiest if I stay here, and you go and show me what you've found."

Devereux nodded. "Makes sense. It's just up the end there, and I can probably move it closer to you if that helps."

In the event it wasn't necessary. Once Devereux had climbed past the ward and carefully moved the screen out of the way, making sure not to accidentally touch the dangerous area with it, Thalia pronounced herself able to see the device well enough.

"Isn't that ward thing in the way?" asked Devereux. "I'd assumed it would be some sort of... magic wall or something."

Thalia smiled. "Not exactly, no. The Pattern of a ward is laid upon a surface- in this case the floor- and then specifies the extent and power of the effect. We are fortunate that whoever created this one went for intensity over coverage. If the attack part of the spell were a little weaker, it could easily have reached the ceiling. Now, let us have a look at this device of yours.... Hmph."

"What?" said Devereux, aware that time was against them. "What does it do?"

"It seems to be a particularly foolish contraption," said Thalia, gazing with her unfocused eyes. "The cylinder is gathering Aether from some source, and feeding it via that silver wire into the Aether-Emerald."

"That's it?" said Devereux, incredulously. "We went through all of this for someone's battery charger?"

"Well, yes and no," said Thalia. "What it does is simple. Why anyone needs it to do it is what confounds me. Not to mention *how* it does it."

"I don't follow."

"You have some of those emeralds in your sword-guard, don't you?" said Thalia. "All that's needed to charge them is for someone to feed Aether into them. You could do it yourself, since you were able to donate Aether to Athas."

"Yeah, that's true," agreed Devereux. "So.. why make this thing to charge one, then?"

"And why do it so gradually?" added Thalia. "This gem is no more than half-full, and it's filling imperceptibly slowly. There's something else, too. I'm having to guess, of course, because the rate is so slow, but based on how much Aether is in this gem and how long Athas has been here, I think someone started to do this shortly after he arrived at the Royal Hospital."

"So what you're saying is that somehow, somebody is using this thing to drain Athas' Aether, and put it into this gem?" said Devereux. "Why the hell would anyone do that?"

"Why indeed?" said Thalia. "And as I said, how they're doing it is a mystery to me. It's a bit like your link with Delys, I suppose- when Aether travels between you two, it can't be seen doing it. It just leaves one of your Patterns and appears in the other, like when we were attuning my staff or when you used the link to stop Jocasta."

"Aetheric Entanglement, the College calls it," said Devereux, and Thalia nodded. "That's it, yes. It ties in to a lot of the most advanced theories on how Aether and Patterns interact, and underpins the functioning of Messaging Crystals, among other things. But you and Delys are the first living beings to have such a link."

"That we know of," said Devereux. "Do you think this has anything to do with the Ague?"

"It certainly has something to do with what's happening to Athas," said Thalia. "But I can't see how it could be done on such a massive scale as the Ague. I can hardly imagine that every Ague sufferer had one of these things hidden in a nearby room, slowly draining them undiscovered for weeks, can you?"

"So someone's using this to fake the symptoms of the Ague, and trying to kill Athas?" said Devereux. "Why?"

"If I had to guess? The Queen," said Thalia, sourly. "She clearly has a personal grudge against me after what my father did to hers, and the.. incident in Dalliance has her fingerprints all over it. Thelen's breath, it's even possible that the ambush was set up by her as well!"

"All right, let's not get carried away with the conspiracy theories," said Devereux, carefully. "Right now, we need to decide what to do about this. If it's not the Ague at all, Alana could be way off in her estimate of how long Athas will take to recover, if he even does."

Thalia nodded. "I agree. Can you bring the device to me?"

Devereux looked it over. "Looks like it's bolted to the desk. There's a catch that would release the gem, though."

The Magister took a deep breath. "Very well. Remove the gem, and toss it to me."

"What?"

"It's not organic, the ward won't trigger," said Thalia.

"Yeah, but isn't whoever put this here going to notice if we steal the gem?" said Devereux. "It's a bit of a risk."

"I plan to return the gem," said Thalia. "I simply wish to charge it first."

Devereux stared at her for a moment, then realisation struck. "Oh, I get it. Right, I'll give you a three count, then throw the gem on 'mark'."

"What?"

"It's so you're ready to catch it," said Devereux. "I don't think you want to drop this thing, do you? Now, 3,2,1, mark!"

She tossed the gem, and Thalia juggled it for a heart-stopping moment before she held on to it. "Thelen's breath! Now, let us see here...."

Within a few minutes, the gem was fully-charged and reinstalled in its mount. Thalia eyed the device critically. "As I thought. Now that the gem is full, the transfer of Aether has stopped completely."

"So.. just to play devil's advocate here," said Devereux, who had climbed over the ward again after restoring the screen to its prior position. "If this was how the Ague usually worked, those people who recovered..."

"..would be those who had enough Aether to fill the gem without dying in the process, yes," said Thalia. "It would explain a lot- why it never killed Royal Knights or Wizards and why the Savalan were able to save so many of their people in the manner that they did. But I still cannot believe that the Abelian countryside was dotted with thousands of these devices and not one of them was ever discovered. Especially by the Savalan, who were actively trying to treat their people."

"Unless Ilia's story was a pack of lies and she really does work for the Queen," said Devereux, as she locked the door behind them.

"But that information helped you keep Athas alive and led us to this, which I very much doubt we were meant to see," mused Thalia. "No, on balance I think my suspicions of Ilia were borne more of paranoia than reason. But still, we should get back before Alana manages to escape from Delys' clutches."

"And before Athas wakes up," said Devereux, hopefully.

80

Thalia's heart was pounding in her chest by the time they got back to the ward. It didn't help that Devereux had chosen the journey back to tell her that she was worried about Jerik.

"And you're sure the device.. exploded?" said Thalia as they entered the ward.

"Yeah, from what I could gather from the last transmission," said Devereux. "But I didn't hear his voice so- shit!"

She suddenly darted forward, as fast as Thalia had ever seen her move. It didn't take long to see why. On the bed where he had been resting, Athas was thrashing frantically, his eyes wide.

"What is it?" gasped the Magister, hurrying over.

"It's the feeding tube!" said Devereux. "It's fed in through his throat, and now he's waking up he's trying to choke on it! I'm going to pull it out, but there might be some sort of incision in there."

"I see it," said Thalia. "Don't worry, compared to most of the healing I've had to do recently this is simple. Remove the tube, but gently."

Devereux did so, and Thalia swiftly healed the damage. Within a few moments, Athas was sitting up in the bed and looking confused.

"Guh," he said, making a face. "My throat feels terrible and my mouth tastes of rotten khile. What happened? The last thing I remember was getting hit by that arrow."

"The Abelians healed you, Athas," said Devereux. "They used a sheep, would you believe?"

"A sheep?" gasped Athas, scrabbling at the bedclothes to expose the new flesh. "Am I... am I going to start growing wool?"

"Honestly?" said Devereux with a smile. "I have no idea."

"Stay with him please, Amanda," said Thalia. "I am going to go and check on Delys and Alana."

She turned and walked off briskly, just in time to hide the tears. Athas was alive and well, and back to his usual self, it appeared. A chink had appeared in the walls of despair that had threatened to entomb her, and she intended to force it wider. A moment later, still drying her eyes, she rounded the corner that led to Alana's office and burst out laughing. Alana was banging on the door of the room, trying to attract attention, and Delys was heading down the corridor towards her, carrying a large potted plant. This object appeared destined to join a collection of other items in the hallway outside the office, which included a broom, two steel buckets, a stack of medical text-books, and an anatomical dummy.

"Delys!" said Thalia, doing her best to sound stern. "What in Thelen's name are you doing?"

"Your Excellency?" shouted Alana from inside the office. "Your bodyguard there did something to my door, and every time I think I've managed to get her to understand that I need her to go to get help, she comes back with... Queen's grace, is that a plant from the arboretum? That's two floors up! Porters! I said get the Porters, you cretinous-"

"Healer Alana, Delys Amaranth is a valuable member of my diplomatic staff," said Thalia, doing her best to summon up the anger that she had felt towards the Queen. "You will refrain from calling her any further unpleasant names, is that quite clear?"

"Y-yes, Your Excellency," said Alana. "But please, can you get me out of here?"

"I will try." said Thalia, looking at the door mechanism. Amanda Devereux's 'little helpers' had done a magnificent job of clogging it with enough dirt to grow the twin of the plant Delys was still carrying. "Your lock is full of filth. I sincerely hope that this is not an example of the level of hygiene your patients can expect. Stand clear, please."

Alana stepped hurriedly back, and Thalia, not feeling any need to be subtle, channelled her Aether into her muscles and kicked the door so hard that it popped off its hinges. It fell in with a crash, landing at Alana's feet and shattering the small window.

"Th-thank you, Your Excellency," said the Healer. "I.. apologise for the inconvenience."

"No apology is necessary, Healer Alana," said Thalia, and meant it. With the week she'd been having, kicking a door down was positively therapeutic. "In any case, I came to offer you my thanks."

"You.. you did?"

"Of course," said the Magister, with a bright smile. "Sergeant Athas has woken up. There was a brief moment of consternation with the feeding-tube, but other than that he seems to be making a full recovery. You and your colleagues are to be congratulated."

"We.. I... thank you, your Excellency!" gasped Alana, before almost jumping out of her skin as Delys dropped the pot-plant and hurled herself at the Healer, enveloping her in another hug. "Get off me! I.. oh, very well..."

"I apologise for any damage, Healer Alana," said Thalia, as the blonde woman flailed under Delys' attentions. "Please send the bill for any repairs or replacements to Herenford While at the Green Palace. We have a treasury now, apparently. Come along now, Delys. Athas will be happy to see you, I am sure."

Delys gave the Healer one final squeeze and let her go, before turning to run after Thalia. Alana watched her go in bewilderment.

"Why did she understand you and not me?"

81

erelar was just finishing his lunch when the messenger arrived. The morning had been a tiresome slog of administrative meetings to begin preparations for the newly-renamed Friendship Games. There had been official announcements to approve, preliminary invitations to various dignitaries and ambassadors to dictate, and more of the sort of diplomatic busy-work that he despised. He had delegated as much of the detail as he could to Magister Stalis, who as Chair of Mendarant was responsible for foreign diplomacy, but it had still taken up far too much of his time.

His breakfast meeting with Anneke, on the other hand, had been more interesting but less productive. The Vice-Chancellor was adamant that if a weakness should appear in the defences of the Kingdom of Abelia, the College should be ready to exploit it, but the losses the Volumes had recently sustained made a prolonged campaign look largely unfeasible. The most optimistic projections that Anneke's people had made suggested that the available forces might be able to take the fortress known as The Knuckle and overrun the Abelian west-coast ports of Emberlain and Antirioch, which would largely cut off the Kingdom from trade with the Daxalai and Freeport. The resulting leverage would be very useful in the ongoing disputes over trade and both powers' colonial possessions in Jandalla. It would hardly match the victories of the First Abelian War, where the Volumes had reached and sacked Abellan itself, but it would certainly help peg back a Kingdom which had recently become increasingly aggressive and assertive. At least the new Ambassador to Abelia, Magister Elsabeth, should by now be on her way with a supply of fresh, secure Messaging Crystals from Anneke's own carefully-vetted stores.

Derelar was still pondering whether the entire venture would be worth the trouble of dealing with the Symposium when he opened the message cylinder. The letter within had been received by his own personal staff on a Crystal reserved for the most private and secret communications, and it was extremely rare that they risked bringing such missives to his office. Whatever it was, it must be urgent. He took out the message, noting with approval that his staff had used fleeting-paper, which would crumble to unreadable dust within an hour, and studied the contents carefully.

"Arch-Chancellor. I apologise for the sudden nature of this message, and for the fact that I did not inform you that I was aware of the existence of this avenue of communication. This message has been relayed via a Crystal held by a trusted associate whom I contacted through a merchant company based in Freeport. My investigation here has been partially successful. In the interest of additional obfuscation, I will refer to all parties by initial rather than name.

I have made contact with 'W', the associate of the man whose death I was investigating ('Y'). W confirms that Y was taken from a vessel sailing to his homeland by Toskan pirates on the morning of his death and was alive when he left W's sight. W also states that they were detained in the custody of the prime suspect in our investigation ('A'), before escaping with the aid of a fellow prisoner ('M'). During the course of the investigation, W and I, along with our associates M and 'J', were assaulted by agents confirmed by W to work for A. Though this assault was repelled, M and J were captured by an unknown third party.

Arch-Chancellor, though I do not expect the agents of A to make another attempt on W and myself whilst I am in Freeport, it is inevitable that A will learn of these events in short order. Should I bring W into College territory to provide testimony, it will force A's hand. If I do not do so, A may decide to act pre-emptively. This decision is too politically sensitive to be taken by a mere investigator, so I ask that if you require me to bring W to Lore for debriefing, you stand at your east-facing office window and press your forehead to the glass of the panel on your rightmost side. If you wish me to remain at Freeport and await further instructions through official channels, rest your head instead against the middle panel. If you wish for me to instead take W into hiding and contact you again once she is safely secured, press your head, as you will already have deduced, against the leftmost panel.

Finally, if none of these options is acceptable, simply do not press your head on any of the panels. In this event, I will contact you again with the location of a dead-drop at which more detailed instructions might be left. Whichever option you choose, I will act on your orders at dawn tomorrow morning.

Yours in Service to the College

Magister Julius Thule."

Derelar set the message down and steepled his hands. So, unless he gravely misunderstood Magister Julius' message, Anneke had been responsible for the death of the Daxalai Ambassador. It would seem, then, that she had indeed defeated the Midnight Tiger, the assassin who had rampaged across the Empire during the Third Mirror crisis, and then arranged another murder using the killer's *modus operandi* to cover the fact up. But why? He could only assume that the power that Anneke so carefully hid came from her true nature as a Dragon, and that she had been concerned that it might be discovered.

The question of what to do next remained. Julius had been quite correct, if also politically cunning, to leave the decision in the Arch-Chancellor's hands. It was certainly true that as soon as Anneke realised that Willow-Sigh Wen had eluded capture by her agents and made contact with a Magister she would do just about anything to prevent the evidence of her actions becoming public. If Julius brought the Daxalai to Lore a confrontation was inevitable, but if he did not there was every risk that the moment to act would be lost. It was even possible that Anneke would act against Derelar directly- she almost certainly knew enough to do so. No. Though he respected Ollan's warnings about how important Anneke was to the security of the College, unsanctioned murders of foreign diplomats were a step too far. It was time to end this.

He strode over to the window, trying to look more decisive than he felt, and immediately ruined any such effect by being struck by a moment of doubt. Was it the panel to *his* right, or the one to the right of an observer? With a scowl of irritation he returned to the desk, carefully checked the wording, and then stepped back over to the window. Where was Julius' man, he wondered? Sitting by a window in some tavern in the Trade Torus, watching for a signal that he might not even know the significance of? Hidden in a watchtower, a spyglass pressed to his, or for that matter her, eye, one hand nervously fingering a Messaging Crystal?

He realised that he was procrastinating, and compounded the sin with a trip to the sideboard for a fresh coffee. In part, though, this was completely forgivable, since staring out of the window with cup in hand was a common ritual of his. No casual observer would think anything of it were they to see him, not that many stopped to stare up at the windows of the High Apartment. After all, there was always the risk that someone would be staring back. Taking a deep breath, he rested his head carefully against the rightmost panel. The cool glass was a welcome, soothing feeling that stood in stark contrast to the chain of events he might just have set in motion.

He stood there longer than he had intended, eyes closed, feeling the cold gradually numbing his forehead. Never again would he be able to confide in his trusted Vice-Chancellor, though in truth that time had probably long passed. Never again would her cunning and her peerless web of contacts, spies and informants help him quietly control a potential disaster. Already unrest in Kathis was rising, and then there was the Dendaril issue, the campaign plans against the Abelians...

Never again would he hear that firm knock on his door and know that Anneke was about to bustle in to dazzle him with her brilliance and infuriate him with her-

There was a sudden, furious knock on the door. For a panicked moment he imagined that his thoughts had somehow summoned the Vice-Chancellor, before his senses rallied and he realised that the sound was heavier, more urgent. With a gesture, he dissolved the fleeting-paper and dispelled the wards on the door.

"Come."

A tall, ash-blonde woman in ornate Guard battle-plate came in almost at a dead run. It took Derelar a moment to recognise her as Ariel Marigold, the Captain of the Belus House Guard, and one of Anneke's most feared enforcers. Instinctively he cast a shielding spell, though he could see that the woman was unarmed and the Scholastic Guards were on duty outside the room as usual.

"Captain Ariel, is it not? What is so urgent that you could not simply-"

"She's dead, Arch-Chancellor!" gasped the tall Guard, and now that she had stopped moving and Derelar could focus properly on her face he could see that her skin was ashen and her eyes red and tear-stained.

"Who? Captain, perhaps we should summon the.... the.. Vice.. no. No, you surely cannot mean-"

"Magister Anneke Belus," said Ariel, shortly. "The Vice-Chancellor, the Matri-arch of House Belus, the damn Boss. She's dead."

Derelar gestured, and the door slammed shut. He motioned Ariel to a chair, amazed that his hands were not shaking. "Sit, Captain, please. Have some wine- no, better yet, there is some excellent Toskan brandy in the sideboard."

As the warrior sank gratefully into the chair, Derelar walked over to the side-board and took out the brandy and two glasses. "The Vice-Chancellor and I used this to toast my appointment as Arch-Chancellor. It seems appropriate that we should use it now to steady our nerves, would you not agree?"

Ariel took the glass, and nodded. "Yes, Arch-Chancellor. The Lily blooms!"

"The Lily blooms," responded Derelar, and they both drained their glasses in one go. The fiery spirit slid smoothly down his throat, and he swallowed, feeling his hammering heart calming. "Now, firstly, who else knows of this?"

"Nobody outside the Manse," replied Ariel, all business now someone was giving her orders. "My Sergeant, Ulla, is keeping an eye on the scene and has strict orders to keep anyone and everyone out."

"Good. We will need to contain this news until contingency plans can be put into place. The Vice-Chancellor had her hand in much of the essential business of the College. I will need complete access to all of her papers, documents and possessions."

Ariel's eyes went wide with panic. "Ah- Arch-Chancellor, I-"

Derelar waved a hand at her in irritation. "Captain, I am fully aware that I will almost certainly find evidence amongst them all manner of misdeeds on the part of you, and of Anneke's other agents. Such would be true of any competent spymaster. Neither you, nor your subordinates, will be held accountable for actions taken on her orders. You will have that in writing before the investigation proper begins."

Ariel noticeably relaxed. "Thank you, Ar-"

"This amnesty will, of course, be contingent on your full, and prompt, disclo-sure of any and all information," interrupted Derelar. "If we discover further crimes that have not been disclosed, they will be prosecuted to the full extent of the powers of my office."

The Captain swallowed, and took a mournful look at her empty glass. "Y-yes, Arch-Chancellor. I understand."

"You may pour yourself another measure if you feel it will help, Captain," said Derelar, magnanimously. "But do not render yourself insensible."

"Hah! Fine chance of that!" laughed Ariel, refilling her glass. "It'll take more than this to put a Belus Guard under the table. Why, we once saw off an entire case of.. of... oh, fuck me..."

She put the untouched glass down heavily on Derelar's desk and buried her face in her hands. "She's really fucking dead, isn't she?"

"That is what you have been attempting to tell me, is it not?" said Derelar, as gently as he could. "What exactly happened?"

"We failed her, is what fucking happened!" snapped Ariel, snatching up the brandy and downing it, her eyes streaming hot tears. "Me, Ulla and a few of the other girls finished loading up the new Crystals for Magister Elsabeth and saw her off, then I went to report to the Boss. I knocked on her office door, but there was no answer."

"Is this unusual?"

"Not really. Sometimes she likes.. liked to take a nap in the afternoon, she'd get undressed and everything. Sometimes she'd be... entertaining. The rule was you knocked at the office door, gave it a few moments, then went through to the back and knocked at the bedroom door, give her time to get decent. Not that she always bothered," Ariel added the last with a small, sad smile. "You'd be surprised, some of the people who visited that bedroom and what they got up to."

"No doubt," said Derelar. Ariel noticed the tone of his voice.

"Yeah, I'll tell you what I know about that but you'd really want Eri- Eri Trevalyn, she looked after the Manse more than me but she fucked off a little while ago."

Derelar nodded, deciding to put the coarse language down to stress. "Very well. Continue your account."

"Yeah. So, I went through to the bedroom in the back of the study and knocked, but there was no answer. So I went in and-"

"Would you usually enter the Vice-Chancellor's bedroom even when not expressly permitted to do so?" asked Derelar, thinking that anyone who did that to him would be lucky to survive the error.

"Not normally, no," admitted Ariel. "But Anneke had given particular instructions that we should tell her once Elsabeth was on her way so she could pass it on to her people in Abelia. Anyway, I opened the door and... and... there she was. Most of her, anyway."

Derelar's eyebrows shot up. "*Most* of her?"

"She'd been fucking decapitated!" growled Anneke. "Some bastard cut her head clean off and just left her there in her night-dress on the bed!" She gave a short, bitter laugh. "Do you know what the first thing I did was? I ran over and tried to stop the bleeding. From her fucking severed neck."

Derelar nodded. "I am reliably informed that shock can cause irrational responses. My own grandmother, when told of my father's death at the hands of Ullarth Tydask, burst out laughing and then spent the rest of the day crying and laundering all of his clothes. What did you do next?"

"I.. I realised that there was nothing I could do for her, so I got the hell out of there and got Ulla to secure the office door. I got washed up, and then came straight here. The Boss had always been very clear that if anything ever happened to her we had to keep it quiet, at least until you knew about it."

"Indeed," said Derelar. "Had I found out about this second-hand, I would have been gravely displeased, Captain." He opened a desk drawer, and took out a small box. "Do you know what this box contains?"

Ariel blinked. "How the fuck would I-, ah, I mean, no, Arch-Chancellor, I do not."

Derelar opened it, revealing a small, hand-carved stone skull. "This is the Sooth-Skull of Thon-Fulush, once a tool of Domedran, often called the High Warlord of Old Damisk. It possesses a simple power, which is that if held in the hand, it reacts to any attempt to lie by becoming super-heated."

Ariel moistened her lips nervously. "Oh. I.. I see."

"The artefact is, however, somewhat temperamental," continued Derelar, mildly. "It reacts to absolutely any falsehood whatsoever, even if the error is one of poor recall, or a sin of omission. It is therefore exceptionally perilous to employ during an interrogation. Pick up the skull, please."

Ariel's eyes went wide. "Arch-Chancellor, I assure you that-"

"Do not be tiresome, Captain," said Derelar. "I will ask you two questions whilst you hold the skull. So long as you answer truthfully- and the questions will require a simple yes or no answer- you will be unharmed. Then you may put the device down and I will be satisfied."

Ariel swallowed. "Y-yes, Arch-Chancellor," She reached out and carefully picked up the skull.

"I recommend you say nothing except your answers to my questions whilst holding the skull, Captain," said Derelar. "Misinterpretations and accidents have been known to happen. Now, for my first question- has anything you told me since you arrived in my office today been a lie?"

Ariel took a deep breath. "No," she said.

"Can I trust that you will now obey my orders as Arch-Chancellor to the letter?"

"Yes," said Ariel, her eyes locked with his. Derelar gave a grunt of satisfaction.

"You may place the skull back in the box, Captain. Carefully, please, it is a valuable and unique device."

The blonde woman did so, almost holding her breath, her hands trembling. Derelar put the box away. The skull was, of course, a completely inert ornament but the legend was historical and occasionally useful.

"Now, this situation must be dealt with, and swiftly. You will gather a unit of your most trusted Guards, and travel immediately to Freeport. Magister Julius Thule will be leaving there in the company of a Daxalai woman called Willow-Sigh Wen. You will present yourself as an escort, give the Magister a message cylinder with which I will provide you, and conduct him to Lore will all haste."

Ariel blanched. "Arch-Chancellor, this Daxalai woman- she was held prisoner at the Belus Manse for some time. Her and Maike Dain."

Derelar nodded. "I know, Captain, but your candour is appreciated and I expect it to continue. Since you and your fellows will be travelling unarmed, you should bear in mind that both Magister Julius and Willow-Sigh Wen could kill you on a whim. I suggest that you do not give them a reason to. Now, this second document will prove your identity to the captain of the *Swift Harridan*, a merchant vessel currently docked at Damisk which has provided certain.. discreet services for me in the past. You will need to make Freeport before dawn tomorrow- see that you do not fail."

Ariel stood up and saluted. "Yes, Arch-Chancellor. If I may ask-"

"Why you?" said Derelar. "Simply put, I am aware that agents of the Vice-Chancellor may still be seeking to prevent Magister Julius and the Daxalai from reaching Lore. There are perhaps others I could employ to protect him, but your position as the right hand of the Vice-Chancellor is well known. If anyone will be able to deter them by their mere presence, it is you."

Ariel nodded. "I understand, Arch-Chancellor. I'll need to return to the Manse to pick up my girls and a fast coach, and we'll be on the way to Damisk within the hour."

Derelar nodded. "Very good, Captain. However, you will not need to pick up a coach- we will be travelling to the Manse in my own personal vehicle which will then convey you to Damisk."

"We, Arch-Chancellor?"

"You, me, and Gisela Dar," said Derelar, already leading the way to the door. "If Magister Julius is to investigate this murder for us, we will need to preserve the scene of the crime with all due haste. Once the High Chirurgeon has formally declared the Vice-Chancellor dead, I will employ Magister Julius' preservation spell until you return with him."

"I don't think it'll take the High Chirurgeon to figure that out, Arch-Chancellor," said Ariel grimly as she followed him out of his office.

She was right, of course. Derelar needed Gisela for something else, but the formalities were a useful excuse.

82

*I*t was well into the evening when the scouting party returned to the Vigil. Magister Haran Dar had been in the middle of a somewhat tense evening meal attended by most of the fortification's senior staff, the Weavers, and the chief Mighty Ones of the various Expelled tribes which he had considered himself fortunate to get through without a fight breaking out. As was often the case, Magister Ollan had proven both infuriating, and invaluable, defusing several quarrels by uniting both parties against himself. It still brought Haran's heart into his mouth every time the old man did it, but he remained in awe of his talent for brinkmanship. Sitting beside him, Magister Kandira did her part, taking Ollan's side or berating him as needed to shift the momentum of the confrontation one way or another. The two veteran Magisters might get on like fire and ice, but the resulting steam was often highly effective.

When Captain Render appeared at the door of the officer's mess hall, however, all such petty concerns evaporated. Swiftly, Haran ordered the room cleared of all but the members of the council-of-war, though at the insistence of Mighty Dokan and Mighty Xaraya the Black Skull was invited to remain. The leader of the Black-bloods had not raised any objection to the scouting party not including a representative of his tribe, but the other Mighty Ones were eager to show that despite his newness in his role, they considered him an equal.

"Are we to assume that your scouting mission was a success, Captain Render?" said Haran, once all was in readiness.

"That depends on your definition, Learned Magister," replied the tall woman. "But broadly, yes. We got out and got back in one piece and we sighted the enemy."

"I get the distinct feeling that we're not going to like what you're going to tell us," said Ollan, filling his pipe.

Captain Render nodded. "Aye, Learned Magister. Second took us to the site of the Mountain Halls, where the last Moot of Kings was held. It was... it was bad.

Shortly afterwards, whilst looking for a way up the mountainside, we encountered a Dendaril, one of the Blackblood tribe."

All eyes turned to the Black Skull, but the Mighty one simply nodded.

"He had completely forgotten who he was," continued Render. He was... help me out here, Second?"

"He was the Second of Blood in Secret places," supplied the Second of the Tree-Searchers, the only other member of the scouting party present. "But he claimed his name was Walter."

"He was surprisingly... friendly," admitted Render. "But it turned out that was because he thought we'd be happy to become like him. He seemed to have some sort of connection to the other Dendaril, even though they were still some distance away. Eventually, though, it became clear we weren't going to get anything useful out of him, so Red Trace in White Snow killed him. I am sorry, Mighty Black Skull."

"Do not be," said the Black Skull, quietly. "What Red Trace slew was no longer one of the Free, but a Fly Lord, and the responsibility for his fate rests with my predecessor."

"And you're sure that none of your patrol was infested?" said Haran.

"The rest of them are being checked over by the Healers now, Learned Magister," said Render. "But the idea of dousing the corpse in lantern-oil worked, as far as we can tell. We were able to burn it before any of the ticks could get out, apart from one which Red Trace crushed. I warned the Healers about that though, just in case."

"Red Trace in White Snow was most wise," said Second, looking surprised to be saying the words. "He slew the Fly Lord by breaking his neck, leaving no open wound from which the Little Ones could emerge."

Mighty Dokan nodded in satisfaction. "It is well. Still, should the Fly Lords arrive at this place in force, we will not be able to simply throttle them all one-by-one. How long do we have?"

"Once we reached a high enough point, we were able to see the signs of their advance," said the Captain. "They don't seem to know how to use the Stone Paths, or even be aware of them, so it looks like they were at least a day's march from the Mountain Halls. Assuming that they stop to rest like any other army would, I'd put them at our gates by dawn in three days time. If they don't stop, possibly as early as the day after tomorrow."

Haran massaged his temples and gave a heavy sigh. "How many of them were there?"

"Hundreds of thousands, at a guess," said Render. "Their formation is ragged—we could tell where they were more by the disturbance to the forest than by actually seeing them, but it looked like they stretched all the way back to the... Shriven Marshes, that was it. They don't seem to have scouts out or a vanguard, even though they've been attacked once already."

"They have?" said Kandira, perking up at the news. "By who?"

"The thralls of dread Ixil," said Second, before the Captain could answer. "He.. spoke to us."

"What?" gasped Mighty Xaraya. "What foolishness is this? Ixil would never stray so far from his domain."

Second stared at her, stubbornly. "He did not need to. He spoke to us through this."

She reached under her war-cloak, and unhooked the Harbinger Skull from her harness. As one, the Mighty Ones gave a sharp intake of breath, and Haran felt a surge of Aether as each of them made a warding sign.

"Umba's teeth, girl!" snapped Xaraya. "You would bring a Harbinger Skull here? Such a thing is forbidden!"

"With all respect, Mighty One," said Captain Render, stepping in front of Second, "I understand that those skulls are considered sacred to you, but this... Ixil spoke to us through them. I'd say that any sanctity they might have possessed was already long-gone when Second took this one. In any event, he talked to us, and told us that his people had attacked the Dendaril and slowed them down."

"Probably buying time for the rest of the Expelled that joined him to withdraw," said Kandira. "His warriors know the terrain and they're supposedly immune to the Dendaril's greatest advantage, so it makes sense. It's what I'd do."

"We still only have.. his.. word that they're immune," pointed out High Vigilant Wilhelmina.

"I believe him, Learned Magisters," said Captain Render. "With the power he seems to have, I can't see why he'd bother lying. There's something else, though, which is far more worrying. According to Ixilinath, the Petard Engines won't stop the Dendaril."

"Blood, ice and fire!" growled Kandira. "I've just got the first of those damned things mounted and a bloody good job we've made of it too!"

"Well," said Ollan, giving her a reassuring pat on the shoulder. "If nothing else we can still use it to blow a few of them into tiny pieces, if that makes you feel any better."

Haran narrowed his eyes. "What exactly did this Ixilinath say about the Engines, Captain? That they would be utterly useless, or that they would merely not have the desired effect as a deterrent?"

"My Sergeant noted it down," said Render, producing a scrap of paper, which was passed around the table. Even this almost caused an incident when Magritte, who had found herself seated next to Mighty Xaraya, offered to read the report for her.

"Nak's skull!" snapped the Mighty One. "Do you think me a child, unable to read?"

"N-no, I-" stammered the Operator, suddenly aware that Xaraya stood almost twice her height and was composed almost entirely of solid muscle.

"Actually," said Ollan, who had appeared behind the two women, "I was having a spot of bother with it myself. Sergeant Tika's handwriting is appalling."

"Th- that's not her handwriting, Learned Magister," said Magritte, as Xaraya glowered at her. "It's the Second Volume's battlefield shorthand. I thought you knew-"

"Never seen it before in my life," asserted Ollan firmly, despite the fact that Haran had watched him read countless documents written in the efficient script. Quickly, with the Mighty Ones listening intently, Magritte read through the report.

"Well," said Ollan, once she had finished. "A fine salad of mystical mumbo-jumbo that was. 'The Dendaril fear potential, not action.' What in Thelen's name is that supposed to mean?"

"Mighty Thalia told us that the Mountain Halls bore terrible weapon-spells of great power," said Dokan. "Perhaps it was that power which the Fly Lords feared."

"Hmph." said Kandira. "In a city as old as Xodan? What were they, bloody thaumaturgic annihilators? There's a reason nobody uses those old weapon-spells any more- they were so inefficient that you had to put in four times the power you got out of them. The only advantage was that they could store a lot of Aether, but if every Magister and Mighty One in this room put everything they had into one, they might get it ready to fire in about a week."

"And yet Thelen the Dragon-slayer used them to bring low the greatest of the Dragons, so the old songs tell us," said Dokan.

"Well of course he did!" laughed Kandira. "Look, you have to understand that as far as we know, Thelen and the Patrons were the only humans in the known world who were capable of effectively using magic at the time. Spell-craft and Pattern manipulation have come a long way since then, but in terms of sheer raw power we're a half-full box of matches compared to a bonfire. And a big bonfire, at that."

"So," said Sir Matthew, who had been listening to the whole discussion in silence. "It would seem that it is that property of those ancient weapon-spells that the Dendaril fear- the ability to store a vast amount of Spirit. It seems to me, then, that all we need do is work out a way to imitate that property."

"YOU WILL FAIL." The eyes of the Harbinger Skull, which Second had placed on the table, suddenly blazed into life again.

"Nak's skull!" gasped Xaraya, her sword hissing out of the scabbard. Ollan held up a restraining hand.

"A moment, please, Mighty One. This is a rare opportunity."

"You are Ixilinath?" said Dokan, staring at the skull with a mixture of awe and revulsion. "How is this possible?"

"I HAVE ALWAYS BEEN WITH YOU, MIGHTY DOKAN," said the skull. "ALWAYS, WHENEVER YOU WALKED IN THE SIGHT OF THE ETERNALS OR THE HARBINGERS, OR STRODE THE FALLEN HALLS OF XODAN, WERE MY EYES UPON YOU. I OFFER YOU ONE FINAL CHANCE. BRING YOUR PEOPLE TO THE TITHING, THERE TO BE CONVEYED TO IXIL-DUNDAL WHILE THERE IS STILL TIME. EVEN TO THE DELUDED IS THIS MERCY OFFERED."

"That's certainly an appealing offer," said Ollan. "I've always wanted to work for a disembodied voice coming out of a dead man's mouth."

"MOCK ME IF YOU WILL, OLLAN DANE," said the voice, unmoved. "BUT I WISH THE CHILDREN OF THELEN THE FOOL NO ILL. THE ANCIENT SECRETS OF XODAN ARE BEYOND YOUR GRASP, AND SHOULD YOU REACH FOR THEM, YOU WILL FAIL AND FALL."

"I disagree," said Ollan, mildly. "After all, Thalia was able to work them out easily enough. You might impress some people with your parlour tricks, dead voice, but we have learned a lot since your time."

"Mighty Lelioko claimed that Ixil was about to stop the black devils when Mighty Thalia destroyed the Mountain Halls," said Dokan, carefully. "It may be that you underestimate-"

"About to!" laughed Ollan. "That's just the point, do you see? This withered old charlatan was 'about to' stop the Daxalai, and a three-leaf Magister with an anger management problem just strolled in and did it in an afternoon! Of course Ixilinath knew how to control the Stepping Mirrors, he was around when the magic was first discovered- but we have come so far since then." He turned back to the skull. "We do not need you, dead voice. We will deal with the Dendaril on our own, just as we did the Daxalai."

"FOR SUCH IMPERTINENCE, THE PENALTY SHALL BE-" began the skull, but Xaraya's sword flashed down and cut the thing in half before the sentence could be completed. In her fury, she also bisected the table and embedded the weapon a couple of inches into the stone floor.

"Thank you, my dear," said Ollan, lighting his pipe. "I might have been about to say something impolite."

Haran looked down at the smashed skull as the fire died in its eyes. For all of Ollan's fine words, they had perhaps two days to find a way to stop the Dendaril and only the vaguest of ideas of how such a thing might be done. Hopefully Ambassador Thalia was having more success.

83

*A*mbassador Thalia Daran looked around the room and marvelled that somehow, her little retinue had managed to make it there in its entirety. Even Athas, released from the Royal Hospital despite Alana's objections, had insisted on coming to the dinner. Herenford had worked wonders searching through the wardrobes of the Green Palace to find College dress uniforms that largely fit everyone, and Amanda Devereux had quietly assisted with some adjustments to improve matters still further. It meant that her three supposed bodyguards were now dressed in matching uniforms of fine green silk, linen and leather, worked with silver thread and decorated with gold epaulettes and lanyards. For her own part, Thalia had to be content with having her best robe laundered. They hadn't exactly originally set out equipped to make state visits.

Herenford had assured her that the wearing of their personal weapons was both permitted and expected at such an occasion, a hold-over from the ancient practice of duelling. Delys' sword, of course, proved somewhat too large to wear without the straps of its baldric interfering with the lines of the uniform- not to mention that the back-sheathe wasn't exactly designed with sitting in a chair in mind- but a little careful adjustment solved the first problem and the appointment of Herenford to the role of official sword-carrier (apparently a well-respected position in pre-Ague Abelia) dealt with the second.

They had arrived at Castle Valour fashionably late as Herenford had advised, Athas' stomach providing great entertainment by rumbling loudly, and were ushered straight into the Queen's personal dining room. It was there that Thalia received her first shock of the evening. As with the rest of the palace, the walls of the wood-panelled dining room were decorated with an assortment of fine art. These particular pieces, though, were distinctly pointed in their intent. One canvas depicted the storming of the Green Palace by the Royal Knights, and showed the fall of Sebastian Vox in impressively graphic detail. Another, much newer piece, was an interpretation of the death of King Tobias and Prince Tobin, who were shown bravely shielding an army of Royal Knights as the mountainside crashed down on them. Thalia didn't need to be told who the flame-wreathed figure with an upraised staff in the background was meant to be, nor did the fact that a group of Royal Knights were bearing down on him with levelled lances escape her. The painting's prominence on the centre of the wall opposite Thalia's seat made it fairly clear that it had been put there for her benefit, but she supposed it could have been worse. She took some comfort from the fact that though it lionised the late King, her own father was at least depicted in a neutral manner in the distance. She wouldn't have been surprised to see his death portrayed with every bit as much relish as the unfortunate General Vox's.

The guest list for the dinner was surprisingly short. Along with Thalia's own party and the Queen herself, attending were Sir Terence, Chamberlain Renholt, Lady Annabelle and a somewhat portly man announced as High Wizard Galantha-ras. This last guest wore a voluminous black velvet robe and a fine white porcelain mask that covered the upper two-thirds of his face, leaving only his mouth exposed. From what Thalia knew of the secretive order, both mask and name were passed down from one High Wizard to the next when one died or retired, as were the long, plain silver staffs that served as their badge of office. Whereas the Wizards in general, much like Magisters, mixed with the general population and leant their skills when and where needed, the High Wizards were reclusive, rarely seen outside of their Chantries and mostly based in the city of Aquila.

After introductions had been made and they had taken their seats at the table, which boasted a pristine white tablecloth and place settings comprising no less than six plates of assorted sizes and as many sets of cutlery, the sommelier brought out the evening's first wine. At a nod from the Queen, Lady Annabelle rose from the table and stepped into her armour, which was decorated in white gold but less extravagantly endowed than Tondarin's.

"As is traditional, Lady Annabelle will draw the first blood of the grape," announced the Queen. Annabelle's right hand flashed down to her left hip, and as it rose again it was followed by a trace of white light that coalesced into the form of her sword. She took the first bottle of wine off the silver tray, and laid her blade against its neck, slicing the top clean off in a single move. As the table gave a polite round of applause, she released the armour and poured herself a glass of the wine, tossing it back in one go as her sword dissolved into Aether.

"This, too, is an important part of the tradition," said Chamberlain Renholt. "If the drawing of the grape is inexpertly done, small shards of glass might be present in the neck of the bottle. The sword-champion of the table stakes their life, or at least their immediate good health, on their skill."

"We have two warriors of the College here who profess to the title of Master, do we not?" asked the Queen, with a sly smile. "Perhaps one of them would be so good as to give us their own demonstration of their abilities."

Thalia realised immediately that Tondarin had set a trap. Neither Amanda Devereux nor Delys had ever performed the trick before and they would be expected to follow Annabelle's example, risking injury if they were unsuccessful. Devereux exchanged a quick glance with Delys, who grinned.

"I'm afraid that my own sword-skills are very much focused on the battlefield, Your Exceptional Majesty," said the Operative. "But Master Delys has been eager to give that trick a go since the moment someone mentioned swords."

"Could she not say so herself?" asked Annabelle, somewhat archly.

"She's not a talker," said Devereux with a smile. "But she'd like you to throw over a bottle so she can try it."

"*Throw* over!" gaped Chamberlain Renholt. "This is a two-hundred year old Orsinio-"

"We're going to drink it, not put it in a museum, Chamberlain," said the Queen with a smirk, her gaze fixed on Delys. "If a bottle should happen to break, so be it."

With a look of extreme disdain, the sommelier selected a bottle from the tray, and tossed it with all the ceremony he could muster in Delys' direction. Thalia suddenly realised that the little blonde's sword was still resting in its scabbard and being supported with some difficulty by Herenford, who was standing against the back wall. She had half expected Delys to do something dramatic whilst the wine was in mid-air, but surely-

The bottle was one-third of the way through its flight when Delys came to her feet. It had covered half the distance to her chair when her sword cleared leather and whipped around so fast that only the position of her arm at the end of the motion betrayed the weapon's path. Amanda Devereux caught the bottle at the end of its flight.

"She.. she missed?" said Lady Annabelle. The Operative lifted the end of the bottle's neck clear.

"No, she got it clean. She just didn't disturb its flight in the process. If I understand it correctly, the technique is called *eikenyu*, the lightning-sword strike, in Daxalai. You aren't usually supposed to do it with such a large sword, though."

"Fascinating," said the High Wizard, quietly. Devereux gave him an odd look for a moment, but was prevented from any further comment by Delys' arrival back in her seat. She retrieved the bottle, and took a large swig direct from the severed neck.

"Ah, sorry about that," said Devereux, as applause and a few chuckles rippled around the table. "Master Delys' mastery of table manners has never really matched her swordsmanship."

"I had heard that a Daxalai émigré now taught at the Imperial Academy," said Lady Annabelle, sitting back down at the table. "Clearly the rumours were true."

If Queen Tondarin was annoyed that her attempt to embarrass Thalia had failed, she showed no sign of it. If anything, Delys' skill had served to break the ice, and the conversation flowed with more ease than she would have dreamed possible. Athas in particular proved to be very popular with the Abelians, his simple honesty and complete lack of nuance winning them over with ease. Thalia noticed the High Wizard paying the big Guard very close attention.

"So, Sergeant Athas," said Galantharas, as the third course was being laid. "I understand you had a narrow escape recently?"

"What, those bandits, you mean?" said Athas. "I was very lucky, Learned- er, what do I call you?"

"Esteemed Sir is the usual form of address," said Chamberlain Renholt.

"Oh, right. Anyway, Esteemed Sir, I was very lucky that Magister Thalia got to me as quickly as she did."

"I was not referring to your arrow injury, though I understand it was severe," said the High Wizard. "I am more interested in your brush with our own.. local affliction."

335

"Er, your what?"

"The High Wizard is referring to the Winnowing Ague, Sergeant." said Thalia, quickly.

"Oh, that? I don't really know a lot about it, Esteemed Sir, if I'm honest," said Athas. "I passed out when the arrow hit me and by the time I woke up I was fine.. just really hungry. These look like really nice bread rolls, by the way." He picked up the one which had been placed on his plate along with a lump of hard cheese, and was about to take a bite when he noticed that the Abelians were laughing at him. "What? What have I done now?"

"This particular course of the meal is not generally eaten," said Renholt, gesturing at the bread and cheese on his own plate. "It is called the Commoner's Course. Traditionally, any left over food from the tables of the nobility was served to the poor and the starving, and during the Great Famine of 1725, when food was scarce, many cooks began serving plain fare for one course of each meal, knowing that their patrons would not eat it. In such a way were at least some of the least fortunate kept fed, even though few families, to their shame, would open their coffers to do so."

"That's.. well, it's quite clever, I suppose," said Athas. "But surely the Great Families should have fed their people anyway? Aren't you supposed to protect them?"

The Queen surprised Thalia by nodding. "You are correct, Sergeant. At times the Great Families have forgotten the debt they owe to the common folk. A throne is nothing without the people it serves. We now observe the Commoner's Course as a reminder of that fact."

Athas looked down at the bread. "But.. I didn't think you had many poor people left any more? Didn't the Ague kill most of them?"

"That is sadly true," agreed the Chamberlain. "Though some still survive, mostly in the ancestral lands of the Savalan family. They do not lack for food, but for coin, so the bread and cheese used in the Commoner's Course is always bought from farms that use exclusively living workers. It is a form of charity, but it allows those who benefit from it to keep their pride."

"So.. this food isn't going to go to the poor after all?" said Athas. "Does that mean it goes to waste?"

"To the horses, usually," said Lady Annabelle with a chuckle. "But I suppose if you were really that hungry-"

Athas took a huge bite from his roll. "My Dad always says that wasted food is a crime against nature," he said, after giving the morsel a hearty chew. "Everything we grow comes from someone's sweat and blood, hard work and the blessing of the land. If I let a good wholemeal roll like this go to waste he'd give me a thick ear."

"A thick what?" said Lady Annabelle, frowning in confusion.

"It's when you clip-" began Athas, but Thalia cut him off in case he felt the need to give a demonstration.

"Thank you, Sergeant. To answer your original question, Esteemed Sir, Healer Alana suspects that Athas had been suffering from the Ague for some time, and the injury he received simply weakened him to the point where the condition became obvious. Feeding him with a tube until he recovered proved effective."

"That khile-goop was really nasty, though," said Athas, finishing off the roll and starting on the lump of cheese. "Not that I'm complaining, because it helped save me, of course."

"And left you with an appetite to rival a Razorpaw Bear waking from hibernation, it seems," laughed lady Annabelle. Athas made a face.

"No, that was the Ague. The stuff in that tube nearly put me off food for life!"

Everyone, even the Queen, laughed at this, and Thalia began almost to think that she could relax. Tondarin chose the arrival of the next course to spring her second surprise.

"By the way, Your Excellency, you should know that your permanent replacement is on the way from the College. You will soon be free to return to your usual duties."

Thalia looked up from an exquisite four-bird roast in surprise. "Really, Your Exceptional Majesty? I hadn't been informed."

"The news only arrived an hour or so ago," said Chamberlain Renholt. "The College is sending Magister Elsabeth Thule. She should arrive within a couple of days."

"I see," said Thalia. "Well, I must say I am relieved. Though this has been an.. educational experience, and it was of course an honour to serve, Magister Elsabeth is far better versed in diplomacy than I."

"We have requested that you be assigned to be our special liaison to the Expelled." said the Queen. "When the expeditionary force leaves, we will be leading it, and you will be by our side."

Thalia glowered at her. "So, you would still like me to personally accompany you, even though I will no longer be an Ambassador? What if I refuse?"

"You will have no such choice in the matter," said the Queen. "Both the Arch-Chancellor, and your new Ambassador, have already agreed to our conditions. We- ack!"

"Your Exceptional Majesty?" said Lady Annabelle, throwing back her chair and hurrying to the Queen's side as the woman winced. "Are you all right?"

"It is nothing," said Tondarin. "One of the babies merely kicked. He is a strong one."

"Then why are you still wearing a corset?" said Thalia, before she could stop to think. "No wonder he's kicking you if he's got so little room to move-"

There was a moment's silence, and then almost the entire Abelian side of the table erupted in laughter.

"The Queen is not *carrying* the children, Your Excellency," said Galantharas, the only Abelian present not too busy laughing to explain. "By the craft of the High Wizards, after the child is conceived by the monarch the pregnancy is transferred to her lady-in-waiting to be carried. The Queen is then free to see to the affairs of state, wage war, or even conceive another child, unencumbered. She will, however, still feel some of the sensations of the pregnancy, and will go through the labour with the surrogate when the time comes. At present, Her Exceptional Majesty is experiencing three such pregnancies."

Thalia gaped at the man. The idea of doing what he had just described seemed at once extremely convenient, and the most arrogant of subversions of nature. The fact that no-one had even mentioned the father, or fathers for that matter, was another factor she was finding difficult to accept.

"Do not worry, Your Excellency," said Tondarin, the look of cruelty returning

337

to her eyes. "We do not anticipate the campaign taking too long. We will have the Dendaril crushed and the savages brought to heel well before it is our time."

"Why are you so determined to conquer the Free Tribes, anyway?" snapped Thalia, finally losing her patience. "You don't need their land, you don't need the labour, it'll make your border with the Empire longer and harder to defend. Why are you doing this?"

The Queen gave her a level stare. "We do not have to explain Ourselves to anyone, much less you, Daughter of the Mountainbreaker."

Thalia stared at her. "That's it, isn't it? Your people respect my father, and understand that what he did was a purely military act, but for you, it's personal. You don't want to conquer the Free Tribes or take their land, you just want to make me responsible for betraying them!"

"Your Exceptional Majesty, perhaps this discussion is best not had at an official function-" began Chamberlain Renholt. Tondarin glared at him, and stood up sharply.

"Chamberlain, you are quite correct. This meal is at an end. Lady Annabelle, see our guests are escorted back to their coach. Ambassador Thalia, I believe we should discuss this in my private sitting-room."

"If that is Your Exceptional Majesty's wish," growled Thalia, practically vibrating with fury.

Swiftly, the various guests stood up and made ready to leave. Amanda Devereux took advantage of the distraction of Athas gobbling the rest of his meal to speak quietly to Thalia.

"Thalia, as soon as I can I'm going to slip away. I need to find out what that Galantharas character is up to. It was him at the Hospital, I'm certain of it. The voice-print is an exact match."

"Be careful," said Thalia, only half listening.

"I should say the same to you," said Devereux. "Are you sure this is a good idea?"

"No," said Thalia. "But if I am to save the Free Tribes without dooming the alliance against the Dendaril, Queen Tondarin and I need to come to an understanding, and quickly."

Devereux gave her a reassuring smile. "I'd like to be a fly on the wall for that conversation. All I can suggest is that you keep being honest with her. These people seem to find your temper quite appealing. Use that."

Thalia watched as the Operative and the rest of her staff were ushered out. Expressing her temper was hardly going to be a problem. Resisting the urge to try to burn the Queen to ashes might be.

84

The courtyard was full of more people than Moon Behind Dark Clouds had ever seen in one place. Over two thousand Free stood before the great ritual altar, led by the most senior Mighty Ones of the Hearth-Tenders. Whatever the Master had said to Mighty Taris must have been extremely convincing, for the leader of the Hearth-Tenders had not only reversed his objection to taking the Brand, but had volunteered to be amongst the first of his tribe to do so. The Hearth-Tenders had never been one of the more numerous tribes, since many young Free left to join other tribes rather than take the Embracing Limbs, the tattoo that marked the bearer as being unable to inflict harm to another human being. Even the Mighty Ones of the tribe bore this tattoo, which served as a mark of free passage through the territory of other tribes in peacetime, and of a non-combatant in war.

To one side of the altar stood Mighty Taris himself, his face an unreadable mask. To the other was the Seneschal, her own impassive visage every bit as inscrutable. The Brands already twisted on Taris' wrist, Moon noticed.

"What do you think will happen, husband?" whispered Night's First Raven from her place on the balcony next to him. Most of the senior Mighty Ones and war-leaders of the Ixildar, as the Master had told them they would now be called, were present, and it was Mighty Lelioko who answered her when Moon could not.

"I believe that Mighty Taris will serve as a conduit for the Master's power," said Lelioko. "From what I understand of the ritual-"

"YOU UNDERSTAND LITTLE, BUT THIS IS NOT REQUIRED," said Ixilinath, as his skull-faced form coalesced from a sudden burst of flame on the previously empty throne overlooking the courtyard. "MIGHTY TARIS KNOWS HIS PART."

Below, seeing that the Master had arrived, Taris swallowed, and turned to face his people. "Hearth-Tenders! Today we perform a great service for the Free, as we accept the Brands and join the ranks of the Ixildar. Never before have so many accepted the Master's gift at one time as will do so today."

Several of the Hearth-Tenders exchanged uneasy glances. Moon could understand why, but it was still a cause for concern. If even one of them were less than certain of their willingness to serve the Master, the consequences could be catastrophic.

"I understand that this will worry some of you," continued Taris. "You fear that we lose the right to call ourselves Free by doing this. That may be so. But you have all seen those who already bear the Brands, talked to them, lived with them. Do they strike you as slaves, or as free men and women? Some of you were also at the Moot of Kings, when the Blackbloods who had been taken by the Woe tried to spread the evil of the Fly Lords to our people. They did not even recognise their own kin, much less respect the sanctity of the Moot or the honour of the Free. If I must choose between that, the silver chains of the Deluded, and the Master's gift, I choose the Master and I do so willingly. So must all of you."

Some of the assembled Hearth-Tenders were weeping openly now, but they were still listening. Ixilinath, his baleful eyes burning, simply sat in silence on his throne, and Moon marvelled at the sight. A being of such power and with unquestioned mastery, content to watch and wait for Taris to convince his people with mere words. It was not like the songs he had learned in his youth.

"I know that many of you also fear that, as Ixildar, we might be forced to forswear our oath of non-violence, which has protected us and safeguarded the Free Tribes since the Great Exodus. And yet recall the words of the *Song of the Hearth*, which tells of our tribe's inception:

> *And for the third tribe, gentle of heart,*
> *The gift of peace unending is given.*
> *To tend the flames of hearth and home,*
> *To guard the child from foolish wrath,*
> *And nurture the shoots of innocent youth.*
> *Within the warm embracing limbs,*
> *And the words of a promise of peace."*

Moon nodded. Each tribe had its own song that told of its founding and its purpose. All the same, he wasn't sure what point Taris was building towards.

"I have spoken with the Master, and He has explained these words to me in a way that no Mighty One has understood them for centuries," said Taris. "The flames of hearth and home that the song refers to are the very flames that burn in Ixildundal, and that burn in the Brands. They are they same flames that protect the Ixildar from the dread touch of the Woe. All know that the tattoos we bear that give us the strength to remain Free are the greatest work of the Ancestors. Now I tell you that the Embracing Limbs are the creation of the Master Himself. We need not fear that the Brands will corrupt the purpose of our tribe, for in truth, they are simply the completion of a work that was begun many centuries ago. The Embracing Limbs prevent us from doing harm to any human being, and the Brands will do the same for all of the Free, one to another."

Moon blinked in surprise. The idea that one Ixildar could not purposely harm another was something that he had never considered, but it made sense. The

Master would hardly wish His people to fight amongst themselves, after all. Below, in the courtyard, the Hearth-Tenders were smiling now, relieved that their tribe's purpose would not be corrupted.

"*MIGHTY TARIS, IT IS TIME,*" said Ixilinath, rising to his feet with the unnerving vitality that Moon had still not got used to. The Master's cadaverous appearance always seemed at odds with the way that He moved, even now. Below, Mighty Taris nodded.

"Yes, Master Ixilinath," He turned to the altar, and took up the first of a stack of large, elaborately carved wooden trays that rested upon it. Each tray contained several rows of small, round wafers. "My people, each of you will be given one of these wafers, called *dareshandalin* in the Old Tongue. This is the Body of the Master, and will serve as a conduit for His power. When the word is given, place the wafer in your mouth, and wash it down with a sip of water drawn from the chalice on the altar. It may seem that there is not enough for all of us, but the water in the chalice is also drawn from the Master's power. It will not run out."

The Mighty One's attendants moved forwards, passing out the wafers and small wooden cups of water. With two thousand people in the courtyard, the process took almost an hour, and darkness was falling by the time the last wafer had been handed out. In the twilight, it seemed to Moon that the *dareshandalin* were glowing faintly in the hands of the supplicants. Ixilinath rose into the air above the gathered throng, his power flaring in an incandescent nimbus around him as his ancient robes fluttered in a breeze that had no source. At Taris' signal, the Hearth-Tenders swallowed the wafers and drank.

Not really knowing why he did so, Moon Behind Dark Clouds reached out, and found his wife's hand questing for his own.

"*NOW, HEARTH-TENDERS, IT IS TIME FOR YOU TO KNOW THE EMBRACE OF IXILINATH. LET THE FLAME JUDGE YOU.*"

Somehow, Moon had expected more preamble, but as Ixilinath spoke his fire blazed even brighter, and leapt in a brilliant arc to Mighty Taris. From there, the flames reached out, hungry tongues enveloping the Hearth-Tenders one after another. For a moment there was nothing but a stunned silence as the flames rolled through the gathered throng, setting shadows dancing on the walls.

Then the screaming started. It was only a few of the supplicants at first, but within seconds it had spread until every Hearth-Tender in the courtyard was writhing and howling in agony. Moon felt his wife's grip tighten. They had seen this happen before, of course, with Fire In Deep Woods and others, but the sound of two thousand people bearing the same agony at once was indescribable. Suddenly, Moon became aware that his Brands were becoming hot on his skin.

"Husband?" gasped Night's First Raven, releasing his hand and staring at her smouldering arms in confusion. "What... what is happening?"

"I do not know," said Moon, through gritted teeth. The Brands were now blazing with fire almost as hot as that which he had endured when he first accepted them, and looking around the balcony he could see that the others were suffering as well. Mighty Lelioko suddenly gave a gasp of shock.

"Look! Look to the Master!"

As one, even as the pain threatened to overwhelm their senses, they looked to where Ixilinath floated above the courtyard. Whereas usually when the Brands were placed on a new supplicant the Master simply watched impassively, on this occasion he was still wreathed in flame. Though he made no sound, Moon could see that the gloved hands were clenched tight into fists and the mouth of his skeletal face was clamped shut.

"The Master is.. serving as the link between all the supplicants," said Lelioko, awestruck. "He feels their pain, as do we. Warriors of the Ixildar!" She shouted, amplifying her voice with her magic so all of Ixildundal could hear her. "The Hearth-Tenders are in need! Steel yourselves, resist the pain, and come to the ritual grounds with all haste!"

"What are you doing, Mighty One?" asked Moon in confusion, fighting the urge to flee and douse his arms in cold water.

"We must aid the Hearth-Tenders," said Lelioko, vaulting over the balcony and dropping to the flagstones of the courtyard. "Come!"

Quickly, joined by increasing numbers of warriors as they streamed into the courtyard from all directions, the Shorewalkers ran to the side of their fellows.

"What can we do, Mighty One?" cried Night's First Raven, desperately.

"We must calm them, help them to accept the Brands," said Lelioko.

"The.. the song of the Trees..." said Mighty Taris, through gritted teeth. "You must remind them.. of who they are.."

"Yes!" cried Night's First Raven. "If anything will calm the Hearth-Tenders and bring them back to us, it is that. All of you, follow my lead!"

She threw back her head, took a deep breath, and began:

> *"The stars are crying, little one, but you are wise,*
> *You make your shelter in the trees.*
> *Their tears are cold, but the hearth is warm,*
> *And I am here beside you.*
> *The wolves are howling, little one, but you are kind,*
> *You wrap your arms around the trees.*
> *Their branches shelter man and beast,*
> *And I am here beside you."*

Moon thought that maybe the screaming was dying down a little, but it was still hard to even hear his wife's voice. Calling upon the Roaring Toad, he added his own bass voice to her song.

> *"The moon is hiding, little one, but you can see,*
> *You find your way in the song of the trees.*
> *Their leaves will show you the way home,*
> *And I am here beside you.*
> *The bears are growling, little one, but you are brave,*
> *You stand before them amidst the trees.*
> *Their trunks are stronger than any foe*
> *And I am here beside you."*

The screaming was definitely starting to fade now, and some of the Hearth-Tenders were even standing up and joining in with the song. Even so, the flames were still blazing unchecked through the courtyard and many of the supplicants were still suffering. Moon felt the Brands burning hotter than ever, but somehow where there had been pain, there was now something else. Power.

> *"The snow is falling, little one, but you are warm,*
> *You watch worlds drift between the trees.*
> *The tribes are proof against all cold,*
> *And I am here beside you.*
> *The night is calling, little one, but you are safe,*
> *You wait for dawn to light the trees.*
> *When comes the sun to Forest Home,*
> *I will be here beside you!"*

The ending of the song was traditionally a crescendo, and Moon put everything he had into the note, which seemed to last for an age, some four-thousand voices joining together and turning it into almost a living, breathing thing. Eventually the sound faded away and he realised he had closed his eyes. He opened them, to discover that the Hearth-Tenders now stood with their rescuers, every one of them bearing the Brands, which were already fading as the fires of their creation dwindled.

"*I LOOK UPON YOU, IXILDAR, AND I AM PLEASED,*" said Ixilinath, descending to stand amongst them.

"Master, we failed you!" cried Mighty Taris, falling to his knees. "Our conviction was not strong enough. Had the Shorewalkers and the other tribes not come to our aid-"

"*YOU FAIL ONLY TO UNDERSTAND, MIGHTY TARIS,*" said Ixilinath. "*FOR THE RITUAL TO SUCCEED, IT WAS NOT ENOUGH FOR THE HEARTH-TENDERS TO HAVE NO DOUBT. ALL THE IXILDAR WERE REQUIRED TO BELIEVE, TO RISE ABOVE THEIR FEARS AND TO UNITE THEIR WILL. THIS YOU MY PEOPLE ACHIEVED, AND I AM WELL PLEASED.*"

"Then this... all of this was part of your design, Master?" said Mighty Lelioko. The skeletal form turned to look at her.

"*NO. I NO MORE KNEW WHAT FORM THE TEST WOULD TAKE THAN YOU DID. BUT I BELIEVED THAT THE IXILDAR WERE EQUAL TO IT, AND THUS IT PROVED. REST NOW, FOR TOMORROW WE MUST CONTINUE THE WORK. IT WILL BE EASIER WITH MORE TO SHARE THE BURDEN.*"

Ixilinath turned to walk away, followed by the robed form of the Seneschal. It struck Moon that alone amongst them, the disembodied thing had not seemed to be affected by the ritual.

"He.. He risked His own life for us..." breathed Mighty Lelioko, watching as the two disappeared into the depths of the fortress.

"What do you mean, Mighty One?" said Night's First Raven. "Surely there is nothing that could threaten the Master? All know of His power."

"It was exactly that which threatened Him," said Lelioko, still looking in the direction that Ixilinath had gone. "During the moment of connection, I felt His power flowing through me- all of His power. Had the ritual failed, I think it very possible that the Master might have been lost to us."

Mighty Taris scratched at his beard thoughtfully. "I concur, Mighty Lelioko. I confess that I believed the Master to be no more than another ancient megalomaniac, like the Dead Lords from the old songs, and I took his bargain only with reluctance at first. But the more that I learn, the more I feel there is a deeper purpose to His actions. He truly cares for the fate of the Free, even though He left mortal concerns in the dust of his flesh many centuries ago."

"The benevolence of the Master is great indeed," said Moon Behind Dark Clouds.

"It is," agreed Mighty Taris. "I only wish that I truly understood why that might be."

85

*T*halia followed the Queen of Abelia down the lavishly-carpeted hallway, barely believing what she was doing. Her state of mind was hardly helped by the resplendent form of Tondarin's armour striding alongside the Abelian monarch, nor by the steady tramp of the Guardian's footsteps behind her. She hadn't been entertaining any sort of attack on the Queen- at least, not in the literal sense- and the two automata presented a strong argument to keep things that way. For the third time that evening, Tondarin surprised her. As they reached a large, ornately-carved wooden door, she gestured dismissively and her armour marched away without breaking stride.

"Aren't you concerned that you might.. need that?" said Thalia, watching it go.

"Hardly," said the Queen, with a cold laugh. "In any case, the Guardian will stand vigil outside. We will not be disturbed. Come."

She stalked through the door, the huge automaton taking station alongside it as she did so, and after a moment to take a deep breath and calm herself Thalia followed. The room they entered was even more sumptuous than the rest of the palace, with a rich, deep-pile purple carpet, more wood-panelled walls, and furnishings of cream and gold. It was also unexpectedly occupied. The three ladies-in-waiting Thalia had seen in the throne room were sitting around a table, drinking wine and sewing, and looked up in surprise as the Queen approached.

"Your Exceptional Majesty!" said the one who was most heavily pregnant, levering herself to her feet. "We had not expected you back so soon!"

"Do not concern yourself, Jelianeth," said the Queen, smiling broadly. "Your Excellency, may I present Lady Jelianeth Egret, Lady Deselani D'Grace, and Lady Titanea Auloux? Ladies, this is Ambassador Thalia Daran, our *temporary* emissary from the Lily College." There was more emphasis on 'temporary' than Thalia thought strictly necessary.

All three women essayed curtsies, Lady Jelianeth with some difficulty. Thalia burned with questions, but her business tonight was with the Queen and she knew

345

she could not allow herself to become distracted. She settled for returning the curtsies with a polite nod.

"The state dinner has concluded somewhat... abruptly," said the Queen. "I require the private use of my stateroom. I will see you all tomorrow."

As the three ladies filed out, with curious gazes at Thalia, Lady Jelianeth suddenly stopped and gasped. "Oh!" She put her hand to her stomach, and the Magister saw that Tondarin copied the motion almost exactly. "I am sorry, Your Exceptional Majesty, he seems to get a little frisky when the wine is opened."

"That is.. quite all right, Jelianeth," said the Queen, straightening up and smiling. "Our son will be a fierce warrior if the strength of his first blows is any guide. Be sure to summon the Healers if you have any trouble sleeping. No- no, that is not necessary, you will injure yourself!"

Lady Jelianeth had been about to try and curtsy again, and gave the Queen a faint smile of gratitude. "Th- thank you, Your Exceptional Majesty. Good night."

The Queen closed the door behind them, and let out a hearty sigh. "Would that I could carry that burden myself, but it does not behove a Queen to show any weakness in these times."

A wooden maid appeared from a corner of the room, heading for the table, but Tondarin waved it over to her. "Leave the wine open, we may have need of it. Take this." There was the faintest hiss of escaping air as the armoured corset of her dress suddenly unlaced itself. The Stickman- Thalia wondered if Stick-woman was more appropriate given that the thing had been carved with a feminine figure and legs shaped to suggest a dress- hurried over and removed the garment, leaving the Queen dressed only in a purple silk chemise and petticoat over her underclothes.

"King's grace, that's better," sighed Tondarin, stretching. "The things I must do for appearances!"

"Not using the royal 'we' any more, Your Exceptional Majesty?" said Thalia, surprised at the sudden change in the Queen's manner.

"That is another thing I must do for appearances," said Tondarin. "In public, I speak as the Kingdom, whereas in private I speak for myself. I do not use that archaic form when alone with my friends, or my enemies."

"And which am I?" said Thalia, daringly.

"Neither? Both?" said the Queen, sitting down on a huge settee upholstered in cream leather and trimmed with gold. "You are a representative of the College, and for the time being at least an ally, though I don't doubt that the twin vipers who nest in Lore are looking for a way to turn this crisis to their advantage. At the same time you are the daughter of the man who killed my father and brother and part of me would gladly strangle you with my bare hands."

"And your own people then killed my father on the same day," said Thalia, her voice low and dangerous. "Do not think, Your Exceptional Majesty, that you are alone in your pain. Or in the... desires it stirs."

Tondarin took up the wine bottle and gave it an experimental swish. With a low grunt of satisfaction, she poured two glasses and patted the space beside her.

"Sit, drink. And for now, call me Tondarin and I shall call you Thalia. It is not our titles that are in conflict here, it is our blood."

Thalia sat down, and took a small sip of the wine. She was already feeling the effects of the drinks she had had earlier, and from the initial taste of it this particular vintage pulled even less punches than the rest. "Is this.. your usual approach to diplomacy... Tondarin?"

The Queen laughed. "This? This is not diplomacy, Thalia. I doubt diplomacy will even commence until whatever this is is concluded. Let us begin, then. I despise you, Thalia Daran. I hate you with every fibre of my being. From the first moment that I heard the College was sending you here, I began to ponder how to hurt you, how to torment you, how to make your very existence nothing but misery."

Thalia did her best not to look away from Tondarin's intense stare, which was being levelled at her from a distance of little more than a foot. Well, she had told Herenford that the Queen would be honest about hating her. She certainly hadn't been wrong. All the same, experienced in person it was less than pleasant.

"Do you know that Talion Daran visited Castle Valour a little before the war?" said Tondarin, after a pause to take a gulp of her wine. "His eyes gaze at me from your face. My father told me that there stood a brave and honourable man, and yet within a few short years he would be dead at the hands of that very Magister."

"Honourable?" said Thalia. "What would King Tobias have known of honour? He attacked while you were sitting down to a peace conference! Had he been honourable and respected the terms of the truce, he would still be alive today!" She took her own large slug of wine, satisfied that she had landed a blow.

Tondarin glared at her for a long moment. A lock of Thalia's hair had fallen down in front of her eyes, but it felt like any movement on her part might provoke the Queen to violence.

"My father," said Tondarin slowly, "did not know about the peace conference."

Thalia nearly dropped the wine glass. "What? B-but if he didn't know, how could you have even signed the peace treaty! Without the authority of the King behind it.."

"Or the authority of the Queen," said Tondarin with a cold smile. "Which was what I had once he died."

Thalia went white, and this time the empty glass bounced to rest on the carpet. "You- you engineered the whole thing? You sent your own father to his death?"

"He was an old fool!" snapped Tondarin. "He was determined to carry on with the old ways, keeping women- keeping *me*, out of the military, using us just as breeding sows! I was twice the swordsman my brother was, and yet he was on campaign whilst I sat being patronised by simpering noblemen!"

"But to kill your own father... for that?" gasped Thalia. "You- you must be insane!"

"He was killing the fucking country!" shouted Tondarin. "There weren't enough Royal Knights to lead the army and he had practically forbidden any women to join them, forcing talented warriors to become Wizards and diplomats and sending high-born sons to their deaths who couldn't even master their own armour! When my mother tried to reason with him, he had her exiled to her death on Shrew Island."

Thalia shook her head, the wine immediately making her regret it. "No. No, this doesn't make sense. You couldn't have known that my father would notice the Abelian army moving through the mountains. And anyway-" she said, triumphantly, "if the whole thing was part of some plan of yours, why would you hate me for my father's part in it?"

Tondarin refilled her glass, and retrieved Thalia's, filling it as well and placing it pointedly on the table. "Two names. Prince Tobin, and Jonal Rill."

Thalia's world felt like it had been tipped on its side and violently shaken. With a trembling hand, she reached out for the wine and took a deep draught. "You- you mean...?"

"My little brother, Prince Tobin. He was with the rearguard, helping protect the Wizards who were keeping the pass stable. Jonal Rill, may Yar curse his name, was supposed to help the College forces ambush the vanguard of the Royal Army, to ensure the deaths of my father and his cronies, the gaggle of festering old bastards who muttered idiocies in his ear. But something went wrong."

"What happened?" said Thalia quietly, barely daring to breathe.

"We captured Rill after the disaster, and tortured him," said the Queen. "He claimed that the College army units that he had planned to warn had been redeployed at the last minute. Because he was a patriot- a patriot who had been bribed by the enemy, perhaps, but still a patriot- he decided to stop the invasion by other means, and so made sure Magister Talion Daran was looking the right way at the right time. From one point of view, at least."

She took a sip of the wine, and laughed bitterly. "He expected Talion to go and summon help, maybe do something to buy some time for the Volumes to move to block the attack. But your father, your brave, honourable... honourable *shit* of a father, decided to stop them all by himself. So he sent all his men away, except for good, trusted, loyal Jonal Rill of course, and then dropped a fucking mountainside on top of the Royal Army! And on top of my baby brother!"

"But.. that was your fault, not my father's!" said Thalia, her face flushing red. "It was your plot that got him killed!"

"It was your father that killed him!" growled Tondarin, her own face inches from Thalia's. "King's grace, you should hate him too! If he had just had the sense to-"

There was a loud crack, and the Queen's head rocked backwards. It took Thalia a moment to realise that the sound, and the mild throb in her palm, were the result of her slapping Tondarin in the face. The Abelian turned back to her with a savage grin of triumph.

"Do you know something interesting about the magic the High Wizards use to transfer a pregnancy from one woman to another, Magister Thalia?" she said, draining what little of her wine she hadn't spilled on receiving the blow.

"I- I didn't mean... what?" said Thalia in confusion, still trying to comprehend the impulsive stupidity of what she had done and wondering if she could blame the wine.

"It is particularly dangerous for a woman under the effects of the enchantment to attempt to use their own magic," said the Queen. "So whilst serving as Royal Surrogates, my ladies-in-waiting eat food and drink wine laced with Jakille Root, picked in the Southern Blastings. Completely harmless, of course, but it does prevent one from harnessing one's Spirit for a few hours."

With mounting horror, Thalia tried to summon up her magic, at least to cleanse the alcohol from her system so she could think clearly. It would not respond- she could feel the power there, but every time she tried to harness it it seemed to slip away. "But... but you drank the same wine as I did..." she gasped. Tondarin laughed, and stood up, a little unsteadily.

"Oh, Thalia, you misunderstand my intent. This isn't some sort of clever plot to murder you- if I'd wanted you dead, I could have had the thing done a hundred times by now."

"Then.. then why?" said Thalia, forcing herself to stand up as well.

"It's so I don't accidentally kill you when I do this," said the Queen, punctuating the end of the sentence with a roundhouse punch to Thalia's jaw. The Magister went reeling backwards, tumbling over the table and knocking both it and the wine glasses over.

"Stand, Daughter of the Mountainbreaker," hissed Tondarin, throwing the table out of the way and advancing on Thalia. "Stand and show me the courage of House Daran. The courage that killed my brother!"

The blow had more surprised the Magister than truly hurt her, and her fall owed more to the wine than to anything else, but she realised she was in serious trouble. Even though Magisters were trained in physical self-defence, Tondarin was a Royal Knight, and was considerably stronger and taller into the bargain. Nevertheless, Thalia managed to get enough distance to rise and bring her hands up, and was foolishly pleased to block the Queen's next attempted punch with her forearm. She kept out two more before the Abelian closed in and hit her with a knee to the stomach.

Reeling back, her mind on fire with pain, her heart thudding in her chest and her fury rising, Thalia felt her magic surge, but the power danced away from her even as Tondarin eluded her clumsy attempt to hit her back. Desperation lending her courage, the Magister followed the Queen as she dodged, and was rewarded as Tondarin stumbled over a fallen chair and lurched into a glancing punch. Still, the blow only seemed to make the Abelian angrier, and she shrugged it off, shoving Thalia back so hard that she cannoned off the settee.

Suddenly, Thalia remembered that though she had left her staff at the Green Palace, her dagger was still strapped to her wrist. Thinking the blade might at least give Tondarin pause, she slipped it into her hand and brandished it.

"Hah!" laughed the Queen. "What do you plan to do with-"

With a shattering boom, the door to the room was flung open. Magister and Queen alike whirled in surprise to see the Guardian advancing on them. Realising her danger, Thalia quickly dropped the knife on the carpet and held up her hands in surrender.

"I- I'm sorry! I didn't mean-"

"I don't think it cares what you meant to do, Thalia," said the Queen, her voice low and threatening. "But now, I think it time for your punishment to truly begin."

She drew back her arm, and Thalia, realising that any further attempt to defend herself was futile, closed her eyes and tried to steel herself. No blow fell, and after a moment she opened her eyes to see Tondarin struggling to free her wrist from the Guardian's grasp.

"What are you doing, you lumbering metal moron?" cried the Queen. "Let me go, damn you!"

Immediately, the automaton released her, but in so doing it moved to interpose itself between the two women.

Thalia frowned in confusion, using the unexpected respite to suck much-needed air into her lungs. "I thought that.. thing was supposed... to protect you..?"

"You could always try picking up that knife again and find out," said Tondarin, archly.

"Oh, I don't think we need that, do we?" said Thalia with a smile, swinging a slap in the Queen's direction. As she had expected, the Guardian's shield rose to block the blow, but her open hand was already slowing down and the impact was only very slightly painful.

"Hmph," said the Queen. "It's not normally so... gentle with people who try to attack me."

"Does it usually stop you hurting them?" said Thalia, her academic curiosity overcoming her pain and anger. She tried to study the Guardian with her Aether-sight, but even that seemed to have been muted by the drugged wine.

"No," said the Queen, her hands on her hips in frustration. "Maybe it's the Jakille Root. The High Wizards told me that the Guardian's sigil-engram is encoded to protect me at all costs, and to obey my orders as long as they do not conflict with that, so I don't see how..."

"Could it be... interpreting that more broadly than you expected?" said Thalia, now fully engrossed by the mystery. "Perhaps it thinks that killing me might weaken you politically, so it's trying to 'protect' you from making a mistake?"

"It doesn't 'think' anything!" laughed Tondarin bitterly. "It's no more intelligent than a War Golem. King's grace, that walking broomstick that serves me as a handmaid is brighter. Anyway, I wasn't going to kill you, just rough you up. I thought it might help us clear the air. I hadn't counted on you being so physically helpless, though."

"Physically helpless?" snapped Thalia, colour rising to her cheeks again. "Just wait until this poison of yours is out of my system and I'll show you just how 'helpless' I am, you... you..." her voice trailed off. Perhaps it was the adrenaline fighting the effects of the alcohol, but suddenly calling each other names seemed ridiculously petty.

"There'd probably be no point," said Tondarin, eyeing the Guardian. "I don't know why, but this thing seems to want to stop us from fighting, even if we both wanted to."

Thalia suddenly slapped her fist into her palm. "Aha! This has happened before, hasn't it?" she exclaimed, triumphantly.

"What?" said Tondarin, but Thalia could see the doubt in her eyes. "What do you mean?"

"In the throne room, when you decided to have me thrown in the dungeon," pressed Thalia, pointing at the Queen dramatically. "You didn't send the Guardian to attack me, did you? You didn't tell it to do anything, but it was moving to protect me from your guards, wasn't it?"

Tondarin sighed in irritation, and walked over to the settee, which had been knocked over in the fracas. "Help me with this, would you?"

Together they righted the hefty piece of furniture, and Tondarin flopped down on it heavily. "Yes, damn it. I didn't know what it was doing and I couldn't stop it. Calling the guards off was the only thing I could think of."

"Were you really going to have me thrown in the dungeon?" said Thalia, sitting back down herself but still acutely aware of the massive bulk of the Guardian watching her.

"Of course. I'm glad it stopped me though. I was having a bad day- three different cases of morning sickness, you know how it is." Thalia did not, and was particularly glad of it, though she had a worrying feeling that tomorrow's hangover was going to come close to giving her an idea.

"I think this was probably a far better way for us to work through everything, even if it didn't work out exactly as I planned," continued Tondarin. Thalia fought back the urge to say that the Queen's plans not working out was what had led to the whole situation in the first place.

"So, what do we do now?" said Thalia. "Given that we can't carry on with... that."

"I imagine we'll just have to talk," said Tondarin. "I shall have some tea brought up- just tea- and then we shall have to try to come to an understanding."

Thalia nodded. This was going to be a long evening.

86

*A*manda Devereux watched the road pass by above her. Of course strictly speaking it was below her, but she had shut down most of the biological senses that would have told her so a few hours ago. Her position, lodged firmly underneath the large coach that housed High Wizard Galantharas, was uncomfortable enough without adding motion-sickness to the deal. She had noticed the black-lacquered carriage when they had arrived at Castle Valour, and the style of the decoration had left little doubt in her mind that it belonged to her quarry.

The crew of the coach that had brought Thalia to the palace had been a concern, but the liveried footmen had been so intent on studiously ignoring the fact that their most senior passenger had failed to appear for the return journey that they had also completely failed to notice her own swift departure. She had visited the vehicle only long enough to remove the dress uniform in favour of the combat jumpsuit that she had worn underneath it. It had taken a few moments of furious signing between her and Delys to convince the little Swordmaster to stay with Athas rather than trying to follow her. In any case, Devereux really couldn't be sure how long she'd be gone and Thalia would need more than just Athas by her side.

She wished she could have taken more time to explain to the Magister why she wanted to follow the High Wizard, but Thalia had been distracted and the situation hadn't lent itself to a private discussion. It wasn't only the voice-print match that convinced her that Galantharas was the key to understanding what was going on in Abellan, though that had been what first attracted her attention. There was also the fact that he appeared to have no vital signs. He had body heat, showing up on infra-red like any other human being, and she would have bet good money that to a Magister, he would have the Pattern of a normal human too, but none of the Hercules suite's more advanced biological monitors could get any kind of read on the man. If a man was even what he was.

There was another thing, which had come to her only whilst half-dozing in her position of concealment. The magic that apparently allowed Queen Tondarin to be vicariously pregnant in triplicate seemed to involve some sort of link between her and her ladies-in-waiting. Devereux's grasp of magical theory was still weaker than she would have liked, but it seemed that such a link must be closely related to the one between the device she had found in the Royal Hospital and Athas. It all pointed to Galantharas, or the High Wizards in general, being connected to whatever had happened to the Sergeant.

The coach had been travelling for several hours now, and based on what navigational data the Hercules suite had been able to gather she must be very nearly at Aquila, the second city of the Kingdom and traditional seat of power of the High Wizards. That certainly chimed with what she'd been expecting. As was often the case in this world, though, she worried that she might be getting into a situation for which she was unprepared. Much though she wanted answers, this was going to have to be a reconnaissance mission rather than an infiltration. If a mere medical store-room had contained a warding spell powerful enough to melt tempered steel, the dangers of trying to sneak into the stronghold of the High Wizards themselves without someone with some serious magical knowledge in support were obvious.

The coach changed direction slightly, and Devereux frowned. Aquila was built some way up the mountain that gave it its name, around the shores of a large lake that served as the source for many of Abelia's major rivers, and so she would have expected the road to start to slope upwards. Instead, the coach was starting to travel down a slope, seemingly taking it into the town of Minat. From what she had learned of the Kingdom's geography, Minat was little more than a hamlet that served as a dormitory for the few living farmers who oversaw the golems that worked the surrounding agricultural land. It didn't seem to be the sort of place a High Wizard would call home. She unlocked her neck joints and took a careful look around. Sure enough, a few small, unremarkable buildings passed by as the coach slowed. Perhaps Galantharas had a country house or was visiting a secret mistress, in which case this whole expedition had been a massive waste of time. Anneke would probably be interested to learn about the mistress though, if she didn't already know.

In a moment, everything changed. The coach left the road completely, rolling along a rough dirt track that tested its suspension before coming to the end of even that crude path and carrying on through rough grass. Devereux saw trees passing to either side, and then something that made her have to fight back the urge to exclaim in surprise. Water. The coach seemed to be driving into the shallows of a lake or pond, but the water then rolled back into two banks that sparkled darkly in the starlight. The carriage kept going, neither slowing nor turning, and a roaring sound ahead alerted Devereux to the fact that they were heading straight for a waterfall. She craned her neck to see, and discovered that a cave entrance loomed behind the cascading water. According to the maps, this should be part of the River Hawksblood, which ran from the lake to the capital and out to sea.

The coach passed through into the cave, the water falling to either side of it without touching the bodywork, and finally slowed to a stop. Devereux had already begun preparing her body to move again, the deadlocked limbs releasing and micro-vibrations gently stirring both her natural muscles and the fibre-bundles assisting them. When the brakes of the coach creaked on and the driver stepped down to open the door, she was ready to act, and she was behind a large boulder in the shadows of the cave by the time Galantharas' booted feet touched the stone floor.

Now was the moment of most danger. Her systems were running in the highest level of stealth, all possible emissions of heat and sound masked and her breathing at the absolute minimum, and the fake Seal Anneke had provided her with was masking her from magical detection, but she wasn't foolish enough to think that she could hide from so powerful a magic-user as a High Wizard if he chose to look for her. The trick was to make sure he had no reason to.

"See to it that the coach is parked well away from the entrance," said the High Wizard to his driver. "I do not want a whinnying horse attracting someone to investigate an apparently solid rock-face."

"Yes, Esteemed Sir," replied the driver. "Will you be staying long, or should I keep the horses ready to move tonight?"

"I will be staying. Once the coach and horses are secure, you may take your leave."

Devereux couldn't stop herself glancing back towards the cave entrance. The waterfall glimmered in the starlight and the dark, distorted shadows of the trees could be seen beyond it, swaying gently in the night breeze.

Apparently solid rock-face? Where?

It suddenly struck her that she had been the only one who could see the black eagle that she had brought down shortly after they had entered the Expelled Territories. The incident had been somewhat forgotten in all the other excitement, but it was certainly possible that just as the artificial nature of her eyes prevented her from using Aethersight, it also allowed her to see through some magical illusions. That was certainly going to be a double-edged sword. On the one hand it might well be useful- and indeed, had been- but there might well come a time when her cover could be blown by not seeing the same thing as everyone else.

Galantharas was walking deeper into the cave now, his long, silver staff striking rhythmically on the stone as he went. Checking that the driver was busy preparing to park the coach, Devereux silently followed at a safe distance, her combat suit maintaining active camouflage. Here and there, glow-crystals set into the roof or walls of the twisting cave lit as the High Wizard approached, and Devereux was relieved to find that they darkened behind him, ignoring her own presence. This was all very encouraging- it seemed that this place, wherever it was, relied on its hidden nature for security rather than wards or alarm spells. Still, it would be deeply unwise to ignore the possibility of such defences, and she paid careful attention to where the High Wizard walked, looking for any sign that he might be avoiding or interacting with anything of the sort.

After a few minutes of walking, for which time the floor of the cave had gradually been sloping upwards, the High Wizard came to a huge chamber, which was almost certainly man-made from the size and regularity of it. But it was not the surroundings that seized Devereux's attention, shocking her so badly that she almost blundered into full view of Galantharas and the robed woman he was approaching. It was what the room had clearly been excavated to contain. Almost the entire cavern, which was at least two hundred metres long and almost as wide, was filled with an enormous machine. It was at once completely incomprehensible, and oddly familiar.

One half of the thing's bulk was comprised of a pair of massive glass tanks, their walls several inches thick, which glowed softly in the gloom of the cavern and contained a familiar-looking liquid which bubbled gently. A mass of twisting glass piping extended from one tank, entering into a colossal mechanism that squatted in the centre of the room. This device was a bewildering conglomeration of pumps, valves, crystals and gears, the function of which defied all reason, and at the bottom of it lay a wide control panel festooned with silver rods and gems that reminded Devereux of those she had seen in the navigation room of Xodan. More pipes emerged from the side of the central mechanism, extending to a series of smaller glass cylinders, and beneath each one was a socket that looked as if it might accept an Aether-Emerald. At the moment, though, it seemed the machine was simply idling, and neither the cylinders, nor the sockets beneath them, were filled. A large alcove in the wall opposite the machine was connected to another, equally empty, receptacle.

"A good eve to you, Galantharas," said the woman as the High Wizard approached, her tone lacking any warmth. "How goes the experiment?"

"It has ended in failure, Anthyana," he replied, his own tone matter-of-fact.

"Disappointing," said Anthyana, curtly. "What went wrong?"

"I do not yet know," replied Galantharas. "The Traitor Mote was successfully grafted and remains in place, though the subject's body will absorb it ere long. The Master Mote was correctly calibrated, and when last checked was drawing Spirit into the Animator."

"And yet?" prompted the woman.

"And yet the subject yet lives. Moreover, he has completely recovered from the Ague with no ill-effects other than a prodigious appetite- which, based on my observations, he may well have previously possessed."

"Odd," said Anthyana. "Was the Animator completely filled? I was led to believe that the subject's Spirit was far too weak for that to occur."

"I have not yet been able to check," confessed Galantharas. "I am not due to visit the Royal Hospital again until tomorrow, and the staff are already curious as to the nature of my work."

"It is regrettable that it was necessary to be so close to the subject," said Anthyana. "After all, the whole advantage of the Reaper is that it works regardless of distance. Were we able to use the master mechanism rather than that portable device, we could monitor it from here and this project would be a lot simpler."

"Aye," agreed Galantharas. "But it took long enough for the Reaper to isolate a hundred likely matches for the Traitor Mote. Without close proximity to the subject it was impossible to discern which one to employ."

Anthyana gave a short, mirthless laugh. "Ironic, is it not? The Reaper made short work of the task of bringing down a kingdom, and yet it struggles to slay a single man. What should we tell the rest of the Concordance?"

"The truth, of course," replied Galantharas. "That in order to precisely strike a single target without error, the Reaper must be able to match Master and Traitor motes in a much closer ratio, and do it quickly."

"It has taken a century to get even this far, Galantharas," said the woman. "How much longer must we wait to fulfil our destiny?"

"I know not," he replied. "But it is of no import. We have all the time we need."

Anthyana looked him up and down. "Well, only if we're careful. You are almost exhausted. Come, take a fresh staff and we will take this report to the others."

The High Wizard nodded, and strode over to the control panel. Smoothly, he · pulled on one of the silver rods, which turned out to be a staff identical to the one he was carrying. His own staff was then slotted gently into the receptacle from which its replacement had been drawn. With this done, the two Wizards turned away from the machine, and headed for a large oak and silver door set into the wall of the chamber. Devereux considered for a moment, but left them to it. She already had far more information than she knew what to do with, and it would serve no-one if she over-extended and got herself caught. She satisfied herself with scanning the huge machine- presumably the 'Reaper' that Anthyana had referred to- in as much detail as possible before retreating.

She needed to talk this over with Thalia, at the very least. This was far too big for her to handle alone.

*M*agister Haran Dar was standing on the battlements of the Vigil, looking east into the Expelled Territories, when Ollan found him just after dawn. Already Kandira had her work-gangs and Weavers busily engaged in mounting the second of the Petard Engines. Wilhelmina had suggested a test-firing of the first Engine before work proceeded on the second, but the Magister had laughed.

"Girl, the Engine will work and the mount will hold. The Choirmasters know their business and the Weavers and I know ours. If there's anyone out there who isn't one of those Dendaril creatures I'd rather not accidentally blow them to bits just to prove something I already know."

Ollan took a quick look around the immediate area, seeing that the nearest sentry was some distance away, and filled his pipe, lighting it with a surge of Aether. In the same moment, he also cast a silence spell so subtly that if Haran hadn't noticed the tell-tale deadening of the dawn chorus he wouldn't have known that the old man had done it. In spite of the fact that Ollan's act suggested he was about to tell Haran something he wasn't going to like, the veteran Magister had to give a grim smile. People got so used to the idea that everything Ollan did was theatrical and overblown that they missed the subtle, and every bit as effective, things he did all the time. Which was, of course, the point.

"A fine morning, I think, eh Haran?" said Ollan, puffing on his pipe with what seemed to Haran to be some satisfaction. "Possibly the finest for some time."

Haran looked out into the morning mist. It was common in these parts, but didn't seem to herald a particularly clement day. "I assume, Learned Magister, that you are not talking about the weather?"

"Oh, on the contrary!" chuckled Ollan. "I am talking about the blowing of a wind. A wind of change, driving out a foul smell, at that."

Haran wrinkled his nose, and drove Ollan's pipe-smoke away with a gust of

Aether. "Such a wind would be a pleasant thing indeed, under these circumstances."

"Hah!" said Ollan. "I can contain myself no longer, though for the sake of the College I will have to continue to do so around everyone else. The Vice-Chancellor is dead, Haran."

Under the circumstances, Haran thought he did quite well to restrict his reaction to whirling to stare at Ollan with his mouth agape. "What? Thelen's breath, man, what did you do?"

"Me?" said Ollan, the picture of innocence. "Nothing. Well, nothing except have a network of very well-paid informers in some very exclusive places. They tell me that someone managed to get into Anneke's Manse some time yesterday afternoon and cut her evil little head off."

"And yet there has been no official news?"

Ollan shook his head. "No, of course not, not yet. Derelar's no fool. Until he has someone else in place to run the Imperial Service and has managed to get at least some control of all of Anneke's little schemes, he dare not admit that she's gone. Her agents would panic or stop doing their jobs, and our enemies would know we'd been half-blinded and strike at us in the shadows." He gave a dry chuckle. "Typical of the damnable woman that even when we get rid of her we're going to be too busy dealing with the repercussions to enjoy it."

"You never have told me exactly what Anneke did that made you hate her so much," said Haran.

"No, I haven't," agreed Ollan. There was a moment of silence that made clear that this was not an omission that the old man planned on rectifying.

"So, what of Captain Render?" said Haran, finally. "She served the Vice-Chancellor only under duress. Do we inform her?"

"No, I think not," said Ollan. "It is very possible that whoever inherits Anneke's agents will also learn the secret that was being used to control the Captain. For her to stop sending reports would be exceptionally dangerous. For that matter, many of Anneke's people probably don't even know exactly who they work for. Most of mine certainly don't."

Haran nodded. "Very well, Learned Magister. I will defer to your judgement on this matter." He gave Ollan a sidelong look. "You know, if I had to pick someone else who had the requisite qualities for the post of Vice-Chancellor and College Spymaster-"

Ollan shook his head, firmly. "Don't even think it, Haran. Espionage is a young man's game. In any case, can you imagine me with the fine ladies of the Belus House Guard at my beck and call..... hmmm."

Haran noticed that the sentry was pointing at something and shouting, though the silence spell was deadening the words so much as to be unintelligible. "Learned Magister-" he began.

Ollan held up a hand. "A moment, Haran, I am imagining myself with the fine ladies of the Belus House Guard at my beck and call. On reflection, they probably don't come with the position anyway- oh, I see."

He dispelled the silence, and a moment later they could hear not only the sentry, but also the alarm horns. In the distance, where the mist was starting to recede from the morning sun, the trees could be seen moving.

"Talk about the timing of Handastalath," groused Ollan. "And it was just starting to look like a good day, too."

The Dendaril had arrived.

88

*A*manda Devereux arrived back at the Green Palace not long after dawn, to find a bleary-eyed Magister poking at her breakfast, accompanied by Delys and Athas.

"You look like you had an interesting evening, Learned Magister," observed the Operative. "Actually, more accurately you look like hell."

Thalia yawned. "You should have seen what I looked like before the Queen's personal Healers were done with me."

Devereux sat down at the table and gave Thalia a quizzical look. "Huh? What happened?"

The Magister sighed. "Amongst other things? Queen Tondarin got us both drunk and dosed with Jakille Root, and then punched me in the face."

"The Magister got her back, though," said Athas, supportively. Thalia gave him a sharp look.

"Sergeant, firstly I got a glancing blow in whilst the Queen used me as a punching-bag in a robe, and secondly, the fact that any sort of physical altercation occurred is something that absolutely must never become known to anyone outside this room. The diplomatic repercussions could potentially be extreme."

Devereux poured herself some coffee. "I'm still trying to get past the part where the Queen hit you. Why didn't you just... set her hair on fire or something?"

Thalia gave a sour chuckle. "Believe me, the thought did occur to me. Even if the Queen were not a powerful Royal Knight fully capable of defending herself against such an attack, satisfying through it might have been, the Jakille Root nullified our magic."

"What, both of you?"

"The Queen wished to express her feelings towards me physically without accidentally killing me," said Thalia. "Even so, if I hadn't pulled my knife-"

"Wait, wait," said Devereux, holding up her hands. "I think you need to begin this story at the beginning and bring me up to speed properly, because right now its starting to sound like the next Abelian War started last night after dinner."

Thalia took a sip of tea, and nodded. When her account was complete, Devereux sat thoughtfully for a moment.

"So, where do you think that leaves you with the Queen?"

"I think we came to an understanding of sorts," said Thalia. "She thought she hated me, but it was more the... *idea* of me that she loathed. I thought I hated all Abelians, but it turns out that my father was as much to blame for his own death as Tondarin or the Royal Knights that attacked him were. I don't know if he was trying to end the war in a single blow out of bravery or arrogance, or whether he could simply have fallen back and called for reinforcements, but in the end he was killed in battle by an enemy he'd just struck a mortal blow against. It's not a happy thought, but it was war."

Devereux nodded. "Does that mean you've forgiven the Queen?"

Thalia gave a short laugh. "Hah! Not in the least. If that damnable Golem wasn't protecting her every moment of the day and doing it wouldn't start another war, I'd gladly pick things up where we were forced to leave off- on my own terms. But in the interests of the College and of this alliance, I think we should be able to at least tolerate each other now."

"Yeah, about that," said Devereux. "There's more going on here than we knew, Thalia. I've got a feeling there's more going on than the Queen and most of the other Abelians know, in fact."

Now it was Thalia's turn to be curious. "Really? You found something?"

Devereux flicked a pointed glance in Athas' direction, and Thalia shrugged. "I've not told Athas anything yet, but we have few enough allies here to be keeping secrets from each other, Amanda. Tell us what you have discovered."

After giving Athas a brief explanation of the device that seemed to have been causing his symptoms, the Operative told Thalia about the hidden machine and the High Wizards attending to it. "After I got out, I used the river to swim back here. I could possibly have gone faster on the road, but there was less chance of being spotted that way."

Thalia tapped at the table with her spoon, thoughtfully. "And they said that this machine- this 'Reaper'- brought down the Kingdom? That certainly sounds like something the Queen wouldn't be very happy about."

Athas was staring wide-eyed at Devereux. "Why would Galantharas want to kill me? What did I ever do to him?"

"I don't think it was exactly personal, Athas," said the Operative, patting him on the hand reassuringly. "I think the High Wizards just needed someone to be brought into the Hospital and you were in the right place at the right time. From their perspective, anyway. With Abellan mostly having a population of noblemen and travellers, I don't think they get many patients these days, so when you were brought in they jumped at the chance."

"I don't think I like being someone's test subject," said Athas, quietly. "I don't think I like it very much at all."

Thalia shook her head. "Nor should you, Sergeant, nor should you. Amanda, ideally I would say we should bring this information before the Queen, but unfortunately at the moment it's not an option. We leave later this day to join with the

Royal Army marching on the Territories, and the High Wizards' support is vital to keeping the War Golems and Stickmen functioning. Without them..."

"The Dendaril overrun the Free Tribes and then the Empire, I get it," said Devereux. "I don't think we can just drop this though, Thalia. From what those two Wizards said, their plans go a lot further than what they've done so far."

"Agreed," said Thalia. "Look, the new Ambassador is due to arrive here tomorrow morning, and she's going to need someone to help bring her up to date on the Dendaril situation, as well as all of this. I'm going to tell the Abelians that you're staying on as a liaison to Magister Elsabeth for a while. Hopefully she can help you work out what's going on and do something about it without jeopardising the alliance."

Devereux looked doubtful. "Can we trust her?"

"She's a politician as much as a Magister, so by definition no," said Thalia with a thin smile. "But if the Arch-Chancellor has appointed her to this post she needs to know everything we do if she's going to do her job, and right now other than me she'll be the only person in Abellan you can take this to without someone finding out."

Delys was looking deeply miserable, and Thalia glanced over at Devereux, receiving a nod in return. "I'm sure the Abelians won't mind if you stay with Amanda, Delys. I'm going to be travelling with an entire army, after all, so I'd imagine that Athas will be more than enough protection. If I take two bodyguards with me the Abelians might think I don't trust them."

"But you *don't* trust them, do you, Learned Magister?" said Athas, quietly.

"No. And they know I don't, but I can't have it *looking* like I don't. Politics, Sergeant. It's like a knife-fight, but with invisible blades and better manners."

Athas took a deep breath. "Don't worry, Learned Magister. I won't let anything happen to you, and if that stupid Guardian tries anything funny I'll... I'll smash it to bits."

Delys laughed. *Big.*

"She's right, Sergeant," said Thalia. "You might change your tune if you see the Guardian. It looks... well, it looks like you might if you had one of those suits of Royal Knight armour and a shield half as big again as the one you have now. But if you remember what I told you, I don't think it'll hurt me, even if Tondarin wants it to."

Devereux frowned. "Yeah, that part's really bothering me, Learned Magister. It's supposed to protect the Queen, and obey her commands, except where that contradicts the first priority. I can't square that with it protecting you. Maybe it's a bug?"

"What?" said Thalia. "You think one of those Shrive-Ticks has-"

The Operative laughed. "No, sorry, that's another bit of jargon. In my world, when you want a device to do something you give it a series of instructions. We call it a program, but the Queen called it a... sigil-engram, yeah? A bug is when the person who writes the program makes a mistake, and because of the mistake the device does something it shouldn't, or doesn't do something it should."

Thalia took a sip of tea. "I see. So perhaps... the Guardian somehow mistook me for Tondarin and thought it was meant to protect me?"

"I think it's a curse or something," said Athas. "We used to read this story in school, called *The Twin-Souled Hunter*. There was this hunter whose was cursed when he surprised a Warlock bathing in a stream. She cast a spell on him that put half of his soul in a rabbit."

"In a rabbit?" laughed Devereux. "Why?"

"Well, the hunter was hunting rabbits at the time," said Athas. "Anyway, the curse meant that if the rabbit died, so would the hunter. The Warlock thought that he'd be so afraid to keep hunting in case he shot the wrong one that he'd starve to death."

"I see," said Thalia. "So you are suggesting..?"

Delys poked Athas hard in the side. *Finish.*

"Oh, sorry Del. Do you mind if I finish the story, Learned Magister?"

Thalia threw her hands up in the air. "Oh, by all means, Sergeant! I had nothing more important to do, after all."

"I'm sort of curious to hear the end, too," admitted Devereux.

"Yeah, so the hunter went several weeks without meat, but he soon noticed that the same rabbit was always nearby when he went out scrounging for nuts and berries or trying to catch other game. So he set a snare, and caught the rabbit, and took it home to keep it safe. The rabbit never grew a day older, and only died when the hunter did of old age many years later."

"What about the Warlock?" said Devereux. "You'd think she'd be a bit angry that her plan didn't work."

"She forgave the hunter and eventually married him," said Athas. "I always thought that bit was strange but it was a kid's story, after all. I wondered why the hunter didn't just go to town to buy food, or if he had to keep shooting foxes in case one of them killed the rabbit, too."

"To return to the point," said Thalia, once it was clear the story was over. "you're suggesting that Tondarin and I are linked, so if she killed me she'd die herself? I hardly think that's likely."

"I suppose it's not impossible, given the other things we've seen the Abelians do with their magic, like that surrogacy spell or whatever the hell that machine does," said Devereux. "But I can't think why anyone would go to the trouble to... unless..."

"Unless?" said Thalia, giving the Operative an expectant look.

"Unless someone was really worried that you and Tondarin would do... well, almost exactly what you did. Maybe not quite Athas' idea, but if the High Wizards were worried about you and the Queen clashing, they might have reprogrammed the Guardian to step in."

"I can't say I like that idea, Amanda," said Thalia. "The idea of possibly owing those... whatever they are my life is not pleasant."

"I don't like the idea of the High Wizards being able to control the Guardian like that very much either, Learned Magister," confessed Devereux. "There was a fad in my world for a while for petty dictators and tyrants to have combat robots-things a lot like the Guardian- as bodyguards. It made the Office's job much easier, because usually there was a vulnerability that allowed us to hack the 'bot's control software and change its targeting profile. More than one potential warlord ended up dead at the hands of his own protector."

Thalia frowned, trying to keep up. "So... much like someone changing the Guardian's sigil-engram to make it attack the Queen?"

"Exactly like that, yes."

"I'll try warning her about the possibility," said Thalia. "But I doubt she'll be receptive. Sergeant, we may well need your shield after all."

89

*J*oniah set down the Elucidated Pilgrim's palanquin with a grateful sigh. The mountainside had been steep and uneven, and the journey through the forest hard, but they had finally arrived at the place of destiny. For all that, the scene did not strike Joniah as particularly auspicious. The clearing they had stopped in was strewn with charred corpses, and a huge, carved stone chair stood incongruously near its edge. From his seat, Pilgrim Toroth looked around in satisfaction.

"We.. are arrived," he said, his voice sounding like that of a man torn between agony and ecstasy.

"Yes, Elucidated One," said Joniah. "The advance party has already pressed on to the Doors of Patros, but as ordered the bulk of the Crusade is amassing around the ruins of Xodan." It had been well that the Pilgrims had detected the subtle surge of magic when a fleeing party of barbarians had activated an ancient Vrae-conduit. The construct was badly damaged and had been corrupted to serve a new purpose, but the Pilgrims had been able to access it to speed the vanguard's progress.

The Pilgrim nodded, and pushed himself to his feet. Joniah felt his Vrae surge, and the old man's bloated, white-robed form floated slowly into the air. For a moment, the Pilgrim hovered, his head thrown back and his eyes closed, and then they snapped open again. A beam of bright white light shot from his staff, converging with similar beams from the staffs of the other two Elucidated Ones at a point some distance away in the forest.

"Mark.. that place.... quickly..." gasped Toroth, his sweating face slack with exertion.

Without any need for further discussion, runners disappeared at full sprint into the woods, heedless of the treacherous scree and jagged rubble. A fading scream from the treeline cut off abruptly to herald the demise of at least one of the scouts, but after a few breathless minutes Toroth nodded in satisfaction and the light winked out.

"It is.. done," said the Pilgrim, before collapsing in a heap on the ground.

"Elucidated One!" gasped Joniah, leaping forward to assist his master. Around the clearing the other Porters were moving to assist their own charges, and charred bones and blackened skulls were crushed and trampled heedlessly underfoot in their haste. Swiftly, the Blessing granting them ample strength, they returned the Elucidated Ones to their seats, though their white robes were now terribly stained with soot and ash. The Porters received no thanks for their actions, nor were any expected.

After a long, anxious moment, Toroth coughed and opened his eyes. Joniah noticed the Pilgrim was bleeding from the mouth, and passed his master a handkerchief.

"Bring forth... the labourers..." gasped Toroth, once he had dabbed the worst of the blood and phlegm from his face. "We go.... to the.... marked place.. and....." He was interrupted by another fit of coughs. The Porters exchanged anxious looks. Toroth was the most senior of the three Elucidated Ones and so far from Sylastine his Ending could not be forestalled indefinitely. But if the Bearers were released here, so far from any who could receive the Blessing...

"...and dig," finished Toroth, finally.

Already, men and women were rushing back and forth, unpacking picks, shovels and other equipment. As the Porters shouldered their burden once more, Joniah dared ask the question that was on the minds of all of them.

"Elucidated One, if I may enquire- for what are we searching?"

"We... search for... nothing," replied Toroth. "For it... is.... already... found. But... there lies.... the means....."

He was silent for a long moment, lying back in his seat, his eyes closed and his breath coming only in ragged gasps. Joniah wished he hadn't bothered his master. Clearly the Elucidated One was nearing the limit of his strength, and needed rest.

".. to bring.... the... Blessing... to.... to....."

"To who, Elucidated One?" asked Jaki, the youngest Porter. Joniah scowled at him. If there was to be an answer, it would come in time. And come it did, some half an hour later, as they approached the dig-site which already rang with the sounds of steel on stone.

"Everyone."

90

"*A*re you really sure you should be sending him out alone?" asked Ollan, watching as the armoured form of Sir Matthew rode towards the treeline.

"Who would you send with him?" said Haran, despite his own doubts. "That armour of his is better protection against those things than anything else, and he's the only person here who can use it."

Ollan pulled at his beard. "I know that, but still, Sir Matthew isn't even officially supposed to be here, much less speaking on behalf of the College."

"There is little to lose in any case," pointed out Haran. "At the moment, we expect the Dendaril to attempt to overrun us and we need to buy time for the Abelians or even this Ixilinath to repel them. If it can be done through words and persuasion rather than with blood and silver, I would rather it be so."

"And if not, at least we get to see a Royal Knight in action without staring down the business end of his lance, which makes a nice change I suppose," said Ollan.

Kandira hobbled over to them. She had been pushing herself hard, as had all the Weavers, and Haran could see the tell-tale signs that she had taxed her Aether too deeply.

"We've got the second engine mounted and ready to go at your order, Magister Haran," she said. "It's a bodge that I'd rather never repeat, but it'll fire and it'll stay put when it does, at least for a time."

"Very well," said Haran. "What of the third engine?"

"Mounting it on the wall or in a casemate is out of the question now," replied the veteran. "With the enemy that close we'd never get away with it. The best I can do is to set up a firing pit on the west side of the wall, angled to fire the blast in a high arc. You won't be able to hit a damned thing with it, at least not on purpose, but if these Dendaril run as soon as we charge one that doesn't matter."

Haran nodded. "I see. Before you start work on that, I require that you take at least three hours of rest."

"Three hours!" laughed Kandira. "What, do you expect them to just sit there while we sleep?"

"I expect you to obey my commands, Magister," said Haran, turning the full force of his gaze on her. "I will not have the most powerful weapon in the College's arsenal set to fire by Magisters too tired to think straight, when the consequence of any error might be an accidental hit on this fortress. You will rest for three hours, then report to the Vigil's Infirmary to satisfy the Healers that you are fit for duty."

"He has a point, Kandira," said Ollan. "You do tend to get short-tempered when you get tired and I'd hate for you to obliterate me in a fit of pique."

Kandira sighed. "Oh, very well. Just be sure to wake me if those things breach the walls. I'd hate to have my brains devoured by some festering insect in my sleep."

Haran had stopped listening. Far below, Sir Matthew had reined in his horse and begun to address the trees.

"Intruders who approach these walls! I am Sir Matthew D'Honeur, of Thecla, and in the name of Her Exceptional Majesty Queen Tondarin II, I command you to state your business!" His amplified voice echoed off the trees and rebounded from the walls of the Vigil almost a thousand feet away. Watching, his magic enhancing his senses as much as possible, Haran vaguely noticed both Ollan and Kandira doing the same.

"They don't seem to be very interested," mused High Vigilant Wilhelmina, peering through her spyglass. "Wait... something's happening."

A woman in a plain white robe emerged from the forest, flanked by two soldiers. Compared to the silver-armoured warriors of the Volumes, or even the Expelled, the soldiers seemed pitifully ill-equipped, each armed only with a simple sword and wearing a steel breastplate, decorated with the Dendaril open-hand icon, over what looked to be civilian clothes. It was the woman, though, who attracted the most attention from the onlookers. The hood of her robe was thrown back to reveal a lined, tanned face and brown hair shot through with streaks of grey. Though the robe concealed most of her body, even to those watching from the walls of the Vigil it was clear that her form was grotesquely swollen.

Haran turned to the High Vigilant. "Order the Choirmasters to begin the Hymnal of Devastation. I want the Petard Engines ready to fire."

Wilhelmina nodded, and called over a runner to send the order.

"Remember that the Engines are not intended as battlefield weapons, Magister Haran," reminded Kandira, quietly. "They aren't like a bow or a trebuchet with a string you can pull back or a pin to remove to fire them. Once the Singers begin the Hymnal, the Engine will fire as soon as it's charged, and nothing will delay or prevent it."

"I am aware of this, Magister," replied Haran, coldly. "But by my estimate, if the Dendaril advance rapidly from their present position they would reach the foot of the walls before we could charge the Engines, were we to wait."

Within the casemate some twenty feet below them, the first Petard Engine was being lined up. Under the supervision of Choirmaster Jarthis, the most senior present, the Singers droned their chant while simultaneously adjusting bearings and working the cranks and gears of a hastily-assembled mechanism. Even with the experience of Jarthis, the expertise of Kandira and the technical skills of a whole Seminar of Weavers, the accuracy of the Engine could still only be relied upon to hit a point within roughly two hundred feet of the intended target. Despite standing some distance above and behind the device, Haran could feel its power building. In roughly twenty seconds, unless he missed his guess, a blast of destructive magic unparalleled in the eastern world would annihilate an area almost five hundred feet in diameter. And there was every chance Sir Matthew would be somewhere right in the middle of it.

"Come on, man!" snapped Ollan. Haran gave him a sharp glance, before realising that the elder Magister was still watching the Abelian. He turned his own eyes on the forest edge, and saw that the Royal Knight was leaning forwards in his saddle, as if straining to hear the words of the robed woman.

"Yar's tits," gasped Kandira. "Don't tell me he's going to fall for that one!"

Ollan grunted. "The old 'I can't talk to you with that helmet on' trick. If he's that stupid, we're better off letting him get killed."

To the incredulity of the watching Magisters, and eliciting no few futile shouts of warning from the walls, the Royal Knight dismounted and removed his helm.

"Archers, stand ready!" snapped Wilhelmina. "If that idiot gets a fly in his head I want an arrow to follow it in through the other ear."

Even as the Archers, Warden, Vigilant and Eagle Hunter alike, bent their bows to aim, the final gambits in the game played out before their watching eyes. A swarm of terrible, black flies suddenly poured out of the robed woman, engulfing Sir Matthew in a dark, impenetrable cloud. No sooner had the Royal Knight disappeared from sight, however, than his body was immolated in a sheet of flame. The swarm was incinerated in a heartbeat even before the hollowed-out corpse of the woman who had borne them had collapsed to the ground.

The two soldiers, driven to a frenzy by the sight of the wanton slaughter of their kin, leapt to the attack as the flames dissipated. The first was sent sprawling by a looping blow from Sir Matthew's helm as he swung it in a wide arc before replacing it on his head. His fellow, perhaps more cunning than his comrade despite his fury, held back a fraction of a second but received no reward for his patience. Even as the Dendaril moved to flank Sir Matthew, the Knight's huge horse reared and a pair of flailing, silver-shod hooves ended his participation in the skirmish along with his life. A roar of outrage, loud enough to be heard even as far as the Vigil, arose from the forest and as the Knight vaulted onto his horse with an agility that belied the bulk of his armour, thousands of people emerged from the trees behind him at full sprint.

"Covering fire!" snapped Wilhelmina. "Bring down the ones closest to him! Leg-shots only!"

Arrows hissed and roared from the battlements of the fortress as Sir Matthew galloped towards it. Those of the College Archers blazed with their silver fire and tore limbs from their targets where they struck, sending running men and women tumbling in bloody, ravaged heaps. Meanwhile, the shafts of the Eagle Hunters flew dark and silent, possessed of an unnatural sharpness that saw many a shot penetrate its target completely, slashing the tendons of one attacker's leg before pinning the foot of another to the stony ground. Even so, the combined fire of five hundred bows could do little to an assault some ten thousand strong except keep it from overwhelming Sir Matthew as he accelerated.

"Blackbloods!" roared the Black Skull, who had watched the proceedings in silence until now. "Unleash the Berserker Teeth!"

Wilhelmina whirled to stare at him. "What? What do you-"

Before she could finish the question, the first few of the Blackblood Eagle Hunters had drawn arrows from a second quiver, and loosed them. Haran saw that rather than being tipped with the black 'blade-glass' normally used by the Free Tribes, these shafts were fitted to what looked like the tooth of a snake. Instead of aiming at those Dendaril closest to Sir Matthew, the Blackbloods fired their volley deep into the mass of his pursuers.

"What in Thelen's name are you playing at, you skin-wearing savage moron?" shouted Wilhelmina. "You might as well spit into a hurricane! Get your people covering the Abelian, now!"

"Were a Blackblood to spit into a hurricane, O door-keeper," said the Black Skull, quietly, "the hurricane would die. See now the bite of the Lurker Snake of the Shriven Marsh."

"Thelen's breath.." gasped Ollan. As the Magisters watched, here and there amongst the onrushing horde men and women suddenly stopped dead, threw back their heads, and screamed at the skies. Almost immediately their comrades, still running full-tilt, crashed headlong into them and swept them from their feet, but the afflicted Dendaril did not lie still when they fell. Instead, they bounded upright, heedless of broken noses and shattered limbs, and hurled themselves bodily at the nearest living being, ripping and tearing at their flesh with nothing but their teeth and nails. All across the mass of the Dendaril, the advance slowed or staggered as venom-maddened men and women rampaged hither and yon.

Sir Matthew had reached the foot of the fortress wall now, against which the Free Tribes had erected a rough camp. Warriors with flasks of lantern-oil stood ready, joined by Mighty Xaraya, Mighty Dokan and their other leaders. With them too were the bulk of the Warden line infantry, their bows drawn, each attended by a young Free warrior acting as their shield-bearer. The Wardens had already started to fire, barely even needing to aim at the dense mass of bodies running towards them, when the Dendaril advance suddenly stopped dead. It didn't take a Magister to tell why. Even as the horde scattered and fled back towards the trees, the first Petard Engine fired, a bolt of pure, incandescent magic hurtling no more than six hundred feet from the casemate before slamming into the ground and detonating.

Haran had seen the effect of an Engine at such short range once before, but on that occasion the mass of the device itself had contained the blast which had so comprehensively annihilated Choirmaster Uthiel that the College still officially listed the fat man as 'missing'. This detonation, though, was unmitigated in its savagery and incredible in its effect. A perfect, painfully bright, white sphere of destruction flashed into being at the point of impact and persisted in his vision for several seconds afterwards, accompanied by an ear-splitting crash. There was no time, however, to worry about the discomfort to either his eyes or his ears, for the impact was followed a split-second later by a shock-wave that shook the Vigil to its very foundations. Several Archers standing too close to the battlements were pitched over the edge, plummeting to crash down on the tents below, and masonry all along the walls cracked and shivered.

Blinking furiously, half-deafened and bleeding from a flying chip of stone, Haran steadied himself on his staff and shouted as loudly as he could.

"Jarthis! Lengthen the aim on the second engine! Quickly, man!"

There was no response. Haran could sense the power in the second Engine building. The device would fire in seconds, and if it had been jolted to aim at a point even slightly closer than the last, the Vigil would not survive.

91

*C*hania Steine picked herself up from the floor and looked around desperately, steadying herself against a wall studded with flickering glow-crystals. One moment she had been standing in the hallway outside the upper mess-hall, the next the world had suddenly tilted and she'd found herself sprawled on the cold flagstones surrounded by dust and rubble.

As a fortification designed to be held in a constant state of readiness, the Vigil had barracks, mess-halls and kitchens on the levels immediately below the upper battlements, allowing a shift of warriors to eat, sleep and relax as near as possible to their battle-stations. Because the mess-halls were large, open-plan rooms with high ceilings and already featured large firing ports to allow a second rank of Archers to fire on any attacker, Magister Kandira had declared them to be ideal positions to site the Petard Engines. The mess just to the north of the main gate-house had been extensively, if rapidly, rebuilt and extended into a casemate for the first Engine, but work on the one to the south had barely begun when it had become clear that time was running out. Instead of the careful modifications that had been made to the northern room, the southern had simply had a sizeable hole knocked in its east-facing wall, and the Engine had been positioned not on a custom-engineered mount, but on the shell of the cart that had brought it to the fortress.

For all that, and the fact that the veteran Magister had loudly decried the whole thing as a 'bodge', the improvised mount had seemed solid enough. With the wheels of the cart removed and the structure of the vehicle bolted to the floor, the suspension system now served instead to act as a shock-absorber for the device. Additional reinforcing struts had been added, and the Engine's built-in pivots and sprockets securely attached to the wagon. It wasn't pretty, but Georg, the Choir-master who had been overseeing the Singers crewing the weapon, had seemed confident that it would serve.

Chania quite liked Georg. Many Choirmasters, especially Jarthis, the most senior of their Role present at the Vigil, were secretive and defensive about their Singers, knowing the discomfort which many Magisters and no few commoners felt about their seemingly mindless charges. Georg, however, had responded to Chania's questions with unusual openness, allowing the Bard to chat with the Singers and see how much free will they retained when not actively using their Seals. He had even let Chania listen to the Gathering Hymnal, the most commonly used chant which speeded the recovery of Aether for those within its area of effect. Out of curiosity, the Bard had tried joining in, the unique ability of her Seal to manipulate and replicate sound allowing her to rapidly harmonise with the chant. Georg claimed that it seemed to be enhancing the effect of the magic, but with no baseline for comparison Chania couldn't tell if he was simply humouring her.

He certainly wasn't doing that at the moment. Georg had been leading his Singers in the Hymnal of Devastation to arm their Engine when everything had gone crazy. There had been a loud crash and several screams from the mess-hall, but at least some of the Singers were still chanting. Meaning to check if everyone was all right, Chania pushed off from the wall, but her head was still spinning and when she touched her hand to her brow it felt sticky and warm. She staggered, and would have fallen but for a bony hand that suddenly gripped her arm.

"You all right, girl? Thelen's breath, you look like I feel."

Chania blinked, her blurry vision trying to focus on the face staring at her. After a moment she realised she was looking at Magister Kandira.

"I- I think so. What happened?"

"First Engine hit too close," growled Kandira, hobbling towards the mess-hall door. It struck Chania that for all the strength of her grip, the Magister was leaning on her as much as supporting. "Damned shock-wave nearly knocked this place flat. I told Haran, these things are siege-engines, not battlefield artillery. Even a near-miss is meant to- Yar's tits!"

They had pushed through the doors, one of which promptly fell off, having been hanging by a single hinge. The room within had been reduced to an utter shambles. In one corner, amidst the shattered ruins of a chair and table, Choirmaster Georg lay pinned to the cracked floor by a massive ceiling beam. If his bloody form showed any signs of life, they were beyond Chania's ability to detect. Two of the beams in total seemed to have crashed down into the room, one injuring most of the Singers and the other glancing off the solid, cast-silver form of the Engine and smashing the wagon supporting it to matchwood. Barely sparing a glance for the human casualties, it was this latter damage that seemed to have alarmed Kandira, and Chania thought that terribly cold-hearted until her reason caught up with her compassion and furiously overruled it.

The wagon the Engine was mounted on had indeed been destroyed, but the Engine had not. The Singers, even those lying at unnatural angles on the floor with broken limbs, were still chanting and the device was still charging to fire. And the mouth of the great bell was sloping down to point at the ground just outside.

Her face grey with pain, Kandira let go of Chania and lurched towards the Engine, laying a hand upon its bulk. "Damnation.. no good. In about twenty seconds this thing will discharge and then..."

"Can't we stop it?" asked Chania.

"He could've," said the Magister, pointing at Georg. "Do you have a knife?"

"What?"

"For them," said the Magister, and despite the peril of the situation Chania almost dropped on the spot from shock. The Singers wouldn't stop chanting the Hymnal unless ordered to by a Choirmaster, and their Choirmaster was either dead or unconscious. The only other way to stop them would be.. would be to...

"N-no!" gasped the Bard, backing away. "I.. I won't do it!"

"Then we're all dead in ten seconds." said the Magister, flatly. She fumbled in her robe for a moment before producing a dagger, which she drew swiftly across the throat of a chanting woman sitting propped against the ruined wagon, her legs twisted beneath her. "Hmph. Fifteen now."

She started to hobble across the room towards the next Singer, and Chania moved to block her path. "No! No, there must be another-" She was distracted by something moving behind Kandira, and didn't see the elderly Magister's hand come around in a slap. She rocked back, but still retained enough presence of mind to grab the woman's knife-hand at the wrist.

"Lift the front! Lift it now!" she almost screamed.

"I can barely lift my bloody feet, girl," chuckled Kandira, bitterly. "I don't know what you're talking about, but you've killed us all."

"Not while Red Trace in White Snow yet draws breath!" roared the huge barbarian warrior who Chania had seen leap up to the mouth of the Engine. He was as big a man as the Bard had ever seen, as large even as Sergeant Athas, the Guardsman who had come through the Vigil with Magister Thalia some weeks ago. Even so, as he bent his broad back to the task he seemed impossibly small against the bulk of the Engine. His tattoos glowed as he strained. Despite knowing she could do little to help, Chania let go of the Magister and ran over, pushing alongside the warrior.

"Eight seconds," cackled Kandira, sagging to the floor and dropping her bloody dagger.

Chania was crying tears of frustration now. The thing just wouldn't move, and her fine-tuned senses could detect it beginning to vibrate as the power within built to a crisis point. Another figure, this one female but almost as tall as Red Trace, suddenly appeared at the opening. Her black hair set in sharp spikes and wearing nothing but the traditional battle-harness of the Expelled, the barbarian elbowed Chania out of the way and leant her own strength to the effort. Incredibly, the mouth of the Engine finally began to rise, even as the woman whispered urgently in her companion's ear.

"Four..." wheezed Kandira, and Chania saw she was dragging herself across the floor of the room. She thought she should probably try to stop her, but if the Magister did kill another of the Singers it would buy them more time. A bestial roar distracted her from the terrible thought, and she whirled to see that Red Trace had sprouted tufts of black fur and grown at least half as big again, his face twisted into a feral mask of rage as a tattoo of a bear glowed blue on his chest.

"The beast has emerged," said the barbarian woman in satisfaction, stepping back as Red Trace lifted the Engine's mouth higher than she could usefully reach. "Now we pray to the Ancestors that he retains control."

Before Chania could say anything in response, the Engine fired. An incredibly bright flare of white light shot out of its mouth so quickly that it seemed to exist only for a fraction of a second, but even that much exposure half-blinded her. The barbarian began to relax, but Kandira shouted at him, pointing a trembling hand at the corner of the room.

"No! Hold it, damn you! You two, get that beam off Georg and use it to prop the blasted thing! It's going to keep firing!" She coughed up blood, and wiped it away with her robe sleeve, grimacing.

Chania and the big woman exchanged a glance, and then leapt to obey. The beam was incredibly heavy but between them they managed to drag it across the room.

"Cross.. cross-prop.." gasped Kandira, pushing herself to her feet. "Wedge it.. diagonally... then the other beam. Quickly!"

Guardsmen and Vigilants were pouring into the room now, entirely too late Chania thought, and with the extra manpower they were able to manoeuvre the two beams into a cross-shape, wedged against the walls with the Engine braced between them. The Magister gestured at the points of contact, and wood fused to stone as if it had been melted.

"Hmph," grunted Kandira, swaying as the Engine blazed again. The beams shook, but held. "It's still a damned bodge. Lucky I had enough left to secure.. to secure the... bollocks.."

She blinked once in confusion, then sank to the floor, supported by Chania. In the bedlam that followed, the Bard realised that there was something else she needed to do. She was just straightening up when the High Vigilant arrived.

"What in the holy ball-sack of Thelen Himself happened here?" said Wilhelmina, gazing around at the devastation in awe.

"The roof beams fell in, High Vigilant," said Chania simply. "They killed Choirmaster Georg and some of the Singers and knocked the Engine off its mount. Magister Kandira and I were.. trying to move it when our new allies arrived and helped us."

"Woe upon this day," grumbled Red Trace, who had resumed his human shape. "Woe upon the day a warrior of the Heart-Eaters takes orders from a Deluded and then has to be aided in his struggles by his wife."

"What happened to this one?" said Wilhelmina, kneeling by the corpse of the Singer who Kandira had killed. "Looks like her throat was slashed?"

"I think she got hold of one of the bread-knives from the mess," said Chania, pointing out the bloody blade lying by the Singer's hand.

Wilhelmina nodded. "Looks like. I wonder why she did it? Both her legs look to be broken, so maybe it was the pain... or maybe she realised that she needed to stop herself Singing and that was the only way?"

Chania glanced over at Kandira, who was sitting up, supported by a couple of Vigilants. The older woman returned her gaze, but gave nothing away. She shrugged.

"I couldn't say, High Vigilant. She was dead by the time we arrived."

92

*T*halia had just finished writing the report that she planned to leave for Magister Elsabeth when Herenford tapped on her door to announce that Sir Terence had arrived to escort her to join the Royal Army. Athas was already waiting in the reception hall of the Green Palace with the bags when she got there, dressed in his recently-repaired battle-plate. The big Guard looked at her wide-eyed as she walked down the stairs.

"Learned Magister, Sir Terence is here, and you should see the coach he's brought with him!"

Thalia rolled her eyes. "Sergeant, we saw the coach the other day, remember? It is a splendid vehicle to be certain, but nothing to be getting so excited about."

Sir Terence, wearing his armour but carrying his helm, was coming through the doors as she spoke. "Ah, Your Excellency, good. Sergeant Athas, I am pleased to see that you are fully recovered and back in harness. It takes a rare man to survive both a gut-shot from a military arrow and the Ague."

Athas beamed with pride before his smile quickly faded. "Thank you, Sir Terence, but it was the Magister and my friends, and Healer Alana, who did all the work. I just sort of lay there and bled a lot."

The Royal Knight laughed. "Hah! Modest as well! Even so, when great art is worked, some credit at least must go to the canvas. Now, Your Excellency, the *Dreadnought* awaits us."

Thalia cocked her head to the side in puzzlement. "The what?" Memories of old, dry history lessens nagged at her. "Wait.. you can't mean..."

They stepped out into the early afternoon sunshine. Amanda Devereux and Delys were already outside, looking over the enormous vehicle that was waiting there. It was almost thirty feet long, riding on six huge wheels and heavily armoured, and pulled by a team of six of the mighty Abelian war-horses. It was painted in the green and white of the Lily College, seemingly quite recently, and

376

bore the three-petalled icon of the College alongside the interlocking rings of House Daran.

"The *Dreadnought,*" announced Sir Terence, somewhat redundantly. "Originally constructed by the Artificer's Guild of Aquila in 1592 as the *Redoubtable* before being commandeered by General Sebastian Vox as his personal command vehicle in the latter months of the First Thelenic War."

"It's certainly pretty impressive, Sir Terence," admitted Amanda Devereux, though Thalia could tell from her tone that she had seen vehicles that made the *Dreadnought* seem positively miniscule. The Royal Knight was too caught up in his story to notice.

"The *Redoubtable* was a Mark II armoured command vehicle, commissioned for Prince Dalant and sister vehicle to the *Valiant,* which serves as the monarch's battlefield transportation to this day. In recognition of the accord between Abelia and the College in this time of crisis, the Queen has ordered the *Dreadnought* returned to its Thelenic livery, with the addition of your own family crest, of course, Your Excellency."

Thalia was still staring at the sheer bulk of the thing. "Is.. is this really necessary, Sir Terence? I am here as an advisor and a liaison. This is the vehicle of a conqueror."

"A conqueror who was himself conquered," pointed out Sir Terence. "The *Dreadnought* will be the only representative of the College in our combined force, Your Excellency. I imagine that the Queen is only too eager to make that fact extremely obvious. Regardless, you and your bodyguards are far more vulnerable to those damnable Shrive-Ticks than the Royal Knights and Golems who form the bulk of the Royal Army. Those Wizards who will be travelling with us to provide additional magical support will be riding in similar, if less ostentatious, vehicles. Please, enter."

He gestured to the door of the enormous coach, which popped open with a faint hiss, a flight of steps unfolding from it to the ground. Devereux raised an eyebrow. "Hermetically sealed? Okay, that I wasn't expecting."

"Just as the armour of the Royal Knights is proof against gases and plagues, so is the interior of any command vehicle from the Mark II onwards." said Sir Terence, as Thalia climbed the steps. "So long as its reserve of Spirit lasts, which will be supplied by the Roads until we leave the Kingdom and can be supplemented by the passengers, it will produce breathable air from the foul. The interior panels can be rendered invisible in one direction only, allowing the occupant to see all around the vehicle in complete privacy without compromising the armour."

"Hmm, so no firing ports," said Devereux. "Does it have any offensive capabilities at all?"

"Only its contents." said Sir Terence with a smile. "Which would usually be a heavily-armed Imperial General and several irate Magisters, when it served the College. I can't imagine why anyone would bother building a vehicle like this and then also attempt to attach weapon-constructs to it with such formidable passengers."

"You might be surprised," said the Operative with a smile of her own.

"I see the driver is a Wood Golem," said Thalia. "Does that mean that I have no control over the destination of the *Dreadnought?*"

"I am afraid so, Your Excellency," admitted Sir Terence. "A human driver would be too great a risk in action against the Dendaril. Rest assured, however, that the *Dreadnought* will be well protected."

"There's even a couple of bedrooms in here, Learned Magister!" said Athas, poking his head into one. "Oh, and a latrine. Probably just as well."

"Of course," said Sir Terence. "The Shrive-Ticks do not sleep, after all. Once we are in hostile territory, you will need to be protected from them at all times. Now, if there are no more questions and you have finished loading, we must be off!"

"Amanda and Delys will be staying here, Sir Terence," said Thalia. "They will be working with the new Ambassador for a time. With Sergeant Athas, the *Dreadnought* and the Royal Army protecting me I am sure they will not be missed?"

The Royal Knight shrugged, and swung himself up into the saddle of his horse. "Her Exceptional Majesty has the nobility's usual disinterest for the affairs of common men, Your Excellency. So long as you attend at her summons she will pay little heed to your retinue. Unless she needs a bottle of wine opened with great haste and aplomb, of course."

Delys grinned at the Knight, and he returned the smile before donning his helm. Thalia settled herself onto the worn purple leather seat of the coach-General Vox had clearly not considered it necessary to have the Abelian vehicle re-upholstered- and tried to relax.

Athas was still looking around the plush interior as the coach began to pick up speed. "Hmm, there's a drinks cabinet here too, Learned Magister. It's mostly just got a bunch of old wine in it though, no beer or anything."

Thalia couldn't quite suppress a smile. "Sergeant, that bottle you are holding is dated 1823. Such a vintage is probably worth more than you will earn in your entire life. For that matter, it's probably worth more than the Daran Manse."

Athas stared at her incredulously. "Er. I.. I should probably put it back then, yeah?"

"That would probably be best," agreed Thalia. "Though if the Queen decides to lock us in here for the whole journey I will take great pleasure in helping you finish off the entire supply."

93

*I*t was early in the afternoon when Captain Ariel, Magister Julius and Wen Lian-Shi arrived at the Belus Manse. The tall Guardswoman had circles under her eyes and showed obvious signs of fatigue, but she and her troops stood at ramrod-straight attention as they presented their charges to the Arch-Chancellor.

"Magister Julius Thule and Willow-Sigh Wen, as ordered, Arch-Chancellor," said Ariel, formally. "Will there be anything else?"

Derelar looked her up and down. He could see why Anneke had trusted the tall woman so implicitly. Even though he knew from reputation that Ariel could be cruel and was something of a bully, her efficiency and determination to serve to the best of her ability were impressive.

"No, Captain, that will be all for now. See to it that the Manse is secure, and then you and your Guards are dismissed."

Ariel saluted. "Yes, Arch-Chancellor. Sergeant Ulla, you heard the man. Get Kat and whoever else is available to set up double guard on all the entrances, then go get some sleep. The rest of you, fall out."

Julius watched them go, and then rounded on Derelar. "Arch-Chancellor, I must protest! After all the effort I went to to keep this investigation quiet, you send the Captain of the Belus House Guard as my escort?"

"There were good reasons, Magister Julius," said Derelar.

"I should damn well hope so," snapped Julius. "She threw my translator into the blasted sea!"

"My orders were specific that you, and your witness, should be the only people that the Captain brought back," said Derelar. "If you require any linguistic services, the College will provide."

The Daxalai woman, who was dressed in a simple cotton blouse and soft leather breeches, barefoot, and yet still retained a commanding presence, spoke a short phrase in her native tongue.

Julius frowned. "Master Wen says that.. there is a disturbance to the natural order here."

Derelar nodded. "Indeed. Though I believe she used the inflection meaning 'perversion' rather than 'disturbance'."

Julius' eyebrows shot up. "You speak Daxalai, Arch-Chancellor?"

"I have acquired a working knowledge," said Derelar. "In these times it does not do to miss conversational nuances. I suspect you have already deduced what it is that she is referring to?"

Julius nodded. "Indeed. After all, the construct is of my own devising. Someone has activated a Preserver in a nearby room. When was the Vice-Chancellor murdered?"

Derelar couldn't completely suppress a grim smile. "You seem very certain that she was the victim."

Julius thumped his staff on the floor in annoyance. "Well of course I am! Given the subject of my prior investigation, the personnel sent to escort me, the fact that those personnel are now taking orders directly from you and the premises in which we stand, it could scarcely be anyone else."

The Daxalai had already started walking down the hallway. "Her lair. This way," she said, using the lowest form of dialect as if talking to a pair of small children. Derelar understood why, but couldn't help feeling somewhat insulted. A few minutes later, the two Magisters and the Initiate arrived outside the door to Anneke's study, Derelar having used the time to bring Julius up to date on Ariel's testimony. Waiting for them were High Chirurgeon Gisela, and Magister Jarton. Derelar had been a little surprised when the Chair of Walanstahl arrived, but supposed he shouldn't have been. After all, many of Anneke's agents theoretically worked for Jarton, even if in practice he had allowed his house Matriarch to usurp his responsibilities.

Julius looked from one Magister to another. "I cannot help but feel like the proverbial fork during the soup course in such esteemed company, Learned Magisters."

"Nonsense," said Jarton, immediately. "Your prowess in the field of investigation is well-known, Magister Julius. Even the late Vice-Chancellor respected it greatly, may Thelen receive her."

Gisela nodded her agreement. "Aye, Magister Jarton. An investigator of crime has more business in this place than a healer of the sick does. I expect my part in this sorry affair to be brief."

Derelar dispelled the construct, and opened the door. For a moment, no-one moved.

"A strange thing, is it not?" said Jarton, peering into the study. "It looks as if she might return at any moment. I have been here many times before, and yet today it feels.. so very different."

"If I may, Learned Magisters?" said Julius, and hearing no objection, he walked into the study. "I expect there will be little of use to my investigation in this room, Magister Jarton, and much that a man of my station has no right to know. If I may, I will leave the inspection of the Vice-Chancellor's documents to you and the Arch-Chancellor whilst the High Chirurgeon and I attend to the scene of the crime."

"Very well," agreed Jarton. "We will, of course, inform you of anything that seems pertinent."

Julius nodded, and headed for the bedroom door. With a wry glance at Jarton, Derelar followed him. The investigator stopped a little short of the door, and pushed it open carefully with his staff.

"Ah, Arch-Chancellor. I did not presume to give you orders, of course. However, if you and the High Chirurgeon could just hold back for a moment... hmm.."

"What is it?" said Gisela from behind Derelar's shoulder.

"Nothing, which is in itself most singular. The Vice-Chancellor was a lover of the finer things in life, which extended to her taste in carpets. Note the deep pile of this example, and that the cadaver on the bed is barefoot. Note also that the carpet is disturbed in a manner that suggests only one set of feet has recently trod it, and that those feet were shod in what appears to be the standard Guard Infantry boot, feminine pattern, size eighteen. This at least confirms the presence of Captain Ariel."

Derelar nodded. "So it would seem."

Julius rose a couple of inches into the air, and floated into the room. "The housekeeping spells of the Manse would typically periodically smooth the carpet of the room as well as removing dust, though the action of the Preserver interrupts this process." He paused for a moment. "Hmm. Yes, the spells of the Manse seem to perform their duties at midnight and mid-day, fairly typical."

"According to Captain Ariel and her Guards, the Vice-Chancellor was still alive at mid-day yesterday and the Preserver was cast well before midnight," supplied Derelar.

"As I suspected," said Julius with a nod, still floating. "We can posit that the Vice-Chancellor took to her bed to rest shortly before the spells went to work, causing evidence of her journey across the room to be removed. The next feet to touch this floor would appear to have been those of Captain Ariel. She crossed to the bed, remained here for some moments, then travelled to the wash-basin in the corner which is notably still bloodstained, before leaving to raise the alarm."

Gisela coughed. "Ah, I hate to raise the obvious point-"

"Then I shall do so for you, High Chirurgeon," said Julius. "This evidence so far would seem to implicate Captain Ariel herself as our killer."

"Unlikely," said Derelar. "She was with other members of the House Guard when Magister Elsabeth left, and another Guard was on duty at the door of the office when she came to report to the Vice-Chancellor. That Guard reports hearing no sound of a struggle and Ariel was inside for less than a minute. In addition, she reports that Anneke could be heard.. moving around in the room after Magister Elsabeth left, which seems also to rule her out as a suspect."

Julius looked down at the bed, and poked it with his staff, eliciting a creak from the springs. "I take it the bedsprings were the sound in question? For someone so.. enthusiastic in their amorous pursuits, the Vice-Chancellor had an unusually vociferous bedstead."

Derelar nodded, and Gisela gave a snort of distaste. "From what I hear, she didn't always even bother with the bed."

Julius lowered himself to the carpet. "I think the floor has told all the stories it will, High Chirurgeon. If you could leave your personal feelings for our victim at the door, I would ask that you lend your considerable skills to a study of the body whilst the Arch-Chancellor and I address the most singular question in this case."

"You refer, of course, to the matter of the Vice-Chancellor's head," said Derelar, following Gisela into the room.

"I refer, more precisely, to the lack of it," said Julius. "Observe the cadaver. The head has been cleanly severed and the act elicited no small flow of blood, as one would expect. We see here also the hand-prints of a woman of roughly six feet in height, consistent with Captain Ariel's account. There are however, two most singular aspects presented by the bed."

Derelar looked and immediately saw one of them. "There is no mark upon the pillow."

"Quite so, Arch-Chancellor," said Julius. "The pillow appears freshly-plumped, as if in preparation for use, but there is no imprint of a head upon it, nor any hairs that I can detect. The second point of note is that there is no mark upon the bed that would suggest the impact of a blade or other cutting device."

"Well, this is certainly Anneke's dead body," said Gisela, her hands on her hips. "She seems to have been that way for a little less than four hours, which would be ridiculous but for that preservation spell of yours. I'd say she died roughly three and a half hours before it was cast."

"If I might make an impertinent enquiry, High Chirurgeon," said Julius, "what was the cause of death?"

Gisela looked at him as if he was insane. "Decapitation," she said, slowly. Julius held up a placatory hand.

"Forgive my impertinence again, Learned Magister, but is that diagnosis based on a medical examination, or upon the obvious physical evidence? To be clear, is it possible that the Vice-Chancellor was killed or incapacitated by other means, and then beheaded *post-mortem*?"

Gisela looked back at the body. "Ah, I see what you mean. There seems to be no evidence of any poison or drug in the blood that I can detect here, but I've taken a sample to study in greater depth. The amount of blood that has left the neck when the head was removed suggests that the heart was still pumping for a beat or two at least afterwards, which also would imply that she was alive at the time. Of course, we're assuming that she's dead at all."

Now it was Julius' turn to look at Gisela as if she were mad. "I beg your pardon? I would think the evidence on that point to be fairly conclusive."

"The Pattern of a living being is made up of two separate, but connected Patterns, as you know, Magister Julius," said Gisela, quietly. "That of the body, and that of the mind. If the body dies, the Pattern of the mind decays quickly, but swift intervention from a skilled Healer or Magister to restore the body will save the life of the patient. In such cases, it is most important to restore the functions of life to the brain of the patient, because that is where the Pattern of their mind is tethered to that of their body."

Julius was looking at her wide-eyed now. "Are you suggesting, High Chirurgeon, that this was not a murder, but an abduction? That our criminal is currently in possession not of the cadaverous head of Anneke Belus, but of her living brain?"

Gisela shrugged. "No. It's purely theoretical, it's never been done in practice, but some of those flesh-constructs that the Royalists used during the War got close. If the head were removed quickly enough and immediately grafted to a new body by a truly skilled Chirurgeon then maybe something of the victim might survive."

"Regardless of such.. frankly terrifying concerns," said Julius, "it seems the most perplexing part of our mystery remains. Where is the Vice-Chancellor's head, and why was it so carefully removed?"

"I should add, in the interests of completeness, that all the evidence suggests that this is the Vice-Chancellor's body," said Gisela. "Her height- to the shoulder at least- is right, her weight, complexion, the colour of her hair."

Derelar looked at her quizzically. "Her hair?"

"Not all of it is on your head, Arch-Chancellor," said Gisela, leaving Derelar feeling deeply foolish. "There are also a pair of crossed lacerations just above her breasts that seem recently healed. They look similar to the injuries that killed the victims of the Midnight Tiger, though those were to the throat."

"If I may?" said Julius, taking a careful look. "Hmm. Yes, there is evidence that these wounds are recently healed and they do match the Tiger's claws."

"Could another, similar assassin have done this?" said Derelar.

"Of course," said Julius. "But if we are to start inventing assassins with super-natural powers we have reached the limits of investigation and moved to the realm of imagination. Given that finding evidence of such a being would be effectively impossible, I will proceed as if one was not involved. Based on everything I have seen thus far, I would conclude that the killer was a Magister or Warlock. The most likely murder weapon would seem to be a plane of pure force, precisely applied to shear off the head of the victim. The killer would have needed to enter the room silently, levitating above the floor to avoid leaving tracks, and once they had killed the sleeping Vice-Chancellor they immediately Committed the head and the head only, before removing all trace of the head from the pillow. They then left as they had arrived."

"What of the Guard on the door?" said Gisela.

"There are two primary possibilities," said Julius. "The first, by the application of Walanstahl's Splice, is that the Guard was an accomplice."

"Walanstahl's Splice?" said Gisela.

"A common axiom amongst investigators, Learned Magister," said Julius. "It posits that in most cases, the simplest possible explanation is the correct one. Walanstahl's Reduction, similarly, posits that if all impossible explanations have been ruled out, whatever is left must be the truth, however unlikely, but I digress. The second possibility is that the killer used mind-affecting magic to prevent the Guard from noticing their presence. The use of such spells is, of course, forbidden to any Magister below the rank of Chancellor, but our murderer would scarcely be concerned with such niceties."

Derelar, who had employed such spells to recently infiltrate the very building they now stood in, kept his expression carefully neutral.

"The most singular aspect of this whole case, I think, is not so much the how or the who, but the *why*," continued Julius. "It is well-known that the Vice-Chancellor had many enemies, some of whom doubtless possessed the capabilities to do this, but why remove the Vice-Chancellor's head and yet leave the rest of the body behind?"

"I may be able to shed some light on that, Magister Julius," said Magister Jarton, from the doorway. "Arch-Chancellor, I've taken a quick look through Anneke's files. They are concise, perfectly ordered, and complete, but they detail absolutely nothing that I was not aware of. We all know that she maintained her own, much darker, network of contacts but I can find no record of them, nor can I find where such a record might have been."

Derelar nodded. Anneke had always prided herself on her exceptional memory. "Then there is only one place where we can be sure that those secrets were held. The mind of the Vice-Chancellor."

94

*S*miling Snake returned to his laboratory in the early afternoon, having spent the day in conference with the other Sages of the clan. Frowning Iron's performance at the Divine Pavilion had galvanised every philosopher, Sage and politically-minded citizen in the city who had heard of it, and Shan'Xi'Sho rang with lively debate as to how the Celestial Harmony might be spread to foreign lands through peaceful means. Swan-neck Tsue, who had been quietly preparing to take over the leadership of the clan in the event of Frowning Iron's death, had reportedly retired to her chambers in fury. This did not concern Rya-Ki overmuch. Swan-neck was yet young and had attained much honour in battle. She would not jeopardise her status by taking rash action against the leader of her clan in a fit of temper. For one thing, she was attended by wise, if unremarkable, Sages. Smiling Snake had seen to it personally.

The only thing anyone could agree on so far was that the Friendship Games, a sporting contest recently announced by the Lily College, seemed to present the best opportunity to begin to develop what the Sages were now calling the Gentle Invasion. There were many, however, who were concerned that the itinerary of the proposed event consisted of disciplines that the *gwai-sen* had been practising for centuries. Few champions of the Daxalai were eager to risk ridicule by defeat in such circumstances. Rya-Ki felt this to be short-sighted, for even the most ignorant child understood that failure taught many more valuable lessons than success, but pride was a difficult beast to slay.

He was about to settle down to meditate when a soft thump came to his ears, as of a body striking a hardwood floor. It did not take the intellect of a Great Sage to tell where it had come from. Rising, he moved swiftly on silent feet to the entrance to the hidden chamber which contained the Tapestry. What he found within sent him scurrying back to retrieve a bowl of *geki*.

Returning to the prone form of White Crocus, he propped the young Sage up against the wall and held the drinking-bowl to his lips. Bai Faoha blinked, and beamed beatifically at him, before his senses rallied and he took a small sip of the enriched liquid.

"May... may the Son of Heaven be thanked for his bounty.." gasped the Sage, recovering his wits enough to take the bowl from Rya-Ki and drain it. Smiling Snake nodded.

"May he be thanked indeed. Are your wits recovered?"

The younger man pushed himself to his feet and bowed. "They are, Great Sage. My thanks."

"Good," said Smiling Snake, delivering an open-handed slap that knocked Bai Faoha sprawling on the floor once more. "And what do those senses tell you?"

"That I have received my just punishment for my foolishness, Great Sage," replied White Crocus, pressing his face to the floor in shame. "I did not heed your warning about the danger of spending too much time in communion with the artefact. In truth, it did not seem to me that I had been meditating upon it over-long, but clearly I was in error."

"When did you begin?" asked Smiling Snake, gesturing for the young man to rise.

"Earlier today, just after you and General Tekkan-Cho left for the Divine Pavilion."

Smiling Snake restricted himself to displaying his surprise by raising a single, finely-plucked eyebrow. "Is this so? You may be interested to know that the General and I left for that audience yesterday."

Less experienced than the Great Sage, Bai Faoha was unable to conceal his amazement, stumbling backwards and sitting down heavily. "B-but.. a day? An entire day?"

"Indeed. I see now that I was wise to choose you, White Crocus, but deeply foolish to leave you unsupervised. Had most Sages attempted what you did, I would have returned to find a shrivelled corpse. What knowledge did the device impart?"

"I.. it is difficult to focus.." confessed Bai Faoha. "There were so many voices, so many stories, so much knowledge... it is overwhelming."

"True," said Smiling Snake. "This is why it is generally best to use the Tapestry only for short periods. Come, let us meditate and see if we can bring some Harmony into the Chaos that disturbs your focus."

They settled down, but after a few moments it became clear to Smiling Snake that White Crocus was struggling. He opened his eyes again. "Clear your mind, Bai Faoha. There is nothing to fear."

"I.. I will try, Great Sage," replied the other. "But it is difficult to cast myself adrift in contemplation so soon after my.. experience with the Tapestry. It seems to me that if I cast my body aside again so soon, I may never find my way back."

"Then focus instead upon my *ki*." said Rya-Ki. "Allow me to be the beacon, the signal fire that keeps you upon the path. Now, try again."

They sat in silence for almost half an hour, before White Crocus spoke again. "I remember... the spider at the centre of the web, she who was hidden from our sight and glimpsed only by the wind of her passing. She is slain, her head taken."

Smiling Snake said nothing, allowing Bai Faoha to focus, but it was an effort not to react. The Most Learned Vice-Chancellor, dead? It seemed impossible.

"There is more... the daughter of he who broke the mountains and the daughter of he who fell at his hand. They travel to confront a great enemy in the forest dwelling of another foe. At a fortified border, this enemy strives to break through, but is kept at bay by terrible powers."

Smiling Snake had become aware of something at the edge of his hearing. It was difficult to meditate and still listen to White Crocus, but this was something else. Carefully, taking pains not to alarm the young Sage, he opened his eyes. As he had expected, the room was full of a swarm of droning flies.

"Great Sage..." said Bai Faoha, quietly. "There is something else.. another message. Not a voice from the Tapestry, but another magic, resonating in harmony with it. I do not understand its meaning. *The bounty of Yaoin-Lao was great, and gleaned at equally great cost, but when the ships of the Tshuh were sighted off Heinlaon, all saw its value.*" He opened his eyes, and started. "What.. what is happening?"

"I do not know," said Rya-Ki, simply. "I have witnessed this only once before. We must endure it. The words you spoke- they were not known to me, but the style is familiar. They are almost certainly a passage from the *Koze-Li-Sen.*"

"The Words of the Sky? Is this, then, a message from the Son of Heaven Himself?"

"I think not," said Smiling Snake. "And I also think that these insects are nothing more than another part of the message. When last I saw them, I was too concerned with what they might be to consider *why* they might be. See now the pattern of their flight- how they seem to emerge from the eastern end of the Tapestry, where the *gwai-sen* Magister stands, and come to rest upon the honourable General at the west. Ah, and there is another detail that I had failed to notice- see the Dragon who stands behind the robe-wearer?"

Bai Faoha coughed, and spat a fly into his hand. "I do, Great Sage, though these noisome irritations seek to hide it from me."

"It is gold once more. When last we communed with the Tapestry, you might remember that it was silver. Previously, the flies emerged from Dragon, now they emerge from man. There is meaning here, for he with the wisdom to see it."

"Do we possess such wisdom?" asked White Crocus. Smiling Snake stood, and clapped his palms together, banishing the flies with a surge of *ki*.

"We do not, but I know where to find he who does."

95

*B*efore they left the Belus Manse, Derelar took Gisela aside.

"High Chirurgeon," he said, noting that Willow-Sigh Wen seemed to have attached herself to him but thinking little of it, "I see you have secured a sample of the Vice-Chancellor's blood. I think, given the circumstances, that it might be pertinent to have a second sample for comparison."

Gisela nodded. "That might be helpful, Arch-Chancellor. With the head missing, much that could be used to decisively confirm the identity of the body is similarly lacking. Do you have such a sample?"

"I may," said Derelar. "Follow me, please."

He led the way to the Messaging Chamber of the Manse, nodding to the Guard on duty outside. Gisela gasped at what they found there. "This.. this is quite unusual, Arch-Chancellor. Is this truly her blood held in suspension?"

"It is," said Derelar, gesturing to the glass-topped table with its crimson decorations. "I visited the Vice-Chancellor shortly after she had encountered a significant reverse and injured herself in a fit of irritation. She chose to commemorate the event in this somewhat unusual manner."

"It is a quite... unnerving effect," admitted Gisela. "The blood is suspended so perfectly that it seems as fresh as that which I have just collected from the cadaver-fresher, even."

"The wise man places his mistakes on his mantel, where he may see them every day and learn from them," said Willow-Sigh Wen, in her native tongue. Derelar looked at her in surprise.

"Master Wen? Is that another piece of Daxalai philosophy?" He spoke in what he hoped was a passable version of the low tongue, but saw the Initiate wince nonetheless. It was truly irksome that the woman would not agree to take part in the Three Gates of Discourse. She did, however, seem to understand him, and held up her left hand, showing a symbol burned into the back of it.

"Yes. We are taught that seeing a reminder of a failure helps prevent another. I placed this mark upon my skin after I failed to protect Silver-Tongue Yue."

"It is the symbol for 'loss', is it not?" said Derelar, persevering with Daxalai both out of pride, and in case he needed to ask a question he was not prepared to have Gisela hear.

"The loss of one who is robbed through their own inattention," said Wen Lian-Shi. "When a thief is caught for the first time, whip the thief. When he is caught for a second time, slay the thief, and whip he who was foolish enough to take their eyes off a known thief."

Derelar grunted. "Hmph. Were we to follow Daxalai traditions, half of the population of Lore would have been whipped raw or executed by now."

"Arch-Chancellor?" said Gisela in confusion, and Derelar realised his last reply had been in Imperial Common. "My apologies, High Chirurgeon. Master Wen was simply instructing me in Daxalai philosophy. Allow me to assist you in retrieving the sample."

He made a point of taking his time, as if considering his method, despite having performed this particular magic once before. He deliberately picked a spot in full view of the entrance to the chamber in which to work, eliminating the possibility of accidentally retrieving the small amount of his own blood he had replaced the previous sample with. As he worked, he considered what Wen Lian-Shi had told him. The philosophy of the Daxalai was heavily influenced by the Dragons, after all, so it made sense if the Vice-Chancellor had thought like they did. Of course, there was always the possibility that she was a Celestial Dragon, as those of the species who dwelt in the west were known.

A soft pop announced that Gisela had sealed the sample within a small tube, which she carefully placed in her bag after marking it with a glowing silver rune. "My thanks, Arch-Chancellor. As well as testing the first sample for any exotic toxins or poisons that might have eluded my initial examination, I will compare it with this one for verification. Will there be anything else, or may I begin my work?"

"There is one other thing," said Derelar, softly. "If there should prove to be anything else... unusual about the samples, or even familiar, please let me know discreetly."

Gisela gave him a puzzled look, but nodded. "Of course, Arch-Chancellor. Now, if you will excuse me?"

Derelar nodded, and she turned and walked briskly out. Willow-Sigh Wen watched her leave, and then spoke a single word.

"Come."

Without stopping to see whether the Arch-Chancellor followed- again- the woman turned and walked off, heading down the hallway. Though not especially tall, the Daxalai walked swiftly without seeming to hurry, and Derelar was forced into an undignified half-jog to keep up with her. She led the way round a corner until she finally halted at what appeared to be a dead-end, hung with a decorative tapestry.

"Door," she said, holding her hands together side-by-side and then turning them side-on. Derelar hardly felt the mime necessary. On the other hand, he also couldn't immediately see what the Initiate was referring to. There was certainly no obvious sign of an opening or a mechanism or spell that would create one.

"I see no door," he said, in Daxalai.

Wen Lian-Shi nodded, and stepped up to the tapestry. Without warning, she threw a lightning-fast blow at the surface, the flat of her palm slapping into the fabric with a sharp crack. There was no reaction from the wall, not even the barest tremor. Derelar frowned. No matter what magic had been used to reinforce the wall, a strike like that should at least have caused the cloth to move. A moment later, the Initiate repeated the blow, this time to the wall next to the tapestry. Watching with his Aethersight now, Derelar saw the shock of the impact vibrate through the stone and yet stop dead at the point where it met the wall hanging.

There it was- the very merest of discrepancies in the wall's Pattern. Now that he knew where to look, he could see it clearly. He sent a questing mote of Aether into the construct, twisting and turning it as a locksmith might a pick, and after a few moments of work the tapestry and the wall behind it vanished completely. The hallway beyond was disappointingly mundane, lit by glow-crystals and leading to a flight of stairs descending to a lower level.

"Here, we were imprisoned," said the Daxalai, leading the way down the stairs.

"By the Vice-Chancellor?" he replied, forced to use Imperial Common, not knowing the equivalent term in Daxalai or even if there was one.

"By *Do-Sou-Roh*, yes. She is a being of great power."

"Is?" said Derelar, copying the inflection Wen had used as closely as he could whilst adding a questioning note. Daxalai viewed time in a particularly precise manner, but the tense she had used was distinctly nebulous and could also have meant 'was' or even 'will be'.

"To seek to slay evil with evil is to seek to slay time by waiting," said the Initiate. "Even if the body of this Dragon is slain, its fangs are deep into the flesh of the world and its fire yet burns."

Derelar was still making sure he had even understood the words, much less begun to untangle their cryptic nature, when Captain Ariel arrived at the run. She was barefoot, clad only in a pair of sleeping-shorts and a cotton tunic. "Arch-Chancellor! One of my Guards came and told me you'd been seen heading this way. How did you.."

"That is none of your concern, Captain," said Derelar, coldly. "What *is* your concern is your explanation of why I was not informed that these hidden chambers existed, which will need to be excellent. You may begin."

Ariel shrugged, stifling a yawn. "I'm sorry, Arch-Chancellor, but this is just a prison area. There's no-one down here now, not since that one and Maike Dain escaped. If you'd asked me for a tour of all the Vice-Chancellor's secrets I'd have gladly given you one. I take what you told me extremely seriously." She smiled, sadly. "The Boss'd be pretty annoyed that you got in so easily, I can tell you that."

Derelar nodded. "You did pass the test of the Skull of Thon-Fulush when you said you would serve faithfully. Very well. You will assign me one of your Guards who is familiar with these secret ways and how to open them, and then you may return to your rest. And on the way, you will tell Magister Jarton about this place and that I require him to search it for any relevant documents."

Ariel pulled herself to a weary semblance of attention, and saluted. "Yes, Arch-Chancellor. I don't think the Boss kept anything of significance down here other than prisoners, but you'll have our full co-operation."

"And what of you, Willow-Sigh Wen?" said Derelar, after Ariel had gone. "Why did you feel the need to show me this?"

"To defeat your enemy, you must know your enemy," said the Daxalai, once again using a dialect that suggested she was quoting philosophy. Derelar had to admit there was a simple wisdom in the words, and one echoed in the Books of Thelen.

He just wished he was certain which enemy he was trying to defeat.

96

*I*t was dusk by the time Amanda Devereux knocked on the door of the unassuming farmhouse. The building was clearly carefully-maintained, but at the same time it, like the surrounding countryside, had an unmistakeable air of dilapidation, of a much-loved home falling into decay due to lack of resources.

"Who is it?" said a familiar woman's voice.

"A friend from the other day," said Devereux. "Someone who hasn't told anyone in Abellan who it was they helped out with a broken-down hay cart. Yet."

There was a startled oath from inside the building, and the sound of a heavy bolt being slid home. *Great. Somebody wants to do things the hard way.* Well, there wasn't time for that.

"Lady Ilia," said the Operative quietly. "You and I both know that locking the door and hoping that I go away isn't going to work. I need your help, and I'm going to get it. You just get to decide how much damage I have to do before that happens."

There was a long pause, and for a moment Devereux began to worry that the Abelian rebel would call her bluff. Even though she was fully capable of knocking down the door and subduing the people inside the house, that really wasn't the way she wanted to approach the situation. There was also the matter of the back door of the farmhouse- if Ilia chose to run, things could get awkward. Not for the first time she wished she could have brought Delys with her, but though the little Swordmaster possessed many talents she couldn't match an Operative at travelling long distances quickly unaided.

++Operative Alert: Monitored rear egress point open. Two contacts exiting.++

This was definitely not off to an ideal start. With the Hercules suite maintaining an active lock on the two targets- one of whom was Ilia given the close match with the signal from the tracker she had placed on the Archer as Thalia threw her out of the coach- Devereux leapt to the roof of the farmhouse in a single bound. A second leap saw her land in front of the two cloaked figures, her right-hand gun levelled.

"King's Grace!" gasped the lead figure, moving as if to draw a sword.

"Hold it!" snapped Devereux. "You know what these things do, Ilia. Don't make me give you another demonstration." She felt a sudden, tell-tale tingle. "And tell your friend that if he even thinks about trying to mess with their mechanism I'll know about it and he *really* won't like the consequences."

Ilia threw up her hands in surrender. "Oh, fucking fine, you win. Alaran, don't try anything stupid."

"Ilia?" said the other figure. "But.. she killed our people!"

"Our people were trying to kill her and her friends, Al," said Ilia, simply. "They fought back. It's a thing that happens, and right now if you don't start acting like a damn grown-up it's going to happen to you."

Alaran sagged. "Okay, okay, Illy. So, now what?"

Devereux looked from one to the other. They stood about the same height, and there was something in their manner that suggested they were related. In fact..

"Are you two twins?"

"Yes," said Alaran.

"No!" snapped Ilia in almost the same moment.

"So yes, then," said Devereux with a smile. "Inside, please."

"But how can you know which of us was telling the truth?" said Alaran petulantly as they went back inside.

"Because if you weren't twins, you'd have no reason to lie about it," pointed out Devereux.

++Operative Alert: Three more contacts within perimeter. Point-defence system locked on.++

Hold fire until ordered. The last thing she needed was Daniel getting trigger-happy. "Ilia, tell your three friends to come out. I told you, I'm not here to hurt you unless you force me to. If I was your enemy, there'd be a bunch of Royal Knights surrounding this place by now and a War Golem trampling on your carrot patch."

The Archer sighed. "Derik, Temis, Miraleth, do as she says."

The three rebels emerged from hiding, casting angry glances at Devereux. There were two young men and a woman, and the Operative recognised all three from the fight on the road. All three bore swords, but at a glance from Ilia they sheathed them.

"Alaran rescued them from that coach guard after you left," said Ilia, by way of explanation.

The Wizard blushed. "Well, if by that you mean bribed him to say they got away, then yes, I did that."

"Take a seat," said Devereux, gesturing to the table. It looked like she had interrupted supper. The table was set with plates- five, she noted with some satisfaction- and a pot of tea steamed upon it. The rebels sat at the table, and Temis immediately picked up a spoon and set to the bowl of soup in front of him.

"What?" he said as Derik stared at him. "I'm hungry. If we can't fight, I don't see why we can't eat."

"Don't stop on my account," said Devereux. "Like I said, I only came to talk. First, let me say I'm sorry about what became of your friends. It was a tragic misunderstanding and it shouldn't have happened."

"Those are fine words," said Ilia, coldly. "But they won't bring Alek and the others back. Did your friend survive, by the way?"

"Barely," said Devereux. "But he's part of the reason why I'm here. Whilst he was recovering from the wound, Athas was afflicted with the Winnowing Ague."

"King's grace!" gasped Alaran. "We've had a few cases recently, but I'd not heard of any in the capital for some time. How does he fare?"

"We were able to save him," said Devereux. "But in the process we discovered something. There's evidence that the High Wizards caused his illness, and it's even possible that they were responsible for the Ague itself."

Temis' spoon dropped into his soup with a plop. "What?"

"What sort of evidence?" said Ilia, her manner suddenly changing. Devereux gave her gun a theatrical twirl, and holstered it. It was a classic trick, called the 'Judas twist' in Office slang. Despite appearances, the SUCS combat software kept the weapon under complete control at all times and could level it to fire in a split second if anyone decided to try to take advantage of the apparent opening. Fortunately for everyone involved, nobody did.

"It's hard to explain, and I'm going to have to show you. But the simple version is that we found a small magical device that drains the.. Spirit of a victim until it's filled or they die. I followed a High Wizard called Galantharas to a cave near Aquila, and they had a much larger version of the device there. The problem is that I need someone with magical expertise to help me figure out what it does, and I need someone who isn't going to go running to the Royal Guard about it. That, and I'm going to need some horses that aren't those giant armoured things the Knights use."

"Who for?" said Ilia. "Other than us, I mean, assuming we decide to help you."

"My Swordmaster friend, and I may need to bring the new Ambassador along, if I think I can trust her," said Devereux. "I'm guessing you don't have many Wizards left, and I'd rather not go into the High Wizards' hidden lair with just Alaran here. No offence."

"None very much taken!" gaped Alaran. "I'm a Wizard, yes, but my training is mostly second-hand, passed down by those who survived the sacking of our family's castle."

"I'm not prepared to risk Alaran," said Ilia. "Without him, we'd have no way to protect our people from the Ague."

"Maybe so," agreed Devereux. "But if we can prove that the High Wizards are behind it, we can stop the Ague for good. Better yet, if the Queen doesn't know about all this and the Savalan family exposes it..."

"It.. it could be the basis for the restoration of our family," breathed Ilia.

"I'm in, Illy." said Alaran, setting his jaw. "This is too important for us to ignore."

"Tell us where to look, and we'll take care of it," said Ilia. "There's no reason for you to be involved, or your Ambassador."

"Unfortunately there is," said Devereux. "Firstly, the entrance to the cave is hidden by magic and I think I'm the only person short of a High Wizard who can get us in there, and secondly, if we do find evidence that they caused the Ague we need to wait a while before we reveal it."

"What?" said Ilia, her eyes narrowing. "Why?"

Devereux sighed. "Have you ever heard of the Dendaril?"

Alaran went white. "I- I have. They were blamed for the Imbal Incident about fifty years ago. It's a colony at the mouth of the Great Rent, mostly independent traders and fishermen- or at least it was. Something happened to it that drove everyone there a little.. strange, and the Royal Knights ended up burning the whole place to ashes. It's been re-established since, of course, but it's never been quite the same."

"That sounds like them. Right now, the Royal Army is marching to drive the Dendaril out of the Expelled Territories, and they're using mostly Stickmen and War Golems to do it. If we do anything to expose the High Wizards before that mission succeeds, both the Kingdom and the Empire might be overrun."

"Nobody is really sure if the High Wizards could really just.. shut down all the Golems," said Alaran. "They've threatened to do it in the past, but nobody has ever dared test their resolve."

"Still," said Devereux. "I'm not eager to put that to the test. So, if we do this, we do it my way and on my schedule. Are you still in?"

Temis picked up his bowl and drained it. "I am. One way or another we get to stick it to at least some of the fuckers who did this to us."

"Let's put it to a vote," said Ilia, to Devereux's surprise. Most of the people she'd tried to explain democracy to in this world had treated it like some sort of collective insanity, though Ollan had said it had provided some interesting lecture material. In the event, approval was unanimous, though she noticed Derik was a little slower to raise his hand than the rest.

"Okay," said the Operative. "There's a bridge about a hundred miles west of here, over the River Distal, you know the one I mean?"

"The Two-Lion bridge?" said Alaran. Devereux nodded.

"Yeah, there's a couple of lion statues on it. Meet me there at dusk tomorrow with at least three spare horses- good ones- and I'll take you to the cave. And Ilia-" she added, looking the Abelian noblewoman straight in the eyes, "remember, this is my operation. I don't want to see any heroics or clever double-crosses."

Ilia nodded. "I understand.. what do we call you, anyway?"

"Amanda will do for now," said Devereux. "Now, I need to get back before I'm missed."

"How did you even get out of Abellan without anyone noticing?" asked Alaran, as she moved to leave.

"I'm the woman who's already sneaked into the most secret lair of the High Wizards, Alaran," said Devereux with a smile. "It's just something that I do."

She stepped out into the night air, but the Wizard followed her. "Might I have a quick word, Amanda?"

She nodded. "Okay, but make sure it really is quick."

"You may need to keep an eye on Derik. He's loyal to our cause and usually a good man, but Alek.. Alek was his.. they were very close. Intimately, if you see what I mean."

Devereux did, and her eyes widened. "I didn't think that sort of thing was common in Abelia, what with the whole population problem."

"It's not," admitted Alaran. "Although no-one much cares so long as you still do your duty by the family bloodline when required. If the family is restored, both Ilia and I will be expected to.. do our part. Anyway, remember what I said about Derik." Blushing slightly, the Wizard retreated into the farmhouse.

Setting her bodysuit to active camouflage, Devereux disappeared into the night. Everything now depended on Magister Elsabeth. Hopefully, she wouldn't be afraid of starting her new posting with a little espionage.

97

*M*agister Haran Dar watched as another bolt of destruction lanced into the darkness, briefly illuminating the entire Vigil from end-to-end. By the time night had fallen on the fortress, the defenders were already beginning to feel the strain. Talya, the Choirmaster of the third Petard Engine, had managed to gain control of Georg's Singers and stop them chanting, and had set her own choir to the task of powering the device. Roughly every thirty seconds, another blast of pure power lanced into the forest, most landing just beyond the tree-line. Few of them hit anything, but the bombardment had forced the Dendaril to retreat. Haran had considered ordering the one Engine that could still be aimed to fire deeper into the forest in the hope of inflicting actual damage on the invaders instead of just deterring them, but the Free Tribes were already ill-at-ease with the destruction of a few of the trees. Deliberately firing the Engine into the depths of their Forest Home might push some of them too far.

The far worse problem, however, was how to maintain the barrage. As Ixilinath- or whichever charlatan had usurped his name- had warned, it proved impossible to prevent the charged Engines from discharging, and in the brief pause when Georg's device had been shut down the Dendaril had immediately begun to advance. Choirmaster Jarthis was already showing signs of fatigue and his Singers were gaunt and hollow-eyed. At Manadar, of course, the College had maintained a steady bombardment for days, but on that occasion there had been enough Singers to operate in shifts. With the losses suffered when the last Royalist bastion had been so spectacularly destroyed, as well as those killed during Jocasta's rampage through Equinox, Singers were in short supply and the Symposium was deeply reluctant to approve the creation of more. Haran had placed an urgent request for reinforcements regardless, and more were coming from Kathis and the work-crews at Fort Tarim, but they would take at least a day to arrive.

Captain Render arrived on the battlements as the next Engine fired, accompanied by Magritte. She gave a weary salute.

"Learned Magister, we have the report you requested. The Healers say that Georg's Singers are almost completely spent. Whatever Talya had to do to stop them has made most of them practically catatonic- they'll eat and follow basic commands, but using them to replace any of the Singers on either Engine is out of the question."

Haran nodded. "I feared as much. When the Singers from the Sixth Volume arrive, we'll have them sent back to Lore. House Daran created them, maybe they can cure them."

Render nodded. "Yes, Learned Magister. The biggest problem at the moment, though, is morale. When these damned things fire-" she began, breaking off for a moment when the south Engine interrupted her by doing exactly that, "the light is so bright it fills the entire Vigil. Between that and.."

There was a distant crash as the shot landed. "..and that, hardly anyone is getting any useful sleep. It's hardest on the Expelled camp, of course, since they're on the leeward side of the wall and get the full brunt of it, but even those Wardens and Vigilants bunked on the far side of the Vigil are suffering."

"I understand," said Haran. "How is Magister Kandira?"

"Still recovering. Magister Ollan cast a sleeping spell on her, but he says she seriously overtaxed herself and... what was it he said, Magritte?"

"The wind is thin, whatever that means," said the Operator. Haran understood the old man's meaning well enough. Ordinarily Magisters and any other wielder of Aether, even those who were Sealed, would recover naturally over time, drawing power from the natural flow of life through the world. Heat, sound, light, even the movement of the planet itself as it span through the cosmos, all imparted small amounts of energy, but the majority was gleaned from the pure Aether that flowed through everything that existed. With two Choirs constantly drawing on that power to feed the Engines, however, and the Vigil neither directly connected to the Road network nor having a Waycrystal of its own, there was precious little Aether to spare for those Magisters and Mighty Ones who were still hale and healthy, much less one weakened by exertion. At Manadar, it hadn't been a serious problem, since the Magisters awaiting the destruction of the city had not needed to use their own power, but here..

"Magister Kandira will need a more conducive location to convalesce," said Haran. "When we send the.. incapacitated Singers away, we will send her as well."

"I don't think she'll like that very much, Learned Magister," observed Render.

"She will not. And as soon as she is able to express that sentiment with her customary vehemence, I will be happy for her to return and do so personally. But a spirit-sick Magister is of no use to us here. What news is there from Abelia?"

"That's more encouraging," said Render. "According to the diplomatic staff at our embassy there, the Royal Army is marching in strength for the Farspan. They should make the Territories by this time tomorrow."

"Another day of this..." mused Haran. "We will endure. We must."

"Beggin'y'pardon, Learned Magister, but that mightn't be enough," said a new voice, as an unpleasant smell heralded the arrival of Alben Koont.

"Scout Koont?" said Haran, carefully muting his sense of smell as he did so. "You have something to add?"

"Yep," said the Scout. "Somethin's up w'them Fly Lord fuckers."

"Well of course something's up with them!" snapped Magritte, wrinkling her nose and stepping as far away from the grimy man as she could without having to shout. "They're infested with those.. those things!"

"Not what I mean, lass," said the Scout. "Look, Cap'n, me an' you and the girls, we saw that lot comin' here, yeah? Remember how many o' the buggers there was?"

"There were hundreds of thousands of them, at least," said Render, rubbing her chin thoughtfully.

"Yep. Now I'll grant yer, there's a lot o' them fuck-sticks out there, but nothing like's many's we saw. And we dint see all o' 'em, neither."

"Are you suggesting, Scout Koont, that this is not the main body of the Dendaril force?" said Haran. "Where are the rest of them?"

"Buggered if'n I know, Learned Magister," said the Scout. "Was thinkin' o' goin' t'take a shufty, see if'n I could find out."

"Out of the question!" said Render. "Even if the forest wasn't crawling with those things, we're firing-"

As if on cue, the northern Engine fired. Haran frowned. It seemed to have taken a little longer than usual.

"-firing unpredictable magical siege engines into it!" continued Render. "If you're not careful, you'll get obliterated."

Magritte made a face. "You say that like it'd be a bad thing."

Alben Koont gave a dry chuckle. "Ah c'mon blondie, y'know y'dream o'gettin' some o' this. Anyways, if'n I'm on me own an' not draggin' some bunch'o clod-hoppers 'n Skinnies about w'me, I reckon I can make it."

"Very well," said Haran, before the most senior 'clod-hopper' could retort. "You leave as soon as you are ready, Scout Koont. Discover where the other Dendaril are, and report back as soon as possible."

"Learned Magister?" gasped Captain Render. "He's defenceless against those things alone! What if he gets infested?"

"As I understand the Dendaril, he will simply not come back," said Haran. "Even so, Scout Koont, on your return you will submit to full examination by the Healers. Failure to do so immediately will see you treated as an enemy of the College and executed on sight, with your remains destroyed by burning. Are we clear on this?"

"Yep," said the Scout. "I'll be off, then. Ladies, I'll be seein' y'later, and Cap'n-thanks fer carin'."

They watched him go, and after the next flare from the Engines faded he had vanished without a trace.

"Are you sure about this, Learned Magister?" asked Captain Render. "Does he even really stand a chance out there alone?"

"That seems to be how Scout Koont prefers to operate," said Haran. "In any case, his abrasive personality and disagreeable odour have an effect on morale that we can ill-afford in this situation, and his usefulness in combat against the Dendaril is negligible. If he succeeds in this self-appointed mission, we stand to gain useful intelligence, and if he fails, we have lost little of value."

The Captain swallowed. "I-I see. Of course, Learned Magister. Will there be anything else?"

Haran nodded, grimly. "Over the course of this conversation, I have noticed the rate of fire of the Petard Engines perceptibly slacken. Investigate this immediately."

Render saluted, and hurried off. Haran watched her leave with a mounting feeling of trepidation. If the Engines failed, by the time the Abelians arrived there might be no-one left to relieve.

98

The Royal Army column halted for the night as darkness fell. They had made good time- from what Thalia could tell they were roughly halfway between Dalliance and Castle Orsinio- but the Queen clearly had no intention of arriving at the Farspan in the small hours of the morning with an army weary from constant travel, even if much of that army consisted of near-tireless constructs. Thalia had attempted to warn Tondarin of the possible danger from the Guardian, but had been dismissed out-of-hand. Clearly the Queen trusted the High Wizards more than her.

She had discovered early on that the large, round table that rose as a solid cylinder of khile-wood from the floor of the *Dreadnought*'s forward compartment was far more than somewhere to place a wine-glass. As befitted the vehicle's role as a command centre, it was capable of displaying a fairly detailed overview of the surrounding area, its magic not dissimilar to that used by College battlefield maps. Whilst those devices had the advantage of portability, being capable of being rolled or folded up as the situation demanded, they conveyed information as largely two-dimensional lines and runic sigils. The *Dreadnought*'s command table, in contrast, presented a stylised three-dimensional view of the area as if from a bird flying at some height above it.

Now, the device was showing that the Royal Army was forming into a defensive circle for the night, the passenger coaches like the *Dreadnought* and *Valiant* in the centre, with the simpler open-topped wagons on which the Golems were transported on the outside. Thalia thought the measure to be more than a little paranoid, but then the memory of a Gestalt Ape rampaging through her own makeshift encampment shortly after the fall of Manadar came to her. Perhaps the Abelians were being over-cautious, but precautions rarely killed anyone they weren't supposed to. Carelessness could.

There was a gentle knock at the door. Along with the command table, Thalia had also worked out the *Dreadnought*'s basic operation, and opened it with a thought.

"Lady Thalia," said the amplified voice of Sir Terence from outside. "The Queen requests the honour of your presence at dinner. Your bodyguard is, of course, also invited."

It suddenly struck Thalia that sizeable though the *Dreadnought* was, Sir Terence would have some difficulty actually getting through the door in his eight-foot-tall battle armour. She knew that the Aether-powered suits were a relatively recent invention, the first having come into general use some fifty years after the vehicle had been built, but it was surprising that no modifications had been made since.

Athas had been dozing in one of the bedrooms, but inevitably immediately appeared at the mention of food. "Are we going, Learned Magister?"

"Do you see anything to eat in here?" said Thalia, slightly crossly. "We will attend, Sir Terence. Am I required to dress for dinner?"

"That is not necessary, My Lady," said the Knight. "Your bodyguard, however, should attend in his armour. It is traditional when meals are taken in the field."

Athas shrugged. "Oh, that's okay, it doesn't take me long to put it on. Do you want to go on ahead, Learned Magister?"

Thalia wished she could have seen Sir Terence's expression inside his helm. "Sergeant, you are present as my bodyguard. The job rather involves being somewhere near me at all times."

Athas flushed, and disappeared back into the bedroom. "Yeah, er, sorry. Just a moment- ow! Bloody thing, who were these rooms built for, midgets? Ouch!"

Thalia gave the Royal Knight's blank face-plate an equally blank smile. "He's a good man really, Sir Terence, just a little... straightforward."

The big Guard finally emerged from the corridor leading to the sleeping quarters, despite a last-minute delay as he manoeuvred his shield out of the narrow passage. "Hey, Sir Terence? How do you get around inside these things? You're a lot bigger than I am when you're wearing all of that."

"We do not." said the Knight, simply, as he led the way. "Our armour stands guard outside the vehicle as we sleep. Once we enter hostile territory, we will be attired for war at all times and the coaches will be used solely for the Wizards and other otherwise unprotected personnel."

"Oh." said Athas. "Well, I suppose it's not like anyone's going to be able to steal it. Are you going to wear that to eat? It seems like that'd be difficult."

"Extremely," chuckled the Knight, his distorted voice giving the laugh an oddly musical edge. "But as I said, there is tradition to observe."

"Wow...." gasped Athas as they came into sight of the dining table. Thalia had to admit that it was an impressive sight. A huge expanse of wood some two-hundred feet long occupied the space within the centre of the camp, made of interlocking pieces much like the palanquin they had ridden to Naxxiamor. Standing to either side of it were fully one-hundred Royal Knights, along with a little over a third that number of Wizards. There was clearly a pecking order- Thalia saw that Tondarin was at the head of the table, accompanied by ten Knights in white-gold amour, whereas she was being guided to the foot of the table which was mostly occupied by the Wizards. Many Knights, however, also sat at the far end, most of them seemingly the husbands or wives of the Wizard they were next to. Thalia recognised Sir Hektor and Lady Ysabella Orsinio a few places down, though mercifully none of their children were present.

It was the Knights' armour, though, that had clearly caught Athas' attention. Thalia had noticed that Tondarin and several of the other female Knights wore long dresses, but hadn't really considered the implications. Now, however, seeing them in their armour, she understood the incredible feats of artifice, tailoring and magic that must have gone into their panoply. The skirt of the Queen's rich purple and gold dress, for example, seemed somehow to protrude through the hips of her armour, though it was slit at the thigh to allow free movement and the suit's extra height prevented it trailing on the ground.

Nobody had sat down yet, and Thalia eyed the simple wooden chairs with more than a little trepidation. They didn't look exactly uncomfortable, but they also scarcely looked equal to the task of supporting the massive bulk of the Knights. Before she could ask Sir Terence anything about it, the Queen tapped a wine-glass with her armoured finger.

"As laid down in the *Treatise of War*, by King Gideon the Brave, we convene this, the Last Feast. From dawn tomorrow until victory is attained, the Royal Knights shall neither eat nor sleep, subsisting on Spirit alone. But tonight, we eat, we drink, and we love, to remind ourselves what, where and who we fight for. Release!"

At the Queen's command, all one-hundred Knights, herself included, stepped out of their armour. Thalia watched, fascinated, as the skirts of many of the female Knights split into ribbon-like segments and retracted themselves through the silver plates even as their wearer moved, reforming into complete dresses without impeding their wearers in the slightest. Each suit seemed to be designed in a subtly different way, their pieces moving and shifting in a unique pattern.

"Pour!" commanded the Queen, and each bottle of wine on the table was quickly seized by eager hands and the glasses filled. There didn't seem to be any feats of swordplay tonight, Thalia noticed, probably because there were so many bottles. Sir Terence passed her a glass, and handed another to Athas. Suddenly suspicious, Thalia took a quick glance at the contents with her Aethersight, in case the Queen had arranged for any more surprises, but found nothing amiss.

"For Queen and Kingdom!" shouted the Queen, which Thalia thought more than a little self-serving. "Valour Defiant!"

"Valour Defiant!" echoed every man and woman present, and downed the wine in a single draught. With this done, the Queen finally took her seat, which seemed to be the cue for everyone else to do the same. Even this, though, was oddly ritualised, and the Abelians sat down in a strict order, starting with those closest to the Queen and ending with Thalia herself at the foot of the table.

"Do not feel slighted, Lady Thalia," said Sir Terence, softly. "It is common for visiting dignitaries at the Last Feast to be seated at the far end of the table. Every part of the meal starts at the monarch, and moves towards the other end, allowing the newcomer ample time to see what is expected of them without having to ask."

"I understand, Sir Terence," said Thalia, stoically, though her stomach spoilt the effect by rumbling loudly. She did not have long to wait, however, for within moments the food arrived, carried incongruously by the armour of the Knights. Unlike the state dinner, there were no formal courses, the ambulatory suits simply depositing plate after plate of roasted meat, pastries, bread, and vegetables of every sort, along with near-overflowing bowls of fruit. Athas' eyes had gone almost as large as his plate.

"You are not expected to over-eat, My Lady," advised Sir Terence, seeing Thalia's concern. "The Knights will indulge tonight in preparation for the campaign fast, but other guests need only sate themselves for the evening. I should warn you, however, that from here on the fare available will be much simpler."

"How.. long will you... go without.. food?" asked Athas, between bites.

"As long as is necessary, Sergeant," said Sir Terence. "A Royal Knight in armour can go for weeks without nourishment if need be, though operating at full seal reduces that time somewhat. The chief weapon of these Dendaril, however, is their ability to infest their victims, and with our armour's immunity to it we should not experience any discomfort before victory is achieved."

"So what happens if you do... run out of time?" said Athas, doing his best to keep pace with the Knights and doing a fair job of it.

"In the extreme case, the Queen will simply declare a halt to the campaign," said Sir Terence. "The Knights will withdraw to encamp and replenish themselves. But such a thing has not happened since the last Thelenic War, and in any case the only time the Last Feast was called during that conflict was prior to the disaster that.. well, that cost both the head and the foot of tonight's table so dearly. But this is not the time for dark thoughts, Sergeant. Tonight, we revel, and tomorrow will look to itself!"

Several other Knights who had been listening cheered and raised refilled glasses at his words, and Thalia found herself relaxing. It was perhaps a stretch to say she felt as if she was among friends, but if even the mention of such a notorious defeat had failed to sour the mood, she certainly wasn't going to do anything that might. She cast a quick look towards the squat bulk of the *Dreadnought*, sitting silhouetted by the moonlight, and another at Athas happily eating alongside her. Perhaps once the meal was done, there might be other things to look forward to before the morning's dangers.

99

"*J*arthis!" said Magister Haran, grabbing the Choirmaster by the shoulders and shaking him. "Snap out of it, man!"

The Choirmaster blinked. "I- sorry, Learned Magister. What was I saying?"

"You were telling me that your Singers were starting to weaken," said Haran, grimly. "I see now that you were not exaggerating."

"I am sorry, Learned Magister," said the thin man. "I know I warned you that we risked over-taxing the Singers, but even I could not have... could not have... have imagined the toll this would exact upon us." He sniffed, and wiped at his nose with the sleeve of his robe. Haran saw there was blood on it.

"How long before the Singers fail completely?" he asked, when the Choirmaster had recovered sufficiently to focus on him again.

"Hours," said Jarthis, flatly. "My Choir has already lost two Singers and Choirmaster Talya's one. The Engines are now firing at a rate of one every forty-five seconds instead of the usual thirty- forty one in Talya's case. Already the lack of synchronisation risks creating gaps the Dendaril could exploit."

"What if your Singers were allowed to rest?" said Magister Ollan, emerging from the flickering half-light of the hallway. "Haran, a word?"

"What do you want, Learned Magister?" said Haran, blinking fatigue from his eyes.

"You. You need to come and talk to Kandira, quickly."

"I hardly have time to-"

"Now, Haran! Damn it man, you may be in charge of this fortress but if you're ever going to listen to me about anything, do it now!"

Haran thought that a little unfair, given the number of times he had taken the old man's advice, but the lack of Ollan's usual playful tone suggested that he was in no mood for his usual banter. "Very well, Learned Magister. Magritte, have a

Healer come to take a look at Choirmaster Jarthis, see if they can do anything for him. If the Engines fail..."

Magritte swallowed, and nodded. "At once, Learned Magister."

Ollan led the way to the Vigil's infirmary. "Was it like this in Manadar, do you think, Haran?"

"What?"

"This," said Ollan, gesturing at the flickering glow-crystals. "Everything they had, put into a last-ditch attempt to protect themselves, knowing that all they were doing was prolonging the inevitable. Of course, on that occasion the Petard Engines were on the other foot, to badly mangle our metaphors."

Haran had to admit that there were unnerving parallels. "The Royalists did not have an army of Golems marching to relieve them, Learned Magister," he objected.

"Then let us hope that we do," said Ollan. "Ah, but here we are. Kandira is still very weak, Haran, try not to let her get too excited, hm?"

"Stop mollycoddling and get in here, you bumbling oaf!" snapped the elderly Magister's voice from within the Infirmary. They entered, and Haran was shocked at what he saw. Kandira's skin was as white as parchment, and her flesh hung off her bones.

"Magister Kandira, I am glad to see you recovering," lied Haran. She snorted.

"Bah! They've got me eating khile and some Jandallan gunge to try to help me recuperate, but it's not working," said Kandira. "Ollan tells me you're planning to ship me out in the morning?"

"I... er.." began Haran, but the old woman cut him off with a smile.

"It's the right decision, cousin. I'm no use to man or beast like this, except possibly as lunch or fertiliser. Get me out of the way and save your Healers for those they can help." She coughed, and Ollan passed her a glass of water with a sorrowful expression. "Stop fussing, Ollan, I'm weak, not dead. Now, Haran, we need to talk about your Engine problem."

"Do not concern yourself," said Haran, softly. "The Choirmasters-"

"Are nincompoops," snapped Kandira. "They know how to drive their Singers and how to set the Engines, and that's about it. At this rate, they'll all be dead before tomorrow morning and then we're royally buggered. And don't tell me to not to bloody well worry about it- if those things break through right now I won't even have the strength to off myself before they take me."

"Very well, Learned Magister," said Haran. "I take it you wish to offer a solution?"

"Yes, but you won't like it."

"I like the alternative less, I think," pointed out Haran. "What do you propose?"

"Simple," said Kandira. "The Magisters and Mighty Ones will need to take over manning the Engines."

Haran blinked at her. "I.. I beg your pardon?"

"You heard me. Look, the Engines may seem inscrutable, but ultimately they're just a massively complicated lens with a funnel attached. They just absorb any Aether directed at them, store it up, then blast it out when there's too much to contain. You just need to.." she broke off, coughing again. "Damn it all. Just watch the flow of Aether into the device, and copy it. That's it- don't you bloody well dare, Ollan Dane!"

Magister Ollan held up his hands in surrender. "What?"

"You know full bloody well.. what," murmured Kandira, her eyelids fluttering. "Save.. save your strength... for what's coming.." Her eyes closed, and she fell into a fitful sleep. Ollan gave her a fond look.

"Stubborn to the last. I suppose I'd better respect her wishes."

Haran had seen Ollan do what he had been about to do to Kandira before, when Magister Thalia was spirit-sick, but he had to agree with the old woman. Giving her a jolt of Aether right now would certainly make her more comfortable, but it would weaken Ollan at a time when they could ill-afford it. He turned, and strode out, the elder Magister following at his heels.

"So, do you plan to go through with it?" asked Ollan.

"As I said to Magister Kandira, the alternative is far worse than I care to imagine," said Haran. "We will study the operation of the Engine, and then test our ability to control one on the third Engine that lies in reserve. And then, should we succeed, we must teach the art to the Weavers and to the Mighty Ones."

"Hmph," said Ollan. "Or we could just try to open a portal to another plane of existence and syphon enough power to keep the Engines firing for eternity."

"That was hardly a great success for the defenders of Manadar, if you recall, Learned Magister," pointed out Haran.

"No, but at least it was quick," said Ollan. "I fear this is going to feel like having our brains sucked out through a straw. Preferable to a symbiont in the skull, but not by much."

Haran nodded. Even if this worked, there was no guarantee that the Magisters would be able to buy enough time for the Singers to recover. If the Abelians didn't strike soon, all could still be lost.

100

$\mathcal{D}$awn found Magister Thalia Daran in a foul mood. Worse, it was a foul mood that she was fully aware was entirely her own fault. Despite knowing full well what effect it would have on her she had happily downed every glass of wine her Abelian hosts had passed her way, and had consequently woken up with the very mother, brother and possibly vengeful Goddess of all hangovers. The last thing she remembered was Athas asking her if she was feeling all right, before waking up in her nightclothes in one of the *Dreadnought*'s two small bedrooms. She probably would have slept considerably longer if the Abelians didn't have the irritating habit of mustering the camp with a loud bugle call. So it was a tired, grumpy, hungover and hungry Magister who went searching for some breakfast even as dawn pinked the eastern skies.

Most of the cooks attending the convoy had returned to Abellan or Dalliance, their services no longer required once the Last Feast had been called, but a couple had stayed to cater to the Wizards and few living human retainers that accompanied the Royal Army. Thalia had retrieved two plates of bacon and eggs, along with a couple of glasses of something sparkling which the cook assured her would settle both her stomach and her head, and was about to start back to the *Dreadnought* when she saw the Guardian. Although swifter than a normal man due to its sheer length of stride, the automaton wasn't fast enough on foot to keep up with the convoy and so rode in an open-topped wagon behind the *Valiant*, but it wasn't there now. It also wasn't by the Queen's side- the Abelian monarch was now mounted on a massive, heavily-armoured destrier like the other Knights and would presumably remain that way until satisfied that victory had been achieved.

"Queen's grace, this bloody thing sometimes!" grumbled a robed Wizard standing next to the automaton nursing a cigarette. "Oh, er, my apologies, Lady Thalia, I didn't see you there."

"That's quite all right.." said Thalia, wincing slightly as the sun broke through the clouds on the horizon. She had almost looked at the man's Pattern through force of habit to learn his name, but the pain in her head made it difficult to focus.

"Hangover, my Lady?" said the Wizard with a smile, flicking the cigarette away. "Ah yes, *piel-de-vitess* with an infusion of ground Kingswort, a traditional if hardly foolproof remedy. If I may assist?"

Thalia nodded mute assent, and the Wizard gave her an almost cross-eyed stare for a moment before tapping her firmly in the middle of her forehead with his index finger. The pain flared briefly, and then fled. Thalia blinked dancing colours out of her eyes, and took a deep breath.

"Agh.. I mean, thank you.. what is your name, anyway?"

"Eldrik D'Alembert," said the Wizard. "At your service, my Lady. It does a man good to do something useful instead of babysitting this... thing."

"What's it doing?" asked Thalia. The Guardian didn't seem to be doing anything much, as far as she could see, other than standing there looking east.

The Wizard shrugged. "I don't know. I'm supposed to be getting its transport wagon ready to move, but it always does this in the morning. Just walks a little way away and stands there for a few minutes. I think it's probably an error in the sigil-engram but the High Wizards surround those things with so many enigma wards that you're not going to catch me, or anyone else, poking our Spirit in there to find out."

Thalia could understand the man's trepidation. Enigma wards were among the most deadly of defences a magical construct could possess, capable of entrancing an incautious meddler so deeply when gazed upon that they would starve to death without even realising it. They certainly weren't something anyone other than the most skilled crypto-arcanists had any business fooling around with. Not that that had stopped her doing something very similar in the past, admittedly, but by comparison accidentally releasing an angry Gestalt Ape was positively fortunate.

Light was beginning to spill over the camp now as the sun broke through, and birdsong filled the air to herald the full onset of dawn. Thalia hadn't considered herself to be a morning person for some time, but she had to admit that the whole thing had a certain calming beauty. Suddenly the Guardian turned on its heel and marched back to its wagon, ignoring the Magister and forcing Eldrik to hop gracelessly out of the way.

"Amaran's tw- ah, I mean, er, bloody thing!" exclaimed the Wizard, strangling the profanity at birth having remembered the company he was in just in time. "I swear it does that on purpose. Sorry, Lady Thalia, I didn't mean to keep you. Your breakfast will be getting cold."

Thalia blinked, and found to her surprise that her eyes were wet with tears. "Y-yes, thank you, Eldrik. I should get moving in case the *Dreadnought* sets off without me."

She hurried off to wake Athas and see if either of them could face the food. But there was suddenly a cold, hollow feeling in her gut that had nothing to do with hunger and which she couldn't explain.

101

"*I*.. I believe I have it.." whispered Magister Hendrik. It was about time, thought Haran. Dawn was beginning to prick at the skies to the east of the Vigil, and as Kandira had predicted the Singers were dropping like flies. In desperation, fully half of the Healers in the Infirmary had given as much of their own Aether as they could to the remaining Singers and Choirmasters. This last-ditch measure had been horribly inefficient and would leave Haran's force danger-ously exposed in the event of serious combat casualties, but it had bought them a couple of crucial hours. He and Ollan had satisfied themselves that they under-stood how to empower the Engines and begun to instruct the Weavers.

"Very good, Magister Hendrik," said Haran. "Now, proceed to the southern Engine and begin showing your fellow Weavers the technique. When you are confident, we will convene at the third Engine and-"

"Thelen's balls!" gasped Ollan, dropping his pipe in the middle of filling it. "Haran! We are out of time!"

Haran whirled to see Choirmaster Jarthis swaying on his feet, blood trickling from his nose. "N-no... no I will be... will be...." the tall man murmured, before keeling over backwards into the arms of the Healer who had been tending to him. His eyes fluttered, then briefly locked with Haran's. "I.. am sorry, Learned Magister."

He closed his eyes again, and after a moment the remaining Singers of his Choir fell silent. Haran almost cried with relief. They had realised early on that the Choirmaster needed to command his Singers to stop before being incapacitated, lest the interference prevent the Magisters from taking over from them until all were dead or catatonic. Already, Haran could feel the power in the Engine ebbing away. Ollan rapped his staff firmly on the floor.

"Now to it, then. Hendrik, you had best hurry. Shall we, Haran?"

Haran nodded. "Aye, Learned Magister. Magritte, send runners to the Mighty Ones. We need them to support this effort, or we are all lost."

"The Mighty are already here," boomed Mighty Dokan, striding into the room with several others at his back Haran didn't immediately recognise. "Magister Ollan, tend to the second Engine. Mighty Haran, there is no time for us to learn the knack of this thing. Rather, the Mighty shall grant you their strength, and allow you to focus it."

Haran almost swore at his own foolishness. Of course, so long as there was a steady supply of Aether the actual number of Magisters communing with the device was irrelevant. "Very well. Magister Ollan, if you would do as Mighty Dokan suggests?"

"I-" began Ollan, looking unsure for possibly the first time that Haran could remember.

"Mighty Xaraya awaits at the southern Engine," said Dokan with a grim smile. "It would not do to keep her waiting.. Mighty Ollan."

Ollan gave a dry chuckle. "Do you really think me so easily manipulated? Thelen damn your barbarian hide, it worked. Good luck, Haran."

"And to you, Learned Magister," said Haran with a nod. Ollan hurried out, and he turned his attention to the Engine. Now it was simply a matter of finding the right part of the device's Pattern, and...

The shock of contact was so savage that it almost felt like it must yank him off his feet. By an effort of will he retained his balance, but the Engine fired almost immediately and he felt a huge chunk of his strength go with it. Too fast, too much, too quickly! Desperately he fought for control, trying to slow the torrent of his power into a simple flow, if not a trickle. Behind him, he felt the magic of the Mighty Ones rising, surging forwards to rush into the void in his self that the Engine had left. He could hear someone screaming, and tried to shout at them to shut up before realising that it was him. Fiercely he clamped his mouth closed, trying to ride the pain, to harness it, to break it to serve him.

It seemed to be working. The Engine's second shot took longer than the first, though it still seemed too fast. He could feel his skin tingling, his hair standing on end and his hands clenching, his left into a fist and his right gripping his staff so tightly that the knuckles were white. His vision had dwindled to a mere point of light as his Aethersight whirled with a blaze of colours. Hands were pulling at his clothing now for some reason but the Engine was the only thing he could think about, its Pattern enveloping his like a lover's. Sound, feeling, thought, all were dwindling, replaced by nothing but the construct's insatiable lust for his power and his own desperate attempts to control it.

Little by little, the being that had called itself Magister Haran Dar was being stripped away. With every pulse of the Engine, something of himself was lost which the power of the Mighty Ones could not replace, like fast-flowing water eroding the rocks of a valley through the mountains. He would endure- he must endure- but for how long?

And once he inevitably failed, would anything of him be left to regret it?

102

*A*manda Devereux had been back at the Green Palace long enough to get some breakfast with Delys by the time Magister Elsabeth Thule arrived. The new Ambassador swept into the entrance hall as if she owned the place, which by some criteria she basically did. She certainly cut an impressive figure, standing a little short of six feet in height and wearing her long, black hair piled up on top of her head in a style that added almost another foot. Her green satin robes were worked with silver and gold-threaded runes, and a mantle of exotic bird feathers adorned her shoulders and trailed down her back. Her staff was of black-stained khile-wood, topped by a prancing horse similar to that on Thalia's but accompanied only by the circle within a circle design of House Thule, with the staff's crystal set within the inner of the two rings. Almost inevitably, her long, black riding boots were high-heeled. The doors of the Green Palace could accommodate a Royal Knight in full battle-armour but even so, her hair very nearly brushed the head jamb. Clearly, power-dressing was an art that had not eluded the new Ambassador.

Herenford While met her at the door, giving a low bow as Devereux and Delys walked down the stairs. "Your Excellency, welcome to the Green Palace. I trust everything is in order?"

The Ambassador looked around. "Mostly, Steward. I had heard that the Abelians had left this place in a state of some disarray, but it seems that you and your staff have done a commendable job of returning it to at least some semblance of order. Kindly have your staff unload my carriage as quickly as possible- in particular, I have brought a consignment of new Messaging Crystals certified by the Vice-Chancellor. The existing ones cannot be considered secure and should be destroyed."

"Your Excellency, if I may?" said Devereux, stepping forwards. "Might I suggest that you hold off on that for now?"

"And who might you be, madam?" said the Ambassador, looking down her nose at her. "I fail to see what possible benefit there might be in keeping them, in any case."

"Amanda Devereux, Your Excellency," said the Operative, adding a small curtsey for good measure. "If the Abelians are listening in to your communications, it might be useful to let them think that they can keep doing it. I'd suggest that you use the compromised Crystal for any business you don't mind the Abelians knowing about, but set up the secure one for confidential matters. That might even allow us to feed them information without them knowing that we want them to know it."

The Ambassador stared down at her for a long moment. "Ah, I remember the briefing report now. You're one of Anneke's people, aren't you? I am a diplomat, not a spy, Master Devereux. Is there any reason to think that such subterfuge will be necessary here?"

"It never hurts to keep the option open, Your Excellency," said Devereux, quietly. "But if you'd like us to convene somewhere a little more private, I do have something pretty important to tell you about."

"Very well," sniffed the Ambassador. "But you will need to be brief. I must attend Castle Valour this morning to present my credentials to the Chamberlain."

Roughly half an hour later, in what had been Thalia's room, Elsabeth leaned back in her chair with a sigh and set down her wineglass. "Do you know, Operative, when you asked me to cast a silence spell before you'd tell me anything I thought that you were being foolishly paranoid."

"And now?" asked the Operative. Her true abilities had been a necessary part of the story.

"Now I'm wishing we were having this conversation in Lore. You are certain that the High Wizards are responsible for the Ague?"

"I'm not certain that they initially caused it," admitted Devereux. "It might be that it began naturally and they turned it to their own ends. But they're certainly involved in it now, and they certainly have plans that they aren't sharing with the Royal Knights or anyone else."

"And you have arranged for a cell of these Savalan rebels to accompany you to the site tonight?" said the Ambassador. "Don't you think that was a little presumptuous?"

"Yes," agreed Devereux. "But both the College and Abelia are relying on those Golems to repel the Dendaril. If there's even the possibility that the High Wizards are planning some sort of betrayal, there's no time to lose finding out what it might be, even if we might have to wait to act on it."

"And you said that they didn't even seem to be alive in the conventional sense?" said Elsabeth. "That does raise the troubling possibility that they plan to let the Dendaril infest Abelia, knowing that they and their Golems will be the only ones immune."

Devereux nodded. "That thought had crossed my mind, Your Excellency. I can't really see why they'd want to do that, though. What would be in it for them?"

"What indeed?" mused the Ambassador. "Very well, Operative. Not only is there a clear threat to the Empire here, it would also be quite the diplomatic coup to expose treachery on the part of such important individuals as the High Wizards. Driving a wedge between them and the Royal Knights would weaken Abelia dramatically, and if we back the right side relations with the Kingdom would greatly improve into the bargain."

"If we *back the right side?*" repeated the Operative incredulously. "Are you suggesting, what, that the High Wizards might just be *misunderstood* magical mass-murderers?"

Elsabeth smiled, and patted her hand. "Of course not. But in diplomacy, it pays to keep an open mind, especially in matters of morality. If the schemes of the High Wizards fall into ruin we might stand to gain more as sympathetic rescuers of the most powerful Gifted in the Kingdom than we would as just another of their enemies. But such a thing would be done quietly and under strict conditions, of course."

"Operation paperclip," muttered Devereux. "All right, I don't like it but I'm not going to argue with you about it. I thought you didn't do espionage, though?"

"I'm a politician, Operative," said Elsabeth with a smile. "We're a lot like spies, but with far better excuses and manners, nothing like the Vice-Chancellor's thugs. Oh, no offence meant, of course."

Now it was the Operative's turn to smile. "None taken, Your Excellency. A few of Anneke's 'people' that I've met fit that description pretty well. For myself, it was more a matter of being in the wrong place at the wrong time and having to make the best of it."

"That's true of many of that whore-monger's agents, so I hear," said Elsabeth, sourly. "She might have had her uses, but I found her methods deeply distasteful."

"In any case-" said Devereux. "Wait, what do you mean 'might have had'? Has something happened?"

"I thought you must have heard, since you worked for her," said the Ambassador. "The Vice-Chancellor was found dead yesterday. The Arch-Chancellor's office is keeping it quiet, of course, but you don't get very far in politics if you don't have someone in place to tell you when something that important happens."

"Fuck me," said Devereux, with feeling. "I can't say I was expecting that. Do you know what happened?"

"I have informers, not spies, Operative," said Elsabeth. "All I know is that she was found dead in her bed at her Manse not long after I left for this posting. It's not that surprising really, someone like her was bound to make powerful enemies. Magister Ollan, for one, blames her for what happened to his family and getting on the wrong side of that wily old man can be distinctly unhealthy."

"What did happen?" asked Devereux. It wasn't the first time she'd heard about Ollan's grudge, but it was the closest she'd come to learning the cause for it.

"Ah, now that I really shouldn't reveal," said Elsabeth. "It's a very personal secret of Magister Ollan's, and I have no desire to suffer the same fate as Anneke."

"You can't be serious," said Devereux.

"No, not entirely," said the Ambassador, shaking her head. "I'm not saying Ollan doesn't have it in him, but he was over a thousand miles away at the Vigil at the time. Still, a diplomat must keep confidences if her word is ever to mean anything, and I would rather not breach this one. Perhaps some day Magister Ollan will tell you himself."

Devereux remembered how much talking about his father had affected Ollan, and decided that she should drop the subject. "OK, point taken. In any case, the most important question is how closely you're prepared to involve yourself with this."

Elsabeth picked up the wineglass again and drained it. "What do you mean?"

"Simply put," said Devereux, "if I go into that cave with just the Savalans and Del, we're taking on the most powerful Wizards in Abelia with only one Wizard of our own, and one who's mostly self-taught at that. Without access to travel magic, Del's not even going to make it to the rendezvous on horseback by dusk tonight unless we leave very shortly. But with a.. six Leaf Magister along with us, that equation changes dramatically."

The Ambassador chuckled. "I think you exaggerate my abilities a little, Operative. I can hold my own in a duel- you don't get far in politics without being able to do that, either- but against ten High Wizards I'd be a pebble thrown at a blizzard."

"I'm not talking about direct confrontation, Your Excellency," said Devereux. "I'm talking about making that confrontation a lot less likely. Ideally we'll get in, find out what's going on, and get out without the High Wizards knowing it. They seem very confident in that illusion of theirs, and the other defences in the cave appear to be fairly minimal. Having a senior Magister along is more a precaution against any Wards or other magical alarms that I can't easily detect than anything else."

"Not to mention someone who might have a chance of figuring out what this Reaper machine actually does, I suppose," said Elsabeth. "Very well, Operative, I will accompany you."

"You might want to wear something a little more.. practical, though." pointed out Devereux. Elsabeth bristled.

"Fashion is always practical, Operative! Though perhaps something with less feathers might be more appropriate."

415

103

*A*rch-Chancellor Derelar Thane had finished his coffee and made a start on the morning's reports by the time his first visitors arrived. At the very top of the pile were suggested candidates for the vacant post of Vice-Chancellor, a position traditionally filled by a close ally of the incumbent Arch-Chancellor. It had only really occurred to Derelar as he looked through the list of names that people he truly considered to be trusted allies were few and far between. Anneke had seen to that. There were very few influential Magisters that at least one of the late Vice-Chancellor's schemes had not affected in some way or another, which had prevented him from forming close ties with most of them. Magisters Ollan, Jarton and Gisela were near the top of the list and he considered all three to be little more than acquaintances. Worse, though Ollan possessed many of the required attributes for the job he had already made it clear that he would be reluctant to take it, and in any case he was over a thousand miles away.

A firm knock on the door announced the arrival of Magister Jarton, who entered at Derelar's call with Julius in tow. As Ollan had suggested he would, the Chair of Walanstahl had taken to the role of head of the Imperial Service with some ease, though he brought none of Anneke's mischievous ingenuity to it. The enemies of the College may no longer have to fear the schemes of the Vice-Chancellor, but they would find it well protected against their own plots.

"Good morning, Arch-Chancellor," said Jarton, nodding to the papers. "Already hard at it, I see."

Derelar gestured to a chair. "As always, Magister Jarton, there is entirely too much of 'it' for me to be hard at. What word do we have from the Vigil?"

"Nothing particularly good, I'm afraid," said Jarton, tugging at his beard. "The final communication we received last night said that the Vigilants were ceasing all non-essential use of Aether in order to keep the Petard Engines charged. Reinforcements are on the way from Fort Tarim, led by Magister Jakob, with more Singers coming from Kathis. I'd prefer that we tried to solve the problem by connecting the Vigil to the Roads rather than just by throwing more bodies at it, but that damnable ravine that guards the west gate of the place presents serious problems for any such construction, even without the time pressures."

"Will they hold?" asked Derelar, simply.

"For now, I think so," said Jarton. "You're talking about some hard-bitten veteran troops, supported by the most cold-hearted Volume in the Guard and led by some of the steadiest Magisters in the College. But in case they don't, the Weavers and the School of Walanstahl have come up with some alternatives."

Derelar nodded. "I have the plans for your 'Striders' here. I thought the art of battle-automata was the exclusive preserve of the Abelians?"

Jarton made a sour face. "It is, Thelen damn them. We can build constructs every bit as powerful as the Abelian Golems- the basic principle of moving a construct remotely is fairly well-understood, if little practised- but we can't make them act independently like they can. The Striders are the best we can manage. Each has to be controlled directly by a Magister but can operate at a distance of roughly a thousand feet from them. A few prototypes were built during the War of Rule as a countermeasure to the Gestalt Apes but the war ended before they could be effectively deployed and afterwards the School rather lost interest."

Derelar nodded again. Though he couldn't admit it to Jarton, the Strider program, along with the Singers and the Petard Engines, had been the direct result of his and Anneke's plan to prolong the War. Several other promising projects had similarly lost impetus with the abrupt end to the conflict.

"When can they be ready?" he asked.

"The two completed and functional prototypes are being brought out of storage now," said Jarton. "We can maybe have them at the Vigil in less than a week. Alternatively, we keep them at Lore and use them to help speed the project along."

"The latter," said Derelar immediately. "If the Vigil falls, it will do so before the Striders could reach it in any case. Are the evacuation plans in place?"

Jarton nodded. "Aye. I had hoped that they would remain a contingency, but lists of essential personnel and plans for their transportation to the nearest ports were already made and waiting for me in Anneke's files. We have agents watching the Vigil from a safe distance and should have enough warning if it falls. The Dendaril are relentless, but not especially swift."

"Grim times indeed," said Magister Julius. "Allow me to simplify your plans a little, Magister Jarton. If I am on any such list of evacuees, kindly remove me. I will not desert the Empire in the face of this threat."

Derelar frowned at him. "This is not a negotiation, Magister. If the Dendaril break through the Vigil, the best we will be able to do is slow them down a little. Any Magister taken by them will simply make our enemy stronger."

"I will not be taken," said Julius, stubbornly. "But I will not leave. I will self-Commit if necessary to prevent my infestation, but without the common folk the Empire is a shell and the College a sham. I will take no part in some... lingering remnant of our people, and that is my final word on the matter."

"Perhaps rather than debate philosophy you might give the Arch-Chancellor your report?" prompted Jarton gently as the other two Magisters glared at each other.

"Very well," said Julius. "As I am sure you are aware, Arch-Chancellor, late last night a woman's head was retrieved from the River Arget, some miles downstream from Lore. Though it was fish-bitten and bloated from immersion, Magister Gisela was able to positively identify it as the cranium of Anneke Belus. If any attempt was made to keep the head alive until the Vice-Chancellor's secrets could be gleaned from it, the High Chirurgeon found no evidence of it."

Derelar rifled through his papers until he found Gisela's report. "Hm, yes, so I see. Also no evidence of any drugs and only traces of alcohol in her blood. For the Vice-Chancellor, such a low level is in itself a little unusual."

"Say what you like about her, the woman could hold her drink," said Jarton with a small smile. "I don't think I ever saw her so much as merry, no matter what she downed."

"Indeed..." murmured Derelar, who had noted with some envy Anneke's exceptional alcohol tolerance on several occasions. There was something about Gisela's report that was bothering him, but he couldn't immediately put his finger on it.

"For my own part," continued Julius, "I found no sign of a struggle in the Vice-Chancellor's bedroom, and no blood spatter other than that on the bed and sink. I am presently working to determine the most likely place and time where the killer, or their accomplice, might have disposed of her severed head in the hope that this may present some fresh leads."

"Have you no suspects?" said Derelar. Julius shook his head.

"None against whom there is anything but the most circumstantial evidence. Magister Elsabeth left the Manse shortly before the body was discovered and is a six-Leaf. She has also, in the past, publicly criticised the Vice-Chancellor's methods, morals, and for that matter dress-sense. But the testimony of the Guards puts her in her coach whilst Anneke was still alive and in any case she was escorted to it by two of them, who would certainly have noticed if their mistress' severed head was in her possession. Magister Ollan Dane similarly has a public hatred of the Vice-Chancellor and is known to have his own network of spies and functionaries. He has also, in some circles, been tipped for the post of Vice-Chancellor if anything should happen to the prior incumbent. But he himself is currently at the Vigil and if agents of his were involved, they left no evidence."

Derelar nodded. "That is unfortunate. Do you have any other leads?"

Julius scratched at his chin. "I find the timing of this murder to be most singular, do you not, Arch-Chancellor? Just as my own investigation of the Vice-Chancellor's affairs was bearing fruit, she is killed, and killed at the exact time of day that will cause her own Manse's housekeeping spells to destroy much of the evidence. What little evidence we have points to an inside man- or given the Vice-Chancellor's proclivities, woman."

"You had previously exonerated Captain Ariel," pointed out Derelar.

"Quite, and I stand by that deduction." said Julius. "Eri Trevalyn would seem to present the next compelling suspect, but she was apparently present at Freeport according to Master Wen- it was she who absconded with Maike Dain and Captain Jerik. However, Master Wen also claims that the former Disruptor Dain is possessed of a mysterious power which she had been helping her learn to control. There remains a possibility, albeit a slim one, that between Guardswoman Eri's knowledge of the Manse's routines, and Maike Dain's new abilities, they had the means to commit this crime."

Jarton snorted. "That sounds more than a little far-fetched. What motive might they possibly have?"

"Per Captain Ariel, the Vice-Chancellor blamed Eri for the escape of Master Wen and Maike Dain from her custody," said Julius. "Accordingly, the same agents who were ordered to prevent me from making contact with Master Wen were tasked with killing or capturing her. Knowing Anneke as well as she did, Eri Trevalyn may have decided to retaliate pre-emptively. On the other hand, Captain Ariel also claims that Maike and Eri bore each other a deep-seated antipathy."

"Peril makes for strange bedfellows, as the poets put it," pointed out Jarton. "Still, I think you may be.. wandering into the realm of imagination, as you put it before."

"I cannot truthfully deny it," admitted Julius. "Arch-Chancellor, I simply require more data. With your permission, I will base myself at the Belus Manse for the duration of this investigation. There are more secrets there to unpick, I am certain of it. I should also like to request that you formally assign Master Wen to my custody."

Jarton chuckled. "You sly dog, Julius Thule. I wouldn't have thought you to be one for exotic women."

Julius flushed briefly, but swiftly regained his composure. "I think you have been in the company of the Vice-Chancellor too often, Learned Magister. Wen Lian-Shi possesses a unique viewpoint and perceptions outside the usual realm of College training. She will be, I believe, a significant asset for my investigation."

Derelar sighed. "Very well, Magister Julius. Magister Jarton, I trust Julius will enjoy your House's full co-operation?"

"Of course," said Jarton. "All levity aside, I want whatever bastard did this on the end of a rope. For all of her faults, Anneke was the Matriarch of our house."

"Indeed," said Derelar. "Now, Magister, we should turn our attention to the continuing unrest in Kathis. With the Sixth mostly at Fort Tarim..."

It was almost an hour later when Derelar finally found himself alone in his office once more. He picked up the papers again, and checked Gisela's autopsy report in more detail. There it was, at the bottom of the third page, tucked away in a summary of the blood analysis almost as an afterthought:

"The blood sample is a perfect match for that taken from the Messaging Chamber of the Manse, which witnesses confirm is that of the Vice-Chancellor. I can therefore conclude with complete certainty that the body is indeed that of Magister Anneke Belus. As expected, there was no match to any previously examined sample."

No match. And yet the blood Gisela had tested before had come from the same source- the blood that had confirmed the Vice-Chancellor to be a Dragon. Had Gisela simply not made the connection, and forgotten to check? Did Dragons even stay in their shape-shifted form when killed in it in any case?

He stood up, and crossed over to his personal library. He had some urgent research to do, and then a visit to pay to the Infirmary.

104

Some miles south of the great city of Shan'Xi'Sho, amidst pleasant, tree-lined fields and gentle rivers, lay the village of Hei-Xishu. The name, which in the most typical usage meant 'the sleep of Harmony', had been gifted to the place centuries ago by the first Son of Heaven, and had not been chosen by accident. Here, those Echoes of Clouds who had successfully served their purpose came to live out their remaining days in peaceful meditation. Echoes were usually well into their senior years by the time that they arrived at the village, and few lingered long, but a small army of attendants saw to it that their final days were pleasant and comfortable.

Bai Faoha reined in his *ryayan* and mopped at his sweating head with a silken cloth. The six-legged lizards used as mounts by the Daxalai possessed neither the elegance, nor the speed, of the horses of the east, but their endurance was legendary and their ferocity in battle formidable. That the Celestial Dragons had gifted their human subjects with riding beasts that so obviously shared their own blood was a fact that had exercised the minds of Sages for generations.

"I fail to understand why we are here, Great Sage," said White Crocus. "Surely, if the matter at hand is of such great importance, we should take the passage before the Son of Heaven Himself."

"An error, but an understandable one," said Smiling Snake, clambering down from his own mount and telling his body to ignore the pain in his back. Comfort was another area in which the Daxalai steed fell some way short of its mammalian counterpart. "Now, you will explain to me why this is so."

"Yes, *Shansenshao*," said White Crocus with a short bow, having similarly dismounted. He thought for a moment. "Ah. Were we to present a passage from the *Koze-Li-Sen* to the Son of Heaven, He would respond with.. the same passage, which the Echo of Clouds would then need to translate."

"A beginning," said Rya-Ki, leading the way towards the village. "But not yet the whole truth. Continue."

"When the passage was dictated to me," said White Crocus, "the Echo of Clouds was different to the present one. Since the interpretation of the *Koze-Li-Sen* is far more complex than some simple cypher, it follows that the translation now would not be the same as the translation that was intended. The Echo yesterday was an old man, who has now retired to Hei-Xishu, and only he can correctly interpret the passage."

"This is my belief," agreed Smiling Snake, "though such a thing has never been attempted before to my knowledge. And yet there is still more that you have failed to consider."

Bai Faoha stopped dead, and briefly released his staff, boxing his own ears and then catching it before it could fall. "Truly is it said that the greatest fool is he who believes himself wise! Were we to take the words before the Son of Heaven, the question of where they had come from would inevitably arise, and the man has yet to be born who can lie to the Emperor Himself. In a stroke, we would lay bare the secret of the Tapestry and throw the greatest advantage of the Hono clan away like rice before hungry birds."

"May the day such a man is born be long in coming," said Rya-Ki. "Nevertheless, it is as you say."

"And yet there is still more to my error?" said White Crocus.

"Perhaps. I am not such a fool as to believe myself wise enough to see every facet of that particular flawed stone. For now, though, it shall suffice. Come."

They walked in respectful silence across the small wooden bridge that led into the village, the soft chiming of their staffs seeming to resonate in harmony with the quiet murmurs of the stream. Smiling Snake had to admit to himself that he was grateful to have an excuse to visit this place. In every direction, the pinnacle of the art of *Koze-Heilin*, the art of wind and water, could be seen. Seven of the greatest masters of the discipline had laboured for seven years to landscape the village, and once their work was complete each had died the following morning, to be buried in the predetermined places in their final achievement.

They entered a wide open square, planted with willow trees perfectly sited to assist the flow of good *ki* into the modest, yet beautiful, houses that surrounded it. After a moment, a wooden door slid open, as close to silently as the immutable laws of nature would allow, and a pretty young serving-girl in a plain dawn-pink robe stepped out.

"This is a place of peaceful contemplation for those who have earned it by their life's service, Sages of the Hono," said the woman, her tone stern though her voice was pleasing. "Such a place is not a destination for the idle wanderer, nor a place of rest for the weary traveller."

"It is well, then, that we are neither," replied Smiling Snake with a bow, his own demeanour respectful. Ordinarily it would mean death for a commoner to speak to a Great Sage in such tones, but the keepers of Hei-Xishu had tended their charges for untold generations, and within its bounds their authority was second only to that of the Son of Heaven himself. He knelt, White Crocus following suit, and laid a cloth-wrapped bundle on the ground in front of him. "I bring a gift of food, comfort, and respect. Here shall you find figs of Ilshan province, known to be the finest ever grown. Here also is a Lakibird of the far east, gorged on exotic fruits until death. Its flesh is known as the sweetest and most tender of all beasts. Here too are smoking-leaf from Heinlan, sweetmeats of the Har'ii and a vial of ancient ambergris from the first Great Deep of the Blue Council. All these I offer in recompense for this most grievous of trespasses."

The young woman regarded him impassively. "Your contrition is received and recognised, Great Sage. Yet the man who goes well-equipped to pay recompense is he who has premeditated his transgression. Do not presume to think that you have escaped your just punishment through simple bribery, however fine your gifts or honeyed your words."

Smiling Snake gently slid the bundle towards the woman, before pressing his face to the ground. "I understand, O keeper, and ask only that my vassal's punishment be laid upon me instead. I am his *Senshao*, and the fault is mine and mine alone."

Though he could not see it, he could hear the woman's manner soften slightly as she spoke. "This is proper. Before your penance, the keepers would know why you have come here."

"A message was received from a source unknown to us," said Smiling Snake. "It is in the words of the *Koze-Li-Sen*, and its meaning may be vital to the security of the Harmony. I wish to present these words to Toh Lonshao, he who was Echo when they were dictated."

"None may disturb the peace of the Echoes," said the keeper. "However, if you will share with me these words, I will ask the honoured Toh Lonshao if it will please him to hear them."

"It is more than this lowly servant of Harmony could have dreamed to achieve, keeper," said Smiling Snake. "Bai Faoha?"

The younger Sage had maintained a respectful silence throughout the exchange, and had to cough to clear his throat. "Y-yes, Great Sage. The message was: *'The bounty of Yaoin-Lao was great, and gleaned at equally great cost, but when the ships of the Tshuh were sighted off Heinlaon, all saw its value.'*"

The woman stared at him intently. "Those were the exact words?"

Bai Faoha nodded. "They were, keeper. I have them in writing, if it will assist?"

The woman ignored the question, and stooped to pick up the bundle. "You will wait here, Sages of the Hono. If you are gone when I return, your clan's lands and titles will be forfeit."

The keeper stepped back into the house she had emerged from, and the door slid shut.

"Can she make such a decree?" asked Bai Faoha, quietly.

"It is made," replied Smiling Snake, his face still pressed to the ground. "Whether it could be enforced is a question I have no desire to learn the answer to. Now, be silent in this place of peace."

105

*I*t was early in the afternoon by the time the Royal Army came into sight of the Farspan. They had passed through Naxxiamor a little over an hour earlier, and had added Sir Jeremiah and Lady Alizabeth to their ranks, along with the Assemblage of Golems under their command. As far as Thalia could make out from the map-table, that put the Royal Army's strength at almost 1300 Stickmen, one hundred and twenty War Golems, and a hundred Royal Knights, supported by thirty or so Wizards. The force certainly looked impressive, but compared with the hundreds of thousands believed to be in the Dendaril horde it felt distinctly small, and she had said so.

"The secret is concentration of force, Lady Thalia," said Lady Alizabeth, who had invited herself to visit the *Dreadnought*. "It's certainly true that these Dendaril outnumber us heavily, and were we seeking to fight a conventional campaign we would find it difficult to prevail. But a single Assemblage of Wood Golems is a match for ten times its own number of the Dendaril, poorly-equipped as they are, and a Demolition of War Golems... well, one of those things would be more than a match for those Gestalt Apes your Royalists used during that unpleasant civil war of yours. Eight of them in concert, correctly commanded, is a force only a full Seminar of Magisters could likely halt. Now, though the Dendaril certainly possess Gifted, for the most part they rely on simple weapons, the raw strength imparted by their... condition, and sheer numbers, as well as the fact that killing them only spreads those horrible little flies."

"But the Golems and Royal Knights are immune to the Shrive-Ticks, aren't they?" said Thalia.

"Quite so. And because the Golems always operate in very tight formations, there's simply no way for enough Dendaril to overcome them to attack them at once. So you see, so long as we prevent them from splitting up to attack multiple important locations at the same time, there's no real way that they can win. That's why Jerry and I will be stopping at the Farspan. With our Demolition, plus an

Assemblage and the ballistae towers, we can hold it against any attempt to slip past the Royal Army and attack the Kingdom directly."

"It... doesn't really seem fair, does it, Learned Magister?" said Athas, sadly. Alizabeth laughed gently, and patted his knee.

"Sergeant, you have a good, kind heart, but this is a war, and the first rule of war is to avoid a fair fight at all costs. Any time two equally-matched armies face each other on the battlefield, someone on both sides has committed a serious strategic blunder. Ideally, of course, you outmanoeuvre the enemy so completely that they realise they can't win and surrender on the spot. The *Treatise of War* calls this a 'white victory', and those generals who achieve one are highly-praised."

"You know a lot about strategy, Lady Alizabeth," said Athas, admiringly. "I just know how to hit people really hard and shout at the lads."

"Both are admirable skills in their own right, Sergeant," said the Abelian, and Thalia began to get an uneasy feeling that she was trying to seduce the big Guard. "For my part, I have been studying martial matters since the Queen made it known that our traditional societal roles were a luxury we could ill-afford. Jerry, I'm afraid, is more a man after your own heart and he's terribly disappointed not to be crossing the Farspan." She sighed. "I can see why. These Dendaril possess little grasp of strategy but they are numerous and determined. Today's victory will not be white, I fear, but crimson."

They dropped the Wizard off at the Farspan soon afterwards, and Thalia studied the map table with some surprise. The Dendaril were here, but they were not attacking. Instead, they seemed to have gathered at a safe distance from the far end of the bridge, well out of range of the ballistae. The Abelians were in danger of being stopped at their own choke-point. From the look of the Royal Army's disposition, the Queen and her generals were of the same opinion.

"That's a lot of.. red blobs," said Athas, frowning at the floating image.

"That's the Dendaril," said Thalia. "If I read this correctly, there's a force ten thousand strong waiting at the far end of the bridge. It's not going to be easy for the Royal Army to break out, but see this blue rune here? That's the War Golems. The Abelians are sending... Thelen's breath!"

"What?" said Athas. "There's a blue blob moving along the bridge. That's good, yeah?"

"It's the symbol for the... fifteenth Demolition," said Thalia. "That means, against ten thousand Dendaril, the Abelians have sent eight Golems. The rest are holding position with the army."

"Wow..." said Athas. "They really must believe that those things are invincible."

Thalia sighed, and flopped back on the padded seat. "You saw them when we first got here. Can you imagine having nothing but a breastplate and a short-sword to fight against them with? Still, I don't see why the Abelians haven't sent more of them into the attack. The Queen doesn't exactly strike me as the subtle sort."

"Maybe the Abelians don't trust the bridge either," said Athas. "I bet those Golems are pretty heavy."

Thalia stared at him. "Blood, ice and fire, I hadn't even considered that! The Royal Knights, these enormous wagons, the Golems- if this entire force tried to cross the Farspan at once..." her voice trailed off. How strong was the bridge's magic, after all those centuries? If it had been built by hands as skilled as those which had constructed Xodan then surely it would hold, and yet..

Suddenly she was on her feet, and heading for the door of the *Dreadnought*.

"L-learned Magister?" said Athas, standing up only to slam his head against the ceiling. "Ow! What are you doing?"

"I need to talk to the Queen at once," said Thalia. "You are at more risk from the Dendaril than I, Sergeant. You should remain here."

Athas shook his head. "I'm sorry, Learned Magister, but I'm your bodyguard, remember? Anyway, those fly-things feed on magic, don't they? If any of them try to eat me, they'll starve to death."

There was no time to argue, and within minutes Thalia was half running, half striding, towards the *Valiant*. Lady Annabelle and the rest of the Royal Guard were standing outside the vehicle, watching the Queen as she studied a projection of the map display emanating from a crystal on the top of the *Valiant's* roof.

"Lady Thalia!" shouted Annabelle as she approached. "To be out of your carriage so close to the Dendaril is most unwise. You should return at once."

Setting her jaw, Thalia ignored the Knight completely, walking straight past her. The woman was so surprised that Thalia was in speaking distance of the Queen before she felt a gauntleted hand close on her arm.

"Queen Tondarin! Your Exceptional Majesty, I must speak with you! Ouch, let go of me, you armour-plated aristocratic cretin!"

At the Queen's side, the Guardian took a single, ominous step forward, though whether to block Thalia from reaching Tondarin or to rescue her from Annabelle's grip was unclear. The Queen clearly couldn't tell either, and raised a hand to her general.

"That will do, Lady Annabelle. If Lady Thalia is determined to risk her own life, we shall allow her to do so, though if this is about the Guardian again.."

Reluctantly, Annabelle released Thalia's arm, and the Guardian immediately stepped back to the Queen's side.

"Your War Golems," said Thalia, without further preamble. "What powers them?"

"Hah!" laughed the Queen. "You've picked a fine time to try and steal our military secrets, Magister. Why should we tell you that?"

"Fine," said Thalia. "Then at least answer me this- do the Golems absorb Aether- I mean Spirit- from their surroundings as they fight, like a living being?"

"Of course they do!" snapped Lady Annabelle. "They could scarcely operate for long if they did not. Your Exceptional Majesty, allow me to-"

Tondarin glared at her. "Shut up, Annie. If we want you to speak for us, we will tell you. What is your point, Lady Thalia?"

"The Farspan is reinforced with magic," said Thalia. "If it wasn't, it would have collapsed long ago."

"It couldn't even have been built without magic!" laughed Tondarin. "But it has stood for centuries and does so on a place of power, so it is hardly likely to fail now."

"The Demolition is almost a third of the way across the bridge, Your Exceptional Majesty," reported one of the other Knights, quietly. "No movement from the enemy as of yet."

"Probably starting to realise what's coming," chuckled another. "Getting ready to break and run, I'll wager."

"I'll take that bet, shit-for-brains," said Athas, suddenly. "Maybe you should listen to what the Magister has to say? She wouldn't come out here like this if it wasn't important, would she?"

"Peasant!" snapped the Knight. "Your Exceptional Majesty, I demand-"

"Choose your next words very carefully, Sir Bryan," said Tondarin, coldly. "Or better yet, still your yapping tongue. A Knight has no need of one to serve. Lady Thalia, continue."

"Y-yes, well," said Thalia. "From what your people have told me about the Dendaril, they use magic to gain strength like a Sealed soldier would. The Golems use it to do.. well, everything. The bridge is using it to stay in one piece. But in a pitched battle, once fatigue starts to set in, the local supply of Ae- Spirit starts to run out. Usually, something as powerful as the Farspan, built on a place of power, wouldn't be able to run out of Spirit, but if it's supporting the weight of your Golems and ten thousand Dendaril, *and* they start fighting.."

"Queen's Grace..." gasped Annabelle. "Could it be true?"

"The Demolition approaches the half-way point, Your Exceptional Majesty," said the Knight watching the display. "The.. the enemy is moving."

"Hah!" laughed Sir Bryan. "There they go, tails between their... no, wait, that can't be right... Sir Ambrose?"

"They're advancing," confirmed the other Knight.

"But that makes no damn sense!" snapped Sir Bryan. "Even in the open field the Demolition outclasses those idiots. In the narrow confines of the bridge they stand no chance at all..."

"Recall the Demolition," snapped the Queen, suddenly.

"Your Exce-"

"Recall it!" Tondarin practically screamed. Thalia could see from the display that the controllers of the Demolition had already heard the Queen's command. The Demolition was retreating, but long-limbed though the Golems were the Dendaril were moving at exceptional speed and were clearly the swifter. Suddenly, the light from the display flickered, and then went out entirely.

"Wh- what happened?" said Sir Bryan.

"The scrying-spell has been disrupted," said Sir Ambrose. "It's often a danger when using them at extreme ranges- enemy Gifted can tamper with the signals. If I reset the sigils for local operation... there."

The display flared back into life, the Golems now appearing right on the far edge of it. "That's as far as I can give you, Your Exceptional Majesty."

"There are Pilgrims abroad, I'll wager," said Sir Bryan. "And yet they do not strike at the Golems?"

"The Golems were never the target!" shouted Thalia. "The Farspan itself is! If this bridge is destroyed, there's no way we could get to the Eastern Vigil fast enough to stop the Dendaril overrunning it!"

Tondarin slammed her gauntleted hand into her palm. "She's right. They must have been hoping that we'd commit more of our force to the attack, that's the only reason they'd have waited. Mounts!"

As soon as Tondarin shouted the word, all ten Knights present closed their helmet visors, and turned to their waiting horses. Thalia stood, mouth agape.

"I- what in Thelen's holy name are you doing? That bridge is going to fall, and there's nothing you can do about it!" She stared at the Farspan with her Aether-sight, but the thing's Pattern was far too vast to comprehend.

"The time for talking is over, Lady Thalia," said the Queen, wheeling her massive horse, purple skirts fluttering behind her. "Now is the time for deeds! Valour Defiant!"

"Valour Defiant!" echoed the Knights, and together they galloped for the bridge, the Guardian running with loping strides behind them but rapidly losing ground.

"Of all the pin-headed, short-sighted, hot-tempered pea-brained blue-blooded idiots ever to command an army-" began Thalia, but Athas cut her off with a whoop.

"Wow, Learned Magister, look at them go! What a jump!"

Thalia's mouth fell open again. The Royal Knights had reached the foot of the bridge at full gallop, but they weren't riding along it. Rather, they had split into two columns, and in a single bound landed on top of the broad side railings of the bridge, their huge horses every bit as sure-footed as Delys had been when she had done the same. Couched lances of shimmering light sprang into being under the arms of each Knight, and were employed to shatter those few intact statues that completely blocked their passage. Within minutes, the entire Royal Guard had disappeared from sight. The map display beside the *Valiant* shimmered, and went out again.

Thalia turned on her heel. "Come on, Sergeant."

"What? Where are we going, Learned Magister?"

"Back to the *Dreadnought*," said Thalia. "Either to see what's happening, or to take cover from its aftermath."

106

$\mathcal{P}$ilgrim Williard watched as the might of the Dendaril surged onto the crude stone bridge. An observer- at least one without the benefit of the Blessing- might think that Williard and his fellow Pilgrim, Maryalla, were trailing at the rear of their forces out of cowardice, or some other desire for self-preservation. They would have been correct only in the sense that both Pilgrims were delaying their Ending for as long as they could in the hope that their Bearers would not be wasted. For the time being, however, they had a more important task even than spreading the Blessing.

He reached out his senses towards the mighty stone structure, feeling the pulse of Vrae running through it. There was such power in the thing, squandered on the simple task of crossing a ravine. As twenty thousand booted feet pounded across its span, he felt the magic surge in response, the heavy stone, brittle with age, demanding more and more support. Every man and woman in the Dendaril horde was pushing themselves to the utmost, straining every sinew, leeching the ambient Vrae of the place away through the hunger of their joined souls. Soon, they would catch the mighty silver war-constructs and the killing would begin, stealing yet more energy from the structure and scattering it in the tiny forms of the Bearers that would be released as the Blessed hurled themselves at the enemy.

This sacrifice alone, of course, would not be enough to cause the bridge- the Farspan, the High Pilgrims had called it- to collapse. The ancient builders of the structure had been far too skilled for that, however simple their work might appear to the untrained eye. No, to bring it down would require someone to directly tap into the bridge's Weave and drain the Vrae from it. Ordinarily, such a feat would require a highly-skilled practitioner of magic, one far beyond a mere Pilgrim's poor talents, but with the strain the Farspan was under its Weave was alight with the flow of Vrae and the weak points were far easier to discern.

In fact, thought Williard suddenly, frowning, they were a little *too* easy to find.

When his people had begun moving, the bridge had resonated with the rhythm of their advance, sending bright pulses through the Weave that were simple to follow, but now that pattern had been accented with a new, more urgent pulse. It was making his task considerably easier, of course, and he exchanged a glance of triumph with Maryalla as they simultaneously latched on to the power and began to strip it away, but there was still something concerning about it. Within a few minutes, the Farspan would be critically destabilised and the route to the Kingdom of Abelia sealed off as the Elucidated Pilgrims had decreed, but whatever was causing the new pulse was moving extremely rapidly. And it was coming closer.

He motioned to the commander of the five-hundred-strong honour guard that stood between the Pilgrims and the end of the bridge. These troops were the cream of the Crusade, wearing helms and breastplates and carrying not only short swords and steel shields, but also long spears. Immediately, the guards stood to, closing ranks into a square around the Pilgrims and presenting their shields, their spears thrust out ahead of them. It was merely a precaution, of course. There was no way any of the Abelians, even their vaunted Knights, would be able to break through ten thousand bodies in minutes, even if most of them were armed only with tree-branch clubs and rocks.

"Valour Defiant!"

The cry jolted Williard out of his complacency almost immediately. In one respect he had been quite correct- the Royal Knights had not broken through the Dendaril. Instead, they had simply gone straight past them. He could see them now, in the distance, coming closer with every beat of his hammering heart. Elucidated be thanked, there were only ten of them, but their speed, and the effortless grace with which their massive steeds galloped across the top of the walls at either side of the bridge, was breathtaking.

"By the golden domes of Tor Goroth...." he gasped, his mouth falling open. After a moment's stunned inaction, during which the galloping figures seemed to at least triple in size in his vision, he realised he was losing control of the power. Quickly, he redoubled his efforts, hoping against hope that between them he and Maryalla could destroy the bridge before the interlopers arrived. It wasn't looking likely. Not only were the Knights accelerating, but someone at the far end of the bridge seemed to have worked out what was going on and started to pour fresh Vrae into the structure's Weave.

"Stand firm, Warriors of the Crusade!" roared the commander of the honour guard. "Keep those spear-tips up! Remember, horses won't charge a shield-wall!"

Williard almost sobbed in relief. Of course, that was true- the Elucidated Pilgrims had been foresighted to allocate a unit of spear-men to this critical mission. The histories were clear on this point- once a horse saw a wall of spears and shields in its path, it would shy away. The Dendaril themselves had never faced horses in open battle, but the essential nature of the beasts could not have changed. He returned his attention to the Farspan. Whatever was going on at the other end was slowing progress, but ultimately it wouldn't matter. So long as even part of the structure was stripped of Vrae it would fail. The Knights would probably get off the bridge before it fell, but they would simply get to watch impotently from outside the square as their only route home- and to their reinforcements and supplies- was destroyed forever.

Then the lead Knight leapt from the bridge, and Williard realised the depth of his error. Everyone knew a horse wouldn't charge a square of spear-wielding infantry that it saw in front of it. The Abelians clearly knew it as well, which was presumably why the all-encasing armour of their mounts had not been equipped with eye-sockets, or vision slits of any kind.

What sort of training would compel a horse to gallop full-pelt into battle whilst completely blind? The question nagged at Williard's mind as the first Knight, a woman in richly-decorated golden armour with billowing purple skirts, crashed into the line. Bodies were flung far and wide like the toys of a petulant child as the Knights came on, spears snapping like twigs before them. Bearers tore themselves free of the ruined husks of their hosts and descended in hungry, angry swarms on the enemy, but against the close-fitting, magically-sealed armour they could find no purchase. The square had disintegrated now, the soldiers casting aside their spears and hurling themselves at the Knights with their short-swords, seeking to bring them down through weight of numbers, and the Pilgrim's heart leapt as he saw a Knight unhorsed, her mount staggering under the weight of twenty men clawing and stabbing at its armour.

A terrible scream from just beside him killed the hope in his breast. He whirled, to see Maryalla impaled on a shining silver lance, lifted from her feet by the impact of the weapon that protruded two feet out of her back. Bearers raged impotently about the Pilgrim as she gritted her teeth and gripped the weapon that had killed her, yanking at it and pulling it further into her body, drawing herself almost face-to-face with her murderer.

"Queen's Grace!" exclaimed the Knight, his helm flaring with light as he spoke. "What-"

With her dying breath, Maryalla clamped her hands on either side of the Knight's helm, and released the sum total of the Vrae she had gleaned from the Farspan. With a sound like a crack of thunder, the Knight's head came apart in a shower of bone, gore and brains, splattering all in the area with crimson. Hungry Bearers burrowed deep into the headless corpse even before it toppled from the saddle.

"Sir Bryan!" shouted the nearest Knight, raising a glowing silver sword to strike Williard down, but the golden-armoured woman held up a hand.

"Hold, Sir Ambrose! Pilgrim, your plan has failed. Your soldiers are slain, and when your people reach the end of the Farspan they will find no thoroughfare. If you will order them to retreat, and remove yourself from this place to your own lands, we shall grant your people clemency."

Williard stared dully at the ravaged corpse of Maryalla. "Who are you to offer such mercy, woman?"

"We are Queen Tondarin of Abelia," said the armoured woman, with surprising gentleness. "We offer our condolences for the death of your companion, but she was engaged in an act of war against the Kingdom and had to be stopped. Now, we ask again- will you yield?"

Williard laughed. He could see what to do now. Maryalla had shown him the way. "Yield? Oh yes, I will yield, Queen of Abelia, but not to you."

"My Queen!" cried the Knight next to her, starting forward. "I think he's-"

The warning came too late. Williard threw every iota of his power into a last blast of Vrae every bit as powerful as that which Maryalla had released, but where hers was focussed, his was broad. It would not slay the Queen and her Knights, he thought in his last moment, but it did not need to. All the Bearers would need was a tiny crack in those suits of armour, and that crack, he would give them.

107

The *Dreadnought* rolled off the ancient stones of the Farspan and back onto natural earth, and Thalia breathed a sigh of relief. The Abelian Wizards, ordered into action by the Queen as she rode, had done all they could to reinforce the ancient structure, but Thalia herself had been forced to simply wait. Unfamiliar as she was with the practice of Abelian magic, any attempt she might have made to assist could easily have done more harm than good.

The Dendaril horde had been almost three-quarters of the way across the Farspan when they hit the retreating Demolition of Golems, which had placed them comfortably in range of the ballistae in the guard towers. Instead of firing the huge bolts that made them so feared, the Stickman crews had loaded less powerful, but no less terrible, ammunition- bundles of simple wooden bolts held together by only the very weakest of spells. When fired, the bundles rapidly separated, peppering a wide area with fast-moving, if mundane, projectiles. The effect of those bolts on the heavily-armoured Golems was negligible, but the densely-packed mass of Dendaril peasant-soldiers had no such protection. With the Demolition turned back to fight, ranged across the width of the bridge with shields lowered and axe-heads raised, there was no way through for the poor wretches. Thousands had finally fled back to the forest, but thousands more lay dead on the bridge, their remains ground into a pulp under the marching feet of the Golems and the heavy wheels of the wagons.

"This is terrible, isn't it, Learned Magister?" said Athas, peering out of one of the *Dreadnought*'s windows as the scene of the Royal Guard's sally came into sight. "All those people killed. They didn't stand a chance, even if they won!"

Thalia nodded. "Yes, Sergeant. It seems the Dendaril considered ten thousand people a small price to pay to destroy the Farspan and prevent the Royal Army's advance. What terrifies me is that most of the time, from what I know of them, the Dendaril are reasonable, pleasant, even friendly. They would far rather spread their 'blessing' to those they meet without violence."

"I don't know about that, Learned Magister," said Athas. "I'd think a fly-thingy burrowing into your head was pretty violent, however they did it."

Thalia nodded. "That's true, though the infestation can also be... sexually transmitted. What I mean, though, is that one moment they seem comparatively sane, and the next.. this."

Athas had blushed bright red. "You mean they can put one of those things in you by... sleeping with you? Yuck. Er.. I just had a really, really nasty thought."

Thalia was looking out of the other window now. There seemed to be a gathering of Knights near the bridge, but she couldn't see what was happening. "What's that, Sergeant?"

"Well, it's just that it's a good thing these Dendaril never got to Dalliance, isn't it?"

Thalia's heart almost froze in her chest. She remembered their discussion about the Abelian Navy, how it protected the coast against the Dendaril. At the time, she had imagined a Dendaril invasion fleet, but it wouldn't take that. All you would need were a few handsome, virile young men in a boat, and the cream of Abelian nobility would be lining up to strengthen their precious bloodlines. Of course, most of the nobles were Royal Knights or Wizards, so they would be unlikely to fall for so simple a trick.

Wouldn't they?

The Guardian was marching over to the group of Knights now, and Thalia recognised the Queen's golden armour amongst them. She picked up her staff.

"Er.. what are you doing, Learned Magister?" said Athas, warily.

"I'm going out there, what does it look like?" replied Thalia.

"B-but, you can't!" stammered Athas. "There's still some of those things out there! The Abelians were really, really particular about this- once we cross the bridge, we stay in the *Dreadnought!*"

"I know," said Thalia. "But something has gone wrong," She turned to look back at the big Guard. "Stay here, Athas. I mean it this time. You can't protect me here, and I don't want to risk hurting you."

"But-" began Athas, starting forwards, but Thalia opened the door and slipped out before he could stop her, immediately sealing it shut behind her. Concentrating, she cast the protective spell known as the Flame-Wreath of Ixilinath by the College. The spell surrounded her with an egg-shaped curtain of flame that made it tricky to see where she was going and made the bloody, trampled grass underfoot smoulder with an evil smell. It was rarely used, especially indoors, but Thalia knew it would keep the Shrive-Ticks at bay. For the hour or so she could keep it up, at least.

Her precautions taken, she strode over to the small group of Knights. Beside them, two bodies lay under Abelian flags, and it didn't take Magister Julius to deduce who lay under them. Only eight Knights remained in the Royal Guard, and two of those lay before their kneeling fellows.

"Lady Thalia," said the Queen, flatly. "Once again, you choose to risk your life for no good reason."

Thalia looked down, recognising the armour of Sir Ambrose and Lady Annabelle. "What happened?"

"We stopped them." said the Queen. "But there was a cost. We lost Sir Bryan

433

and Lady Tiliath in the fight, but that was only the beginning. The last Pilgrim.. he.."

Tondarin stopped talking, and despite the all-encasing armour Thalia could tell she was crying.

"He spat in the face of Her Exceptional Majesty's offer of truce," growled Sir Ambrose, struggling to rise despite his shattered helm and the blood streaming from his nose. "Even as she offered mercy, he released his stolen power, seeking to crack our armour and leave us exposed to those.. things. Agh... Queen's Grace, it hurts."

"He partially succeeded," said Tondarin, recovering some composure. "Had Sir Ambrose and Lady Annabelle not realised the peril and thrown themselves in the way, all of us might have fallen. As it was, only they suffered enough damage to their armour for those evil creatures to get in."

Thalia looked from one Knight to another incredulously. "Then.. why aren't you doing something?"

"We are," said the Queen. "We will attend our faithful Knights until the end, and then see to it that they do not rise again as Dendaril. After that, their remains will be repatriated with honour so that their families might make the appropriate arrangements."

"You gold-plated, cold-hearted harridan!" snapped Thalia. "I mean why don't you save them?"

"Only a Healer could do that," said Tondarin, so deep in her misery that she ignored the insults. "And no Healer can step into the presence of these creatures and long survive. This infestation is beyond the simple medical skills of a Knight or a Wizard."

Thalia threw up her hand in exasperation. "Thelen's breath! Sometimes, with all your magnificent devices, I forget most of you Abelians have the magical knowledge of a third-year Twig. Stay there, and for Sherenith's sake don't do anything until I get back. You two- fight this, damn you!"

When Thalia returned several minutes later, she was accompanied by Eldrik, the Wizard she had met the previous day, Lady Ysabella, Sir Hektor and Sir Terence. The two Wizards looked distinctly nervous, but both had cast flaming shields of their own. Sir Hektor had refused to let his wife out of his sight on such a "damned fool errand," and Thalia had a particular need for Sir Terence.

"Your Exceptional Majesty!" gasped the Knight, rushing forward. "Are you all right?"

"We are," replied the Queen. "Though we are displeased that two Wizards have ignored our specific commands."

"Blame me for that," said Thalia. "But I thought you might want to keep your Knights alive more than you want your every command followed. If I'm wrong about that, you can always have me whipped or something later. Now, you two, move to the side of the Knights and do as I showed you."

"Be careful, my love," said Sir Hektor. "I cannot lose you to this."

Lady Ysabella smiled. "Stop playing the fool, Hektor. Eldrik- now!"

Quickly, the two Wizards dropped their fire-shields, hurried to the side of the fallen Knights, and cast them again, but this time combining their power into a larger, dome-shaped shield that extended for a radius of some ten feet around them. Thalia nodded, dispelling her own shield.

"Well done. Remember to warn me if you begin to weaken. Sir Terence, keep that flask of yours handy."

"I did mention to you how long it takes to distil this liquor, didn't I?" grumbled Sir Terence, but he did as he was bid.

"Right," said Thalia. "Sir Ambrose, can you still release your armour? I need to get a better look at you."

"I... no, damn it," said Sir Ambrose. "The control sigils were completely scrambled by the blast. I can barely even move."

"My apologies to your family, Sir Ambrose," said the Queen, reaching down and tearing the breastplate of the Knight's armour clear. "Will that be sufficient, Lady Thalia?"

Thalia blinked. "Er.. yes, thank you. Now, let's get a look at what we're dealing with."

She trained her Aethersight on Sir Ambrose, studying his Pattern. Yes, there the evil little thing was. The Shrive-Tick had burrowed all the way through the Knight's ear, and was already starting to bore into his brain. There was no time even to warn the Knight what she was going to do. She sent a questing tendril of Aether into the man's ear, seized the loathsome thing with it, and yanked. Sir Ambrose screamed in agony, sat bolt upright, and then passed out, crashing down into the bloody earth again.

"Sacred blood of Thecla!" gasped Sir Hektor. "Is.. is he?"

"He'll live," said Thalia. "Though he'll need treatment from your Healers to deal with any bleeding in there or any bits of that thing that I missed. Now, on to Lady Annabelle."

Annabelle's treatment proved easier than Sir Ambrose's. The captain of the Royal Guard had been unhorsed in the fighting and had conjured a shield to go with her sword, and had managed to get it in between her and the Pilgrim just in time. The blast had still destroyed the shield, her left gauntlet and two fingers, but her armour was still functional and the Tick had failed to get as far as her brain, instead working its way along the flesh of her arm. She managed to stay conscious throughout the procedure, and stepped back into her damaged armour afterwards.

"Right," said Thalia, noting that both Lady Ysabella and Eldrik had taken a sip of Sir Terence's flask. "Now all we need to do is get Sir Ambrose back to your Healers. Which carriage are they in?"

"There are no Healers with the Royal Army," said Tondarin. "As I said, they would be in danger here, and in any case, it is rare for a Royal Knight to be injured in battle."

Thalia gaped at her. "What? Do you really think you're invincible, even after this?"

"No, Lady Thalia," said Annabelle, gesturing with her damaged hand. "It is rare for a blow powerful enough to penetrate our armour to not kill the Knight instantly. As it is, only the Artificers of Aquila can repair it."

The Queen nodded. "Lady Annabelle, you are relieved. Take Sir Ambrose in the *Indefatigable* and return to Naxxiamor for treatment, then convey his armour and your own to Aquila. If it can be repaired swiftly enough, return afterwards and aid Sir Jeremiah in the defence of the Farspan. Valour Defiant!"

"Valour Defiant, Your Exceptional Majesty," replied Annabelle. The Shrive-Ticks had largely fled by now, driven away by the magic of the Wizards and their hunger for easier meat, but Thalia was still relieved when she reached the *Dreadnought*. Before she could board, the Queen rode up to her.

"Lady Thalia! There is still the matter of your punishment for disobeying my orders. Furthermore, you caused two other Wizards to risk themselves without my express permission."

Thalia drew herself up to her full height, which just about brought her up to the top of the Queen's armoured boot. "Yes, I did. I'm not going to apologise for it, either."

"I see." said Tondarin, quietly. "It seems that the hot blood of the Daran line runs through your veins after all." She produced a bottle from her saddlebag. "This is a bottle of Kingswater Chêrelle, a particularly fine sweet, sparkling white that also happens to be staggeringly alcoholic. Before you retire to sleep tonight, I expect you to have personally finished the entire bottle. This is a royal command, Lady Thalia, and I will not tolerate you disobeying me again. Is that clear?"

Thalia nodded, solemnly taking the bottle. "Yes, Your Exceptional Majesty."

"Good," said the Queen, wheeling her horse. "I expect the resulting hangover to be more than sufficient punishment. Good day to you, Lady Thalia... and thank you."

108

The Magister became aware of someone trying to get his attention, and shook them off in irritation. The only thing that mattered was the Engine, he had to make sure the Engine kept firing. He couldn't really remember what an Engine was, or what 'firing' was or why the first needed to keep doing the second, but that wasn't important.

The only thing that was important was making sure the Engine kept firing.

"Haran! Damn it all man, snap out of it! Haran!"

Haran? What was a Haran? Suddenly, without any warning, the world exploded into a flash of light and pain. The Magister- no, Magister Haran Dar, that was who he was- sprawled on the cold stone floor and spat blood.

"Thelen's breath, was that really necessary, Captain?" said Magister Ollan, looking down at the other Magister as he blinked himself back into awareness.

"It worked, didn't it?" said Captain Render, putting her armoured gauntlet back on. "After all, Mighty Xaraya did much the same to you, or so I hear."

"Er, not exactly, she didn't," said Ollan, quickly. "But that is a tale for another time. How do you feel, Haran?"

Haran sat up on the floor. "Like my Guard Captain just slapped me very hard around the face, Learned Magister. What happened?" He reached for his staff, which was lying on the floor a little distance from him, but Ollan slid it further away with his boot.

"I wouldn't, Haran, not yet. Your staff is totally drained and you need to get your strength back before you even think about touching it. The reinforcements arrived- a little late, I might add, but welcome."

"That would be my fault, I fear," said a voice Haran recognised from behind him. He turned, to see the slender figure of Magister Pieter, the enigmatic Chancellor of Verge. "I persuaded Magister Jakob to allow me to lead the reinforcements in his stead. Ah, excuse me, Magisters, but the Choirmasters must begin their work."

437

The three Magisters stepped aside to allow the robed Singers and their Choir-master to file in, the Singers already chanting the Hymnal of Devastation.

"I was, I am afraid, guilty of an error of judgement," said Pieter. "I believed that as the former Chair of Yar, Magister Jakob was better employed securing Fort Tarim against Dendaril invaders whilst my own talents in healing would be of more use to you. I did not anticipate that the extra hours of delay this caused would have such a.. dramatic effect upon you. For that matter, I expected to find the Singers still operating the Petard Engines, not an *ad hoc* alliance of Magister and Warlock."

"It certainly wasn't my preferred option, Chancellor Pieter," said Haran, wincing. His head was pounding and even the dim, fitful illumination of the flickering glow-crystals seemed far too bright. Pieter suddenly gasped in alarm.

"Magister Haran, your nose is bleeding! We should take you to the Infirmary at once. Magister Ollan, Captain, your assistance, please. Quickly, now!"

Pieter's voice seemed to be coming from very far away, and Haran suddenly realised that the floor was at an odd angle. In fact, on closer inspection, it appeared to be coming his way at some speed.

When he awoke some hours later, Magritte was at his bedside. She quickly sent a runner to fetch Magister Pieter, and passed Haran a glass of ice-water.

"What happened," said Haran, and then, realising that this was becoming a habit, added "this time?"

"Magister Pieter says your Patterns briefly separated," said Magritte. "Your mind had sort of.. come unstuck from your body, and it knocked you out. At least I think that's what he meant."

"Your adjutant has it close enough, Learned Magister," said Pieter, arriving with Ollan and Captain Render in tow. "You had entered such a state of deep focus that your body had begun to shut down. Impressive, as a feat of magic, but deeply unsatisfactory for a man planning to continue living in the traditional, corporeal sense."

"You did a better job than me, Haran," chuckled Ollan. "It turns out that the habitual pipe-smoker can't get away with that sort of thing- I had to stop every hour or so to try to cough my lungs out."

"You have been suppressing a distinctly unpleasant tumour in your left lung with your magic, Learned Magister," said Pieter. "As soon as you began to enter a deep state of focus on the Engine, you stopped doing so and suffered the consequences. I suggest that once this whole affair is over, you pay a visit to High Chirurgeon Gisela- completely removing a growth of that magnitude would challenge a Healer of lesser skill and is certainly beyond mine."

Ollan's eyebrows shot up. "Have I really? Thelen's breath, and there I thought I was just a little out of shape."

"I would be remiss to not point out that this is also, in fact, true," said Pieter with a wry smile. "Regardless, Magister Haran, Magister Ollan has updated me on the events leading up to my arrival. Under the circumstances, I must say you have conducted yourself with the utmost skill and honour in the highest traditions of the College."

Haran blinked at him. "I.. thank you, Chancellor."

Pieter waved a hand dismissively. "Please, Learned Magisters, that title is meaningless here and frankly practically meaningless even in Verge. Magister

Pieter is all I would lay claim to. With no faculty, I am no more a Chancellor than a man in an empty field is a shepherd."

Ollan chuckled. "Not that meaningless, Pieter. It meant you could lay your hands on two more Choirs at short notice. Haran, we have four full Choirs now, working in rotation. The Vigil should be able to hold the Dendaril at bay almost indefinitely."

Haran swung himself out of the bed, noticing for the first time that someone had changed him into a sleeping robe. "I- where are my robe and mail?"

"The robe is in the Vigil's laundry, being washed," said Ollan. "You had a... bit of an accident when..."

"And the mail?" interrupted Haran quickly.

"You're going to need a new mail-shirt, I'm afraid," said Ollan. "When you started communing with the Engine there was apparently some interference and it started to heat up pretty dramatically. Magritte and Render got it off you, but it was fused beyond repair."

"That was certainly a new experience for me," admitted Captain Render. "Damn thing was fizzing and sparking all over the place."

"Notwithstanding your state of dress, Learned Magister, you are physically recovered and whilst your reserves of Aether are low, they are no longer dangerously so," said Pieter. "I see no reason why you should not return to duty as Gifted in residence, and place myself at your disposal. I should caution, however, that had I not persuaded Jakob to stay at Fort Tarim, things might have been somewhat different."

"How so?" asked Haran, taking a sip of the water. "Other than the obvious, of course."

"Magister Jakob, along with many other older Magisters and Guard officers who are veterans of the last Incursion, is deeply sceptical about your.. arrangement with the Expelled," said Pieter. "They believe you court disaster by allowing any of them within the walls of the Vigil, and as for standing alongside them in battle..."

"Had we not done so, the banner of the Dendaril would now fly above the Vigil, if it even stood at all," said Haran, flatly.

"I concur. However, the potential political damage to your personal career, and to the reputation of your House, is significant." said Pieter. "I have taken the liberty of suggesting in conversation with some of those Magisters who, in their ignorance, object to your strategy, that I advised you in this course during your recent visit."

"What?" said Ollan and Haran practically in stereo.

"I have no House, no particular power, and no reputation," said Pieter. "Accordingly, I see no reason why I should not shoulder some of the burden of responsibility for events here. Should any Expelled transgress or raid into the Empire, I will arrange for the blame to fall upon me, rather than you, Magister Haran."

"I need no scapegoats, Magister Pieter," said Haran, firmly. "I will accord to you responsibility for your own actions, and nothing else. Your service, however, will be much appreciated, especially in the Infirmary."

Pieter gave a short bow. "Very well, Learned Magister. I also brought several of my best Healers from Verge with me, and took the additional liberty of sending those who had been weakened by their efforts here to Fort Tarim to recuperate. You need have no fear that your wounded will be well tended to."

"Things are finally looking up, eh Haran?" said Ollan, beginning to fill his pipe before glancing at Pieter and putting it away again with a grimace.

Haran nodded silently. It certainly seemed that the Vigil would now be secure, and with a hard-bitten veteran like Magister Jakob commanding the next line of defence the Dendaril would find infiltration difficult- as, for that matter, would any opportunistic Expelled. All the same, he couldn't shake the nagging feeling that all of this was too easy, his own experience notwithstanding.

He hoped Alben Koont would succeed in his scouting mission. There was something critical that they were missing.

109

*M*oon Behind Dark Clouds motioned to the rest of his war-band, and the Ixildar warriors froze into immobility. Though the process of binding the Free Tribes to the Master's will was not yet complete, with the addition of the Hearth-Tenders to their ranks there were sufficient numbers in Ixildundal that warriors could be spared to return to the Forest Home. From what they were seeing now, it hadn't been a moment too soon.

He signalled to his Eagle Hunters, and the three sisters flowed up the nearest trees like gliding-snakes. They were only a few miles from the Tithing, and yet from the disturbed birds in the distance it was clear that someone was heading their way. Whoever they were, they were both clumsy in their wood-craft, and extremely numerous. Sure enough, a moment later the silence was broken by the call of a green-crested gull from the forest ahead. The Third had sighted the enemy.

Moon considered his options, glad that Night's First Raven was by his side this time. It wasn't that he was concerned about the Dendaril discovering his war-band. The Fly Lords were poorly equipped and no more than mediocre fighters, though the Woe gave them significant strength and endurance. More importantly, few of them showed any skill or talent in tracking or wood-craft of any sort. If the Shorewalkers simply melted into the forest now, their enemies would certainly pass right by them without ever knowing how close they had come to death.

Unfortunately, unless he missed his guess, the route that the enemy force was taking would lead them straight to the Tithing. The ancient, ruined fortress was still defensible after a fashion, but the Ixildar had deliberately avoided rebuilding it or holding it in strength. A half-collapsed, time-eroded castle on the edge of a stinking swamp and bordering nothing but barren wasteland held little interest for all but the most curious scavengers, and those few bold enough to investigate its depths could be quietly dealt with by the guards. If the Fly Lords discovered the portal stone, however, that would change quickly. The precautions Ixilinath had

441

taken made it extremely unlikely that the Dendaril might be able to attack Ixil-dundal directly through it, but the destruction of the Tithing or its loss to enemy hands would effectively cut the Ixildar off from the Forest Home. The Free Tribes knew many arts of survival, but a march across some four hundred miles of barren tundra would be too much for all but the strongest. No, the Fly Lords could not be allowed to find the Tithing.

He gave the call of the hunting grebe, summoning his scouts to his side. After a few moments, the Third loped towards him from the deepening shadows of the trees, and Small Fangs in Shadow, the eldest of the Eagle Hunter siblings, slipped smoothly down from her perch to join them.

"How many?" said Moon Behind Dark Clouds, quietly.

"A hundred, perhaps, in this rabble," said the Third, not bothering to cover his nakedness. The young warrior, as yet unmarried, clearly had his eye on the sisters of Small Fangs and wasted no opportunity to show them his boldness, along with his other attributes.

"Many more further to the south," said Small Fangs. "There are at least nine more war-parties like that one out there, and all of them are moving north-east."

"Umba's teeth," hissed Night's First Raven. "Husband, at least one of them is going to find the Tithing, however stupid and clumsy they might be."

Moon nodded. "Aye, Wife. Third, I fear I must ask a thing most terrible of you. Are you prepared?"

The Third nodded eagerly. "Anything for the Free, First. Speak, and it is done."

"Ah, the easy valour of youth," smiled Small Fangs. "I fear you will not like this task, young buck."

"I will rise to any challenge!" snapped the Third, hotly.

"That is good to hear," said Moon. "Third, you must flee to the Tithing with all haste. Return to Ixildundal, and tell the Master and the Mighty that the Fly Lords threaten the Tithing. In the meantime, we will attack their advance party, and seek to lead the rest of them on a hunt for shadow rabbits."

The Third flushed red with annoyance. Though he had acquitted himself capably in the last clash with the Fly Lords, he had yet to earn true renown and had clearly hoped to do so in this battle. That was another good reason to get rid of him- a war-band of thirty had no business getting involved in the sort of pitched battle the Third might desire. Nonetheless, the warrior had given his word and was too determined to impress to go back on it.

"Very well, First, though I shall run with my belly dragging on the ground from my heavy heart," said the young man. "Can you tell me, at least, to where you will lead the Fly Lords, that I might tell the Master where you are to be found?"

"We shall lure them north, towards the sea-caves of Dran's Refuge." said Moon. "The blue-hairs moor there from time to time, and it would please me to set one foe at the throat of another. Go now!"

The Third nodded, and shifted into his wolf-shape, wasting no further time in loping off into the forest. Moon turned to the two women.

"We shall swing around to the north, and take the first group as silently as we can. Once they are wavering, I shall give the call of the Roaring Toad, which will be the signal for the full force of our fury to be unleashed. Kill them noisily and violently, but let a few flee to summon their allies. When their reinforcements appear, we begin to fall back towards the coast. Small Fangs, I leave it to you and your sisters to slay any Fly Lord who tries to restrain their pursuit and enrage the rest. Slay the strongest, slay the most beautiful, cripple the fastest."

"With the way these Dendaril think, perhaps we shall simply slay the fattest," said Small Fangs in Shadow with a grin that exposed her pointed teeth.

"Whatever serves," said Moon. "Now, let us begin."

110

*T*halia watched the map display with a certain amount of trepidation. The Abelian approach to forest warfare probably shouldn't have surprised her, but that didn't mean she had to like it. The Free Tribes certainly weren't going to. It was, she supposed, at least fortunate that the route from the Farspan to the Vigil only skirted the edge of the Forest Home rather than going straight through the middle of it. Even so, if it were possible for the trees that stood in the way of the Royal Army to regret where they had chosen to grow, regret it they would.

She had wondered how the Abelians planned to handle an army that consisted largely of heavy cavalry and wheeled vehicles in a dense forest which would eliminate many of the advantages of the former and seriously hamper the mobility of the latter. It turned out they had no intention of doing so. Instead, on entering the forest the Golems, both War and Wood, had dismounted from their transport wagons and moved to the fore of the convoy, forming a flying wedge with the War Golems at the tip and leading edge, their heavy hammers rotated into striking position. Then the whole mass simply pulverised anything that stood in the way. The map table gave only the barest indication of the trail of smashed trunks and trampled undergrowth in their wake, but Thalia had to imagine it was a sight that would not gladden the hearts of the Mighty Ones.

She chose, given her complete inability to do anything at all about the Abelian tactics, to deal with the situation by getting extremely drunk. As well as the bottle of wine the Queen had given her as part of her 'punishment', the *Dreadnought* had been loaded with several large preserving hampers of food before the army had left the Farspan, as had the other carriages carrying the Wizards. The fare was perhaps a little more elaborate than she was used to, especially when served as trail rations, but she certainly wasn't complaining. Working their way through the food and alcohol might not be productive, but it was certainly enjoyable.

"Hey... Thalearned Magister.." said Athas, his voice a little slurred. "Don't.. don't you know a spell.. thingy to make... us less... drunk?"

444

Thalia looked at both of him sternly. "Yes.. yes.. I do, but.. you don't want to be.. doing magic when you're... you're.."

"Pissed?" suggested Athas.

"That's it!" said Thalia, triumphantly. "You remember.. Kaine?"

"Magister Kaine? Yeah."

"He.. was clever.." murmured Thalia. "Very... very clever.."

"Why?" said Athas, trying to pour one more glass from the empty bottle. "Oops, looks like it's all gone.. shame."

"Why what?" said Thalia, gazing at him with narrowed eyes.

"Huh? Oh, why was he.. clever?"

"Who?"

"Kaine! Oh, I remember," said Thalia, wondering how they'd got onto the subject. "He.. cast his sobr.. sobby.. not-being-drunk spell before he.. got drunk, you see."

"Well, couldn't.. couldn't you do.. that?" asked Athas. "You know.. you're very pretty, by the way."

"I'm very pretty, *Learned Magister*," admonished Thalia.

"Huh? I'm not a Magister!"

"No, I mean... anyway, yeah, I could've, but I... didn't. Er, I don't think I did, anyway."

Thalia finished off her glass, tried to stand up, and found that she couldn't. Athas reached out a hand to help her and gave a mighty heave, succeeding only in depositing the Magister in an untidy heap in his lap. Giggling, Thalia tried to disentangle herself. Of course, the distant, serious part of her mind pointed out, Kaine's method had been unsuitable because it had relied on the subject getting incredibly drunk before triggering the sobriety spell. Even if she'd wanted to, Thalia would have found it impossible to make the spell trigger after only half of a bottle of wine, even such a potent one. Failing completely to regain any sort of balance, she reached out for something to lever herself to her feet, finding her staff leaning against the wall, and discovered two things in quick succession.

Firstly, the distantly-remembered, stone-cold-sober version of Magister Thalia Daran had indeed taken the precaution of casting the sobriety cantrip before getting started on the wine, in case of a crisis. Secondly, anticipating what an even extremely drunk Magister would do in an emergency, she had bound that spell to trigger when she next touched her staff. She had used the more subtle version of the spell, but it turned out that whatever you did to shock a person's system from extreme inebriation into sobriety there were going to be consequences. Her faculties returned as if someone had violently shoved them into her face and her stomach turned several cartwheels before violently rebelling against the cold roast chicken that had recently arrived in it. Scrambling to her feet, her elbow causing the surprised Athas no little inconvenience, she scurried to the privy and only just made it.

She was just emerging some ten minutes later when someone started banging on the door of the *Dreadnought*. A headache had been the final side-effect of the sobriety spell and the racket certainly wasn't helping. She shot a quick glance at the couch she and Athas had recently unwittingly shared and found that the big Guard had fallen asleep. There was no help to be had from that quarter. Wincing at the effort of focusing, she commanded the door to open, taking the illumination of the *Dreadnought's* glow-crystals down a little as she did so. The stench hit her immediately and she had to force down the urge to vomit again. For a moment she thought that another horde of Dendaril had been put to the sword whilst she was too drunk to care, but there was something oddly familiar about the smell.

"Scout Koont? Is that you?"

"You recognise this man, Lady Thalia?" said Sir Terence's voice from outside. "He emerged from the forest claiming to have come from the Eastern Vigil but we have no way to check his credentials."

"I'm still alive, ain't I, y'tin-plated ponce?" said Alben Koont. "Ain't many could say that after dodgin' them buzzing bastards and their goons f'r a day an' a bit."

"That," said Thalia, smiling despite herself, "is definitely Alben Koont. What in Thelen's name are you doing out here, Scout?"

"Clues in t'name o' t'job," chuckled the wiry man. "Thought them Fly Lord wankers was up t'summat, so Magister Haran sent me t'go see what."

"And what, sir, might the.. Dendaril be 'up to?'" asked Sir Terence. "Speak quickly now, I mislike leaving the door of a carriage open with our miniscule foes in the wind, even with the camp secured for the evening."

"Fucked if'n I know, yer lordship," said the Scout. "But I can tell yer what they ain't doin'. They ain't tryin' t' get into t'Vigil, and they ain't tryin' t' get around 'er, either. There's some moved south t' try t' cut your mob off, a fuck-load what went north-east, best I can tell, an'n even bigger fuck-load mobbed up round that big pile o' shit mountain in't middle."

"The Mountain Halls?" said Thalia. "But they were destroyed. What could the Dendaril possibly want there?"

"S'good'n high up," said Alben. "They c'n see what's goin' on fer miles, so there's that. Couldn't get eyes on 'em, anyway- found out most 'o this by earwiggin' on the cunts what've put down roots outside t'Vigil."

"I have heard it said that the directness of the common folk can be a refreshing change from the niceties of Court." observed Sir Terence. "I see now that it is possible to have entirely too much refreshment. Speaking of which, I believe your man is waking up, Lady Thalia."

Athas sneezed, and sat up, wrinkling his nose. "What.. what's that horrible.. oh, it's you. Wait, what're you doing here?"

"Not now, Sergeant," said Thalia, quickly. "Sir Terence, we need to take this information to the Queen."

"We do?" said the Knight. "Forgive me, Lady Thalia, but our task is to prevent the Dendaril from overrunning the Vigil, is it not? It seems that our enemy has simply made that task considerably easier through poor tactics."

"Bloody hell," said Alben Koont. "And I thought soldier-boy there were thick. Does that helmet y'wearing squish yer brains or summat?"

"How *dare* you, you foul-smelling... peasant!" growled Sir Terence. To Thalia's surprise, Athas moved to block the door.

"I'm sorry, Sir Terence, but I can't let you hurt him, even if he is really rude and smells like a shit-farmer's socks," said the big Guard. "He's right, you know- not about you being stupid, but... ow, my head.."

"What the Sergeant is trying to explain, Sir Terence," said Thalia, once again stepping in quickly to prevent disaster, "is that it's no good just killing a few thousand Dendaril- we need to drive them out of the forest. We were heading for the

Vigil because we assumed that that was where the main force would be, but if they aren't there, we'd be wasting our time and exposing ourselves to attack for no good reason."

"S'like stabbin' a bloke t'death with a really little, really fuckin' sharp dagger," said Alben Koont. "You can hurt t'bastard easy enough, but you've got t'get 'im in a bit he's really gonna miss 'fore he grabs y'arm."

"Yeah, like his heart or his eyes or something," said Athas. "Hey, that actually made sense!"

Thalia wondered what Sir Terence's expression looked like under his blank-faced helm. Finally, however, the Knight shrugged. "Very well. If I understand correctly, you are saying that we need to strike the Dendaril leaders, and they are unlikely to be where we expected them to be based on this intelligence. I will take this to the Queen along with your counsel, Lady Thalia. I will also, of course, entrust this... gentleman to your custody and place him under your parole."

"Oh, wonderful," said Athas, wrinkling his nose again. "There goes my appetite."

"Don't y'worry, soldier-boy," chuckled the Scout. "Tell y'Queen I ain't stayin', tin-head. Magister Haran's waitin' on me report an' I can't have all them fine ladies at t'Vigil thinkin' I'm dead or anythin'. Reckon t'High Vigilant'd top herself if'n she thought that'd happened."

Thalia eyed him doubtfully. "Are you sure you should travel again tonight, Scout Koont? You don't look like you've slept or eaten for some time."

The wiry man laughed. "Yeah, sleepin' ain't f'r me. See that sorry bunch'o wankers I used t'run with every time I close me eyes. I'll take a leg o' that chicken t'munch though, if's all t'same t'you."

"Here," said Athas, tearing it off. "I'd prefer you didn't touch anything I might want to eat later."

"Fair'nough," said the Scout, ripping a chunk of the white flesh off with his teeth. "See y' about, Learned Magister. Don't go getting y'self with a fly in y'bonce."

"And safe travels to you, Scout Koont," said Thalia, as he disappeared into the darkening night. She wondered what the Queen would make of the news. It probably wouldn't be a critical mistake to carry on to the Vigil, but she wished she knew what the Dendaril were doing.

111

*S*miling Snake had spent the last three hours contemplating a small crack in the earth. There was, after all, little else to look at when one was lying face-down on the ground and dare not move for fear of causing grave offence. Even so, the crack was quite interesting, given the context. The square at the centre of the village was immaculately maintained, the close-packed, hardened earth raked daily to the exact specifications of *Koze-Heilin*, and yet even in this ordered perfection a small flaw persisted. He wondered if it was an oversight, or a deliberate statement by the ancient masters who had built the place, for truly was it said that even in the most perfect Harmony there could be found Chaos, and even the most dire Chaos harboured tiny motes of Harmony.

He had spent at least an hour vigorously debating with himself as to whether the crack being deliberate or accidental more perfectly reflected that axiom.

In the meantime, they had been gently tortured by the smell of roasting meat- the Lakibird, unless his nose was too clogged with carefully-raked soil to speak truth to his mind- and taunted by the faint sounds of music and conversation. Bai Faoha had spent the majority of the time in silent meditation, but as dusk fell he finally spoke.

"Great Sage," he said, quietly. "Are you still awake?"

"Given the grave discomfort of my posture, I could scarcely be otherwise," replied Smiling Snake.

"I fear the Keeper will not return," said White Crocus. "She has left us here to rot, or until the morning sun rises and questions of your absence are asked in Shan'Xi'Sho."

"That is your second understandable error," said Rya-Ki. "But there is no time to contemplate it. Be silent."

To his credit, Bai Faoha did not argue or ask questions, immediately doing as · he was bid. A moment later, the door to the nearest house slid open again, and the Keeper emerged.

"I have your answer, Sages of the Hono. Oh, Great Sage, have you remained like that all this time?" She laughed, musically, and Smiling Snake found the sound soothed his aching back like the finest unguent.

"I was not given leave to move," he replied, simply. "And therefore, out of respect, I did not."

"Then please, rise now, and sit as your vassal does," said the Keeper. "The Echoes consider your discomfort to be punishment enough for your trespass, Smiling Snake of the Hono. I will not explain to you the process of deciphering your message- suffice it to say that it took more than the wisdom of Toh Lonshao to unravel it. The Echoes were concerned enough at its importance to insist that I write it down upon a scroll, rather than relating it verbally."

She held out the scroll, and Rya-Ki gave a quick bow of thanks before taking it. Swiftly, he unravelled the message and read it. The next moment he was on his feet, aches, pains, hunger and thirst forgotten. Bai Faoha scrambled to follow him.

"Great Sage! What-"

Smiling Snake ignored him, turning to the Keeper and bowing again. "Thank you, Keeper. Please convey my additional thanks and most humble apologies to the Honourable Echoes. Come, White Crocus."

He left almost at the run, not stopping until he reached the outskirts of the village. Placing his staff firmly butt-first on the ground, he forced himself to focus, and tapped the third chime once with his finger. Bai Faoha followed suit, and a few moments later their *ryayan* emerged from the shadows of the trees. They mounted swiftly, and began the ride back to Shan'Xi'Sho.

"Great Sage, what was the message?" asked Bai Faoha. "Clearly it was of grave import."

Smiling Snake tossed the scroll-case over to the other Sage, who caught it deftly. "Read it for yourself."

"*The ancient doom moves in the East. It seeks to plunder the secrets of the fallen city, and through them to conquer the Heavens. It seeks the stolen Heart of Yoshan'Ru, below the First Gateway,*" read White Crocus. "*By the third way must Harmony come to the broken mountain.* So, the answer to our riddle is.. another riddle?"

"Did you notice the calligraphy?" said Smiling Snake.

"I.. I had not, Great Sage. I thought only the words important, not the characters."

"The brush-work is, of course, exquisite," said Rya-Ki, "But you will notice that the style is Imperial High Script, in the honorific cursive, as befits a message of great importance. But what else is noteworthy about Imperial High Script?"

Bai Faoha frowned. "I apologise, Great Sage, but my knowledge of this matter is poor. All I can think of is that in ancient times, before the Yellow Curse War, it was customary for any text written in High Imperial to feature *kanoi* that, when read in the base form rather than in the continual form, spelt out a prayer of thanks to the current Emperor. Once the Son of Heaven ascended the throne, of course, the practice became meaningless."

"And do you see such a sequence of *Kanoi* in this message?" asked Smiling Snake.

"Of course there is not.... no, wait... no, this is impossible. The Keeper must have made an error."

"No scribe with brush-skill of that perfection would mistakenly write the wrong *kanoi*." said Smiling Snake. "Why do you assume otherwise?"

"Because the *kanoi* spell out the phrase 'All praise to His Benevolent Majesty, Emperor Shon Quaolin,'" said Bai Faoha, in wonderment. "And Shon Quaolin died some two centuries before the Yellow Curse War, almost two thousand years ago!"

"The Tapestry was originally woven in the reign of Empress Yanshoa Quaolin, mother of Shon Quaolin," said Smiling Snake. "This choice of script is no accident. You did not receive a message from the threads of the Tapestry, Bai Faoha, but from the very essence of the artefact itself- and that message awaited your coming for two millennia."

They rode on in silent contemplation, racing the dawn back to the capital. They could only hope that two thousand years was not a moment too late.

112

*N*ight's First Raven laid open the throat of the man in front of her with a curved dagger and cast a quick look over her shoulder at her husband. "There are too many! Fall back to the caves!"

Moon Behind Dark Clouds swept up the fallen knife of the foe he had just impaled on his spear, and caught his wife's eye as he brought his arm back. She read his meaning as he had known she would, and rolled smoothly to the side as he threw. The knife was crude, little more than a cooking tool, and did not fly true, but it hit the woman who had been leaping at his wife in the throat hilt-first with enough force to flip her over backwards in mid air. Night's First Raven moved in quickly to finish her before turning to run deeper into the forest.

Already, some way behind them, a new line of Shorewalkers waited, and over-head shadows danced in the treetops as the Eagle Hunters moved to new positions without touching the ground. As they passed the line, Moon glanced at the tattoos of his warriors. As he had feared, many had long-since ceased to glow a bright, healthy blue, and several were now a dull, angry red. They would not be able to keep this up much longer. The Shorewalkers had been fighting and running for what felt like several hours by now, and were still not even in what had been their own territory, much less anywhere near Dran's Refuge.

As he turned, ten more Fly Lords emerged from the gloom of the night, led by a young, strong-looking woman with flowing red hair who wore an armoured breastplate and carried a sword of some quality. She opened her mouth to scream encouragement to her fellows, but fell back with a choking gasp as a dark-fletched arrow sprouted in her throat. The other nine hesitated for a fatal instant in dismay, and the Shorewalkers picked that moment of confusion to fall upon them. As the unequal struggle raged, Moon heard the cry of a mountain wren from the trees behind him. Small Fangs in Shadow and her sisters had used the last of their ammunition.

He felt the first stirrings of despair in his heart as his warriors finished off their foes, noting in concern that an attacking force of seven had been reduced to five warriors. Angry Little Ones swarmed around the survivors as they fell back, small bursts of flame marking the moment when the Master's power repelled them. They had put many miles between themselves and the Tithing, this much was true, and the Dendaril rampaging through the forest had become so completely caught up in the chase that it was doubtful they would soon find the ruined fortress, but he had hoped to preserve his war-band and leave the enemy lost within the trees. That had not come to pass, for what the Fly Lords lacked in war-skill and weaponry they made up for with sheer stamina and persistence.

Another bird call echoed through the forest, this time from further behind- the green-crested gull- and Moon's spirits sank still lower. The enemy had somehow overtaken them, and now lay between them and the shore. It was likely that they had surrounded the Shorewalkers completely. The warriors looked at each other, their expressions grim. Night's First Raven stepped forwards to the corpse of the red-head, pulling the arrow that had slain her out of her throat and dipping two fingers into the open wound. She spread her fingers wide, and painted two streaks of fresh blood down from her forehead to her chin.

"If I fall here," she growled, "I fall with the blood of my foe as my trophy," She whistled, and tossed the retrieved arrow to the tree-tops where it was deftly caught.

Moon followed his wife's example. "Aye, now we paint for the final stand. Reclaim any other arrows you can see, and recover your strength as best you can. They will be upon us soon. Let these curs have good cause to regret the day they trod the soil of the Forest Home."

In truth, most of the warriors were already covered in enough of the enemy's gore that Night's First Raven's gesture was fairly redundant, but the seven or so retrieved arrows and the respite from running and fighting was certainly welcome. By the time the next wave of foes came running out of the shadows of the forest, the ten remaining Shorewalkers were ready for them. Or so they thought.

"Nak's Skull!" muttered one of the warriors as they fanned out into a loose circle. "How many more are there?"

"Stand strong!" snapped Moon, but in his heart he shared the man's concern. There had to be at least another hundred in the war-band that was bearing down on them, and from the sounds coming from the forest there were more beyond those.

"More behind..." growled Night's First Raven, hefting her knives. "May we meet again in the Ancestor Glades, Husband."

Before Moon could reply, the enemy was upon them. Perhaps a more disciplined foe might have restrained their attack upon seeing the loose circle of gore-smeared warriors, their tattoos glowing and their sweat-soaked hair plastered onto their heads, but the Dendaril were no such enemy. The first wave died with blade-glass in their hearts almost as soon as they reached their intended victims, but the next fared better, the reckless impetus of their predecessors driving their carcasses so firmly onto the Shorewalkers' spears that several warriors were unable to withdraw their weapons in time. Moon saw the woman to his right borne to the ground by ten foes, their crude cudgels and knives descending to rise again stained bright crimson though four joined their prey on the bloody earth in the process. To his left, a warrior speared another Dendaril, pushing the corpse from his weapon with his foot as Moon's own spear covered him.

A cry of outrage from behind him distracted his attention, and he whirled to see Night's First Raven struggling in the grip of a giant warrior, a man standing almost seven feet tall. Both the bald man's thick arms were wrapped around the woman from behind, though each streamed blood from deep cuts. Eagerly, two more Fly Lords closed for the kill, rusty blades glinting in the moonlight, but the Second was not so easily taken, and a booted foot lashed out, driving the closest man's nose into his face with shocking force. Unable to reach the struggle in time, Moon hurled his spear, transfixing the other Dendaril to a tree. The bald giant, still squeezing, turned slowly to face him, which proved to be a fatal mistake, for the movement presented his eyes to the bows of the Eagle Hunters and both were replaced in quick succession with the dark feathers of their arrows. The man swayed on the spot for a moment, relaxing his grip as he did so, and then pitched over backwards as Night's First Raven kicked free.

"The blood-price is high this night, Husband," said the Second with a savage grin, sweeping up her knives and tossing one to her husband. Moon nodded wordlessly, and they turned to face the next mass of enemies. Behind the advancing line, men began to haul themselves clumsily into the trees in search of the Eagle Hunters. No arrows flew to deter them, but Moon knew the fleet sisters would elude the artless pursuit for now. There would be no such escape for the last two Shorewalker warriors still standing on the ground. For a moment, however, their enemies hesitated. So high were the bodies piled, and so dark had the forest become, that it was difficult to tell friend from foe, only the dull glow of their tattoos giving the two warriors away as the Fly Lords closed in on them.

Suddenly a bright flash of flame lit the night sky, followed a moment later by a thunderous detonation from the rear of the advancing force. The Dendaril were hurled into confusion as fresh warriors, Shorewalkers and Stonesingers both, tore into them before the surprised eyes of the exhausted survivors. Yet still greater was Moon's shock in realising who led the newcomers. Striding through the melee, staff striking left and right and the brands blazing on her wrists, came Mighty Tyrona.

"Well met, First of the Shorewalkers," she said, as the remaining Dendaril scattered. "It seems we reached you not a moment too soon."

"Aye," said Moon, gazing sadly at the slaughtered remnants of his war-band. "Too many brave sons and daughters of the forest were lost this day. My Third got through, then?"

"He did," said Mighty Tyrona. "He is resting at Ixildundal, having run himself nigh unto death. It is my great sorrow that his haste was in vain, for when he arrived we were in the midst of the final binding ritual. We came as soon as we could."

"The-" began Night's First Raven, but she was interrupted by a shrill scream of terror from above, followed almost immediately by a body that crashed to the ground next to them. A moment later, Small Fangs in Shadow landed feet-first on the moaning figure, crushing the last vestige of life out of him.

"That was the last of those dogs who thought themselves to be cats," she sniffed. "These Fly Lords climb even worse than they fight."

Night's First Raven looked up at the tree-tops. "Your sisters?"

"They live, though Second of Twisting Leaves took a dagger to the arm," said Small Fangs. "We will see to it that she keeps the scar as a reminder to be faster in future."

"Mighty Tyrona, you said the final binding ritual was complete?" said Moon, finishing his wife's interrupted question.

"Aye," said Mighty Tyrona. "The Free Tribes are no more- we are all Ixildar now. Ten thousand warriors now march from the Tithing to reclaim the Forest Home."

"Forgive me, Mighty One," said Moon, "but even the full strength of our three tribes is a mere flea on the back of an angry bear. There are hundreds of thousands of these Woe-bearers, perhaps even more. Can we truly prevail?"

"Alone? No," said Mighty Tyrona. "Though the Fly Lords would long rue the day we tried. But the Master has a plan, and Mighty Taris will explain it to you. Come."

"Mighty Taris?" said Night's First Raven. "But he is a Hearth-Tender, sworn never to wage war! What is he doing leading our war-bands?"

"He is not," said Tyrona. "But he will make the greatest of sacrifices to bring us victory."

113

Joniah watched as the winch-teams worked, turning the massive, crude handles with painstaking slowness. Darkness had fallen some time ago, and the forest was alive with the calls of night creatures. Some of those calls, the Dendaril had learned to their cost, came not from the throats of simple beasts, but from far more dangerous creatures. They were terrifying, these tattooed barbarians, not just for their prowess in battle in their home territory, but for their blasphemous rejection of the Blessing. Such a thing had never before been encountered in the history of the Hegemony, and many in the Crusade wondered at what it might mean.

Seemingly unconcerned despite the loss of a scouting expedition over a thousand strong in the northern forest, the High Pilgrims had simply ordered large crystal beacons unpacked and erected to light the excavation site, and kept digging. Now, the first prize was slowly emerging from the reluctant earth, lifted by four great winches, each lying horizontally like a ship's capstan and worked by a team of two hundred strong men and women. It was huge, a globe of crystal some fifty feet in diameter, its surface dirty but otherwise completely unmarked by its time below ground.

"Hold..." gasped Pilgrim Toroth, "Now... we.. see..."

Gratefully, the labourers banged in the pegs to lock their winches, which groaned under the load even though they were reinforced by the magic of the Elucidated Pilgrims. The Porters carried the three Dendaril leaders to the edge of the huge shaft, and once more beams of white light shot from their staffs, this time converging on the crystal sphere and filling it with a bright glow. Joniah could feel his hair standing on end as the air crackled with Vrae.

"Release!" cried Toroth, his frailty briefly eased by the working of his power, and the winch-captains banged the pegs free, their crews scrambling clear in anticipation of the winches starting to run out of control. And yet, they did not. Slowly, to the awe of the watching workers, the glowing sphere lifted out of the shaft, and began to float above their heads towards a shallow corpse-pit dug into the centre of the camp, the slack ropes trailing behind it. As the huge crystal began to descend, Mother Dorcas, the eldest of the Elucidated Pilgrims, suddenly let out a gasp and collapsed, flopping back into her palanquin chair as if she were a marionette whose strings had been cut. The light from her staff winked out, and that in the globe began to gutter and fade. Even as Dorcas' Porters leapt to her aid, the glow was completely extinguished and the crystal dropped the last few feet into the hollow with a wet splat, pulverising the dismembered bodies below.

There was a terrible, breathless moment as one of the winch-captains ran over to check the damage. "It is unharmed, Elucidated Ones!" he announced, triumphantly. "It was most wise to cushion the bottom of the receptacle."

None chose to comment on the nature of the cushioning. It was enough that those who had fallen over the course of the Crusade could still serve, after a fashion. Already the labourers were hard at work with long swabs, cleaning the worst of the gore and effluvia from the sphere.

"How fares.... Mother Dorcas?" asked Toroth, slumping back in his own seat in exhaustion.

"She lives yet, Elucidated One," replied the head of Dorcas' Porters. "But she is gravely taxed. Her Ending will not be much longer delayed."

"Then... there is no... time..." murmured Toroth. "Take us.. to the.. deepest shaft."

Joniah nodded. "Aye, Elucidated One. And the other shafts?"

"Continue the... work," whispered Toroth, as men scrambled to detach the ropes and dismantle the winches. "Recall.. our forces... to the camp... and gather... the Pilgrims."

"Which Pilgrims, Elucidated One?" asked Joniah. There were Pilgrims spread out across the entire forest, including those leading the forces keeping the unwitting enemy bottled up in their fortress to the west. Toroth's answer came in a barely audible murmur as he fell into a fitful doze.

"All.... of them.."

114

*T*halia was jolted out of her sleep as the *Dreadnought* abruptly began to move. She waved a hand at the window-panel of the small bedroom, activating its enchantment so it turned invisible from the inside, and for a moment it almost seemed as if nothing had happened, so black was the night. Then her eyes adjusted enough to confirm that the Royal Army was on the move. She dressed quickly, and carefully made her way down the narrow corridor to the map table. She had taken more time to study the device, and now understood how to operate the Messaging Crystal built into it. The crystal was small, and primitive by modern standards, but it was able to communicate with similar crystals in the other coaches over a fair distance. She considered trying the *Valiant*, but Tondarin would almost certainly still be travelling on her horse- the Royal Knights, true to their oath, had not slept or eaten since the Last Feast. Instead, she touched the rune for the *Formidable*, the vehicle carrying Lady Ysabella and her family's Wizards.

"*Hello?*" sent Thalia. "*Is anyone there?*"

"*Of course we are, Lady Thalia,*" responded the crystal after a brief pause. It wasn't exactly accurate to think of the process like hearing a voice, but Thalia was fairly sure she was talking to Lady Ysabella herself. "*It does not do to slumber when the Queen calls us to war.*"

"*We're going into action now? In the middle of the night?*"

"*The report from your Scout rather set a fox among the Queen's chickens,*" replied Ysabella. "*She wants to finish this in a single, dolorous blow, and knowing that the enemy's head isn't where it was supposed to be made that a little difficult. About half an hour ago, though, we started seeing lights on the mountainside to the north-east, and given that the ruins of Xodan seem to be the most important strategic position in this benighted place the Queen has decided to take them.*"

Thalia wasn't entirely sure that she had actually told the Abelians about Xodan, but they had spies and informers like everyone else, and from what she'd heard

457

Magister Fredus' last communication with the College had been less than discreet. In any case, there was no need to worry about that now.

"The Royal Army is going to attack an encampment on a mountain?" she sent. *"Isn't that going to be difficult terrain for cavalry and wheeled wagons?"*

"Yes," replied Ysabella. *"But the Queen was unimpressed by the prowess of the Dendaril in the last engagement. The Royal Knights will now use bows to engage the Pilgrims in case any more decide to try to go out in a blaze like the one at the Farspan did, but other than that the plan is to send the Golems in to crush anything in front of them before the Knights finish off their commanders. The wagons will have to remain at the foot of the mountain, most likely, but that will be close enough to command the Golems."*

"I see, thank you Lady Ysabella. How long before we meet the enemy?"

"That depends on them," replied Ysabella. *"The Golems aren't at their fastest when they're clearing a path like this, so it'll take about half a day to get to the mountain, but unless these Dendaril are complete tactical dunces they'll try to head us off before then."*

"In that case, I'll try to get some sleep and leave you to yours, Lady Ysabella," Thalia sent. *"Good night."*

"We'll be up all night directing the Golems," replied Ysabella. *"But you should sleep while you can."*

Athas appeared at in the corridor, half-dressed, as the link closed. "Learned Magister? What's going on?"

"Nothing we can do anything about from in here," replied Thalia. She didn't like the idea of a critical battle taking place whilst she was cooped up in a metal box, but with the Shrive-Ticks around there was little other choice.

115

*J*t was after midnight by the time Amanda Devereux, Delys and her new allies approached the cave outside Minat. It still impressed the Operative just how quickly even mundane horses could move when supported by the travel-spells of a Magister, and Elsabeth had proven every bit as adept at the art as her six Leaves would suggest. Alaran, who had used a similar spell to get the rebels to their rendezvous with Devereux on time, was in awe of the older, better-trained Magister.

They had left Abellan openly, Elsabeth telling the gate guard that she planned to visit with an old friend in the northern city of Thecla for a couple of days. The new Ambassador had brought her own coach, a College design less elaborate than those used by the Abelians but no less swift, along with a pair of bodyguards and a maid. The latter was somewhat shorter than the Ambassador and had blonde, rather than black hair, but Elsabeth had packed a wig that perfectly imitated her own unusual hairstyle and with that, a spare pair of the Magister's high-heeled boots, and her best robe the woman was a fair double for her mistress. The plan was for the three to go to Thecla and visit a merchant with whom House Thule had several lucrative trading contracts.

"Of course it won't fool any truly talented spies," the Ambassador had admitted, as she made the final adjustments to her maid's disguise, "but it'll mean that if anyone asks, casual witnesses will think they saw me where I was supposed to be."

Devereux wondered about the three members of the decoy team as she approached the water's edge. They had certainly looked like Guards, the taller one in full armour and the smaller sitting next to the coach driver, bundled up in a travelling cloak, but something about their manner seemed a little off. Perhaps it was simply that none of them seemed particularly concerned at their unusual assignment. Then again, judging by the wig Elsabeth might pull this sort of trick fairly often. Certainly, the speed with which she had left the coach as it passed the Two-Lion Bridge suggested it wasn't the first time she'd slipped away in a hurry.

The night was cloudless and star-lit, and beginning to turn chilly. Alaran eyed the roaring waterfall cautiously, his eyes losing focus and then regaining it as he tried to penetrate the illusion. "Well, I give up. If there is some sort of entrance there, I can't see it, nor any sign of the magic disguising it." He cast an expectant gaze at Elsabeth, but the Magister shook her head.

"Don't look at me, young man. Operative, I've seen glamours cast by Gheris Falon himself, but if there's one here, it has been created by a master whose knowledge eclipses his."

Devereux frowned. "That's odd. Like I told you, I can't see the thing at all. As far as I'm concerned, there's a cave opening behind that waterfall in plain sight." She glanced at Delys, wondering if their link might allow the little Swordmaster to see the cave, but the blonde woman just shrugged.

"I can do something about the waterfall, at least," said Elsabeth, gesturing at it. "There's a fairly simple spell on it that divides it into two streams that fall to either side of where it is now.... there. Someone doesn't like their coach getting wet."

"Are we safe out in the open like this?" asked Ilia, looking around warily, her bow nocked. "If the High Wizards can see out like you can see in, the whole damn Concordance could be staring out at us right now and we'd be none the wiser."

"I'm not seeing anyone in there," said Devereux. "Stay here a moment, I'll head in and check that we're clear."

She had forgone her armour, and now wore only her bodysuit and weapon-belt, along with *Liberty* in its back-sheathe and a combat knife. She shifted the suit to active camo, acutely aware that the sword would be a giveaway if viewed from behind, and stole quietly into the cave. A quick check confirmed that there was nobody in the entrance chamber nor in the first access corridor, and she went back outside to confer with the others. Her appearance caused no small amount of consternation- in fact, Alaran fell to his hands and knees at the water's edge and vomited noisily.

The Operative stared at him in confusion. "What the hell's the matter with him?"

Even Elsabeth was looking a little green. "Amanda... please step forward a little... ah, thank Thelen for that. You obviously couldn't tell, but as far as we could see you walked straight through solid rock."

"Okay, but why did that make Alaran throw up? It can't be the first time you've seen someone do something that should be impossible."

"That's just it," said Alaran, wiping his mouth and taking a canteen of water from his sister before drinking greedily. "Usually when something like that happens a Gifted can sense the magic working. With this... whatever this is, there's nothing like that, and the effect on the psyche is deeply disturbing."

"Lady Ilia," said Elsabeth, "would you mind going over there and knocking on the stone?"

"Why me?" said Ilia, glaring at her. "Do it yourself!"

"I could," said Elsabeth. "However I'd rather not ruin these boots for no reason. You're better dressed for this than I, and in any case I need to see what happens from a distance."

"Let's try this first," said Alaran, picking up a small pebble from the water's edge. He threw it firmly at the cave, and as far as Devereux could see, it bounced off empty air before disappearing into the water with a plop.

"Okay.." said Devereux. "What if I do that?" She followed suit, the Hercules suite targetting the exact same spot Alaran had hit for good measure. Once again, the stone bounced off nothing.

"Now *that's* interesting," said Elsabeth. "I take it that the wall hasn't suddenly appeared for you?"

Devereux shook her head. "Nope. Still not there."

"I have an idea," said Alaran, suddenly. "Everyone turn your back to the waterfall- except you, Amanda. Right, now none of us are looking, try another stone."

Having no idea what to expect, Devereux did as she was bid. Surprisingly, the stone flew into the depths of the cave and splashed into the shallow water within.

"It went straight through," she reported.

"Impressive," said Elsabeth, turning around. "This isn't an illusion of light and sound, it's an illusion of the mind. No wonder we can't see the magic that creates it- not being able to see it is part and parcel of the magic."

"You've lost me, Learned Magister," said Devereux.

"It's like I was saying," said Alaran. "Our minds are being tricked by the magic into believing the wall is there, and the deception is so powerful that that even extends to looking at its Weave. But if we can't see it, our belief stops reinforcing the illusion."

"So how come I can walk through it even when you're looking?" objected Devereux.

"This sort of illusion only works on.. a personal level," said Elsabeth, slowly. "Anything living that can't see it can't be affected by it in any other way, but an inanimate object has no will of its own and will react to whatever the perceived reality is."

"All right," said Devereux, deciding to just accept the explanation and move on. "So how do I get you in, then?"

Alaran and Elsabeth exchanged a glance. "Close our eyes?" said Alaran.

"I'd prefer a blindfold," said Elsabeth. "Just in case of any surprises."

Devereux looked from one to the other incredulously. "You can't be serious."

"Of course we are," said Elsabeth. "As long as we can see the illusion, we won't be able to pass through it. The same will probably apply if anyone else can see it. So one of us will need to be blindfolded, and the rest will have to turn our backs as you lead us through. I volunteer to go first, by the way."

"You?" snorted Ilia. "Why? I thought you were worried about your boots?"

"Only about ruining them for no reason," said Elsabeth. "Anyway, I'm the best equipped of any of us to defend myself if anything happens whilst I'm in there alone."

Delys gave the Magister a challenging look, and she held up her hands. "My apologies, Master Delys, but I am a six-Leaf. If nothing else, I'm better trained to deal with any magic we might find in there. Now then, Amanda, let's get on with this before anyone finds us here, shall we?"

Miraleth, the small, brown-haired woman who bore the Seal of the Operator, had also brought a simple medical kit for emergencies, which contained amongst other things a length of bandage. Swiftly, she covered Elsabeth's eyes until the Magister pronounced herself to be quite unable to see.

"You'll need to resist the temptation to peek with your Wizardken," reminded Alaran. Elsabeth chuckled.

461

"Wizardken! Oh, the names you Abelians come up with just to avoid referring to College training. Don't worry, Wizard, I won't cheat. Now that I think about it, though, it's probably better if I deliberately dampen all of my senses, rather than just relying on the blindfold."

"What? Why?"

"So I can't subconsciously count my paces or anything like that," said Elsabeth. "Amanda, you'll need to lead me in, but don't go in a completely straight line. I don't want to give my subconscious any clues as to when I reach the illusion. Now, turn your backs, all of you, and no looking until Amanda tells you it's safe. I don't want to end my days stuck in an illusory stone wall."

"I'm still not certain that this makes any sense, Learned Magister," said Alaran, thoughtfully. Elsabeth sighed at him, pushing up the bandage.

"Young man, I am a six-Leaf Magister and you are barely a Twig as far as your magical education is concerned. This should work, and if it doesn't I risk only damp boots and possibly a couple of bruises. In fact, here-" she said, slipping off her footwear, "take these, if you're so concerned. And don't get them wet, hmm?"

She pulled the bandage back over her eyes, and turned in the Operative's general direction. "Now, I'm going to suppress my senses for about two minutes. Amanda, you need to lead me through the illusion before that time expires, starting from... now."

"What a jumped-up, overbearing bitch," grumbled Ilia, as Devereux took the Magister by the hand and led her towards the water.

"Hey, that's not really fair, Illy!" gasped Alaran, before smiling knowingly. "Oh- you were testing to see if she could still hear us, weren't you?"

"Yeah, if you like, Al," snorted Ilia. "Come on, we need to look away whilst they go through."

Carefully, Devereux led Elsabeth towards the cave entrance, turning left and right and generally doing all she could to obfuscate the route they were taking. After perhaps a minute, and at least one narrow escape when they came perilously close to the falling water which might possibly have shocked the Magister back into awareness, they crossed the threshold into the cave without further incident. A few moments later, the Ambassador pulled the blindfold off, and nodded in satisfaction.

"Ah, excellent, it worked," said Elsabeth. "Hmm, as I suspected. From this side the illusion is far less subtle and I think that... there."

"There what?"

"I've disabled the illusion. The others should be able to get in without all that elaborate messing around, now. I imagine it got a little interesting with the water-fall, didn't it?"

Devereux nodded. "Yeah, I was worried that if it soaked you, it might ruin the whole thing." She turned to the cave entrance. "Come on in, everyone, it's clear."

"I must admit, I usually do all I can to know everything that's going on, rather than trying very hard to ignore it," smiled Elsabeth as the Savalan rebels trooped in, their leader bringing up the rear.

"What did you do, Magister?" said Ilia, stepping into the cave, dripping wet. "The rock face disappeared, but just as I got to the cave entrance the waterfall returned to its original course. It's fortunate I packed up my bowstring before I came in just in case."

"Did it really?" said Elsabeth, innocently, retrieving her boots from Alaran having dried her damp stockings with her magic. "I must have accidentally done that when I disabled the illusion. Ah, but I see everyone is here- I'll restore it now, then, in case a passer-by notices."

"Shouldn't we set a watch outside?" said Temis, eyeing the cave entrance warily.

"In here, perhaps," said Ilia. "Outside, they'd have no way to come in and warn us even if they did see someone coming. Miraleth, hide yourself in here and keep an eye on things."

The Operator nodded. "Yes, Ilia. I doubt I'll be much use if you run into a High Wizard in there, anyway."

"Okay," said Devereux. "That's fine, but from now on I'm in charge. We communicate in hand signals like I showed you on the way here, and we don't waste time with titles or anything like that when we do talk- first name terms only for speed. Elsabeth, you're in front with me watching out for magical traps I can't spot. Alaran, you take the rear in case anything triggers behind us. The rest of you go in the middle. Keep your eyes open and your weapons sheathed- that means you, Del. We aren't here for a fight, we're here to figure out what the High Wizards are up to. Clear?"

Ilia nodded. "Fine with me. We'd never have even found this place without you, much less got in here. Just don't get us killed, Amanda."

Elsabeth smiled. "And with me- and for once, I agree completely with Ilia. I'd just as well not get myself killed on the first day of the job. Or cause a major diplomatic incident for that matter."

Devereux nodded, and led the way towards the Reaper. It was finally time for some answers.

$\mathcal{T}$he assembled war-bands of the Ixildar had fallen back to cover the approach to the Tithing, and convened a Moot in a forest clearing roughly mid-way between it and the Mountain Halls. The war-leaders of the Stonesingers and Shorewalkers were there, along with their Mighty Ones and all five-hundred Guardians of the Halls. Present too were the Mighty of the Hearth-Tenders, who stood with Mighty Taris, their expressions sorrowful but determined.

"Do you know what is going on?" said Moon Behind Dark Clouds to the First of the Stonesingers, a tall, burly warrior simply called Rocks Falling. Like many of the Stonesingers, the man bore a weapon made entirely of enchanted stone from head to haft, in his case a large, solid stone battle maul. Through the craft of their Mighty Ones, the tribe's weapons were both lighter, and stronger, than their materials suggested. Moon had seen a single blow from the hammer shatter a man's skull like an egg.

"I know only what we have been told," said the tall warrior. "That we shall have a war-leader to drive the Fly Lords from our lands, and that leader shall be born of Mighty Taris' sacrifice. It is pointless to worry about it, in any case." He raised his hand, allowing Moon to see the Brands twisting on his wrist. "Now we are sworn to the will of the Master, we could not oppose his design even if we knew what it was."

Moon wondered at that. They had been told that Mighty Taris was making a noble sacrifice of his own free will, but now that they bore the Brands could any of them truly know where their own will ended and the Master's began? Did the very fact that the thought could cross his mind prove that that mind was still his own?

Night's First Raven snapped him out of his reverie. "Husband!" she whispered. "Look!"

Entering the clearing were a procession of grim-looking figures. At first glance, they could have been mistaken the skeletal warriors who had guarded the entrance to the Mountain Halls, but these dead things, true Eternals, moved with a born warrior's grace, each hefting a huge, ancient two-handed sword over one shoulder. Their gilded bones were protected by golden chain-mail, and the Master's fire burned in their eyes. Before them came the Seneschal, seeming to carry a small, obsidian box in front of her, though those few who dared look closely saw that though the robes moved to suggest arms, no hands gripped the container.

All conversation in the clearing ceased, the Mighty Ones stepping respectfully out of the way of the procession as it approached Mighty Taris. Standing proudly, he turned to Mighty Endeo, the next-eldest of the tribe's Mighty Ones.

"I leave the Hearth-Tenders in your hands, Endeo," said Taris. "Continue to lead them in the old tradition, as the Master has decreed."

"It shall be done, Mighty Taris," said Endeo, his face wet with tears. "Are you truly certain you wish to go through with this?"

"The Master has shown me the peril we face," said Taris, as the Seneschal approached. "Enemies of the Ixildar- no, of all the Free, and all who value life, love and home- stand close to a prize that will re-shape the world into a new form that would doom us all. For this reason, the Master must take the field, and a Mighty One who could take no part in the battle is the obvious choice to aid him."

The box opened, and Mighty Taris withdrew something that made Moon's blood run cold. It was a gem, burning with the Master's fire, much like the one Moon himself had been entrusted with for the delaying attack on the Fly Lords.

"Umba's teeth..." hissed Moon. "Surely he cannot mean to...."

"Honour the passing of Mighty Taris!" shouted Endeo. "May the Roaring Toads sound the Call, and may the Larks cry! Split the heavens with your grief and your joy at this, the final apotheosis of a man of peace, transformed to a champion of war!"

As one the gathered throng roared, shouted, screamed and sang as they were bid, the sound starting in the clearing and rippling out to the satellite camps as ten thousand warriors took up the cry. The sound was so intense that it became an almost physical thing, and at its apex Mighty Taris opened his mouth, screwed his eyes tight shut, and swallowed the gem whole. Almost as soon as he closed his mouth, it opened again in a scream. From his face, the man was in pure agony, but the sound was lost amongst the general cacophony.

As the Ixildar watched in awe, lungs burning from exertion and ears deafened by the din, Mighty Taris went completely rigid, fire streaming from his mouth, ears and eyes. His Brands flared, their flames twisting and growing until they covered his entire body, as the Eternals knelt before him. More flames rushed up the Mighty One's staff, immolating the simple wood and leaving behind a spiralling rod of black iron, topped by a blazing gem. The gem pulsed once, emitting a flash of incandescent light so intense that all watching snapped their eyes tight shut and turned their faces away. The cry of the warriors stilled, and Moon blinked furiously, trying to restore his eyes to function to look upon what change the Master had wrought.

When vision finally returned, a robed figure stood in the place Mighty Taris had been. Though the body looked the same, and the face still bore the same features, all the weariness of age and care had been stripped away, leaving only a cold, stern countenance. And in the eyes was nothing but fire, which blazed so bright that they left traces in the vision of any who looked upon them.

"MIGHTY TARIS IS NO MORE," said Ixilinath. *"I NOW STAND BEFORE YOU, RETURNED FOR A TIME TO A PHYSICAL VESSEL. FOR A NIGHT AND A DAY SHALL THIS FORM ENDURE, AND IN THAT TIME SHALL THE DENDARIL, THE FLY-WREATHED INVADERS, BE DRIVEN FROM OUR LANDS. FIRSTS, RETURN TO YOUR WAR-BANDS AND MAKE READY. MIGHTY ONES, ATTEND AND RECEIVE YOUR BATTLE ORDERS. FOR IXILDUNDAL AND THE FOREST HOME!"*

"For Ixildundal and the Forest Home!" echoed the assembled warriors, awe-struck at the terrible, glorious sight. Moon Behind Dark Clouds turned to leave and prepare his tribe for the battle to come. This would be no hit-and-run raid, no spoiling attack, but a death-blow aimed at the neck of the foe. But as any warrior knew, such a strike against an enemy who had not first been crippled ran a serious risk of exposing the attacker should their cut not land.

Now, they could only hope that the Master's aim was true.

117

*J*oniah looked around the Dendaril camp in awe- if it had been busy before, by now it was positively teeming. Though many of the more far-flung forces would not arrive until at least the following morning, several hundred thousand members of the Crusade had rallied to the mountain at the Elucidated Pilgrims' call, along with almost a hundred Pilgrims. Some of the newcomers, in particular the few soldiers among them, thronged the slopes of the rubble-strewn mountainside in defence, whilst others were directed to help the work-gangs in their excavations. There were many more eager hands than there were picks and shovels, and some resorted to daggers, sharp rocks or even their bare hands to dig. The Pilgrims, too, leant their magic to the task, drilling into the stone and earth with beams of light or transmuting rock to more easily-dug soil, depending on their talents.

The Elucidated Pilgrims had chosen to conserve their strength by meditation, passing on their orders through the Communion to the Pilgrims. At a distance, the link was nothing more than an instinctive drive, but with three of the most powerful Elucidated in close proximity they controlled their subordinates like puppets on a string. Already two more of the great crystal spheres had been exposed, but it was the prize at the bottom of the deepest shaft that seemed to interest the Pilgrims the most. The excavation was perilous, filled with sudden voids that sent labourers plummeting to their doom without warning but were yet welcome, for they sped progress considerably. Three-quarters of the way down the shaft, the workers now toiling in pitch blackness, disaster struck as some buried stream or other water source was breached and the entire shaft promptly flooded.

In answer to this setback, the Pilgrims themselves descended into the shaft, heedless of the freezing cold water and utter darkness. Using their magic to create a pocket of air, they blasted away the last hundred or so feet of rock, despite no less than ten of their number being slain by falling rubble dislodged by the forces unleashed to do so.

Suddenly a titanic explosion erupted below the surface, sending shock-waves through the camp so fierce that all three Elucidated Pilgrims were toppled from their palanquins. Screams rose up from the forested slopes as the winches holding the other two crystal spheres that had been raised failed, becoming whirling pin-wheels that smashed themselves asunder and broke bodies and shattered trees as they went. And yet none of that mattered, for a glowing light in the depths of the shaft signalled that the greatest prize had been claimed. Moments later, a shining white crystal bobbed up to the surface of the flooded excavation. It was far smaller than any of the others, no more than two feet across, and was more an irregular mass than a worked shape, yet even as Joniah and his fellow Porters struggled to right Toroth's palanquin they could feel the power radiating from it.

"It is found," said the Pilgrim the Elucidated had chosen as their Voice. "The Heart-stone of Xodan, claimed by Thelen in ancient times and harnessed to power his capital. With this he threw back the Dragons and claimed the soil and all that walked and crawled upon it for himself. In his hubris, he placed it at the summit of his great city, knowing its might made his greatest work all but invincible."

"Then how did his city come to fall, Elucidated One?" asked Jaki as they care-fully settled Toroth back into his seat.

"Simple pride," replied the Voice. "Thelen and his progeny flew higher and higher, meaning to chase the Dragons to the very edge of the sky, but failed to look below them. They did not see one Dragon, Helieachoates, slip beneath them and strike at the crystal spheres that lifted the city. At the furthest extreme from the Heart-stone its power was at its weakest, yet even so Helieachoates was wounded nigh to death even as she struck one single blow against the spheres. But never in the history of the world has a single blow had such effect, for it disrupted the magics controlling the city's flight, causing it to topple from the sky. Had the youngest of Thelen's children, the Patron Amaran, not arrived and leant her power to soften the impact, all six of her kin and their father would have died that day."

Helieachoates. All Dendaril knew that name. She who was the First, the Mother Dragon, who to this day slumbered beneath the golden domes of Tor Goroth. Joniah gazed at the crystal in renewed wonder. Not only was this an arte-fact of great power, it was directly connected to the very genesis of the Dendaril themselves.

"It is an irony, is it not?" said the Voice. "A thing of such power and importance, yet so small and light that a child might lift it. We must- guh..."

The Voice stopped mid-sentence, and a moment later Mother Dorcas' Porters shouted in alarm. "The Elucidated Mother.. her Ending is upon her!" cried their leader. It was true. As Joniah watched, the old woman slumped in her seat and then simply came apart, disgorging a swarm of Bearers larger than any he had ever seen. Only the tiniest ruined scraps of flesh remained of the Elucidated Mother, and Joniah marvelled at the sight. To have clung to even a semblance of life under such circumstances must have taken a truly colossal effort of will.

"We are diminished," said the Voice, sadly, "And yet Mother Dorcas' Ending is not entirely in vain. Behold!"

Joniah had expected the swarm of Bearers to simply mill about or disappear randomly into the forest, as usually happened when no suitable host was present at the time of an Ending, but instead the entire thick mass suddenly hurtled skywards. Never had he seen Bearers so large or so fast, and as he watched they disappeared into the night sky. A moment later, a gout of flame erupted in the heavens.

"Antorathes comes to hinder our work," said the Voice. "But she reckons without the Bearers of Mother Dorcas. See now as she withdraws- the mightiest single beast in all creation, set to flight by the very least. Such is the power of the Gift."

Joniah would have to take the Pilgrim's word for that. His own eyesight could see nothing in the dark sky, but there were no more blasts of fire and no giant, taloned beast of nightmare swooping on the camp.

"Now," said the Voice, seemingly satisfied that the threat of the Dragon had receded. "Bring forth the vessel for the Heart-stone. To touch a thing of such power is fatal, and we must prepare to bear it away from this place."

Joniah watched as the camp returned to action, labourers carefully pushing the Heart-stone to the side of the flooded shaft with long poles where Pilgrims awaited with a large wicker basket. All was proceeding as the Elucidated Ones had planned. The wind carried the distant sounds of battle to his ears, but with so many Dendaril defending the mountain and the greatest prize now in their grasp, victory must now be certain.

118

*A*manda Devereux led the way down the darkened corridor, Elsabeth at her side. The glow-crystals set into the walls remained dark, and whilst the Ambassador was fairly confident that she could light them without alerting the High Wizards to their presence, it was agreed to be too much of a risk. As it was, with Devereux's own enhanced vision supported by the Aethersight of the Magister and Wizard, along with Ilia's own superior eyesight from her Seal, they were able to find their way in the darkness with some confidence.

As the Operative had expected, they encountered neither resistance nor any significant magical defences. The illusion at the cave entrance, after all, should have been completely impenetrable to anyone the High Wizards might have expected to be dealing with. Eventually they came to the huge chamber containing the Reaper, and Alaran let out a low whistle.

"King's Grace, I've never seen anything like this. What do you think it does?"

"That's why we brought you along, remember?" said Ilia. "You and the Ambassador here. Get to it- we need to uncover whatever dirty little secret the High Wizards are hiding in here and get out again before they come back."

Alaran was still gazing at the machine in awe. "Whatever it is, I'd hardly call it little."

Elsabeth was also staring at the device with her Aethersight. "Well... we can see a few things immediately. Those silver rods in the lower panel are charged with Aether, for one thing."

"They seem to be the staffs of the High Wizards," said Devereux. "When I was last here Galantharas took one of them and replaced it with his own staff."

Elsabeth frowned. "He did? That's extremely unusual. A Magister is very closely bonded to her staff- I've certainly never known any to keep more than one of them. I wouldn't touch that, if I were you." She added the last to Temis, who had wandered over to the rods. He shrugged.

"Hey, can't we just smash this thing up or something? Whatever it is, if it's that important to the High Wizards we could strike a pretty good blow for the cause like that."

"You'd be more likely to get yourselves killed," said Elsabeth. "Now that I know what I'm looking for, I've had a better look around the area, and there are at least three more of those staffs in the rooms behind that door over there, which probably means three High Wizards are about five minutes' walk away. You start damaging their... whatever this is, and I'd be very surprised if they didn't come running."

"Yeah, so maybe we take advantage and ambush them too?" said Derik. Elsabeth sighed.

"You and you friends couldn't successfully ambush Magister Thalia with three times as many people as we have here. And let me remind you, three High Wizards are far more powerful than a single three-Leaf Magister and a few bodyguards. If we were very lucky, with my power, Operative Devereux and Master Delys, along with your own.. contributions, we might defeat one of them but it would be neither easy, nor quiet."

"Okay, so we're not breaking anything, at least not yet," said Devereux. "Ilia, get your people set up to cover that door. Del and I will support you. I should be able to give you a heads-up if anyone's coming, so watch for my signal and for fuck's sake don't attack anyone without my order. If we have to hide from these High Wizards we mustn't give them any reason to get suspicious and start using their magic to search for us."

Ilia nodded. "I understand. If one of them notices us, though, I'll try to put an arrow in them before they can cast a shield."

Alaran shuddered. "I don't even want to think about challenging a High Wizard. I've heard stories about what happens to people who try."

"Then let's get on, shall we?" said Elsabeth, brightly. "It's not every day one gets to study a device as complex as this. If only Magister Jarton were here, he'd be happier than a Toskan pirate in Dalliance."

Devereux waited nervously as the Magister and Wizard examined the huge machine. All of her active and passive sensors were at full gain, to the extent that until the Hercules suite filtered them out she could hear the heartbeats and breathing of all her companions. Oddly enough, though, even though the door they were watching seemed fairly mundane she couldn't pick up any signs of life beyond it. Of course that tied in to the fact that she hadn't been able to read the vital signs of Galantharas either, but she also couldn't hear any footsteps or other sounds, other than a very faint moaning of wind.

"Thelen's breath.." muttered Elsabeth, finally. "Amanda, I think we have the beginning of your answer, and it's... well, it's terrifying. When you were telling me about this place, you mentioned Master Motes and Traitor Motes? Well, I think we now know what those are."

"Those tanks up there," said Alaran, pointing. "They mostly contain simple water, but each also holds untold millions of tiny living cells. One tank is designed so that a single cell can be decanted into one of those lower containment cylinders- that's what the main body of the machine does. The other is connected to the water pipes coming into the room from above."

"Okay," said Devereux. "But what does it do? Where do these 'motes' come into it?"

"This is more of a guess, based on what you've told me about Athas," said Elsabeth. "But from what we can tell, each cell, or mote, in one cylinder is entangled with a cell from the other. The Master Motes stay here, while the Traitor Motes are piped out into the mountain lake that Aquila stands on the shores of. That lake supplies the drinking water for half the cities in the Kingdom via the rivers it feeds. Once someone drinks water with a Traitor Mote in it, the cell is absorbed into their system and they become entangled with a Master Mote."

"Fuck me," said Devereux, with feeling. "I think I'm beginning to see where this is going. The Reaper can tell when that happens, yeah?"

"In a manner of speaking, yes," said Alaran. "The Master Motes are pumped through the machine, and subjected to a drain of Spirit. Those which have an active corresponding Traitor Mote will supply a steady stream of Spirit, and are then decanted into those cylinders. An Aether-Emerald is placed in the connected receptacle, and the Spirit of the victim is gradually drained into it."

"The Winnowing Ague," said Devereux, grimly. "It was in the water all along, but because those mote things aren't dangerous in their own right no-one spotted it."

Elsabeth nodded. "Yes. In Athas' case, I suspect the Wizards tried implanting a Traitor Mote directly with the new flesh. They must have already narrowed down the corresponding Master Motes to a few possibilities, which was why they used that portable device- they'd have had to test each Mote separately and the Reaper's not designed to do it."

Devereux frowned. "I still don't get it, though. This machine charges up the High Wizard's staffs for them, and it's a really, really slow way to fill those emeralds that also sometimes kills people. Why? I've got three of the fucking things in my sword and Del can fill them just by touching me!"

"Three?" said Alaran, peering at the sword. "I only count two. One of the sockets is empty."

"Well, yeah," said Devereux. "That was the one that Magister Fredus....."

Her voice tailed off, and she took an involuntary step away from the Reaper in horror. "Oh. Oh fuck me. Fuck. Me."

Alaran raised an eyebrow. "I'm not saying it's not an inviting prospect, but I'm guessing that's not what you meant. What?"

Elsabeth and Devereux both glared at him for a moment, before the Ambassador turned back to the Operative. "He's a young man, Amanda, and there is always the temptation to show off around beautiful women. I take it you have come to an unpleasant realisation?"

"M-maybe," said Devereux. "Look, I was there when Magister Fredus Dane self-Committed, and somehow part of him got... stuck in one of the Aether-Emeralds in my sword. I was even able to talk to him occasionally. Eventually he ended up controlling Xodan, and helped us destroy it, but the gem broke in the process and I think he.. died? Again? But what if... what if you drained all of someone's Aether into one of those gems and they died. What happens to them?"

"Well, the Pattern of the body would detach from that of the mind," said Elsabeth. "The physical body has to be Committed to return to Aether, but that of the mind scatters almost immediately. But if the draining effect was ongoing... oh."

Alaran looked from one to the other, askance. "Are you telling me that those gems don't just contain a person's power, but their... their *soul?*"

Elsabeth shrugged, though the look on her face belied the nonchalance of the gesture. "Well, that's how the Breathers might put it. I'd imagine it's more a.. debased copy of the Pattern of their mind. It wouldn't be capable of more than simple.. tasks... no. No, surely they wouldn't. Surely they didn't!"

"Oh, I think they did," said Devereux. "It's the fucking Golems, isn't it? The College could never work out how the Abelians make them move independently. I'll bet if we broke one of those damn things open, there'd be an emerald stuck right in the middle of it. Fuck me, there was even a Stickman in that store-room right next to the device!"

"The first Golems were simple, almost totally mindless," said Alaran, quietly. "It was only after the Ague started that High Wizard Ranthalian presented ones that were actually useful. Now I understand why."

"I certainly understand why this machine was so well-hidden," said Elsabeth. "The question now is what, if anything, we do about it."

"If anything?" replied Alaran incredulously. "The High Wizards killed millions with this thing to create the Golems! They must be exposed!"

"And what then?" said Elsabeth. "The Abelian economy is completely depen-dent on the Golems. Do you think exposing the High Wizards will bring any of their victims back? What if they threaten to disable or destroy the Golems to protect themselves?"

"B-but... we can't keep using them, knowing what they are!" stammered Alaran.

"So what would you do with them? Destroy them? You're talking about Abelia's entire labour force and the bulk of its military."

"If nothing else," said Devereux, as Alaran floundered in confusion, "I think we can all agree that this... thing needs to go. I've made up a charge of explosive that I can detonate remotely. Where's the best place to put it that'll wreck this thing without bringing down the whole cave?"

Even as she spoke, Daniel was giving the Operative a detailed structural analysis of the chamber. The small pack of C-6 explosive she had nano-manufac-tured over the last few hours had a significant yield but so long as the Reaper contained the blast, the Hercules suite was optimistic about the integrity of the cave itself.

"You can do what?" said Alaran. Elsabeth seemed less surprised, but given that Devereux had briefed her on her capabilities that was to be expected.

"I'd go with the console at the bottom," said Elsabeth. "It's the nexus for most of the Aether running through the device and the Patterns of most of the control spells run through it. How powerful is your device, exactly?"

"That's.. not easy to answer in a way you'd understand," said Devereux, calling up some comparative simulations. "But there's roughly enough here to completely destroy... hmm.. a War Golem. Not that I'd like to try it."

Alaran let out another low whistle. "That's some explosion. I agree with Elsa-beth- if you place it under the console, near those staffs, it's near enough to the most critical parts of the Reaper to completely destroy it. Most of the rest of the machine is just plumbing."

Devereux worked swiftly, closely watched by Elsabeth. Finding a suitable spot, she shaped the C-6 charge to direct most of its force up into the very heart of the Reaper.

"It doesn't look like much," said the Magister, having studied the greyish putty with both her natural and magical vision.

"That's the point," said Devereux. "This stuff was developed from a previous explosive which was already very hard to detect and difficult to set off accidentally. I don't know how it looks to your Aethersight, but to all but the most advanced chemical sniffers it reads as completely harmless. But once I put this detonator into it, I can trigger it remotely from a mile or so away, depending on the terrain."

"Fascinating," murmured Elsabeth. "Your world must be a very dangerous place, Amanda Devereux, when something so powerful can be so easily concealed."

Devereux slid herself out from under the machine, and nodded. "It is. Threats like this stuff are exactly the reason the Office- my old employer- was created. We used the most cutting-edge stealth warfare technology available to make sure it never fell into the wrong hands."

"That sounds like trying to win a race against your own shadow," said Elsabeth. "Why even create such things in the first place?"

Devereux shrugged. "Science moves forward whether we like it or not. Medical technology, A.I., nanotech, advanced chemical engineering- they've massively improved the lives of people in my world, but also exposed it to all sorts of new dangers."

Elsabeth smiled. "I'm not sure I understood half of that, but it sounds like you're talking about Walanstahl's staff."

"Huh?"

"Walanstahl's staff- an illustration that Patron used to use. Take a six-foot long wooden pole, and what do you have? To a Magister, it's a staff, both tool and weapon. To a warrior, it's a quarterstaff or spear-shaft. To a labourer, it's a lever or a prop. To a fisherman, it's a fishing-pole. You can't give a person one of those things without also giving them all of the others."

Ilia came over, having been brought up to date by Alaran. "So, Amanda, what's our next move? I agree with Elsabeth that we can't just decide what to do about the Golems on our own, so we need proof of what the High Wizards have done to take to the Queen."

Devereux nodded. "I assume you also agree about destroying this thing?"

"Alaran says it won't affect the existing Golems, so yes," said Ilia. "I may think that keeping them around might be a necessary evil, but no way in all the stinking fucking jungles of Jandalla am I letting those robed bastards make any more of them."

"Good," said Devereux. "I don't like suggesting it, but I think we're going to need to go deeper into this place. We need some proof- documents, schematics, anything."

"Not to mention we should find out if the High Wizards really could disable the Golems," said Ilia. "They've threatened to do it before."

"Okay." said Devereux. "But you need to understand this is going to be incredibly dangerous. I've set the charge in a fail-safe mode, so if I die or go out-of-range of the detonator, it'll blow an hour later. It'll also go off if anyone tampers with it."

"Why so long?" said Alaran.

"Because there's always a chance that something will interfere with the signal," ·

said Devereux. "If that happens, I need enough time to get back into range. We don't want the charge going off if I lose contact for a couple of seconds, after all."

"Not to mention it gives us time to get out of here if something goes wrong," pointed out Elsabeth. "So, Amanda, same plan as before- you and me in front, Alaran at the back?"

Devereux nodded. "Yeah,"

"What if we run into any of the High Wizards?" said Alaran. Delys, who had been watching the door silently, pointed to the sword on her back.

"Like Del says," said Devereux. "We know now that they're a bunch of murderers. If one of them spots us, we hit them fast, hard and quiet and try to take them out before they can defend themselves or raise the alarm. Anyone who doesn't like that idea had better stay behind."

"Not like it?" growled Temis. "It's the first thing you've said since we got here that I really *have* liked."

Ilia nodded, grimly. "Let's get this done."

he warning horns echoed through the Vigil, rousing Magister Haran from the first even vaguely decent sleep he'd managed to get for some days. He dressed quickly, remembering in irritation the loss of his mail-shirt, and hurried to the battlements to investigate, finding Sir Matthew and the High Vigilant already there.

"What's happening, High Vigilant?" asked the Magister, trying to keep his irritation out of his voice. Have the Dendaril mounted a fresh attack?"

Earlier in the night, the white-clad horde which had been lurking in the distant forest had withdrawn. It had been this which had prompted Haran to call a halt to the Petard Engine bombardment to allow the Singers to rest and his troops to get some much-needed undisturbed sleep. Even so, the sentries had been set with care and the Choirmasters had assured him that they could recommence firing in minutes should the need arise. From the fact that the Engines still lay silent, he presumed it had not.

"Not them, but something's certainly up, Learned Magister," said Wilhelmina. "There was a flash of flame in the skies far to the east a few minutes ago, and-"

"There's another!" shouted one of the sentries, pointing into the air. Sure enough, some distance away over the forest a gout of flame had suddenly appeared, vanishing almost as soon as Haran saw it.

"-and there've been several more since, each one closer than the last," continued the High Vigilant. "We don't know what to make of it, but I've ordered the troops stood-to as a precaution."

"Closer and lower," said Sir Matthew. "Whatever it is, it's descending as it approaches. If it carries on at that rate, I'd wager it'll hit the ground some way short of the- Queen's Grace!"

The exclamation was prompted by a final burst of fire that erupted above the forest just short of the Vigil's killing field. For a moment, not only the trees were illuminated, but also the source of the flames. A huge, gloss-black, scaled and winged form, twisting and flailing awkwardly as it fell.

"It's a fucking Dr-" began Wilhelmina, but before she could finish the huge body slammed into the forest with such force that Haran felt himself bounce an inch into the air. Trees were shattered and smashed asunder by the impact as the creature disappeared into their midst before finally coming to a halt.

"Well," said Magister Ollan, pausing at the top of the stairs. "That's certainly not something one sees every morning."

Already, below, the Expelled camp pitched against the east-facing wall of the Vigil was clamouring into life, warriors rousing from their bedrolls and casting off their war-cloaks. Striding to the edge of the battlements, Haran looked down to see the Mighty Ones rushing to the fore, seeking to restrain their kin.

"I wouldn't like to be that Dragon if the Expelled get hold of her," said Ollan. "They should be bound by the Decree of Fire like everyone else, of course, but there's no telling if they intend to honour it."

"We need to get down there!" snapped Haran. "High Vigilant, take charge here. Runner! Send word to Captain Render to have a Dispensation meet us at the gates, then tell Magister Pieter in the Infirmary to safeguard the Vigil until I return."

"I will accompany you also, Magister Haran," said Sir Matthew, stepping into his armour. "I will collect Nemesis and meet you below."

As they ran down the stairs, Haran found time to ask Ollan the question that had occurred to him. "You said *her*, Learned Magister? Do you know which Dragon that is?"

"If... I guessed..." puffed Ollan, face red with exertion, "I'd say... Antorathes. Certainly... not the first.... time she's visited."

They reached the main gates in time to meet up with Captain Render and her troops, led by Sergeant Tika. As they swung open, Mighty Dokan was waiting for them.

"It is well that you are here, Mighty Haran. There is little love between the Free Tribes and the scaled ones, but our songs remind us of the ancient pact between man and Dragon. Still, no few of our young-bloods relish the thought of being the first Dragon-slayer among the Free."

"The consequences of such an action would be dire, Mighty Dokan," pointed out Haran. "The Decree was signed in the blood of Thelen and the Patrons, as well as that of the mightiest Dragons and Whales. If broken, the magic will slay the transgressor, as well as many of the most powerful of their kin, chosen largely at random."

"And then it'd probably start a war into the bargain," said Ollan, who had recovered a little of his breath. "We're hardly in a position to deal with that, even without an unspecified number of our best and brightest suddenly dropping dead on the spot." His eyes widened. "Great Thelen- that could actually include *me!*"

"This, too, the songs teach us," said Dokan. "And yet the Free will not stand idly by while a thing of such wonder lies so close at hand. A war-band will investigate, but if you will lead, we will follow."

A clattering of silver-shod hooves announced the arrival of Sir Matthew. "I shall ride ahead, Magister Haran!" he shouted. "Valour Defiant!"

Before Haran could object, the Knight had already galloped off, heading for the ravaged tree-line.

"Very well," said Haran. "Mighty Dokan, your most capable Mighty Ones should accompany us. Even if the Dendaril have withdrawn, those damnable flies may still be abroad."

"You speak, and it is so, Mighty Haran," said Dokan, pointing. A war-band was approaching, led by Mighty Xaraya and the Black Skull. Haran also recognised Fleeting Deer, Red Trace in White Snow, and the Firsts and Seconds of all three tribes.

"Just be sure to remind them that we go to investigate, not to kill," said Haran. "We already have one potential disaster looming in this forest, I would sooner not precipitate another."

120

*T*halia was woken from a fitful doze by a jolt as the *Dreadnought* came to a stop. It was a testament to the vehicle's excellent engineering that she'd been able to sleep at all, even as the Royal Army convoy crossed the trampled undergrowth and pulverised trees left in the wake of the Siege Golems. Bleary-eyed, she wondered what time it might be- they were far too far from the Waycrystal of any city she knew of for her to easily find out. A glance at the window-panel revealed that it was still pitch black outside.

She rolled clumsily off the bed and padded through to the command room on bare feet to consult the map-table. From what she could tell, the coaches were once more being formed up into a defensive circle, but with one important difference to the previous occasions. With the exception of a single Demolition of War Golems and an Assemblage of Stickmen, the rest of the automaton infantry was redeployed in a huge column, with the Royal Knights at the centre of the formation. For a moment, she thought she was misreading the display, for there seemed to be double the number of Knights that she was expecting. Rubbing her eyes and looking closer, she saw her error. Each Knight was represented with a small blue depiction of their personal crest, and what she had taken for another group of Knights was in fact a similar symbol that represented their horses, which had been corralled in the middle of the camp.

The reason for this change of tactics was made immediately clear by the topography. Though the Royal Army had been travelling uphill for some time, the previously gentle slope had become far steeper and strewn with rocks. It was almost completely impassable for the wheeled coaches, and would restrict the movement of cavalry mounts so much as to eliminate any advantage they might usually have conferred. Therefore, it seemed the Royal Knights intended to advance on foot. Whilst it seemed to Thalia that this must be taking a terrible risk, she was acutely aware that her knowledge of the Knights' capabilities, not to mention Abelian battlefield tactics in general, was distinctly limited. A single Three-Leaf College

Magister, especially one of no more than mediocre ability at Impose, was unlikely to have more tactical acumen than the Royal Army's entire command staff.

Athas appeared in the corridor, wearing only his soft leather breeches. "Oh, er, good morning, Learned Magister. Er. Is it morning?"

Thalia gestured at the window-panel. "If so, it's only in the most literal sense. I think it's still some hours before dawn."

Athas looked at the map-table. "But we're getting ready to attack?"

Thalia snorted. "*We* aren't getting ready to do anything, except possibly have an early breakfast. The Royal Army is preparing to advance on the Mountain Halls, or whatever's left of them, and once they've finished killing every Dendaril they find and trampling all over the Free Tribes' most sacred ground, they might just decide to let me out to try to persuade them to surrender to the Queen."

"Oh," said Athas. "Yeah, I suppose with those fly-things out there going outside's probably not a very good idea."

"I don't know if any of this is 'a good idea', Sergeant," groused Thalia. "We- the Abelians- were expecting to be hitting the Dendaril from behind whilst they were pinned against the Vigil, not advancing uphill against an enemy who've had days to dig themselves in. Whatever's going on here, Queen Tondarin is just marching blindly into it."

Athas shrugged. "Well, from what we've seen of those Golems in action, not to mention the Knights, they can probably handle it. I remember something Captain Gantis used to say when he was playing Impose- 'They can't fool you if they're dead.'"

Thalia frowned. "What did that have to do with Impose?"

Athas smiled at the memory. "He was really good at beating Magisters at it. If he couldn't figure out what their plan was, he would just settle for taking as many of their pieces as he could as efficiently as he could, even if some of them didn't seem to be doing anything important."

The Magister sighed. "Sergeant, that hardly counts as tactics. Any Magister who knew that he was trying to do that could easily mislead him."

"Yeah," nodded Athas, "but the thing was he was *also* really good at the game anyway. So a lot of the time he'd see the real plan, but if he couldn't, he'd do something so direct that any Magister trying too elaborate a strategy often got caught out. I'm not explaining this very well, I know, I was never any good at Impose. Or Chasten, for that matter. I'm not very good at tricking people."

"I understand what you're trying to say, at least," said Thalia. "Ultimately, if the Royal Army can force their way to the top of that mountain and defeat the Dendaril there, it should weaken their position at the very least, if not drive them completely out of the forest."

They watched as the runes denoting the Royal Army units advanced swiftly up the mountainside. Thalia had walked the ground there herself fairly recently, and couldn't help but be impressed by how easily the Abelians were coping with the treacherous terrain, judging by the speed they were moving at. If the Dendaril had expected the surroundings to give them a tactical advantage, they looked to be in for the rudest of awakenings.

"It's funny, though, isn't it?" said Athas, suddenly. "You remember what you told me Lady Ysabella said?"

"About what?" said Thalia, as the last runes moved out of the range of the map display.

"About the Dendaril probably attacking us before we got to the Mountain Halls unless they were.. complete dunces? Well, we're here, and so far, they haven't."

Thalia looked at the map again. "That's a good point. It's possible that they just decided to make a stand on the mountainside, where they'd have the high ground."

"If I was them," said Athas, "I'd wait for the Royal Army to leave the camp and then attack it, try to kill the Wizards controlling the Golems. If I- I mean, the Dendaril- managed to take this camp and fortify it, it'd make the Golems a lot less useful and catch the Royal Army between their forces above, and a hostile camp below."

Thalia stared at him. "I think perhaps you were paying more attention to Captain Gantis' Impose lessons than you give yourself credit for, Sergeant. In any case, I suspect the Abelian generals agree with you. That's probably why they left a pretty significant force of Golems behind here."

"Yeah," nodded Athas. "Those War Golems are bloody nasty, and anyway there's thirty Wizards here. You'd need to have totally unwoven your basket to attack this place without a fuckto- er, I mean without a lot of troops."

"You're forgetting that this camp also contains a Magister and one of the strongest men in the College Guard," said Thalia with a small smile, only really noticing Athas' state of undress for the first time as she did so. "Er, speaking of which, we'd better get properly dressed and see to some breakfast, just in case we need to.."

"In case we need to what, Learned Magister?" said Athas, already standing up, half-stooped to avoid the ceiling.

Thalia shrugged. "I have no idea. But whatever we might need to do, we at least need to be wearing appropriate clothes for it."

Athas nodded, his expression serious, and Thalia watched him go to change into his armour. Of course, there was one thing for which they were both appropriately dressed, but now was hardly the time.

481

121

*L*ed by the imposing form of Ixilinath, the skin of whose borrowed body was already beginning to burn away, the Ixildar warriors struck with the ferocity of a tree-lion defending her cubs. At first, their progress was swift, covering several miles of forest opposed only by scattered enemy war-bands that seemed to be retreating and put up little serious resistance. Indeed, only the fact that the eastern forest through which they advanced bordered the territory of the Blackbloods caused any impediment at all. The Stonesingers, whose own lands lay on the northern side of the vague border, took the lead, and were able to direct their kin to avoid the worst of the various venomous beasts that the Blackbloods had allowed to flourish within their domain, they themselves being immune to most poisons.

Moon Behind Dark Clouds wondered what the fate of the remaining Black-bloods, not to mention the stout Tree-Searchers and fierce Heart-Eaters, had been. Had they successfully fled to the lands of the Deluded, or might his warriors soon face enemies bearing the war-tattoos of the Free, if not the knowledge to properly employ them? The fact that the title of Free Tribes might now fit the exiles far better than it did his own people came once more unbidden to his mind, and he suppressed the unworthy thought savagely. They had acted as they must.

Mighty Lelioko, who led the Shorewalkers alongside him, suddenly turned to Moon. "First, order your Eagle Hunters into the trees. We approach the Mountain Halls, and the true battle."

Moon nodded, and issued the Call. The Eagle Hunters, Small Fangs in Shadow and her sisters among them, had been given very specific instructions by the Mighty Ones. They were to save their arrows for either dire emergency, or for the white-robed Pilgrims of the Fly Lords, who served as the Mighty Ones of their kind. Though their knowledge in the ways of magic was poor compared to the Mighty, the Pilgrims outnumbered their forest-dwelling counterparts almost ten-to-one and would probably be defended with fanatical devotion. A single well-placed arrow from an unexpected quarter might easily save hundreds of lives, even as it ended one.

Mere moments later they struck the main enemy battle-line, and the northern forest erupted in fire, smoke and pandemonium as the Ixildar pressed home their attack. Moon had led many a war-band in his time, and stared death in the face more than once, be it in the form of the blue-haired coast raiders or rival tribes of the Free. But nothing in those years of combat, of silently stalking prey and being stalked in turn, of struggling breast-to-breast and blade-to-blade with the foe, had prepared him for this. It wasn't just the sudden improvement in both the tactics and co-ordination of the enemy that was disconcerting, but the sheer scale of the battle. Even the largest inter-tribal conflicts had usually been resolved by confrontations of war-bands no larger than fifty strong, but this clash featured some ten thousand warriors on the Ixildar side alone.

As for the enemy- it seemed that every rock, tree and shadow had suddenly sprouted limbs and seized a dagger. There were so many of the white-clad fanatics, their ragged tunics now stained a muddy brown, that their poor weapons became almost an advantage, for the thick forest and sheer press of bodies would have hampered larger, more imposing blades. The Ixildar, though, were well-versed in fighting in their home terrain, and wielded spear and curved knife with accustomed skill. Here and there, those warriors whose choice of weapon required more room rampaged through the Dendaril lines in berserk fury, long-hafted axes and heavy mauls simply felling trees on top of their foes where they might otherwise have been impeded. Moon saw Rocks Falling send ten men flying to their ruin with a single sweep of his weapon, before a bolt of lightning transfixed the First of the Stonesingers and sent it spinning from his grasp. Before the white-robed Pilgrim responsible could finish her prey, three arrows slammed into her breast and she fell as surely as any of her kin.

"With me!" roared Moon, and his warriors advanced, spears jabbing and knives slashing. Mighty Lelioko brought wide sheets of flame down on those Dendaril foolish enough to try to stand in her way, and within moments they had reached the side of Rocks Falling.

"Can you stand, First?" said Lelioko, dropping to her knees next to the warrior as the elite of the Shorewalkers pushed the foe back further.

"Aye," said Rocks Falling, sitting up and spitting blood. "That robed wench struck firm, I'll give her that, but no firmer than my wife when I overcook the stew."

Moon passed him his maul, and his fellow First levered himself to his feet. "Still, Mighty One, I mislike this. These Fly Lords have grown both a spine and sharp fangs, and we are yet some distance from the Mountain Halls."

"Aye," agreed Night's First Raven. "Before they fought only to slay, once they realised the Master's gift made us immune to their Woe. But now- now they fight for territory. They are trying to hold us back, and they care not what the blood-price might be to achieve it."

"If they are so determined to die for this patch of ground, I say we help them," snarled Rocks Falling, hefting his maul. "For myself, I intend to live for it. Stonesingers! Onwards! For the Forest Home!"

With a great shout the Stonesingers leapt forwards once more, spears jabbing as Rocks Falling's maul went about its red work. Some paces behind, Mighty

Renjka lent her power in support. The chief Mighty One of the Stonesingers was not famed for her battle-prowess, but instead focused her power into the weapons of her kin-folk, giving already deadly spear-tips of knapped, enchanted flint a still-keener edge. More Pilgrims emerged to attempt to stem the rush, lightning flaring, but Renjka's magic was equal to the challenge and bolts that would have slain whole ranks of warriors instead pattered harmlessly from her defences like summer rain. Though they tried, few of the Pilgrims were able to deflect the Eagle Hunters' swift retribution.

The night air was still darker now with Little Ones, the tiny insects darting back and forth, searching for victims to infest. Though every warrior they bit was protected by the Master's fire, the mindless flies swarmed in such great number that more than one was felled by the sheer number of tiny entrance wounds, each injury smouldering in the aftermath of cleansing fire that staunched the flow of blood but did nothing to replace the missing flesh.

"Umba's teeth!" hissed Mighty Lelioko. "These things have not the sense to avoid their doom at the Master's hands, and no few of our kin will pay the price for their ignorance. Mighty of the Tree-Searchers!" she shouted. "Redouble your efforts- we must repel at least some of these beasts, less we suffer a death of a thousand bites!"

Hearing her words, the Mighty Ones began to lay down sheets of fire, burning some of the insects to ashes and sending the rest surging away in terror, or at least some mindless semblance of it. But this change of tactics was not without cost. More Pilgrims began to emerge, death crackling from their fingers, and few Mighty Ones had power to spend to repel them. Worse, the thick clouds of flies, gouts of fire, and smoke from both wood and insect corpses obscured even the exceptional vision of the Eagle Hunters. The enemy spell-casters were surviving too long, and inflicting almost as many casualties as the Little Ones had.

"Stalking Wolves!" roared Moon, despite a throat raw from the smoke. "Strike low!"

In answer to the call, those warriors bearing the Wolf slunk forwards in their beast-shapes, bellies low to the ground and fighting their beast-mind's instinctive fear of fire. Almost invisible in the gloom, they struck at the Pilgrims' ankles and loins from below, bringing many down in a screaming mass of flailing limbs. Though few were able to finish off their prey before being forced to withdraw, the enemy magical assault slackened considerably.

As they drove forward, Moon Behind Dark Clouds wondered what the wider situation might be. They were the tip of the Ixildar formation, the strongest and most experienced warriors of their tribes, and yet their forward progress was slowing as more and more of the enemy, including some armoured troops, mustered to oppose them. If they were unable to make headway, surely the situation on their flanks must be worse.

Then the Master entered the fray, and Moon understood his error. Ixilinath had deliberately committed His apparent vanguard ahead of His main battle-line, holding back His flanks, and the Dendaril had taken advantage to bring their greatest strength to bear in their centre, thinking to shatter the Ixildar advance, slay their leaders, and split their forces in two. They had reckoned without Ixilinath. Striding forwards at the head of His Eternals, supported by Mighty Tyrona and the Guardians of the Halls, the Master brought his terrible fire to bear on the

Fly Lords. Ten Pilgrims, whose magic had repelled hundreds of arrows and threatened to challenge the Mighty Ones, were blasted to ash in mere seconds. A thousand Dendaril, screaming in outrage, hurled themselves at the advancing Eternals, but the fleshless warriors were indifferent both to the Little Ones and to their frantic hosts, and cut them down methodically. Behind them, the Guardians' spears brought low any who tried to flee or threaten the flanks of their advance.

"Nak's Skull," gasped Night's First Raven. "To see the Master's wrath unleashed so- what use has such a one for we mere mortals? Why does He even care about our fate?"

"It is enough that He does, Wife," said Moon. "But you heard the Master's words- Mighty Taris' body can contain His power for only a single fleeting night and day, and the dawn fast approaches. See, our kin in the other war-bands advance, and we must follow- there is far yet to go, and many foes yet to slay before the Mountain Halls are ours once more."

"Aye," said his wife, nodding. "For the Forest Home!"

The other Shorewalkers took up the cry, and drove forward in the Master's wake. Around them, the forest burned, its air filled with the buzzing flies and its soil stained red with blood. Not for the first time, Moon wondered if they were truly saving the Forest Home, or destroying it.

122

*I*t was still late at night when Smiling Snake and Bai Faoha arrived at the Great Sage's laboratory. As soon as they had reached the outskirts of the city, Rya-Ki had sent word to the Hono estates for Frowning Iron to meet him as a matter of some urgency, and was relieved to find his brother waiting for him when he entered. He was not alone, which presented certain challenges, but also certain opportunities.

"Brother!" said Tekkan-Cho, rushing forwards with a rattle of armour. "Your aspect bears the greatest concern! How may I aid you?"

"You are leader of our clan, General Tekkan-Cho," admonished his companion, Swan-Neck Tsue. "It is not seemly for you to be at the service of a subordinate."

"Silence!" roared Frowning Iron. "Leader of the Hono I may be, but Brother Rya-Ki is my elder, and worthy of the greatest respect that I might offer. Only the Son of Heaven stands higher in my regard, and that is true only through duty."

Swan-Neck bowed, chastened. "I humbly apologise, General. I meant no disrespect."

Smiling Snake banged his staff on the floorboards. "Enough. Tsue Tian-Jin, your intent was pure but there is no time for such trivialities as pride this night. I see you have brought blade, armour and a desire for honour to my chambers. Have you the courage to use them?"

Swan-Neck lifted her head proudly, displaying the elegant throat that had given her her name. "Always, Great Sage. Name he who must be cut, and cut he shall be."

"Would that I could," said Rya-Ki. "Brother, we have received a most dire portent this night through the whispering shadows. The Dendaril, foul hosts of the Mind-Stealers, stand on the cusp of a great victory, and it falls to the Hono to thwart them." He tapped the second ring of his staff, and his attendants swiftly hurried into the room, leading before them the three remaining sacrificial vessels that he had kept in reserve in case of such an emergency.

486

"Brother..." said Tekkan-Cho, eyeing the drugged vessels worriedly. "These... can it be that you intend once more to attempt the Third Mirror? There is no time to rally the troops, much less to perform the ritual of the Dragon's Spear."

"Neither will be necessary," said Smiling Snake, as his attendants uncovered the mirror. "And in any case, I would not seek to turn your wise words in the Divine Pavilion to dust in your mouth. We go not to conquer the Chaotic East, but to deprive the Dendaril of their ill-omened gains."

"And what of the vengeful *kami* that repelled our previous assault?" said Tekkan-Cho. "Will he not be moved to still greater wrath when we flout his mercy so blatantly?"

"I believe that the spirit of the Most Learned Magister Fredus has passed on to.. whatever fate awaits the children of the Devil Thelen in the beyond," said Smiling Snake. "If he has not, I shall offer him reason. Should that fail, I shall offer him my head in recompense."

"Great Sage!" gasped Bai Faoha. "You cannot do such a thing! Let me face the fury of the *kami* in your stead!"

"Who is this worm that barks like a dog, Brother?" said Tekkan-Cho with a scowl, his hand flashing to his sword. "If you require that he be taught his place, I shall gladly oblige."

Rya-Ki smiled. "That will not be necessary, Brother. Like Tsue Tian-Jin, White Crocus speaks thus only out of concern for the clan's future." He turned to the younger Sage, who had dropped face-first to the floor at the first sign of Tekkan-Cho's displeasure. "Rise, Bai Faoha. Your offer is noble, though it would be wise to refrain from using the imperative form with your betters in future if you should desire a long life. In any case, the bargain originally struck was mine, and if the *kami* requires it, recompense must be paid by the transgressor."

White Crocus gave a short bow of acceptance, and Smiling Snake turned back to the two warriors. "Now, Brother, Lady Tsue. Bai Faoha and I must see to the unpleasant task of opening the way, which is no sight for the valorous. I beg you retire to my antechamber and meditate until the call to action comes."

"Very well," said Frowning Iron. "But when that call comes, what is our goal? To rush into battle knowing neither the terrain nor the objective is as sure a path to defeat as seeking to wrestle fire."

"You are most wise to say so," agreed Smiling Snake. "In this case, though, other than knowing that we seek an object of great value, I can tell you little. In this action we must be like rain in the wind, ready to react to circumstance in an instant. The foe will be unaware of our coming, so we shall strike as lightning strikes and be gone as swiftly as the thunder fades."

Tekkan-Cho nodded. "It shall have to suffice. Come, Tsue Tian-Jin, let us fill our minds with thoughts of honour and victory, for when next we open our eyes it shall be to make them reality through our valour."

The two warriors strode away, and Smiling Snake waited until they had entered the antechamber before turning, for to show two such esteemed guests his back would have been a grave insult. He found Bai Faoha and the attendants ready for him. In the event, it took only one sacrificial vessel for the Third Mirror to respond, and Smiling Snake had time enough to be satisfied that this must mean that the corresponding device had not been moved far before he became aware that something was amiss.

As he had expected, the scene that met his eyes was that of a mass of rubble. Considering that when he had left the ancient chamber in which the stone circle lay the ceiling had been collapsing, he had been expecting this, and had been prepared to unleash a blast of *ki* through the portal to dislodge it. Then it would simply be a case of determining where the Dendaril excavation lay and forcing their way into it. What he had not expected was for the rubble to almost immediately begin to quiver, as if acted upon by some great force. Even as he stepped back in alarm, rivulets of water began to trickle between the stones before the whole mass burst through the portal, rocks bouncing dangerously across the lacquered floor as dirty water flooded in.

123

*O*perative Amanda Devereux stole across the dimly-lit laboratory, fighting-knife at the ready. Once the small party had got past the door that led into the High Wizards' lair, it had become apparent that the three members of the Concordance present each had a set of chambers that adjoined the central corridor, which gradually led up towards the city of Aquila. Ordinarily, the goal of an infiltration would be to get into the target area silently, achieve the objective, and leave, but since no-one was exactly certain what they were looking for it had been agreed that a thorough search would be necessary. And that meant, much to the undisguised glee of the Savalan rebels, that anyone who might potentially raise the alarm needed to be dealt with.

There had been no shortage of volunteers for the task, but Devereux had exercised her command prerogative, knowing that her unique skill-set made her ideally suited to carry it out. Now she was mere metres away from the unsuspecting back of the first of the High Wizards, which looked by the robe to be the woman, Anthyana, who she had seen before. That made sense, given that she seemed to be in charge of the Reaper. Ideally, they'd take her alive for interrogation, but Devereux had seen enough of Magisters and Wizards to know that without extremely specialised equipment subduing one in such a way that they couldn't use their magic was almost impossible.

The complete lack of vital signs from the High Wizards was another concern. Even at a range of less than a metre, Anthyana seemed to have no detectable pulse or heartbeat, though her thermals suggested her organs must be in the right places. For a non-augmented assassin, this might have been a serious concern, since most silent-kill techniques involved striking the target in a vital spot whilst silencing them, but for an Operative, more extreme measures were both available, and often necessary. Treating the woman as if she were an augmented human of the very highest threat level, Devereux swiftly executed an Office-standard silent take-down, known colloquially as the 'belt-and-braces'.

Assassins and infiltrators throughout history, from the medieval enforcers of Persia through to the Comanche braves of the American Old West and Commandos of the Second World War, would have recognised the first motion- a swift seizing of the victim's head from behind in such a way as to throw them off-balance and muffle any attempt to call for help. But where those predecessors might have then struck at one of a variety of vital points to finish their victim as swiftly and efficiently as possible, the enhanced strength and speed of an Operative allowed for a more thorough approach. Within the space of less than a second, the monomolecular-edged blade had sliced cleanly through Anthyana's throat before moving on to rapidly penetrate every significant bodily organ that could be reached from behind. Heart, lungs, kidneys and liver, all were precisely impaled in what would have seemed like a mere blur of frenzied violence to any onlooker, should the Operative be incautious enough to allow such an individual to be present.

Even with the kill complete, for even the most heavily-augmented human could not survive such treatment for more than a few seconds, Devereux did not release her victim's corpse, instead swiftly sheathing the knife and transferring her grip to hold the High Wizard's dead hand closed about her staff without touching the thing itself. The next step would be to carefully lower the lifeless body to the ground, making sure to avoid any tell-tale clatter of weapons or equipment which might otherwise alert anyone nearby. It was at this moment that the Operative realised that something was horribly, terribly wrong. Far from collapsing, the High Wizard was struggling in her grasp, her free hand reaching to try to pry Devereux's own from her face as the other worked to wrench free of the Operative's grasp. Nor were these the feeble efforts of a dying woman, for their strength was sufficient to tax, if not overcome, Devereux's own.

What the fuck is going on?

Grimly, the Operative reflected that she must be feeling much like Jocasta had, when the Red Witch had sliced her throat as part of a ritual sacrifice and stabbed her heart, not understanding that the distributed physiology of a Desdemona-class cyborg reduced such usually fatal injuries to the level of an unpleasant inconvenience. Even so, whatever Anthyana was seemed to be even harder to kill. The High Wizard writhed in her grasp, twisting her body around and kicking back with legs so powerful that the stamp that Devereux narrowly avoided cracked the flagstone beneath the grappling women's feet. Then Delys arrived, moving with steps every bit as swift and almost as silent as Devereux's own.

With a speed and precision not significantly less than that of the Operative's knife, the great-sword struck, the first blow severing Anthyana's right arm just short of the shoulder and removing any chance of her using her staff. The High Wizard's body twisted again, now no longer fully under Devereux's control, but before she could act on her liberty Delys' eyes met the Operative's. Immediately, she released her grasp and ducked away as a decapitating strike put the outcome of the unequal struggle beyond any further doubt. The body tilted sideways, and Devereux caught it, the staff-bearing hand still held in her right as she cradled the rest of the corpse with her left, looking like some sort of macabre dancer. The severed head, meanwhile, struck the floor with an oddly-solid thud, though the sound was muted by the robe hood that still attended it.

Elsabeth and the rest of the rebels stole into the room, Ilia motioning Temis to watch the corridor before closing the door.

"We should be fine in here," said the Magister, quietly. "There's a privacy spell on the lab. Just don't make any loud noises."

"I thought you said you were a professional at this?" said Ilia. "What the fuck happened?"

"I-I don't know," said Devereux. "The injuries I inflicted should have killed her three times over, but they barely even seemed to slow her down." Grimacing, she laid the staff, and the gloved arm that held it, down on the floor. "I assume it's probably not a good idea to touch this thing?"

"You'd better not, no," agreed Elsabeth, kneeling down to inspect the body. "Ka- !" she began to exclaim, before putting her hand over her mouth quickly.

"What is it?" asked Devereux.

"That's a very accurate question, Amanda," said Elsabeth, seeming to have regained her composure. "*It* is... well, see for yourself."

Swiftly, the Ambassador stripped the remains of Anthyana's robes from her corpse, leaving her decapitated remains naked on the cold stone floor. The sight was less gruesome, yet somehow more horrifying, than it should have been.

"She's... she's made of wood," gasped Ilia. "She's a fucking Golem!"

"King's grace!" exclaimed Alaran, who had picked up the High Wizard's head. "Look at this!"

"Shh, idiot!" hissed Ilia. "What's the matter?"

Alaran held out the severed head. "There's a bit of skin here, sort of attached to the front of her face below the mask. There's even a working mouth and throat, with teeth and everything, even though the rest of her is wooden."

Devereux nodded. "Yeah. That must be so they can appear to eat and drink in public, like Galantharas did when I first met him."

"Fascinating," breathed Elsabeth. "They must use their magic to discorporate the food in their throats. Look, the body is almost completely solid.. aha."

"What?" said Ilia. "What have you found?"

"High Wizard Anthyana," said Elsabeth, opening the concealed panel she had found over the place where the body's heart should have been. "Or at least, what's left of her. I wouldn't even have found this, but the cover had been jolted loose a little, probably from when you stabbed her in the 'heart', Amanda." She withdrew a large Aether-Emerald. "There's still Aether in this thing. I'd wager that if we put it in a new body, the late and unlamented High Wizard Anthyana could yet live again."

"Fuck me," said Alaran, sitting down heavily in a padded wooden chair by the lab table. "I've just realised what the High Wizards were doing all this time."

"What do you mean?" said Ilia.

"Look at this... thing," said Alaran. "There's nothing living about it, it's just a mind and some Spirit attached to an automaton. I'll bet it can't restore its own Spirit in the usual way- that's why they need to use the staffs. The Reaper charges the staffs and the High Wizards replace theirs from it when they run low. But even that wouldn't allow them to feed more Spirit into the gem- for that, they'd need a living donor."

"Why do you say that?" said Elsabeth. "The Golems can gradually restore their Aether by resting, can't they?"

491

"Only very slowly, nowhere near fast enough to use magic," said Alaran. "And in battle, they're recharged by their controlling Wizards. But anyway, that's not what I'm getting at. Remember what happens when a High Wizard dies or 'retires'?"

"The most powerful Wizard is selected to become a new High Wizard," said Ilia. "Then they take on the name and mask of the old... oh hell."

"Yeah," said Alaran. "The High Wizards don't 'die', but when the gem starts to run low, they find some poor bastard Wizard and suck them dry to fill it up again. It's not a new High Wizard with the same name, it's the same damn automaton bastard it's always been!"

"Probably," said Elsabeth. "Maybe sometimes it works the other way, if one does die in an accident or battle or something. Perhaps then the new Wizard gets to become immortal. It'd be quite appealing, if you picked the right one."

"Appealing?" snapped Alaran. "Are you mad?"

Elsabeth chuckled. "I'm talking about an old Wizard, one with no family, who just wants more time to study the deeper secrets of magic. I've known a few Magisters like that- some of them even allowed themselves to be Sealed to buy a few more years. Rarely a good bargain- compared to that, becoming an ageless wooden man would look quite attractive."

Alaran stared at her. "I- I'd never even consider such a thing!"

"Really?" said Elsabeth. "What if you'd given your entire life to studying magic, and you were *this* close," she pinched her fingers together in front of his face, "to completing your life's work when your body started to fail you. Your memory starts to go. Spells you used to know slip away when you try to use them. The words of your books blur on the page, and food and wine start to taste like ashes. And then, when you're staring at ending your life having achieved nothing of note, someone offers you... this. Can you say for sure that you wouldn't say yes?"

"I.." said Alaran, before lapsing into a thoughtful silence.

"Anyway," said Elsabeth, brightly. "Let's see if we can find anything else useful in here. I almost think that this is proof enough of what the High Wizards truly are, but some schematics of that infernal machine would certainly help too."

124

$\mathcal{T}$he trembling body of the Dragon would have been almost a hundred feet long, though it seemed the mighty creature had curled herself up in her agony. Any questions as to why she had landed so abruptly and clumsily were answered almost as soon as Magister Haran and his *ad hoc* Dispensation came into sight of her- from head to tail, the silvery-black scales were cracked and pierced, and dark blood streamed from a hundred tiny puncture wounds. The terrible scene was lent a still more gruesome aspect by the fact that the main illumination came not from moon or starlight, but from trees that had been set on fire by the Dragon's desperate, flame-spurting passage.

"Thelen's breath!" gasped Haran. "Is she.. is she infested?"

"Not yet," said the Black Skull, stepping forward from amongst the Free warriors. "The might of a Dragon is enough to repel even this many Little Ones- not for nothing are they the rulers of the skies."

"And yet she lies at our mercy," observed Mighty Xaraya, her sword in hand. "It is sorely tempting to not grant it, whatever the cost might be. Such a glorious act would be remembered in song for generations."

"Aye," said Mighty Dokan. "And they would name that song 'The tale of Xaraya the foolish.' The affairs of Dragons are not for men to meddle in, even the Free."

"And what, then, would you have us do?" snapped Xaraya. "Nothing? What if she dies anyway- what might our fate be then?"

"I don't think that's what we need to worry about," said Magister Ollan, having recovered his breath. "We should be more concerned about what happens if she lives."

"What?" said Xaraya. Ollan held up a hand.

"To be more precise, what happens if the Dendaril manage to infest her. Even if she is able to resist the parasites already within her body, do you think those things are going to just leave her alone here to rest? I think that's why she came this way in the first place."

493

"She.. was trying to get over the Vigil?" said Haran. "She hoped that if she made it back to College territory, the Dendaril wouldn't be able to follow her?"

"I-" Ollan began to respond, before wrinkling his nose. "What in Thelen's name is that terrible smell?"

"Beggin' y'pardon, Learned Magisters," said Alben Koont, seeming to appear from nowhere. "But y'know them Fly Lord wankers what was leggin' it back ter the mountain? Seems they fancies themselves a bit o' Dragon. There's a fuckload o' the cunts headin' this way, and they ain't out fer a midnight stroll."

"You!" snarled the First of the Tree-Searchers, thrusting his spear at the Scout. "You were warned what would happen if I ever saw you again in the Forest Home!"

"Yer welcome t'try, y'tattooed fuckwit," chuckled the grimy man, "But y'might want ter wait 'till that lot what're comin' this way've had a go. Reckon they's thinking t'save y'the effort, yeah?"

Looking to the east, Haran couldn't see the advancing Dendaril yet, but he had no doubt that the Scout was telling the truth. "Enough bickering. We cannot slay the Dragon, and we must not allow more of the Shrive-Ticks to infest her. Wardens! Defensive positions! Oil-bearers to the fore!"

"The Free shall stand with you also," said Mighty Dokan. "First, put aside your oath for now. There will be time enough for such things later."

The First of the Tree-Searchers nodded. "As you command, Mighty One. Yet there is a problem- the Eagle Hunters require a high vantage to strike from, but those trees that are not burning are wreathed in wood-smoke."

"We use the Dragon," said the Black Skull, simply.

"What?" said the First of the Tree-Searchers. "Mighty One, you cannot mean..."

"He's right," said Xaraya. "This is a thinking creature, at least as wise as any Mighty One. She will understand that those that stand upon her do so to protect, not to attack."

"Aye," said Mighty Dokan. "Yet it might be well that you do not do so, Mighty Xaraya. Dragons also have very good hearing and excellent memories for those that speak of taking their heads."

"Hah!" snorted Xaraya. "Hear me, lizard, I do this for the Free, not for you or your scaly kin! If I live through this night, your kind will owe me a boon!"

If the Dragon heard her words, she gave no response, nor did she react as the Eagle Hunters nimbly clambered up her flanks. Even the highest ended up no more than fifteen or so feet from the forest floor, for the creature's body was long and slender and lay mostly upon its side, but as warriors formed up before it Haran felt that they at least had a semblance of a defensible position. Quickly Captain Render and Sergeant Tika marshalled the Wardens, forming a front-line of some fifty shield-bearing Guardsmen backed by the twenty dedicated Archers of the small Dispensation. Behind them, each guarded by a loose ring of Free warriors, stood the Mighty Ones and Magisters, along with the few Healers who had been available.

"You know, Haran, this is a terrible plan," grumbled Ollan, fishing out his pipe. "In fact, the only good thing about it is that it's better than anything else I can think of. It's not like we can use a flame-wreath to protect something this big, at least not for any length of time."

"I have sent a runner to the Vigil for the third Petard Engine and Singers to crew it," said Haran. "If we can hold long enough, we should be able to set it up nearby and deter the Dendaril more surely, though it may take time to reassemble the wagon. You are back to that evil thing?"

Ollan shrugged, lighting the pipe. "It's not going to kill me before those bloody flies do, Haran, and with luck if they do turn me into one of those drooling thralls the cancer'll get me before the foul things breed." He chuckled. "Dire peril does rather put thoughts of long-term survival into perspective, eh?"

A loud crash from the forest drew everyone's attention and at least one nervously-loosed arrow, before Sir Matthew burst into view on his armoured steed. "The foe approaches!" he shouted, his helm amplifying his voice. "I have blooded them as best I can!"

"Make ready!" shouted Captain Render. "Keep it tight and don't let them close. Watch out for the man beside you, and report any insect-bites to the nearest Gifted or Healer immediately. The Lily Blooms on blooded ground!"

With a terrible scream, the first wave of Dendaril emerged from the darkness, less than a hundred feet from the front line of Guardsmen. Almost immediately, Sir Matthew wheeled his horse and charged into their flank, his shimmering lance levelled. Scarce few of the attackers got past, and those were immediately brought down by arrows or blasted to ash with magic. To Haran's surprise, even Mighty Xaraya had sheathed her sword and was using a small wooden wand. The Magister had heard tales of the wands of the Expelled, which unlike the versatile but limited tools given to young Acolytes were focused solely on the casting of a kill-spell. From the dark bolt of energy that streaked from the device and utterly eradicated its target, he could see that the stories had not been exaggerated.

The Royal Knight wheeled, and entered the fray again, but this time without the impetus of a full charge. After his lance struck home, Sir Matthew drew a shining silver sword seemingly out of nothing and began to hack his way into the press, but rapidly began to get surrounded. Captain Render saw the danger immediately.

"Shield wall- forward! Break the Abelian out! Shield-strikes only!"

Swiftly the Warden infantry advanced, Seals flaring, crashing into the mob of Dendaril with shattering force with the faces of their shields, seeking to disable and scatter their enemies without killing them and causing the release of their parasites. Render and her Swordmaster skirmishers followed closely behind, oil-flasks at the ready. It was well that they did, for Sir Matthew showed none of the restraint of the College troops and continued to cut down his enemies on all sides, sending great clouds of Shrive-Ticks swarming into the air faster than the Wardens could bring fire to the corpses.

"Damn it all!" snapped Ollan. "There's no way the Wardens can deal with that many of those flying pests. Haran, we'd best do something."

"Agreed," said Haran, advancing towards the battle, staff in hand. Not to be outdone, Mighty Xaraya and Dokan followed them, their bodyguards falling in a step or two behind. All four, even Ollan, unleashed their magic as flame, driving the Shrive-Ticks back, though too late for several of the Wardens. Unbidden, Red Trace in White Snow surged forwards, his wife and several other burly warriors at his side, dragging the injured Guardsmen to the waiting Healers at the rear.

"Sir Matthew!" shouted Haran. "Fall back, damn you!"

Even then, the battle-maddened Knight would not retreat, seeming instead to be intent on forcing his way still further into the press. Suddenly a voice rang out, so impossibly loud that it seemed Haran's eardrums must burst.

"The Queen of Abelia is a stinking whore who lies with dogs!"

"Who dares?" shouted Sir Matthew, turning in the saddle to look in the direction from which the shout had come. Standing some way in front of the Dragon was the First of the Tree-Searchers, the Roaring Toad still flaring on his chest. "Damn your eyes, savage, you shall pay for that!"

Spurring his massive horse, the Abelian cut his way clear of the press and galloped towards the Dragon, but the First had already melted away into the mass of warriors. As the Wardens fell back, the Black Skull shouted an order, and the Eagle Hunters of his tribe loosed the last of their Berserker Teeth arrows, each picking a Dendaril warrior deep in their ranks and causing them to fall upon their fellows in a death-frenzy.

"Where is that slanderous cur?" roared the Abelian as the defensive line reformed. "I demand satisfaction!"

"He's fucked off," chuckled Alben Koont. "But it were me told 'im t'say it."

"I- what?" snapped the Knight in confusion, his blade still raised.

"Look over there, y'jumped-up, tin-headed prat," said the Scout, his tone hardening as he pointed at the Healers working their desperate triage. "That's three good lads won't be goin' home t'their mammies 'cos some glory-hoggin' wanker thought he was too important t'do as 'e was told. Y'want t'spit me with that shiny sword, y'go right ahead. What's one more, eh?"

"I-" said the Knight, "Damnation." He turned to Haran. "Learned Magister, my deepest apologies. The lust for battle was upon me and I failed to appreciate the danger of my position."

Mighty Xaraya laughed. "Ah, so there is a man under the metal after all! Fear not, Great Knight, there are foes aplenty for all of us!"

"Mighty Xaraya speaks truly," said Haran, eyeing the mass of Dendaril warily. "All I would ask is that you consider your tactical value, Sir Matthew. Uniquely among us you can engage the enemy at close range without succumbing to those creatures, and we can ill-afford to lose such an asset."

"Here they come again!" shouted Sergeant Tika. Sir Matthew dispelled his sword, and summoned up his lance again.

"I shall strike their flank, and then disengage," he said. "With your permission, Magister Haran?"

Haran nodded. "Valour Defiant, Sir Matthew."

"Valour Defiant!" shouted the Abelian, charging into the fray again. This time, when his charge carried him through the enemy ranks he wheeled away, falling back to let archery and magic do their work.

"There may be hope for him yet, eh Haran?" said Ollan. "Though I seem to have dropped my pipe in all the excitement, more's the pity."

125

he Dendaril camp was a hive of frantic activity as dawn began to prick the eastern skies. In the sparse forest clinging to the lower slopes of the mountain, fierce fighting had erupted. To the north-east, the savages who denied the Blessing were pressing hard, and more and more Pilgrims and warriors had been dispatched to repel them. Worse still, it seemed the terrible creature who had attacked the Crusade when they first reached the forest had returned even more powerful. Even so, the native warriors had not had the battle all their own way, and it seemed they could be held back for at least another hour.

The same could not be said for the horror that approached from the opposite direction. Joniah had heard whispers of the Golems, the soulless, fleshless constructs of wood and silver that marched in the armies of Abelia, but he had found them hard to believe. Yet now, from the vantage of the camp, the things could be seen battering their way up the slope. Only the roughness of the terrain was slowing them- the automata seemed almost impervious to daggers and swords. In desperation the Pilgrims had set fire to the forest, hoping that the conflagration would damage or destroy the wooden men, and where the trees were sparser or destroyed work-gangs took their pry-bars to the largest rocks they could find, sending them careening down the mountainside. These tactics had accounted for many of the constructs, but there were many more, and following in their wake came the silver-clad Knights. These combined the might of a Golem with the cunning of a veteran warrior, and no mere ruse could slow them.

Yet still, the Elucidated Pilgrims were unconcerned. Hundreds of thousands of Dendaril still stood between their foes and the camp, and the excavations were completed. All three of the intact crystal spheres had been loaded onto litters, each manned by a Pilgrim who had been instructed in the art of channelling Vrae into them, allowing a single man to pull the entire thing as it floated above the ground. The Heart-stone, meanwhile, was simply to be carried in its basket by two strong men holding it suspended between long poles. Within a few minutes the Crusade would begin the retreat to Sylastine, even as yet more reinforcements poured into the forest to delay their enemies.

"This is a great day," said the Voice, looking around as the preparations were completed. "But it is the harbinger of a greater day to come. With these ancient treasures shall we complete the construction of Tor Goroth according to its true purpose- a great vessel, able to bring the Dendaril into the skies where none since Thelen have dared venture. We shall bring the Blessing to the Dragons, and through them to every sentient being that lives on the land or flies in the air- and finally, with the power of Man and Dragon combined, to the seas. Then shall this war-ravaged, blood-soaked world finally know true peace."

Joniah felt tears of joy streaming down his cheeks, even as he hefted his burden on his shoulder once more. Truly was the cause of the Dendaril the most noble of endeavours- who were these savages, these arrogant Knights, or even the Dragons to oppose such a design? And yet, in this exultant moment, he felt a sudden prickle of concern.

"What.. what is that noise?" said Jaki, hampered by the palanquin and unable to turn his head far enough to look in the direction of the strange rumbling, gurgling noise echoing around the camp. Joniah, standing at the front-right of the team, was able to twist a little further, enough to discern that the sound was coming from the water-filled shaft that the Heart-stone had been retrieved from. There was another sound now- a faint, arrhythmic tap, tap, tap that seemed to be getting louder.

"Protect the Heart!" screamed the Voice, suddenly, before dropping to the ground like a puppet whose strings had been cut. The two surviving Elucidated Pilgrims instantly snapped out of their meditation and began to rise into the air above their palanquins, staffs upraised. Joniah's dagger, never before drawn in anger, had still not completely cleared the leather sheathe his wife had stitched for him when the first figure flew out of the shaft. The man- for a man it was, despite his terrifying aspect and inexplicable presence- was clad in blue lacquered armour that covered him almost from head to toe, of a design unlike anything Joniah had ever seen before. His face was obscured by a snarling metal mask, and a shock of long, blonde hair streamed from beneath his wide helm. He was large, well over six feet in height, but landed so gracefully that he might have been a dancer.

His elegance in motion was matched by a similar perfection of action, and even as he landed next to the shaft his hands blurred, a long, slender blade leaping into them and striking in a smooth movement that made a sound like thunder. The heads of the two labourers standing nearest to him had not even struck the ground when the next man died. More figures were emerging from the hole now, and the second was armoured similarly to the first, though she was more slender of build. If any had thought that this, or the fact that the black-skinned woman wore no mask or helm, made her any less deadly than her predecessor they were swiftly disabused of the notion. Her hands crossed twice, the first time to draw a long and a short blade from her belt and the second to strike with both in a scissoring cut that bisected the nearest Pilgrim as if he were made of snow rather than flesh.

The other two intruders left the hole more slowly, and Joniah suddenly realised why. The two warriors had climbed the narrow shaft by springing rapidly from one side to the other- he had seen the woman complete the last leap as the first enemy had emerged- but the other two, bald, black-skinned and dressed in strange golden robes, simply floated out of it, levitating much as the Elucidated Pilgrims were, their ring-topped staffs jangling softly.

For a moment, even as men and women rushed to block the intruders' path to the Heart-stone and its bearers, Joniah wondered why the Elucidated Ones had not struck the enemy down. Realisation struck immediately afterwards, as the first few Bearers emerged from the slaughtered corpses. Whoever these strange, dark-skinned interlopers were, they were human, and would surely make fine hosts. The bald men were clearly Gifted but could only resist for so long, and warriors, however skilled, were nearly defenceless against the Bearers.

The hope died in his heart almost as swiftly as it had risen. The lead warrior, seeing the swarm approaching, reached to his belt and brought forth a wide, paddle-like wooden fan. His left hand moved with a speed Joniah could not believe possible, creating a gust of wind so strong that the insects could make little head-way. The woman, both hands full of blades, took a more direct approach. Standing with her back to the other warrior, she struck every last Bearer from the air with a flurry of furious blows.

With this, the Elucidated Pilgrims had clearly lost patience. A titanic bolt of lightning arced from Toroth's staff, to be met by a Vrae-barrier hastily erected by the younger of the bald men. Another bolt came, and still a third, first from one Pilgrim's staff and then another, and whilst the barrier held the strain on the face of the man maintaining it was clear, though his dark features were hard to discern in the early dawn light.

For a moment, there was a stalemate. Though the two warriors were able to defend themselves against the Bearers and struck down any who came against them with ease, they could advance only slowly, wary of the wrath of the Eluci-dated Pilgrims. For the Dendaril's part, as more and more men and women rushed to the aid of their masters the situation was looking better by the moment, even though the sight of so many Bearers being slain moved every heart to fury. Soon, the intruders would be overwhelmed, and they would know fear and pain before they knew the holy peace of the Blessing.

Then Joniah realised he had been ignoring the older golden-robed man. The warriors were striking men down left and right, and the youngest was repelling the Pilgrims, though as the Porter watched another blast drove him to one knee. But the other man had simply stood watching, before abruptly dropping into a low stance. He moved slowly, and gracefully, yet each tiny motion seemed somehow full of power, tension, and terrible potential. Even so, Joniah was not greatly concerned. The Elucidated Pilgrims had repelled even the dread magic of the savage, dead god of the natives- whatever blasphemous sorcery this fool was working would not save him before his companions' own defences collapsed.

Without warning, Toroth's palanquin suddenly pitched backwards, as if Jaki had released his grip. Joniah twisted, struggling to regain control of his burden, and saw the young man leap forwards, his dagger drawn. His first jump took him to the back of Toroth's chair, and his second, with a terrible inevitability that Joniah was powerless to stop, carried him into the air, the blade already whipping down to plunge into Toroth's unprotected back.

126

"*Now!*" roared Frowning Iron as the first of the lightning-hurling enemy Sages fell. The ranks of the thralls had been thrown into confusion by the sudden act of incomprehensible betrayal, but the moment would not last long. Bai Faoha had already pointed out the place where the artefact lay, though it had hardly been necessary- although his senses were nowhere near as finely-honed as a Sage's, Tekkan-Cho could feel the powerful waves of *ki* being emitted by the thing held captive in a wicker basket supported by two peasants.

Swan-Neck Tsue, by a hair the faster, had been granted the honour of taking the prize, and leapt to do so with her customary grace. Her first light-footed step saw her briefly alight on the snarling, upturned face of an enemy peasant-warrior before flowing away again, springing across the throng like a stone skipping on water. Ever had the weapon of the mindless been sheer numbers, but the hundreds of wretches who had formed a human wall to block the Daxalai's progress had instead merely given a peerless performer a stage upon which to dance. Daggers thrust up and hands clutched at air, but none succeeded in even getting close to the duellist.

Yet still there was terrible danger, for whilst the first of the enemy commanders had fallen to Smiling Snake's strategy and his mastery of the Fivefold Conquest Step, the remaining one had wisely lifted himself higher into the air, beyond the reach of any of his followers. Swan-Neck Tsue had reached the artefact-bearers, but still needed to retrieve her prize and return with it, and Tekkan-Cho could feel the enemy Sage's *ki* swelling as he gathered his might for another strike. Marshalling his own *ki*, Frowning Iron charged, screaming his challenge at the top of his voice.

"Sorcerer! Thrall-taker! I, General Tekkan-Cho Hono, shall take your head this day! This I swear upon the throne of the Son of Heaven!"

Perhaps the Dendaril leader spoke a little Daxalai, or perhaps he simply felt the surging of Tekkan-Cho's will as the General rushed towards him, battering those .

who tried to impede him aside with blows of his command-fan. Whatever the reason, self-preservation overcame strategy and the next bolt of lightning was directed not at Tsue Tiane-Jin, but at Frowning Iron himself. Perhaps, had the enemy been a true Sage and not some ignorant eastern mockery of one, he might have understood his error in seeking to slay one trained to the pinnacle of the Path of Lightning with a bolt of that very same energy. Perhaps in the heat of battle, he might even have retained the presence of mind to remember this knowledge and act upon it. But he was not, and could not, and did not.

As the bolt of lightning streaked towards him, Tekkan-Cho's *eiken* swept up, its point to the ground as its edge faced forwards. In a single movement, the sword flowed upwards, catching the full force of the enemy's power and containing it before streaking down again in a cut that seemed to strike only air, but ended with the Dendaril's own attack returning whence it came with redoubled fury. Utterly unprepared for the violence of his own assault, the corpulent wretch exploded in a mass of gore, viscera, and terrible, swarming flies.

The shocking violence of the unleashed *ki* forced the Mind-Stealers back for a critical moment, and despite his warrior blood raging at the indignity of the thing Frowning Iron took the opportunity to withdraw. Whirling, he sprinted for the excavation shaft, seeing as he ran that Bai Faoha and Brother Rya-Ki were introducing those few thralls still fighting to the finer points of the Gentle Path, sending their enemies flailing backwards with open-palmed strikes and staff-blows without adding still more flying menaces to the already perilous air. "It is done, Brother!" he shouted, seeing Swan-Neck Tsue approaching with the basket tucked under her arm. "Go!"

Somehow finding a moment to bow in acknowledgement, Smiling Snake leapt into the shaft, followed a second later by Bai Faoha and Tsue Tiane-Jin. Tekkan-Cho was the last in, hoping with all his heart that his brother had retained enough *ki* for the final act. As they fell down the shaft, he felt Rya-Ki's *ki* rise, the Great Sage sending a shock-wave hurtling down ahead of them. The blow dislodged the portal stone, which immediately began to tumble down into the darkness, giving tantalising glimpses of home as it did so. Having already built up more speed than the artefact, the four Daxalai were gaining on it quickly and mere moments after the stone circle wedged itself in the shaft Smiling Snake passed through it, followed closely by the rest of the raiding party.

They emerged with considerably less grace than they had entered, having fallen some thirty feet and then abruptly transitioned to sideways motion. Tekkan-Cho, exiting the Third Mirror last, narrowly avoided clattering into Tsue Tiane-Jin as she sprawled on the soaking-wet, rubble-strewn floor. Similarly unable to maintain his balance, it took Frowning Iron crucial seconds to regain his feet, and as he did so he became aware of screaming and buzzing from behind him. His command-fan had been lost in the scramble and his armour battered, but as a warrior should he had retained his sword, and whirled to face the new threat. That from the thralls who had flung themselves in desperate pursuit was soon ended, for those few who managed to survive their arrival in any fit state to fight were still no match for two Generals, but the Mind-Stealers were a graver concern. Bai Faoha put the matter beyond doubt with a surging blast of *ki*, hurling the flying menaces back to splatter against the walls or career uncontrollably through the portal whence they came.

Smiling Snake, drained from his exertions, forced himself to his feet and struck his staff once on the floor, the action robbed of its usual dignity by the spreading pool of shallow, filthy water. Nonetheless, the Third Mirror responded, the portal closing and being replaced with the black, glossy surface as if it had never been there. In the silence that followed, Tekkan-Cho became aware of a pounding at the door to the laboratory. The most senior of Smiling Snake's attendants, her plain blue robes soaked, stained and clinging to her skin, hurried to the entrance to answer it.

"The Most Honourable Sage Gao-Tse requests that you cease whatever experiment you are conducting, Great Sage," she said, after a moment. "The noise is most irksome, and a tide of muddy water threatens the purity of his meditation chamber."

127

*D*awn was fast approaching, and there was no mood among the infiltrators to linger any longer. Magister Elsabeth had spent longer than Devereux would have liked loading Alaran's arms up with books, tomes and scrolls, but had at last pronounced herself satisfied.

"I may not have enough here to completely understand the Reaper," she announced, "but there is sufficient to prove both what it is, and what it does. If we present this to the Royal Guard they'll have no option but to throw the High Wizards down a very deep hole, drop the smashed remains of that damnable machine on top of them, and bury the lot."

"I agree, Amanda," said Alaran. "I don't understand half of these texts, but their overall meaning is clear enough."

"Good enough for me." said Devereux. "Let's get the hell out of here before the sun comes up."

"You should know, Amanda," said Elsabeth as they headed for the door. "There are documents here that suggest the High Wizards were planning to introduce Traitor Motes to the rivers of the Empire."

"I'd have been more surprised if they weren't," admitted Devereux. "I hope this genie will go back in the bottle, Ambassador. This magic could be the basis of a whole new type of warfare, and not a pleasant one."

Elsabeth nodded, grimly, before everyone lapsed into silence. Quietly, Devereux pushed open the door to leave the lab, checking the coast was clear before motioning the rest of the little group to follow. They were a few steps down the corridor when the omission hit her. Temis. The rebel soldier had been left on guard outside the lab, but there was no sign of him. She exchanged a quick, worried glance with Ilia, who shrugged, her face a mask of concern. Turning to Elsabeth, she signed, quickly,

Staffs?

None. Elsabeth signed the word back, looking even more worried than Ilia had.

If the Magister could no longer sense the staffs of the two remaining High Wizards, that meant either that they were no longer present, or that their owners were doing something to prevent her finding them. Devereux doubted they would be so lucky as for it to be the former. Her fears were confirmed almost immediately.

"Come out, scurriers!" rasped a voice from the Reaper chamber. "We have your friend, but I would see the faces of all of my guests, that I might furnish proper hospitality."

They emerged from the door to find three figures waiting for them. Two were already known to Devereux- High Wizard Galantharas and Temis. The latter was hopelessly trapped, gripped by the throat by the masked man and lifted a foot into the air. The other was more elaborately-dressed, his mask golden rather than white porcelain and his black robes decorated with bright silver runes. Alaran gave a gasp of recognition.

"H-High Wizard Ranthalian!"

"The very same, at your service," said the Wizard, with a mocking bow. "Alaran Dolan Savalan, is it not? And your sister, Lady Ilia, no less." He turned to study the rest of the party. "Ambassador Elsabeth Thule! I was not informed of your visit, Your Excellency! Master Delys Amaranth, protégé and ward of Yu-Kan Toha, and... hmm... now you present a tantalising puzzle-"

"Die, Wizard!" shouted Derik, hurling himself at Ranthalian, sword raised. It was, thought Devereux, a fair attempt, and one she had been considering herself. The High Wizard was clearly distracted studying the Patterns of his visitors, and might possibly have failed to react in time. Unfortunately, it seemed High Wizards, like Magisters, were trained to have excellent combat reflexes and Derik crashed insensible to the ground as his intended victim casually raised his hand. Nor did the Wizard's response stop there, for it rapidly became evident that the paralysis spell had extended to the entire raiding party.

++Operative Alert: Motive functions compromised by unknown energy field. SUCS unresponsive, standard countermeasures ineffective++

The warning wasn't particularly helpful, other than to confirm that the spell seemed to be physically holding her in place rather than anything more complicated. The High Wizard looked down at Derik in disdain.

"I had hoped, young man, that we could have had a civilised conversation. Most people would have shown more concern for the life of an imperilled comrade. Galantharas, it would seem that that particular piece of leverage is no longer required."

The other High Wizard nodded towards the alcove opposite the Reaper. "Aye, Ranthalian. Perhaps the transference chamber?"

"I think not," said Ranthalian. "There is no demand for more Golems at the moment, and once our plans in the Empire come to fruition we shall have power aplenty. Dispose of that one."

"As you wish," said Galantharas, snapping Temis' neck with a simple flick of his wrist.

"Murdering.. filth!" growled Derik, with great effort.

"I agree," said Elsabeth, obliterating Galantharas' chest with a bolt of pure power from her staff. The robed body stood motionless for a moment, before collapsing in a heap next to Temis' own corpse.

"What?" snapped Ranthalian, a shield of magic springing up around him. "How did you...?"

"I had a little help from High Wizard Anthyana," said the Magister, holding up the glowing Aether-Emerald in her free hand. "That hold spell of yours is impressively potent, but not enough to keep all of us under control, especially not with this in my possession. Hmm.. it seems that might have taken a little too much out of her, though. I wouldn't try putting this gem in anything more complicated than a Wood Golem after this. Or possibly some sort of lamp."

"High Wizard Galantharas has served me faithfully for a century!" said Ranthalian, menacingly. "For this, I will see that you suffer a thousand screaming torments!"

"Elsabeth!" gasped Ilia. "He's gripping us tighter! Free us!"

The Ambassador looked from one to the other. "Oh grow up, both of you. You especially, Ranthalian. I mean, Ilia there is a silly, vengeance-obsessed little girl but you must be well over a hundred and fifty years old. I'd have thought you'd have more sense."

"What do you mean?" asked the High Wizard, warily.

"I know what you are," said Elsabeth. "That much should be obvious by now. I also know how powerful you are. Ilia, dear, I certainly could free you and the others but all that would achieve is to weaken me enough for Ranthalian here to kill me. I have something else in mind."

"Such as?" said Ranthalian.

"Well, it occurs to me that you have a couple of... sudden vacancies in the ranks of the High Wizards," said Elsabeth. "I'm a six-Leaf Magister who would very much like a taste of immortality- and that is well within your gift, is it not?"

Ranthalian glanced down at the smouldering corpse of Galantharas. "It would appear so. Of course, you would need to take the name of Anthyana and study her mannerisms and history-"

Elsabeth crushed the emerald in her hand. "I've got most of that already. It turns out using someone's entire life essence to power your magic teaches you a lot about them. She hated Galantharas, you know- I think that was probably why it was so easy to use her power to kill him."

"Very well," said the High Wizard. "You realise-"

He was interrupted by a thud as Ilia passed out. From the looks on their faces, Delys and Alaran were also struggling to breathe, though for now Devereux's augmentations were coping.

"You are unconcerned with the fate of your friends?" asked Ranthalian.

"Them? Means to an end," said Elsabeth. "Oh, but you might not want to kill the Wizard before you've had him put Anthyana's books back. Now, you were saying?"

"You realise that once you enter the transference chamber, you will be entirely at my mercy, do you not?" said the High Wizard, gesturing to the alcove. "Were it my desire, I could simply absorb the power stored in your Animator as easily as you did the unfortunate Anthyana's."

Elsabeth snorted. "Well, of course. I'd already gleaned that much from her memories and those books. But you need ten High Wizards, and you know that I'd never have enough power to challenge you, so why would you do so? If you're worried that this is some sort of ruse, well.." She shrugged, and laid her staff down on the cave floor. "There. Now you could easily overpower me, should you so wish."

"You are taking a grave risk, woman," said Ranthalian. Elsabeth shrugged again. "The prize is worth it, High Wizard. Now, the dawn is breaking and I'm not getting any younger. Shall we?"

Ranthalian reached into his robe pocket, and withdrew an Aether-Emerald. "Here. Place this in the receptacle next to the transference chamber, and then step within. I warn you one final time- if this is a deception, it will fail. And do not think," he said, with a glance towards Devereux and Delys, "that my hold upon you will weaken during this process. The Reaper will do all the work."

"I do hope you're not going to be like this for the next century, Ranthalian," sighed Elsabeth, walking over to the alcove. "We understand- if this is a trick, it's just going to blow up in our faces."

Devereux thought that to be overdoing it a bit, but the High Wizard didn't seem to notice anything unusual in the phrase. She waited until Ranthalian was bending over the control console of the Reaper before detonating the charge. The blast was shatteringly loud in the confines of the cave, and they were all standing far closer than they should have been. The Operative, Ilia, Delys and Alaran were sent flying backwards, and even Elsabeth, who had started to move away from the alcove, was shoved back into it. None of this, however, compared to the ruin that almost a kilogram of C-6 explosive wreaked on High Wizard Ranthalian at near point-blank range. Yet, incredibly, even this was not quite enough to destroy him. As Devereux regained her feet and held out a hand for Delys, the smoke of the explosion cleared to reveal the tottering automaton advancing.

His robe was gone, as was most of his head and right arm. The wooden body that remained was scorched and blackened, and yet somehow he still lived, still moved. Worse, a blast of fire from Elsabeth intended to finish the thing struck a shield of magic- not only was Ranthalian still alive, but he was still a threat. Reacting immediately, Devereux drew both guns and opened fire, even as the Magister redoubled her own efforts. Shot after shot crashed home, two, six, twelve, and yet the shield still held, though it seemed be contracting. The last two bullets were stopped perhaps an inch short, and Devereux made to reload, only to discover that the spare clips attached to her gun-belt had been torn away by the force of the explosion.

Delys charged, but the High Wizard flung out his one remaining hand and a blast of force knocked her sprawling. The construct's mouth was moving, but no sound came out, even as he gestured again, pinning Devereux's arms to her sides. She almost cried with frustration- all this, everything they had done, and yet still it seemed not to be enough. She thought of her sword, but was unable to reach for it. Perhaps if she had used that first, rather than the guns-

There was a sudden hiss, followed immediately by a solid thud. The High Wizard's shattered head, one wooden eye lolling crazily in the socket, flopped down as if to stare at the hole in its chest. Before it could take any further action to defend itself, Ilia sent another arrow into the same place, this one tearing its way clean through in a blaze of silver fire. She stood from the shooting crouch she had risen into, and covered the distance to the smouldering thing in two quick strides, before spitting on it.

"That's for Temis, you fucking abomination!" she shouted. "And this-" she kicked the head clean off the ruined body, "is for Derik."

Devereux looked over towards the wreckage of the Reaper. "Is he..?"

Ilia shook her head. "He was too close. At least it was quick, and with luck he had just enough time to see that wooden bastard get blasted in the face before he died. Al, are you all right?"

"I'm.. I'm fine, Illy," said Alaran, sitting up. "Looks like most of the books are, too. They must have protective spells on them."

"That's fairly standard for any tome of note," said Elsabeth, walking over to them. "I'm sorry about Derik, Ilia. I lost my staff in the explosion, but that hardly compares to-"

Ilia whirled, nocking an arrow. "Traitor! I should kill you where you stand!"

Elsabeth sighed. "Well, I certainly can't stop you. I wasn't lying to Ranthalian about that- that feeble little blast of fire I threw at him after the explosion was all I had left."

"But you were lying about wanting to become one of those.. things, weren't you?" said Alaran. "I mean, it was all a trick to get him close to Amanda's explosive, wasn't it?"

"Of course," said Elsabeth. "But Lady Ilia is going to have to take my word for it. I didn't have enough power to stop Galantharas and Ranthalian, girl, and that's the truth. Moreover, I was fairly sure that his hold spell wouldn't stop Amanda from detonating her bomb and that he wouldn't notice that it was there. After all, her.. unusual nature was enough to fool the Red Witch. Now, I think we really should be leaving."

A crash, followed by the tinkle of shattered glass and the sound of rushing water from behind her emphasised Elsabeth's point. Already put beyond use by the explosion, the Reaper had started to collapse in on itself.

"Those pipes.. lead up to the High Font," said Alaran, pointing. "So... er..."

"Run!" shouted Devereux. The warning came almost too late, and as it was they were no more than halfway down the passage to the entrance chamber when a wall of water hit them and swept them off their feet.

"Thelen's breath!" gasped Elsabeth, spitting out water. "Alaran! The illusion! You must dispel it before we-"

"Wh-what?" stammered Alaran, trying to keep his head above the water. "I- I can't!"

"You must!" shouted back Elsabeth. "I'm too weak! It's easier from this side, just concentrate, damn you!"

The mouth of the cave was fast approaching, and Devereux could see the water crashing into what seemed to her to be an invisible barrier. They were being swept along with some speed now, and the others would probably hit the illusory wall hard enough to do some serious damage. Worse still, the cave was filling fast and showed no sign of stopping.

"You can do this, Al!" shouted Ilia. "I believe in you!"

"I...." gasped Alaran. "I... can't.."

At the very last moment, just as Devereux was passing through the illusion, Elsabeth gave a shout of triumph. "Yes!"

Together with the extremely confused Miraleth, who they had left watching the entrance, the surviving members of the raiding party were dumped unceremoniously in the shallow pool outside. They splashed to shore, the Operator helping Alaran gather up the spilled books and scrolls, which fortunately also appeared to be water-proof. Delys suddenly grabbed at something floating in the water, which turned out to be a fine necklace with a single, large pearl set in silver on it. She grinned, and pocketed the trophy.

"Well," said Elsabeth. "You certainly cut that very close, young man."

Alaran blinked. "I- I'm not sure I even did it. Perhaps the magic failed because of the death of those three High Wizards. Look, the waterfall is failing, too."

"The lake is draining too fast, I'd imagine," said Elsabeth. "It'll probably recover once the pressures sort themselves out. I wonder if the same can be said for your Kingdom."

"What?" snapped Ilia, turning to face the sodden Magister. "What do you mean?"

Then the sound of distant screams came to their ears.

128

With dawn, Thalia had decided to have a proper breakfast. Things in the Royal Army camp had been fairly uneventful since the main force left to assault the mountain, though several times during the night large rocks had crashed down the slope, sometimes carrying the mangled remains of a few Golems along with it. Few had come anywhere near the camp, and those that did had been running out of impetus long before the nearest War Golem had intercepted them with its huge shield.

Sipping a cup of tea- heated in the kettle by her magic since the *Dreadnought* was not equipped with a stove- she was exchanging morning pleasantries with Lady Ysabella in the *Formidable*.

"Well, it seems that the Dendaril are in full retreat," said the Abelian over the link. *"It was tough going until about half an hour ago, but then there was some sort of commotion at the camp higher up the mountainside and now resistance has greatly slackened."*

"Is there any sign of the Free Tribes?" sent Thalia.

"Some," came the reply. *"Another force was pushing the enemy from the north-east, from what we can tell. It may be your services will be needed soon."*

Thalia nodded, having already taken some precautions in that regard, before realising foolishly that Ysabella couldn't see her response. She was about to rectify the mistake when the Abelian sent again, her tone far less confident.

"Lady Thalia.. something is amiss. We... we've lost contact with the Golems we were commanding."

"What?" replied Thalia. *"Which ones?"*

"Ah.. all of them," came the response, and Thalia could tell now that Ysabella was deeply worried. *"Even.. even the ones that are.. no, no, that's impossible. Even the ones defending the ca-"*

The link cut off abruptly, and almost at the same moment a deafening clang rang out, followed immediately by a terrible clamour from outside. Athas, who had been shaving in the small wash-room attached to the privy, emerged.

509

"Learned Magister? What's that horrible noise? It sounds like fighting!"

"Yes, it does, Sergeant," said Thalia. "Get your armour on, quickly. We're going out to see what's going on."

"What about those fly-things?" said Athas, shrugging into his breastplate.

"Lady Ysabella thinks the Dendaril have mostly retreated," said Thalia. "Even so, stay close by my side so I can defend you if there are any about."

"Isn't that... sort of the wrong way around?" said Athas, with a small smile.

"Rest assured, Sergeant," said Thalia. "If a horde of angry Daxalai are somehow attacking us, the fore will be all yours. Now, hurry up!"

They emerged a few moments later to a scene of utter confusion. Whilst most of the command coaches, with the exception of the *Formidable*, were largely intact, the transport wagons which formed the perimeter of the camp had been smashed to splinters. Thalia opened her mouth to comment, but was abruptly shoved forwards from behind.

"Look out!" shouted Athas, raising his shield to block the attack of the Wood Golem that had served as the *Dreadnought*'s coachman. The construct was unarmed, and hadn't even tried to form its carved hands into fists, but the force of the blows was still sufficient to drive the big Guard back several feet. Not wanting to take any chances, Thalia hit the Stickman with a blast of fire from her staff and burned it to ashes. Athas stared as the blazing figure subsided. "What in Thelen's name... it just went berserk!"

"It's not the only one," said Thalia, grimly. "Look!"

All around the camp the Golems were running amok, War Golems and Stickmen alike. Here and there the Wizards attending the camp were banding together to repel the constructs, though they simply fled before the War Golems, which after all had been designed to repel hostile magic. Indeed, the only thing keeping anything in the camp alive seemed to be the fact that the automata were simply attacking anything near them, be it a wagon, a luckless human, or another Golem. Two War Golems had even rampaged off into the nearby forest and started felling trees seemingly at random. In the corral in the centre of the camp, the horses of the Royal Knights pranced and snorted.

Thalia ran over to the *Formidable*, which was lying on its side, battered and dented. Lady Ysabella and several other Wizards were huddled in its shadow, pale and shocked.

"Lady Ysabella! What in Thelen's name has happened?" said Thalia.

"I- I don't know!" said the Abelian. "One moment we were commanding the Golems, making the final assault on the Dendaril encampment, and then.. this! Queen's Grace- there were over a hundred War Golems alone in that force and the Knights were advancing in their wake!"

"We can't worry about that now," said Thalia, as firmly as she could. "The first thing we need to do is stop those damn things killing everyone in the camp."

"With what?" snapped one of the other Orsinio Wizards. "Those things are almost impervious to attack spells, that was the whole point of their design!"

Thalia thought quickly, remembering the battle of Equinox. "What about other magic? Illusions, for example?"

"They don't really see like human beings," said Ysabella. "Illusions won't work on them."

"It's a shame you can't just make them fight each other," said Athas, eyeing the rampaging constructs warily. Thalia stared at him.

"Lady Ysabella," she said, slowly. "Do you and your Wizards study levitation magic?"

"Of course," replied the Abelian. "It's a fairly basic... aha, I see."

In the event it took several Wizards acting in concert, directed by Thalia, to pick up each War Golem and basically drop it on the next nearest. The impact did little damage to either construct- it would have been necessary to lift them far higher than anyone present had the power for to do that- but it effectively presented both Golems with an ideal target on which to vent their inexplicable rage, and they battered each other into scrap in short order. With the task all but completed, Thalia turned to Athas.

"Sergeant, oversee things here. Help Lady Ysabella gather up the wounded, and make sure no other Golems are around. And if any of those damn flies appear, get everyone inside the coaches as quickly as you can- including you."

Athas saluted. "Yes, Learned Magister. What are you going to do?"

Thalia swallowed. "Me? I'm going to find the Royal Army."

"Alone?" gasped Lady Ysabella. "That's insane!"

"No, it's not," said Thalia. "There are still some of those flies up on the mountainside, and your Wizards are barely capable of defending themselves against them. Anyone I took with me would just be a further drain on my resources- and that goes double for you, Sergeant."

Athas stuck out his jaw, stubbornly. "I still don't like it, Learned Magister. Why do you have to go up there, anyway?"

"Someone has to," said Thalia. "We and the Abelians are allies, remember? I could hardly go back to Abellan having left a hundred Royal Knights to die up there, including the Queen."

"Then at least allow us to give you some measure of aid," said Ysabella, gesturing to the other Wizards and closing her eyes. "Everyone! Lady Thalia is going to try to help the Queen. I ask you, grant her what power you can spare!"

Almost immediately, a wave of Aether washed over Thalia, and she marshalled it as best she could, filling her own reserves and storing the rest in her staff.

"Thank you, Lady Ysabella," she said, turning to leave.

"The Lily Blooms, Lady Thalia," said Ysabella, with a curtsy of respect.

"Valour Defiant," responded Thalia, with a nod. She only hoped that the Abelian battle-cry didn't turn out to be her last words.

511

129

"*D*rive them back!"

It was, thought the Second of the Tree-Searchers even as the First shouted the words, not exactly the most tactically insightful of commands. No-one in the mixed Dispensation of Wardens and Free Tribe warriors was under any illusions about what needed to be done or the urgency of doing it. Despite terrible casualties, the lack of any of their Pilgrim leaders and Sir Matthew's repeated, devastating charges, the Dendaril kept coming. Had the warriors known that their own personal theatre of battle was the only one in which the parasite-ridden foe continued to attack, they would not have been greatly cheered.

Twice already, through nothing more than sheer weight of numbers and determination, the Dendaril had reached the Wardens' shield-wall. The first time, the enemy had been hurled back in disarray by Red Trace in White Snow, who had fully assumed his massive bear shape and rampaged through their lines. The swarms of Little Ones released by the attack had very nearly taken their prey, prevented only by a desperate magical barrage launched by Mighty Xaraya. The flames she had blasted the flies with had driven Red Trace, lost as he was in the beast-mind, into a frenzy of terror, and it had taken all of Fleeting Deer's guile to shepherd her husband back behind friendly lines.

The second clash had been even worse. Few of the Mighty Ones had enough strength left to continue to repel the swarms, and supplies of arrows for both the Eagle Hunters and the Archers of the Wardens were running low. The two Magisters had come to the fore in this dark moment, the superior construction of their staffs and their greater battlefield experience granting them endurance, at least in magical terms, beyond even the mightiest of the Free. The First of the Tree-Searchers had also chosen this moment to return to the fray, having decided that Sir Matthew was probably too busy to take revenge for his previous insults. Ironically, it had been the Royal Knight who had proved the decisive factor. Reaching the limit of his own endurance, he had ridden his horse to the rear and

512

dismounted to join the shield-wall, armed not with his shimmering magical blades but with a sword and shield borrowed from an injured Warden. His presence at the centre of the line had allowed the Magisters to concentrate on holding the flanks, with the few remaining flasks of oil employed against those corpses that threatened to unleash parasites in a poorly defended area.

For all the valour, guile, and might of the defenders, it was clear that another assault would sweep them away. The tattoos of the Free Tribe warriors were mostly glowing an angry red, and the Seals of the Wardens shone brightly through their armour, both signalling in different ways that their bearers were nearing the end of their strength. Captain Render, her own Seal glowing, shouted to the Magisters.

"Word from Magister Pieter at the Vigil! The Petard Engine is coming with reinforcements- we need to hold perhaps another ten minutes."

Magister Ollan jerked his head towards the enemy, who were massing in greater numbers than ever. "That is excellent news, Captain, but I fear it will be some eight minutes too much. Does anyone know any good jokes?"

"What?" snapped Mighty Xaraya, resting on the hilt of her bloody sword as if it were the only thing holding her up. "What are you wittering about, old man?"

"Well, if we could just make them laugh so hard that they don't attack for a few more minutes..." said Ollan.

"Perhaps now would be a good time for you to adopt the raiment of a Mighty One," said Fleeting Deer. "I know that would make *me* laugh."

Ollan shuddered. "Perhaps I should just settle for offending Mighty Xaraya enough that she kills me before they get here."

"Do not flatter yourself, old man," sniffed Xaraya. "This blade has become irksomely heavy, and I'll not waste my last good swing on your scraggy neck."

"Woe upon this day," growled Red Trace in White Snow, who had returned to human shape. "Woe upon the day that foes remain living, and yet the beast has been lulled to sleep."

"If it hadn't been, you'd be halfway to Abelia by now," said Fleeting Deer. "If I am to die, my husband will be by my side, and it is well that this be so."

The Second had shifted to her wolf-shape before the last attack whilst she still had strength to do so. The fangs and claws of the wolf were good for hamstringing and crippling enemies, allowing the oil-bearers time to prevent any Little Ones from emerging from their bodies, and so the few Stalking Wolves present had been harrying the enemy advance, relying on their swift paws to outdistance any of the insects that did threaten them. As the Dendaril began their final charge, it was the keen senses of the wolf, rather than the form's natural weapons, that suddenly proved invaluable. She became aware of the subtle changes in the Dragon's posture mere seconds before the Eagle Hunters still perched upon her, but it was enough. Shifting back to human shape, caring nothing for her nakedness, she screamed a warning.

"Back! Get away from the Dragon! Now!"

The archers were already moving as she finished the sentence, but the Wardens and other members of the shield-wall were slower to respond. Captain Render made the difference, issuing commands in a clipped tone that brooked no debate.

"Shield wall- part!"

Almost immediately, the Warden line split down the middle, swinging backwards to alter formation to two files. The manoeuvre was not executed with the Volume's usual precision, since the command was usually issued in two stages, but given the urgency of the situation Render had decided speed was more important than perfect drill. Within a second, only Sir Matthew was left in the centre of the line, staring left and right in confusion. Behind the Royal Knight, Antorathes' huge head swung around to face the advancing enemy.

"Down, fool!" shouted the First of the Tree-Searchers, hurling himself at the Knight even as the Dragon's mouth yawned open. He crashed into the armoured figure with an impact that usually would not have been sufficient to dislodge the Abelian, but Sir Matthew had been in the process of turning around and was off-balance. They clattered noisily to the ground as a jet of white-hot fire blazed out above them.

There were few living creatures who could claim to have witnessed a Dragon unleashing the full force of its breath. There were fewer still who had done so at a distance of less than ten feet and survived. Even though none of the nearby warriors was directly in the path of the flames, the heat was unbearable. Hair and beards caught fire, armour was superheated and fur singed. Men and women scrambled backwards, Seals and tattoos flaring, dropping near-molten swords or throwing aside bows that had burst into flames. But their plight, and their pain, was as nothing compared to the apocalyptic destruction that ensued at the far end of the jet of magical, primordial fire.

The leading edge of the Dendaril charge was perhaps thirty feet away and closing fast, and at that distance the conical blast had not widened to its fullest extent. Even so, three-quarters of the front rank disappeared in flaming ruin, reduced to ash in a heartbeat. These victims, however, could count themselves fortunate compared to their fellows on the extreme ends of the line, who were instead merely set alight to run screaming and flailing in all directions for several agonising seconds before falling to lie still and silent. For the next hundred feet or so, the area of blazing obliteration widened, before finally dissipating some way beyond the last few warriors.

A terrible silence fell, filled only by the groans of the injured and the metallic pings as weapons and armour heated by the flames cooled in the chill dawn air. From the place where he had fallen, the First of the Tree-Searchers coughed.

"Healer!" shouted Sir Matthew. "Healer, quickly!"

The two Healers who had survived were already running over, heedless of the massive form of the Dragon even as it settled into a sitting position.

"This worthy saved my life!" said the Knight, as they approached. "But I fear he may be beyond your aid."

Second, who had wrapped herself in her war-cloak despite the fact that it smelt of charred fur, hurried over, as did the Mighty Ones and Magisters. Sir Matthew was still lying on the ground with the First sprawled on top of him, the latter's flesh seared almost black. The first Healer, kneeling by his side, shook her head.

"Do.." began the First, before being interrupted by a fit of coughing, "Do you forgive... me, Great.. Knight?"

"Wh-what?" gasped Sir Matthew. The Knight had managed to remove his helm, but didn't otherwise seem able to move. "Why would I need to forgive a man who saved my life? Your name, Sir, shall be inscribed on the D'Honeur roll of valour in Thecla for all to learn."

"Even after..." began the First, another fit of coughing stealing the words, ".. about.... Queen?"

"That was you? Yes, of course, you are forgiven!" said the Knight, quickly. No response came.

"He is gone," said Mighty Dokan. "And yet in its own way, this is well."

"Who was he?" asked the Knight, desperately. "I must know his name, at least! Honour demands no less!"

Second felt tears pricking at her eyes, already irritated by the wood-smoke. The First had died without Joining, his name a secret only known to the Mighty Ones, and they would never-

"His name," said Mighty Dokan, "was Ashes in Dawn Winds."

130

*M*oon Behind Dark Clouds looked around the wrecked camp in awe. It was clear that the Fly Lords had worked great feats of magic in this place, and they had left the mountainside dotted with several deep shafts of various depths. They had defended the place tenaciously, before suddenly seeming to lose the will to fight altogether and retreating to the east. The Master, intent on reaching the site of the Mountain Halls, had let them go. Now, His borrowed body reduced to little more than burning bones, Ixilinath stood at the rim of the deepest excavation, which was filled with dirty, stinking water.

"*THE DENDARIL HAVE FAILED,*" said the blazing avatar. "*AND YET, SO HAVE I.*"

A strange noise came from the Master's form, and it took a moment for Moon to realise that it was laughter, of a sort.

"*ALL OF THIS,*" said Ixilinath. "*ALL OF THIS, AND THE GREATEST PRIZE IS STOLEN BY THAT BALD SOPHIST. DOES HE EVEN UNDERSTAND WHAT HE HAS, I WONDER?*"

"Master?" said Mighty Lelioko, worriedly. "Have we displeased you?" The burning skeleton- for such was all it now was- did not immediately respond, instead looking at its left hand as a finger dropped off it and plunged, hissing, into the water.

"*FEAR NOT, MIGHTY LELIOKO,*" replied the avatar, eventually. "*THE IXILDAR HAVE DONE ALL THAT WAS REQUIRED OF THEM. MIGHTY TYRONA, COME FORWARD.*"

"Yes, Master," said Tyrona, doing as she was bid.

"*THE HALLS ARE YOURS ONCE MORE. WE SHALL RAISE A NEW HOME FOR THE MIGHTY HERE, AND THE GUARDIANS AND ETERNALS SHALL DEFEND IT. FOR NOW, TAKE THE TRIBES TO THE SITE OF THE LAST MOOT. THERE IS ONE LAST TASK FOR THIS BODY, AND IT WOULD BE WELL WERE YOU NOT HERE WHEN IT IS ACCOMPLISHED.*"

Mighty Tyrona bowed. "Y-yes, Master, but what-"

Before she could finish the question, the burning figure, its flames growing brighter and hotter by the moment, stepped forwards to drop into the water-filled shaft. Immediately it sank out of sight, the water bubbling and steaming. Moon suddenly realised what the Master's last words to them had meant, and shouted frantically.

"Everyone, get back, now! Run!"

Several of the warriors with him had been in the first encounter with the Dendaril, and were already scrambling away. The rest, the Mighty Ones included, heard the urgency in his tone and were swift to follow. They had been running for perhaps thirty seconds when a dull, roaring boom split the early morning air. From the site of the excavation camp, a column of boiling water shot into the sky, filling the surrounding atmosphere with steam. Moments later, small shards of rock and rubble rained down into the ravaged forest.

"Umba's teeth!" gasped Mighty Lelioko. "I see now why the Master ordered us to flee!"

"Is... is He...?" began Mighty Tyrona, looking at the brands on her wrists.

"Gone? No." said Lelioko. "It is merely that Mighty Taris' body could no longer contain the Master's power. When we return to Ixildundal, He will be waiting for us."

"I shall not return to that place," said Mighty Tyrona, firmly. "Not unless the Master commands it. You heard His intent, did you not? The Guardians will once again defend these sacred grounds, for the Ixildar and the Free, should they desire to return."

They came to the site of the Moot soon afterwards. It was in a state of utter disarray, most of the trees burned or smashed. Mighty Renjka was already there with several of the Stonesingers, including Rocks Falling.

"This place shall once more be one of meetings and peaceful talk," said Tyrona, looking around. "This I swear upon my ancestors."

Renjka chuckled. "Then the other tribes will have to make new Thinking Seats. Truly, it would serve you well to learn the secrets of stone- see, only ours survives."

"Would you ever want to sit that Seat again, knowing what transpired the last time?" asked Lelioko, quietly.

Renjka turned to look at the Seat, its stone charred black. Broken, burnt bones still lay in pieces around it. With a gesture, she reduced it to rubble. "No," she said. "No, I would not."

"Then perhaps the permanence of stone is not the boon you would have us believe," said Lelioko. "Now, the majesty of the seas, and their glorious bounty-"

"Wait," said Night's First Raven suddenly, pointing down the forested slope. "What in Umba's name is that?"

halia made her way up the mountainside as swiftly as she could. Though many of the trees had been smashed by the Golems or by the rocks the Dendaril had rolled down in attempt to stop them, many more still stood unbowed despite the battle, as well as the changes wrought on the landscape by the destruction of the Mountain Halls. Thalia wondered what their secret was- whatever it might be, she could certainly use some of it. If Athas were here, he'd probably think of it as some sort of metaphor.

Even though she felt terribly alone and exposed, she was grateful that the big Guard had accepted her orders to stay behind. So close to the site of the Dendaril camp, the air was still thick with Shrive-Ticks, and she was forced to maintain a flame-wreath to repel them. Extending it to cover two people would have greatly reduced the time she had available to search, not to mention increasing the risk of setting more of the trees on fire.

The thought brought with it a sudden realisation- there was more she could do to increase the efficiency of the spell. At the moment, she was keeping it out at a distance of several feet from her skin, aware of the risk of setting her own robes on fire, but underneath them she was wearing the leather straps of her Mighty One outfit as a precaution in case she ran into any of the Free. Not that that seemed likely at the moment. Picking a distinctive tree so she could find it again later, she dispelled the flame-wreath, shrugged off her robe and hung it on a branch, before stepping away and casting a new defensive shield. Carefully, she contracted the area of the spell, until the flames were close enough to her skin that they were making her sweat. She nodded in satisfaction- that had bought her at least another half-hour. The fire was neither particularly hot, nor all that danger- ous, but it was enough to keep the Shrive-Ticks at bay and that was all that mattered.

Her attention was suddenly diverted by a dull boom from higher up, near where the encampment must be. She couldn't think how it could be related to the

Royal Army- unless one of the rampaging Golems had exploded- but redoubled her pace anyway. Almost immediately, she came across the first evidence of the Knights' fate. Cresting a low ridge, she found a hollow piled high with Stickmen, their halberds and armour strewn in heaps in all directions.

"Thelen's breath.." she muttered, realising that walking through the pile of splintered wood whilst surrounded by flames, even mild ones, was deeply unwise. Looking around for a way past, she found yet more Golems, though most had been shattered into pieces making it impossible to count them. From the number of weapons, it seemed several Assemblage's worth had been halfway across the hollow when the disaster that had afflicted the Golems in the camp had struck them. Despite the terrible scene, there was one consolation that could be drawn- from the look of it, the Abelians had continued to use the tactic of marching the Golems in very close formation, relying on their perfect synchronisation when directly controlled by a Wizard. When they had gone berserk, that would mean that they were most likely simply to have attacked each other.

Finding that the flame-wreath was all but blinding her Aethersight, she looked around quickly for Shrive-Ticks. Seeing none were nearby, she dispelled the wreath again and searched for any signs of life or magic in the pile. As she expected, there were none, but looking further up the mountainside she saw a powerful mass of Aether. It was too far and too confused to make real sense of, but it was there. Throwing caution to the wind, she began to run, scrambling over the Golem wrecks and using her magic to increase her strength and speed, allowing her to swiftly climb the far side of the hollow. She could hear sounds now- shouts on the wind, clashing metal- and ran on, doing her best to control the twin feelings of worry and euphoria that rushed through her. The latter was a known risk when enhancing one's physical prowess directly with magic- being stronger, faster and tougher was enjoyable, and could easily become addictive. Such a fate had befallen the late and unlamented Crown Princess Myrka at Equinox.

A low, droning buzzing brought Thalia skidding to a halt. Swiftly she brought up the shield again, noting that her exertions had significantly depleted the reserves of Aether in her staff. There were Shrive-Ticks ahead- many of them. It was even possible, she thought sourly, that the tiny, faintly magical insects were the only thing she had been sensing, though if so they were making some unusual sounds. Well, the peak of the next ridge lay ahead and she would soon have her answers.

And then she did.

Ahead was the apparent site of a battle the likes of which had never previously been fought in history. In the centre of a forest clearing, a group of Royal Knights were huddled, some twenty strong. Surrounding them lay the sundered remains of at least twelve War Golems. It made sense, of course- there had been two whole Demolitions guarding the centre of the Royal Army's formation, and the Queen's bodyguard had been almost directly behind them. Thalia stared in concern- it seemed most of the Knights were still alive, even if they weren't moving, but she couldn't immediately see Tondarin. The swarm of Ticks was dense here, denser than she'd ever seen, and she certainly dared not risk lowering her defences to get a better look.

Another clang from the far side of the huddled Knights drew her attention, and she saw the Guardian stagger back, having taken the blow of a Golem's hammer on its massive shield. Once again, she was struck by how smoothly the Queen's bodyguard moved- where the attacking Golem lumbered, the other construct seemed almost to dance, despite its great weight. As she hurried forward, she saw the Golem attack again, but this time the Guardian stepped back from the downward swing, slapping the flat of its huge sword into the oncoming weapon and driving it into the soft earth. Immediately, the bodyguard construct riposted, stamping on the hammer's haft before bringing its shield up into a slam that lifted the massive War Golem completely off its feet to land with a crash. Unable to withstand the colossal strain, the construct's weapon arm came off in a shower of sparks and remained where it lay. The Guardian twirled its sword in its hand elegantly, bringing it up before slashing down to remove the Golem's head.

One of the Knights in the huddle looked up as Thalia approached, and she saw to her relief that it wore the crimson of Sir Hektor. "Back, savage! Oh, ah, Lady Thalia, I did not- look out!" shouted the Knight, his tone changing from alarm to relief and back again in one breath. Thalia had already heard the clumping footsteps and threw herself aside as a one-armed Stickman lurched at her from behind. She gathered her power to burn the thing to ash, but before she could do so Queen Tondarin emerged from behind the wreck of a War Golem and struck the construct down with a blow of her shining sword.

"Thank you, Your Exceptional Majesty," said Thalia, with a curtsy that felt deeply out-of-place given the circumstances and her attire. "I had thought I was coming to rescue *you*, but-"

Before the Magister could finish the sentence, the Queen staggered and fell to one knee- or rather, Thalia suddenly realised, her armour did. A muffled feminine cry of pain emerged from the huddle of Knights at the same moment, and the Magister realised that the Queen's skirts were not protruding from the waist of her ambulatory battle-gear. Most likely, this was because she was not inside it.

"What in Thelen's name is going on here?" she snapped, advancing on Sir Hektor and the other Knights. "Why.. why are you all piled up on top of the Queen like that?"

"The Queen is.. unprotected," said Sir Hektor. "And those creatures are thick in the air. We were forced to pack ourselves as tightly as we could to defend her against them."

Thalia blinked in surprise. It seemed impossible that the Knights could have formed so dense a huddle that the Shrive-Ticks couldn't penetrate it, but the creatures had clearly learned that they could not infest a Knight while his or her armour was whole. It seemed that they were unable to tell that a more promising victim lay under the pile. Another gasp of pain cut short her musing.

"You must be crushing her to death under there!" said Thalia, hurrying forwards. Once she was close enough, she dispelled the flame-wreath and cast an expanded version, forming a dome much as she had directed the Wizards to at the Farspan. "There, that will keep those things away. Now get off her, all of you!"

For a moment, no-one moved. Then Tondarin's voice, sounding weak but still commanding, issued from the depths of the mound of bodies. "Do as she says."

"But your Exceptional-" began Sir Hektor.

"Do.. argh.. do as she says!" gasped the Queen. Reluctantly, the Royal Knights obeyed, each peeling him or herself off the pile one-by-one. Watching, Thalia saw that at least some of her fears had been unfounded- the Knights had carefully arranged themselves to avoid their weight bearing down on their monarch. Then the last few Knights, clad in the white gold of the Royal Guard, moved away and Thalia saw the reason for their actions, and for their concern. As she had expected, Tondarin lay on the muddy ground dressed in the same finery that she had worn for the Last Feast, though her corset had been removed.

What she had not expected was the fact that the Queen was now obviously, visibly and painfully pregnant.

"It happened shortly before the Golems went berserk," said Sir Hektor by way of explanation. "The Queen suddenly stopped, complaining of stomach pains. They are an occasional side-effect of the spell of the High Wizards, so we halted and waited for them to pass. Then suddenly... this."

"I.. barely got out.. of the armour in time," gasped Tondarin, her sweating face pink with exertion. "The.. pain is incredible. I think something.. something is wrong.."

Biting back a sarcastic comment, Thalia peered at the woman with her Aether-sight. "Blood, Ice and Fire, Tondarin, you're right about that. There's not just one baby in there- it's all three!"

"Wh-what?" gasped Tondarin. "How?"

"I have no idea," said Thalia, "But it makes more sense than only one of them being in there. Whatever disrupted the spell has affected all three pregnancies. It's the suddenness that's the problem- because the babies have just suddenly appeared in there and your womb is quite small, it hasn't had an opportunity to stretch naturally, so there's no room for more than one child, however tiny."

"You mean-" began one of the female Knights. Thalia nodded.

"Yes- we need to get the most mature baby out as soon as possible, otherwise it could die. Worse, the strain on the Queen's body is such that if we don't act quickly, *she* could die!"

"I don't understand-" began Sir Terence. Thalia exploded.

"You don't understand? Well neither do I! All I know is that three babies in various stages of development have all appeared in the womb of a woman who barely has space even for one! Does that sound like a good thing to you?"

"Ah.. no?"

"Then shut up and let me think!" snapped the Magister. Healing magic was one thing, but delivering a child was quite another, and lay well beyond her limited medical knowledge. She knew that in order for a baby to be delivered the mother needed to be in labour, and certain bodily orifices needed to relax and dilate in order for muscular contractions to push the child out. None of these were happening, presumably because until very recently the Queen had not been preg-nant in any meaningful sense. By the time her body caught up with the situation, at least one of the babies would almost certainly have died and it might well take its mother with it.

Suddenly there was a shout from one of the Knights. Thalia looked up, angry words already on her lips, but immediately saw that the man's warning was justi-fied. Emerging from the early morning mist were a large number of figures. For a terrible moment Thalia thought that they were Dendaril, but as they came on she recognised them as Free Tribe warriors. Even so, there was something wrong and she rapidly realised what it was. They were walking, undefended by magic, through a swarm of Shrive-Ticks.

"Look out!" she shouted. "Protect yourselves!"

"There is no need, Mighty Thalia," said the leader, who Thalia suddenly recognised as Mighty Tyrona, the head of the Guardians of the Halls. "We of the Ixildar are protected against the Woe even more surely than the Great Knights."

Even as she spoke, one of the Ticks surged in to bite at the flesh of a warrior at her side. Immediately, a flash of flame consumed the thing's body, though it left a small wound in the skin of its would-be victim. The other insects, already agitated by Thalia's own magic, whirled away in alarm.

"*Mighty* Thalia?" murmured Sir Hektor. "I wondered why you were dressed so.. exotically."

"Now is not the time, Sir Hektor," admonished Sir Terence. "Madam, I am Sir Terence Egret of Abellan, Custodian of the West Gate. We came to this land on a righteous quest to rid it of the Dendaril foe, but now find our Queen in dire need of aid- aid which we simple Knights are ill-qualified to give."

"So I see," said a woman wearing open-toed bearskin boots. "Which of you lucky dogs did it?" A chuckle arose from the war-band, but the man standing next to her waved them into silence with a scowl.

Mighty Tyrona peered at Tondarin. "Mmm.. what fool thought it wise to bring a woman great with child on campaign?"

"It's.. a little more complicated than that, Mighty Tyrona," said Thalia. "But if we're going to save her or the child, we need your help."

"You are intruders in the territory of the Ixildar, Knights," said Tyrona, sternly. "Yet we do not make war on children, much less those unborn. If we do this thing, you will withdraw to your own lands and not return."

"I-" began Sir Hektor, turning to look at Tondarin. Grimacing, the Queen nodded. It wasn't that onerous a condition, thought Thalia- the Royal Army, such as was left of it, was hardly in a state to fight the Free Tribes, or whoever these new 'Ixildar' were.

"Very well," said Mighty Tyrona, as two other female Mighty Ones moved to flank her. "Then dispel your barrier that we might approach, and we shall begin."

"I'll need to cast it again once you're inside," pointed out Thalia. "The Queen isn't protected like you are."

Tyrona nodded, and the three Mighty Ones began to walk forwards. Immediately, the Guardian strode to block their path.

"What is this treachery?" roared the warrior leading the war-band. Tondarin gasped in pain.

"Th-Thalia.. I can't command the Guardian, not since the Golems... it won't respond to me any more!"

"Blood, Ice and Fire!" groaned Thalia. "Mighty Ones, it's just trying to protect the Queen. It thinks you're dangerous."

"It is correct," said the sea-shell wearing Mighty One, who Thalia remembered was Lelioko of the Shorewalkers. "Yet if we are to save your friend, we cannot waste our Spirit battling this... thing."

Thalia stood up, walking towards the Guardian. For some reason, the construct had protected her before. She could only hope that whatever had changed, it still would. The huge metal figure watched her as she approached, and she saw for the first time that it had sustained some damage in the fighting, the armour of its chest cracked and battered. Carefully, she interposed herself between the bodyguard and the Mighty Ones.

"They are here to help, Guardian," she said, dropping the flaming barrier as the trio recommenced their advance. "Please, allow them to approach Tondarin."

The Guardian didn't immediately respond, and took a single, hesitant step forwards. Instinctively, Thalia thrust out her free hand against its damaged chest, hoping against hope that the gentle contact would persuade the thing to halt.

It did, but the secret she learned in the process sent her mind whirling into furious darkness.

132

$\mathcal{M}$oon Behind Dark Clouds watched in alarm as Mighty Thalia fell to her knees, her face a mask of anguish. Though the Ixildar war-band outnumbered the Abelians by almost ten to one, all knew the battle-prowess of the Great Knights, and the huge silver... thing she had been talking to looked if anything even more dangerous. Now was not the time for the only person known to both parties in such a delicate situation to take leave of her senses. Worse, the protective spell she had been maintaining, and had dropped to allow the Mighty Ones to approach, had not been re-established. If a Little One should manage to take this Tondarin, the wrath of the Knights was likely to be terrible.

"Mighty Thalia!" snapped Mighty Renjka, dropping to her knees beside the weeping woman. "Whatever ails you, now is not the time!"

Thalia seemed to come back to herself at the Stonesinger's gentle touch. "I-what? Oh.. oh, of course."

She picked up her fallen staff and stood, and a moment later the flaming barrier sprang back into being, incinerating several Little Ones which had been slowly flying nearer.

"There," said the woman, who Moon noted was dressed more in the simple straps of a warrior than the finery of a Mighty One. Even so, her power was without question. "Do what you can to save the child."

"And the mother, of course," said Renjka with a nod, moving to join the other Mighty Ones at the Queen's side. Thalia did not respond to either agree, or disagree, instead simply standing red-eyed, staring at the metal man and ignoring the drama behind her. Almost immediately after Renjka joined them, Mighty Lelioko stood up again.

"Second!" she shouted. "Throw us one of your knives!"

Night's First Raven nodded, and tossed one of the razor-sharp, curved blades through the flames. One of the Knights caught it, and turned to the Mighty One.

"What in all the sacred vessels of Thecla do you intend to do with this, barbarian? If you harm a single hair on the Queen's head-"

"Silence, fool!" snapped Lelioko, the shells of her harness rattling. "Delay us further and you risk worse than that! Give me the blade, quickly!"

"Oh, I'll give you the-" began the Knight, hotly, but another, this one female from the shape of her armour, held out a hand to restrain him.

"Don't be a fool, Sir Terence! They're trying to help!"

"Aye," agreed the man standing next to Sir Terence, taking the knife from him and handing it to Mighty Lelioko. "I have seen this done before, when my own wife struggled with our second. Curse me for a fool for not thinking of it myself!"

"You would have killed her," said Lelioko, matter-of-factly, kneeling down beside Tondarin again. "The birth of blades is not a thing to be undertaken lightly."

"Umba's teeth!" hissed Mighty Tyrona. "See how swollen she is! How in the Master's name did she ever reach this state?"

"This is no ordinary child-bearing," agreed Mighty Renjka. "There is magic at work here, magic unknown to the Free."

"And yet, there is no more time," said Lelioko. "Already, the hearts of both mother and child toil, constricted beyond measure. This must be done, and quickly. Knights of Abelia, I give you this warning once, and once only- interrupt our work once it begins, and your Queen dies."

"We understand, Mighty One," said the Knight who had reassured Sir Terence. "On the honour of the name of Sir Hektor Orsinio, you shall be free to work undisturbed."

"Then we begin," said Mighty Lelioko, wreathing the blade in a brief burst of flame to purify it before setting to work. It seemed to Moon to take an age, but in truth only minutes later the efforts of the Mighty Ones bore red, wailing fruit.

"He is small," said Mighty Tyrona critically as Lelioko cut the cord. "How many moons?"

"Er.. five, I believe," said Sir Terence.

"Hm. Then it is well," said Tyrona with satisfaction. "For one ripped free so early, he is of fair size. His father must have been mighty indeed. Here," she said, passing the severed cord to the nearest Knight. "This should be made into a broth for his mother, to restore her strength."

The Knight, who had opened the helm of his armour once Thalia's shield had been restored, turned visibly green. "Ugh.. is that truly necessary?"

"It is, especially when the normal course of nature has been interrupted," said Lelioko. "Not only will it bring strength to your Queen, it will help restore the bond between mother and son."

"See.. that it is done.." whispered Tondarin, pale with pain and exertion. Clearly a warrior, she had refused sleeping-herbs.

"How many is this for you?" asked Renjka, eliciting a snort from Lelioko.

"Hah- see how firm she is. This is the first."

"Eight," said Tondarin. Mighty Lelioko was so shocked she nearly dropped the child, but she rallied magnificently.

"Then look upon the world with your new eyes, Eighth of Tondarin. Your mother knows your true name, and you shall learn it when you Join."

"His name is-" began Tondarin, but Renjka quickly laid a hand on her mouth.

"No, do not tell him yet, at least not within our hearing. Such is not the way of the Fre- the Ixildar."

"There is yet a problem," warned Mighty Tyrona. "She is dry."

"What?" said Lelioko. "When she was so swollen? How?"

"The how matters not," said Renjka. "But the child must be fed, and quickly. Born so small, he must have sustenance."

"M-my wet-nurse.. is in Abellan..." groaned Tondarin. "This... was not supposed.. to happen.."

"Well are your people called the Deluded!" snapped Lelioko. "Fortunately the Ancestors sometimes take a liking to fools. First they sent us to you, and then they caused Small Fangs in Shadow to be among our number. She has recently borne a child, and should yet have milk enough for Eighth of Tondarin."

After some prompting, for she seemed to have lost all interest in the proceedings, Mighty Thalia was persuaded to drop her flaming shield. The Shrive-Ticks had mostly been driven away by now in any case, which was just as well. The Magister, as Moon had heard the Mighty Ones of her tribe named, seemed so lost in grief and fury that she would have been unlikely to be able to cast it again. Soon, Small Fangs in Shadow was feeding the child, and cooing in appreciation of his strength.

"I wonder, Mighty Tyrona," said Mighty Lelioko, "If one day this little prince will lead an army of his kin into our lands once more."

"He.. will not.." murmured Tondarin, "if his.. mother has any say.. in it."

"It matters not," said Mighty Renjka, standing up. "No child can be judged by what he might become, only by what he is, and Eighth of Tondarin is an innocent."

Mighty Thalia strode over to where Lelioko was tending to the Queen. "Thank you for your assistance, Mighty Ones. Will both mother and baby be all right?"

"They will, Mighty Thalia," said Lelioko, standing. "The baby will require regular feeding, so we will escort you back to your own lands, that Small Fangs in Shadow might continue to do so."

Thalia nodded. "We accept your kind offer, Mighty One. How soon will Queen Tondarin be able to fight?"

As a warrior himself, Moon Behind Dark Clouds recognised the dangerous tone of Mighty Thalia's voice, but before he could act on his knowledge Lelioko responded.

"It will not be necessary for her to do so, Mighty Thalia, for we will respect the peace. But she will be fully recovered by this time tomorrow, if I am any judge, for she is yet young and strong."

"Eight!" put in Mighty Renjka, shaking her head in disbelief.

"Good," said Thalia. "Because Tondarin, as soon as you are able to defend yourself, I am going to kill you."

133

*T*here was an utter, shocked silence in the clearing. *Good*, thought Thalia. *Let them know a little of how I feel.* Her righteous indignation was immediately punctured by Mighty Lelioko, who raised the obvious flaw in her reasoning.

"There are two more children as yet unborn within her womb, Mighty Thalia," she said, drawing herself up to her full height. "To strike her down now would be an act of murder against an innocent, and the Ixildar will not allow it."

Thalia clenched her fist and ground her teeth in fury. "I.. I know, damn you. And yet.. do you have any idea what she has done?"

"*I* don't... have any idea... what I've done.." gasped Tondarin.

"Have a care, Lady Thalia," cautioned Sir Hektor, gesturing at the Guardian. "Whatever the cause of your indignation, it is unwise to speak such words when standing next to that."

"Or when standing before the Royal Guard," said Sir Terence, sternly. "I would think, Lady Thalia, that you would have more decorum."

"Indignation?" snapped Thalia, rounding on the Knights. "Decorum? You have no idea, do you? None of you know why the Guardian defended me in the audience hall, or why it still responds to me now, do you?"

"Er.. no?" said Sir Hektor, glancing around at the assembled Knights and receiving only confused shrugs in response.

"Do you not wonder why only the Guardian has remained sane, when every other Golem has gone mad?" said Thalia, her anger cooling a little. "Do you not ask yourselves why it moves the way it does, fights the way it does? Have none of you ever seen that manner of sword and shield work before?"

"Well..." said Sir Terence. "I had never considered it, but the warriors of the College Guard use a similar style.."

"They do," nodded Thalia. "As do those Magisters that train in armed combat, like Magister Haran Dar, a friend of mine."

"I.. do not understand, Lady Thalia," said Sir Hektor. "What are you suggesting we should have seen?"

"Oh, you could never have *seen* it, Sir Hektor," said Thalia, with mock sweetness. "You would have to feel it, and even then, you would have to be... well, me. Or possibly my mother."

Tondarin had gone white. "No... I remember watching him spar with my father. But.. how?"

"Don't pretend you didn't know!" screamed Thalia, her eyes streaming hot tears and fire blazing in her hand. "You fucking bitch, don't even try to tell me you didn't know!"

"Mighty Thalia, please!" said Mighty Renjka. "You are scaring the child, and a new-born's first sights and sounds should not be full of wrath and sorrow, lest they infect his soul. What are you trying to tell us?"

"That.. thing!" said Thalia, turning to point at the Guardian. "That thing is all that remains of Magister Talion Daran, my *father*!" She spat the last word at Tondarin as if it were an arrow, as if the very force of it could kill its target. "You hypocrite! All that talk about losing your father, when you had done this to mine!"

"I." gasped Tondarin. "I didn't know! Thalia, you must believe me!"

"No wonder the Guardian defends her," said Sir Hektor. "Whatever the cost, whatever condition he finds himself in, any father would move the mountains themselves to protect his daughter."

"Aye," agreed the leader of the Shorewalker war-band, who Thalia had learned was called Moon Behind Dark Clouds. "In this, the Free and the Deluded are not so different."

Sir Terence, moving slowly and carefully, interposed himself between Thalia and the Queen. "Lady Thalia, I understand your rage, and it is well-founded. And yet, despite your savage attire, are you not still a Magister of the Lily College?"

Still furious, Thalia was brought up short by the seeming irrelevance of the question. "I... of course I am. What of it?"

"And are you not taught, in the Lily College, to consider the facts without the distorting influence of emotion?" pressed the Royal Knight. "I ask only that before you take your vengeance, you do so now. What transpired the first time you met the Queen?"

"She ordered me thrown in the dungeons," said Thalia, defiantly. "I find it hard to see how you could put a positive twist on *that*, Sir Terence."

"I would not seek to," said the Knight. "But why was the order not carried out?"

"The Guardian stopped her," said Thalia. "Or at least, the fact that she didn't want to reveal what it really was did."

"So the Queen, in her desire for vengeance upon you, deliberately provoked the Guardian to defy her command?" said Sir Terence. "Do you believe anyone would take such a risk, when there was no need to?"

"I-" began Thalia. Before she could say more, the Guardian was standing by her side. Not even knowing why she did so, she reached out again to touch the place where the light of the Aether-Emerald buried deep inside the construct seeped out. Once again, there was the rapid flash of images that had overwhelmed her, but this time she was prepared for it. She saw the last few moments of her father's life, the Knights closing in and dragging him before a robed figure in a golden mask. She saw him screaming in a dark, dismal cave as his life was ripped away by a massive, arcane machine. And she saw the moment his new form was presented to the Queen.

"*This construct is unique, Your Exceptional Majesty,*" said the robed man. "*Its sigil-engrams are bound to serve and protect you, and you alone.*"

She felt the Guardian's- her father's- helpless rage as it/he struggled to strike down the monster who had trapped him in this prison of metal, but could not.

"*It is a fine gift, High Wizard Ranthalian,*" replied the young Queen. "*How is it that it is so much more powerful than a War Golem?*"

"*A combination of.. unique materials and exacting magic, Your Exceptional Majesty,*" said the High Wizard. "*It would be neither feasible nor necessary to fill your armies with such things, but for the vital task of defending our beloved monarch, no expense or effort is too great to expend.*"

The vision faded, and Thalia found herself back in the clearing, all eyes upon her. "She.. she's telling the truth," she said, quietly. "She didn't know."

"But she does now," growled Tondarin, trying to stand. "Ranthalian, that robed charlatan! That vicious, repulsive, infamous fraud! When we return to Abellan, I'll have him and all nine of his damned Concordance hung by the heels!"

"You'll have to get to them before I do," said Thalia, grimly. Mighty Lelioko looked from one to the other.

"I know not who this Ranthalian is," she observed, with a crooked smile. "But I think he shall have cause to rue this day."

134

*I*t was well into the morning by the time the last of the guests arrived for the Committal of the Vice-Chancellor. Having satisfied himself that as many of Anneke's loose ends as possible had been tied up through the diligent work of Magisters Jarton and Julius, as well as some discreet enquiries of his own, the Arch-Chancellor had allowed the news of Anneke's death- though not the exact circumstances of it- to be released. The official College explanation was that the Vice-Chancellor had died in her sleep of a serious attack of night terrors. This was less unlikely than it might have sounded to those ignorant of the perils of studying advanced magic. A Magister plagued by nightmares could, in extreme cases, begin to work magic in their sleep, either attempting to defend themselves against imaginary threats or even inadvertently making them real. Such occurrences were rare, but were part of the reason why most citizens were Sealed rather than being trained to wield the full extent of their potential power.

In pre-College times, night terrors had been a far more common cause of death amongst the Warlocks who had risen to dominance after the disappearance of the Patrons. Modern training had almost completely eliminated the condition, but falsified records that Derelar had arranged to be stored securely- but not *too* securely- in the wing of the Archives attached to the Infirmary would show that High Chirurgeon Gisela had been aiding Anneke in dealing with them for some time. Certain medicinal herbs and potions often used to aid in controlling the condition had also been quietly planted in the Vice-Chancellor's office in quantities suggesting that she had been neglecting to take them. They had, Magister Julius had remarked bitterly, managed to make it look like a beheaded woman had committed a form of suicide.

Derelar wondered about the man, who was taking his assigned place for the ceremony accompanied by Willow-Sigh Wen. Like Magister Jarton, Julius was a man who bore a deep-seated love for the truth, but unlike him he also had the guile to understand how and when to bend it. Only his three Leaves made him unsuitable- at least, as of yet- to fill the vacancy that Anneke had so recently left. That, and his potentially dangerous relationship with the Daxalai woman. Already, Julius' fluency in the tongue of the vast western empire had improved significantly, and according to the men Derelar had watching him the investigator was also receiving instruction in the martial arts practised by his ward. At some point soon, the Arch-Chancellor considered, he may need to be reminded of the College's prohibition against interbreeding with the Daxalai. Derelar thought the law archaic and pointless, and had discussed its repeal with Anneke several times, but for now at least it still stood, and failing to respect it could destroy Julius' promising, and potentially useful, career.

That was the greatest paradox of Anneke Belus, he considered, as he regarded the simple khile-wood coffin the Vice-Chancellor's body had been placed in for the ceremony. Though in many ways actively malevolent, possessed of a blatant disregard for the sanctity of life and pragmatic to the point of sociopathy, she had been a strong force for modernising and strengthening the College. Few present, even those allies of Ollan Dane and other enemies of the woman, could deny that the Empire was weaker for her passing. Even her much-remarked upon sexual proclivities and excesses had had the surprising effect of making those strong enough to force their attentions on others wary of doing so, lest they fall into one of her traps.

Anneke would certainly have relished the morning's news, and would have relayed it with far greater panache than Jarton had. The Dendaril were in full retreat from the Expelled Territories. It was rumoured that they had retrieved some artefacts from the ruins of Xodan, but all reports suggested that they had fallen back in some disarray having suffered heavy losses at the hands of both the Abelians, and a mysterious new faction of the Expelled known as the Ixildar. That the latter claimed to be led by a Warlock unheard of since the Foundation Wars simply reinforced, in Derelar's eyes, the reputation of the Expelled as superstitious barbarians.

The rescue of Antorathes from the clutches of the Dendaril had been a significant coup. Though Derelar had not yet heard from the Ambassador since the event, he had no doubt that the Dragons would be impressed by the victory. The casualties inflicted by Antorathes herself on her defenders were regrettable, but it was the opinion of Magisters Haran and Ollan that had she waited even a fraction of a second longer, the range to the onrushing horde would have been so short that the collateral damage would have been far worse. The effort had caused the Dragon to lapse back into a healing slumber, but no further attacks had come and the local Expelled tribes were guarding her diligently, putting their antipathy aside for the time being. The only concern from that quarter came from certain traditionalists who were deeply uncomfortable with the presence of the Expelled at the Vigil. The anger of these malcontents, however, was mollified by the fact that no-one seemed certain which out of Magister Haran or Chancellor Pieter of Verge had been responsible for the situation.

The forest itself was already beginning to return to normal. High Chirurgeon Gisela was certain that any Shrive Ticks released during the fighting would by now either have died, or made a home in the beasts of the forest, within which they would become effectively harmless. Though many trees had been destroyed, burned, or flattened in the fighting, vast areas of the forest had escaped completely unscathed. The scars on the land might take decades to heal, but heal they would. The High Chirurgeon had less useful news on the subject of the Dragon blood. She remained adamant that it could not have come from Anneke, and according to the few sources Derelar had managed to find on the subject a shape-shifted Dragon would indeed revert to its natural form upon death. When Derelar had finally directly asked Gisela about his evidence, she had suggested that Anneke had dripped Dragon blood on his desk in an attempt to deceive him, though could not suggest a motive for so bizarre a ploy.

Other news was also distinctly mixed. Contact with the Abelian Royal Army, including Queen Tondarin II and Magister Thalia Daran, had yet to be established, either by the College or by the Abelians themselves. Most incredible, though, had been the sudden request by Chamberlain Renholt, acting as Regent, for military assistance from the College Guard. Apparently, in the early hours of the morning every one of the millions of Golems serving menial and military roles in the Kingdom had simultaneously run amok, causing untold damage though mercifully few actual human casualties. All attempts to contact the new Ambassador, Magister Elsabeth Thule, had so far been unsuccessful, and Magister Jarton had as yet been unable to find the Messaging Crystal corresponding to the one set into Amanda Devereux's sword pommel. He did, however, report that the Operative appeared to be somewhere in central Abelia, near the city of Aquila. The High Wizards who made their lair there were strongly suspected of being involved in the Golems' rampage, so Derelar doubted that the Operative's presence nearby was a coincidence.

Regardless of the exact reason for the request, those Volumes which had been working on preparations for the Friendship Games were now marching for Abelia, ready to embark on altogether more direct diplomacy. Though Derelar did not intend to use them to conquer the Kingdom, he also intended for it to be extremely difficult, not to mention expensive, to dislodge the Volumes once they arrived. The Abelians had to expect such a consequence, so for them to directly request what was practically an invasion suggested that the situation in the Kingdom was dire indeed.

The actual Committal of Anneke's body would, as these things invariably did, take mere moments. However, due to the Vice-Chancellor's seniority, both with regard to her position in the College and as Matriarch of her House, there were certain formalities to observe. Every Symposium Magister who could find a way to do so had attended, along with the entire High Seminar, and many had taken the opportunity to say a few words about Anneke when that part of the proceedings arrived. Even Captain Ariel, serving in her position as head of the Belus House Guard, had spoken in tribute, though she had carefully avoided alluding to the true circumstances of her mistress' death as she had been warned to do. There were also certain rituals to observe surrounding the Vice-Chancellor's staff, which were complicated by the fact that it had not been found with the body, a detail which had greatly interested Magister Julius. A facsimile had been swiftly fashioned and then equally swiftly broken, with the excuse that the woman had destroyed it herself in the throes of her self-inflicted demise.

Finally, the speeches drew to a close, and Derelar presided over the last, and most important, act of the ceremony. "From the Aether you came, and to the Aether you return, Anneke Belus," he intoned, as the coffin and its contents glimmered away into dust. "May Thelen receive you."

"May Thelen receive you," echoed the congregation, including, Derelar noted with interest, Willow-Sigh Wen and Master Yukan. The latter had spoken with customary Daxalai flourish on the merits of the "Most Learned Vice-Chancellor," with whom he had formed something of a rapport during the affair of the Third Mirror. Derelar had not yet dared mention to him that his adoptive daughter was also missing along with Operative Devereux. As the Daxalai himself had observed, the two were a potent combination and there was no reason to believe that they had come to any harm. At least, not yet.

There was a reception afterwards, allowing the Magisters and other guests to mingle and share quiet gossip about the deceased that perhaps they might not have dared to speak out loud to the full company. Derelar had, of course, ensured that the Acolytes serving food and drinks kept their ears open and reported anything useful that they heard directly to him. It was, he thought wryly, what Anneke would have wanted. In the course of his mingling, he found himself standing next to his mother, Marike. Though he had carefully avoided his brothers and his aunt Kyria, the former because they were unremittingly tedious and the latter because she was unapologetically ambitious, he always made time for Marike Falon. His mother, who had kept her prior name out of respect to her small, but proud House, now served in the High Seminar as the Chair of Leaves, responsible for the training of Acolytes, having become too old for her previous position as Chair of Amaran. Even so, with the latter post currently unfilled many looked to her to also serve as Voice of the Voiceless.

"Derelar, my son," said Marike, looking him up and down. "How are you faring? To lose Anneke so suddenly must have been a terrible shock."

"It was.. certainly regrettable," said Derelar.

"Thelen's breath, look," said his mother, gesturing subtly to direct Derelar's attention to the corner of the room. "Poor Isadora. Practically the anniversary of Talion's death and now Thalia is missing too. You were considering her for Amaran, were you not?"

"Magister Thalia? Yes," said Derelar. "She has the.. independent streak the Chair demands. I have hope for her yet, Mother," he continued, surprising himself with his own sincerity. "Thalia Daran has come through trials she had no right to survive before. I fully expect that she will do so again."

"Let us hope so," said Marike. She sighed. "Do you know, I remember the first time that I met Anneke?"

"Oh?" said Derelar, not listening particularly closely. He was scanning the room, watching for any sign that the carefully-constructed cover story was threatened.

"Yes," said Marike, almost to herself. "It was in the Symposium chamber, on the day Empress Hypatia died. Thelen's breath, the fury of that Ritala Daran! If Thalia shares any of *her* blood I fear for anyone who gets in her way."

Derelar raised an eyebrow. He had heard the story of Hypatia's death before, of course, but hadn't known Anneke had been present, and said so.

"Oh, she wasn't at the High Seminar meeting," said Marike. "She was waiting just outside- I think she had brought a message for Hypatia but obviously the reason for her visit was rather forgotten in the excitement. No- no wait, it was Orton Belus she had come to see, that was it. Ritala sent her flying in the Processional corridor before she stormed in and killed Hypatia."

"And then.... the High Seminar destroyed her," mused Derelar. Something was stirring at the back of his mind, but it felt like if he tried to grasp it, it would slip away.

"Oh yes," said Marike, shuddering at the memory. "Almost immediately, in fact. She must have used everything she had to destroy Hypatia. When the smoke from the explosion cleared, there was nothing left but a few scraps of cloth."

"And... she died in the Symposium chamber, did she not?" said Derelar, mentally snatching at realisation as it flashed through his subconscious.

"Yes, that's right," said Marike. "Right on the threshold."

"Or what is not here, that should be?" muttered Derelar.

"What?"

"My apologies, Mother," said Derelar. "I was... remembering something a friend once said to me." That was not entirely true, of course. Though she had been wearing the form of Anneke at the time, it had been Jocasta, the Red Witch, who had spoken those words to him outside the Symposium chamber during the Revenant crisis. He had been looking at the ghostly remnants within the chamber, every man and woman who had died within recreated on the spot where they had fallen, which given the events of the War of Rule had left the place quite crowded. Empress Hypatia had been there, her hollow-eyed ghost staring at him.

Lady Ritala Daran had not. Nor could he possibly have overlooked her- had her Revenant appeared where Marike insisted she had died, she would have been right in front of him. Ritala Daran- impetuous, powerful far beyond any training she should ever have received. Known to have been mother to the three Tydask siblings who had proved to be both Magisters of exceptional power, and hopelessly, impossibly insane. And in the place where she had supposedly died, mere moments later, had appeared Anneke Belus.

Anneke Belus- impetuous, possessed of knowledge and power far beyond her apparent years. He had suspected, until Gisela's fresh analysis of her blood seemingly proved otherwise, that she was a Dragon who had taken human form. Yet if a Dragon could do such a thing- and everything he had learned about them suggested that they indeed could- why would it necessarily be restricted to one form? And if it were not so restricted, what would it do if it believed itself to be on the verge of being exposed?

Ritala Daran had died on that day, that much was certain, but only in the sense that her name had. The real Ritala had probably perished long before that, if she had ever existed at all. No, the disguise had died, but the Dragon had lived on, this time in the form of Anneke Belus. Derelar wondered what had happened to the real Anneke. For that matter, he wondered who she might have become had she lived. At least he would have an answer for Magister Ollan the next time they met.

Of course, this still left a vital question unanswered. If Anneke, or whatever the Dragon was called, had once more faked her death and taken a new identity, who had he just Committed? And who had she now become? Ariel? He discounted the idea immediately. For the Dragon to pretend to be a human of so little power and influence, especially one who was not even a Magister, would be intolerable. No, there was only one possibility, and he, Derelar Thane, had practically personally selected her.

"Please excuse me, Mother," he said, turning to leave. He needed to find Magister Elsabeth Thule. He needed to find her very, very quickly.

ACKNOWLEDGMENTS

As always, this book would not have been possible without the help and support of my friends and family. I'd also like to thank the staff and regulars of Wyldstorm Games in Great Yarmouth, particularly Chris, Andy and the Mitchell brothers. (Not those ones.)

Once again, Sean Harrington has stepped up with a cover that really captured the scene in my head, and Tiffany Munroe has drawn a beautiful map at very short notice to bring Abelia to life, largely the reverse of what I've spent this book doing to it. In both cases, the artists were working closely to my brief so any egregious errors of layout, topography or geography are mine and mine alone.

Finally, thank you- yes, *you*- for reading this far, talking to me at events or conventions, and generally being interested. A book is nothing without a reader.

Printed in Great Britain
by Amazon

27295874R00308